KT-558-785

Margaret Graham

A FRAGMENT OF TIME

THE FUTURE IS OURS

This edition published by Arrow in 2002
an imprint of The Random House Group
20 Vauxhall Bridge Road, London SW1V 2SA

Papers used by Random House UK Ltd are natural
recyclable products made from wood grown in
sustainable forests. The manufacturing process
conform to the environment regulations of the
country of origin.

A catalogue record for this book is available from
the British Library

Printed and bound in Great Britain by
Cox & Wyman Ltd, Reading, Berkshire

ISBN 0 09 189098 5

A FRAGMENT OF TIME

Margaret Graham

My sincere thanks to Sheila Doering,
Nancy Copas, Daphne Folyer,
Thelma Kazda and Margot Loomis –
all now of the United States –
without whom this book could not
have been written. My thanks also to
Sue Bramble, Martock Branch Librarian
with Somerset County Library,
whose advice and help has been, as always,
above and beyond the call of duty.

Part One

CHAPTER 1

The lichen was dry beneath her fingers, dry and warm. It crumbled as she rubbed her hand along the top of the old bridge; some had caught beneath her nails which were cut short and square as her mother insisted. Helen smiled because soon it wouldn't matter what her mother thought. It was 1931, she was eighteen and at last it wouldn't matter.

She lifted her face to the sun. It was hot although it was early May and through her closed lids she could see only red but she felt Heine near her, next to her. She could hear his breathing, smell his skin and here was his hand, firm on hers. Through her closed lids she could picture him; tanned, his hair golden.

'I love you, Heine,' she said and it was not until she felt his lips on her neck, his breath on her skin that she turned, looking into his face, touching the lines beneath his eyes, kissing his mouth, stroking his hair. Although he said there were grey hairs she could see none, he was too blond.

'And I love you, Helen,' he said. That was all but it was enough.

She turned back to the parapet, her arm in his.

'I used to come here with my father,' she said, the index finger of her other hand tracing the figure six, round and round in the lichen. 'Before he died, of course.'

Heine nodded, leaning over to look down into the stream. 'In the trenches, I suppose?' His voice was tense and Helen lifted his hand to her lips. There was dirt on his palm from her fingers.

'Mother wishes that he had. It would be so much more proper somehow but no, it was the flu. In 1919 when I was six. But I can remember coming here with him, I know I can, although Mother says I can't possibly. I was three the first time when he was on leave.' She stared hard at his hand. 'I can remember coming here while she stayed at home to cook the joint on Sundays. He would hold my hand as we walked from the Avenue, across the fields, along by the hazel trees to this exact spot.'

She turned and smiled at Heine. 'To this exact spot,' she repeated, 'and the lichen was here then too. The weather always seemed warm and dry and the minnows darted in and out of the shadows just as they're doing now.' She paused. 'I haven't been back for years.' She thought, but did not add, that she could not face coming alone, or with her – her mother.

Helen leaned over the parapet, her shoes digging into the stones and turf of the lane which had never been tarmacked. There was no need, no traffic, just us, her father had said. The minnows were darting and now she remembered how they would each drop a stick into the water from the other side of the bridge and race back. Her father would lift her so that she could see whose had won and although her head and body had been well over the water she had never been afraid. He had been thirty when he died and she hadn't been back since then.

Would he be pleased at her news, she wondered, as she looked again at Heine, and felt that he would because she could remember him saying, Be happy, to her in that room, the spare room where her mother had moved him the moment he had become ill. Just be happy when you can, life is so short.

The room had a wet blanket soaked in disinfectant draped in the doorway day and night. Her mother had said it was to stop the germs and Helen was not to enter; on no account was she to enter. But on the first Sunday of his illness she had pushed past the heavy Army issue barrier. Its wetness had soaked into her blue summer dress, staining it darker where it had touched. Its smell had saturated the room. She bent forward and kissed him by his eyebrow. He was so hot and dry and there was a pulse beneath his skin. I love you, Daddy, she said, and he smiled. I won't let you die. Every day she had crept into that bleak room and kissed him there and said, I will not let you die. But one day he was dead, and she was alone with her mother.

Now she couldn't remember what he had looked like, though there was a photograph on the mantelpiece in the dining-room of him in his Pay Corps uniform. But somehow it was not the father she had known, the father whose smile had been slow and whose voice had been kind.

'We also had the flu in our land, Helen.' Heine's voice was gentle and she nodded.

'Yes, I know, my love.' But she pushed the thought of his land away, just for now. There would be enough said about that when they arrived for tea in the house in the Avenue where she still lived.

'Are you sure your mother will receive me?' Heine asked, the lines deepening around his eyes and across his forehead.

'Of course she will.' But she looked away because she did not want him to see her face as she said those words. She touched his arm. His sleeves were rolled up and his hairs were golden in the sun, thick and golden, and she wanted to bend her head and press her lips against his flesh and forget her mother as she always could with him.

She turned then and ran down from the bridge squatting beneath the hazel trees which grew almost to the banks, looking over her shoulder as she scooped her grey cotton skirt clear of the ground.

'Let's drop sticks into the water and see who wins the race,' she called. 'Come on, Heine. Choose your own or I'll pick one with branches which will snag on the rocks and you'll lose.'

She watched as he limped down to her and flushed. She hadn't forgotten that Heine could no longer run, it had just got lost somewhere in her head, just for a moment, the moment when she had smelt his skin, wanted his body. She turned away, seeing the roots which rose from the bank and then the field beyond. It must be hard when the sun was so warm, the grass smelt so fresh, the birds sang and the breeze wafted. It must be so hard not to be able to run but then – and now she paused as she searched for a thick straight twig – but then perhaps men of thirty were too old to run. Had her father ever run? She could not remember.

Heine stooped, his leg would not bend. 'That one, my darling. It is short and thick and will race and win.' He pointed to a stick just to the left of her foot buried in long grass. She picked it up; it was cool and the bark was damp, torn and pungent. She handed it up to him, narrowing her eyes as she looked into the sun.

Why had he chosen her? Of all the women he must have met, why had he chosen her? Helen reached for a stick, any stick, it didn't matter now. She felt foolish, a child beside his maturity, his beauty, his intelligence.

She pushed herself up, not looking at him now.

'Let's not do this. You must think me such a child and I'm not. I might be younger than you but I'm not a child.' The sun cooler now, she rubbed her arms with her hands and the stick streaked her skin with mud. There was a mark on her new pink blouse. She moved out from the grass, from the hazel trees, looking across the fields to the backs of the houses half a mile away. Her mother would be waiting.

'You are beautiful and I wish to race our sticks,' Heine said.

He smiled as he looked at her short dark curls, so gloriously dark, not like the heavy gold plaits of the women of his land. She was so young and fresh and strong, all that he no longer was. It was this which had drawn him to her when he had photographed the new premises of the bank where she worked. In her, this young girl, he could see no harshness, no brutality, no reminders of the land he had been forced to leave. He knew he must have had a childhood but somehow he could not see past the darkness which was crawling in the streets of the towns where he had once lived. Would he regain the sights and sounds of youth with this girl whose skin was flushed and smooth? Ignoring the ache in his leg, he held out his hand and smiled as she took it. Together they walked back to the bridge and dropped their sticks far out into the running current, then hurried back over to the side which still had a number six rubbed in the lichen.

Helen leaned over, seeing again the small child, feeling her father's hands as he lifted her. Heine's was out first, the short thick one, and he laughed and kissed her and said into her hair, 'Faster on water than on land, my darling.'

And she wanted to ask him yet again how he had been injured, for it was not in the war, that much she knew, but he would never tell her. The girls in her office thought the limp romantic and she smiled at the feel of his arms around her, not embarrassed as his body pressed against hers, though she had felt awkward when she had danced with the boys at the St Matthew's Christmas dance five months ago. She remembered the hot sweating hands which had made her skin wet through her gloves, the conversation which had spluttered and died. Heine made her feel safe, made her feel full of love.

'Isn't it time that we faced your mother?'

Helen put her face against his jacket, not wanting to think of the world in the Avenue, her mother, the past.

'Just a little longer. It's not quite three-thirty,' she replied, knowing that today there would be meringues. On this occasion there would definitely be meringues and she shivered.

It was a million years since her mother had bought her ribbon and green knickers in the large store two weeks after her father had died. They had travelled in a lift to the restaurant where mannequins had paraded and a chamber orchestra had played on a small stage fronted by imitation palm trees. Her mother had ordered tea for two and one meringue and one toasted teacake. A waitress dressed in black with a small white pinafore had served the large meringue on a bone china plate with a white paper doily.

It was as white as her father's face had been the last time she had seen him.

Her mother's teacake oozed butter. She cut into it with a knife, carrying it to her pursed mouth with her small plump fingers, watching the mannequins, listening to the music, her head nodding in time, her black felt hat firm on her head. Helen had watched the butter drip on to her chin and wondered how her mother could eat when her own heart seemed to fill her body with the pain of loss, leaving no room for food, leaving no room even to breathe properly.

Helen had dug her fork, prongs first, into her meringue and it shattered, spraying the table-cloth and her lap, and she had been glad to see it destroyed, because that was how she felt too. Daddy, she had thought silently.

Her mother leaned forward then. Eggs and cream are good for you, she had said, and Helen could smell the tea on her breath. Eat it, or I shall put you in the cupboard. And her mother had smiled a strange smile, one that did not reach her eyes. Mother knows best, she had said, and I am all you have now. Now he is dead.

Her stomach had swayed in the lift but she had not been sick until midnight and then she had cried out, 'Daddy'. Her mother had come and taken her downstairs and put her in the cupboard, the dark black cupboard under the stairs. She had cried into the blackness, holding her father's coat against her face until it was wet, because her mother must not hear her sobs.

Every holiday her mother had taken her to the same restaurant and if she was displeased she would buy her a meringue and the darkness of the cupboard would be close.

'Oh yes,' Helen said as Heine touched her arm. 'Oh yes, perhaps we'd better go now.'

She turned and rubbed out the number six on the lichen, rubbed and rubbed, then shook her hands, smiling as Heine gave her a crisp white handkerchief. She handed it back before taking his arm and walking at his pace down the lane towards the houses they could see over the two fields. He was her sunlight, but she would have to struggle for him.

Lydia Carstairs brushed the table-cloth with the silver-plated crumb brush and dustpan which she told people had been a wedding present but which she had bought in Kingston-upon-Thames after her husband had died. There had been some money then, for the first time ever. Clerks did not earn a great deal but he had been very wise, she had to say that for Ernest, very wise in the matter of insurance. Perhaps that's what came of dealing with little bits of paper for a living. So in a way it was as well he had died of flu and not in the line of duty, because she wasn't sure just how his insurance would have stood in those circumstances. Mark you, there was no telegram, was there, with flu? No valour.

Lydia moved across to the mantelpiece and dusted the photograph of Ernest with a corner of her flowered apron. He had been a very ordinary little man, but steady, her mother had said, and he had of course owned this detached house and on a corner too, which made it rather better than the neighbours'. There was also a bit of extra land at the side which Ernest had used to grow cabbages and potatoes. He had liked potatoes straight from the soil; small and translucent, he used to say, with the scent of nature in every bite. What nonsense he talked. She stood back from the photograph. Good, no dust.

She hadn't missed him, and no, she didn't feel that was a sin. As her mother had said, no woman liked a sweating body in her bed. Men were better dealing with wars, better at being with other men. When they were home they interfered. And she'd been right. They spoilt their children, came between mothers and daughters. She looked again at the photograph. No, she didn't miss Ernest because she had Helen.

Lydia turned and looked at the table. The best cloth was on, the white cotton covered by the white over-lace. Scones, sandwiches, but not those with egg yet because they smelt so. Lydia smoothed her hands down her apron and then touched her hair, looking in the wrought-iron mirror over the sideboard. Her grey hair was in place, her face powdered, but very lightly. She wished her eyes were not such a pale blue and her face was not quite so plump. She sucked in her cheeks. Perhaps she should have less jam on her scones. There was dust on the mirror frame and she licked her finger and ran it round the wrought-iron edge.

The clock in the hall chimed three-thirty and Lydia took her apron off, carrying it through to the kitchen, hanging it on the hook which Ernest had put up on the inside of the pantry door when he seemed a little better from the flu. And while he was doing that it had seemed sensible that he should just finish off the shelf for the new meat safe. He wouldn't do the second one though; stubborn, yes stubborn. He had collapsed the next day.

She moved to the sink. Where was Helen and why had she invited this friend? The girl knew how she felt about the weekends. After all, the weekends were family times, they always had been and they always would be. It was lonely when she was away in London during the day. She was becoming a selfish girl again. Lydia picked up the dishcloth and polished the splash marks from the cold tap before looking up at the clock. She should be back from the station by now. She polished harder, pushing the rage down, pushing the fear of loneliness down. She did not want to think of the word that Helen had used, that had taken the breath from her body. Him, she had said. I will go to the station to meet him.

Helen rang the door bell because she was not allowed a key. Her hands were cold now and the porch seemed foreign to her. There was a broken tile in the right-hand corner, and the lead which swept upwards on the stained glass window was thinner at the top and cracked with age.

The door was opening and her mother stood motionless, her smile fixed, her hair newly permed. Helen could smell it from here. It was crimped and tight, hard like her mother's eyes as they looked past her.

'Mother, I'd like you to meet Heine.' She could only move slightly aside in the cramped porch but her mother had not yet opened the door wide enough for them to enter.

'Heine, this is my mother, Lydia Carstairs.'

'Mrs Carstairs,' her mother said, still with a fixed smile. 'How do you do. You had better come in.' She shook Heine's outstretched hand but looked at Helen. 'Go through to the dining-room.'

They walked down the dark hall and through the first door and Helen wished that she had been able to be honest with her mother. She had wanted to tell her that Heine was her life now, that at lunchtimes she had been walking in the park or sitting in a Lyons Corner House with him but she had been unable to. She had been too afraid that it would all end, that she would not be strong enough to fight for him.

She heard her mother go on into the kitchen. She could hear the kettle humming through the hatch, then its whistle, abruptly halted as her mother lifted it from the gas and poured water into the teapot. It would be the silver one, she knew.

Helen smiled at Heine who raised an eyebrow.

'Do sit down,' she said and wondered why she whispered.

'Did your mother not know of my existence?' Heine also spoke quietly, his face serious.

Helen flushed. 'You don't understand how difficult it can be. I am all she has. She depends on me too much.' She was still whispering. She rubbed at her hands, at the lichen dust, the dirt from the stone parapet, the bark stain.

'My darling girl, you are not that frightened of the situation are you, or of her reaction? I didn't realise.' His voice dropped almost to nothing. 'I should not have put you in this position, you are too young, too fresh.'

Helen caught one of his hands. 'I am not too young. Just nervous, that's all. It needs to be put to her gently.' Her voice was still a whisper but she must not think of herself as frightened or she would be lost.

'Then I will be careful, but I just wish it need not be this way. There seems to be no end to obstruction.' His voice was still low but it now sounded tired. 'Go and wash your hands now, leave me alone with her for a while.' He kissed her hand, holding it to his mouth for a moment. 'And now I have dirt on my lips?'

'No, my love.'

In the bathroom Helen scrubbed her hands and then her nails and soap sprayed on to her pink blouse and even when she wiped it with the towel the marks still showed. He had spoken to her as though she were a child and she was, inside she still was. He was right, she was frightened; so frightened that it would all be destroyed, that he would go and leave her here with her mother. Alone with her mother whose voice was not kind, whose hands had never shown her the stream but had pushed her into the darkness.

She held the towel to her face. She must not cry, she never cried, and today if she did it would show in her eyes and her mother would say that all men did this to you; that mothers were the best companions. She looked in the mirror, she could not go down yet. She opened the window and stared out across the garden, across the fields they had just passed through, breathing in the spring air, letting the breeze cool her face.

They were both sitting at the table when she re-entered, her mother pouring tea from the silver pot.

'So your father is a solicitor, is he?' she was saying, her face stretched into a smile. 'And you have a studio just a few yards from the Underground station. Cannon Street did you say? Alton Mews? Most convenient.' She turned to Helen. 'Do take a scone, Helen. Heine says that he has not tasted anything like them ever.'

'Indeed they are quite delicious, Mrs Carstairs.' Heine smiled at Lydia and then at Helen. 'Really, Helen, you did not tell me you had such a talented mother. I should have insisted on visiting you before at this . . .' he paused and looked around the room. 'At this comfortable and tranquil home.'

Helen watched her mother smile, not at her but at Heine. She could see that he had already eaten three sandwiches and she knew he did not like egg.

'Yes, my father is a solicitor and of course is kept extremely busy. And my mother too because unfortunately our home is not as cosy as yours. It is big, too big.'

Helen watched as her mother looked again at Heine, her face thoughtful, but Helen knew she was just waiting.

'And how large is your studio in London, Mr Weber?'

'It is integrated into the flat I have. There is a pleasant garden and in the flat there is a spare room for guests. And of course I am not very far from Waterloo.'

'And they're bringing those new trolley buses in soon, aren't they, the ones they use in Yorkshire? You know, Helen, those trackless trams. They're cheaper, the paper says, and don't interfere with the traffic so much. That will make it easier for you won't it, Mr Weber? For your business?'

'You are quite correct, Mrs Carstairs,' Heine took a sip of tea from the bone china cup with pink flowers. Her mother's best, Helen noticed. He set the cup carefully in the saucer, before looking up at Helen and her mother.

Helen also looked at her mother who was patting her mouth with her napkin then back at Heine. His smile was sincere, his voice anxious. She felt warmth flood over her. Perhaps it would be all right. Perhaps Heine was going to make her like him.

'Helen, the meringues are on the kitchen table. Now pass me your cup and I shall refill it for you, Mr Weber.'

Helen rose, looking from her mother to Heine. It would not be all right. She understood her mother's words. Helen carried the plate back into the room together with the silver-plated cake tongs and placed it beside her mother. She could not look up.

'Now tell me more about yourself, Mr Weber,' her mother asked as she chose the largest meringue for Helen and placed it carefully on a small white plate and then passed one to Heine. 'I think from your accent you must be Dutch.'

Heine did not falter, he did not look at Helen who had stopped and turned. Her chair was still two paces away from her.

'I was born in Germany, Mrs Carstairs.'

Her mother held the plate quite still, her fingers whitening. She said nothing but she smiled and there was satisfaction in her eyes. It was the smile she used when Helen came out of the cupboard.

Steam was coming from the spout of the teapot, a slash of light caught the lid. Heine reached forward and took the plate from her mother's grasp, saying as he did so, 'Do you mind if I begin? It looks too delicious to ignore.'

Her mother said nothing. Helen moved to her chair now but

did not eat her meringue. Didn't Heine know what had just happened? Couldn't he see from her mother's eyes? But no, of course not, no one could but her.

Heine looked at Mrs Carstairs, his face gentle, his voice firm. 'I know that it is difficult to divest ourselves of the past. Of the pain that both our nations experienced. There are some who cannot forgive or forget but I know that those of us with compassion and tolerance, such as you, Mrs Carstairs, can see beyond that. I have chosen to live in England because I prefer it to my own land. I prefer its people, its tolerance. Its essence. I know that you will understand what I mean.' He was holding her mother's arm now.

Lydia Carstairs was looking at him, feeling the weight of his hand, hearing his words, hating him for thinking that he could take her daughter from her. She is mine, she wanted to shout into his face, but she said nothing.

'I wish to marry Helen, Mrs Carstairs. I love her and I will take care of her but I will not marry without your approval.' He looked at Helen who still did not eat. Heine smiled at her but she could only look at him and then at her mother who had still not spoken, still not moved.

Heine pushed back his chair. 'I feel it would be too impolite to smoke in your home, Mrs Carstairs. I shall go into the garden if I may.' He rose and smiled again at Helen but his blue eyes were dark and the lines were deep across his forehead and around his eyes and as he left the room his limp seemed more pronounced.

When his footsteps could no longer be heard her mother turned slowly to Helen, her lips thin.

'How could you do this to me? After all your poor father's suffering you expect me to accept a German into my life, into the Avenue.'

There was no steam coming from the pot now, or was it just that Helen could not see it in the fading light, for the sun seemed to have vanished. There was no gleam to the silver, just this hard lump in her throat which obstructed her breathing, her vision, her words. She clenched her jaw, pushing away the plate with the meringue as far as she could reach.

'Mother, I love Heine. Even if he were English you would not be pleased. You would not let me go. I know you are using his nationality as a reason to stop my marriage. You can come and stay often. We are not too far away. He is of the right sort of family to please you. Mother, I love him.'

She could feel her throat thickening, aching, and knew that tears were near but she must not cry. There was no time in her life for tears, she had told herself that years ago.

'You love him more than your own mother?' Lydia's voice was harsh, her hand had bunched into a fist.

Helen sat back. She picked up the crumbs around her plate, one by one, placing them in a neat pile along the blue painted edge then she looked up at her mother. The ache in her throat was gone and there was a coldness in its place, a strength, and she spoke clearly as she picked up the plates, laying the knives side by side, neatly, quietly.

'I love Heine as a woman loves a man. You must let me go, Mother.'

'You are disgusting.' Her mother was shouting now, opening her hand and striking the table. 'He is so old. You are only eighteen. The neighbours, what will they say when they know he is a German? Mrs Jones lost Albert, Mrs Sinclair her husband.'

Helen stood up now, standing above her mother, realising that she was taller than the other woman. 'Tell them he is Dutch.'

She wanted to strike her mother for daring to use the grief of her friends to hurt her daughter. The grief of Mrs Jones who had once been plump, of Mrs Sinclair whose eyes were deep set now when they had not been before.

'Tell them he is Dutch,' she repeated, suddenly tired. 'I shall come and see you often, you must come and see us but I shall marry him, and I shall do so in the autumn.'

Her mother spoke again. 'But . . .'

'Mother, I will marry him, even if I have to become pregnant in order to force you to agree. It is your decision.' Helen's mouth was hard and set. Heine would not marry without her mother's consent and she had spent too many years waiting to be loved, waiting to be free. She would say and do whatever was necessary.

Heine stood beyond the patio, on the grass. It eased his leg to stand on something which accommodated the difference in length between the right and left, slight though it was. He drew on his cigarette before holding it away, watching the ash as it fell. He could feel and taste a shred of tobacco between his lips. He removed it with his thumb and forefinger.

He looked at the forsythia which grew up against the wooden fence surrounding the garden and at the two apple trees near to the gate which led out across the field. Had Helen walked through that with her father, he wondered.

It seemed strange that there were no lime trees as there were in his garden. He corrected himself – in his parents' garden. Momentarily he could smell their scent. He drew on his cigarette again and the memory dissipated but at least it had existed and he felt warmed. For the first time for what seemed like years he had found his way back beyond the darkness.

He turned and looked back at the house. A dog barked somewhere in the neighbourhood. The tea had been difficult. Helen should have told her mother, it was not correct to approach their marriage in this way and fear rose in him that he would lose her, this girl who pushed shadows away. Should he go back in? But no, it was for the mother and daughter to decide, as he and his mother had decided.

Yes, you must leave Germany, she had said, her face pinched and anxious, her voice low as they sat before the tiled stove. You must leave for the sake of harmony in this house. Your father is a good man. You are also good, but impulsive. He will not change and you will make his position awkward. We love you, Heine, but you must leave.

Heine walked across the lawn, across the path to the forsythia. He threw his cigarette in an arc on to the damp earth to one side and bent to the shrub. There was no scent.

He had left Germany.

He turned and stood, his hands deep in his pockets, his jacket rucked beneath his arms. The dog was still barking in one of the gardens further down the Avenue. He looked up at the sky, it was still blue though the sun was going down slowly. And then he remembered how his own dog had barked like that when his parents had taken him as a child on holiday to one of the North Sea islands. It had barked and barked as his parents waded into the sea in red swimming costumes which reached to their knees. His mother had clasped his father's short sleeve as she tried to keep her balance against the waves but she had brought him down as well. He and his cousin Adam laughed until they ached, and his father and mother had laughed too.

Heine took another cigarette from the packet, tapping it on his nail before lighting it. This time there was no shred of tobacco to become caught between his lips. Again and again he heard that laughter and he knew that his father was a kind man, a precise man, but a man who could not see that the order he craved would only be achieved at great cost. That such order would only be achieved through black boots and brown shirts kicking and pulling and punching until the most common German words would be '*Vorsicht*' and '*Leise sprechen*'.

'Careful and speak softly,' he repeated aloud in English, turning again to the house. Still there was no sign of Helen, but she was here with him, because it was through her that his love for his family had come back to him, for a moment at least.

If they married – but then Heine corrected himself – when they married, for he could not bear to think that they would not, he would take her to Germany because she had made him promise that he would. He touched his leg. He would take her to Hanover, his home town. He would take her to the forest near his home. They would walk beneath the elm, the ash, the beech and the linden and his leg would be less painful there, walking on the softness of mulched, shaded, ground. He would take her to one of the rest houses which were scattered through the forest. They would eat food cooked by the woodsman's wife. Maybe they would see elk, or deer. Yes, he would take his '*Frauchen*', his little wife, to the beauties of his land while they were still untainted.

He drew on the remains of his cigarette, the heat of the enflamed tip warmed his fingers. He would take her to the Kröpcke as he had promised today by the stream and they would sit within that glass-domed café and he would order her coffee topped with whipped cream and shavings of chocolate and watch while she ate enormous cream cakes. He would relax in her pleasure and her youth.

And yes, Helen, he said silently as he ground out his cigarette on the path, yes, I will take you to the land of my birth but I will not take you to Munich where my friends live; where something else is being born which will go far beyond law and order and decency, unless we protest again and again. And I am not there to do my share, because my mother made a decision for me. Or did she, my love? Was I just scared of being hurt again?

The sun was fading now and still Helen had not come for him and so he moved to the low wall which edged the patio. Yes, his father was a kind man and would welcome the wife of his son even though she was English because, after all, she was Aryan. Yes, he was a kind man but was he still proud of his National Socialist membership? Did he still quote Herr Hitler's every utterance as the Austrian toured the country electioneering? Heine was not sure whether he had spoken aloud, shouted aloud.

'*Vorsicht, leise sprechen!*' This time he knew that he spoke aloud but only in a whisper.

Then he heard the back door opening, and turned but did not move, could not move as he saw Helen coming towards him, because he could not tell from her face what their future would be.

CHAPTER 2

Helen waited in the car as Heine walked to the German customs office carrying their passports and the international carnet. They had driven at a leisurely pace for several days through Belgium and it had been the honeymoon they had not yet had time for because Heine had been inundated with work. Only nine months late. She smiled as she ran her hand along the walnut dashboard of the motor car Uncle had lent them for the trip. She had not known life could be like this, that such happiness existed; that there were such nights of love, such days as gentle as a stream in full sun.

The wedding had been quiet. It had not taken place in Hemsham but in London, away from the neighbours. Her mother had not smiled even when Aunt Sarah and Uncle Harry had said how much they liked Heine.

He looks a good steady sort, they had said, with a damn sight more breeding than most and it's something to have a thriving career these days. Helen had seen her mother looking at Heine, her pale eyes hard, but it did not matter now, she had Heine and their future, so full, so good. It swept memories to one side.

Now the birds sang from the branches of the trees, which were too far from her to give shade as she watched Heine talk to the German border officials. He had become quiet as they approached the customs post and she had watched as he gripped the wheel, his face becoming still, and she had heard him say through lips that barely moved, 'So my darling, we enter the land of my countrymen, most of whom seem to have pebbles for eyes and cauliflowers for ears.'

Helen turned now to look at the slender pole which hung between two posts and barred their entry to Germany. What was this country like? What were his parents like?

She heard his uneven footsteps on the road and turned,

watching as he walked back to the car, his limp rather less noticeable than it had been last year. She smiled because he was smiling, the tension gone from his face, his body. The hot June sun was burning in through the windscreen of the car but it did not matter for soon they would be moving again. And soon she would meet the woman who had sent letters greeting her into the family and bone china handled fruit knives as a wedding present which her mother had sniffed at and polished up on her apron. Heine would meet his father again, and last night beneath the light sheet she had said that he should be gentle, for, after all, it was only politics which divided the two men, not years of struggle. She had not understood his silence but he had promised, and said bless you for being nineteen.

Heine eased himself behind the steering wheel and drove her past verges full of poppies, cornflowers, brown-eyed Susan and Queen Anne's lace and entered villages down avenues bordered by orchards flushed with cherries, apples and pears. They swept through streets of black and white houses with window-boxes of petunias or geraniums. They stopped and ate sausage and bread in the car watching girls with coiled blonde hair throwing corn to geese, before easing themselves from their seats and walking to the village ponds, throwing their crusts to swans and brown ducks.

They stayed overnight in a room with a balcony and the next day they drove alongside fields of tall rye which swayed in the breeze and darkened as the clouds swirled briefly between earth and sun. Over to the east of the road hay was being pitched into wagons drawn first by horses on the lower slopes then oxen as the fields became steeper. Helen wished that she could take photographs as Heine was doing and he promised that on their return he would show her. He pushed strawberries into her mouth and kissed her and she could taste the strawberries on his lips too.

Soon they drove through sugar beet fields where women and children hoed between the rows and Heine said that they would be at his parents' home soon and fell silent. But Helen would not let him sink again and made him tell her of the beet women. He told of how they had come after the war from the East; from Poland and Silesia to work on German farms during the beet harvest, for here they did not starve – not quite. He told of how they had married farmworkers and settled in condemned farmhouses where they were secure as long as they stayed bound to the farmer. He stopped the car and pointed to a plot of land on which a woman and two children worked.

'I used to watch them before I went to Munich, wondering how they could bear it. In the spring they single out the small plants. In the summer they hoe the weeds as they are doing now and in the autumn they pull out the beet.'

Helen peered forward, trying to see past him but there was no room so she opened the door and stood looking. She preferred the fresh air, it made her feel less nauseous but she would not tell him about that, not yet. The wind was brisker now, across the flatter lands. Heine turned off the engine and he too came and stood and looked.

'I took many photographs, especially of the children. They start work at the age of six and here our winters come early and are not like English ones. I would see them tossing the beets into the carts in the snow and ice and hear their coughs. I exhibited the photographs in Munich but what can be done? It is, and was, work in a time of no work. It is food in a time of no food.' He looked over to a clump of cottages in the distance. 'I took photographs inside too, of the one large stew pot in the centre of the table, the spoons which were dug in all at once by thin armed, thin faced people.'

He turned again to the beet fields. 'I felt so fortunate that I was not a beet picker, that I had the time and energy to think; something which is denied to these people. But now I wonder.'

Helen grasped his arm. 'Come along, my love, the sun is out, this is our honeymoon. Or would you perhaps like us to move back here; pull beet, hoe, plant?' She shook him and smiled, willing him to laugh and he did, and he kissed her and said against her mouth that no, no one in his family would ever have to hoe or pull beet and that while she was with him she kept the shadows from him.

The village where his family lived was to the west of Hanover and his mother met them at the door, holding Heine to her, her blonde-white hair folded into a pleat, her face buried in his shoulder.

'Mutti,' he said. 'Oh Mutti.'

Helen knew then just how much Heine loved his mother because he cried.

She turned and looked over the village, at the church, the

barns, the tall poplars, the houses, the window-boxes and wondered what a mother's soft arms were like. She looked to either side of Heine's tall house and saw the lime trees, those same trees that Heine had talked about throughout the winter and as spring approached.

She looked up at the long eaves which he said dripped heavy thawed snow in the spring and knew that when they entered the house they would go into the sitting-room and sit on red brocade settees with carved wooden arms, and that there would be a portrait of his grandfather above the sideboard. She knew too that the room would be dark because of blinds drawn halfway down the window to protect the red carpet from the sun. And it was just as she imagined it would be when they followed his mother into the room from the hall except for the muslin curtains which she had forgotten would be hung in the summer.

That night they slept in the room which had always been Heine's. The bed was large and there was a shelf full of lead soldiers.

'Painted by me,' Heine said, 'when I was nine.'

'So clever, my love,' she murmured against his neck. The moonlight was bright in the room and she could see the stove clearly but not the colours of the tiles. The brass knobs of its doors gleamed as she listened to him telling her of the *Zuckertüte* he had carried to school on his first day and she imagined the rolled cone of cardboard filled with sweets and laughed when he said it had not lasted much more than an hour. 'Pig;' she said and laughed again when he told her how he and his cousin Adam had hunted for acorns to feed the pig which was growing larger and larger down in the orchard at the edge of the village.

He did not talk of his father who was away until tomorrow night but of the forest he wanted to take her to and then he kissed her, then again more strongly, and she felt passion rise in her until it matched his because she no longer heard her mother's words. You are disgusting.

The moon was behind cloud while Heine slept and she lay full and relaxed, with the feel of him still on her skin. She stretched, and knew that Heine had been right to marry according to old German country customs. She had laughed when he had insisted that a rising moon promises good fortune while a moon on the wane drains it from you. How Wednesday and Friday were reserved for widows, and she had said that Saturday had been in her mind anyway.

So they had married when the moon was rising and she knew without doubt now that good fortune was to be theirs; her pregnancy had been confirmed before they left England. But it was news which was hers alone for she had waited to tell Heine until they arrived. He would hear in his beloved forest tomorrow.

At breakfast his mother smiled at Helen and spoke in slow but clear English.

Ilse, who helped in the house, brought a jug of coffee, smiling and greeting Heine.

He smiled at her. 'How is Hans?'

'Very well, Herr Weber,' Ilse replied, placing the coffee jug before Frau Weber. 'He keeps the garden as nicely as ever, I think. Still a few weeds but not too many.'

They all laughed.

'You slept with comfort?' his mother asked as Ilse left the room. She poured coffee into large cups and held her hand to Heine's face as he stopped to kiss her.

Helen answered. 'Oh yes, thank you. The bed was fine and we didn't wake until we heard the cart go down the lane. It is very quiet here.'

There was cream for the coffee and Helen poured it from the white jug, watching it sink then swirl as she stirred. The coffee was hot and strong and the steam dampened her face as she drank.

Frau Weber turned to Heine. 'My dear, your father rang late last night. He will not be back now until tomorrow. He is sorry, so sorry, but he has a meeting.' She paused and Helen watched her place her hand over her son's as he stretched back in his chair which was at her right hand, opposite Helen. Her full sleeves were gathered at the wrist and a Zircon brooch was fastened at her throat. 'Just a meeting, you understand, but one he cannot miss, the election is too close, you see.' She paused as Heine nodded but did not speak and then she smiled at Helen.

'And now you still take your beautiful young wife to show her our forests, our woods?'

Heine looked at his mother. 'No, Mutti, not now. We will go

tomorrow. Today perhaps we shall go by train to Hanover. As you say, the day for casting votes is close and maybe my English wife should see how we in Germany conduct our elections, while we still have them?'

'Heine.' Helen's voice was loud, for she could see the darkening of his mother's eyes, the tension in her full face. He was so like his mother; the same lips, the same blue eyes, blond hair, proud face. The same lines around the eyes and mouth.

'Heine,' her voice was softer now. 'Yes, I should love to go to Hanover, to drink coffee topped with cream as you promised a year ago, do you remember?' She remembered the parapet, the sticks racing on the current and from his softening face she knew that he did too. Perhaps her news should not wait until the forest, it was needed today to lift the darkness which was easing into his face.

The train journey took little time and as they rattled and jolted he pointed to the forest in the far distance through a window which was dust spattered. She could not see the trees, just a darkening of the horizon but there was such longing in his face.

'Why don't we go there today?' Helen urged. 'You want to go so much.'

'No, I will need the forest on the day that I meet my father again. It gives me strength, I think.'

Helen grasped his arm. 'I'll be with you, my darling.'

'I know, and for that I thank God. You are my lightness, a breeze that sweeps the dark shadows away.' Suddenly he laughed, a loud long laugh and the old man who sat in the carriage with them lifted his head from the paper but could not follow their conversation for it was in English.

'I think perhaps I get, how you say, carried away. Dark shadow is altogether too poetical, my love. Let us just say that I look forward to seeing my young wife drinking her first glass of coffee at the Konditorei.'

Helen laughed now, poking his arm. 'Just because you want to see me with a white moustache, you bully.'

Hanover was busy, but not as busy as London and there were no trolley buses, just trams and cars which, it seemed to Helen, barely missed one another or the pedestrians, especially this nervous English girl. They crossed the Ernst-August-Platz and then the Georgstrasse and Helen pulled at Heine to make him hurry because of the noise and speed of the traffic. She could not adjust to looking for cars coming towards them on the right-hand side of the road.

There was no free table at the glass-domed Kröpcke but Heine spoke to the Manager who smiled and shook his hand, because, Heine told her, Herr Busch knew that in the past he had brought many beautiful young women here and had greatly increased the profits of the Kröpcke. They all laughed and the Manager's eyes darted about the room until he saw a movement to their left. He signalled to a waiter, and bowed, and they were ushered to a table whose occupants were leaving.

It was so light beneath the glass dome – for that is all that the building was, just one large glass dome – and Helen thought that her father would have loved it for his vegetables. As she smoothed the napkin on her lap she noticed the women at the surrounding tables; so groomed, so immaculate, smoking cigarettes in ivory and jade holders through pursed red lips. Their perfume thickened the air. Helen felt young and gauche until she saw Heine watching her and heard his words.

'You will always be more beautiful than a hundred of these women put together.'

How did he know what she was thinking, how did he always know? But she was glad that he did. The waiter brought coffee heaped high with whipped cream and topped with shavings of chocolate and Helen laughed, using her spoon to scoop some into her mouth.

'But no, Frau Weber, with the mouth. It must be with the mouth.' Heine's smile was broad.

'You are a cruel man, Herr Weber,' she replied but she did lift the glass by its silver-plated handle and drink, feeling first the cool cream and then the hot coffee. She knew that she had a white moustache because Heine laughed and leaned across, wiping it with his napkin as he told her of his first such coffee, when he was young and in a sailor suit. Young and clean to begin with, young and dirty when he was finished. His parents had laughed too and this time his face did not tense as he spoke of them. They ate cakes which squeezed cream but left some because they were too large.

Later they walked past shops which were smart and rich and in the Post Office she dampened a stamp with a small sponge before writing a card to her mother: 'Having a wonderful time, Love Heine and Helen.'

She did not put, 'Wish you were here'. They walked on towards the Markthalle, a large building with yet another glass roof where it was also light and so full of noise that it seemed to ring around inside her head.

Heine bought her an orange from a stall which had citrus fruits piled high in precise displays. Vegetables were scrubbed and placed in neat rows unlike any she had seen in England. Sausages were hung above the delicatessen counter and Heine told her of the smoking room in the attic of his mother's home and the sausages which she made herself.

'She will take you up there tomorrow to cut some sausage for the picnic before we go to the forest.'

There were lobsters, and shiny black smoked eels which made Helen turn away. There were *Kieler Sprotten* packed as tightly as she and Heine were in the flowing and ebbing crowd.

'My favourite,' Heine said. 'Smoked spratts to you, my non-German-speaking wife.'

Helen stopped and pulled him round. 'But you won't let me learn your language,' she protested.

'I know.' His face was tense again and she wished she had not spoken. 'I do not wish you to become German in any way.'

They walked again, out of the market to a café with a small orchestra playing where Heine ordered *Fleischsalat*, which Helen discovered was meat salad. She was tired now but he was smiling again. It was early afternoon and soon she would tell him of his child; but not here, it should be when they were alone. Heine drank beer with his meal; too much, she thought, as she asked for more coffee. People sat at other tables talking, laughing; the men with napkins tucked into their collars and beer foam around their mouths. Fans whirred lazily above the room, lifting the hair gently on an old man's head. He patted it with a blue-veined age-spotted hand.

As she stirred her coffee discordant sounds stabbed at her thoughts, intruding into the background music, and through the window Helen saw a van with posters on its sides. She heard a metallic voice, distorted by speakers, shouting harshly, but could not understand the words. It moved slowly down the street before pulling in further along into a small square. And now she looked up, shaken, as Heine, his lips drawn tight, suddenly shoved his chair back, scraping it across the tiles. He threw money on the table and pulled her up.

'Let's go and hear too, shall we? Perhaps you should listen to some German.' It was not a question but a statement and his voice was harsh and rapid, as discordant as the metallic voice had been. He stared at her but did not see her.

Helen held back, reaching for her handbag on the table. People were looking and now the fan disturbed her own hair.

'Whatever's wrong, Heine?' she asked, but quietly because they had already created too much fuss.

'For God's sake, just come on.' He grasped her hand, knocking the table as he brushed past the waiter, and now she followed because silence had fallen in the café.

He did not let go of her as he rushed along the street towards the crowd that was gathering around the parked van. He did not let go even when they were standing amongst the crowd which stood still and listened as the man with short hair spoke. But her hand hurt because he was holding it so tightly and he did not hear when she asked him to be gentle. She could smell the beer as he breathed hard.

'What is the matter, Heine, for heaven's sake?'

He looked at her then but his eyes were not seeing her.

'Nazis are the matter.' His voice was low and cold.

'Heine, you promised. Your mother. Our honeymoon. You must not cause trouble.' Helen clutched at his sleeve but only with one hand for he still held on to the other.

No, I must not cause trouble, Heine thought. No, none of us must cause trouble, or we get hurt. Yes, we get very badly hurt. He could hear Helen, he could feel her hand and he must not let go, no. He must never let go because she was sanity in this world which was around him again and which was reaching out, engulfing him, suffocating him.

He started to return through the crowd, turning from the man who spoke of a Germany that had been betrayed in 1918 from within. Who spoke of the armistice which meant that the war was not at an end for Germany. Heine pulled Helen along too but there were more people now. He pushed, twisted and turned, always moving towards the thinning edge that he knew was there. He could still hear the voice, even though he did not want to.

'Germany will regain its lost territories. Herr Hitler will end unemployment, end despair. End the contamination of the Aryan race by the *Juden* traitors. You voted for us in 1930, you gave us a National Socialist landslide in the Reichstag elections. Vote for us again so that we can restore law and order. Restore economic stability. Cleanse our nation.'

But they were through now, there was room to breathe, there was light, and Heine moved quickly, still holding Helen's hand until he could no longer hear the man who told people what they wanted to hear. Yes, that was the danger; jobs, stability, pride – but at what cost? Dear God, surely they would not gain more power? Surely to God, that could not happen?

Heine turned now and looked at the growing crowd standing silently around the speaker.

'It's all the other things,' he shouted at Helen, holding her shoulders now. 'It's all the other things that are written, all the brown-shirted thugs who kick and push and kill. It's that maniac Hitler. If they vote for him in July then it is the beginning of the end. There will be no more freedom, no more Germany, just brutality.'

His breath was full of beer and Helen shouted back.

'You're drunk. You're drunk. Why can't you stop being so serious? We love one another, think of that. This is all just politics. Only politics.' Fear stirred deep inside her because she was outside his life when he was like this. She could not reach him. She was alone.

There was silence then between them until Heine held her to him. 'I'm not drunk, Helen. But you are right. I should think of love more often. You are also right that this is just politics. Please God, that it stays just that.'

They walked on back to the station now, with the sun lower and the breeze cool and Helen did not want to tell him of the baby, not today, not like this. Perhaps tomorrow.

Heine held Helen's arm, feeling her warmth, her flesh beneath the blouse, and loved her. With her he could learn to laugh as he had once done and was beginning to do again. And after all, she was right, it was just politics and he was living in England now. He wouldn't think of Munich. Perhaps, after all, it had not really been as he remembered it, perhaps there had not been any violence, perhaps the *Kampfzeit*, the Nazis' time of struggle, had been just a nightmare he had imagined but his leg ached as they hurried for the train.

The next morning Helen followed Frau Weber up steep stairs to the attic which ran the width of the large house. The windows at either end let in the light from the fine June day and as they entered Helen breathed in the smell of stored fruit from the orchard which she could see when she peered through the window. The village looked so small, the trees even smaller and she could hear no noise.

'Through that small door is the linen cupboard,' Frau Weber said, smoothing her hands down her apron. 'It is there that we keep the winter quilts and over there in that corner is our store for all that we need each year for Christmas. Perhaps you can smell the candles. They are special; they are honey wax.'

Helen smelt them as she approached the corner; their scent hung rich on the air.

'One day perhaps you can come back to our land for Christmas. I would like that. This . . .' Frau Weber paused. 'This difficulty between father and son cannot go on. Their squabble will die as the politics die. It is just a silliness between them.' Helen stopped, she could not go where the eaves sloped. It was too dark, like her mother's cupboard. She turned, holding on to the post, feeling its roughness, wanting cool air.

'Yes, it will pass. You're right, I'm sure it will pass,' she said, breathing deeply, watching as the older woman took down a small muslin bag which hung from a hook secured to a beam.

'These apple slices will make a cinnamon tart for you tonight. It is Heine's favourite, but then you will know that, my dear Helen.'

Helen eased herself over to the window; it was light here, so light. The window ledge was warm, the grained wood worn smooth. She rubbed her hands along it, pushing the darkness away. A butterfly was beating its wings against the glass and she opened the window, cupping her hand around it, feeling it fluttering against her skin. She opened her hands and threw it out into the windless air, watching as it flew its jagged path to safety.

'Come now, my child. I will take you to the smoke room and then we shall cut some sausage for your picnic. I am glad that you go to the woods. It is good for his soul.'

Helen shut the window, still looking at the butterfly until it disappeared against the green and brown of the lime trees; only then did she turn and follow her mother-in-law.

She was glad that today they would be far from other people.

They drove the motor car to the forest and walked down clearly marked paths. Heine carried the rucksack with two folding canvas chairs strapped to it but Helen knew that she would lie on the ground when they stopped and look up at the sky through the branches of the chestnut, beech, elm, lime and ash. They passed beech trees which had been felled in November and left to bleach. She climbed over a newly hewn pine and her shoes and stockings became coated with sawdust which brushed off easily for it was so dry, and the trees' scent, so fresh and clean, clung to her hands and clothes. She lifted them to her face and breathed in deeply.

Heine laughed and kissed her and his happiness loosened his face. He showed her where the plantations of spruce were being grown for Christmas trees and she hoped that one day they would come for Christmas. But she said nothing because she did not want to draw any shade close to him today.

He reached into the rucksack and pulled out two apples, tossing one to her. She bit into the crisp flesh and juice ran down her chin. He reached forward and wiped it with his finger before taking her hand and walking on again, limping less on the soft ground.

'The Germans care deeply for their forests,' he told her. 'In ancient times we stripped our land almost bare but the wind punished us and blew away soil and seed, as is now happening in the middle of America. We learned that we must restore our forests to coax the wind to drop its rain. The forests then held back the water so that it did not rush away and so now the trees have a special place in German hearts.'

'Especially in yours, my love,' she said as she took another bite, watching his face as he looked at the sawn logs neatly stacked in piles to their right.

'Yes, I have always loved the forest. It is cool, and no matter how many people there are, it is quiet. I love the mythology also. Did you know, my English Helen, that the beech is Wotan's tree and the oak belongs to the god of thunder? Then there is the raven who has the task of flying through the trees warning both man and beast that the gods are about to ride past and they must flee to their homes and not intrude on holy secrets.'

'And you of course have seen this raven?' Helen laughed.

'Indeed, everyone has seen the raven, and heard it too. It comes in the form of a storm, with wind blowing and the skies exploding in thunder and lightning. And who stays out to see the gods? No one.' Heine had lowered his voice and now swung round. 'Do you?'

His arms were round her, and he blew into her neck, dug his fingers into her ribs until she pleaded for mercy. They ate their picnic beneath the trees, not at one of the rest-houses, and then Helen lay on the ground, her green skirt and shirt dusty and spiked with pine needles, but she did not care and neither did Heine, for he lay with her. They had not used the canvas chairs.

He stroked her hair, pulling at the curls which sprang back as they had been.

'I love your dark, dark hair, your dark, dark eyes, your lips, so full, your skin so smooth,' he breathed into her neck.

'And I love your blond hair, your eyes, your mouth,' she whispered, looking up at the sky through the conifer branches. The raven was far away today, she thought. Far far away.

'I am having our baby,' she said into his hair. 'Will he have blond hair and dark eyes, I wonder?'

Heine made no movement. She could not even feel his breath on her neck and then he gripped her tightly.

'I should have known. How stupid of me, my precious darling. I should have known.' He sat up then, looking down at her, his eyes taking in the darkness beneath her eyes, the thickening waist. And then he held her so that she should not see his face, because how could this child, this girl he had married, have a child? It was a miracle somehow, a joy, an anxiety. Would she be all right? Was she strong enough?

He gripped her tightly, seeing the trees and the shadows that played beneath their branches. He had never thought in terms of a child. Just in terms of Helen. How could he bear to share her?

She turned to him then. 'I love you so much.' She looked into his eyes and saw pleasure, but something else as well. She kissed his lids, his cheeks, his lips. 'Are you pleased my love?'

She waited as he turned on to his back, throwing his arm over his eyes. 'It's just that it's such a surprise. And of course I'm pleased.' He paused then turned and kissed her again with his eyes shut.

Later they walked slowly back to the motor car. Helen loved the feel of his arm around her. Would it be a boy or a girl, she wondered, able now to think of the baby, now that she had told Heine, now that it was a shared joy. They passed a rest-house and flaxen-haired children were running round the hewn tables and chairs: their parents were drinking beer and watching. Helen turned to Heine who was also watching.

'In December, my love, we shall know our child. We shall hold it and know it,' she said and he bent down and kissed her.

Heine's father kissed her on both cheeks and shook his son's hand, holding his arm, squeezing it. They sat down at the heavy oak table in the dining-room. It was a dark panelled room which seemed to suck away the light from the yellowed shaded lamps set above the table and on the walls. They ate soup made from locally grown asparagus, though not from their own garden, Herr Weber told Helen. He asked if they had seen the *Jagdtrophäen* in the rest-houses. The antlers of the buck and the elk, Heine explained when she turned to him, puzzled.

Herr Weber told of the time he had been *Jagdkönig*, the Hunt King of the day, but that now he had little time, and at this point Frau Weber broke in.

'Heine has some excellent news, Wilhelm. There is to be a grandchild in December.'

Herr Weber placed his spoon back in the bowl and pulled down the serviette from his neck. 'My dear son, this is marvellous news. Quite marvellous. We shall drink brandy after the meal but not the little mother, I think.' He smiled at Helen and his face was gentle and kind and she saw a look of Heine in him. Flowers filled a large blue vase on the sideboard behind him.

They ate veal and there was too much for Helen so she sat back and listened to the talk between the father and the mother which she could not understand because it was in German. She looked at Heine who was watching her and she smiled and mouthed, 'I love you. I love you.'

And Heine knew that she did and smiled as he drank the dry

cool wine, feeling the crystal against his lips, remembering the clear ringing sound the glass had made when he had licked his finger as a child and run it round the edge. In that moment his anxiety faded and all that remained was joy, for she had opened up his past to him through her love and would continue to do so. It was a love which would expand to include the child rather than dividing itself into two.

The cinnamon tart was good, very good and Helen knew she must learn how to make it.

Herr Weber had been speaking to his wife and now he turned to Helen but spoke in German until he corrected himself. His wine glass was empty and he reached for the bottle as he began again, this time in careful English. He also refilled Heine's glass.

'I was saying before I so rudely forgot your language, my dear, that it is important for an English person to appreciate that Herr Hitler is very concerned with the legality of his actions because, of course, we Germans are a very correct race. I am a solicitor after all. His rise to power will only come about through the due process of law. By the vote. Look at the landslide in 1930.'

Helen looked at Heine. He was holding his glass to the light, turning it round and round in his fingers. She drank some of her own wine.

'I know nothing of politics, Herr Weber,' she replied.

'Indeed, my dear. Helen is too tired to think of such things.' Frau Weber intervened. 'Will you have a little more of the cinnamon tart, my dear? You are eating for two, I think you say in England.'

Heine smiled at Helen and hoped that his father would not now turn to him but he did.

'Heine, you and I have had our differences but even so you must now see that it was through pursuing the legal line that Hitler won over one hundred seats in the Reichstag.' His speech was eager, his face concerned. 'And you must see that he offers us what we need. Law and order, progress, stability. July is going to be a month of greatest importance for us. We expect over thirty-five per cent of the vote, my son. Is that not saying something to you? The people want it, Heine. Six million unemployed, a world slump. Strength is what we need.'

'Yes, Father,' Heine said for he had promised his wife, his mother.

'A strong man who is mindful of legality.' Herr Weber paused, sitting up straighter, his hand reaching out towards Heine.

'Yes, Father,' Heine said but his thoughts replied that until now there was no punishment without law. Will it be the same when your leader is in power? Will there even need to be a crime? Won't there just be punishment? I can remember Munich too well and I think you do too. That is why you are speaking to me like this. Trying to make sense of it too. I hope so.

'You see, dear boy, there is anarchy on our streets. We need strength to combat the unions, the dissidents. Our young people are leaving as you have done. We will become a land of old people, defenceless against our enemies both inside and out.'

'Yes, Father.' But silently he groaned. Don't you know why I left? And can't you see, can't you read? What about the solution Hitler propagates for racial purity? What about *Lebensraum*; living space? What about another war? What about Munich? What about the exhibition which was defiled by your brownshirts because my brilliant photographer friend is a *Jude*, a Jew? What about my arm which is still stiff from the beating they gave me because I interfered?

What about the socialist meeting I attended in Munich? what about the iron bar wielded oh so legally by your party members? It broke my leg in three places, Father. How can you excuse that? It was a real question which Heine asked in his mind. One that he had asked his father in January 1930 which was when his mother had sent him from Germany.

His father's kind, honest face had been confused, had been desperate because he had not been able to excuse what had happened, but neither could he believe that it was anything more than an aberration. He would not listen when Heine told him it was the norm.

Heine leaned over to his father now and covered his hand with his own. 'I love you, Father. Be careful. Be very, very careful.' He rose. 'Helen, you look tired, my darling. I'll take you up to bed now.'

He turned to his mother and father. 'Please excuse me from

the brandy. I also am tired and I have my family to think of now.' He smiled at them, at Helen, at his child.

Helen held him close and at last he slept, but she could not for he had told her about Munich and now at last she understood the reality of politics. She did not want to though. Oh God, no, she did not want to, because she was nineteen and in love and pregnant. She wanted her husband for herself, she wanted the peace of their lives to go on. She wanted the photographs they took, the child they had, the walks, the laughter to be everything. She held him tighter still. How much of his life would it take?

CHAPTER 3

In England in August 1932 Heine received a letter from one of his Munich friends telling him that German voters had handed Hitler's brownshirts an election victory on 31 July and the Nazis now formed the biggest party.

'But he doesn't have a majority?' Helen asked because she had been listening to Heine since they had returned to England and now understood the political situation.

He put down the letter on the kitchen table. 'No, at least he does not have that.'

'So, there is still hope,' she insisted, shaking his hand, leaning over and stroking his face. 'Come on, Heine, you must be brave, you must go on. We must go on.' Because she had decided that whatever battles had to be fought they would fight them together. She paused. 'Listen, you were telling me about the changing mood of photography. If you want me to be able to help with the work, we must concentrate.'

She rose from the table and moved round to him, putting her arm along his shoulder. 'This baby is getting bigger and bigger. He won't wait for something that might never happen. And it might never happen, you know. Hitler can still be defeated – contained. If he's as bad as you say the German people won't let him take power.' She held his head against her. 'Now, my love, what were you saying about imagery.'

She felt his hand on her swelling abdomen and then his voice, muffled as he spoke into her body. 'I try for a greater range of imagery. I like strong direct photographs with the emphasis on design instead of soft focus and tranquil scenes. Now is a time for realism.' He sat up straight now and used his hands to express his ideas and Helen felt relief ease into her. She had caught his interest, kept him away from the shadows for now.

He told her that he had been taught to use an overall soft focus to provide atmosphere, to use a sombre tone for mood landscapes, to use soft and subtle nuances of light and shade, but in Munich he had become interested in the 'New Objectivity' which he thought had grown out of the harsh reality of the war. He told her that Martin Weiss, his Jewish friend whose photographs had been defiled, considered it wrong to allow the ego of the photographer to come between the camera and subject and, though others thought that this technique was too cold he did not.

'I would want a picture to say something about myself, my views, my feelings, the feelings of others involved,' Helen said.

'Well, that is another style and a successful one. Perhaps it is as well that we have different opinions,' he said.

They walked to the darkroom which had originally been the dining-room. 'We should have another lesson with the Leica. I have no appointments scheduled for this afternoon so we shall do it then, but now, my darling, let us go through again the procedures of developing and printing.'

He stood at the door as he waited for her to repeat all that she had learned throughout the last two weeks.

'You must understand the principles, you must have knowledge,' he told her as she protested.

And so she explained how black and white films contain light-sensitive crystals which darken after exposure, and how development is required to make the image visible.

'The longer the exposure the greater darkening of the crystals,' she added. 'Development is required to make the image permanent and visible.'

'Good girl.' Heine moved into the darkroom showing her the wet and dry areas, the enlarger, the processing equipment, the dryer, pausing at the print finishing area. There was still some work left to do on the photographs he had taken last night at the introduction of the trial floodlighting of some London buildings. He told her how he had concentrated on the traffic chaos because it was important to see a situation from an unusual angle.

'You can help me,' he said, setting the working surface at thirty degrees. 'I want to get them delivered to the magazine office at lunchtime, then we can spend the afternoon in the park with the camera.'

'Remember Mother is coming to stay for the weekend. She will be arriving tonight.' Helen settled herself on to the stool, peering at the photograph of black cars and angry drivers. She reached for the trimmer from beneath the bench, confident, sure, eager to begin work, work that she could share with him. She eased her back which ached more each day as her child grew within her.

'My love, how could I forget that your mother comes?' Heine shook his head but his smile was visible in the dim red light of the room. 'Every time I go into the spare room I am reminded of her.'

Helen laughed and had to put the photograph to one side. 'I know, she has certainly staked her claim, but how could I say anything?'

She pictured the dressing table with her mother's brushes, her photographs, her pots for hairnets and pins. She had stayed on their return from Germany after Helen had written to ask her, saying she was to become a grandmother and they would like to see her. It had seemed impossible to do anything else. Her mother had turned the spare room into a replica of her own bedroom, saying as she did so that it was as well to be comfortable since she would be spending so much time here, especially now there was a grandchild on the way. She had been brisk but not unkind and Helen had remembered Frau Weber's soft arms and wondered if there would be a future after all for mother and daughter.

Christoph was born on 1 December and Heine looked down at his son and marvelled at the perfect fingernails, the perfect feet and the softness of his skin, the lightness of his hair, while Helen looked at her husband and saw love in his eyes for his son and wondered if her father's eyes had been the same.

When Christoph was nearly two months old, on 30 January, Hitler became Chancellor of Germany, and while Helen held the baby, stroking skin she could hardly feel, kissing hair which was gossamer fine, she reminded Heine that all was not bad in the world. Hadn't the British Prime Minister ordered a review of the Government's policies on unemployment after the marches and riots? Hadn't Roosevelt won the United States elections with a landslide and promised a New Deal? Hadn't two of his photographs been taken by an American magazine? And after all, in Germany it might all pass.

'And look,' she said, 'Christoph is smiling, I'm sure he's smiling. Here, hold him and see for yourself.' She pushed the baby towards Heine who took him and looked but did not seem to see, and Helen touched the fine crocheted shawl, feeling its pattern, its warmth. 'I'm sure he's smiling,' she said again, touching her husband's hand, feeling him at last lift hers and put it to his lips, but despair still remained in his eyes and Helen knew that she was still outside his pain.

When Christoph was nearly four months old the Enabling Act was passed in Germany allowing Hitler, rather than the President, to rule by decree.

'It sets him above the law, you see,' Heine said, his voice flat, his eyes dark, and Helen wondered what Herr Weber must be feeling but Heine would not write to him; he would only pace the flat, leaving work unfinished so that Helen felt she must work until midnight in the darkroom to complete his assignments for him after she had put Christoph to bed.

When Christoph was nearly six months old books were burned in the streets of Germany, unions were harassed and in London the blossom bloomed and Helen printed and developed films and delivered them because Heine did not have time. He was too busy writing letters to Munich and meeting friends in dark pubs.

When Christoph was seven months old he reached forward and pulled Helen towards him and laughed but Heine did not notice because opposition parties had been ousted from the Reichstag in June and a month later Hitler announced plans to sterilise imperfect Germans. Helen took a Leica and carried out two of Heine's assignments and the results were as good. And so, increasingly, she took over his workload too and did not mind because she had told herself that she would join the battle if that would help this man she loved so much.

In August her mother came to stay and Helen had to take her out to photograph damage caused by the gales which had hit England, and that night, when the wind blew again and the thunder roared and her mother was asleep, she crooned to Christoph and told him of the raven who was warning them to stay in in case they saw the gods go by. She looked up and smiled at Heine when he came home wet and cold.

'Did you see the gods going about their holy business, my

darling?' she whispered, lifting her face for his kiss. Knowing that for her he was the god.

He laughed. 'Only one of your English coppers getting very wet as he paced his beat.'

Helen made him tea and he sat by the gas fire which plopped and spluttered, cupping the drink in his hand.

'Your mother is asleep?'

'My mother would sleep through a deluge of ravens,' she said softly. 'Christoph has not woken since nine and I have finished trimming the hotel photograph. Did you have a good meeting?' Helen sat down on the worn carpet in front of the fire. The heat was comforting. She clutched her knees, seeing the dust lying on the mantelpiece, on the hearth.

'Yes, we are trying to find firms that will sponsor those that are going to have to leave Germany if it goes on and on. So far in America and to some extent here we have been fortunate. But there is a great deal to do and unemployment is a problem in both countries. I think the time we have and the dissidents have and the Jews have, is short.'

He put his mug down on the table and leaned back, his hands clasped behind his head.

'Oh God, it's the studio portrait tomorrow, Helen. I know I said I would do it but I can't. I have to be at the Embassy by ten. Darling, can you?'

Helen nodded, laying her head on her knees. Yes, she would do it, as she did so many others. She would have to tell her mother that Heine was out on another assignment again. It seemed easier to lie than to try and make her understand that some things were more important than making a profit. And they were, in this case they were, because people were being saved and Heine's eyes were no longer dark, his steps were no longer heavy. At last, he had told her in the spring, he felt as though he was doing something again, actually helping people threatened by Hitler's regime.

In September one of his Munich friends arrived at their flat with no money and few clothes but many bruises and cuts because storm troopers armed with revolvers and piping were roaming the German streets looking for Jews and Communists and liberals. He told them of a concentration camp which had been opened for these 'dissidents'.

'It is at Dachau,' he said.

Helen made up the bed for Isaac in the spare room and listened to his story and cried. That evening they ate a stew which she had padded out with vegetables and she told them that Christoph had said 'dada' and that Heine really did need to make sure he arrived at the art gallery promptly at ten tomorrow because they were leaving up the paintings until he arrived. They particularly wanted him because he had produced such fine work for the catalogue last year. She said nothing when he explained that he had other more important things to do; just nodded and smiled at Isaac and handed him more rice. She had overcooked it and it clung to the spoon in a lump; so white against the old stained table spoon.

That night in bed she told Heine that he must do tomorrow's assignment because she could not, she was already booked to cover the meeting at Whitechapel. Her voice was calm but high as she told him that they would have to earn more money if the bills were to be paid and there was Isaac to feed now. He became angry and told her that she was being trivial; there was a vast problem, or was she too much of a child to see? His voice was tight but low, because they were not alone in their flat, were they?

Headlights flashed across the ceiling and walls from the passing traffic and Helen watched as the brass picture frame over by the door glinted, caught by the lights of one car and then another.

Her voice remained calm as she answered but the effort made her hands clench. She breathed slowly.

'Is it childish to deal in reality?' she said. 'If we are to help your friends we need to work to pay for it or our child will suffer. You prefer reality. You told me.' She pointed to the glinting frame which held the photograph he had taken of London Bridge. 'You have used no soft focus there, Heine. There is no place for it in our lives at this moment. We need to eat, and in order to do that we need to work. We both need to work. You have responsibility to your family as well as your friends.'

That night she did not sleep but lay on her side, tense with anger and disappointment, aware that he was not asleep either; but she could not touch him, she could not bridge the distance between them because suddenly she was tired. So tired and the sun of their German honeymoon seemed too far away.

That morning they dressed without speaking and neither looked at the other's nakedness. Her tiredness hung heavily on her. In the kitchen she poured his tea, watching the tea leaves fill the strainer. Still they did not speak. She fed soldiers to Christoph, then watched as Heine went to the studio and returned with his cameras.

He stood in the doorway, leaning against the doorpost, his eyes watching Christoph as he dropped his toast on the floor and smeared butter all over his face. His shrieks and banging were the only noise between them.

Helen leaned back against the sink. It was cool across her back. She looked at the brown lino which was worn in the far corner, the strands of hemp showing through.

Heine spoke. 'You are right, my little wife. I'm sorry.' He blew her a kiss and she watched him as he left and thought, I am not a little wife, I am an adult.

In December 1934 Christoph was two. In 1935 conscription came into being in Germany, Hitler took possession of the Saar, and Helen's house became even more full of frightened, thin young men. Her mother no longer came to stay because it was not proper amongst so many foreigners and there never seemed to be the time to try and make her understand how necessary it was. How it would not last for ever because Hitler would fall. Surely he would fall?

But her mother should have known it was necessary, Heine told Helen. There wasn't time to make him understand that the distance between mother and daughter was still too wide to discuss such things.

There were camp beds in the sitting-room and the spare room and others were folded up ready for use if necessary in the studio. Heine was eager and young, his limp hardly noticeable. He talked until the early hours with the refugees until they left to go to jobs and countries Heine and his friends had organised. But always new ones came, occasionally bringing wives, sisters, children, and the sunshine of their honeymoon seemed never to have existed.

The refugees were 'placed' but sometimes it was difficult as the flood of those escaping the swastikas and black boots increased and so some stayed on. Each night when she returned from carrying out commissions and Christoph was in bed, they talked over wine and sometimes remembered to speak in English until Helen left to work again or sleep, but she never slept soundly now and her dreams were bleak.

Full of the horrors she had listened to, steeped in loneliness, one night she dreamed of a lichen-covered bridge and hands which held her safe and she woke up crying.

At night Heine crept in beside her and sometimes he would hold her but he was tired, so tired, and so was she. Christoph was passed from one to another and did not know that his father was different to all these uncles.

At the beginning of May in 1935 they had only four staying and on Silver Jubilee Day she helped the neighbours set out trestle tables in the street while red, white and blue bunting hung across the road, and she asked Heine who was sitting at his desk to carry down some cakes and to come and join her and watch his son enjoy himself.

'I am so busy, my darling. I have letters to write.'

He had said that too often and Helen felt the anger come. It crept from every pore of her skin and she knew now that it had been there for months and months but it had not formed into words in her head until now. But why this moment? She did not know, except that she was English and this was an English celebration and she asked nothing of him but that he should join her, as she had for so long joined him. She turned to the window, where they were on a level with the bunting. She watched Mr Frazer who lived above the tobacco shop hauling on a line festooned with flags which stretched from his flat window to Mrs Briggs who lived opposite. Heine had never met them, he did not even know their names.

All she asked was a little of his time for the world which she and their son lived in and he would not give her even that. There were so many other people in their lives, so much that needed doing; but there should be time for happiness as there once was. She smoothed the curtain between her fingers, rubbing up and down, up and down. Then she turned, looking at Hans, Georg, Hermann, Ernst who had been with them for two months.

'You will all come to see how we in England celebrate, and you, Heine, you will come too.' And her voice was firm. She walked to the desk and covered the notepaper that he had pulled towards him. 'You will come because you are part of

England now. You will come because your English-German son needs you there.' The paper was cold and dead, the room was quiet.

Heine looked at her, his eyes puzzled, surprised.

'You will come because you are my husband and I need you there.' Her voice was calm but the anger sounded in her own ears and she wondered when the child inside her had gone and this woman had taken her place.

Helen turned then, walked past Hans standing awkwardly by the door, his face turned from her in embarrassment. She stooped and picked Christoph from his playpen, sitting him on her hip. She did not look back but walked from the door to the studio where she picked up her Leica, for she never went anywhere without it now.

'You will come,' she said as she walked down the stairs feeling so much older than twenty-two. The stairs needed painting. The pushchair had marked the walls and too many hands had felt their way up. Perhaps she would ask Hans and the others to help, and Heine too. But, of course, he would be too busy. As she reached the street the daylight hurt her eyes. The flags were thrashing on their poles in a burst of wind and she turned and looked up at the windows of their flat. Would he come?

He came with the cakes and the jelly and the hats she had cut from coloured paper, and Hans, Georg, Hermann and Ernst came too and they danced throughout the afternoon and evening and Heine bought wine for the street because Helen had worked on five studio portraits in two weeks and for once all the bills had been paid on time.

Helen laughed with Marian, the girl who was married to the greengrocer and gave Helen yesterday's vegetables without charge for the rabbit they both knew she did not have. She had a daughter of four and Helen had photographed her in return. Heine drank with her husband Rob and learned of this for the first time. He kissed his wife though she did not know why, and then sat Christoph on his shoulders and danced him up the street and back again along with the surging crowd. For the first time he met and spoke to their neighbours in the street.

That night he helped Helen to bath Christoph and he said he had not realised he had grown so much and bent over the cot to watch him fall asleep. He had not looked at him for so long; he had not looked at his wife for so long. He must remember that they existed. He must remember that he loved them; that he was responsible for them.

Helen stood in the doorway, glad that at least this room was safe. Its ornaments of trains and dogs and bricks in place on the mantelpiece. This was family territory, to be kept secure for her son. There would be no sleeping bags here, no camp beds.

That night Heine made love to her, slowly, gently, and she wept and told him how much she loved him and he said that she would always be loved by him.

'Will I?' she asked against his shoulder. 'Will Christoph?' She dreamed of the dark cupboard that night.

Helen's photographs of the Silver Jubilee celebrations were bought by an American magazine and she celebrated with champagne. She and Heine had one glass only for there were three others with them, but what did it matter? Isaac's cousin Joseph laughed with them and Wilhelm and Günther too and it was good to see their eyes full of fun, their pain, which tore at Helen daily, gone for just a moment. But then Heine left to meet a contact. Helen watched him leave without surprise for what else had she come to expect? She pushed the bottle with one more glass in it towards the bruised, thin boys who were as young as she was and went to bed alone, for that also she had come to expect.

In 1936 during a January that was dank and cold George V was laid to rest and Helen and her mother lined the route. Christoph was warm in his knitted suit and coat and he wore a black arm band like the rest of the crowd. The mood was sombre. Helen was thoughtful as her mother pointed out King Edward VIII walking behind the gun carriage pulled by sailors because she had read in the letters which came from America of the liaison between Edward and Mrs Simpson. She brushed the hair from her eyes. So even the succession seemed as uncertain as the rest of the world, which darkened as Hitler and Mussolini growled and raged. Peace was never more fragile, Heine had said, and Helen feared that he was right and what would happen then to a German who lived in England?

Her mother held Christoph's hand as Helen lifted him high on to her shoulders.

'That's right, then he can see and tell his own children, poor little mite,' her mother said, glaring at the man behind who clicked his teeth and moved so that he could also see.

'But he won't remember surely? He's only three,' Helen commented.

'You always said you remembered your father taking you to the stream at that age. He was on leave,' her mother said with an edge to her voice, a voice which had been more mellow since Helen had begun to take Christoph to see her every two months. Alone of course. Her mother was looking back at the procession now; it was almost past.

Helen looked up at the grey sky. She must go to the stream and take Christoph. She touched his knee briefly with her ungloved hand. The wind was sharp now and her fingers were becoming numb. She lifted her camera to her eye again and took more photographs because she did not want to think about why she had not thought of going to the stream with Heine.

'You'll get the backs of all these people,' her mother protested.

Helen smiled. 'I know, Mother,' she said as she took more and more, glad of her interruption. 'That's what I wanted to do, to somehow catch the bowed shoulders of the people, the hats being removed, the sadness against the pomp.'

'Oh really, Helen, you don't sound like a mother at all. What is this poor boy growing up into. All he'll know about is camera angles, public meetings, distant views. It's not right. And all those men cluttering up the house. It's just not decent, you know. I can't imagine what your neighbours think.'

Helen didn't know either because she did not ask them. She covered the lens with the cap and shrugged, lifting Christoph down, holding him close.

'We do all right, don't we, my darling? You have lots of uncles and I take you to the swings. And he has his books and toys and his own room when they smoke too much.' She did not add that these days she too stayed in her own room when the processing was finished for there seemed no place for her. But her work was becoming more popular and it enabled them to help more of those persecuted by that mad Austrian.

She lifted him into his pushchair, brushing the hair out of her eyes. 'Anyway, tonight there is no one there, not even Heine. He's taken three of them to Liverpool to board a ship.' Helen pushed a way through the crowd for them both and did not see the smile on her mother's face. The pushchair caught on a lamppost and she heaved at it, pulling it clear.

That night they sat in front of the fire and Helen enjoyed the clean air, the sound of the gas spluttering and hissing, the click of her mother's knitting, and for the first time since last winter she too picked up wool and needles and began a jacket for Christoph. They did not talk but listened to the wireless and then they drank cocoa and said goodnight. Helen was glad that she had replaced the hair brushes, stacked away the camp beds and made the spare room her mother's, just for tonight. As she watched her close the door she realised that this evening she had not been lonely.

As she lay in bed she felt her limbs relax and grow heavy and again she wondered why she had not thought of taking Heine to Hemsham, to the stream. She watched the clouds gust between the moon and earth, blocking the light and releasing it, and faced now the separateness of their lives. She did not ask for Heine's company these days because, with a blown kiss, he would refuse. Too much to do. Too many important things to do, he would say. Some other time when it is over. But when would that ever be, Helen wondered, turning over and holding his pillow to her, pushing back despair, breathing in his scent.

A New York magazine bought Helen's pictures but addressed the letter to H. Weber, Esquire. Heine was pleased at the news and said the cheque would pay the telephone final demand and the extra food bill which was larger still this time.

By August 1936 unemployment was falling in Britain but Hitler's troops had entered the Rhineland and Mosley's Fascists were pinning up anti-Semitic posters in the East End. Helen left Christoph with Marian and went to photograph these and was hit across the face by one of the blackshirts and called a Jewish bitch. She told Heine as the pain throbbed through her face and he said that now she knew how his friends felt, but that their treatment was much worse, and he did not turn from the letter he was writing.

She looked at the back of his head and wanted to scream that she already knew how his friends felt, hadn't she listened to them and cried with them, cooked and washed for them, soothed their nightmares and not resented one moment? No, it was not that she resented but she said nothing, just turned from him and bathed her face in cold water and then slept that night with her back turned to his still body.

The next day she took Marian and her daughter Emily and Christoph on the train to Eastbourne for Bank Holiday Monday. The sun was hot and soaked deep into her skin, reddening her arms and her legs where she had pulled up her skirts. The deckchair dug into the backs of her thighs but she watched Christoph hold his face to the sun and forgot the ache in her cheek. But the sun could not warm the coldness she felt deep inside.

They ate sandwiches curled at the edges and ice-creams which a man in a red and white-striped apron and cardboard top hat dug out of a round tin container with a scoop which he dipped into a jug of water first. Christoph smeared his across his face and up into his hair as well as his mouth but Emily licked hers carefully and her dress was not marked either. Helen took photographs of them both and of Marian and Marian took one of Christoph and Helen together and as the sun at last lost its heat they straggled back to the station.

They took an Underground train from the station and Helen waved goodbye to Marian before climbing the stairs to the flat. No one was there and in Christoph's room his small bed had gone and there were two camp beds. For a moment she felt as though the air had gushed from her body but then something deeper than rage gripped her, mobilised her.

She turned and walked through to her own bedroom and there was the small bed jammed tight next to theirs with his toys on top. She laid her child on their double bed and washed his face and hands, gently soaking his hair while he was asleep. She eased his loose limbs into his pyjamas, then draped the sheets and the two blankets around him, kissing him, smelling the sun still on his skin. And then she left the room.

She walked to the small bedroom and picked up the camp beds, the blankets folded on top, and threw them across the sitting-room, not looking where they fell, not hearing the crash of the vase they hit. She moved then to the darkroom, not able to spare the time to shout the anger that she felt, the outrage, the hurt.

She heaved at the hinged board which Heine had left on one end beneath the sealed window, saying that they had no need of it. But oh God, they had need of it now. Yes, they damn well had need of it now. She dragged it into the bathroom, sweeping Christoph's rubber duck on to the floor, wedging the board on top of the bath. She moved the developer into the bathroom, came back for the enlarger, the chemicals, everything she needed. Finally she dragged the cabinet across the frayed carpet, across the cracked lino in the passage-way into the bathroom too.

She took the chisel, hammer and nails from the cupboard under the sink and wrenched the hardboard from the dark-room windows, going back for the saw when she saw that it was too big for those in the bathroom. Leaning on the hinged top, she sawed the boards to the correct size, then, holding the nails in her mouth, she stood on the edge of the bath and hammered them in. Heine came in then. He stood in the doorway and said, 'What in God's name are you doing, Helen?'

She did not turn but said, 'Get out. Get out before I kill you.' She leaned her head on the wall. It was cold. 'Get out and only come back when I have finished.' There were others there. She could hear them and so he left because she knew he would not care to be embarrassed.

She had to keep the electrical equipment away from the water so she used an extension lead which could be plugged into the hall socket when power was needed. She hung a heavy opaque curtain from a rail above the doorframe. There was already a louvred vent above the door. She turned out the light to check that it was lightproof and it was.

She turned on the light again and ran her hands down her dress. She had not put on an apron and she was dirty but it did not matter. Sweat was running down her back but that did not matter either. She carried in the stool so that she could work at the hinged board comfortably. She lifted the board easily, peering into the bath, knowing that it would be adequate for the wet work, for the cascade system which she had made for herself. She set up the trays one above the other beneath the taps, then watched the water fall from one level to the next and realised that she was crying.

She put the board back and set up the portable red light then went to collect her camera. Using the changing bag, she loaded the film on to the tank reel inside the bag, then put the reel in the tank. Later, much later, she had developed, printed and enlarged the photograph that Marian had taken of her and

Christoph. It was lopsided but they were both smiling, holding hands, and it was full of love. She carried it to the bedroom and took from its frame her wedding photograph, throwing it on the bed. She then inserted the one of herself and her son and placed it on her bedside table. Then she took Christoph's mattress through to his old room, and dragged his bed after her. It caught on the door but she unscrewed the feet and there was room. She took the toys, the books and finally her son, carrying him close to her, whispering into his hair before placing him in his own bed, in his own room. She then sat in the sitting-room, which was also their dining-room, and waited.

Heine came in alone at two in the morning, his face white, his lips tight. His grey jacket was unbuttoned and he smelt of cigarette smoke and beer. He threw his hat on to the square table.

'How dare you?' he said. 'How dare you shame me before my friends? Are you a child that you behave like this?'

He stood before her, looming large, but she was not intimidated. The smell of beer was stronger now and she could hear his breathing, heavy but fast. His keys bulged in his trouser pocket.

'Sit down, Heine,' she said. Her voice was not hard or cold. It held nothing. 'Sit down.'

But he did not and so she stood, pushing herself up from the chair, feeling its wooden arm beneath her hand as she did so. 'I am not a child. Your child is in that room, in his bedroom where he will remain. Is that quite clear?'

Heine shook his head, shrugging his shoulders. 'What a fuss about nothing. Does it matter where a child sleeps?' He pointed to Christoph's room. 'In there, or in our room. What does it matter?'

'It matters to me. I am his mother, he is my responsibility.'

'I am his father, he is mine too. I love him.' Heine's voice was rising, his hand gripped her arm.

'Do you, do you really?' Helen was shouting now. 'So where were you today? Where have you been for the four years of his life? We love you but we don't know you any more.' She pulled from his grasp. 'We were going to fight the battles together.'

He grabbed at her, spun her round. 'You are a child, you see? It is only yourself you care about. Only yourself. Can't you see that we are just fragments in comparison to this great tragedy? Just fragments.' His face was close to hers now and she could smell the cigarette smoke on his breath and the beer, stronger still.

She reached up and gripped his lapels, shaking him backwards and forwards. 'How dare you call my son a fragment? Or me. We are not fragments, we are people. We are your family. You will not ignore us, you will not watch me cooking for your friends, working for money to feed them and then call us fragments.' Her knuckles were white, her voice high, loud, insane. What was she saying, for God's sake? Whose mad voice was this coming from her mouth, shaking the man she loved? What had happened to them?

He slapped her then, breaking her hold on his jacket and she fell across the chair, and for a moment there was silence until Helen turned awkwardly, pushing herself up, aware that the grunting noises she heard came from her. That she was crying like an animal, that her mouth was open and mucus from her nose and eyes were running into it and past it. That she tasted blood in her mouth. She pushed him from her as he came to her, his face shocked.

'I love you, Heine.' Her voice was strange, she could not find the breath to end her words. 'I love you but I wonder whether you love me.'

Heine came towards her again, his arms outstretched, his own eyes full. 'I do love you. I love our son. I'm sorry, so sorry.'

'Don't touch me,' Helen said and backed towards the hall. He mustn't touch her until she had finished. She did not want hands on her, pushing her into cupboards, gripping her in anger. She was tired of it. No, she was not a child or a fragment but a person.

'I insist on becoming a partner. I produce more work than you. I earn more than you. I want it to be offered under my own name.' It was important to her now that she had something of her own, something that would keep her son safe for she could not trust her husband to do so. Somehow she feared that she could not trust him at all any more and it broke her heart because of the loneliness that the thought brought.

He came to her then, holding her, soothing her, stroking her hair which was damp with sweat. 'My love, my love. Forgive me. I love you, love you. Believe me, I love you.'

Helen nodded in his arms, wanting to be soothed, wanting their lives to go back to the sun-filled days when it was simple. But those times had gone, for now at least, and so she said again, 'I must be a partner. I can only rely on myself.'

CHAPTER 4

Helen watched Heine as he turned over the second page of his father's letter. It was a colourless November day in 1938 and her husband looked older, and very tired, but then they both did. His eyes met hers and he reached across for her hand which was already stretching to meet his. The new flat was smaller, the kitchen had damp walls but it had not known their bad years, the pain of a life too full for them to reach out and touch one another as they did so frequently now. It had not heard the blows of that night, the grunting despair of a woman she could not recognise as herself. It had only known Heine as a man who loved his wife and child, who held them as though they must never leave him. A man who had said as he had looked at his wife, sweating, bleeding on that dark night, that life was too short to wait for a time for themselves, that time must be carved out, no matter what else needed doing. That he had been a fool. That he would prove to her that she could trust him.

That night when her lip had split and blood had flowed on to the carpet he had held her, but she had fought. He had soothed her but she had shouted. He had promised her that it was over, that he would make room for her, for his son. That they would be loved as they should be loved but she had not believed him, seeing only the loneliness of the life she had led with her mother and then again with him. Each day, after that night, she had watched and listened as he spoke to her and Christoph. Each day she held herself upright, and had merely nodded when he brought the partnership papers to be signed. Each day throughout 1937 and into 1938 she had watched and waited until, with the coming of spring she had allowed herself to love again and be loved. To trust in this man.

Helen watched now as Heine put the letter on to the small

pine table they had brought from the other flat. They had moved from Alton Mews after Chamberlain landed at Heston Airport in September, two months before, waving his piece of paper, calling to the waiting press and photographers, 'Peace for our time'. Heine had taken no photographs but had driven without stopping, back to London.

He had rushed up the stairs, into the sitting-room, wrenching his coat off, calling out to her that they must now sell the flat as they had talked of doing. It was time to buy the cheaper flat near Stepney and send the balance of their capital to America with Claus, the refugee they were sheltering. He had held her as though he needed support, his hands cold, his face pinched. Chamberlain has not opposed Hitler, he had groaned into her neck before moving past her to the desk, picking Christoph up from the floor, holding him on his knee as he searched for the sale agreement in the large compartment. He had scattered papers on the floor as Helen watched.

We must do as we agreed, he had said, his hands shaking. Hitler will never believe that anyone will stop him. There will be war, but when?

Helen remembered nodding, feeling the chipped gloss paint of the door frame, watching, wondering how much longer peace would remain. Wondering whether England would allow the Weber family to remain in its midst once war was declared or would its people be like some of the neighbours they had danced with at the Jubilee – those who had no longer stopped to talk as the Munich crisis had deepened?

She had watched her husband as he scanned the papers he had prepared for partnership with Claus. There might not be war, she remembered saying. Russia has sided with no one yet, but Heine had not heard. She had run her hand up and down the paintwork again. She would sandpaper and paint and the smell would take thoughts of war away, for a moment at least.

Claus will take our money to America when he goes in April, Heine had said, turning his head, talking to her over his shoulder. He will establish the studio that will support us too. We will go to America if we have to; if war comes and Germans are really not welcome here. But only if you can bear to leave, my darling.

She watched now in her smaller kitchen as Heine put the letter from his father back into the envelope, his face set.

'Is it bad news?' she asked, coming to him, holding him against her, wondering when Claus would be back from the ticket office, when Joseph would wake. He had arrived from Germany only last night, carrying just the ten marks refugees were allowed to take but a firm in the city had been persuaded to sponsor him and so he had been allowed entry. He had cried for his Jewish parents who would not leave their house because it would be confiscated and they would be aliens with no pride, with nothing. He cried for his parents who thought the whirlwind would pass. Would it pass, she wondered. What would Russia do?

'When do you need to collect Christoph?' Heine asked. 'It's band after school today, is it not?'

'We have time. Tell me what is wrong.' Helen looked at the clock. She had one hour until four.

'Father has written, after all these years he has written. He would like us to go and see him before it becomes impossible. He would like to see his grandson and so would Mutti.'

'I'm so glad,' said Helen, speaking carefully because Heine's face was still set and she did not know whether he cared for his father at all. Whether he could forget that they stood on opposing sides. 'But is it safe?'

'Oh yes, it is safe enough because he has vouched for us with officials. He is a Nazi Party member, do you not remember?' But Heine's voice was not bitter as it usually was but quiet, thoughtful.

He pushed her back and looked into her face. 'I promised you after that night when you re-arranged the darkroom' – he grinned now and she did too – 'I promised you that you could always trust me to look after you. I have tried to do that, but now I have something to ask of you.' He took her hand. His cuffs were frayed and a thread of cotton drifted on to her green flowered overall.

He looked away now at the clock. Helen checked too. There was half an hour.

'You have done so much for me and my countrymen. I have to ask you to do one last thing. Father wants us to go, but he also wants us to take something to him that a man will bring, if we agree.'

Helen picked up the letter taking it from the envelope but it was in German.

'Something has happened to my father. He has changed but he has to be careful with his words.' Heine took her hands in his, crushing the letter as he did so. His voice was slow. 'He has, he says, realised the meaning of my words on our last visit. That he hopes my leg has healed as well as his sight and his hearing. He wants us to take a camera, my love. He doesn't say so but I know what he means, and I know which one he wants. It has a wide aperture lens which takes photographs indoors without flash. Ideal for working inside courtrooms, at meetings.'

'But won't we be stopped at the border? Photography is allowed only with a permit, isn't it?'

Heine did not answer and there was only the sound of the clock. They had fifteen minutes and then Helen realised what Herr Weber had meant and she sat down, her hands cold. The camera was for secret work. His sight was better and his hearing. Of course she knew what he meant.

'You see what I mean when I say I cannot promise to keep you safe – but I need you with me. You are English, they have to be more careful with foreigners. We are not yet at war.'

Helen picked the white cotton thread off her apron, curled it round and round her finger, watching her fingertip turn to purple. It was four o'clock.

'But most of all I need you because you will give me courage.'

She walked alone to the school and stood at the railings waiting for Christoph. The children called him Chris and thought his father was Dutch. He ran towards her, past the white-chalked hopscotch squares, his cap on the back of his head, his blond hair too long. His smile was wide and his eyes were her father's: dark brown.

'Did you bake the conkers today?' she shouted as he reached her but did not kiss her cheek because none of the other children did and, after all, he was nearly six. She laughed and nodded and they walked back through the park. Other children trailed in front and behind with their mothers. Helen held his sandwich tin which smelt of Marmite when she opened it. They stopped by the swings with their rusted chains. He ran to one and pushed off with both his feet.

'So you ate everything today then,' she called as he swung himself high, his socks down at his ankles, his knee black. One dark woman pushed her son on the swing next to Helen and turned and smiled.

'Said I would if you baked 'em for me.' He was slowing now. 'Hey, I bashed a tenner today, so now mine's the king. It's got sixteen so far. Is Dad home? Did he get any good shots today? Did you?' But he wasn't listening, he was scraping his shoe along the ground as he slowed the swing, ready to jump from it before rushing to the roundabout.

'Chris, for goodness sake, don't do that and come on now. It's time to get home.'

'Man and boy, they're all alike,' the other woman said and laughed. Helen smiled, the tin was cold against her skin. She put out her hand to steady the swing after Chris ran off. The chain links stained her hand.

'Yes, man and boy,' she echoed and added silently, German and English too; we're all alike. She waved to the woman. 'See you again,' she called and hoped that she would.

They walked down the path which ran alongside beds which held no flowers now that summer was gone, just heaped dark earth. Chris kicked a stone, scratching his toe-cap but Helen said nothing, just breathed in the smoke from the bonfire that the greensman was fanning by the tennis courts. There were hardly any leaves left on the trees and the sun seemed to have been sucked from the face of the earth.

'How would you like Grandma to come and stay with you for a bit? Daddy and I have to go away, just for a while.'

There had been no decision to make really, she had known from the start she would go because a father's love was too important to let slip through your fingers, too important to waste. And besides, Heine had said he needed her.

Chris would not stay behind. He did not like his grandmother, he told Helen as she read to him that night. She was always too close, always wanting to take everyone away from him so that it was just the two of them. Helen listened but she already knew. That night in bed she told Heine that the three of them would go and that it would be all right. She dreamed of a sun-filled stream and she woke in the morning crying.

Four days before Christmas Helen sat next to Heine as he drove slowly up to the border posts, his eyes on the slush-covered road, his hand wiping the inside of the windscreen where his breath had condensed and begun to freeze. Helen took out the leather from the glove pocket, leaned across and helped and then did her own. This time there were no birds singing, only snow which dragged down the branches of the trees. Neither of them spoke of the camera, of the search that must come when they stopped.

There was no '*Grüss Gott*' from the young blond border guard dressed in his green jacket and black trousers with his high black boots. This time he stood erect and snapped '*Heil Hitler*' while Helen smiled, her shoulders tense, willing Heine to reply in kind which he did, but only when he had climbed from the car, because she knew he did not want her to hear him say those words.

Chris eased himself up against the back of her seat, leaning his elbow along the top. There was a box of Christmas presents on the seat beside him and another box with the remains of their picnic beside that. They both watched Heine walk to the customs post and then climbed out at his gesture. Another guard came and searched the car, picking up and shaking the presents and opening some. Would he find the camera? But even if they did, they wouldn't hurt a child, would they? Helen felt her headache throb more deeply. It had clenched down one side of her neck and head since they had left Britain.

She took Chris's arm and pointed down the road. 'That's Germany, where Grandfather and Grandmother Weber live.' She must look natural, at ease. She must not appear afraid.

She looked at the Nazi flag which hung limp at the top of the pole, at the trees which had been cut back so that it would be clearly visible from a great distance. She looked at the scarlet background, the white circle and the hooked cross marked out in the deadness of black and her hatred of it gave her courage.

She smiled at her son and he took her hand. She could see his breath in the crisp cold air. Behind him the guard was looking at the picnic box, his face full of distaste at the apple cores, the banana peel, and he turned from it and nodded to the officer who waited with Heine. She smiled again at Chris and told him to stamp his feet to keep warm and knew that for now they were safe.

They drove without stopping through verges no longer full of poppies or brown-eyed Susans but heaped with snow stained by slush and dirt. They saw no blonde-haired maidens, just iced ponds. No window-boxes, just inches of snow on ledges and long daggers of ice hanging from pointed eaves. They stayed on the first night at a country inn and the second in a town, but in both they said little because the people might have been Nazis.

On the third day they drove through the flat beet fields and Helen told Chris of the boys his age who picked beet through the snow and ice. There were no commercial advertisements as they approached the outskirts of Hanover because the Nazis did not approve. They skirted around the city and as darkness fell they drove into Heine's village.

'Why wouldn't Grandmother come? She will have Christmas on her own now.' Chris's voice was sleep-filled, his lids heavy.

Helen shrugged. 'Older people get set in their ways,' she answered and was glad that her mother was not here because the older woman's eyes had been hard since Heine had come back to them.

She climbed out of the car and opened Chris's door, holding out her arms to him, breathing in his warm scent as he clung to her. The picnic basket was on the seat and Heine reached in past her and picked it up.

'Clever girl,' he said. 'I thought he was going to look in there for one moment.'

Helen laughed quietly, her headache gone now that they had arrived. 'Men don't like dirty nappies or mess, surely you haven't forgotten.'

He pulled a face and Helen remembered the woman in the park.

'Man and boy, you're all alike,' she murmured and as he kissed her the front door opened, flooding the garden with light, and she was glad they were spending Christmas in Germany.

They sat at the dining-room table eating by candlelight. Frau Weber had brought down from the attic two honey wax candles to celebrate their arrival, and their sweet Christmas aroma was everywhere, mingling with the pine of the Advent candles. Chris sat next to Helen, smiling because his Oma, his grandmother, had said that he could light the last Advent candle on Christmas Eve. They ate asparagus soup, as they had on their last visit, oh so long ago, Frau Weber said. Venison, chestnuts, sprouts and potato puffs followed decorated with sliced orange. The Bordeaux was thick and strong on Helen's tongue and she smiled when Heine's mother said she must call her Mutti.

Heine and his father spoke quietly when they spoke at all, but both seemed content to share the sight of the child and the women talking of St Nicholas and Christmas stockings. Chris leaned his head on his mother's arm when he had half eaten his venison. His lids were heavy and the talk spun around him. There were strange smells and sights and voices but the German was familiar and it made him remember the men who had come to his home, the men with thin faces and shaking hands who had been kind, who had sat him on their knees and seemed to drink in his laughter as though it was something they had never heard.

He turned to his mother. 'My uncles liked me to laugh, didn't they?'

She didn't hear and so he pulled at her sleeve. It was silk, so soft and smooth and he wanted to sleep. His mother turned and smiled. 'My uncles liked me to laugh, didn't they?'

Her face was close to his. 'Oh yes, my love. It was a sound that was very sweet to them.'

He saw her look across to his father but his chair was empty and he felt panic. Had he gone again? He had always been away, but not for months now. He turned again to his mother and she was there. She was always there and he leaned his head against her again. But then he felt strong arms around him and his father's rough chin against his cheek. His Oma rose and kissed him and then they left the warm honey-scented room and climbed the stairs, and his face was against his father's chest as he drifted in and out of sleep.

Helen went ahead, into the room which was to be Christoph's for the next two weeks. It was cold, so cold. There was ice frosted on the inside of the double windows and she scraped a finger from top to bottom, collecting frost beneath her nail.

She marched from his room into theirs. It was warm from the stove. She walked quickly to the top of the stairs, hissing at Heine to stop, pointing towards Chris's bedroom. 'There is no heating in there. It's freezing.'

Heine stopped. 'In Germany the children sleep in cold rooms.'

She turned. 'In my family, children sleep in warm rooms even if it means the adults go into the cold one.' Her hands were on her hips, anger in her voice.

Heine shifted his son's weight slightly and then laughed. 'My darling girl, do not prepare to do battle. I am too tired and too intelligent to risk my life fighting over something which is easily remedied.' He passed Chris to her, walking quietly into their room, riddling the stove as she stood behind him and watched, feeling the heat from the ash and red-hot coals as he drew out the pan. He moved ahead of her into the smaller bedroom and heaped them on to the kindling and coal already laid in the stove, leaning down to open the draught doors at the base, and she saw his long thin hands on the brass knob, his wrists against his good shirt cuffs, his eyelashes casting shadows on his cheeks in the dim overhead light. The Nazis seemed far away in this room. War seemed an impossibility.

When the room was dark and warm and Helen and Heine had kissed Chris goodnight, he watched as they left the room, then waited because he knew she would be back. She always was. The door opened again and his mother was there. 'Sleep tight, my darling boy,' she whispered and only then did he close his eyes.

Herr Weber's study was lit by a small table lamp which cast a circle of light that barely reached Heine and Helen as they sat in their armchairs. They watched in silence as the older man laid old shirts against the gap at the bottom of the door, pushing hard until it was plugged. They watched as he pulled the telephone plug from the wall but still did not speak because he had held his fingers to his lips. Only when he was completely satisfied did he sit near to the low fire, opposite them but close so that his whispers could be heard by them.

'You see, Hans has been with us for twenty years and Ilse too but we dare not trust them. The telephones can be tapped too. I am not suspected. Not yet. But now as I said in my letter I can see and hear all that Heine saw and heard. But it is too late really. I know it is too late.'

Heine laid his hand on his father's knee. 'Be careful, Father.'

'Oh I am most careful.' Herr Weber laughed softly. 'I carry

out my duty to my utmost ability. I am in and out of the courts. In and out of interrogation rooms and so I need your little present very badly.' He raised his eyebrows to Heine, who nodded at Helen.

She lifted her handbag and took the camera out. 'Please, do be careful. We see the refugees. We hear such stories.' The camera was cold in her hand as she passed it to him. His hand was thin, with veins which knotted and bulged. He had been a strong, fit man. He was that no longer.

They did not watch as he took it and moved behind them. He did not want them to know more than they had to and it would be elsewhere by tomorrow. He started to speak only when he had returned and again in a whisper.

'I have taken the post of *Blockwart*. I am now the leader of a local group of Party comrades. I am, my dear son, honoured to serve at the lowest level of the Nazi political system but I know what is going on. I can, with this camera you have brought me at such risk to yourselves, take photographs with a view to recording crimes and, as importantly, blackmail.'

Helen looked at this old man who had held legality above all else.

He laughed but there was no amusement in the sound. 'Yes, my dear. Legality loses its appeal when it is used to remove from society "vermin" such as gypsies, Jews and parsons. I use the Nazis' vernacular, of course.' He was still whispering. Helen looked at Heine, who took her hand, holding it tightly, and she saw in his face love and fear for this man.

Herr Weber leaned forward, his face sharply etched in the dull dim light, and started to speak, but Helen interrupted.

'Parsons. I didn't know. Why parsons?'

Herr Weber clasped his hands together. He was still leaning forward. 'Because according to our noble leader God was a Jew, and so one does not allow a faith which worships such as he. But also because Christians owe an allegiance to something apart from our dear and glorious Führer. We Germans, the master race, must ignore such superstition. We must follow the Nordic beliefs.' He lowered his head. 'I feel such disgust with myself. I did not protest soon enough. I looked at the promises he had fulfilled. The orderly streets, the employment, the national pride and then I saw Herr Weissen beaten to death and his small son too, on the street, and people laughed and I did nothing then. I was too frightened.'

His voice was so steady, Helen thought. So cold and steady, and her hands were steady too, because she and Heine had lived with the knowledge for years now. But always, inside, the anguish coiled and lashed.

'The Nazis had such a glorious party in November, my dear. It was far more spectacular than, what do you call it – ?' He paused. 'Ah yes, your Guy Fawkes Night. We called ours *Kristallnacht*. Such flames, such delightful bonfires, such sharp glass, such ruin. Such disgrace.' His voice became tight and hard. 'And now the officials are angry because the insurance companies have to buy imported glass with precious foreign currency to replace the damage the verminous Jews brought upon themselves.'

Helen could not listen to any more of the words which were pouring from this old man in the small dark room and she rose, but before she left the two men together she went to Herr Weber and said, '*Ich leide seelisch*,' and kissed him. Knowing that he also was 'sick in his soul'.

When Heine came to bed he held her and said that his father had saved some people already and would save others too with the camera, with his courage, and she asked him if he were not afraid for him.

'It is his gesture,' he said. 'What more can he do?'

When Helen rose in the morning snow was falling from the dark sky, big flakes which fell faster and faster, settling on the already white earth. The room was light, everything was quiet. A cart passed but it could not be heard as it ground through the soft clinging snow. She could see the horse's breath, its shaking head and then she heard Chris and took him out into the snow, dressed in his grandfather's fur hat and his father's old fur boots. Heine found a sledge and as the snow stopped falling he pulled his son along and there were deep fresh grooves carved in the cold whiteness.

Then Hans came and shovelled the path and so they helped, nodding and smiling, and wondering if, one day, he would betray Herr Weber. Ilse came with ashes, salt and sand and scattered them on the ice which had been beneath the snow and in moments it became soft and brown and ugly and Helen turned from it, watching the sundial far out across the garden near the orchard. Children passed behind the hedge which looked foreshortened against the depth of the snow and Helen listened to their laughter and made herself ignore the ugliness of the path.

Later they drove to the forest on roads cleared of snow and chose the Christmas tree and took the toboggan down a thirty metre slope again and again. The snow clumped in Helen's hair and scarf and trickled down her neck but all she could feel and hear was the laughter of her husband as he watched, his leg too stiff to participate, and that of her son mingling with her own. On and on they went until the sky turned pink and the sun lost its weak warmth. She and Chris took the last run together. Chris in front, then Helen, and as the wind caught her cheeks and the toboggan jarred and flew, she held Chris tightly and did not want the slope to ever end because now, this minute, she had her family safe and close.

That night they watched a torchlit procession from the window and Chris thought it was pretty, like a moving Christmas tree but his father said that sometimes things were not as they seemed and then Chris saw that they were soldiers.

On Christmas Eve Chris went with Helen and Oma to the attic and she showed him the decorations, the electric candles, the crib and its figures, the provisions. They carried boxes down and decorated the tree so that it was ready for the evening, for it was tonight that they would have their presents, Helen told him. Frau Weber smiled and said that it was because it was the German way and, after all, he was half German.

Chris looked at her and then at Helen. 'I can't say that at school,' he said.

Helen looked away and then at Mutti who touched her shoulder. 'I know. I know,' was all she said.

That evening they opened their presents before they ate. They were set on low tables either side of the tree which shimmered with silver strips, baubles and electric candles. Set before the tree was the crib. Hans and Ilse came to receive their gifts and there was the sound of paper crackling and laughter until Hans turned on the radio for the Government's Christmas Eve broadcast and Helen heard in this room, so full of gifts and light, the voice which had changed so many lives.

She looked at the tree and counted the candles, she breathed deeply ten times and then counted the candles again because she wouldn't listen. No, she would never listen, not even to the sound since the words would escape her anyway. She looked at the Advent wreath of fir branches which was hung from plaited blue, green and red ribbons suspended from the ceiling in the dining-room. Christoph had lit it before they started to open the presents, his arm steady as he reached forward, held up by Heine, his face red from the cold of the day. She had kissed him when Heine lowered him and he said that she smelt of ginger. She laughed because she had baked ginger biscuits most of the morning, cutting him out a Hansel and Gretel for his stocking which she would put on his bed tonight because he was also half English.

Before dinner, before they left the tree, Herr Weber went to the piano which stood in the corner of the room and played carols for them and when he came to 'Silent Night' Helen sang it half in German half in English as her present to the Webers. Her voice was pure and strong and there was silence for a moment when she finished.

During dinner the smell of ginger and honey mixed with the cool white wine and took away the strong taste of the carp and horseradish which Helen had found strange and Chris could not eat. She smiled, doubting if he could have eaten even his favourite food, bacon and eggs, after the tea of toast and honey and the cakes, and she felt the flush in her own cheeks from the afternoon's tobogganing. Talk flowed gently and quietly and for now there was peace for each of them.

Herr Weber told Christoph of the Opera House in Hanover where Heine had been taken as a child to see the children's play. How the chandeliers had sparkled and the seats had pricked him so that he wriggled all the way through. How the gilt boxes full of officials and their families had glistened. He told him how his father had taken the toboggan out one day with his friends and come back so late that there were icicles on his mittens, his hat, even his nose. He laughed gently when Christoph said that today he had gone down on the sledge with his mother because his father was an old man with a stiff leg who could only watch.

Helen did not laugh at the words which dropped from

Chris's mouth, wondering if Heine felt the pain of them as she did, but he looked at her with his eyebrows raised.

'This is how you bring up your son is it, Frau Weber? To show such scant respect for his father?' He was laughing, his blue eyes clear and without hurt.

Helen laughed then and lifted her glass to him, to the man he now was, looking from him to their son. So like Heine except for those eyes and she looked up at the Advent candles. One, lit on the first Advent Sunday was burnt almost to a stub. The wax from today's was burning with a strong firm flame. She could smell the pine and the honey.

She could not remember a Christmas with her father. Would he have laughed? Would he have sat on a toboggan? She thought so. Would her mother? She knew she would not.

She thought of her mother on Christmas day when they walked through Hanover. She had left presents and cards with her but her mother had sent none out to Germany in the car.

Frau Weber had said this morning that she sent a card each year but never heard in return. As they walked in the air which was so cold it hurt her lungs, Helen felt the tension knot in her shoulders but pushed it away because it was Christmas and she was happy. She kicked at the ice which had chipped and protruded up into the road. Frau Weber took her arm.

'Come, Helen. Do not be left behind, they miss you.'

Helen looked up and waved as Heine and Chris called.

'Yes, I was just thinking,' she said, smiling at Frau Weber.

'There is much to think of these days,' Frau Weber said as they walked along down the alley into the centre. Heine and Chris carried the red ball which had been in his stocking from Father Christmas. It showed up clear and shining against the snow, the grey buildings with icicles hanging like witches' fingers from the eaves. Would her own mother have wanted to hurry to join with everyone else? She knew she would not. She would have tried to hold her back and would not forgive her when she pulled away. But that was all in the past. She could not hurt her ever again. This was Christmas and she was far from England.

As they reached the men, Helen smiled and looked at her mother-in-law; the daylight showed up the lines around the eyes, the hair which was almost white. She looked fragile, strained, her skin almost translucent. Did she know of Herr

Weber's activities? It never seemed safe to ask. There were many people in the city centre, walking, nodding, and Helen moved to look into the window of the toy shop where the shelves were now half empty. She turned to call to Chris and saw an old man slip and fall in amongst the milling crowd. She moved to help but Heine caught her arm.

'Leave him,' he said, pulling her round, back to the shop.

His hand was tight on her arm and she stared at him and then twisted round again. Chris was staring as the old man struggled on the unsanded ice near the road. He was still on the ground, his black coat and hat smudged with white. His earlocks too.

'Are you mad?' Helen said. 'Let me help him.'

Chris was looking across at her now, his face puzzled. Helen looked at Herr Weber, at his wife. They did not move to help but turned away as though they had not seen, but they had seen because Herr Weber's face was white. Those in the square did not help either but passed either side. Still the old man could not rise.

'He is a Jew. If we help him Father could be in danger. There is too much to lose, too much work yet to be done.'

Again Helen looked at the old man and then at Heine. She looked at Chris then and saw him move to help but he was only six and not strong enough.

'Let go of me, at once,' she said to Heine. 'I do not bring up my child to pass an old man who has fallen, or is he just a fragment?' Helen turned to Herr and Frau Weber who were standing with their backs to them, looking in the window. 'Move on, don't be seen with us. I shall try to protect you.' Her voice was quiet but firm.

She followed Chris, lengthening her stride, holding his arm, talking, and then Heine saw him nod and throw his mother the ball which she missed. He saw its redness against the black of the old man's coat, saw it land by his leg, saw Helen's hand reach for the ball, saw Chris stand on his other side, shouting for his ball. And then the man was up, walking away quickly. Too quickly for him or anyone else to have seen what had happened in the crush. The Webers had no need to fear.

Helen held her son's hand as they walked towards him but she could still feel the thin arm, the smell of poverty, the cultured voice which had said, '*Danke*,' while she had said, 'I'm so sorry. So sorry.'

She stood before Heine now, her face gentle. 'I was the only one who could go. Chris and I were the only ones who could go and there was no possible way we could have walked on. It was our gesture. Do you understand?' She didn't touch, just stood there and waited, still feeling that thin arm.

'I love you,' Heine said and kissed her, turning from her only when Chris called.

'Catch,' and the ball hit his arm.

Heine had wanted to help too.

Her mother's telegram arrived the next day.

'Return immediately. Stop. I am unwell. Stop. Mother.'

CHAPTER 5

They arrived in the Avenue at midday on the 30 December having travelled almost without stopping. It was cold. A heavy mist coated the trees, the last few skeletal leaves hung like rags and the houses looked grey.

Her mother was sitting up in bed eating a lightly boiled egg, which, she said, a neighbour had kindly cooked just a moment ago. Helen just looked at her, at her pink cheeks bearing no trace of illness, at her permed hair tucked into a hairnet.

'Just a touch of flu, after all,' her mother said and her smile was the same as it had been when Helen came out from the cupboard.

Helen turned, and left the room, straightened the pictures on the stair wall, placing her feet carefully on each stair, concentrating on this, not on her anger which was so intense that she felt sick. She walked into the kitchen where Heine was lighting the gas under the kettle. There was a smell of sulphur from the match, a smell of gas from the front ring.

'Stay in here,' she said. 'Whatever you hear, stay in the warm.' She smiled at Heine, at Chris, but did not stop and explain.

She returned upstairs, made up the spare bed in that bleak room and then told her mother that she would stay for three days so that the neighbours did not have to boil eggs for her and watched the smile increase.

'Heine will stay with me and you will move to the spare room, as you felt Father should. There is no room for Heine unless we use your bed.'

The smile disappeared, the eyes were dark, and Helen was glad. She took her arm and led her without speaking, without listening to the harsh voice. She helped her into the bed and now she spoke again.

'Should I hang a damp blanket to contain the germs?' she asked. 'Would that be wise, Mother?'

She left her then with the anger hanging in the air between them.

In the front room on 31 December, she and Heine saw in the year of 1939 with mulled wine, praying that peace would endure, that somehow Hitler could be stopped without great carnage; that hostility would not blossom in England towards Germans and Italians. That in Germany, God was with Heine's parents.

As they drank quietly together Heine touched Helen's hand and said, 'Your mother is widowed and lonely. We have our lives before us and one another. We should be generous, my darling. Ask her to join us, please.'

She said nothing, just looked at the fire and the flames which lurched round logs and coal. She did not want her mother down, she did not want to see in the New Year with her in case, somehow, she tainted it with her presence.

'Please,' Heine said again. 'There is enough bitterness and pain throughout the world without continuing a feud within our own family.'

So Helen helped her mother down the stairs although she was not fragile enough to need help. She eased her into a chair, handed her a glass of warm wine, feeling the heat from her own as she sat and watched her mother smooth her satin dressing gown and sip with pursed mouth. Yes, all right, Mother, she thought as she sipped her own wine, tasting the warmth in her mouth. All right, I shall do as Heine says and be generous tonight and in the future, but I will never let you spoil any part of my life ever again.

In January the gas mask drills which had been desultory for the past year took on a new urgency in the schools, and in Germany Jews were banned from cinemas, theatres and concerts. They were banned from being vets, pharmacists and dentists and so the refugees continued to pass through Helen's flat.

In February her mother complained that she earned too much from Ernest's pensions to claim a free air raid shelter and Helen said that she was not in one of the priority target areas anyway, as she, Heine and Chris were.

Helen was glad when Heine began digging in early March when the soil was frost-free and easier to work. It helped to feel they were doing something as the tension in the press mounted, as people grew edgy and ignored the warm spring. She watched as he sliced the spade deep into the earth at the bottom of the narrow strip of garden behind the flat, heaving cold heavy sods on to the lawn. She was glad that her arms tugged at the shoulders when she and Chris put them into the rust-smeared wheelbarrow and then transferred them to the left side of the garden where the sun struck in the afternoons. She was glad to be working, to be doing something to protect themselves, glad too to be creating from that need a rockery which would thrive. For she wanted flowers to bloom; even if bombs fell from black-crossed aeroplanes she wanted flowers to bloom, then some sanity would remain.

She watched as Heine dug again and again, the sweat soaking his shirt, his hair. There was a smell of fresh earth; there were old pennies, pipes, bottles, tiles and Heine smiled each time they fell from his spade and then threw them up to Chris who would hold them, turn them, then put them to one side to take to school for the 'precious table'. Worms bored holes in the straight glossed sides of the pit as the weekend passed and Helen took them to the rockery which now held small, wide-spaced plants, and it seemed almost a game as the sky turned blue and the trees budded and blossom bloomed. Almost.

At three feet Heine stopped and helped Helen drag in the fourteen steel sheets which had been dropped off on the pavement by council lorries to each building in the street. Her hands tore through gloves and her shirt was ripped at the shoulder as they dragged them one by one through the narrow passage-way into the garden.

Sandbags had been left also and while Heine fixed the sheets in the late afternoon Helen and Chris doused the bags with creosote to stop them rotting and the smell sank into their skin and their hair and their lungs and although they slept with their windows wide that night they could still taste it in their mouths the next morning.

Helmut arrived that morning and so Heine was too busy to ease the sandbags against the shelter and Helen was taking photographs in the studio, but the next week, with Helmut helping, they pushed and carried and kicked the sandbags into place and Helen's back felt as though it would break. Chris threw earth on the roof of the shelter with the spade he had taken to Eastbourne and Helen did too, but with a large shovel. It would be added protection against blast and shrapnel. She called to their neighbours, the Simkins, who then did the same. She lifted Chris who would not be seven until December – but already weighed enough to be twenty, she whispered into his neck.

'Higher, Mummy, I can't reach,' he called.

She growled and he laughed but she lifted him higher still and then he threw the seeds – forget-me-nots, love-in-the-mist, marigolds – across the shelter roof, and for a moment Helen wondered whether they would be at war when the flowers bloomed.

They painted the inside walls white while Chris broke cork tiles into pieces with his fingers, leaning over, watching the pile of bits grow on the upturned dustbin lid. An ant ran over his shoe and then on into a crack. Some bark was caught under his fingernail and he dug it out, rolling it between his fingers. It was bouncy and warm.

'Smaller, Chris,' Heine called and so he worked for another hour and then he climbed down into the shelter and threw the cork at the wet paint, again and again until the cork stuck to the sides. And he nodded as his father said that the pieces would absorb the moisture and prevent condensation.

'It's going to be a good play-house, Dad,' he said.

They had to hang a blanket not a door, the inspector said when he called. 'Don't want to be shredded by splinters now, do we?' Helen looked from him to the rockery. Would the alpines take root and bloom, she wondered, not wanting to hear the words.

In the middle of March Hitler took over Prague and spring-cleaned the country, Heine said between thin lips. Czechoslovakian Jews now began to come and the flat was full again. Claus had written from America that he still had not established an agency for the partnership but was working for another firm to make some contacts. It would take at least two years, he said, and Helen had been glad because England was her country. Heine had been worried.

Helen smiled and kissed him. 'There is no war yet, there

might be no war. Look, the Russians still have signed no pact with anyone. Hitler needs that signature to neutralise Russia before he can bite into Poland. And in the street there has been no unkindness towards us, no anti-German feeling.'

'Do they know we are German?' Heine asked and Helen did not answer because she could only have said no.

In April conscription plans were endorsed after Britain and France pledged to defend Poland and that weekend Heine and Helen took Chris to the Avenue and dug her mother's shelter. They bolted, doused, heaved, while Helen's mother told her neighbour that Heine was too old to be called up and had an injured leg and later told Helen that perhaps they would think he was Dutch.

On Sunday evening before they returned to London, Heine and Helen took Chris to the stream and floated sticks, swearing that the winner was the one which Chris had thrown even though it was not. Helen watched as Heine lifted his son over the parapet, saw the strong hands, the fine blond hairs. Saw the green lichen which stained Chris's coat. Saw her father, quite clearly now, his face, his shoulders, his hands, and remembered the horror of that war and its legacy for the women who waited and the men who never returned. She prayed that another war would not come.

May was hot and the British Government declared again that it would side with Poland in the event of a German attack to the East but negotiations were still being conducted between Russia and Britain with a view to a pact and so hopes for peace remained. Helen watered her rockery and sewed Chris's initials on his shoe-bag and swung him in the park, talking to other mothers whose faces were strained as they listened to their children talk of the evacuation practice or the gas mask drill. She stood and watched as Chris played cowboys and Indians with the other boys, seeing him load his pistol with a roll of red caps, hearing the snap as he fought his battle, smelling the blackened roll when he gave it to her to carry home.

She was asked to photograph the trenches being dug in the parks, the builders reinforcing the basements, the brick surface shelters which were going up in many London streets. She did but she would not think of them afterwards.

In July a local boy won a big boxing match and Mr Simkins, their neighbour, drank until he passed out in the street. Heine carried him up to his flat above his tobacconist's shop which also ran beneath theirs. It was then that Mrs Simkins asked if they would be evacuating Chris. She clicked her tongue and said that she supposed the Government was right to want to remove anyone who would get in the way but it seemed very hard and would the bombs really come? Heine said he did not know.

That night he and Helen talked as they did every night about Chris, their love for him, their need to keep him with them, but they spoke also of his right to safety, to a billet in the country. But then they thought of him with a stranger, of his face as he woke, soft and full, his arms which hugged them. They thought of his fear of the dark. Would foster-parents understand? They drank him in as he came home each day, listening to his voice, his ideas, hearing his laughter, watching him grow, holding him when he fell, kissing him when he was asleep, and knew they could not bear to be parted, not even for a week, let alone for the years of his childhood, for who knew how long a war would last?

And then in the darkness of night they talked again of the bombs that had fallen in Spain, of the buildings which had crumbled and killed, of the shrapnel which had sliced, the blast which had destroyed, and knew that they could not bear any of this to touch their son.

They talked then of them all moving to the country but Heine said, 'How can we? We need to stay, to work for the nation as everyone else will do.'

'But he is our child,' she whispered, watching high clouds nudging in front of the moon.

'How can we run away?' he replied as he held her, his breath moving her hair. 'I've done too much of that. And we must earn a living, darling. As photographers we need to live in London, we have our contacts now. I can work as an air raid warden, earn my place in your society.'

On and on they talked, night after night, but neither spoke of the question to which there was no answer. What would happen to a German in this country if war was declared?

After a hot dry summer the children of the neighbourhood were tanned and Helen's arms were brown from weeding the rockery. In August negotiations between Russia and Britain collapsed and on 23 August, as Helen and Heine listened to the wireless on a hot still evening, it was announced that Germany and Russia had signed the Nazi–Soviet Pact. Helen cried while Heine held her but she did not feel safe, even with the feel of him so close because it meant war. She knew it meant war but what would that mean to them?

On 31 August Helen packed Chris's bag. They had bought an enamel cup, a knife, fork and spoon and the list of allowable clothes had been ticked and folded into the case because Christoph's school was to be evacuated tomorrow and Helen and Heine had decided that he must go. He must be safe, but they were numb with grief.

The next day they took him to school, walking past police cars which crawled the kerbs telling parents through tannoys to take their children to the schoolyard where they must assemble in front of their form teachers. Helen kissed her son at the gate, smoothing his hair with her hand, and somehow, she let him go. They joined the other parents outside the playground and watched through railings which held none of the summer heat. They saw the register being taken and the children being formed into columns two abreast. They saw him labelled by a teacher, saw him not look at them as they pressed with other parents against the school railings. Helen gripped the flaking metal, feeling the cold hardness, thinking of that, not of her heart which seemed to fill her chest and which was destroying her.

Helen did not hold Heine's hand, could not move hers from the railings until they marched from the playground and then she thrust them into her pockets where they were bunched into fists, trying to keep the pain clasped inside them.

The children marched with their gas masks banging against their sides, their cases in their hands, following the Headmaster who held a banner with the letter 'S' and the number '60' inked on. Along the streets they marched, with Heine and Helen and the other weeping or silent parents.

They crossed the road in waves as they had learned to do in the summer practices, the parents waiting as their children queued up along the pavement in lines two hundred yards long before turning to face the road and crossing quickly at a teacher's command. The traffic was held up by police for three seconds only.

So efficient, Helen thought. They are taking my child from me so efficiently. Old men and women stood outside their doorways watching the children followed by their despairing parents, and their eyes were full of the knowledge of what war really meant.

At the station the children marched past the barriers to the waiting area, where there were other schools milling or sitting on cases talking. The Stepney children stopped close to the entrance and Helen watched as Chris stood quite still, looking across at the group beneath the clock. His face had been still and quiet all morning and now she saw it close, saw his shoulders drop, his head turn but not before she heard, 'It's that bloody German.' It was a high voice and she turned and looked and there were the Alton Mews children from Highlands School, standing behind their banner, carrying the same gas masks as Chris, the same cases. But they were not the same; they were English and at the flash of fear on her son's face, she moved.

She felt Heine hold her arm but she heard the call being taken up as it had been in 1938 when faces grew ugly and words even uglier.

'It's that bloody Hun.'

'What you doing 'ere, boy? You should be over with that Hitler.'

The other children were turning now, staring first at the boys from Highlands, then over to Chris.

Around them women were looking, talking, pointing.

Helen moved again, pushing forward and this time Heine was with her. She passed the woman she had talked to in the park.

'Please let us through,' she said and the woman looked at her and then at Heine. Her own face was blotched with tears.

'Please let us through. I have to reach my son,' Helen said, clutching her arm.

The woman wrenched away. 'I didn't know you were one of them,' she said, her mouth twisted in her face. 'If it wasn't for you, our kids wouldn't have to go.'

Her words were taken up then and Helen was pushed and so was Heine but they got through, somehow they got through into the station, and saw Chris yards and yards away, standing with space between him and his friends who were no longer his friends. A teacher was there, his face cold, his hand on Chris's shoulder. A train was pulling in now and there was hissing steam and shrieking brakes and the harsh engine smell all around them.

A guard came towards them, his hat large, shouting at them to go back.

'You've made your decision. Stick by it.' His teeth were rotten and his breath smelt. Heine put his arm out and pushed on by. Chris was crying now, watching them but moving, always moving towards the train, the children still shouting, the teacher herding his column onwards.

A WVS woman in a hat intercepted them. 'Go back, please, behind the barrier. If we let you through they'll all come.' Her voice was loud but the shrieking brakes were louder and Helen pulled free of the hands which held her, dodging past the children as they turned to look for their parents one last time, and now there were tears from many children and they were on her face too.

Still she could hear the calls of 'German' 'Hun' 'Murderers', and she wanted to scream at them and at Heine because it was all his fault.

A boy with red hair shouted at her, 'Bloody Hun.'

'Stinking German.'

Christoph's column was moving now. His face was white and pinched but the tears were still there and they were too far away. He was getting on the train and suddenly she saw that he must not because now she knew what it was going to be like being German when England was at war.

A teacher was taking Chris's shoulder, pointing to the door, and she wasn't going to reach him, there were too many children, too many teachers, too many hands pulling at her but then she was through and Heine was with her. She reached Chris and he felt her hands on his arm, her voice.

'Chris, come home.'

He turned and pressed his face to hers. The boys were shouting at him because he wasn't Dutch as he had said, he was German. The teacher told her that there were many who would be kind, it was only a few and she knew that he was right but a few was too many and so the three of them went home to a city almost without children.

That night she whispered to Heine, 'I'm sorry, my darling,' because she couldn't forget that she had blamed him and part of her still did.

At eleven-fifteen a.m. on Sunday 3 September, Chamberlain announced over the wireless that Britain was at war with Germany, and fifteen minutes later Helen heard the air raid siren and stopped with a duster in her hand, fear making her mouth drop open, making her scream come as though she were a child in pain. Heine picked up the gas masks and turned her, pushing her towards the stairs, calling Chris, shouting at her to hold her son's hand, get him to the shelter, get him to safety, and then she moved, pulling her son, her head down, waiting for the whine of bombs, the crash and splinter of glass.

She ran down the garden, hearing nothing but the siren, hearing their neighbours rushing down their path, hearing Heine running behind. Her mouth was open and saliva ran down her chin. She felt a fear deeper than anything she had ever known. She looked up but could see no planes, no black crosses, no falling bombs, but they would come. She thrust aside the curtain and went down into the dark, the bloody dark which she could not bear, which her son could not bear. She took the masks from Heine, watching as Chris put his on, his chin in first and then the mask over his face, the straps wrenched over his head, and still the siren filled the air.

She pulled hers on; it was hot and smelly and pulled at her hair. She felt that she could not breathe, that she would die here and now in the noise and the fear. She held Chris to her, watching Heine who sat with them but then the mask clouded up with her breath and she could not see his face. They waited but no bombers came that day though the liner *Athenia* was sunk on the third and then the letters from German-haters began to drop through the letterbox, harsh, cruel and accusing.

Internment also began. Men were taken from their homes, locked away where they could do no harm to Britain. Their friends went, those who had come to escape the Nazis and who loved Britain. They went in police cars, handcuffed, interned without trial but no one came for Heine and they dared not think of it or even talk.

There was no school now because there were so few children, but Helen asked Dr Schultz who ran a small private school a quarter of a mile away if he would have room, and because he knew of Heine's work and was Austrian he took Chris. He would only charge half the fees because Heine had been visited by the police and told he could no longer use a camera because he was an alien and they soon found that he could find no other work for the same reason. Dr Schultz offered to approach a bank manager he knew who might find essential work for him so that they could live once their savings had gone. They felt exposed, impotent and afraid.

Each morning Helen walked Chris to school past alley-ways where children who had not been evacuated and who did not now go to school waited. They never hurt them, just shouted and Helen told Chris to ignore their talk because they knew no better, but they made her tremble and see only greyness around her. Even the rockery had bloomed then faded.

In the afternoon Heine collected him and walked back to the swings but Chris did not want to stop where people could see him with his father because his father, Herr Weber, was German, wasn't he, and the British were fighting the Germans, weren't they? So Grandfather and Grandmother were their enemies and planes would come and blow them to bits and those planes were flown by Germans, by people like his father. So one day he went screaming from the park and when Heine ran after him he shouted, 'Leave me alone. Why can't you be English? I hate you. I hate you, you're a Hun.'

In November they heard that Heine had to appear before a tribunal which would decide whether he was to be imprisoned.

That night they did not sleep but then neither of them slept any more. Helen listened to their son crying and she could not do anything to help because nothing could be altered. Heine had cried too because he was the cause of all their tension and she had held him and said, 'Sshh, it doesn't matter. It will be all right. Everything will be all right.'

But she wondered how it could be because already he was not allowed to travel more than five miles from the house. Already they had swept up shattered glass from the stones hurled through their window. Already their son was weeping because he did not want his father to bring him home from school but neither did he want him to be kept from them in a prison camp.

In the morning there was a letter from the bank manager that Dr Schultz had spoken too. He offered Helen a job, not Heine. It would be deemed war work and keep her in London with her family. Heine had kissed her as she left for school with Chris holding her tight, looking at her face, the lines, the eyes, and loved her more than life itself and tried not to feel humiliated, just as she was trying too.

His son would not kiss him but pulled away and went from the house but then ran back and hugged him.

That night Heine was home again. He was not considered a danger to the country, he told Helen over a glass of wine, sitting Chris on his knee, explaining to him about Category A and Category B but how much could a child who was not yet seven understand?' He looked back to Helen.

'I'm Category B, my love. I'm not dangerous enough to be interned immediately but unfortunately I didn't merit refugee status, Category C. I was not deprived of my occupation by my government or deprived of their protection. I merely ran away from them.' His laugh had no humour in it.

Helen gripped his hand. 'But they must know how hard you've worked to save people. They must know you won't do anything to hurt this country.'

Heine hugged Chris to him but the child pulled free and went across to Helen.

'I want to go to bed, Mummy. Will the German bombers come tonight?' He did not look at his father and Helen could not either because of the hurt she would see there.

Heine was not allowed to register at the Labour Exchange and so Helen earned for them while he washed their clothes, swept the flat and made sure their supplies were ready to take into the shelter if there was a raid. But there was no raid. There was no real war. Just hostility, just fear and pain. He was refused as a warden. He could only walk his son home and try not to feel that his life had no worth any more.

In the evenings the lights were dim, the voltage reduced as a wartime measure. The blackout was in force. Helen asked her mother to come and stay because she felt she should but Mrs Carstairs refused because Heine was at home all day and he was a German, wasn't he? She told Helen that she did not want to be whispered about, did not want a brick to be thrown at her.

Helen met Marian one day and smiled but she walked straight past, the collar of her coat drawn up, her gloved hand holding it together at her throat. Her brown shoes scuffed the leaves which lay on the path outside the park. Emily was with her because Marian had not been able to face the thought of evacuation either.

'Hello,' Chris said.

There was no answer because Marian dragged the child along too quickly. Helen didn't watch her go, but took her son into the park and watched him on the swing. It was so quiet with no children.

At the end of November her mother came to stay and Helen was surprised.

'It's Chris's birthday and he must have a party,' her mother said. 'For the children at that nice little school.' Helen looked at Heine and smiled and was touched at her mother's efforts.

Her work at the bank was not interesting but it kept her from the war factories outside London and earned them just enough for party food but not enough for a present for Chris. So each night she sewed in the dim light of the sitting-room lamp as her mother drew up plans for games and made hats out of cardboard with Heine, sticking the seams while he held them together.

Chris came out of his bedroom looking at his father as he drew coloured circles on the paper hats and then he walked over and leaned against his leg, taking up a pencil, colouring in the circles, and Helen turned away because she did not want him to see the tears which would not stop running down her face and into her mouth. It was the first time he had touched his father for weeks.

All that week she came home from work into a house full of secrets and excitement and voices which stopped when she entered the room. The first of December was a Friday and so the party was planned for Saturday.

In bed on the night when their son was seven, in a room guarded from the moonlight by the blackout, Heine held her, telling her that he wanted to give her something to show how much he loved her, how he would never, ever stop loving her. That tomorrow he would be away for the morning but would be back in time for the party and Helen said he must because it would be the first one he had attended and they loved him so much. She stroked his smooth skin. His warmth and his lips were on her body and as the night wore on they loved one another as though there was no tomorrow.

Helen baked on the morning of the party, while her mother talked and her son played in the cowboy outfit Helen had sewn during the evenings while her eyes ached with the strain of wartime Britain. He drew his cap gun in and out of his holster, firing at Mrs Simkins in her garden and then at his grandmother. She would not play dead but Helen did, gurgling and groaning until he shrieked with laughter.

Before lunch her mother put on her coat and hat and said that she would walk for a while in the fresh air to build herself up for the next few hours. She had a slight headache. Helen laughed and watched her mother walk down the street, her gas mask in a tin box hanging from her arm. The war had pulled them together, she thought, watching through the windows which were criss-crossed with strips of sticky paper to protect against stones as well as bombs.

The children arrived at three o'clock and her mother's head had cleared. She was laughing and joking in a way which Helen had never known. There was a happiness in the older woman which warmed the daughter. Some of the children who came were English, but some were the children of refugees and it was good to hear laughter from other children, not hissed profanities. It was good to see Christoph's face loosen and hear his laugh too.

At four o'clock Heine had still not returned and Helen could not watch the children for more than a few minutes before going to the window and looking down the street. Dusk was falling, a chill mist was settling and soon the parents called to take their children home before dark. They were friendly and kind before they left and Helen wished that Heine could have been there to feel the warmth of friendship. She must talk to him, they must meet these people again, but where was he?

She walked again to the window, wiping her breath from it with her hand. Beads of moisture remained. Worry tore at her. She looked towards the High Street and then towards the Church but no one stirred. Chris stood by the window now, watching, crying, and her mother said, 'He'll be fine. He's just been held up I expect.'

'But where has he gone? Where would he have gone?'

Then Chris turned. 'Grandma knows. I heard her tell Daddy what you would like more than anything.'

Helen turned to him. He was rubbing the window where his breath too had condensed. She held his hand still and turned.

'Nonsense, Chris.' Her mother's voice was sharp as she carried plates from the table to the kitchen. 'Come now and help me carry these things.' Helen watched as she pointed to the hats which the children had discarded by their plates.

Chris walked across and picked them up, then looked at his mother.

'Daddy made nice hats,' he said. 'I wish he had been here.' It was dark in the room now. Helen pulled down the blackout blind, and then the curtains before putting on the light. She walked to the kitchen.

'Where has he gone, Mother?' she asked because fear made her cold.

'I don't want to spoil his surprise,' her mother said without turning.

'He said he would be back. He promised. It was important to him.' Helen knew she was shouting. She could tell from the look on Christoph's face. 'I'm sorry, my darling. I just want to know where Daddy is.'

'But Grandma knows,' Chris said, standing by the sink as his grandmother ran the tap, her flowered overall pulled tight across her breasts.

Helen turned again to her mother but then the knocking started on the door, started and did not stop, and Helen ran to it, seeing Chris behind her, seeing her mother turn.

It was the police. They had come to tell her that Heine had been arrested in possession of a camera in Hemsham. He would not be returning. He was in custody and would be interned, probably on the Isle of Man. He was considered Category A now, a danger to the country.

'The police had acted on information received,' one of the policemen told her because he was a friend of theirs and had drunk wine with them last month.

'But you can't just take him,' Helen said, holding Chris in front of her, keeping her voice calm. She must stay calm or she would not get Heine back and she could not go on without him.

'But you can't just take him. He's not dangerous. Bill, you

know he's not.' She wanted to reach out and touch Bill Rowbottom's arm but he looked different in a uniform.

'We can, I'm afraid, Mrs Weber. We don't need a judicial warrant for his arrest. We act under the Royal Prerogative. There is no charge necessary to imprison enemy aliens.' He paused. 'But, Helen, what was he doing outside the five-mile limit? And with a camera? He'll be interrogated. This is very serious.'

Helen just looked at him, at his eyes which were not unkind, at the badge on his collar, the helmet which he had not removed.

She gripped Chris tightly. An enemy alien. How could Heine be an enemy alien? And she wanted to shake this solid, kindly man but instead said, 'When will he be back?'

'I don't think he will be, my dear. Not until all this is over. Not until the bloody war is over.' He nodded at the other uniformed man who left to wait downstairs. Helen knew he was there because she had not heard the front door open.

'Now I need his passport and some clothes.'

His passport was in the top right-hand drawer, beneath the letters from his father. She packed pants, shirts, trousers, pyjamas, toothbrush, shaving kit, mirror, hairbrush, saying the words aloud. She carried the case back to Bill. It wasn't heavy, she told him. 'It really isn't heavy,' she said again and again, until he prised the case from her and left.

But she didn't see him go. All she could see was Heine's face, tired and drawn and full of love, all she could feel were his lips on her body and now they had taken him.

She stared ahead at the door and saw that it was dirty. There was jelly on it. There was red and green jelly on it, bloody jelly.

Her mother was there behind her, holding her arm, shaking her.

'It will be all right now, Helen. I am here. I can look after you. It will be all right. It will be just the three of us now.'

'There's jelly on the door, Mother,' Helen said, pulling herself free, sitting Chris in the chair, reaching for a cloth from the table, rubbing at the marks. How dare they take him? How dare they take Heine? He was good and kind. How could she cope without him? How could she face the stones, the hate? Oh my God. But what was he doing there and with a camera? How could he do it? He should have been at the party.

'What was he doing there?' she said, leaning her head on the door, crying now, shouting the words. 'What was he doing there?'

She turned, leaning her back against the wood, seeing the fire flickering low, the debris of the party, her son sitting curled against the dark red cushions of the chair, his eyes large and alone. She went to him and held him, stroking him, telling him it was all right and then he was crying and talking and his words came together into a sentence.

'Grandma told him to go and get a picture of the stream for you.'

Helen could not move her body but her mind became clear, rapid and cold, and she remembered Bill Rowbottom's words and now she looked at her mother. At the smile which was playing on her face, at her happiness this afternoon. At the words she had spoken – 'There will be just the three of us now' – and knew without a doubt where her mother's walk had taken her; knew who the informant was.

And then she screamed, 'Mother.'

And all the hate in her body was in that word.

CHAPTER 6

The plain-clothed police had been waiting for Heine when he stepped from the train. They grasped him by the elbows, pushing him over towards the waiting-room, pressing him up against the red-brick wall, his back flat to it. He felt the strap of his gas mask digging into his shoulder, saw the faces of passengers as they paused, looked, then hurried on. The train drew out, noisily with sparks flying from the wheels.

'Your registration card, sir?' the uniformed policeman said, stepping back, taking it from Heine's hand together with his ticket; looking, nodding to his companion who tightened his grip on Heine's arm. 'It's him.' They did not give him back his registration book.

'Your camera?' The policeman spoke again and this time there was no 'sir' and now Heine knew what Helen's mother had done. He knew that, for him, at this moment the war was over and he was filled with anguish because he could not bear to be parted from Helen, and fear because he knew that the bleakness of imprisonment was all that waited for him. There was no anger yet.

They took him to the local police station, locking him in a bare, cold cell with no blackout blinds because there were no windows. They removed his shoe laces and his belt and he walked backwards and forwards in stockinged feet because he could not stand the slopping of his shoes. He wouldn't kill himself, he wanted to shout. He had done nothing wrong. He had a wife and child. They brought him cocoa with grease floating in blobs and bread and margarine on a tin plate and then he tried to sleep but could not. He tried to think but could not. Nothing stayed still, there were just flashing images of party hats, rust-streaked wheelbarrows, toboggans which sped down slopes. He asked the policeman when he came to check that he was still alive if he would tell Helen, and he said that he would ring his local police station because they needed his passport anyway. So his wife would know when they arrived, wouldn't they? His voice had been hard and his eyes too.

In the morning they returned his registration book and took him by car back to London, the handcuffs uncomfortable on his wrists. They had not charged him at the police station and they did not charge him now.

'No need,' the policeman said. 'There's a war on, mate.'

Heine knew they were right. He thought of the stream which he had not reached, he thought of the party he had missed. He looked out of the car window at the houses which crowded the roads more densely now; they were approaching London. He knew exactly where they were going but he would not think of anything except this moment; only the house they had just passed with the red roof, the sandbags at the windows of the Town Hall to the left. The churches into which people hurried and which were tolling their bells. For him? Yes, it should be for him.

His mouth was dry. It was hours since he had eaten because he had been unable to face breakfast. It was hours since he had spoken to another person as a free man and that weighed like a stone around his neck. Now he was an enemy, a man to be grunted at, to be ignored, to be treated as though he was nothing. But he was someone. He was Helen's husband, Christoph's father, but he could do nothing for them now and so, therefore, they were right. He was nothing, just an enemy alien. He belonged nowhere.

Heine clasped his hands together, feeling the cold of the handcuffs, wanting to stretch out his arms, roll his shoulders, but the policemen sat either side of him, and as they drove up to Olympia at last he wanted to break free of them, run through the streets, back to his home. Because what would they do without him? And what waited inside the sandbagged entrance for him? But he knew the answer to that question. There would be Nazis waiting for him at this huge building which was now the collecting centre for enemy aliens. He did not move from the car at the policeman's command because fear had taken his strength from him and all he could see were the brown shirts of Munich and feel again the pain of his leg.

'Get out of this bloody car before I make you,' the policeman still sitting at his side shouted, pushing him.

Heine moved then, side-stepping his way along the seat, stumbling from the car because his hands were latched together and he could not find any purchase. The soldiers with fixed bayonets standing in a line outside the building did not look as he passed through the entrance. They just stared ahead as if he did not exist. The hall was in semi-darkness, the light excluded by the blackout, and Heine remembered the decorations and the noise of curious crowds at the exhibitions before the war and it seemed as unreal as he now felt. There were people, but they were milling aimlessly beyond barriers which marked off the area nearest to the door. There was a low murmur, that was all.

The policemen pushed him forward towards a dimly lit table behind which two British Intelligence Officers sat, heads down, pens writing on paper. In shadow at the edge of the desk was an inkstand and two mugs which were coffee-stained and half empty. The badges on the officers' hats glinted on the chair at the left of the table.

They did not look up as Heine stood there, his shoulders aching from his immobility. The police stood too, sighing, coughing, until one of the men looked up, but not yet at Heine, only at his companions.

They nodded and the police left but the handcuffs were still on. Heine raised his arms and the Intelligence Officer nodded and called the men back, watching as the key was inserted and the metal fell from Heine's wrists and the police left again. Heine did not look round but he could hear the fading click of their shoes.

The Intelligence Officer did not ask him to sit and Heine rubbed his wrists where red marks hurt.

'I'll have your registration book, please.' The Intelligence Officer was not rude, just cold. His eyes were pale, expressionless and his hair was thinning on the crown. Heine wanted someone to speak to him as though he was a person.

He took the police registration book from his pocket and passed it across to the officer who didn't smile or speak while he examined it and then he looked up.

'Category B is a bit out of date, Mr Weber, isn't it?' he said, his lips barely moving as he spoke.

'I was only in Hemsham to take a photograph of a stream behind my mother-in-law's house. One that my wife is very fond of,' Heine explained but it sounded foolish, absurd.

The man just nodded. 'We'll discuss all that in a moment, shall we.' It was not a question but a statement and Heine felt totally helpless.

He was not carrying his passport and so the man nodded to his colleague who telephoned, speaking quietly into the mouthpiece before placing it carefully on the rest and returning to his work.

'Can I tell my wife, please?' Heine asked.

'I dare say someone will be telling her soon. We have to have your passport, don't we? Can't just go in and take it, can we?' His voice was crisp. 'Any more than we can just have people taking photographs, especially Category B aliens.'

Heine said nothing. He emptied his pockets when he was asked and watched as a list was made, but it was short because he only carried one handkerchief and some money. He was allowed to retain these and his watch. Then the questioning began and always the murmur of the other detainees ran like a river around him.

It was not until midnight that Heine was allowed to sleep. He was marched up to the gallery where three-tiered bunks were set up, row upon row. The guard pointed to one. There were no blankets and he did not know where to wash and so he lay down amongst the snores and mutters of a night which was dark and lonely.

In the morning the blond middle-aged man in the next bunk sat up, swung his naked legs to the floor and looked across at Heine.

'So, another joins us, eh?' He laughed and stood up in his underpants, snapping his heels together, raising his arm. 'Heil Hitler, my friend. I am Hauptmann Meiner.'

He wore a vest, his lips were full and his belly sagged. Heine turned from him but felt a hand on his shoulder, pulling him back. It was not Meiner but another man, blond and young with anger in his face. He wore blue-striped pyjamas and his hair was cut so short that Heine could see the pink of his scalp.

'You do not return our salute?' he said, his face close to Heine's. His night-time breath was stale.

Heine stood up now, pushing the hand from him.

'Surely, my dear Hauptmann Meiner, you are incorrectly dressed for saluting. You have no hat. You look ridiculous,' he said, his voice heavy with contempt.

He walked from them past bunks where men loitered, some half dressed, some fully dressed, some still asleep. It was as dark as it had been last night. No daylight came past the blackout. It was so large, so full of so many people. His head was aching and in the cloakroom a man was shaving, peering into a metal travelling mirror, pulling his face to one side as he ran his razor down his cheek. His voice was distorted as he said, 'Good morning.'

He was English surely, Heine thought, and replied, 'Good morning,' as he drenched his face and hair with water so cold it numbed his hands.

'So, you are not newly arrived from Germany?' the other man asked.

Heine shook his head. 'I've been here since 1930. Had a bit of trouble in Munich.' He smiled slightly and dried his face on the corner of a sodden towel hanging from a hook. The other man had his own. It was blue and thick, not like the one Heine held which was threadbare with a red stripe running down the centre.

'Ah, Munich.' The man sluiced the shaving soap from his face and Heine ran his hand over his own chin. It was rough but he had nothing with which to shave or clean his teeth.

'My name is Isaac Stein. I have been in England since 1919,' the man said, watching him carefully. 'I have a spare razor if you would care to borrow it.'

Heine looked at him, at his face which was narrowed and wary and recognised the look. It had been on the face of the fallen Jew in Hanover.

The door was opening as he said, 'Thank you, that would be most welcome.'

He reached across as Isaac handed it to him but a hand with thick hairs and raised veins gripped his wrist and as Heine turned he saw the young blond man and Meiner.

'Aryans do not use Jew-boys' razors.' It was the young man again, his hand gripping tighter still. Heine looked at Isaac who said nothing, just waited.

Heine at last felt angry, a deep fierce anger which slashed at Mrs Carstairs, at himself, at the world for tearing his family apart, at this blond young man who dared to touch him and speak such filth and he turned, lifting his knee into the German, bringing down his free hand against his neck, then sweeping his fist round to catch the side of his face and nose.

The grip on his wrist was gone and the German lay on the tiles, his nose bleeding, his mouth slippery with saliva, his throat heaving as he gasped for air, and there was no pity in Heine because it had all gone on for long enough. Meiner had been watching from the door.

'Hauptmann Meiner, I met your brownshirts in Munich. You taught me many things. Now your friend knows some of them too.'

Heine turned back to Isaac and kept his hand from shaking, though he did not know how, as he began to shave.

'Did you know that in Southern France and Northern Italy they call brown the colour of the beast?' Heine said, fighting to keep his voice level whilst Meiner pulled the German boy over to the sink, washing him, throwing water on him.

'You will pay for this,' Hauptmann Meiner said but Heine would not look at him. He washed the soap from his face, handed back the razor to Isaac and followed him from the room. He felt cold now but not frightened. He was tired of running. Just so damn tired of running, he told Isaac, and so angry.

Breakfast was bread and margarine and stewed tea which coated his teeth, but his hands shook so much that Isaac had to lift the cup to his lips. His hands were throbbing now and he kept seeing the blood and hearing the gurgling, and was angry that he shook so much. It was not through fear, it was just reaction. He looked at the men who ate around the table. They were quiet as Isaac told them what had happened and then one old man turned to say, 'It is good to hear such news.' His eyes were dark and his face drawn.

Heine was glad that for the first time he had fought back.

After breakfast he was interrogated again and it lasted until the evening when he moved his bunk to be nearer Isaac and the non-Nazis who had accumulated at the far end.

For the next two days he was questioned but on the fourth he was left in peace for a day.

By then the Nazis and Hauptmann Meiner had been transferred to another camp but there were other Nazis to take their place and they talked in loud voices of the victory that would soon be theirs: of the Dachaus they would build in

Britain when Hitler came. They sang the 'Horst Wessel' at night when the others wanted to sleep, they jeered the *challahs* which a new internee brought in for the Sabbath, telling them that the plaited bread was like the blonde hair of the Aryan maidens who were the women of the master race.

Heine talked quietly to men he met; those who had fled from the terror which was now Germany, Austria, Czechoslovakia, who moved away from the raucous noise and tried to understand why they were here, locked up with those whom they thought they had escaped. At night, only at night, Heine allowed himself to think of Helen and Christoph.

When the police had been to collect his passport they had brought back clothes and shaving kit, a mirror, a hairbrush, and it helped to know that Helen's hands had held them but he could hardly bear the loneliness which tore at him.

The questions stopped in the second week and the next morning his section of the gallery was told they would be moving, that they must gather their luggage together. They were taken in unheated lorries away from London, sitting quietly, huddled together for warmth. They were driven to the siding of a railway station, jerking past large heaps of coal until they stopped and were ordered out, jumping to the ground on numb feet, reaching up to help the old men down. They stood near discarded sleepers beside the track, letting the elderly sit on the stacked wood, turning their backs to the wind, collars up, hats pulled down with their gas masks hanging from their arms, their cases at their feet.

A train arrived after half an hour and the guards formed them into columns, marching them along the chippings. One old man stumbled and Heine caught him before he fell. They embarked from a deserted platform at the count of three and then they rumbled off to an unknown destination.

Isaac was not with him. He had not been transferred yet but there were other friends. There was Albrecht who had fled in 1938. There was Werner whose parents were in a concentration camp. There were Georg and Wilhelm who had lived in England since they were six and were now twenty. There were the Nazis too.

In the carriages they were forbidden to lift the blind or open the window. Neither could they move about. Drinking water was not available and though they travelled throughout the day they were not allowed to buy tea at any of the stations that the train eased into.

They arrived at four p.m. at an unnamed station, parched and no longer talking, but they knew it was near the sea. They could tell from the gulls and the smell in the air. They were marched through the town with the Nazis holding up their arms in salute. The crowd jeered and Heine wanted to explain, to tell them that all Germans were not like this but as the sounds of the 'Horst Wessel' drowned out the gulls he knew it was no use.

They marched out of the town and down a lane where leafless hawthorn grew and the December wind was chill. It was darker now but there was light enough to see the gates that Heine and his friends straggled towards though the Nazis still marched.

There were low white painted wooden huts set in neat rows behind flowerbeds containing hard pruned roses and an empty swimming pool with a solitary spring board. Lichen grew on the tiles and momentarily Heine saw Helen marking in the number six on the bridge parapet. The guards pointed towards one large single storey building.

'Down there,' they said. 'Assemble in there.'

Heine took Willi's arm, a boy of eighteen who had walked alongside him from the train. He had told Heine quietly, his voice hesitant, his eyes anxious, that his father was in Sachsenhausen concentration camp, where he too had been but had escaped. He was glad to be back in a camp, he told Heine, because the English guards would protect him when the Nazis came and Heine did not point out that there were already Nazis here. He just patted his arm and kept close to him, because he would want someone to take care of his own son.

The lounge they filed into was carpeted and there was no longer the sound of crisp Nazi boots marching and Heine was glad to see their militaristic fervour thwarted by a piece of worn Axminster. The settees were comfortable but everyone was still hungry and thirsty. They were not given anything yet but were called in groups of ten to see the doctor.

Heine was called with the boy, Willi. He was examined and interrogated but only for two or three hours this time. They were escorted in groups of eight to huts by two soldiers with bayonets fixed who told them that they were at a bloody holiday camp.

'Comes to something,' one had said to the other, 'when you put these buggers into a bloody holiday camp.'

Heine said nothing because there was nothing to say.

They were pushed into a hut filled with four two-tiered bunks and no one moved as the door locked behind them. They still had not eaten or drunk. There was a mirror, a wardrobe and hot and cold running water and Heine felt proud of the British. Proud that they treated their prisoners as they did and he smiled at Willi and nodded.

Two hours later they were called back to a large hall where they were served tea, cheese and bread from two trolleys, each with an urn, one of which dripped on to a folded dishcloth. Nothing had ever tasted so good. Willi ate too, tearing at his bread, hiding some in his pockets until Heine told him that this was not a concentration camp, that the British would feed him again.

The Camp Commandant spoke to them when their meal was finished; explaining that they could only leave the fenced sleeping quarters under military guard. That they would only leave those quarters in order to eat in the dining-room.

'A camp leader must be chosen to be responsible for the performance of your obligations and your conduct as prisoners-of-war. He must be able to take the necessary measures to see that any orders I may give are complied with, and put any complaints or suggestions before the Commandant of the Camp. This leader must form a committee which will be responsible for the cooking arrangements, education, recreation, even hairdressing.' He paused. 'One last point. Everybody who wishes to can appeal to the Home Office for release and Advisory Committees have been set up to examine cases.' His voice was crisp and professional.

Heine sat quite still, hope in him once more. There was more than a murmur of conversation. People were laughing, slapping one another's arms, and the Commandant smiled before he left.

The Commandant stopped at the door and called back, 'You have three-quarters of an hour to hold the election for your camp leader. You will then be escorted back to your quarters.'

There was a pause in the talk then and Heine ran his hand

along the wooden table. The grain was straight and smooth from the scrubbing of many years. He would appeal as soon as he could and be home. Perhaps by Christmas. He watched as a tall man stood up. He was not young, and his voice was loud as he called for quiet, moving towards the back of the room where he could be seen by everyone. He stood next to an urn that still steamed.

'I propose Captain Rettich for Camp Leader,' he said into the quiet which had wrapped itself around the room. 'We must show these British how efficient the Germans are. We must run the camp along clear lines for the short time we will be here. Our Führer will destroy these British before long. We all know that.'

He pointed to a man who sat smiling quietly. Another man stood up. 'I second Captain Rettich.'

Heine looked around at the nodding heads knowing by now that the vast majority in the room were Nazis, most of them prisoners-of-war whose ships had been sunk. They would win any election but they must not be unopposed. Oh no, they must not be unopposed again.

He looked down the table. The men with him were liberals, Jews, refugees, all were non-Nazis.

He said quietly, 'We must not just let them take control. They must know there is opposition; that their authority will be questioned. Someone should stand against them.'

Heine waited for an answer; there was none. He looked around the room. The Nazis were talking and laughing now. They must announce a nomination soon or it would be too late, there would not even be a vote.

Herr Thiene said, 'I have a wife, you see, and she is unwell. I want to be fit to argue my appeal. However, I will stand if no one else will.'

Others nodded, shrugging, talking, and at the next table it was the same. Willi said as he leaned back in his chair, 'I have seen the Nazis in the internment camp I started in. They beat a man to death who stood against them.'

There was silence and then a cheer was heard from across the room and Heine thought of his father in Hanover, his friend in Munich, but then he thought of Helen and the life he owed her, her grunting tears when he had hit her what seemed like years ago.

There was not much time now. The Nazis were beginning to raise their hands, their laughter was louder still.

Friedrich, who sat at the end of the table, leaned forward. 'We should not ask our friend, Herr Thiene, to challenge these people.'

Heine knew that this was true and as he heard the Nazis he spoke. 'Nominate me, Willi, second me, Herr Thiene.' He felt he could not breathe.

Willi looked at him. 'You know what you are doing, Heine? They could hurt you.'

Heine pushed him up. 'Quickly now, there is no time.'

He listened as Willi called out the nomination, listened as Herr Thiene seconded him, and knew that this would make him the spokesman against the Nazis. He listened hard to the words, watched closely the hands which voted for the Nazis, the fewer hands that voted for him. He pushed away the thought of Helen's face if she ever came to know what he had done.

He had not won the election but the wire fence around the huts did not suffocate him as it had previously done. The guards with their fixed bayonets meant nothing because he was fighting back. At last he was fighting back and he felt strong again.

The next day he bought camp notepaper which the inmates called eggshell paper and wrote to Helen restricting himself to the twenty-four lines they were allowed.

He told her that they were by the sea. That the gulls woke them in the morning. That he loved her. That he was going to appeal. That smoking was not allowed outside the dining-hall, that he would miss her and Chris at Christmas in five days time. That he worried about them and the hostility that they lived amongst in their street.

He did not tell her that he had been punched in the stomach as he left the dining-hall that morning and warned to keep away from his *Moishe* friends but that he had caught his assailant across his cheek as he turned to leave.

The next day was 21 December and the Nazis held a festival, for it was the day the Teutonic pagans celebrated the solstice. Timber was set ablaze for this occasion with the Commandant's permission, but Heine wondered whether the man ever saw the Nazis' salute raised in the light from the bonfire.

On Christmas Eve Willi sang 'Silent Night' and Heine remembered Helen's voice soaring as they listened to her in the candlelight of his parents' home and that night he wept but so did many others.

In January the snow was heavy and it was cold, so cold, and Heine stood with Willi and watched the Nazis build snow swastikas and Herr Thiene said that when the thaw came they would melt as, in time, the Third Reich would.

'But when will that be?' Willi asked and no one answered.

The Camp Committee was set up in January under the direction of the Camp Leader and it was in charge of the food distribution as arranged. There seemed never to be enough for the non-Nazis. Heine lodged a complaint with the Camp Leader. It was ignored. He lodged a complaint for the Camp Commandant through the Camp Leader. It was not passed on.

He stopped the Camp Commandant one day and told him and knew that Nazi eyes were watching. The next day the food improved but he was beaten in the latrines. After that the non-Nazis stayed together, close together, and Heine's eyes and lips healed but they had kicked his leg and that still did not mend.

In late January he received his first letter from Helen.

> My darling,
> At last I know where you are. Your letter only arrived in the second week of January. We are well. Christoph continues to go to Dr Schultz and so far there has been no bombing.
>
> I know it was my mother who caused all this. I cannot speak to her now, or see her. I am happier this way but miss you so much and long for you to be at home with us. How is your appeal going? Please write and tell me.
>
> It is a relief to know that you are safe, away from the hostility which you would otherwise face. That comforts me each night.
>
> I will write again soon, my love.
>
> Helen.

*

In March Heine received leave to attend the Advisory Committee. Herr Thiene had already been released and Heine missed him and Wilhelm too. He stood at the window looking out at the snow as he pulled on gloves that Willi lent him and hugged the boy to him before he left. He had taught him English and mathematics and anything else that he could because he needed to feel useful as much as the boy needed the attention. But could he really be called a boy? Willi had seen too much to ever be young again.

The guards were knocking on the door now and Heine walked down the snow-cleared path, dirty with ash and sand and laughed at the shoes and slippers that were thrown at him by his friends for good luck. It was like being in Germany again, the Germany of his youth. He did not look at the huts where the Nazis lived and from which came the sound of jeers. He knew they were at the windows and he would not look at their faces.

He travelled by train under guard, and then by Underground to Piccadilly Circus and wanted to run to Helen, he was so close. They walked through to Burlington Street and his breath was visible in the cold. People passed them, hurrying, busy, free. There were posters on the newspaper stall and he saw the headlines: 'US peace mission fails.'

He wanted to stop and buy one, to see newspaper ink on his fingers again because they were not allowed the sight of one in the camp and lived on rumours. He looked again at the headlines. Britain would need the United States in order to survive. Would they ever join in?

As he sat before the panel of ten his feet and hands hurt with the warmth and he held Willi's gloves and told them where and when he was born. What his business had been, his present address.

'How often have you been abroad?' they asked and he replied with the truth.

'When was your last visit?'

Again he replied with the truth.

Here they stopped and the Chairman looked at the others, slowly. Again and again they took him back over that journey.

'Why did you go?'

'To see my parents.'

'Yes, but why then? War was so close. Wasn't it strange?'

Again and again they asked and he held the gloves tighter each time because he could not tell them why. To do so might injure his father. Word might get back. Oh God, Helen, he thought as he looked at the dark panelling, at the Chairman's face, so set, so dark. Oh God, I'm not going to come home now. I know I'm not. He pushed down the panic. Could he tell them of the camera? His knuckles were white as they held the gloves. He knew he couldn't. 'But you see, it was because war was so close that I went. I needed to see them again. Surely you can understand that?' He watched their faces. Would it be enough?

It was dark when they left and the guard held a torch whose slit of light barely picked out the path shovelled through the snow and Heine looked at him and wondered how far he would get if he pushed him to the ground and ran. But he didn't because it would be pointless. He would not be able to go home, for that is where they would look for him.

At the station the guard bought him tea and the steam rose into his face, blurring his eyes, warming his skin. He pushed his gloves into his pockets and held his hands more tightly round the cup. He sipped, knowing that Helen was not far away, that his son was there too. Knowing that his appeal would be rejected because he must not betray his father. They left to board the train but it was late into the station and the guard looked around. He was young and looked kind and Heine had told him about Germany, about Munich, about Helen.

'There's a phone over there, mate,' the soldier said. 'Give your wife a ring. I won't listen.' He handed money to Heine and walked behind him to the booth.

Heine lifted the receiver, dropped in the money, pushed the button and heard her voice and for seconds he could not speak. Then he said, 'Helen, it's me. I'm just about to get on the train. I've had my appeal hearing. I'm going back but it's breaking my heart, my darling.' He didn't know where the sobs were coming from in a grown man.

'Heine, I'll come. I can come. They've told me I can come and see you. Don't cry, darling. Don't cry. It will be all right.'

But on the train with its meshed windows, its black out blinds, the dim lights, he knew that it would not be all right because he had set himself up in opposition and now he was not going to escape the Nazis. Would he ever get home again?

CHAPTER 7

Helen sat on the wooden seat. The brass plaque which had been screwed into the wood was dull. What would Sir Reginald Potter think of that, she wondered, as she watched Chris swing high into the air, lifting her face to the spring sunshine of 1940, and who was he anyway to warrant a park bench as a memorial? It was Sunday, her day off, and there were other children here after a winter bare of young voices. The children were trickling back from the countryside because no bombs had fallen. Nothing seemed to be happening and people were kinder to her now that Heine had gone and no invasion had occurred.

Chris laughed at the boy on the swing next to him. He had grown since Christmas, he was tall for seven and mature and he smiled more now that the schools had opened in the mornings and the boys no longer had time to lie in wait for him en route to Dr Schultz. He was happy there, secure, and Dr Schultz had said that it would not be a good idea to move him back to the old school where hate might still lash out at him in snarls and punches.

Helen fingered the letter which had arrived from Heine yesterday telling her that visits could be made twice a week for two hours. He knew she could not come so frequently but if she obtained permission it would lighten his days and his nights.

She looked up at the sky again, where white clouds drifted against the blue, where no aeroplanes had yet roared, bucking and firing; bombing. Yes, she had obtained permission and would go soon to see him and the thought filled her with joy.

Shading her eyes, she watched the barrage balloon which was anchored by wires in a corner of the park. The airmen who were always there now, guarding, winding, checking, sat outside their metal hut smoking, occasionally talking, sometimes laughing with the children who hovered near. Perhaps they were reminded of their own families, thought Helen. Did Heine ever speak to children?

The balloon's elastic sides heaved in the slight breeze; its floppy ears trembled. It was never still, always fighting to escape, to climb higher still. In February one had broken loose, its wires snapping as the wind had torn and snatched at the air-filled hulk above. It had floated off, its wires breaking tiles and chimney pots but it had not escaped. It had been shot, sinking airless and powerless to the ground, covering the road and the gardens. You should know you can't escape the war, Helen had said, and knew that she had spoken aloud because a man who was walking his dog paused and laughed.

Would these lumbering balloons really force aeroplanes up into the sky so that accurate bombing was impossible, so that strafing of civilians would be impracticable? 'We shall see,' Helen murmured, beckoning now to Chris because she felt sure the bombers would come. But when?

'Time for lunch.' She smiled as he shook his head. 'Come along, no arguments.'

He came then and they walked home past the Wardens' post where they too sat outside in the sun, their overalls unbuttoned at the neck, ARW embroidered in yellow. Mr Simkins from the flat next door was there, his tin helmet resting on one of the sandbags which lined the walls. There were more bags on the roof and a post with the number '51' stuck out from them. Mrs Simkins, who looked after Chris until Helen returned from work, said that a bit of power had turned her old man into a right little 'itler.

Helen nodded and waved and Ed Simkins smiled, flicking the ash from his cigarette on to the ground before throwing her a half salute. They had always been kind and helpful, and other neighbours were too now that Heine had gone. Helen lay awake at night and felt guilty at the relief his absence brought. She lay awake too because of the pain that absence also brought and could make no sense of anything any more.

Chris did not hold her hand now as they walked. He was too big, he had said, and Helen had been pleased at his confidence. They passed posters stuck on the wall showing them how to remove distributor heads and leads, how to empty petrol tanks or remove carburettors in the event of an invasion. They were torn now and discoloured, one hung by a corner only and folded over on itself. Chris swung his gas mask at the sandbags which were heaped at the foot of the lamppost outside their house.

'Careful, Chris. You might need that.'

He just grinned. 'It's good for putting my lead cowboys in, Mum. They fit in beside the mask. There hasn't been any gas, has there? No bombs either. Nothing's happening, is it?'

Helen turned the key in the lock. No, nothing was happening.

They sat quietly in the evening, either side of the small fire because, though the days were warm and blossom hung from the trees in the park, the heat vanished with the sun. Helen could smell the smoke which hung above the coal which she had wrapped individually in damp newspaper to make it last longer. Smoke drifted out into the room but she could not open the window wider because the blackout would be broken.

She knitted, her hands sore from digging up the lawn for vegetables as everyone else was doing. More things would be rationed soon and she would grow potatoes and cabbages.

Chris was making a balsa wood aeroplane and the sharp, clean smell of glue cut through the bitterness of the smoke. His lips were set together, a frown dug down between his eyebrows. He was eating well, though meals were dull and repetitive with only half the usual food being imported. At least now everyone had two ounces of butter, and in the grocer's yesterday afternoon one woman had said that she had never tasted it before in her life and that if this was what war did to you, it was a bloody good thing. She had laughed then, showing blackened teeth and gaps where there were none and Helen had smiled but felt angry that so many people who lived in this part of London were tasting butter for the first time and that it took a war to distribute food fairly.

She watched now as Chris took out the Oxo tin which he kept in the cupboard under the wireless. There was a concert playing quietly and he should really go to bed but it was good to have someone else in the room.

He took a cotton reel from the tin and cut notches in its high rims.

'What on earth are you doing?' she said, setting down her knitting, pushing back her hair. 'Be careful.'

Chris did not look up but said, 'I'm making a tank.'

Helen did not want him to be taken over by the war. 'What about your cowboys and Indians, the lead ones? A head came off, didn't it? Have you repaired it?'

'Of course, Mum, like you showed me. I stuck that match you gave me into its head and pushed it down into the body.'

Helen poked at the fire and flame flickered up, clearing the smoke, giving off heat. She looked at her son kneeling on the floor, his socks down by his ankles, his shoes off and under the table. She wished she had her camera but they had all been confiscated.

'But why a tank?'

'Because the other boys are making them, that's why.'

He was poking a hole in a stub of candle now, then making a slight groove along the top side. He pushed an elastic band through the hole and tried to keep it in place with a matchstick which lay in the groove. It would not stay and so Helen came and settled on to her knees too, holding it for him, hearing his breath as he concentrated. He threaded the band down through the reel, keeping the candle stub on the top, and pinned it fast to the bottom with a drawing pin.

She watched as he wound up the elastic band and laid the reel on its edge with the matchstick touching the small table. The frown was still there and so was the heavy breathing but slowly the tank began to move, unevenly but inexorably, and now he looked up at her and smiled. 'That's good, isn't it?'

'Very good,' she replied. 'Daddy would be proud of you.'

He just smiled and wound it up again.

The next week the warehouse behind the bank was filled with *papier mâché* coffins and the man who usually worked next to her was absent, arrested for filtering the red pool petrol through his gas mask filter and selling it on the black market for 6/6 a gallon.

On 9 April, the war which the Americans called phoney became real. German troops entered Denmark and moved into Norway, taking Oslo, Bergen, Trondheim and Narvik. The British newspapers claimed that the collapse of Norway was due largely to betrayal from within and Helen felt the tension knot in her back.

In May one Borough Council dismissed in the interests of

public safety seventeen enemy aliens who had been engaged in Air Raid Protection work for the previous five months. A stone was thrown at Helen's window but did not break it because of the gummed tape. She began to walk Christoph to school early, before work, because the boys were going later to school and waiting in the alleys again and her son grew drawn and tense and took a safety candle to bed each night, carrying the saucer it stood in, sheltering the flame with his hand as he walked, smiling to his mother, but the smile did not reach his eyes.

On 10 May Germany invaded Holland and Belgium and Chamberlain's government fell during a debate on the Norwegian campaign. Winston Churchill became Prime Minister. On 12 May, it was declared that in the interests of safety male Germans and Austrians over sixteen and under sixty who lived near the coast were to be interned. The newspapers called for more action against the fifth-columnists who were probably signalling to aircraft, who were making plans behind their blackout curtains to betray the British nation to Hitler.

Each day there were more calls against the aliens and Mrs Simkins looked worried, though she still looked after Christoph because Heine was already interned, wasn't he, dear, she had said, and could do no mischief. Helen had wanted to snatch her son from her but she needed her job and anyway would not be allowed to resign as it was necessary work.

Other aliens, from non-coastal areas, had to report daily to the police station in person and not use any motor vehicle, except public transport. They had to observe a curfew between eight in the evening and six in the morning. On 15 May, Helen had to appear before a tribunal because she was married to a German but was exonerated and that night she thought her head would burst with the pulsing pain and wondered who had written to the authorities. Who was trying to ruin her life?

Mrs Simkins heard in the greengrocer's that one of the mothers in the park had reported her for taking too much notice of the barrage balloons and Helen just nodded but did nothing, for what could she do?

Helen washed the curtains that night, and the carpet, the paintwork, wanting it clean and fresh and new, wanting an end to it all but it had not even begun. She knew that, as the rest of Britain knew, because the bombers were waiting, somewhere they were waiting, and so were those in her area who hated the aliens. Despair was close.

She worked later now because there was so much to do and came home aching with tiredness, but Chris was crying in the night again and she told him that soon they would be able to go and see Daddy but he would not go. He didn't want to because it was his daddy who made him different, who made people throw stones, and shout and spit at him, he sobbed. Each night he cried and each night Helen held him, angry that her son was frightened and confused. Angry at these people – angry at Heine. And then, when Chris slept, her anger faded because she loved her husband and wanted him, but still the anger was there, and the pain, and the tiredness. And still there were no bombers.

She travelled to the internment camp on 25 May after receiving permission to enter a coastal area. At each change of train police stopped her and everyone else, checking their identity cards, their driving licences, before allowing them to proceed. She bought weak tea on the platform, sipping it, watching people waiting on platforms for trains. They were normal, fighting a war, an enemy they could see clearly, and she was envious because she remembered Heine's parents and friends and wished she did not know so many good Germans for then it would be so much easier.

Her tea was nearly finished and now she could hear the train. She talked to other passengers as they lurched and rattled away from the station. She did not tell them why she was travelling but talked instead of her son and an old woman asked, 'Will you evacuate him?'

'Perhaps.'

As the wheels rattled she looked out of the window but could see little through the mesh. Perhaps, she thought to herself, because evacuation had been in and out of her mind since 9 April, not because of the planes which still had not come, but because of the boys who shouted and attacked. But Chris could not go where he was known, he could not go where the other children had gone, so where? Joan who worked beside her at the bank had an aunt in Norfolk who was kind and tolerant and had said she would have him, but how could she let him go? He was only seven and she loved him, needed him. How could she let him go?

From the station she walked through the town, asking in a shop where the internment camp was, and ignored the stares and the hostility because she was used to it. She walked past the houses, the barbed wire which seemed to be everywhere, coiled in long rolls along the beach. Past the empty ice-cream stands, the rows of boarding houses, some shuttered, forlorn. Past the gardens which still held flowers. She heard the gulls which Heine had written of, smelt the sea breeze, saw the hawthorn in full leaf as she walked down the lane, heard the birds, full-throated, melodic.

There was a high wire fence at the bottom of the lane, and gates guarded by sentries. More barbed wire was rolled on top of the squat huts. It was like nothing that she had seen before and Heine was here, barricaded like a criminal. Helen showed her pass and was escorted to a hut by a soldier with a bayonet that glinted in the sun. It was two-thirty p.m. Behind that door would be her husband but she must not tell him of Chris crying, or of the boys, because he must think that they were safe.

He was there, sitting at a table, but then she saw that it was not one table, but two pushed together. He looked older, thinner and she went to him but was waved back by a guard.

'Sit there,' he ordered, pointing to a chair at the other side of the two tables. 'And you must not touch your husband.'

Helen walked towards the chair, looking at Heine, not at the two tables that had been pushed together so that she could not reach him, could not touch his thin hands, his tanned skin. Could not smell his skin or kiss him. She sat, clasping her hands together and they said nothing yet, just looked, and then he smiled.

'Hello, my darling.' His voice was the same.

They talked then and another prisoner brought coffee in a tin mug and she told him of the bank manager who dealt with all the munitions and war factory accounts and how she worked until late because records must be kept, details must be logged, or production would falter. She told him of the balloon in the recreation ground and how it had torn free. She told him of Mrs Simkins's kindness. All this he already knew from her letters but it did not matter because they were speaking words which reached over the distance between them.

She did not tell him of Chris.

Heine told her of the English he taught Willi. Of the hairdresser who had opened up in one of the huts. He told her of the concerts which were held every Tuesday. He did not tell her of the barbed wire which had pierced their roof, letting in the water when it rained. He did not tell her of the Nazi sailors who were picking flowers to make victory wreaths. He did not tell her that they sang in the evening of Jewish blood dripping from Nazi steel, shouting also that Hitler was very close. He did not tell her that he had been beaten again for taking the scissors from the hairdresser because he would not cut Jewish hair. Neither did he tell her that she was too thin and her eyes were sad.

'You are so beautiful, Helen. You are so very lovely.'

'And so are you, my darling. You will be careful. You will think of us, remember that you must come home to us.' Helen could see the bruise on his neck which he had not spoken of. But she would say no more because they both had their war to fight and when she left she didn't cry or look back until she was far along the lane and all the time she wondered if she could bear to come again, only to leave him so thin, so hurt.

On 28 May Belgium surrendered and the evacuation of the British Expeditionary Force from Dunkirk began. Small boats, big boats, ships; anything that could float took men from the beach and the sea and filled up the stations, the trains, the camps, the hospitals in Britain. Helen saw them in lorries being driven from Waterloo, dazed and defeated, and wondered what would happen now, and she was frightened, as everyone she met was frightened. Invasion could be only weeks away, the press said, and so did the girls she worked with and the passengers in the tram queue as they craned to see the illuminated number which had been moved from the front top to the side to avoid attracting enemy aircraft and Helen wanted to run home, snatch up Chris and hide. But where?

Then the newspapers began again. Act! Act! they screamed. Lock up all refugees from Austria, Germany and Czechoslovakia. Lock up those of British nationality who could be considered in sympathy with the enemy. And so they were locked up, including the British Fascists, and so too were German and Austrian women between sixteen and sixty. Many of those had escaped from the threat of concentration camps, from the terror of the Nazis, and Helen wondered whether she would be sent for again and could not sleep for the fear which ran through her because of what would happen to her child.

By June there was still no invasion though Italy declared war on Britain, German troops entered Paris, and on 23 June Britain stood alone.

'Got rid of those bloody frogs. Now we can get on with it,' Mrs Simkins said.

No one had called to take Helen away and she spoke to Bill Rowbottom because she could not bear it any more and he told her that she was safe. She was British, she had been cleared once and that was enough. She went home and weeded the garden, digging down into the earth for the dandelion roots but snapping one off in error, knowing that next year a dozen would come in its place. Would there be a next year? She threw them into Chris's small wheelbarrow, watching as he took them to the compost, putting her hand on her aching back and lifting her face to the breeze because at least she was free.

In the summer small-scale air raids occurred but not near them. Signposts came down. Road blocks were put up, ringing of church bells was banned and Heine's camp was to be moved but when? For weeks she heard nothing from him though the newspapers told of prisoners being evacuated and interned in Canada and she wondered if he would be exiled. But he wrote to say that he would not.

On 2 July the *Andorra Star* was sunk by a German torpedo. It had been carrying internees bound for Canada. Nearly six hundred were drowned and now, at long last, the newspapers said, 'What have we done to these friends of ours?' Overseas internment ceased and people began to think rationally, not with fear. Neighbours were chastened and left lettuce on the doorstep, not stones, and Helen showed the paper to Christoph who was glad it was not his daddy who had drowned and said to Helen that he loved his father and she held him close because he had not said these words for far too long.

Marian, from Alton Mews, came round and said she was sorry for everything she had not done. She came each week after that and sat with Helen in the evening and read stories to Christoph because Emily had now been evacuated to her grandmother in case Germany started bombing, and without her child she could not sleep or eat.

In July the police drew up outside and Helen watched as they knocked, gripping the window ledge, wondering if they had come for her but they had not. They had come to tell her that her mother had been knocked down in the blackout and killed. She stood quite calmly while they told her, watching the clouds scudding through the sky as white as the gypsophila which she had picked from the edge of the garden that morning.

When they left she sat in the chair and thought of her mother; the tight curls, the smooth skin, the eyes which were hard so much of the time but which had softened when she saw her grandson; the hairbrushes on the dressing table; the young refugees whom she could not condone, and Helen wondered if she would have been able to at her age.

She thought of the evening they had had together when Heine had gone to Liverpool, the loneliness which had been assuaged for those few hours. Then there was the day of the Jubilee, the laughter, the talk and now regret crept in and guilt.

But then she thought of her father; the damp curtain, the bleak room. She thought of the telegram to Hanover, of the sight of her mother's smile when she arrived home from Germany, the same smile when Heine had not returned from Hemsham that day. That smile which had played across her mother's face each time she was released from the cupboard. That night she didn't sleep but sat up stirring weak tea, not knowing what to think or feel but knowing that there was a loss inside her. She heard the ticking of the clock on the mantelpiece, the twelve chimes of midnight from the church tower. Then one, two, three, four, five, six o'clock and still she did not know what she felt.

She arranged the funeral but did not take Christoph, and on a hot sunny day she buried her mother next to her father, standing with Mrs Jones and Mrs Sinclair while the vicar spoke, his voice calm and quiet as the bees nuzzled the flowers from the Avenue and her wreath. As she threw a handful of earth warmed by the beating sun on to the coffin, she cried, but not in grief for now she knew what she felt. She cried for what might have been; for the companionship they might have found together, echoes of which had reached them both but which had been destroyed.

She cried for the woman her mother must have once been; for the loneliness she must have experienced especially when Helen turned away from her finally but in the end she could feel no guilt because her mother had betrayed Heine. She turned from the grave as the vicar finished and now there was a sadness which bit deep and would be with her always.

In a dark cool office, sitting behind a dark cool desk, the solicitor read the will, his voice as dry as his lips, and Helen received the rocking horse her father had made for her before he died. The house and all other effects had been bequeathed to her mother's cousin.

She walked then from the office to the untarmacked lane where her father and Heine and her son had walked, down to the bridge where the stream barely flowed on this hot dry day. She leaned over remembering so much, wondering why the world had gone mad. She rubbed the lichen, dry and crumbling, and felt her father's hands around her waist, saw Heine's hands firm and strong throwing the stick, heard her son's laughter as he peered to see who had won the race, and then she turned and left the bridge. Would she ever come here again?

As the summer grew hotter the hospitals took pilots whose faces had been burnt beyond repair as they fought the Luftwaffe in the skies above the fields of south-eastern England. Still no sticks of bombs fell. Chris did not have to pass the boys because it was not term time and Marian or Mrs Simkins stayed with him while Helen worked.

She thought of evacuation as she walked to the tram, to the shops with her ration book. She thought of it in the evening but who would hold her hank of wool while she wound it into balls, she asked herself as she looked at her seven-year-old son, so big now with the fear gone from his eyes. Who would smile and warm her heart?

At the end of August bombers got through to London, but not over them. Lying in bed, her hands limp at her sides in the heat, Helen feared that the time was close for Chris to go because his safety must be everything, but how could she bear it? And so sleep would not come because she knew that she must cope, as so many other mothers were having to, and so many children.

*

On Saturday 7 September at five-fifteen Helen was peeling potatoes in the kitchen, watching Chris in the garden, kicking the ball up and down the ash path, missing the potatoes by inches but not the cabbages. She opened the window to shout and then she heard them, droning, rumbling, inexorably following the Thames and then there was the air raid siren, rising, falling, rising, falling and she knew that at last they were coming and her son was down there, playing on the path.

She dropped the knife into the bowl and water splashed up at her, cold, so cold and she could not shout as she saw Chris stop and look and turn to her and then back towards the sound which was everywhere. The siren and the unsynchronised beat of the bombers wrapped around her head but the sun was out; it was Saturday, people were shopping; how could they come? The noise grew louder, and now she moved, reaching for the gas masks, for the bottle of water she kept for the shelter as instructed and then she ran down the stairs, along the path, picking Chris up, her breath hard in her chest and then through the curtain of the Anderson, into the darkness, and still there was noise, nothing but noise and no one to hold her. Heine was not here. She must not moan and cry with the fear she was feeling because her child was frightened too. She must smile and say, 'It's fine. It's fine. We're in the shelter Daddy built. It's strong. It's fine, Chris. It's fine.'

On and on they came, hundreds, darkening the sky, thundering, and Chris began to cry and so Helen told him of the ravens, telling people to hide until the gods had gone by. But these were not gods, her mind screamed, these are black-crossed monsters and then the thunder of the aeroplanes was overhead and the thud of the ack-ack was louder. The noise was like nothing she had ever heard, pressing into her, tearing her mind from her. Now she pulled Chris's gas mask up over his chin, his nose, his hair, and then hers, the straps catching at her hair, suffocating her, and the bombs began to fall, screaming, crashing, shaking the ground, and her breath was clouding the mask so that she could not see Chris and she tore hers off so that he could hear her talk, hear her sing to him, as she held him on her knee, leaning over him in case they were hit.

The shelter moved with each juddering crash but at the end

of one hour they were unhurt and the planes were gone and no bombs had fallen near but the docks were ablaze. The all-clear wound on as Helen waved at Mrs Simkins who was crying. Smoke was rising above the docks and there was a smell of destruction in the air which was quite new to her and to her neighbour.

Helen forced herself to walk up the path, leading Chris, calling to Mrs Simkins to come too, because neither of them wished to be alone. It was good to be back in the flat, away from the rising palls of smoke, but inside the ceiling of the kitchen was cracked and plaster lay in the bowl of potato peelings. She picked the knife out of the water. The wooden handle was cold. Fire engines were driving past the flat and ambulances and lorries, then more fire engines, bells clanging, and while Chris watched and counted from the window, calling out to her when they reached ten, Helen tried to scrape the potatoes but her hands shook too much. She boiled them in their jackets and made Mrs Simkins eat with them because Ed was on Warden duty, though neither of them was hungry.

Helen sat watching Chris eating fast, eating theirs too, and Mrs Simkins spoke in bursts and so did Helen and what they said made little sense. The siren went again at seven and the bombers came in 'V' formation and they walked to the shelter because Mrs Simkins could not run.

'I don't want to die alone,' she whispered as she sat on the bench looking at Christoph picking at the cork, but not seeing him.

'We won't die,' Helen said against the wail of the siren.

She was right, they did not die, but others did in the two hours when the bombers flew and targeted and dropped their loads which screamed and crashed until darkness fell. When they pushed the curtain aside this time the sky was red and Helen could see the cabbages quite clearly in the light from the burning docks and the smell was everywhere.

The fire engines came again and the ambulances and the lorries for the bodies and they ran along the road towards the greengrocer's – which was no longer there, just rubble and dust that caught in their throats. Helen turned Chris away as Mr Taylor was dug out, dead, and fire roared up suddenly in what had been his home.

'So this is war,' she whispered.

The bombers came again that night, blasting and searing, and at three a.m. a bomb tore and whistled too close and the shelter shook and shrapnel banged on the roof as the ground lifted and dust choked them. The curtain billowed and they felt the blast. Mrs Simkins cried out that they should wear their gas masks but Helen could not bear to breathe in the smell of rubber and Chris screamed and kicked and would not have his put on his face. But Helen could not hear the scream only see the lips pulled back, the fear and rage, because the planes were circling now, their engines drumming, the bombs pounding, drowning out all other sound and she knew that the next one would hit them, but it did not.

Again and again the ground shook and fear became less sharp though it was just as deep because the bombs fell for hours. There was a sourness in Helen's mouth and her breath was shallow and remained so until the all-clear went at dawn.

They climbed up the steps of the shelter into a dawn which was dust-filled and like no other that Helen had known. There was the smell of burning still heavy on the air, the crackle of fire, the screams of people, but the drumming was gone. At least the drumming was gone, but for how long?

In one hour, while Chris slept on the settee and they waited for the siren yet again, Mr Simkins came to fetch his wife. He was drawn and white and covered in dust but people had used the shelters and that pleased him, he said, as he helped his wife down the stairs and then he stopped and turned, saying quietly, 'The Hopkins boy has been killed. A direct hit. He was eleven.'

Helen watched as Mrs Simkins seemed somehow much older in a matter of seconds. Her lips were quivering, her head wobbling, and Helen knew that now it was time for Chris to go to safety and she knelt by the settee and laid her head on his, not waiting to see if Mr Simkins and his wife had left.

CHAPTER 8

The train stopped and started throughout the November night and morning but Heine could see nothing of the country they jolted through because the blinds were pinned down but he heard the planes, drumming overhead, coming in waves. He looked at his cards, his matchsticks in a small pile on the cases they had piled up to make a table and smiled when Willi won, but there was little talk. They were listening for bombs to fall and split the train apart, to crash and tear into their bodies.

How many had fallen on Britain since September, Heine wondered. How many on London where Helen still struggled in to work over craters where roads had once been and water spouting from broken mains, round cordons, fire engines, ambulances? And he wished that she too could have moved to Norfolk as Christoph had done.

As the train stopped yet again he put his cards down, shaking his head at Willi and Leopold. The noise of the planes was too loud and Wolfgang threw his hand down too, his face intent as he eased the blind away from the window, levering it from the pins with his pen.

'They fly high still,' he said. There was relief in his voice.

They had become complacent, Heine thought, tucked up in their holiday camp by the sea. They had heard the bombers day after day, night after night, but always they were going somewhere else, weren't they? And now we too are going somewhere else, but we don't know where, and perhaps we shall feel the judder of the ground which we have only so far had to imagine as we listened to the wireless or read the newspapers or received letters which told us our families were dead.

Not mine yet though. Not mine.

They were travelling up through England to another camp,

the guard had said as they had embarked before daylight in alphabetical order. Leaving the train is forbidden even in the event of a raid, he had continued, so that when the first formation of planes overrode the rattling of the train on the rails, their hands had become too wet with sweat to deal, and Heine hoped that the Nazis who had cheered when Martin Stein had heard that his family had been killed in the first raids felt the same fear.

It was not until midday that they reached the covered station that their guard told them was Liverpool. So they must be bound for the Isle of Man, Heine thought. Their mouths were parched because the water had run out at eight in the morning but there was nothing to drink, just soldiers with bayonets pushing and shouting, herding them into columns, marching them from the train.

Heine fastened his grip on his case, printed with a 'P' for prisoner. He did not look at the passers-by who stopped, their faces tired and drawn, darkness dug deep beneath their eyes. He did not turn as they cursed the column; he looked ahead but then he could see the raised hands of the Nazis, their swagger nurtured by their months in safety by the sea, their chants of 'Heil Hitler, Heil Hitler, Heil Hitler' ringing out in rhythm to the march until the guards shouted and thrust their rifles at them.

Now there was just the sound of feet; the clanging of train wagons, the barked orders, the coughs as they reached the landing stage and the grey cold entered their lungs and the dampness from the riverside seeped into their clothes and their bodies. But at least the sky was above them and they could feel the wind in their faces. They marched in step until a floating stage was reached and then they were ordered to stand at ease. Heine looked at the small grey steamer tied to bollards with thick hawsers which dripped wet slime. The river was stained with fuel oil, rainbow splashed in the cold shrouded sunlight.

'It is the Isle of Man we go to now, so says the guard,' Willi said, turning to Heine.

'We will not all fit on that boat?' Wolfgang asked from behind.

'He says that there is another coming. They have already taken an earlier load,' Willi replied, not turning his head but looking towards the boat as the gangway was secured.

Heine was watching the gulls as they wheeled in the wind which licked at the river, and wished that Helen was here, travelling with him, away from the mainland, away from the bombs. He thought of the letter he had received from her and reached into his pocket, feeling it with his cold hands, feeling closer to her because of it, because her hands had also touched it.

He drew it out, reading it again as the wind snatched at it.

> My darling,
> I have just returned from the station where I saw Christoph leave for Norfolk. He has gone to Joan's aunt, Laura Manners who moved there to live with her husband many years ago. He is dead and she is lonely and Joan tells me she is kind. I wanted to go with him so much but Mr Aster would not allow me the two days away from work that I would need.
>
> He was so very brave, so very small, and I could hardly bear it but at least he will be safe. Mrs Manners knows that he is partly German but to her it doesn't matter. She thinks it better though, not to tell the villagers because the vicar's wife is a 'patriot' and there may be others.
>
> Oh, Heine, I miss you so. I miss our son. When will it ever end?
>
> I love you,
> Helen.

The siren began then, a penetrating sound which silenced the clamour of voices, the shuffling feet. On and on it went, striking into their shocked silence and then they heard the planes, drumming with that German beat, louder and louder, but they were not allowed to move towards shelter. Instead, as the sky darkened with wave after wave of wide-winged, heavy-bodied, black-crossed planes and the drumming seemed to press the air from Heine's body, the first of the men clambered up the gangway.

'Come on, get going. Move it along.' The guards were shouting but they could not be heard now against the bombs thudding, bursting, whistling. The ack-ack was stabbing up into the sky and Heine held Willi's arm, his own shoulders hunched as the stage shook, even though it was not part of the battered earth. He pushed the letter into his pocket, unable to believe the noise.

Soon no sound existed other than the crash of bombs, the crackle of the burning riverside, the explosions of warehouses, the clamour of fire engines and ambulances. No cold air filled their lungs now. It was hot from the flames and their fear.

The guards were waving the men forward, always forward, their mouths working, no words audible. Bombs dropped to either side, ceaselessly, the noise filling Heine's head, stretching it, hurting it. The heat was greater now and the birds were no longer wheeling but had gone. Gone where? Where was there to go?

Some men were crouching and shrapnel was flying through the dust-laden air. The soldiers wore tin hats and pulled at the men, then pushed them on to the gangway.

'You can't take shelter. There's nowhere to go. We must sail, go quickly, out to sea,' the sergeant mouthed at Heine and Wolfgang, rushing forward, hurrying those at the front.

Shrapnel clicked and slapped on to the floating stage, hot and jagged. It clicked and slapped into backs and arms and soon men were being dragged back on to the quay, blood staining the ground, no cries audible, just faces and twisted mouths.

They were at the steamer now, the gangway rope rough in Heine's hand as he pulled his way up, his case banging against his leg, his gas mask in the way and still the raid went on and on until at last the Manx steamer cast off and moved away from the noise, the destruction, the inferno. Sailing down the Mersey, away from the red flickering flames reflected in the river, away from the roaring heat to the open sea beyond the bar.

Heine took hold of Willi who was crying, throwing their cases against a bulkhead. He passed Martin Stein staring wordlessly back at the conflagration and took hold of him too; pushing and shoving through the jam of men until he reached the side, until they all reached the side. He looked each way and then he saw what he wanted. He dragged them both towards the lifeboat.

'Come on,' he said, again and again, as Martin turned to

look at the flames, which reddened the sky, at the planes which flew in 'V' formations, at the gaps which appeared as the ack-ack found their targets and a burning mass plummeted to the earth.

'Come on,' he said, forcing a way through until at last they were there, resting up against the lifeboat tackle, breathing heavily. At least they had a chance now if they were hit. Still Martin looked back and Heine did too, knowing now what Helen went through each day, each night, and he felt ashamed because he had been safe and would be again.

He looked at Martin, at the dead eyes which had seen nothing since the letter had come, at the lips which never smiled, and knew that now he had seen how his family had died. His father, a successful manufacturer, had left Germany with nothing. His mother, cultured and refined, had played the violin. They had died in an air raid pushing their vegetable barrow because they had been Jews in Hitler's Germany.

He put his hand on the young man's arm but there were no words. What words could help?

The Nazis came then, shouldering their way through, standing before them.

'No Jews allowed near lifeboats, *Moishe*,' one with broad shoulders and blue eyes said, standing with his hands on his hips.

Heine looked at him, moving forward, and words leapt from his mouth, burning as hot as the Mersey had done. He was shouting, his fists were coming up, and Nazis were laughing. But when he called them 'Pigs, not worthy to lick the boots of my friend' they did not laugh, but shouldered closer and Heine wanted them to. He wanted to crash his fists into their faces and their bodies and fight their bestiality.

''Ere. Break this up. There's enough bloody trouble back there!' The guard was pushing in with his rifle, moving Heine along and Willi too. Martin just stood but Heine reached for him, pushing past the guard.

'Why do you not move your real enemies along?' he shouted, pointing back at the Germans. 'Why do you not move those swine?'

The guard took his shoulder and turned him forward, pushing him from behind.

'Because there's too bloody many of them, chum, and just three of you. For God's sake, keep your nose clean.'

Willi had his arm then, pulling him along, through the men who patted him, told him not to fight. It was not worth it. It was pointless. Such a small thing.

A small thing? Heine thought as he turned and looked across the sea wanting cold air on his face; wanting his wife, wanting her love, wanting his son. Seeing the old Jew on the ground in Hanover. He closed his eyes for a moment and then leaned on the rail thinking back over the months of his captivity, the endless battles with these Nazis who shouted and laughed and waited for the invasion. He thought of the words, the fists which had struck at him in the dark because he fought back. He was tired of it, and frightened, but he would not stop. No, he would never stop. There was a war going on, wasn't there? A damn war.

He stood there until they drew into Douglas Bay. It was still light. Willi pointed to the white building standing in the middle of the promenade and the square dark one on the hill behind the town.

'Look, Heine, Martin. Look, it must be a church up there, see, it has a tower.'

Heine looked and nodded but Martin did not.

They berthed at the pier, straggled on to the firm ground, their legs uncertain, their heads heavy with tiredness, following the guard who marched them, slowly this time, along the promenade. They marched to the right of the tram lines which ran between the sea and the tall boarding houses. This time there were no passers-by, just other prisoners, other guards and barbed wire which was tangled on the beach to their left and strung tautly between posts on their right where it surrounded clumps of houses, converting them into camps.

They marched past three camps, each with great locked gates guarded by soldiers, but the fourth was theirs and as the gates opened and then swung shut Heine wanted to clasp his hands to his ears because he could not bear the sound.

He was allocated a house called Sea View, together with Martin and Willi. Wolfgang and Leopold were at The Croft. The House Leader met them at the door and showed them to their room. It overlooked the sea and he explained that this had been a choice room in the days before the war when these were all holiday hotels.

Heine looked out through the salt-stained windows. There

were only four strips of brown gummed paper forming large diagonals and through these he could see the gulls wheeling again and grass on the lawns which fronted roads blocked by the barbed wire which ringed their group of houses.

'The islanders wanted evacuees, not internees,' Johann the House Leader said as he showed them the wardrobe space. 'So they were paid extra to sweeten the pill. I will see you downstairs when you have unpacked. Bring your palliasses with you.' He nodded and left.

There were five single beds in the room, each with two blankets, a pillow and three with empty palliasses. A mirror was suspended above the basin in the corner of the room and a picture of Douglas Bay hung above the door. On the cupboards by two of the beds were photographs and books. The others were clear.

Heine unpacked, then helped Martin who just sat on the bare springs of his bed. He took his clothes, shook them, then put them on to hangers. He placed the Hebrew Bible, his yarmulka, the photograph of his parents on the bedside cupboard. Nodding at Willi to follow, he carried his palliasse downstairs making Martin do the same. They filled them with straw, coughing at the dust, pushing, smoothing, then struggling back upstairs, laughing as they felt the sharp stalks through the canvas, but Martin did not laugh.

A meal was served in the dining-room while Johann explained that all the houses had to work together as a whole to ensure the successful running of the camp. There were schools, lecture halls, even a sports area. Within each house the jobs were shared, each taking a turn to cook and clean.

He told them that goods could be sent in by relatives, and Heine wished that he had not said that because Martin's eyes had flickered then. There was no English money allowed in the camp, he went on. The authorities took it and exchanged it for camp currency which consisted of celluloid discs for anything under sixpence and the rest was paper. No more than ten shillings was allowed to be drawn per week from the camp bank.

Willi asked, 'But what can it be spent on?'

There were about forty men in the room and they laughed. One called out, 'There's the coffee shop. The tailor's. You might like a nice haircut. In fact, you should have a nice haircut, my boy.'

Willi laughed and ran his hands through his hair. It was long, too long, and Heine smiled.

'You might have noticed that big white building as the steamer came in?' Johann said. 'Well, that is the old cinema which is used as the depot for camp food. Bread, meat, fish and milk are supplied locally and the military authorities allow us the same rations as the soldiers. You are each allowed four ounces of sugar a week, half of which must go to the cook.'

He paused. 'Now, we have a great many prisoners-of-war here. German sailors from ships sunk by the Royal Navy, airmen and so on. Many of these are Nazis. We have none in this house but they *are* in the camp and we find that it is sensible for Jews and non-Nazis to keep their distance, though for some it is difficult. There are taunts, surreptitious attacks which sometimes cannot be ignored. Be sensible, that is all I say.'

That is what they had said in the other camp but sometimes it was too hard, Heine thought. Later after roll-call, Johann came up to their room, nodding to Heine to follow him out to the landing, asking him if it would be better for Martin to go to the camp hospital. But Martin, who was only twenty, would not go. He wanted to stay with his friends, Willi and Heine, and so he did on the understanding that Heine watched over him.

That night in bed Willi called softly to Heine, 'Can Britain ever win?'

Heine lay on his back. It was very dark though there was a bomber's moon on the other side of the blackout. The mainland would be hurting more than ever tonight. 'Not unless America comes in, and so far they don't want to.'

'So the Nazis will come and we will be lost,' Willi said, his voice still a whisper remembering the camp he had left in Germany.

'No, Willi. Finally they will come in. I'm sure of it.' But he wasn't.

Each day was full with food preparation, chores, lectures and long country walks along the cliffs where the wind hurled at them, pushing them backwards until they leaned into it and strode on. He was pushed as he walked to the lecture hall by the Nazis from the boat. Georg, the leader, kicked at his leg when he would not return the Nazi salute. Heine dodged the next kick, elbowing him, taking the breath from his lungs before walking on. He talked with other non-Nazis and walked with them, Martin alongside and Willi too.

He wrote to Christoph on his birthday and wondered what it must be like to be eight in a strange house in a village you did not know, with your parents far away. He thought of his father in Germany. Was he well? Had he survived? Were the bombs falling on Hanover? Had the Nazis discovered him? He thought of Helen each day and each night and he wanted to hold her just once more. To stroke her skin, feel her lips open beneath his, her breath rapid against his mouth, her body moving, eager, but he could not write and tell her this because the censor in Liverpool read each word, and these words were for her ears alone.

She could not visit, she wrote, but had sent a parcel. Work was busy, travel too difficult. He must wait for the spring to come and the bombers to go. But each day she loved him more.

He gave a lecture in the large hall, talking of photography, of clear images, abstract images, telling them of his wife who preferred to use images to reflect her feelings and how that could be just as effective and, for a moment, he felt closer to her. He walked round the compound with Martin twice a day, talking, always talking. Asking, hoping for a reply, but there was none.

At the start of the second week in December he walked with Willi to the school hut and spent two hours explaining about film processing to a class of seventeen-year-olds. It was cold when he left, cold and brisk, and he walked along by the wire, looking out across the sea, watching the white foaming waves peak and trough, pulling his coat tightly across his chest. His hands were cold, almost numb but the air was fresh and no one else was there but then he heard the shouts, the laughter, and turned and there by the corner of Sea View was Martin.

He was being forced by Georg to kneel. Those large hands were gripping his collar, pulling it tight while five other men laughed. Heine ran, pounding across the ground, the breath was pumping in his chest when he stood close to the men and his leg was aching but that didn't matter.

'Put that boy down.' Because now Martin was being hauled up higher and higher, the collar wrenching tighter and tighter until his toes were almost off the ground. The slats of the wooden fence behind him were broken and the shafts lay on the ground. Heine reached for one but was held from behind.

'Well, our little Nazi hater,' a big German said, 'you don't like the way Georg holds your friend?' He turned to the other men who were laughing still, their faces red in the cold, drips on their noses. 'Do you like the way Georg is holding this dirty little person?' He laughed as they nodded.

'*Ja. Ja. Ja*,' they said, clapping their hands and chanting.

Heine looked from them to Martin whose eyes were not blank any more, but filled with a fear which was not human. Saliva was running from the corner of his mouth and Heine could hear his breath gurgling in his throat as he struggled to suck in air. Georg pulled harder.

Heine struggled against the hands, there was no time. For God's sake, there was no time. 'Let him go, you animal. You God-forsaken animal. You bastard. You're worse than your bloody Führer.'

He wanted Georg angry, wanted him to drop Martin, to turn on him, but he didn't. Heine relaxed then, slumping into the arms which held him, and then he moved. Quickly, sharply away, pulling out, shouting, 'Johann, Wilhelm, help, help.' Leaping across at Georg and Martin, reaching for the whistle Johann had given Martin in case he ever needed help but he had never understood. He ripped at the boy's pocket, thrusting aside the man who came from the side at him. He had it, cold and shiny in his hand, then his mouth.

He blew but it was jerked from his mouth. Martin was choking now and Heine fought free of the hands again, ramming his head into Georg's side, belly, hearing the groan. He brought up his hand, smashing into his face, seeing Martin drop and fall limp to the ground as Georg sagged backwards.

The hands were on him again, but again he struggled free, using his feet, his head, his fists, reaching for Georg again as he in turn reached for Martin, bringing his fist up on to his jaw, feeling the pain shoot up his arm, and then they were on him, punching and kicking and gouging and for a while he fought back until a kick caught his leg and he screamed. But then the others came from the house, shouting, calling.

'Heine, where are you?'

'For God's sake, where are you?'

He could not call, his mouth was full of blood but then the

Nazis were gone, running before they could be seen, hauling Georg away, his feet dragging limply on the ground, turning to tell him that this was not the end. They would come for him again.

Johann found him and called the others, wiping the blood so that he could talk but all Heine did was to point at Martin. Back at the house Heine spat blood into a bowl while Johann bathed his broken nose, his split lip, the torn eyebrow, but he hardly noticed as he sat in a chair watching Martin rock and moan like a wounded dog. At midday a guard arrived and arrested Heine for fighting.

He was accused of assault on Martin Stein and taken to a cell, while his friends objected. He was frisked before the door was locked and bolted. There were brackets on the wall supporting three loose planks of wood which separated when he lay on them so he sat on two blankets on the floor and did not sleep that night. Not because of the pain but the despair.

When he came before the Commanding Officer at eight the next morning evidence was given by Georg's friend that he had witnessed the unprovoked attack. This was substantiated by three others. Martin could not give evidence. He had been taken under escort to the hospital where he was to be committed to an asylum for the insane. He was completely and utterly deranged, the Adjutant said. His Sea View friends could not give evidence because they were not witnesses to the attack.

Heine was sentenced to four days at Camp Easterley where the punishment block was based. It was a light sentence, the Commanding Officer said, because he was not convinced of the accuracy of the statements but had to accept them. The cell was six feet by three with a small ventilator, no window and a damp cobbled floor. There were eight cells, one of which was the lavatory and the smell permeated the block but Heine did not care. Nor did he care that he had to sit or stand until blankets and a palliasse were brought by another prisoner at ten a.m. All he cared about was that the Nazis had broken Martin's mind. Each day as the guard paced outside that was all he cared about.

Christoph had been eight for almost two weeks when Heine was released but he could not think of his son because he was too full of anger, too full of hate. Instead he watched the orthodox Jews walking and talking. He watched the non-Nazis discussing the war. He read his letters from Helen and received a food parcel from her which had been held up at the administration office run by Hauptmann Rusch, a Nazi. The food was rotten and smelt and Heine sat and looked out of the window, thinking of Helen, bombed, frightened, sending food she could not spare to the Camp where provisions were more than adequate. Thinking of Hauptmann Rusch knowingly destroying her gesture.

He thought of her sending money each week. Money which she earned and he could not. His anger was so deep that he could no longer sleep or eat properly. The next day he walked through the country and ran in the sports field but still he could not rest. He thought of his father, so tired and old, so brave, and on 14 December he gave a lecture entitled 'Democracy versus Totalitarianism', in which he publicly castigated Nazism and everything it stood for.

That night a stone was thrown through his window wrapped in paper on which had been drawn a skull and cross-bones. Willi swept up the glass and the other men helped while Heine burnt the paper but knew that nothing could erase its message. The death sentence had been passed, one which the Nazis gave to those they considered arch traitors to the Fatherland.

CHAPTER 9

Christoph lay in bed listening to the silence. There were no bombs, no aeroplanes, no ack-ack, no cold damp shelter, just a warm bed, a stone hot-water bottle at his feet, and silence. Each night the quiet lay like a blanket around him in this room with the sloping roof, the dark beams, the fireplace which was boarded up. Each night Laura kissed him, pressing the sheets and blankets tightly round his neck to stop the draughts. Each night he lay straight and still and safe and could not sleep because his mother was not there.

The candle in the saucer flickered, shadows catching the dried flowers which hung from string wound around the nails driven deep and rusting into the overhead beam. Marian had given him a string bag full of vegetables when he left London. She had stood with his mother on the platform crying, but his mother had not wept. Her face had been still, her lips barely moving as she said goodbye, bending to kiss him, to hug him, pulling his arms from her shoulders when he clung, pushing him to the WVS lady who stood at the open door.

Other children were all around, crying. He had not cried but he had clung again because he could not bear to leave her. She had pushed him again and her eyes had grown red and full and her lips had trembled as though she were cold. He had gripped her coat and still she had pushed and said, 'Darling. I love you. You must be safe.'

Her lips had not moved around the words, they had just gone on trembling and her voice had been thick and he knew it was with love. He moved away then towards the door and the fat lady, climbing up the step, smelling the train, the soot, the steam. Sitting on a seat that itched, sitting too close to a boy whose gas mask dug into his side, watching as the WVS lady lifted his case on to the rack, looking at the children who sat opposite, wanting to rip off the linen labels which had been pinned on at the collecting post outside the Town Hall. He knew none of the children. They did not know him, did not know that he was German.

As he lay in the soft bed, Christoph pulled the sheet up around his ears. It was cold but warmer than the shelter where his mother would be. The light from the candle caught the flowers again and Christoph felt the string bag once more, full of vegetables and sandwiches, so heavy, cutting into his hand. He had not let go until they had been travelling for two hours because the pain had stopped his tears.

He had shared his sandwiches with the fat girl who only had two of her own. She had travelled on with him and four others by bus to this village and was nice, but she smelt. He didn't mind though because of her smile, and he would not let the others shout at her because Mary was his friend. She could throw stones that hit the targets and laughed when he pulled faces behind the teacher's back. She didn't ask questions about his parents or talk of her own like the others did all the time.

At six the next morning Laura called him, but he was already dressing, pulling on the grey socks with diamonds down the side that his mother sent for his birthday. He lifted the blackout hardboard from the window and saw hoar frost whitening the stunted apple trees in the bottom orchard, stiffening the grass into frozen clumps and knew that today his knees would be frozen again.

The stairs were narrow and dark but the smell of porridge was warm in the kitchen and so was the black-leaded stove which burnt with the logs he had helped Laura to bring in from the woodshed yesterday. She had said that it was good to have a man about the house and he had smiled, liking her grey hair which was wound round her head in a plait, her cheeks so red and full, her laugh which made her chin wobble. His mother would like her, he knew.

He did not stop at the table but walked on through and out of the door, laughing as she flicked at him with the tea cloth. The latch was stiff and Laura called, 'You can use the pot under the bed.'

But he didn't turn. He didn't want to talk about things like that with her. He was not a baby. He was eight now. He closed the door behind him. She had baked a cake and sung 'Happy Birthday' on the first and it had almost not mattered that his mother was not there.

He ran up the garden path, the cold air sharp in his nose and mouth, catching in his throat. He passed the outhouses, hearing first the pig in her sty, then seeing the sawdust outside the woodshed, hearing the hens in their shed. The latch on the door was frost-coated and his fingers stuck to it for a moment and he knew that the seat would be covered with ice again and shuddered. As he sat he could hear the hens calling, forever calling.

'Wait for a moment,' he called back. 'Just wait.'

Laura smiled and pointed to the sink as he returned, and he nodded, washing in cold water which felt warm to his frozen hands.

'Give 'em a good rub with this,' she said, passing him a rough towel. He wanted to sidle up and reach out towards the fire but she would not let him because it would give him chilblains. His mother had always told him that too, so Laura must be right.

He sat at the oilcloth-covered table, smoothing it with his hands, wishing it was white, not black, watching Laura as she ladled porridge into a bowl. She passed it to him, the steam rising, curling bits of hair which were too short for her plait.

He poured thick milk from the jug into the hole he had scooped in the middle and then she spooned honey on top with the same smile that she had used when he handed her the vegetables in the string bag. She had kissed him in front of the WVS lady who had brought him last of all to Laura's cottage. How kind, she had said. How very kind. And it was only later that he had seen the long back garden filled with sprouts and potatoes, swedes and parsnips but he did not feel foolish because Marian had given him the only things she had and Laura had been pleased.

He watched as she moved from the stove, carrying the kettle to the draining board, pouring boiling water on to the bran mash in the chipped enamel bowl, mixing it up with the old dented spoon. Her arms strained beneath her sleeves and her face grew red. She hummed. She always hummed, Chris thought as he took another mouthful of porridge and then stirred his spoon round and round until the honey and milk were mixed completely. She was a happy widow, not like his grandmother.

'Are you a grandmother?' he asked, licking his spoon.

Laura did not turn from her mixture. 'No. I had no children, but your dear mother works with my niece, young Joan. She is almost the same as a daughter to me and no doubt I shall one day be a great-aunt. When I'm wrinkled like a walnut,' she laughed now, turning to him, her cheeks shiny from the mixing.

'You'll never be like a walnut,' Chris said, running his finger round the inside of the bowl. 'You're like a plum.' He wanted to lean against her, feel her arms around him because his mother wasn't here but he was too old for that.

'Look here, while we're chatting away, those hens are getting hungry.' She held out the bowl to him. 'And don't you be cleaning your porridge bowl like that. Your mother would have my guts for garters. Now be off with you.'

Chris took the bowl, feeling the heat of the mash through the sides. 'What about the potato peelings we roasted last night?'

'I'll bring those, but you put your coat on first. That's a bad frost out there.'

They fed the pig next, leaning over the pen door, watching the steam rise from the manure on the other side of the sty, watching the pig snuffle and breathe great belches of warm air. Laura pulled her jacket hood up round her head, tapping his shoulder. 'We'll clean Peggy out after lunch. Pigs are clean if you let them be. We'll get her down to the orchard. She likes a bit of exercise.'

Chris nodded. It was too early to go yet. He was meeting Mary down by the blacksmith. It was Saturday, no school.

'You meeting Mary, are you?' Laura said as they moved to the woodshed to fetch wood in for the fire.

'Yes, by the blacksmith. It's warm and we like the smell and if I'm not there she just wanders about on her own because her lady doesn't like her in the house, under her feet.'

He looked at the pig again. Would his mother let him stay with someone like that? He knew she wouldn't.

He did not see Laura frown as he bent to pick up the spliced logs, loading four into the crook of his arm, not bothering yet to brush off the sawdust and splinters, but breathing in the clean smell of the wood. He followed Laura in, heaping them by the stove, then walked into the sitting-room, lifted up the willow basket from the inglenook and eased it through the door and back out to the woodshed.

Laura was there already, bending and throwing logs into a bucket.

'How are you sleeping now, Chris?' she said, looking at him, rubbing her back with her hands.

'Better,' Chris said, leaning down now, throwing the logs into the basket as Laura moved away. Last night he had not lain awake as usual until the dawn came. Last night he remembered nothing after thinking of Mary laughing in the carriage which had no corridor as one boy had peed out of the window. He had not dreamt of the bombs either.

'You bring that Mary back for lunch. It's rabbit, and if the frost keeps up, we'll have ice-cream as well.'

He walked down the lane past Laura's neighbour Mr Reynolds, who tied his trousers with string at the knee and came after dark every day to empty the night soil from the earth closet and put it on the ash pit beyond the orchard. For the tomatoes in the summer, Laura had said when Chris had thought the neighbour was a spy who came each night because his father was German. When she told him what Mr Reynolds was doing he almost wished he had been a spy instead, and knew that he would eat no tomatoes in the summer.

He was glad it was Saturday but school was quite good. They were taught with the village children, not separately as most of the evacuees were. There were so few so far, Laura had said, and Chris hoped it would stay that way. It was nice and the village boys swapped baked conkers for spent bullets, flattened like mushrooms where they had hit the road. He had picked up pocketfuls in London and so had the other boys. Mary had shrapnel which his mother had not allowed him to bring because it could have sliced his skin. Mary had no mother or father and her sister did not care. He sometimes wished he had no father.

He passed the cottages which were built of grey stone. The women hanging out washing nodded and waved. Would they if they knew what he was? He waved back, then walked quickly on. Were people shouting at his mother, cursing her husband, his father? Was she safe, were bombers dropping their loads now as he walked along safely, as his father sat writing letters safely? Chris kicked at a stone, his feet cold in his boots. He dug his hands into his pockets, his gloves not keeping his hands warm. Laura said that they thought his dad was the same as the others, a British soldier.

He looked back at the women. Laura had also said there was no point in putting out washing today, it was too cold and there was no sun.

He stopped at a gap in the houses, leaning on the stile. The trees were wild and free not like the club-like ones which lined the London streets. The fields stretched into the distance gently rising into a sloping hill. White frost streaked the brown earth and the straw stubble which lay in furrowed lines. The beetfields were further from the village.

He kicked at the post and watched the ice in its cracks shatter and whiten. He kicked again then stood still. Ice covered the fence too and each head of dried cow parsley, each twig of the hedge, each blade of grass. The puddles in the road were thick with it.

'I hate you, Daddy,' he said and knew that he was speaking aloud because he could see his breath burst into the cold air. I hate you, Daddy, he said again, but to himself this time. I hate you for making me different, for making Mummy have to listen to people who shout. For making Mummy have to work in London while the bombs fall and you sit on an island and I stand here, safely. I hate you for making me lie, making me say you are a soldier, making me want the bombers to be hit by ack-ack but when they are I hate you again because I think of Grandpa and can't cheer. He dug at the puddles with his heel, again and again until the ice was crushed and shattered.

But I love you, too, he thought as he walked on and so he pushed the thought of his father away because it was too difficult, all just too difficult.

Mary was waiting by the forge, the hem of her smock dress hanging down at the back. Her mackintosh hem was down too and her cardigan sleeves hung below the cuffs. Her wrists were red from the cold and her gloves had holes in the fingers. She waved and beckoned but he couldn't run because it was too slippery.

They stood beneath the awning and watched as Ted the

smith talked to the carthorse. It was tethered to an iron ring in the wall. He nodded at Chris.

'Come to see us again have you?' he said as he reached down and lifted one large hoof between his knees, bending double, paring with the knife, his leather apron stained and burnt.

He grunted as Chris nodded.

'Got your postal order too, I reckon, my old boy,' he said, his head down, his voice muffled as he eased back.

Mary looked at Chris and then away but he caught her arm, pulling the postal order for sixpence from his pocket. 'We'll go to the shop afterwards. Mrs Briggs won't say the sweets are all gone. Laura went in and told her that they should come out from under the counter. Sweets weren't just for village children.'

He smiled at her and was glad his mother sent him this each week for his pocket money and that there was enough for Mary to share. 'And come to lunch. Laura said you must.'

The smith was pressing a red-hot shoe on to the hoof and they heard it sizzle and watched the sweat run off Ted's nose and down his face to his shirt. The heat from the fire reached them and warmed them. They moved closer. Ted lifted the shoe off and doused it in the water tank and the smell came up with the steam to mingle with that from the charred hoof.

They waited until all four were done and then Chris moved to the grindstone near the wall and wound the crank, sharpening his penknife, though he seldom used it.

They moved on then, to the bottom of the lane, shouting back at Tom and Joe who had moved down from London too. They waited for them, walking with them, sliding on the ice, passing the goat which was tethered by an iron ring to a thick stake in the middle of a field between Teel's Lane and the crossroads. Chris pushed his hands into his pockets. He wondered if Mrs Briggs would be cross after Laura's talk.

The Post Office was open and smelt of spices and tobacco. It was dark after the whiteness of the frost and the mahogany counters gleamed. Chris asked for a quarter of gobstoppers after he had cashed the order, knowing he would get six and some liquorice. It was Mr Briggs in the shop today so it was all right after all.

He passed the gobstoppers round and then they slid down Nag's Lane, balancing, waving their arms, wobbling on the stream of ice. They did not speak much and when they did they dribbled pink saliva and laughed. Joe told Chris how his foster-mother had rushed out last night to bring in the washing off the line in case a German bomber came and the whiteness guided him to her cottage.

They laughed again but then walked quietly for a while, round the back of the pub where sometimes a packet of crisps could be found, unopened. There was none today and so they leaned against the wall, still not talking but thinking, because they knew the bombs were dropping on their homes in London whilst here people knew nothing of the noise and the dust and the screams.

The village boys came then, kicking a football up the back lane and so they made up two teams and the village won 6–2, but it was five boys against four, Joe said, squaring up as Ted's grandson laughed. But then they squatted, while Joe pulled out a Woodbine packet, squashed and flattened from his coat pocket, lighting up and talking of his father in the Army, waiting to kill some of those German bastards.

'You shouldn't smoke. You're only ten,' Mary said, taking another gobstopper from Chris, pushing it into her mouth, wiping her hand across her lips. 'You only do it to look big.'

'You don't need to smoke to do that, do you?' Joe said, drawing on the cigarette, blowing the smoke up into the air while the others laughed.

Chris wanted to push him back so that he fell and pull his cigarette from his mouth, because Mary had flushed and dropped her head, and because Joe had called the Germans bastards. But he just pushed himself upright and walked away because Joe was much bigger and he was scared.

He took Mary back for lunch, eating the pie slowly at first, watching Mary looking at the pastry and the meat, then the knife and fork until Laura showed her how to eat.

'I only have chips at home and eat 'em with me fingers from the newspaper,' Mary said, her elbows wide, her hands awkward. 'My sister's too busy. She's got a job. It takes her out a lot, that and her boyfriend.'

'You must miss your mother,' Laura said.

Mary shrugged. 'I don't remember ever having one. She died when I was two. You can't miss what you don't know, can you?'

'What about your father?'

'I don't remember him either.'

After the pie Laura took them out into the garden, round to the north side to the rain butt where they watched as she scraped the ice and frost off the top. They brought it into the house where she showed them how to crush it, then mix it with milk, cornflour and honey from Mr Reynolds's hive. They ate it from dishes in front of the inglenook fireplace and Laura nodded when Chris asked if the slates were in place in the chimney ready for the evening. He and Mary were frightened that the firelight would beckon to bombers which might fly overhead.

They stayed in all afternoon, playing snap and dominoes, laughing at Laura who lost, watching as she fell asleep in front of the fire, whispering, not shouting, 'Snap'. And then they just sat sprawled in chairs, feeling the heat of the fire, listening to it crackle and Chris almost told her about his father because he didn't want to lie to Mary but he did not because neither did he want to lose her.

CHAPTER 10

Helen walked through the streets, glass crunching beneath her feet, shrapnel lying on the ground still warm from the afternoon raid. She thought of Chris's letter telling her of his conker swaps and was glad that normality existed somewhere.

She was tired, more tired than usual today. The warehouse behind the bank had been hit last night. The coffins had gone up in flames and the plate glass windows of the bank had shattered from the blast and the heat. Water had poured in from the fire hoses which had been used to stop the bank from burning. Helen had arrived in the morning to see Mr Leonard in boots and coat, his bow tie immaculate and his face red with fury, standing on a chair directing the staff as they brushed at the water, the glass, the dust which filled the banking hall.

He had handed a broom to Helen, pointing to his ground floor office which he felt she, as his secretary, should deal with but she had passed it back to him, telling him he should do that himself while she helped in the bucket chain which was bailing out the basement strongroom. She had not listened to his protests but had smiled as Joan and the others turned away to hide their laughs because Mr Leonard did not care to deal in practicalities. He had come in from another branch to take over the position of manager two months ago when Mr Aster, Dr Schultz's friend, had been killed during a raid. He always wore a bow tie and would not allow gloves during office hours, though he wore them himself. He hated Germans and Jews.

All day there had been no gas or electricity and daylight was kept out because the windows had been boarded up, the hammering piercing their headaches. They had been cold and wet and the dust had hung in their hair and throats but by eleven o'clock in the morning the bank was open for business, though Mr Leonard had complained that his hands were quite ruined.

'In spite of your gloves?' Helen had asked.

The accounting machines were out of operation and most of the typewriters were no longer serviceable. All entries had to be made by hand in the light of candles whose flickering was reflected in the pools of water which remained in some areas of the banking hall. All letters had to be handwritten and as they worked, the frost cut through the staff so that they felt sick with cold.

Helen had gone out to a café and arranged that jugs of coffee should be sent into the staff, sending one in to Mr Leonard who smiled until she told him that she had billed it to the bank. He did not protest, though, but insisted on Helen staying late to finish urgent correspondence. Tit for tat, she thought as she passed dark shops, walking in the middle of the pavement, feeling her way past sandbagged lampposts, Belisha beacons, and other pedestrians.

A lorry had given her a lift this far, the driver asking if she knew where he could find a Christmas tree for the second festive season of the war. Helen had shaken her head, not knowing. She did not want to know either because she would not be able to see Chris. Mr Leonard had refused her request for leave which was why she had thrust the broom at him. He knew, of course, that Heine was German but now she was fighting back.

Number eight Warden Post was on her right; she could see it quite clearly now that the wind had carried the clouds clear of the moon. It was bright and the clouds had almost gone. A bomber's moon, she thought, and then the air raid siren rose and fell and the man walking behind her increased his stride as she did, hurrying towards the Underground station which was just ahead. The planes could be heard beating in the air and she ran. Joining all the others who pushed into the entrance of the station and down the steps, but she wanted the District Line and so she turned, forcing her way through the people, taking the route she needed, then on down the corridor.

It was warm on the platform and camp beds were already set up for the night, row upon row with women guarding two or three until the family arrived. So few children, Helen thought, standing and watching. So few men out of uniform. She smiled as two women danced to an accordion player. They lifted their skirts, kicking their bare, mottled legs high as three sailors whistled and clapped.

Joan spent each night in her local station with her mother, she had told Helen. It was safer, more fun than on their own. More women were dancing now, their laughter ignoring the raid above them which was pulverising the city, perhaps their homes, but what else could they do? What else could anybody do? Helen watched as an old woman took out her Thermos flask and poured tea into a cup, tilting back her head and drinking. Helen watched as she placed it on the ground, taking her paper packet of sandwiches from a shopping bag on her camp bed, tearing the bread and scrape of butter into bits before eating them. She looked up at Helen and smiled, holding out a piece to her.

''Ere you are, dearie. Have some bread and butter.'

Helen smiled back, shaking her head. Knowing that the woman would need it for herself because she would not move from here until the morning.

She walked along, away from the blankets which hung from a wooden frame around the toilet buckets. The stench was still strong down at the other end of the platform and it was too warm, fetid. She undid her coat. A train came and although it was not hers the draught it caused was welcome and she wondered how these people could bear the airless stench once the trains stopped for the night.

She put her hands in her pockets and eased her feet in their boots and thought that anything was better than being crushed beneath the rubble of your home.

Her train came then and she could find no seat but did not expect to. She hung on the strap, feeling bodies close against her, hot and heavy, but when she reached her station and the fresh cold air she was sorry to leave the company of others.

The raid was over but the sky burned red as she knew it would. Rescue lorries ground past her as she walked on down deserted streets which had not been hit tonight. But there was still time. Yes, there was still plenty of time.

There were gaps in the terraces where houses had once been and through these she could see that the warehouses in Mill Street had been hit. She could see and hear the flames leaping high into the sky and then there was an explosion and she ducked instinctively, knowing it must be the spirits exploding. She held on to a lamppost, watching as more fire engines clanged and roared down the street towards the conflagration.

She saw more flames shoot into the air and the timber yard which stood close to the warehouse caught fire. Then there was a whoosh as the draught from the flames sent timbers up into the air to fall and set other areas alight. Over to the right a man ran past telling her the gas station was ablaze and that burning rats were running from the warehouse, and now Helen wanted to get home, to shut the door on all this, not to have to see and hear the destruction. And so she ran, knowing as she did so that there would be another raid, and another and another, and perhaps, next time, she would burn.

She ran until the breath pumped in her chest and hurt her throat. It was light now from the fires and she jumped over hoses which curled across the road and round people who came to stand and look. The road ahead was cordoned off and so she turned right, then left, but her way was blocked by an ARP rescue lorry which roared as it backed up to a pile of smouldering rubble. She turned again, crossing down a narrow footpath, then out into Kendle Street but she was walking now because her legs were weak and she wished that there was someone at home waiting for her.

She could not hear the sound of her footsteps against the noise of ambulances, rescue lorries, fire engines. She passed old women who pushed food from baskets into the mouths of rescue workers who could not stop to eat or drink. Further along a dead fireman lay on the pavement. Further along still a queue was forming at the Town Hall for missing relatives. She wanted to go up and shake them. Tell them to go away because there would be another raid and they would be dispersed and have to begin queuing all over again. But she did not because it happened every night and they all knew it did.

She looked at her watch. It was nine o'clock. She had left work at seven and not eaten since midday. Her mouth tasted sour and dry. She wanted to get home before it all began again. She started running once more down a street where no fires burned but it was darker because of this and so she slowed, moving out past a car slewed into the kerb, but a hand caught her arm and stopped her. She swung around, her hair in her eyes, her breath shallow. She pulled but could not break free.

'It's all right. It's all right. I'm a doctor.' The man's voice was calm and so Helen stood still. She could not see his face clearly because his back was to the burning sky.

'There's a man in there, down in the basement.' He was pointing to a house which no longer had a front, just floors which hung limp and wallpaper which was torn. 'He's not good but we can't get to him. We're too big.'

The doctor pointed again but this time two ARP wardens – one of them Mr Simkins – came over and guided her to the building over scattered rubble, glass and shrapnel, showing her a small gap at the base of the destruction.

'Can you get down there, Helen? Talk to him, see how he is? We can only hear noises.'

Helen stood there, the dust from the fallen masonry making her cough. I'm going home, she wanted to say. I want a drink. I want a hot cup of tea. I'm cold and I want to go home. And I don't like the dark. I don't like the dark.

'Be a good girl,' the doctor said, taking her arm again.

I'm not a girl, she wanted to say as he started to take her coat off, pulling it from her arms because there would not be room for her to pass through the gap while she still wore it. I'm not a girl, she repeated to herself, I'm a woman of twenty-seven but then women of that age shouldn't be frightened, should they?

'You'll need to go in head first. We'll hold your legs, drop you as far as possible. Call to him, see what it's like down there.'

Mr Simkins took her arm. 'It's Frank, the grocer,' he said.

She went, of course, head first down into the dark where the air was so full of dust she thought she would die, feeling the bricks scrape her legs and she cried out. 'My coat, put it under my legs.' She could feel them pushing it between her skin and the bricks, and the pain eased but it had made her cry.

Down into the dark and it was her mother's cupboard again, coming and closing itself around her and she cried, silently. It was dark, so dark.

'Call Frank,' the doctor said. 'Call him, see how he is.'

'How can I see? It's dark. Pitch dark, you bloody fool.' Helen shouted these words and anger drove the fears away. Along with the anger came surprise because she seldom swore. Ladies didn't, did they? 'Send down a torch, for God's sake.'

'Ssh, Helen,' Mr Simkins said. 'Don't disturb anything. We don't know how safe it is.' He paused and Helen felt the blood coming into her head. She closed her eyes. There was a scrabbling sound and then something cold brushed her face and she opened her eyes, seeing the beam of weak light catching the particles of dust, those same particles which caught in her eyes, her nose, her mouth. She gripped the torch, feeling the string round the handle.

'Don't take the string off. You might drop the torch,' M Simkins called.

She could hear grunts still and turned the torch towards them. There were just bricks and beams and one arm and one leg visible.

'Frank, Frank, it's me, Helen. How badly are you hurt?' There was no proper reply, just grunts and gurgles, but if they lowered her just a little more she could reach down and touch the hand and perhaps move the bricks.

'Drop me a little further,' she gasped, the dust thick in her mouth. Her ankles were breaking. 'Shall I move the bricks? All I can hear are grunts.' She started coughing now and her legs bucked as she did so and she dropped the torch, but it was still on its string so the doctor pulled it up and it was dark again.

She called 'Pull me up. Pull me up.' And now she was screaming because it was so dark and there was a man grunting, but he wasn't a man, he wasn't Frank any more. She had seen the blood as the torch swung, the bones and his head and knew why he grunted. They pulled her up but she couldn't stand, just sat with her head in her hands. And then she was sick and her mouth was sour as she told them again and again what she had seen.

The doctor wiped her face and held her head and told her he wanted her to go down again and give Frank an injection because no one should bear that sort of pain. But she couldn't. How could she go back down into the dark? How could her mother make her? How could this man make her? Where was Heine, why wasn't he here helping her? Keeping her safe. He had promised, hadn't he? She lifted her head. There was still the noise of the flames, the timber, the ambulances but up here at least there was some light.

It was dark down there. Didn't they know that? It was dark and there was a man with no face, grunting and gurgling, and she wanted to go home to her flat but there was no one there, was there? God damn it, there was no one there.

She was crying but it was inside and it was hurting her.

Mr Simkins helped her up, handed her the torch.

'Be a brave girl,' he said.

But Mrs Simkins wasn't brave, was she, Helen wanted to shout. She had left London, hadn't she? She had left and gone to live where bombs don't fall.

She took the syringe and listened as the doctor told her what to do when she got close enough to the arm. They held her legs again as she eased through the hole, her arms out before her, dropping down into the darkness, breathing the stifling air, the dust, hearing no crackling flames, just those grunts, and then the torch was lowered on the string. She caught it, using the light to guide herself back to the rubble, but she had to release it to move four bricks, slowly, carefully, hearing the creaking above her, feeling a sudden fall of dust, but nothing else moved. She groped her way forward. The torch swung round and round on its string, its light not reaching this far and so she felt over the jagged mortar, the splintered wood. She touched a hand. It was still warm and fingers closed around hers and the grunting stopped, just for a moment.

The crying inside her stopped too then, and so did her fear of the broken head and face and it was Frank who held her hand and for a moment they gave one another strength.

Then his groans began again and she talked through the dust in her throat. She talked of the shop and Christoph; the shrapnel he had swapped; Mary, the friend he had made. 'They're both outsiders you see,' she murmured gently as she plunged the needle into his arm, pressing the morphine into Frank.

Mr Simkins called, 'Shall we bring you up now?'

The blood was pounding in her head but it was not until the grip on her hand relaxed and the grunts ceased that she called, 'Yes, bring me up.'

The rescue team was there as she was dragged back through the hole and the doctor took the syringe from her, checking her carefully, making her sit, but this time she was not sick. This time she waited, breathing in the cold air, heavy still with the smell of burning and floating with ash fragments.

'Will someone be worrying at home?' the doctor asked. 'Shall I drop you off?' He turned as an ambulance stopped and a nurse called to him.

Helen shook her head. 'No. I shall be quite all right. You're needed again,' she said, clambering to her feet, moving out of the way. She waved to Mr Simkins as he answered a call across the street. 'Shall I wait?'

Mr Simkins turned. 'No, Helen, you get back. This'll take all night. Get your head down before the next wave comes.'

The flat was dark and cold but she did not light the fire. There was no point. There would be another raid soon. She lit the gas under the kettle, cut sandwiches, rinsed out the Thermos. Then she shook her coat out of the window, clearing it of brick dust, and did the same to her skirt. Her lisle stockings were torn and her legs grazed but before she stepped into the bath she poured water over the tea in the strainer. It had only been used once this morning and so was not too weak. She filled the Thermos and used what was left for a cup now, sipping hastily as she did so because the sirens might go and she must get clean today for the first time.

After her bath she put woollen stockings and socks on and then her boots. There was a candle in the upturned flowerpot in the Anderson from last night for warmth but she would need matches and so she put them in her pocket. She was talking aloud, listing her shelter provisions but that was better than the sound of nobody's voice. She had missed the nine o'clock news but the wireless was playing music and that was some sort of company. She did not put on the light in the sitting-room but instead eased back the blackout. Her hair was still wet from her bath and lay cold on her neck. She picked up a towel and rubbed it. Marian was coming tomorrow for lunch.

How was Frank? She paced to the kitchen, pouring more boiling water on to the tea leaves, drinking as she walked, frying rissoles in the pan. Listening, always listening for the siren, for the planes, and she was glad Christoph was not here but she missed him and paced again to push away the ache. She sat down and wrote to Heine by the light of the red sky and the moon, telling him of Chris swapping shrapnel for sixers, and for a moment she could smell the rotten conkers which they had found in the park beneath the tree. She told him of the bank because she hoped he would laugh, and of Marian coming tomorrow because it was Saturday and they had the day off. She told him she missed him and loved him, because she did, but she did not tell him that she wished he was British and that they were the same as everyone else. She told him she was so glad he wasn't here, that he was safe.

She did not tell him of Frank, of the dust and the darkness, because he blamed himself that he was not here and part of her did so too.

At eleven the bombers had not come back and she put on her coat because she wanted to see what had happened to Frank. She had walked as far as the corner of Ellesmere Road when the sirens went again and this time the bombers were close, roaring in, wave upon wave, and there was no time to go back to the shelter in the High Street, no time to go to her own. She pressed herself back against the wall of the gutted house behind her. It had been bombed in November.

The noise grew louder, spreading itself around her, trying to force her to the ground, and then the bombs came again, flashing, crushing and juddering. Helen crouched, knowing that the whimpering she heard was coming from her. She looked up at the black wide bodies, the bursting ack-ack, the two parachute mines floating down in the direction of the park.

She flung herself down, holding her fist to her mouth. She must not scream. She was not a child. She must not scream. Two long dull roars came and the barrage balloon stood out in relief against the blaze that came. Fire bombs were hurtling down now and white magnesium fires leapt up to turn red as buildings caught fire. The thuds of heavy oil bombs followed and now she could feel the heat. The bombs were getting closer.

She lay on the ground, rubble digging into her. She could hear glass shattering. More incendiaries fell; small, pretty. They did not blast, they just burned where they fell. A warden ran by, stopping, shouting at her as she lifted her head.

'Get into a bloody shelter.' His voice was harsh, impatient. Then he ran on.

But where was there a shelter? She scrambled up now, looking each way, then running to the corner, hearing the shrapnel falling all around. There was no safety anywhere. She ran blindly now, across the road, down a lane, but everywhere there was heat and falling walls, shouts and screams, and then she came to a crossroads and there on the opposite corner was St Bede's; dark, black and solid, and she ran in through the gate, past the gravestones, into the porch, panting. Gasping for breath. Holding her arms tightly round her body.

Was there ever a time when life was quiet, when nights were

for sleeping? It was madness. Absolute madness. She felt the ground juddering, heard the hiss of the falling bombs, and even here the shrapnel came and so she ran again, keeping close to the walls of the church whose windows had been boarded up when war was declared. She was stumbling now, tripping on the graves, falling on frozen grass until she came to the clump of lilac trees which bloomed each summer and there was a large door down some steps and Helen stopped. She turned, feeling her way down until she reached the bottom. There was someone else there, an old woman who caught hold of her, pulling her against the door.

'Bless you. Gave me a fright you did,' the old woman said, pulling her scarf tighter round her head.

Helen looked at her, at the camp stool she sat on, the knitting she was doing out here in the open air. On her hands she wore fingerless gloves. Helen pushed at the door. There was a crypt here. She remembered now because they had held the vicarage fête in the gardens before the war and the tables and chairs, the bunting, the stalls were carried in here afterwards. Heine had laughed because the vicar had been so busy directing everyone he had become jammed behind the benches and they had to move everything back again to release him.

The bombers were coming in another wave now, overhead. The noise was loud, the explosions close and over to their left. Shrapnel still fell, clattering down the steps, against the door. Helen ducked and pushed again.

'No good doing that, ducky. The vicar keeps it locked.' The old woman laughed but her voice trembled and Helen touched her shoulder.

'Why are you here?' she asked, crouching beside her, looking up at the sky, wincing as a bomb dropped nearby.

'Nowhere else nearby, is there, love? I ain't got no shelter, the station's too far and the brick one in Maine Street got hit last week.'

Helen ducked as the run of explosions drew closer still. The ack-ack thudded nearby.

'There's more poor souls out past the lilac bush. They got bombed out earlier. They've got nowhere else to go. They don't want to leave the area, see. It's their home.'

There were fires crackling and ash being blown across from the nearby streets. Helen eased herself up, pushing once more at the door, and then again. It gave a little each time but not enough. She eased herself up the steps.

'Have you asked the vicar to unlock it for you?' She was shouting now against the noise.

'He's too busy, isn't he? Rushing around seeing all these dead people.'

Helen was up the steps now, running round to the back of the church and on towards the vicarage. She knocked but there was no reply. She ran round to the Anderson, too angry to fear the bombs. Too damned angry.

There was no one there. She ran back, wrenching at the upright garden fork stuck deep into the soil, dragging it along behind her so that it clattered on the path but that was just one more noise in the bedlam.

She dragged it past the lilac bush, shouting at the people there to come down; the crypt was going to be opened. She carried it down the steps, forcing it into the gap between the door and the frame, just below the handle, pushing on it. It gave further this time but still not enough. Helen threw her weight on it but still it did not open. She turned then as old gnarled hands added their weight and an old man nodded. Together they tried it and then the wood of the door splintered and the lock gave way. The door was open.

Helen turned. 'Get in here. Quick.' A bomb dropped outside the churchyard.

'Get in quick!' She was screaming now, grabbing at the old woman, who dropped her ball of wool and went back for it. Helen pulled her, running for the wool herself, pushing at two more people who came running down the steps from the graveyard where they had been sheltering. The wool caught in her fingers, she dropped it again, picked it up once more and this time held it to her, backing into the crypt, slamming the door shut.

'Everyone away from the door,' Helen said, her voice hoarse now, remembering the inspector who had insisted on a blanket for the shelter because of blast splinters.

It was pitch black. There was no light and almost no noise.

'Can't see to move,' the old man said.

Helen was fumbling in her pockets. She had her matches. She struck one, cupping it in her hand, moving forwards and then sideways to get out of the line of the door, hearing the shuffle of feet as they followed her, feeling a hand clinging to her coat for guidance.

There were benches piled high and a stuffy feel to the air but no shrapnel clicked and cut. One of the old women had a candle in the bag which held all that she now owned.

Helen lit it and with the old man who smiled a smile without teeth she left them in the dark on seats they had found while she moved amongst the vicarage fête material looking for more candles.

The old man found a new packet, long, thick white ones, which Ruth, the woman who had dropped her knitting, said they could not use because they were for the altar. Helen looked at her and at the others.

'I will speak to the vicar in the morning,' she said, burning the bottom of the candle so that the wax melted and then setting it down on the lid of a tin of old powder paint they had found. They sat or lay on the benches which Helen pulled round into a square until the all clear at four-thirty a.m. They had been cold but safe and Helen had not been alone.

She was tired and angry as she watched the others leave, walking out into the grey dawn. But then she called, 'Come back tonight. It will be open and there'll be hot tea. Bring some bread and butter and some tea if you can.' She went round to the vicarage again and knocked on the door, and when there was no reply she waited, sitting on the step until the vicar came up the path, his face grey with tiredness.

Helen stood up; she held out his garden fork. 'I broke into your crypt last night.'

He paused, his hand in his coat pocket, where he had been searching for his key. 'Why?' was all he said.

'Because we needed shelter,' she said, but what she meant was that she was tired of people locking doors in her face, dropping bombs, making her send her son away, making her feel anger at her husband.

'Come in, we need some breakfast.' He was an old man, bent and tired, his face thin. His tea was as weak as hers but his toast was warm and she was hungry in the cold green kitchen with its half empty meat safe on the windowsill.

She told him that she had people who would come back again tonight. That there was no other shelter and she would break the crypt open again if he barred it to them.

He smiled, stirring his tea and told her that she could use it. They needed a rest centre in the area as well as a shelter; a refuge for those bombed out, for those unable to endure loneliness any longer in this world which had once known peace.

'Do you understand what I mean?' he asked, his eyes heavy-lidded and dark. 'War is lonely as well as dangerous.'

Helen nodded, for she understood too well.

'We'll need toilets, primus stoves, cups, blankets,' Helen said, washing her cup in water poured from the simmering kettle.

He nodded as she continued, drawing up a verbal list because she had used the hours of the raid to channel her rage into this. There was no work at the bank on Saturday this week and she was glad because she had to go to the ironmonger's for rubber gloves and a hurricane lamp but the first one would not sell them to her because Heine was a German. Helen was too busy to speak to him as she would have done yesterday.

The second one smiled because Heine had taken his son's photograph shortly before he had been killed in a car crash. He sold Helen two hurricane lamps and filled them with paraffin though he would not sell her a can because of the risk of fire. She could come each day for more. He gave her the gloves because she had no more money on her.

She carried them back to the crypt, kicking away the rubble from the path in the churchyard, clearing the shrapnel from the steps with her boots. The vicar was there already, pushing back the benches, setting out tables. He had found two camp beds in his attic and had spoken to the Red Cross about chemical toilets.

Helen looked across at the bucket she had found last night and which was now full. She grimaced and the vicar moved towards it but she stopped him.

'Go and get some sleep,' she said, pulling her rubber gloves out from her pocket.

'But you must be tired too,' he objected.

'No, I'm not. I'm not at all.' And she wasn't. She carried the bucket to the door, walking behind him, watching him climb the steps.

'I should have done this before,' he said, turning. 'Somehow there wasn't the time to stop and think.'

Helen nodded. No, there was never any time to stop, never

any peace to think. She turned then, carrying the bucket down the side of the church to the back, pouring it down the drain, scrubbing with a brush while the smell made her retch but as she did it she thought of the letter she would write to Heine, telling him of the crypt, telling him of the people who now had shelter, of the buckets instead of toilets, of the altar candles which the vicar had laughed about, of the sign he was going inside to write, pointing people towards the new Rest Centre. But first he must speak to the authorities.

She would tell Marian of the work that needed to be done. The tea that needed to be brewed, the advice that needed to be given about lost ration books. Marian would help. It would stop her brooding over Emily. Over Rob, her husband, who had been posted to Scotland.

She scrubbed the bucket with disinfectant and stacked it beside the door which the vicar had said was to remain unlocked at all times. At midday she left because Marian was meeting her at the flat where they would heat thick soup and talk of their children and their husbands until the next siren went.

She picked her way through debris and chaos, turning left as a cordon blocked the street. The air was thick with smoke but then it always was. She came into the street and her flat was still standing but the one opposite was down and Mr Simkins stood waving pedestrians past.

'Did Frank survive?' she asked him and was not surprised when he shook his head. She remembered the clasp of that weak hand and was filled with the waste of it all.

She was tired now, and pushed at the front door which was singed by the heat from the bomb which had dropped so close. There were blisters on the paint. She eased it open, hearing Marian call as she came down the street, so she turned, her hand on the doorpost and saw the telegraph boy riding his bike, then stop by Mr Simkins and ask directions.

She saw her neighbour point to her, then stop the boy and take the telegram from him, carrying it himself, his overalls dirty, his yellow initials blackened by dust. She watched as he came, but slowly, oh so slowly. She watched as though from a distance as his ankle twisted sideways on a piece of brick. 'It's for you, Helen,' he said, his voice cracked and dry from the nighttime dust.

She knew it was for her. Of course it was for her, she had seen him pointing, hadn't she? But Heine was safe from the bombing, wasn't he? And so was Chris, wasn't he? So it was a mistake. She shook her head, pushing the envelope from her. She turned but Mr Simkins's hand pulled her round and pressed the telegram into her hand.

'It's a mistake, you see,' she said, still shaking her head. The paper was cold and limp in the frosty air. She could read her name, Mrs H. Weber. The type was black against the buff. She knew she must open it, she knew that she must lift the flap and read because Mr Simkins and Marian were standing there and it was cold and she mustn't keep them waiting. Mrs Tomkins hadn't kept Helen waiting when her telegram had come last month.

But it couldn't be news which would tear her heart from her body because both of them were safe. They weren't here as she was, living next to fire and death. No. Neither of them could die. They couldn't die. She wouldn't let them die.

Marian came to her side. 'It might not be bad news.' Her hand was on Helen's arm.

So Helen peeled the envelope open, lifted the telegram out and read, aloud, that Heine was dead.

Killed in a fall from rocks while on a walk. Stop.

CHAPTER 11

For over an hour Helen stood in the doorway, pushing Marian and Mr Simkins from her because they were not Heine and he was all she wanted but how could she tell them that when the only noise she could make was this moaning from deep within her? When the only sound she could hear was his voice? There was no cold piercing her coat, no war in front of her eyes. There was nothing but him; but he was gone and she couldn't bear it.

And then she said, 'How could he die like this? I don't understand how he could die like this?'

She turned and walked over trailing hoses, only now seeing the firemen on the top of ladders, hearing the coughing from all sides from the smoke which hung over the city, over them all. How could he die when he wasn't amongst all this? It was wrong. They must be wrong. She walked on towards the vicarage, towards the only phone that worked, because she had to tell them that they were wrong.

The telegram was damp in her hands and it still held the words which told her Heine was dead. It still, still held them but she was not going to cry because they were wrong. She picked her way round the brick wall which had run round the back of the grocer's but now spilled across the pavement. She listened to Marian who held her arm and talked of how bad the trains were and how she shouldn't think of going up for the funeral, she really shouldn't.

Helen cut through these words because they were wrong, weren't they? She said, 'I've opened the crypt. Why don't you come and help? It will need a committee to get things running smoothly.'

She eased between the cordon and the rescue truck. Its rear bumper was ripped from its nearside support, hanging suspended by only the right-hand screw. There was a jagged hole in the bodywork. She crossed the road, passing the queue of people waiting for a new delivery of eggs. They all seemed so clear this afternoon, as though they were etched in glass.

Marian was shaking her arm now. 'Yes, I'll help. Of course I'll help. It's so lonely with Rob away.' And then she suddenly stopped talking.

Helen crossed the road to the vicarage. Yes, it will be lonely with Rob away, she wanted to say. But neither of them are dead, are they? She wanted to shout it, scream it so that it would reach the Isle of Man. She hurried because she must tell them quickly – but they were at the gate now. Soon they would reach the telephone.

She pushed at the gate, leaning her weight on it, looking again at the telegram in her hand, hating it, tearing it, again and again and again as she hurried forward, throwing it, watching the wind take it, piece by piece, fragment by fragment, because it was wrong. But why was there this terrible pain inside her when it was so wrong?

The vicar came when she knocked and now she was holding her arms around her body because she hurt so badly.

'They say Heine is dead but he can't be. I must ring them and tell them. I have some hurricane lamps but Mr Simkins has taken them for now.' It was important that he should know about the lamps.

The vicar looked at her, and led her to the kitchen but he wouldn't hurry. His voice was gentle and kind but why wasn't he hurrying? He made her sit while Marian boiled the kettle, lighting the ring which burnt blue. They said nothing while they listened to the kettle rattling on the stove, while they listened to the vicar talking on the telephone in the hall, for he was ringing for her.

'Yes, I understand.'

'Yes, I shall explain to Mrs Weber that it was a tragic accident – a fall from the rocks – into the sea.'

'I see. Yes, I'm sure she'll understand.'

But Helen did not. She did not understand when the vicar told her that the telegram was true. That Heine was dead, drowned before he could be rescued. His body had been recovered and he had been buried yesterday. That the delivery of the telegram must have been delayed due to the bombing. That she would never, ever see him again.

She walked up and down the kitchen, listening to the kettle, seeing Marian taking it from the stove with a tea towel round the handle. She watched the steam rise from the teapot before the lid was put on and then it escaped from the spout. She watched Marian's hands holding the pot, watched the vicar fetch cups from the cupboard.

And then she said, 'They've won,' her voice calm and cold. 'They've won. I thought when we took the camera through that we had won. But we hadn't. They have.' Because now she knew. Somehow she knew that they had killed him.

She turned and walked out of the house and down the path, and then she ran; hard, fast, past the Heavy Rescue Truck which was jagged and torn – jagged and torn – jagged and torn – like her life was now. Her legs were running in time to this until she was home, back in the flat, back in their bedroom and then she lay on the bed which would never feel his weight again.

Marian came and bathed Helen's face and the cloth was cold on her skin but it did not touch the pain inside. Marian left at four because the vicar wanted to prepare the crypt. Helen watched her leave the bedroom, heard the front door click. Her arms felt heavy, her legs too. Her mouth was dry and in the silence she thought of his arms, tanned and strong, that would never again hold her. His voice, slow and deep, which would never again speak to her. His skin which would never smell of the summer, never feel the sun. Skin which had been made wet and cold by the sea, and she thought she would die.

The light faded as the minutes passed. How many minutes, how many lifetimes? She had to move at last because there was banging on the door and it wouldn't stop. It pounded and pounded, and wouldn't leave her to die too. She pushed herself from the bed, feeling old and tired and still the banging continued. Didn't they know the bombers would come soon and then the pain might go because the bombs might find her? Her hands hung limp at her sides and her feet seemed too heavy to move towards the door but then there was the sound of a key in the lock.

'Heine,' she called, turning to the door.

It was Mr Simkins who held out her hurricane lamps and told her that she had things to do. He was kind but his voice was firm as he brought her coat, guiding her arms into the sleeves.

'You must not give up,' he told her. 'Heine would not want that. He was a good man. I liked him and I am so sorry he's dead. But the raids will begin soon and you have a son to live for.'

He took her to the crypt, walking in silence with her, and she was grateful for that because she was listening to Heine's voice inside her head. She could see his face, so tanned; his hair so fair.

The vicar and Marian were gentle when she arrived and she knew now that they had arranged for Mr Simkins to come for her. They asked where they should set up camp beds, benches, chairs, and somehow she knew, pointing to an area well away from the door. She reminded them that they must make definite aisles between the rows but to her own ears her voice sounded dead.

The vicar held her hand and asked, 'Would you rather just lie down, my dear?'

'No,' she said because then she would have time to think and then she might cry and her mother had taught her not to cry, hadn't she?

The vicar had brought down two old paraffin stoves which they lit to try to build up a bit of heat before the sirens began.

'We'll have to turn them out when the raid begins. How much paraffin is in them?' Helen's voice was quite level but slow, so slow. Her lips could hardly form the words but nobody seemed to notice and she wondered how the world could keep on as though nothing had happened. But what else was there to do?

'Not much, Helen. So it should all burn through by six. It would be a fire hazard.' The vicar heaved at a pile of blankets, walking down the rows of camp beds, dropping one on to each.

Helen nodded slowly. 'It would help if we had some old carpeting or something to stop the cold seeping up from the floor. And what about the chemical toilets?' She could still hear Heine's voice and she hugged him to her.

The vicar handed the blankets to Marian and stood looking towards Helen, his face thoughtful.

'Let's get back to the house. There are carpets and rugs up in the spare room at the top. Quick though. It's five-thirty.'

They passed people coming in through the door. Helen wondered how she could be quick, her legs were so heavy. She stopped near two women of her own age.

'Can you come and help?'

They did and two others joined them. They carried three carpets back and Helen asked Marian to organise a party of people to unroll and lay them before placing the camp stools and benches on them, watching herself work as though she were outside her body. Others came to help and soon there were carpets beneath some of the camp beds too. But there were no chemical toilets, the vicar said, because so far they were not a designated shelter.

As the siren started Helen slung the stage curtains used in the peacetime pantomimes over bamboo poles which she tied horizontally between two pillars. She tipped disinfectant into three buckets and lined them up behind the curtains listening to Heine.

'There'll be a bit of a bloody performance going on behind there soon,' cackled Ruth, the old woman from last night who had brought her knitting again.

'Just so long as there's not a round of applause every time,' Helen replied, smiling, and was surprised that words like these could come while she was listening so hard to him.

The vicar came and stood behind her. 'Helen . . . what about the men?'

'That's a point, ducky,' Ruth said, cackling again, her arms waving as her hands wielded needles and wool.

Helen sighed, then looked up at the vicar and smiled. 'Come on, you can help.' But she didn't want him to talk because then she would not hear Heine.

She bent and picked up the remaining two curtains from the floor, collecting up twine and another bamboo from the storage area. The vicar carried the ladder to the other end of the crypt, walking in front of her. She could hear his breathing, heavy and laboured and knew this man of sixty felt much older because of the sights he had seen over the last few months and remembered then that her grief was one amongst many, but somehow even that did not give her any relief.

The raids had begun now. They could all hear the bombs, feel the earth as it juddered, see and taste the plaster as it fell in narrow streams from the ceiling but the conversation continued as before. Or almost as before. There were moments of silence, of tension when some of the crumps were too close, too loud, too violent, and they had drowned Heine's voice for the moment and she couldn't bear it. Helen stopped, her hand to her mouth because she mustn't cry or she would go in the cupboard.

She must follow the vicar, she must reach forward to move that chair from his path and slowly it was all right again. She coughed as plaster dust fell on to her head, catching in her throat. It itched on her scalp but she had no hands free to scratch and it was important that she did. Why was it so damned important? Her husband was dead, wasn't he? Dead. And she wanted to scratch. Her head was aching now, throbbing, and her mouth was dry and again Heine had gone.

The vicar looked behind.

'Whereabouts, Helen?'

She pointed to the two pillars over in the corner and he opened the ladder as wide as the rope would allow then started to climb, but she shook her head.

'I'll do it. I know how to fix the pole.' His breathing was laboured. He was too tired.

He held the ladder while she climbed on legs which felt like lead but she tied the bamboo, then hung the curtains, listening while he told her that the Red Cross had been very pleasant but they would just have to manage for now.

Helen shook her head. 'Oh well, we'll see about that,' she said, anger surprising her, raging through her, cracking in her head, making her hands clasp the ladder, bringing sweat coursing down her back. 'We'll see about that.'

Marian walked down the centre aisle carrying one bucket which she had found by the bamboo poles. It would not be enough.

'There are more in the vicarage,' the vicar said.

Helen put her hand on his arm as he moved to the door. 'Let me,' she said, because in the vicarage she might hear Heine again and when she heard his voice it was as though he had not left her.

'But surely we've enough?' Marian asked. 'There's a raid going on. It's dangerous.'

Helen listened. It was drawing away. There had been no plaster trickling down for the last ten minutes. She looked at the people sitting and talking. At the two young children running up and down the aisles.

'No, it's not going to be enough,' she said. For her there

would be no danger, but there would be peace. The vicar put his hand on her arm.

'Wait until it is quite quiet,' he said and so she did. Sitting on a camp stool watching Ruth knit, finding comfort in the regularity of the needles. Counting the stitches because it filled her head with numbers, not his poor, lonely, cold, wet body which had begun to nudge at her mind.

Ruth handed her a red jumper and scissors. They were rusted but sharp and Helen picked away at the sewn seams until it was in sections and then she pulled the kinked wool, watching row after row unravel, winding it round and round her hand; red upon red. Had there been red on his face? Had he felt pain?

'It should be all right now, Helen,' the vicar called.

She rose then, smiling as Ruth smiled, but her face felt stiff and unreal. She nodded to the vicar and slowly edged in front of the curtain in the doorway, then opened the door, knowing that there would be no light showing. She could not run, there was no strength in her legs. She watched the searchlights stabbing the skies, saw the puffs of flak, and drowned in the noise of the aeroplanes, the bombs and shells away to the south. Had he been afraid as the water entered his lungs?

She heard the revving of the auxiliary fire engines from the yard behind the vicarage but then she was inside the house, feeling her way down the hall, into the kitchen where there was a sort of peace and she stood for a moment but his voice did not come back. But neither did the image of his body.

She dragged two pails from beneath the sink and then a third from the scullery, searching for him in her mind, feeling her way back into the darkness of the hall, hearing the bombs, not him. And then as she moved past the telephone table there was a hush, a silence, a moment of utter calm, and she called his name then but there was no answer, just a tearing endless sound that filled the space around her and the ceiling dropped, and great timbers crashed to the ground and Helen was swamped with a blackness which took all pain, all thought away.

It took the rescue party over two hours to pull her free and take her to the first aid point where nurses pulled splinters of glass from her hands and arms, for the wedged timbers had protected her. It was now that she cried and cried and thought that the whole world must hear over the sound of the bombs and shells and alarm bells. But it was not for the pain and the blood, but at last for Heine.

Her leg was not broken but badly cut and bruised and by the time it was dressed the all-clear had sounded and Marian helped her back to the flat where the vicar was waiting. His house was ruined and so Helen asked him to use her spare room and was grateful when he agreed because she did not want to be alone any more. Marian came too and used the studio because she could travel more easily from here and she too was lonely.

The vicar put a hot-water bottle in Helen's bed but she was not ready for sleep yet because there was something to be done. She walked steadily back down the stairs, pushing aside for now the pain in her leg, hugging close to her the thought of her husband.

'I could have died and I didn't. I thought I wanted to die but now I know I don't,' she told Marian who had tried to stop her. 'I felt fear when I had thought I would not feel anything but grief again. They mustn't think they've beaten him or me.'

At first the woman at the Red Cross was annoyed at Helen's interruption, at her dust-covered clothes, at her description of scrubbing out dirty buckets. Helen lifted her hands; the blood from her splinter wounds had seeped through the bandages.

'I want those chemical toilets. The vicar has been assured that we are to become an accredited shelter. I want those toilets and I want them now.' Her voice was still and slow. She stood in front of the desk; her leg was throbbing and her hands too. 'I will not leave until I have them.'

The woman came round the desk then, taking Helen's arm, drawing her to a chair, calling for a drink.

'My dear, you shall have them.' Her voice was kind and her face was too, and Helen's anger was gone again and only the despair was there, coming out in endless tears, and she wondered if grief was always like this, hard and fast, then ebbing for a moment leaving life to run on as usual until the next bout of tears. She cried on and off all that night in the crypt, lying on a camp bed while more than sixty people sat or slept around her.

Ruth came and held her. 'You 'ave a good cry, my dear. It

helps you know. My old Albert never came back from the last lot. My grandson's in this one. His dad's dead.'

Helen told her then that Heine was German and had not been a soldier but a prisoner because it seemed unfair to accept sympathy unless she was honest. Ruth just smiled.

'They're all young, poor little buggers. They all bleed just the same and we cry, just the same.'

Helen lay in the dark, feeling the pain of her hands and arms, of her leg, wanting the comfort of the only person who could not give it. Thinking of the bombers who flew over London, dropping their bombs, thinking of the bombers who flew over Germany, and wondered how she could tell Heine's parents that their son was dead.

The next morning she received a letter from Willi.

Dear Frau Weber,
I ask a friend of mine who is being today released to post this to you when he reach the mainland. I want you to have knowledge of how Heine is killed. He had stood against the Nazis you see, too loudly, too strong and in the end they hurt his friend. Martin now is insane. It is something which makes him want to fight them with more effort.

We walk near the sea on a cold rough day. He had been sent the death sentence but it not stop him from speaking out on that walk too. The guard was in front. I was behind Heine and was pushed to ground from behind. I saw these men come to Heine and push him hard, over edge, on to the rocks, into the sea. They had promised they would, Frau Weber, and I do not tell you this to pain you further but to tell of his courage.

I was with him the night before he died. Perhaps he had knowledge of it in his heart. He said, if he die, I must tell you that he make his gesture as you did in Hanover with the old man on the ground. That these years are just a fragment of time in the great age of the world and that they will pass. Tell her it will all pass, he said to me. And tell her that I love her.

Your husband was brave man, Frau Weber. We

shall miss him, miss his spirit. He was honoured amongst us. He was loved.

Your obedient servant,
Willi Weiss

Helen was late into work. She walked in the icy drizzle of that Monday before Christmas to the Red Cross and spoke to the woman who had brought her tea and kindness. She was able to assure Helen that a message could be conveyed through the Red Cross to Herr Weber informing him of his son's death in an internment camp on the Isle of Man. It was 23 December and Helen wondered whether there would be carp for the Christmas Eve dinner in Hanover or just bombs and tiredness as there was here. She wondered how long love lived when there was no one to accept that love.

She felt the drizzle turn to rain on her face and was glad she had sent presents for Christoph two weeks ago: a carved catapult for knocking targets off the wall as he had asked and books which she had bought from the stalls which still opened down many side streets. It seemed too much of an effort to think of Christmas now. Before Heine's death she had hoped to travel down for two days but the vicar had rung the rector in Greater Mannenham to tell him to pass a message on to Laura that the trains were too difficult. But it was not travelling that was too difficult, it was the knowledge of Heine's death which would be too hard to hide from her son and he should at least have peace this Christmas. It would be time enough in January to tell her son of his father's death. She stood still and looked at a smouldering ruin, pushing a brick with her foot. Who knew if there would ever be another Christmas free of Hitler's rule?

On Christmas Eve people still came to the shelter although raids had almost ceased for forty-eight hours. They had found companionship and safety down here beneath the church and had no wish to spend Christmas alone in houses, flats or Anderson shelters. Helen dragged out old bunting and everyone helped to hang it round the crypt. There was no midnight service in the church but beneath it they sang carols and Helen found that her voice was too uncertain to sing 'Silent Night'. The vicar said prayers for all those under attack; those in the provinces, those in Germany. Afterwards he pumped the primus and as a light raid continued outside they made tea and soup, using goods that people had brought.

They ignored the crump crump of bombs and Helen pushed the pain of her leg and her hands from her as she listened to the groups talking softly. Sometimes they laughed and sometimes they cried because a father, a son, a husband had died and Helen did not feel alone in her suffering any more and there was some comfort in that but still each day and night seemed to last a lifetime.

On 29 December when there was due to be a tidal low-point in the Thames the Luftwaffe came again. The water mains were damaged at the start of the raid by high explosive parachute mines and then at least 10,000 fire bombs plummeted from the planes. In the crypt they could not feel the heat of the fires which raged unchecked until water was available again from more distant mains but in the morning they smelt and saw the devastation and that night there were more people who had been bombed out arriving to stay in the crypt. The next day, which was Monday, Helen was late in to work because she took them to the Town Hall to get coupons until their ration books could be replaced.

Mr Leonard could say nothing because so many were late, unable to force their way through the havoc which had once been London. Some never came because they had been killed.

That night the vicar explained as they all sat talking that a fire-watching rota was to be drawn up at the request of the authorities and those in the shelter were eager to put their names down. Helen decided that there should be soup available at one penny a cup and Marian volunteered to organise it. The old lady, Ruth, stood up and said that she thought there should be a knitting group to make socks and hats for the soldiers.

'All you need to do is pull out old jumpers,' she said, holding up a dark green one. 'Just pull it out and knit it up again.' And so a knitting group was formed, but Helen could not yet bear the thought of wool being drawn across her cut hands and so, instead, she formed a small choir at the back of the crypt and found solace in the music.

The days passed and December became January. Britain and Australia's attack on the Italians in the Western Desert proceeded. Nits became a problem in the shelter and Helen bent her head over newspaper and combed out several lice. One of the women was a hairdresser and soon most of the women had bobbed hair and Helen looked at herself in the mirror and wondered how Heine would have liked it. She did not cry this time but put her arms round the young mother whose husband was missing in action and, instead, held her while she wept.

By 17 January Helen's hands and control were improved enough for her to leave London to see her son.

The train journey took six hours and was cold, so cold. Again and again the train was shunted into a siding to allow troops or goods wagons to pass but there was no raid as they travelled and little to see through the mesh of the windows. There were other mothers on the train, travelling to see their children. They were pale, tired. Their eyes sunken. No one talked very much but some slept, jerked awake with each stop only to fall asleep again within minutes. But Helen couldn't sleep.

She caught the bus from Thetford and dusk fell after twenty miles. The journey took one hour more, the slitted headlights picking up the white line painted at the side of the road but nothing of the flat countryside beyond. Helen eased her leg, flexed her hands, glad that her gloves covered the red scars. The bus stopped three times but each time another village was called out and Helen watched as the women she had travelled with on the train stepped down into the darkness. Would there ever be a time when they would see the welcome of lighted windows, she wondered.

At last the bus pulled up again and the driver called, 'Greater Mannenham.'

Helen rose, lifting her bag from the seat beside her. She had brought Christoph a knitted hat from Ruth and some more books and one change of clothes for herself because she could not stay more than a night. She thanked the driver and stepped carefully from the bus to the road; her leg was still stiff, still sore. For a moment she couldn't see Chris but then he was there, his arms around her, holding her, and she knew she must not cry but she did when she heard him say, 'Oh, Mum, I've missed you.'

She heard the bus move off, smelt the exhaust, and saw

Laura standing behind Chris, but all she felt was his arms around her, his head pressed into her body. She dropped her bag and held him, stroking his hair, bending to kiss him, wondering how she could have forgotten the sound of his voice but somehow it had indeed become lost.

They walked back through the centre of the village. It was cloudy so there was not even the light from the moon or stars to light their way. Laura held a torch covered with tissue paper and gripped Helen's arm, guiding her along the lane while Chris held her hand tightly, causing pain to stab right up into her arm but it didn't matter now that she was with her son.

There was a fire in the inglenook and Helen sat on the settee, keeping her gloves on, saying that she was cold. One of her cuts had begun to bleed and Chris must not see. But Laura saw and beckoned her out to the kitchen while Chris sat on the rug in front of the fire and looked through the books. She bathed and dressed the cut and all the time there was the smell of stew in the air and Helen realised she was hungry. She realised too that she had not felt hunger since his death. She looked at Laura and knew she should tell her about Heine but the words hurt too much in her throat.

Laura smiled at her, pointing to a chair, calling to Chris to come in and wash his hands. He ran through and Helen thought again how much he had grown, how strong and straight and tall he was. He ran the tap and it splashed up and over the sink but Laura just laughed and threw him a towel and Helen felt excluded.

This was her child but she did not even know where the towels were which dried his hands. She didn't wash them, or any of his clothes. She didn't serve up his meal, as Laura was now doing, heaping rabbit, carrots and potato on to his plate and then on to theirs and now jealousy surged into her throat and chest and she was appalled.

She looked down at her plate, not wanting to see familiarity between her son and this kind, plump woman.

'Chris talks of you every day. There is no one in his life but you,' Laura said.

Helen looked up and saw Laura looking at her and then at Chris and knew that after all she was lucky to have placed her son with this woman.

'He knows that it hurts you much more to let him stay here

than to take him back with you to London,' Laura continued, and Chris looked up at her and smiled.

'I think you're very brave, Mum. You have to stay there. I know you do because we need the money. Laura has explained it to me and Daddy told me too, in one of his letters.'

Helen picked up her knife and fork now, tasting the rabbit, the thick gravy, the potatoes, but there was no appetite again. Later she must tell him about Heine. Later.

She listened while she ate sparingly as Chris told her how he had pulled the carrots and stored them in sawdust. How he fed the chickens and the pig and how they had called one of the piglets Heine and one of them Helen. She listened as he told her of the fat girl called Mary who was his friend and who lived in a cottage where no one cared. She listened but he did not talk of his friends at school. He did not talk of the games they played and he lowered his head and told her about the butterfly net Laura had found in the attic and she thought she saw a darkening in his eyes when she asked about his school friends and he did not answer.

Later she asked Laura if the boys knew of Chris's German heritage but she said that they did not. How could they? Only she and the rector's wife knew. Helen looked closely at her son as they sat in front of the fire and could see no shadows now in those dark eyes so perhaps there had been none earlier?

They sat and talked in the quiet of the cottage and Helen was restless. There was no normality in the hissing of the fire, the voice on the radio reading out the nine o'clock news, the hoot of the owl. There was no normality to this quiet evening which came from the peacetime past.

She read to him in his room that night. A room warmed by logs burning in the grate, their light shielded from the sky by more slates, like the inglenook downstairs, Chris told her. She sat by his bed, holding his hand with her wounded one and she told him it was nothing and then asked him if everything was all right in the village. If the boys were his friends too, as well as Mary? He kissed her hand and held it to his cheek and told her she must be careful of the bombs because he loved her so much. He loved Laura too but more as a grandmother, not as he loved her.

Again Helen asked him if there was any trouble but this time he said, 'No, Mum. Everything's all right. Honestly it is.' And most of the time it was. Most of the time.

In the morning Helen fed the hens and the pig, watching the squealing piglets born too early.

Laura said, 'Too impatient, couldn't wait for the spring. It's because old Reynolds let his damned pig into the orchard.' Helen laughed then walked with Chris along the lane, watching him as he stamped on puddles. Laughing as he slid on frozen skid paths. Listening as he told her about the blacksmith at the forge.

He showed her the goat, their school and pointed to the copse in the distance to the left of a line of elms.

'That's where I'll go with the net. Mary said she'd come. I wrote to Dad about it.' He kicked at the frost-stiffened verge. 'Mr Reynolds says the Germans are buggers. They drop bombs on you, hurt our animals, kill our people. They've hurt your hands. They're buggers. That's what Mr Reynolds says anyway.'

Helen stood next to him, staring over at the copse, seeing the rooks' nests high in the bare branches, hearing his words drop into the still air. Her face was pinched and cold. She wet her lips, clenching her hands, wanting to feel the pain.

'It's war that's the bugger, Chris. Most of the people in it are like us. Doing things we don't want to do just because we have to. No, I don't hate the Germans but I do hate the Nazis and that's the difference that you and I must remember. The Nazis hurt other Germans too. They've somehow dragged everyone into the war.'

Chris turned to her. 'But it's easier to hate them all, isn't it? It makes us the same as everyone else here.'

Helen put her hand on his shoulder. His coat was getting too small. His sleeves were too far up his arms and his wrists would get sore from the cold wind soon. She must find him another.

'But it's not always best to take the easiest course, Chris, and we're not the same, are we, darling? Daddy was born in Germany.'

Helen gripped her son's shoulder hard because now, in the cold brisk air while the frost lay white on the ploughed fields, she must tell him. She turned him to her, holding his face in her hands.

'It's all so difficult, Mum,' Christoph said. 'I wish you were here.'

Helen nodded. 'Yes, Christoph. I wish I was too because we

are going to need one another more than ever now. Darling, listen to me; I have some terrible news.' She paused. 'Daddy died before Christmas.' Her voice was not level, it was full of tears and she stopped for a moment, watching the blankness of her son's eyes change to shock and then disbelief. He pulled away, snatching at her sleeve, breathing fast.

'What do you mean, died? What do you mean? How could he? There were no bombs there. I never had to worry about him, only about you. I never worried about him. Never, never.' He was shouting now, stepping away from her. She moved forward and grasped his shoulders.

'And why have you had your hair cut? You look silly. You look stupid.' He was hitting at her arms.

Helen would not let go of him; she hung on, feeling the blows on the splinter cuts but understanding his pain, his rage, because it was the same as hers. Perhaps they also shared the same guilt at resenting Heine's nationality.

She hung on and hung on until at last he was tired and then she showed him the letter and he knew that his father had been brave and honoured and they clung together and mourned him properly, here, in private, where the wind was now blowing cold and sharp.

They walked and remembered their lives together and Helen told her son of her anger at Heine when stones had been thrown, but she also spoke of her love. She hoped that Chris would talk to her but he didn't.

She stayed another night because her son needed her and the next and the next because she didn't care what Mr Leonard said – this was more important – but then she had to return because she must earn her money and there was no work down here, Laura said, shaking her head. The farm had all the workers they needed and there was nothing else.

The night she left Chris did not sleep. He lay looking up at the ceiling, seeing the beams in the glow from the ashes. He was glad his dad was dead. He was glad because now he could tell them at school that his father had been killed by the Nazis and maybe Joe would stop asking questions. So many questions. Would the stones start again if he knew?

He turned on his side, the pillow was wet. He couldn't stop crying because he wanted his dad. Wanted him to be here, to hold him, to be warm and alive; to hear his voice. He was brave, so brave, and what would he think of a son who said he was glad he was dead but who loved him so much that it hurt? Chris knew he would not sleep tonight because there was so much else in his head that was wicked and he could not tell his mother because she had the bombs and that was enough.

Winter turned to spring and in the evenings Helen took her turn at fire-watching and in the crypt she arranged further education classes for the regulars. She smiled when the old man offered to teach boxing and listened when he told her he was a southpaw and had fought in all the booths in the country during the depression. She watched as he shadow-boxed and was glad when others did too because his dignity returned during those nights and did not leave him.

The vicar arranged for a piano to be hauled from the church hall to the crypt and one of the young mothers taught Helen the tango and on Ruth's birthday they had a party and the vicar danced with Helen. The raids grew fewer but every night the crypt was open and the flat was seldom slept in. She wrote to Chris each week and slowly found that she could sleep now, though she still woke in the small hours and wept for Heine and wished that it had all been different. That they had been born in another time when war was not a consideration and they had been free to love.

In March Roosevelt signed the Lend-Lease Agreement with Britain and the crypt had another party and this time they did the hokey-cokey, with Ruth leading them. On 17 March Bevin announced the first steps in a massive mobilisation plan to release men for active service and Helen wondered if any of the farm workers in Greater Mannenham would be called up. She wrote to Laura and asked her to let her know because she knew that Chris would need her. Somehow she just knew.

In April Germany invaded Greece and the bombing of Britain continued in earnest again. Throughout the long nights they listened to the crump of bombs and sometimes Helen led the choir in a sing-song and everyone followed, but not every night because relatives were killed and people needed comfort.

On fire-watch duty Helen watched the flares being dropped and then the showers of incendiary bombs falling and knew that low level bombing runs would follow. Bert, the old boxer, was with her and said, as ack-ack hit one bomber which was flying in a straight line throughout his run, 'He was a brave one all right. Poor bugger.'

They both watched as the plane plummeted from the sky, a flaming mass to fall into the furnace of its own making. 'Poor bugger,' she echoed.

At the end of April the British were pushed out of Greece and Chris wrote to tell her that the piglets, Heine and Helen, were now his. Laura had given them to him. Laura wrote to her to say that he seemed to be sleeping better and was glad that Helen had left the letter from Willi with him. It was folded in his top bedside drawer and she knew that he read it every night.

On 11 May there was a brilliant bomber's moon and over 500 German planes dropped hundreds of high explosive bombs and incendiaries within a few hours. It was claimed to be a reprisal raid for the methodical bombing of the residential areas of German towns and Ruth said, 'The whole bloody world's gone mad. These are people in planes dropping bombs on other people. They're all dying. They're all somebody's sons and daughters. It's a crying shame. That 'itler needs to be strung up.'

Helen unpicked the jumper seam and pulled out wool, winding it around her healed hands. The hurricane lamps were dotted all over the crypt now; many had been brought by the people who sat around her and she was comforted by the smell, though the light was weak. As the hours passed she wrote a letter to Chris, telling him what Ruth had said and asking him to write to her because Laura had written that he was sleeping better, but was he really? Remember you can tell me anything, darling, she wrote.

In the morning they trooped up the steps of the crypt and wept at the devastation everywhere. Helen passed through a shattered city on her way to work and arrived three hours late and wanted to slap Mr Leonard because he was on time. Joan did not arrive until the afternoon because their house had been hit, but they had been in the Underground railway shelter.

There were cheers in the crypt on 28 May when the news came in that the *Bismarck* had been sunk the day before and Marian put a big notice on top of an old box.

SCRAP
Jam Jars, Iron, Bottles,
Paper, Rubber

Help to build planes and ships to
sink the enemy

The next day she and Marian brought aluminium pans from the flat and put them in the box because, as dawn had come, Helen had decided that it was her role to keep the Nazis and the Germans apart in her own mind and in her son's. The Nazis must indeed be sunk.

In the first week of June an exploding gas main ripped up the pavement outside the flat and they clambered through and into the hallway, but only to pick up the mail because they had to reach their offices. Laura had written to say that there was still no sign of the men leaving the farm but that Chris seemed to be fine and was looking forward to seeing his mother in the summer.

On 22 June the Nazis broke their pact and invaded Russia and that night Helen lay on her camp bed and thought of Heine; heard his voice saying, We'll be all right as long as Russia joins us.

She rolled over on her side, whispering aloud, 'Perhaps we'll make it now, Heine. But we still need America on our side.'

She cried though to think that he would not be here if they did survive and knew her grief, though dulled, still remained but it was mixed with anxiety for her son.

Part Two

CHAPTER 12

Chris sat on the old mac which Laura had handed him. He looked across at Mary and smiled; the egg sandwiches tasted good. The hens were laying well this week. They must have known it was spring. He looked up at the branches of the elm. He could see the blue sky through the leaf buds. There were bluebells in the copse, not many but enough to colour the ground.

'What did your mum say?' Mary asked, pushing a piece of crust into her mouth. 'Is she coming down yet? Did you say thank you to her for getting me out of old Ma Turnball's house and into Mrs Simpson's?'

Chris dug deep into his pocket, pulling out the letter he had received this morning. He read it to Mary.

London
May 1942

Darling Chris,

Well, though the bombs have tailed off I can't say that it is quiet here in London. As Mr Leonard grumbles, 'The Yanks are over-paid and over here.' We seem to have foreign soldiers everywhere now. Not just the Free French, the Poles but all these Americans. It is wonderful to see them. At last the end must be in sight, though of course it won't be as soon as we would like.

I was so pleased that it is working out better for Mary at Mrs Simpson's. Laura seemed to think that she was a kind person and believe me, the money I have to pay does not matter at all.

I am almost allowing myself to believe that I will be able to get to Norfolk soon. The Labour Exchange have said that it should be possible to exchange one form of war work for another but I need the permission of my employer and a replacement. They suggest that I apply for work in a sugar beet factory for the winter when even the permanent farm workers are laid off and then start work on Mr Jones's farm in the spring because I have his offer of a job in writing. If I apply to the Land Army I could be put to work anywhere and I can't be parted from you for very much longer. I will be able to get over to you every weekend once I start at the factory.

It seems a long time until the winter – another six months – but I have somehow to get Mr Leonard's agreement and you know how very difficult that will be. I will come though. I promise you that.

The vicar is still staying at the flat and is a constant support to everyone in the area and Marian is well and so too is Rob. He is stationed in Scotland still, in the Stores, and sometimes comes home on leave.

London is no longer the place you knew. In fact, I wonder if you can remember it. There are so many buildings destroyed. A bomb landed on the park and blew up the balloon and the horse-chestnut tree.

Write to me with your news when you can. Are you all right? Really all right?

All my love,
Mummy

Chris put it back in his pocket. She was coming. Not until the winter and then not to the village but he would see her every weekend.

'I'm glad she's coming,' Mary said, reaching forward and taking the last piece of bread. 'You need your mum. You'll have to tell her, you know.'

Chris crunched up the greaseproof paper, smaller and smaller but when he threw it to the ground it sprang out into a larger ball. 'Shut up', he said. 'Just shut up. She mustn't know. No one must know.'

He took a drink of water from the bottle, wiping the top before passing it to Mary. She took it and drank and now there were crumbs in the water but he didn't want any more anyway.

'She should know because they'll get you one day. They won't be satisfied with a postal order soon, you know.' She passed the bottle back and he pushed it down into the canvas bag which Laura had packed the picnic in.

'I don't want to talk about it,' Chris said, getting up. 'Come on, let's see how they're getting on.'

He didn't wait for Mary to catch up but picked up the canvas bag and walked to the edge of the trees, looking out towards the fields which had once grown wheat and barley but which were now churned up as men built huts at one end and hangars at another. The row of elms was still standing, though, hiding the airfield from the village. The runway markers stretched and stretched across three fields and Laura had said that they would never get it back as it used to be once the war was over. Chris looked back into the copse. Mary was coming, bringing the old butterfly net. It was too early but sometimes if the spring was really warm, Laura had said, you could be lucky.

He looked back again to the airfield and then to the village. There was no sign of Joe or the gang on the road. Maybe they wouldn't be waiting by the crossroads today, but he knew they would. They always were on a Saturday. He felt the postal order in his pocket. They would be there because today was the day he had to give them his pocket money or they would tell the whole village that his dad had been a German.

'My sister says the Yanks are good fun. They give her stockings and gum. Chewing gum, you know. And comics and cigarettes.' Mary stood next to him. 'When they come d'you think they'll give us gum? I've never 'ad it.'

Chris turned towards her. It was only two o'clock. Joe wouldn't be there until four and maybe today he'd be brave enough to stand up to him. Yes, maybe today he would but now he wanted to see the toad spawn. Yes, that's what he wanted to do. They walked round the edge of the copse to the pond and there, in long spotted strings were the spawn, stretched out in the water, crossing and recrossing one another.

'Blimey, I thought they was in one big blob like tapioca,' Mary said, and Chris laughed.

'So did I but Laura told me last night.'

They lay on their stomachs, their hands in the cold water. The moss on the stones was close to him, like a miniature forest. His breath blew up puffs of dry earth and there was a smell of spring in the ground. In the summer, Laura had said, fly agaric grew here, the red and white spotted toadstool which was poisonous for humans but which slugs loved.

'Maybe I should push one down Joe's throat,' he said to Mary and smiled when she laughed.

They walked over to the hollow which was where the badgers had a set. Where would they walk to now that the airfield had been built across their path? They looked for the long scratch marks on the other bank and there they were, made with the long digging claws.

'I never want to go back to London, do you?' Chris asked as they walked on down the deep rutted track where the cart-wheels had churned the earth.

'No, it's lovely, ain't it? Just so quiet and lovely, except when it's harvest time. Then it's too bloody busy. Like Piccadilly.' They had reached the larger pond now, where the old tin bath was still stuck, half submerged out in the middle. Chris crouched, and together they discussed whether they could get a rope out to it and bring it back and have another go this summer.

'Maybe it won't sink this time if we put a couple of empty drums either side,' Chris said.

Mary was breathing heavily next to him, sucking at a new blade of grass. 'How d'you fix the drum, clever clogs?'

Chris shrugged. 'Well, how about a plank going across the top and tie everything to the plank?' It sounded good to him and she smiled.

'All right, but how do we get it back? I'm not going in after it.' Mary was scrambling to her feet, dusting off her dress which hung from her shoulders like a sack.

Chris pushed himself up too, taking the butterfly net from her, heaving the canvas bag on to his shoulder. He didn't want to go in either and feel the sticky mud under his toes again, the soft wriggling which could have been anything.

'Oh well, we'll think about it,' he said, walking on.

They didn't take any eggs from the nests today. Laura had said they must only take one or two otherwise there would be no birds for the mothers to hatch. Somehow they had not thought of the eggs turning into birds before and now they did not want to take any at all.

Chris felt the jam jar filled with diced laurel leaves in his pocket and wondered if he would really be able to catch a butterfly if he saw one and ease it into the jar with the bitter almond smell, leaving it to die. He remembered Mr Reynolds's butterflies pinned into position with their wings fixed so that they were beautiful. But were they really? Weren't they only beautiful in flight or resting on a plant with the sun on their wings? Would he ever be able to bring his net down and capture them, kill them, mount them? He didn't know but saying that he would gave him a reason to come out into the woods, to leave behind the games of Germans and British convoys, not cowboys and Indians. It gave him a chance to keep away from Joe and his gang.

It was four o'clock now, they could hear the chiming of the church clock from here and Mary had to be home for tea. They walked towards the village. There were fresh young nettles growing on the verges and Joe was there, in the distance, down by the crossroads. Mary had seen them too.

'Tell your mother, Chris, or Laura, or someone. There's too many of them to fight, you know.'

But he couldn't tell anyone because Joe had said he would tell the village and Chris couldn't bear the thought of the stones again and the shouting. Not here, not in this countryside that he loved.

He shook his head. They were closer now. He could see Joe swiping at the verge with his stick, and Chris stopped, staring at Joe and then he slowly and deliberately bent and gripped the nettle by the side tightly, jerking his hand upwards, knowing that this way it would not sting you. He pulled it from the earth, holding it up so that Joe could see.

He watched as the other boy laughed and did the same but he pulled it downwards, touching the top of the leaves, stinging his hand and his fingers.

'Blimey, that was a good one,' Mary said.

Chris nodded, looking with satisfaction at Joe's red face, at his hand which he clutched between his arm and body and it didn't matter so much when the boys came and grabbed him, digging in his pocket for the sixpence, but not Joe. Joe was holding his hand and swearing.

*

In August the sun was hot, so very hot. Chris had sat up with Laura last night, making another butterfly net from a forked oak branch and thin hoops of hazel which they threaded through the hem of an old net curtain sewn to the correct shape. He had then twisted old fuse wire round the hazel and the oak, fixing it into place with wire. Chris did not tell Laura that since the nettles Joe had been waiting for him more often. He had beaten him twice and then broken his butterfly net, but his father had suffered too, hadn't he, in the internment camp, and so he must be as brave.

'Are you going out to the copse with Mary today?' Laura asked, frowning when he said no.

'But why? You're spending too much time on your own. You're only nine. You need friends.'

Chris took up the canvas bag. 'She's a girl,' he said. 'She can't keep up.' But that wasn't the reason. It was because she cried when she saw them waiting for him and it made his eyes water too.

He walked through the long grass of the two meadows leading to the copse. The cornflowers and red poppies hung limp in the hot sun and the Common Blues rose in front of him. He stopped, waiting for them to settle again and they did, with closed wings, the undersides of which were a medley of orange and black spots and rings on a grey background. The female was dark brown touched with blue, edged with orange rings and she lifted up into the air and then settled. Chris didn't catch them. He never did. Laura knew it, he knew it, but nothing was ever said.

The copse was cool and dark and nightingales used to sing when he and Laura walked in the evenings but that was before the bombers came, two weeks ago. They had thundered over in wave after wave, coming in low over the village and the evacuees had thrown themselves on the ground, some screaming, while the village children laughed. But they had never been bombed had they, the teacher had said, his face white with anger at the village children's laughter.

Where had the nightingales gone, Chris had asked Laura but she didn't know. He looked around. The fly agaric were bright against the greens and browns and he wondered if Mary came to the copse at all. He walked to the larger pond. The tin bath was still half sunken. He missed her. Really missed her.

It was dark, too dark here, he felt suddenly. He wanted the sun on his face, pushing the shadows back, away from him. He ran through the wood, leaping over gnarled roots, skidding round trees, going faster because there could be Indians. Faster and faster. Quick, the arrows could be coming. Thwack, thwack into the trees, but missing him, always missing him. He was out into the daylight now, the breath was heaving in his chest but he felt better. He walked towards the airfield, seeing the great dark shapes of the planes behind the elms.

The planes were so huge and dark and, at dawn each morning, seemed to claw through the air, climbing higher and higher, but so slowly and heavily, pushing their noise down on to the earth, the village, the cottage, his bed, until the buildings shook. This morning he had watched from the window and seen the planes turn at last into silver specks in the clear blue sky.

He walked up to the perimeter fence, seeing the heavy equipment and vehicles running more easily over the heavy clay ground now that the summer was here. A jeep roared along the edge of the tarmacked runway, skidding to a halt beside a towering B-17. Nissen huts clustered together and there were Quonset huts too with flat roofs and straight sides.

He had cycled up to the wire with Laura and Mary when they were building the airfield. They had watched as the curved corrugated iron plates of the Nissen huts were buckled together and Laura had said they would hold twenty or thirty men. Chris had listened to the shouts, the laughter of the men, seen their mouths endlessly chewing the gum, some of which they had thrown through the wire for them, though Laura had forbidden them to pick it up.

It was a disgusting habit, she had said, but Mary had slipped it into her pocket when Laura blushed and turned away as the men whistled at her.

They had watched all morning as they heaved the panels up and locked them together and he remembered how his father had built the Anderson shelter and he had cried, standing there at the wire he had cried, then ridden home when Laura had seen. He had cried all night and she had stayed with him but did not know that it was more than grief, it was because he was still too afraid to let the village know about his father and he was ashamed.

Chris felt the sun on the back of his head, his back. On his hand which held the butterfly net. He was thirsty and moved off, down the road waiting for two jeeps to pass before crossing. The horse manure had been squashed flat and dry by so many trucks and he smiled. Each morning he had to collect the cow pats from the field behind their cottage to put on the vegetable garden and on dry days it was easier. Today had been a dry day.

He sat on the edge of the copse again, watching the air base. They were only training, the publican had told Laura. The Americans came into his pub each evening and on the first night they had drunk him dry.

The water in Chris's bottle was warm but he drank it, taking deep long gulps, watching the rolling walk of the airmen in the distance as they strolled about the airfield. They didn't march like the English. They had rubber soles which were quiet and they rolled their feet. He stood up, rolling his, slipping his hands into his pockets, chewing his sandwich as though it was gum. He didn't hear the man until he laughed.

'Well, I guess that's a pretty good imitation,' he said, and Chris turned, whipping his hands from his pockets, standing silent, fearful, watching the flyer who stood in his uniform, his back to the trees, the sun on his face.

'Hey, ease up, fella. I was just out taking in some of the countryside. It's different. You know. Kind of different.' The man turned and looked out over the flat fields to the low undulating hills in the distance. He had his hands in his pockets and his leather jacket was unbuttoned, his cap was slipped back on his head. He turned back to Chris who was chewing his sandwich, trying to make it small enough to swallow.

'You like candy?'

Chris shrugged. He didn't know what candy was.

The man laughed again. He had dark eyes like Chris with deep lines running down from them, like Chris's father. But he had a moustache too; it was brown like his hair.

'Well, I guess I mean, would you like a sweet?' The man rounded his mouth and said again. 'Would you care for a sweet?' He almost sounded English.

Chris watched as he brought out boiled sweets, a bag full, from his pocket. He hadn't tasted sweets for over a year because Joe had taken his pocket money for that long.

Chris took one but the man said, 'No, take the pack. There's plenty more on base.' He pushed them at Chris, nodding to him. 'Thank you,' Chris said, reaching out, feeling the bag heavy in his hand. 'Would you like one of my sandwiches? They're egg. Straight from the hen this morning.'

The man laughed again. 'Is that so? Sure. That'd be great.'

He looked round sizing up the ground, then sat next to the canvas bag, picking at the long grass while Chris took out the sandwiches. He unfolded the greaseproof paper and offered them.

'Have two if you like,' he said. The man's hands were brown and strong and his nails were short and square. He wore a heavy wrist-watch which glinted in the sun.

'One'll be more than plenty. I guess I was just coming out for a stroll and here I am, eating homegrown hen's eggs. My name's Ed. What's yours?'

Chris was chewing the sweet, swallowing its sweetness. He wiped his hand across his mouth before replying.

'Chris,' he said. 'Chris Weber.'

The man tipped his hat even further back on his head. 'Well, Chris Weber, you must be mighty proud of where you live. This is a nice little corner.' He waved his hand across the view. 'You born here?'

Chris was drinking from the bottle again and now he hesitated, wiping the neck with his sleeve, looking at the man. Then he passed it to him. Ed took it, looked at him and grinned, and then drank. Chris smiled, taking it back, burrowing it back in the canvas bag out of the sun. He brought out a stick of rhubarb and a twist of sugar saying as he did so, 'No, I wasn't born here. I lived in London but when the bombing started I was evacuated here. I like it.'

He broke the rhubarb in two and handed a piece to Ed. Then he spread out the paper. 'Dig the end in the sugar and then eat it.'

Ed did and Chris laughed at his face, at the strings of rhubarb which hung from his mouth.

'Jeez, what the hell's this?' Ed said, his face screwed up.

'It's a bit sour, makes your teeth feel funny doesn't it? But it's nice when there's nothing sweet left to eat.' Chris was smiling and now Ed was too. Chewing but asking for more water.

'I forget that there's rationing over here. You must excuse us if we tread on your toes. We don't mean to but little England sure takes some getting used to.'

'My mum says we're very lucky Mr Roosevelt decided to come in after all, even if it took Pearl Harbor to do it. She says we can't win without you.'

Ed threw the remains of his rhubarb right across the field and Chris watched. He threw the remains of his too but it fell far short of the man's.

'Your mom is here with you, is she?' Ed asked, stretching out his arms, flexing his shoulders.

'No, she's in London. How do you throw that far?' Chris said, kneeling now, looking out across the field, trying to see where the rhubarb had landed.

'I was a pitcher back home in college. You know, baseball. You call it rounders.'

Now Chris did know but the boys at school called it a girls' game and sniggered at the American comics which showed pictures of the game. But this man wasn't girlish.

'I'll show you one day. How about it?' Ed leaned forward, pulling up another grass shoot, chewing it. He turned and looked at Chris who was nodding, his blond hair bleached almost white by the sun.

'So we're both away from home then, Chris Weber? Get's kind of lonesome, doesn't it?'

Chris nodded, packing up the sugar carefully, to take home and use again tomorrow. 'I'd like to learn to throw,' he said.

'Well, we got a deal then. You don't bring me any more rhubarb and I'll teach you to pitch.' Ed stuck out his hand and his teeth were strong and white when he smiled.

Chris shook his hand. It was big and warm and it felt good to be touched by a grown man again. It reminded him of his father.

'Where you going now then, Chris?' Ed was standing up, wiping his forehead with the back of his hand, lifting up his cap then brushing off his trousers.

A formation of bombers was coming in to land and Chris could not talk against the noise so they both stood and watched.

'I was just going to look for some butterflies. You can come if you like.'

They walked slowly through the meadows and Chris asked Ed if he flew.

'Yeah, I fly one of the Fortresses.' Ed stopped as a Nymph rose from the wheat. 'Say, is that one of those things that fly into the lampshade at night, banging itself to bits? Can't stand the things.'

'No, it's a Nymph, a butterfly. You can tell them from moths because butterflies' antennae have knobs on the end. Moths tend to hold their wings horizontally when they're at rest too.'

'You know a lot about this then? Do you collect 'em?'

Chris shrugged. 'No. I don't like the idea of killing.'

Ed nodded and started to walk again. 'I guess most of us are like that.' He wasn't smiling now but then a Red Admiral flew up before them and Chris held out his hand to stop the man.

'Isn't that beautiful?' Chris said. 'I mean, it's just so beautiful.' They stood quietly for a moment watching as the butterfly wove its way over the wheat.

'They get drunk on the rotten apples in the orchard, you know,' Chris said, talking to this man as though he had known him all his life. He was so easy. Not like the English grown-ups. Were all Americans like this?

Ed's laugh was loud.

'Do you get butterflies where you live?' Chris asked, moving the bag on his shoulder, then feeling it lifted from him as Ed took it.

'Not much. We live in Montana, ranch country. Down in the valley they come but not up near the sage brush. We keep horses, cattle, sheep. Herd them, and there's some hay too. It's kind of beautiful there. Mountains all around with deep snow in the winter and hot sun in the summer.'

Chris stopped. 'Do you ever brand them to stop the rustlers? And are there Indians?'

They were on the old cart track now and Ed sat on the oak which had been felled by lightning four years ago.

'Sure we brand them, but we don't have a big herd and it grazes behind fences now but in the days of rustlers there was a real need for branding. You ever seen it done?'

Chris shook his head.

'Well let me tell you something you can tell your friends.

Come the spring the cowboys would bring in all the cattle on the ranges, sort them out into the different owner herds. Then they'd brand the calves with a red-hot iron. Say, you got a blacksmith here?'

Chris nodded.

'Well, the iron has to get that hot, then you press it against its hide and the smell and the sizzle is just something.' Ed took a packet of Lucky Strikes from his pocket, tapping the cigarette on his fingernail, then striking the match on it too. Chris breathed the scent of sulphur pretending it was the smell of burning hide.

'Now, there are all sorts of brands, put on with a stamp iron. Usually no more than four inches long, not more than seven inches in any direction but they grow with the animal you see. Now a brand's made up like this. If it's the Lazy M Bar you would lay an "M" on its side with a line underneath. Kind of neat eh?'

He flicked the ash off on to the ground. 'But, oh my, did those cowboys know what they were doing, kid. They would have to drive a mile-long herd you know. They'd keep the stronger cattle forward and out of the way so they didn't trample the weaker ones. They'd call that keeping up the corners. The cowboys would keep the herd together, signalling by hand, using Plains Indian sign language.' He paused. 'Hey, should you be back at home by now? It's past four o'clock.'

'No, go on.' He could tell Mary and the others, but not Joe or his gang.

'Now did I tell you about a running iron for branding? That's what those darned rustlers would use. A straight poker drawn like a pencil to make any brand.'

'But what about the cowboys. Did they shoot the rustlers?'

'Yeah, they sure did. They were taking something which wasn't rightly theirs, you see. And the West didn't have the kind of laws you Britishers have. You've been here so darned long.' He laughed.

'What about stampedes? Have you ever been in a stampede when you've been moving your cattle?'

'Not moving our own but I have when I worked one summer down in the south. You have to churn them around to the right when they're spooked, always to the right and you have to have a good horse, one that ain't going to run out on you. You just got to squeeze that circle smaller and smaller until the herd becomes compact and stops. It's kind of spooky, I'm telling you. And there're no Indians any more near us but there were some on the plains. They got real mad when the white man came but who can blame them?'

He lit another cigarette. 'It all seems very far away now.'

'Is flying as exciting as being a cowboy?'

Ed smiled. 'Exciting isn't the right word. We go up into the sky and try to find the assembly ship which is shooting off flares so that we can see it. This can take an hour, Chris, and then we fly in formation at high altitude, hoping our bomb aimers are going to do their job properly. And we won't know whether any of us are going to turn out right until we actually try it and who knows when that will be. No. It's not exciting. It's tiring, it's worrying. Ships collide, crash. It's not exciting.' His voice was flat now and he stood up.

'I guess maybe being a cowboy is better. But I reckon I'd better be getting back now. I'll see you again, Chris, teach you how to pitch, eh?' He passed back the bag and punched Chris on the arm. 'Nice meeting you, kid. You take care now.'

Chris watched him go, his rolling walk, his cap on the back of his head and turned, his hand at his belt, wishing he still had his cap gun. He formed his hand into a gun and shot into the hedges that he passed. The shadows were longer now, the sun not so hot and his watch said it was five o'clock.

Joe was waiting at the edge of the village, beyond the grey stone wall where no one could see. Chris had forgotten him. How could he have done that? How could he have forgotten? He tightened his grip on the butterfly net and kept his hand as a gun. It gave him courage.

Joe lounged out into the lane, kicking a stone.

'I want to talk to you, you German swine,' he said, using a drawl he had copied since the Americans arrived.

'I don't want to talk to you,' Chris said, pushing past because it was not the postal order day. The gang came out from behind the wall then and they had nettles in their gloved hands. They grabbed Chris and he fought but Joe hissed, 'Keep still, or I tell the whole bloody village.'

He kept still while they rubbed the freshly picked nettles over his face, arms and legs as far as his shorts would allow. They then broke his butterfly net, again.

That week Laura wrote to Helen to come because Chris would not tell her what was going on, but something was because his limbs were covered in nettle rash and she was sure he hadn't fallen, as he was insisting.

Ed walked on back to base. No, he thought, it was not exciting. He had not expected it to be somehow, maybe because he was older than most of the kids who volunteered or were drafted. For Christ's sake he was thirty, so why the hell was he here? To get away from the ranch, from his father, his mother who loved him too much? Out of a sense of duty maybe? Who knew, who cared? He was here, wasn't he?

He looked over the meadows. England was so green, that was what had struck him when they finally landed at Liverpool and travelled out from the bombed city. It was so damn green. But Liverpool hadn't been green, neither had the run through bomb alley off Greenland on the transport ship because he'd travelled over by ship, not flown one of the Fortresses like some of the others. It had been cold and grey at sea and cold and grey in Liverpool.

Barrage balloons were moored to barges in the river the guys called the Mersey. There was a freighter with a torpedo hole, women with scarves round their heads. There were little trains with hooters, not whistles. Red tram cars but hardly any cars. Red Cross girls with doughnuts and coffee at stalls on the station. On the train there were closed blackout curtains, on the trucks which wound through these tiny little lanes there was just a wooden rail to hang on to.

At the air base there were only showers with cold water which shot up from the centre of a wide concrete dish and you washed yourself in the downfall. It was crazy. What a way to run a war; but as he walked he knew that he was thinking of these things rather than the daylight bombing runs they were training for.

Why daylight? He knew why. So that the Air Force could become a service in its own right, separate from the Army. They wanted to bomb accurately in daylight and win the war in a few months. Ed shrugged. But he wasn't being fair. After all, the Allies did need to put the pressure on day and night but they'd forgotten there was no proper long-range fighter cover. They had forgotten there were a lot of enemy planes up there, a lot of anti-aircraft guns. They'd forgotten that the people flying these damned Fortresses were skin and bone.

He thought of the boy, the butterflies, the pitching. Yes, he'd show him how to throw. He was a nice kid. It was better to think of that than assembling at altitude, flying in formation, dropping bombs, spotting Messerschmitts, hearing the stuttering of guns, feeling the shudder of bullets hitting the fuselage. He was thinking in time to his footsteps and now he stopped, his hands in his pockets, breathing deeply, wishing there were just a few mountains around, making himself stop thinking of aeroplanes and battles.

Making himself think of the Red Admiral getting drunk on apples, tasting again the rhubarb. Crazy people, these Britishers, but kind of nice.

Helen came down when she received Laura's letter. The trip was quicker now that the bombing was almost non-existent. The bus drove quickly down the lanes in the long evenings made longer still by double summer time.

She talked with Laura in the kitchen and with Mary too who would not say what was happening but only that one boy and his friends were ganging up. Helen fed the hens with Chris while Laura prepared salad and after they had eaten she walked with him, letting him take her towards the base, walking along the tarmacked road which was slippery with melted tar from the hot afternoon sun. They walked on the grass verge and stopped as Chris pointed out the hangars, the aeroplanes, the baseball pitch which had been marked out off to the left.

She listened as he told her of Captain Ed McDonald who was showing him how to pitch in the meadow near the pond; of Mary who came and watched. He talked of the butterflies he still watched and led her over the fields to the pond where they still had not recovered the tin bath. But he told her nothing of his fears, though she hugged him and said that she knew there was something wrong. He would not tell her about Joe though. No. His father had told no one of his battle so he mustn't either.

Helen stood at the edge of the pond watching her son flick his hair from his face. The shadows were there in his eyes and they had been there for too long.

'Right,' she said, walking over to him. 'Listen to me. I can't make you tell me but I am going to teach you what an old boxer taught some of the lads in the shelter because you must fight back, Chris. Whatever is going on, you must fight back.'

She turned him round. 'Now watch me. You hold your hands like this, see?' She stood with her right hand forward and her left in close to her chin. 'You lead with your right and then hit hard with your left. Now, you've got to keep your feet moving. Don't stand still. You mustn't stand still or they'll be able to hit you.'

She stopped. 'Do you understand?' She was panting.

Chris nodded.

'Good, now put your hands up and try and hit me.' Her fists were up again and her feet were moving.

Chris just stood. 'Come on, Chris, hit me.'

He put his hands up too but it felt awkward. He moved his feet but he couldn't hit his own mother and so she hit him on the cheek and it hurt. He still couldn't hit her and she hit him again, on the ribs, and now he circled her and jabbed at her, hitting her on the chin.

Helen stopped, her eyes blinking. It had hurt. It had really hurt. She smiled. 'That's right. That's absolutely right. Come on. Again.' They circled and jabbed for the next hour and both walked home with red faces but they were laughing and when Ed drove by in the jeep and hooted, Chris said to his mother, 'That's my friend.'

That night Chris slept because his mother had come and looked so funny trying to help.

CHAPTER 13

It was September, a month after Chris had first met Ed and each Saturday when the American was not flying they met out on the grass patch near the big pond to practise pitching. The tin bath was now up on the bank but neither Mary nor Chris had clambered in to drag it out. Ed had brought it in.

Chris had stood on the bank with Mary while the American threw out a four-pronged hook attached to a line. It had landed in the bath with a muffled clang and they pulled the line gently, hearing the hook scrape against the sides but it had caught on the rim and they were able to drag the bath back.

It had smelt and Ed had swirled water in it, then called them to help him tip it up and left it to dry. Chris had a plank now and Ed had brought along two empty drums from the Airbase and, after pitching practice this afternoon, Chris was going to lash it all together and see if it would float properly this time.

'Come on then, Chris, let's get going,' Ed called from his position ten yards in front of him. 'Now remember what I said last week. The pitcher's got to deceive the batter, right. He's got to produce pitches which are fast or will swerve or dip because the whole aim is to get that man out. Now I want you to throw me a fast ball, OK? Mary, you get ready too, because I'll be sending one to you soon.'

Chris looked at Mary. She had begun to come with him again because he had told her that he could fight now and one day he would and she was not to cry when she saw him with Joe. So far, though, he hadn't fought. But the sun was too hot to think of all that now and Ed was waiting.

He was wearing a pitcher's glove which Ed had given him. It was padded leather with a webbed pocket to help to catch the ball.

'Remember to keep that foot in contact with the back plate

when you throw.' Ed called and Chris nodded, checking that his right foot was on the square that Ed had marked out with a stone earlier. He held the cowhide ball with his thumb underneath and his first two fingers on top, and close together. The ball was warm and smooth.

'Blimey, it'll be time to go to bed before he gets going,' Mary called and Ed laughed.

Chris threw the ball then and Ed scooped it out of the air, curving his body, moving his legs.

'That was great, really great. Real quick. Try catching this.'

As he threw it Chris saw the twist of his wrist and the ball came at him from right to left and dipped at the last minute but he caught it, hearing Ed's shout of praise and Mary's cheer.

Ed came over and stood next to Chris. 'Right, Mary, you get ready to catch the next one. Let's see if boy wonder can throw a curveball like that.' He checked Chris's grip. 'OK, the grip's the same as the fastball but the fingers are parallel to the seam. That's right. Now get that twist right. Like this, see?'

Chris watched as again and again Ed twisted his wrist but did not throw the ball. The American had tossed his jacket over on the grass when he arrived and rolled his sleeves up above his elbows. He had left base for two hours only today because there was a briefing at 14.00 hours.

'OK. Now try that.' He ran back, standing towards Chris. 'Move in a little, Mary. Ready to go when you are, Chris.'

He threw then; the grip was right and the twist. They both missed it and the ball rolled to a halt yards behind, near to the trees.

'You're going great,' Ed said, picking up the ball, showing Mary how to hold it and now Chris leaned forward, ready to catch. Again and again they did it until the sweat was rolling down Chris's back and his shirt clung to him. Ed was hot too and Mary had flopped down on the grass in the shade.

Laura had made them ginger beer and they sat in the shade at the edge of the copse, hearing the bees in the grass, drinking it from enamel mugs which Chris had brought. Laura had told Chris to ask his American if he would like to come home for tea.

'That's kind of you all but I have to get back to base and I reckon maybe I won't be back out again this evening.' He reached across and dug into his jacket pocket. 'Have a cookie.'

'Why?' Mary said, taking one of the biscuits, and then another. 'Why won't you be back out?'

The American shrugged.

Chris looked at him and asked, 'Is the training over? Are you really going to fly properly now?'

'Well, I guess maybe that's what's about to happen soon.' Ed grinned but the smile didn't touch his eyes and Chris looked away towards the pond.

He knew that look. It was how he felt when he saw Joe at the end of the lane and suddenly he didn't want this man to go up in those big dark planes, dropping bombs, being shot at. He didn't want the training to finish.

'Maybe they'll think you're not ready,' he said, looking down into his ginger beer. It was warm and not very nice. 'Maybe the war will be over by tonight. Will it be tonight you fly?'

Ed drank back the last of his ginger beer, holding the mug in his large hand, not using the handle. Chris copied.

'No,' his voice was short, clipped. 'Not tonight. We only fly in the daylight and as you say, Chris, maybe the war'll be over by tonight.' He grinned at the boy and reached out, flicking his hair. 'But somehow I don't reckon it will be. Sometimes you just got to get on with things.'

They sat watching the heat shimmering across the freshly harvested fields in the distance, seeing the wind brushing at the reeds near the pond, rippling the surface. A fly came and settled on Ed's empty mug and a Red Admiral danced in and out of the cowslip until they could no longer see it.

When would they start the real thing, Ed wondered. He had just sent a V-mail letter back to his folks telling them that it was great over here. That he flew and trained, drank in the pub and taught baseball to an English kid. He asked them again to look after his mare because he wanted her fit when he got back. When he got back, when he got back. If he got back. He picked up a stone from the grass beside him and threw it from hand to hand.

'No,' he repeated. 'Somehow I don't think this war is going to be over by tonight.'

Chris swatted at the fly, holding out the bottle to Ed and shaking his head. 'I guess not.' He liked speaking the way the American did.

Ed looked at Chris. 'So when's your mom coming back dowı then?'

Chris shrugged. 'I don't know. When she can, I suppose. He laughed and looked at Mary who was giggling.

Ed asked, 'So what's funny then?'

Chris was laughing still so Mary told him that Helen hac shown him how to box last time she was down.

'Your mom? But why not your pop?'

Chris stopped laughing then and turned away. The wind was brisker now and there were ripples on the top of the pond and the reeds were shaking. There were clouds coming up from the east.

'My dad's dead,' Chris said, still looking away, but then he turned and faced the man who was running the rim of the cup over his lips, backwards and forwards. 'He was German. He was in a camp. They killed him. He was brave.' The words were high-pitched, clipped, but they were out, for the first time they were out and what would Ed do? Would he move away from him, pick up his ball, his jacket and go?

Ed touched his shoulder. 'That's tough, real tough.' That was all. He didn't move, he didn't shout. His voice had been kind. Chris looked across at Mary and she smiled. He pushed his hand into his pocket and took out Willi's letter which he always carried now. It had seemed too dead somehow, in the top drawer.

He pushed it into Ed's hand and then got up and walked to the tin bath, rubbing at the dried mud with a stick, clearing it off the sides, watching it drop as fine as sand into the bottom. He rubbed and rubbed and tipped the bath upside down, banging the base and then he rolled it over again. It was clean.

He picked up the plank and straddled it across and then he heard Ed walking towards him and Mary was there too. He didn't look round but took the letter and shoved it in his pocket.

'I thought I'd tie the drums on, then we can see if it floats,' Chris said, still not looking round.

They worked on the raft, tying, knotting, securing, and nothing was said until it floated out across the pond, tethered by the frayed rope which they had kept hidden in an old wooden box in the reeds.

Chris stood with his hands in his pockets, grinning at Mary and then up at Ed, who smiled back. 'That's going to be great,' he said, putting his hand on Chris's shoulder.

Mary took the rope from Chris. 'I told 'im,' she said. 'I told him about Joe. He wants to see what your mum taught you.'

Chris bit back his anger. How could she tell? It was their secret. Ed mustn't know he was afraid. How could she tell? He snatched the rope back.

'You should shut up,' he hissed at her. It was cooler now. There were goose pimples on her arms. He hoped she was cold.

'No, she shouldn't shut up.' Ed's voice was firm. 'She should have told someone a lot sooner. You need to give this Joe guy a good lesson, one he won't forget. Like your pop gave those Nazis, like your grandpa is trying to do out there in Germany.' He nodded at Chris's surprise.

'Yeah, Mary told me that too. But you need the tools to do the job, kid. You need to know what you're doing or how can you fight back? No one can expect you to. Britain couldn't do it. It needed all this stuff from the States. How can I fly without a plane? How can you fight back against this kid without knowing how? You're just like the rest of us. Brave enough but scared too. It's crazy not to be scared. It keeps you alive sometimes.'

Chris felt the American's hands on his shoulders. They were gripping too tightly and he remembered the look in Ed's face earlier. He was frightened too. That's why he was digging his fingers in like he was. Ed was frightened, and if a big man like that was, it didn't matter so much that Chris Weber was scared too.

So he showed Ed his right hand out in front, his left hand close in to his chin and the position of his feet but he still didn't feel comfortable. He stood up and shook his head when Ed asked if he was a southpaw. 'You know, left-handed.'

He shook his head and Ed smiled. 'Well,' he said. 'Your mom is some sort of special lady but she's learned from a southpaw. You need to put your left hand forward like this.' Ed's eyes had lines at the corners when he smiled and the sky was blue above. The trees from the copse were throwing shadows far out across the grass and Chris felt happy right down to his fingertips to be here by the pond with him.

Pitching was forgotten for the next half-hour while Ed taught Chris and Mary too, because she did not want to be left out.

It didn't matter hitting Ed. He was big and strong, not like his mother and so his shoulders loosened and his head came down and he pretended Ed was Joe and landed punches, getting through Ed's guard.

He was stronger now from the pitching. He could feel it and he was quicker too. But it was something else as well. This man knew that he was half German and it didn't matter to him. Gee, he had said. Some Americans are Germans and Italians. How d'you think they feel fighting their own people? And should we hate them because they're Germans or Italians? It's what they are that's important, isn't it? It's the ideas we're fighting against, isn't it?

Chris punched harder, rhythmically in time to that last sentence, It's the ideas we're fighting against, isn't it, isn't it? until Ed called to him to stop, yelling at Mary too who was shadow-boxing just two feet away. He showed them then how to use judo throws because boxing sometimes wasn't enough, but it was getting late. Before he left, though, he kicked Chris's feet out from beneath him, quickly, neatly and the grass was close to his face and smelt fresh and clean. Ants were running in amongst the stems.

'Remember that one,' Ed said, breathing heavily as he bent to pick up his jacket, looking at his watch, then breaking into a jog. He had reached the copse, ready to run through it out on to the fields and then down the road to the base but stopped and turned. 'Hey,' he called. 'When's the next drop for the postal order?'

Chris sat up and cupped his hands round his mouth. 'Next Saturday; ten hundred hours.'

Ed waved. 'Keep practising and watch out for Mary. She swings a mean punch.' He turned and was gone and Chris realised he hadn't wished him luck.

All that week it was overcast, the cloud hung low over England and Europe.

'The summer's finally over,' Laura said as she ironed before the kitchen stove on Thursday afternoon.

Chris could smell the fresh hot linen and was glad of the cloud because it meant the bombers were not flying; that the training had not turned into something more dangerous. It meant Ed was safe.

He practised all that week, sparring against Mary near the

pond but he couldn't bring himself to hit her. She hit him though, and once he got angry and stalked off through the flattened grass, hearing her laugh, and he wished that Joe would walk round the corner that very minute so he could knock his block off while he was still angry.

He had to meet Joe in the woods because the crossroads was too busy with American jeeps and on Thursday he felt tired and taut because there were only two days now before he must stand up to him. He had decided that he could not wait any longer because his father had been brave and there were men out there in bombers with the same feeling in their stomachs and they went, so he must. On Friday he felt sick and his head hurt but there was only one day and night left.

Mary came round and she dodged and weaved in the garden and made him angry again but it didn't last. It was only the fear that was left as darkness fell and he climbed the stairs to bed on legs that felt too tired to carry him. He wrote to his mother that night in the candlelight of his bedroom, bending low over the paper, his hand tight on his pencil. He liked the flickering light, it gave off heat and a waxy smell which was comforting.

He told her that tomorrow, Saturday, he was going to face the boys. That his friend Ed had shown him how to do some judo throws. He did not tell her that she had taught him as a southpaw, because 'she was some kind of a special mom' and he loved her so much. I miss you, Mum, he wrote. I miss you.

The next morning was cold and dull and as he ate an egg which tasted strange and the toast which was too hard, he looked out of the window and hoped that the cloud cover was thick and deep again today and that Ed was kept safely on the ground.

He had not seen him since last weekend. The Americans had been confined to the air base all week but that didn't matter. It only mattered that the aeroplanes had not roared off from the runway at dawn, flown by men with frightened eyes.

'Eat up then,' Laura urged him, coming round the table, looking into his face, her flowered apron stiff from the ironing. 'Are you all right? You don't look too good.'

Chris nodded. 'Yes, I'm fine.'

He heard the postman come and walked to the door, picking up his mother's letter. He opened it and took out the postal order, putting it on the hall table but pushing the letter deep down into his pocket. He took his coat from the hook and left the cottage without saying goodbye, without seeing the geraniums along the path. There was no time.

He walked down the lane. The mist was thick and damp all around and the leaves lay sodden on the road through the village and smoke rose straight up from the chimneys because there was no wind. Jeeps came up and down the road, steering round him, clipping the verges so that grass became mud. Mary was waiting for him outside her cottage. He did not want her to come. He didn't want her to see his eyes, or to see him beaten.

'Stay here, Mary,' he said, heaving his collar up round his neck but she wouldn't. She trailed along after him and he was glad really because he liked her round face, her smile, her voice. His arms ached and he loosened his shoulders as Ed had told him to do. They were on the track now and it was muddy but he hadn't worn boots because he wanted to be able to move fast. He stepped from the mud of the track to the grass which was firmer but water splashed up the back of his legs and he wished he was old enough to wear long trousers. He stopped and pulled up his socks. Mary stopped too.

'It's so damp, ain't it?' she said, pulling her coat round her.

In the copse it was quiet and they didn't talk but edged along the path through the tangled undergrowth. Water dripped from the branches and leaves fell slowly, damply to the ground. The leaves were catching in his shoes and he ducked down, pulling out an oak leaf which had caught beneath his arch. His fingers were trembling and his arms still ached. He was angry with himself and with his fear. He stood up suddenly, hurrying now.

Mary followed and he whispered, 'Stay here. For heaven's sake. Stay here. It's my fight.'

'Oh no it ain't. He's a little snot and he deserves a bloody good hiding.' She grinned and came along beside him now.

The clearing was just beyond the holly tree and they moved slowly forward but there was no one there. Chris stood, his fists clenched, ready but unsure now. He looked at Mary and then all around.

'They're late,' Mary said. 'They got lost in the mist or had another slice of toast for breakfast, greedy pigs.' She walked over to the sawn logs which were piled near the edge of the clearing; brushed at some sawdust and some damp leaves and then sat, her chin in her hands.

Chris stood motionless. His head was still aching. He flexed his arms, then took off his coat, throwing it towards Mary. It didn't reach her and he started to walk across but then they came, bursting from the woods, swinging glowing cans round and round their heads, holding on to the wire and Chris knew that inside the cans were sticks doused in paraffin because he had seen them do it before, but never near another boy. Round and round they whirred, burning brighter and brighter as the air entered the holes which Joe and the gang had pierced in the sides. They were surrounding him now and one boy rushed forward and Chris had to dodge the can, leaping back, fear high in his throat.

Mary was calling out, trying to get through but Len dropped out of the circle and grabbed her, his can hanging limp as he coiled the wire up round his hand.

Chris turned this way, that way, seeing the brightness of the cans, one coming close, and then another. One nearly hit him and he scrambled back but lost his footing and fell. There was laughter now. Loud mouths and the burning cans were all around and over his head and it was like the torches in Germany that he had watched with his father.

'Daddy,' he whispered and then he heard Joe call.

'Don't think we don't know you took lessons from your Yank. We saw you, didn't we? Been on your boat yet? No, because we've sunk it, haven't we? Sunk it proper this time. You didn't know, did you?'

Chris pushed himself up, crouching because the cans were still above him, still too close. If they hit him, the lid would fly open and the wood would burst out and he would burn.

He was dribbling, he knew he was dribbling because it was running down his chin but he wasn't crying. They wouldn't make him cry but he could hear Mary. She was. She was crying and shouting and he tried to crawl beneath the whirling cans to her but then the boys were spreading out and he was up again. He could smell the paraffin in the air, see the trail of black smoke and then there gripping two of the boys was Ed, his face set and calm, his eyes hard and angry.

Chris spun round. There were two other Americans holding

a boy each, gripping them by the collars so that their feet almost left the ground. They were chewing gum and smiled at Chris but their eyes were angry too. The cans lay on the ground, the leaves steaming from their heat. They would not burn now that the wind was not tearing through them. The boy who was holding Mary ran off into the darkness of the wood.

Joe was the only one left and he stood uncertainly between Ed and Chris.

Chris wiped his chin.

'You OK, Chris Weber?' Ed asked.

Chris nodded, waving Mary away.

'I'm OK,' he said. 'I'll fight you, Joe. I'll beat you and then you leave me alone.'

They fought then but Joe used his head to butt and his teeth to bite. Chris did not. He punched and then he flicked Joe's feet from under him but Joe caught at his ankles and brought him down too, punching his ribs, his legs, biting his arm, butting his face. There was blood in his mouth but he could see Ed standing there, holding the two boys, watching closely, never speaking. Just watching.

Mary spoke though. He could hear her shouts, her groans, her cries.

'Kill 'im.'

'Oh Chris.'

'That's not fair.'

'Stop it, Ed. Stop it.'

But Ed didn't stop it. He watched as Chris fought, blood staining his cheek and he wanted to grab Joe and slap him because he was a bully and he was hurting the kid, like he'd been hurt when he'd broken his first horse in. His father hadn't stopped that and afterwards Ed had been glad.

He watched as Chris tried the uppercut but from the ground. He made contact, and again, and then he was on top, his knees resting on Joe's shoulders. Keeping his body on the ground, twisting his hair until the boy cried and told him to stop.

Ed let the others go then and didn't watch as they ran through the woods. He nodded to Earl and Mario who loosened their grip on the other boys, letting them push away, and follow the others.

He walked to Chris, helping him up, letting Mary come and grip Chris's arm, lead him to the logs. Then Ed dragged the other boy up, checked him over and led him from the clearing, right through to the edge of the copse. He told him that if there was any more trouble of any sort it wouldn't be Chris who dealt with it next time. It would be somebody much bigger. Did he get the picture? He watched as Joe ran back down the track to the village. He'd not be back.

Chris was sitting on the logs. His head hung down. It was still aching, banging and banging inside his skull. His hands felt swollen and his mouth was sore but he looked up when Ed came and stood in front of him.

'You did real good, Chris. Your pop would have been proud of you. And your mom too.' He held out his hand and Chris shook it, standing, feeling his legs trembling but he smiled. He felt so good inside.

'It doesn't matter if he tells the village,' Chris said, though it hurt to talk and spit had filled his mouth. He swallowed it.

'He won't. Don't you worry about that. You tell them when you're ready.' Ed was passing his cigarettes to Earl and Mario, then lit one himself. 'I guess it was lucky we were passing but I figure you could have dealt with it anyway.'

He smiled at Chris and they both knew the truth.

'You'd better get along home now. Get that face cleaned up, spend that money. Give Laura a heart attack.' Ed laughed. 'You can make it can you?'

'Sure the kid can make it, Captain,' Earl said, helping Chris to his feet. 'Someone who's as tough as this can manage just about anything.' He bent down and picked up Chris's coat, letting Ed help him on with it.

'By the way, this is Earl whose family came from Hamburg, and this other guy is from some strange hot place where they eat a lot of pasta.' Ed winked at Chris.

Chris pulled his coat around him, but he was hot, really hot. He looked at the men.

'Thanks,' said Chris. 'You know, thanks.' His voice was fractured now and small.

'I know,' said Ed, punching him lightly on the arm. 'Be seeing you then.'

He turned and walked back with the other two men and this time Chris remembered to call.

'Good luck.'

*

The next day Laura called the doctor who said that the headache was not schoolboy tension or the result of a scrap but rheumatic fever and an ambulance came. But Chris knew nothing of that, he just knew pain and illness.

He lay in the hospital bed, his legs aching too much to keep still even though the woman in the white apron told him he must not move so the nurses came and put iron bars across his calves and his forearms and the pressure of their weight hurt him even more. He cried and Laura held his hand but her hand was too heavy on his flesh. He was so hot and the screens around the bed were too bright. He wanted it dark, no light, nothing to blind his eyes.

The nurse came again, forcing his lips apart but they were cut. Couldn't she see they were cut and the medicine was bitter and scoured his throat. He was so hot.

'Mum. Daddy.'

He was so hot. The screens were still there. They were like Laura's knickers on the washing line, all gathered, but they weren't blowing. They were just white, glaring white. His legs hurt. Why wouldn't they take these bars away, these screens?

'Mum. Daddy.'

He was crying. He knew he was crying because he was shaking but it hurt his head. Where was his mummy? She'd been away for so long. Where was she?

Helen came on the first train. She took the bus to the hospital and ran in. The nurse at the desk called the doctor who took her into the side office, calling for a cup of tea for Mrs Weber.

'He has rheumatic fever and is holding his own, Mrs Weber. He has been delirious for two days and we have attached him to a heart monitor. Unfortunately we have had to restrain his limbs to prevent any unnecessary strain on the heart. This of course is the danger with rheumatic fever. It can affect the heart you see.'

He turned as the door opened and the nurse came in with a cup of tea. He was a small man, with lines of tiredness running from his nose to his mouth but then, Helen thought, the nurse had them just as deep.

And yes, she did know that rheumatic fever affected the heart but it must not affect Chris's. She loved him too much. She mustn't lose him, not after sending him away. Not after leaving him here without her. No, she mustn't lose him; she had lost too much of his life already.

She said, 'Yes, I see. What can be done?' But she couldn't drink her tea because she was gripping the cup and the saucer too tightly.

'The remedy is rest and aspirins in fluid, twice daily. A tablespoon at a time.' He smiled. 'Try not to worry, Mrs Weber. It is usually most effective.' He took her then to see Chris. He lay behind screens and seemed so alone in the large room, but then she saw Laura and Helen was glad that she was there.

Helen smiled as the doctor moved back the screen, lifting it so that there was no noise. She touched Laura on the shoulder, then sat in the chair that the doctor indicated.

Chris was so small, so fevered. His face was red and beaded with sweat and the iron bars were there, pinioning his limbs.

'He's doing very well,' the sister murmured, taking the place of the doctor.

Helen touched her son's hand, slipping hers beneath his, folding her fingers over lightly.

He opened his eyes. 'Mum,' he said and smiled. 'Where's Daddy?'

He drifted in and out of delirium for one week and Mary looked in through the window, anxious, unsmiling. Laura stayed some of the time but Helen stayed every day and every night wondering if the flight of planes each morning and evening disturbed him. At the end of the week his fever broke but his limbs still hurt and one moment he was sweating and the next he was cold but now Mary could come in too.

She sat with Helen and talked to him of the boat which Ed had fished for and found. Chris smiled.

Helen left for two hours when Laura came. She walked into the town where the hospital was situated and bought blackout material which was not rationed. She sat and sewed each day and night, sitting at his bedside telling him of the crypt, of the vicar, of Marian. Telling him that it looked as though there would be victory in the Western Desert. Unable to talk of his village and his life but determined that soon she would be able to.

She brought her old lace blouse into the room and cut and hemmed a collar from it and cuffs for the dress which was to be for Mary and listened while Laura talked of the hens and the pigs and Mr Reynolds who had to gather in the cow dung now.

On the tenth day Helen was helping the sister to ease another pillow behind her son and watching as they removed the iron bars because there was no more delirium, no more asking for his father. She lifted the cup with a spout like a teapot to his lips, not allowing him to move at all because the doctor was still concerned about any strain to his heart.

'There is a murmur, you see, Mrs Weber,' he said as he watched her wiping Chris's mouth. 'A weakness. It is imperative that he rests.'

His words were over-hung with the roar from the aeroplanes as they returned from a flight. Helen looked not at the doctor but out of the window.

'Yes, I see,' she said. 'I will make sure he rests.' She looked at the temperature chart hooked on the bottom of the bed; the thin red line was more even now. She smiled at her son but he wasn't looking at her, he was looking at the door which had opened.

'Hi, Ed,' he said and there was such pleasure in his eyes.

Helen turned and saw the man, so big in his uniform, his hat slipped back on his head, his grin wide.

'Hi, Chris Weber. So, got yourself a bit of trouble, hey?' He walked over, his shoes silent on the waxed floor, his left hand in his pocket.

He walked to the bed, tossing some candies on the blanket. 'You'd better get out of here soon, that boat's going to get pretty rusty out there and the pitching's going to go downhill.'

Helen walked to the door with the doctor then turned and watched this big man talking to her son, his hands strong and kind. He picked at some fluff on Chris's sleeve, rolling it into a ball and flicking it into the dish on the beside table and Chris smiled.

'Well, that's the kind of aim you get when you've pitched as much as I have.' Only then did he turn to Helen, only when Chris was tired and his lids were drooping and for that she already liked him.

He rose and walked with that ambling stride to the end of the bed where she was now standing.

'I guess you must be Mrs Weber. That's a fine boy you have there.' His handshake was firm and his smile broad but there were the same lines of tiredness on his face that there were on everyone's.

'I think I have much to thank you for, Captain McDonald,' Helen said, because Laura and Mary had told her everything.

'Not a lot, most of it he did himself. Look I can't stop long, I've got to get back to base. We should be training tomorrow.' He paused. 'I wanted to get over much sooner but we've been kind of busy.' His smile was wry.

'It's enough that you came. He's been waiting for you,' Helen said, hearing him rattle the change in his pocket, hearing the hoot of the car outside the window. He moved across and looked out.

'There's my lift. I got to go. I'll come again, if I may?' He was looking towards Chris and she saw the fine cheekbones, the flickering left eyelid.

'Please do. Chris would be very grateful and so would I.'

He nodded and smiled at her. The jeep hooted again and he turned towards the door, waving as he went.

Helen watched him and then as she moved towards Chris again she saw the material lying folded on the back of the chair, the lace collar draped across it, and she went running out after him, down the corridor, calling, 'Captain McDonald, Captain McDonald.'

He stopped and turned.

Helen blushed. 'I'm making something rather special for somebody but I can't get any elastic and I've heard the Americans have everything.'

She laughed when he spread his arms wide. 'Well, I guess that's as good a war aim as any, Ma'am. Leave it with me.'

He came back every other day for the next three weeks and they sat by the bedside as Chris woke and talked, or slept.

He brought the elastic on his second visit and Helen sewed it around the waist of the dress she was making, listening as he told her of the farm in Montana, of the mountains which looked pretty much like Chris's earlier temperature chart, of the mare he was hoping to breed from. He told her that his mother loved him too much and Helen knew what he meant and so she told him of her own mother but then he said, 'Oh no, Mom's nothing like that.'

Mary came the next time, driven by Ed in his jeep. Helen

gave her the dress and she held it up against her and then turned to Chris, who smiled at her and then at his mother.

'It's got a waist. I've always wanted a waist but my sister said I was too fat. How did you know I wanted a waist, Mrs Weber?' Mary's face was eager.

'Every woman wants a dress with a waist, my dear Mary,' Helen said. 'And you have been such a true friend to Christoph. It is so little.'

She sat back then and listened as Ed told the children of the heat a cattle herd would build up, of the cowboys' fear of storms because they spooked the cattle and he asked Chris how a stampede could be halted. Chris told them and Ed laughed and called him a clever kid for remembering.

Then Chris told Ed the German story of the raven coming ahead, warning by thunder and lightning that the gods were coming and everyone should hide and Helen was glad to hear her son talking of his heritage so naturally.

The next time they talked of the Flying Fortresses because Ed's hands were shaking but he didn't say why. But when Chris was asleep he told her of the punishment a ship could take, his face pale, his uniform dark against the white walls.

'The rounds of gunfire, the blasting of an engine and still the old bus will get us home, or some of us.'

They talked or rather Helen listened as he told her that already there were not enough spare parts, not enough spare crews.

He told her how the planes were pouring from the Detroit plants but they would soon be pouring from the skies too, over Germany. That the crews were so young, too young to be killed, too young to kill. That though they would fly high they would fly in daylight and they would not have fighter escort the whole way. That they had twenty-five missions to accomplish before they could go home. He had flown in a British bomber as an observer last week, and now he knew what they would be facing when the training was finished. The next time he came he brought her candies because he had talked too much, but she didn't think he had.

It was October before Chris was able to sit up, and Helen left him for two days to travel to London and when she returned she told him that she would not be going back. She had spoken to Mr Leonard and insisted on him releasing her because

Laura knew someone at the beet factory and they would take her now.

She did not tell him that she had threatened to tell Mr Leonard's wife that he took flowers each Friday to a lady who lived in Harrow but she told Ed, who laughed and said that he reckoned that even if she did box like a southpaw she was a dangerous dame to meet on a dark night.

Helen did not understand but she laughed with him. When Ed left, Chris woke and picked at the crisp starched sheet with thin fingers, his striped pyjamas caught up above his elbows.

'Mum, I've got to tell the village you know.'

Helen took his hand. 'No, darling. I must tell them. I'm going to be living here too, permanently soon. I shall tell them, but when the time is right. Now, shall we finish this puzzle?'

She carried over the tray and put all the blue pieces to one side. There were planes coming over again.

'Mum.'

'Yes, Chris?'

'Ed's great, isn't he?'

'Ed's a very kind man.' Helen said.

'But he's more than that, isn't he?'

Twelve planes had flown over now.

'Yes, he's more than just a kind man,' she said but he couldn't be more than that for her, because she couldn't live with the threat of another loss and she still loved Heine.

CHAPTER 14

Helen signed an official contract to work in the laboratory of the sugar-beet factory on Friday 30 October. She had dropped her cases in the small room at the top of the boarding house on the main street of the town. She had stuffed newspaper in the rattling window frame and beneath the door which had been cut to ride over a now non-existent carpet and then left to spend the days of the weekend at the hospital with Chris and her nights at the cottage. She talked to him of the new Commander in North Africa, General Montgomery, who was beginning a big offensive along the coast at El Alamein, of the Russians who were hanging on grimly in Stalingrad, of the American Marines who had made a successful landing on the Solomon Islands.

She fed him ice-cream which Ed had brought and left earlier in a big container filled with ice. There was too much for him and so the nurses took the remainder for the other patients. Helen had not seen Ed, she had arrived too late and Chris asked why.

She told him of the boarding house, the rattles and draughts. The girls who had been smoking in the small kitchen and stubbing their cigarettes out on a tin lid and who had wanted to talk. So she had not been able to arrive any earlier, had she? She didn't tell him that she did not want to see the big smiling American who made her feel things that she thought had died with Heine.

She arrived back at her digs on Sunday evening carrying the dungarees that she would need for tomorrow. She had heard the planes straggling back as she travelled on the bus and counted, knowing Ed was flying his first mission, knowing that if he didn't return Chris would tell her, somehow he would tell her.

She climbed the stairs and slept from ten until five without waking. She was satisfactorily full because Laura had brought a picnic lunch into the hospital; chicken and bacon pie and eggs from the hens. The bacon had been a surprise but Laura had said little, only smiled slightly and said that the government allowed the killing of people not pigs in the war but after all, wasn't it strange how one animal could go missing and turn up in separate joints in villagers' houses? Helen had felt uncomfortable for a moment but then hunger had triumphed.

She walked to work through cold, wet, dark streets, stepping over mud spun off the wheels of the incessant beet lorries. Overhanging everything was the heavy smell of beet pulp which the boarding housekeeper had told her belched out from the chimneys twenty-four hours a day during the beet campaign. Others were walking with her now but nobody spoke, they were too tired.

She arrived at six a.m. and walked from the cold into a barrage of heat and noise. Within seconds she was too hot and she shrugged herself out of the heavy greatcoat, holding it as she knocked on the forewoman's door. It was opened but the woman could only nod, the noise was too great to hear any words. Her hair was wound up inside a headscarf and her breath was nicotine-heavy as she came up close and shouted, 'Follow me.'

The smell of beet pulp was thicker inside the building, too thick to breathe but somehow Helen did, following the woman who did not look behind her once. They passed machinery which roared and rocked and women who smiled before turning back, sweat running from their bandana-wrapped hair and from their faces and arms to drip on to the floor. They climbed up an iron stairway, slippery from the dripping overhead pipes and now there were men who wore no shirts and whose backs were beaded with sweat. One turned and whistled. Helen saw his lips but heard nothing but the clang and the clatter. Her short-sleeved shirt was sticking to her now and she held her coat away from her body.

How could these people work like this, how could they bear the noise, the smell? How could she? The woman was walking more quickly now, lengthening her stride, checking her watch, walking down half a flight of stairs, turning left. Helen caught up, taking shallow breaths, looking at the small grey office they were approaching. There were white stencilled letters on the door and she saw that they said 'LABORATORY'.

The supervisor walked in and Helen followed, shutting the door, reducing the noise by a fraction, but even that was welcome. The woman was beckoning to her, talking to a small man in a paisley tie and starched collar, soiled now where it rubbed against his neck. When Helen approached she shouted into her face again.

'This is Mr French. He is in overall charge of the laboratory. You will take your directions from him.' Her fingers, which she ran through her damp hair, were nicotine-stained but her grin made Helen smile. 'I'll see you down in the canteen for lunch. Half an hour, that's all we get.'

Helen stood watching as Mr French tucked his pen behind his ear and pointed to her coat and then the rack on the wall. He smiled as she walked back, having heaped her coat on top of two others.

'Tea break of ten minutes at nine o'clock. You'll need that on the first day.'

Helen nodded, looking round. Three other girls were working in dungarees and short-sleeved shirts, their heads down, their hair lank and wet.

Mr French tapped one of them on the shoulder and when she turned he said, 'Take Mrs Weber through the procedures please, Marjorie, I have to get on.' He smiled. 'Marjorie's our charge-hand.'

Marjorie rose then and stuck her hands into her pockets, leaning back against the bench she had been working on. She grinned.

'Right, they'll already have told you how long you have to put up with this bedlam. We knock off at two p.m. sharp and leave prompt for our breaks. That way maybe we stay sane. They'll also have told you that there are three shifts. We do two weeks on each. The graveyard shift is ten p.m. to six a.m. but I'm not going to tell you about it, I'll let you wait and enjoy its delights at first hand.' She laughed but it was sucked away by the noise as Mr French opened the door and left the room.

Marjorie jerked her head in his direction. 'He's OK. Pinches a few bums from time to time but he's never tried mine. Fancies them blonde and giggly.' Helen smiled and watched as Marjorie waved her hands along the benches.

'We're supposed to check that there is the correct standard of sugar in the beet and not too much going out into the waste products. Each result you get should be within just a few degrees of the standard.'

One of the girls rose from her bench and left and again there was an increase in noise as the door opened. Helen's head already felt as though it were bursting.

'Frances has gone to collect the samples. We have to take turns; it gets to be quite an art arriving back not dripping with the damn stuff. Once we get them here the waters are filtered and polarised, the beet pulp is dried out and weighed, then we record the results in the book. Sweet water and diffusion juice are brought up every couple of hours and five diffusion juices in bottles once every shift.'

Marjorie crossed her arms and nodded towards the other girls. 'That's Penny and Joan. Frances will be back soon and then I'll show you what to do.'

It was twenty minutes before Frances appeared. The waters and juices were thick; cloudy and dark grey. Like the weather, Helen thought, but thank heavens the East Anglian clouds didn't smell like this mixture. She watched as Marjorie added lead and distilled water to the samples, leaving them to filter, after which the liquid came through quite clear.

She wrote it all down on a notepad, her pencil slipping in her sweaty hand. It was HB and smudged black across the paper.

'Don't worry too much,' Marjorie said. 'It all seems strange at first but you'll soon get used to it.'

Helen thought she never would. She looked round at these people she didn't know and missed London, the crypt, her friends, the routine of the bank. The noise drilled through her head, the strangeness made her feel like a new girl at school. For now she had no home, just a room with newspaper stuffed in the cracks but her son was close, his heart murmur was improving and that was all that mattered.

She watched now, pushing her discomfort from her, making herself pay close attention as Marjorie poured the samples which had given a low reading into a polarimeter through a long tube with a funnel at the end. Those samples which had given a high reading were poured down a shorter tube with a funnel in the middle. She wrote this down. Then Marjorie took a reading by looking through an eyepiece which was like a telescope and turned a screw on the polarimeter until no shadow was in evidence on the screen. She copied out the reading from the scale at the top.

Marjorie made her do it too and then it was nine o'clock and time for the break. They rushed down through the factory without coats and out into the air where the cold and the quiet was like another world. They ran down the alley to the canteen where there was only time to take a cup of tea, already poured, from the trolley and sit and drink. Marjorie smoked, exhaling through her nostrils and mouth, talking, wafting it across the table, telling Helen that she would soon get the hang of the work, that she worked on a farm during the summer, though she was from Manchester and hadn't known one end of a cow from the other at first. Then she looked at her watch and they ran back because their ten minutes was up. Up the steps and into the factory where the heat, the smell, the noise hit Helen again like a bulldozer, sucking her breath from her.

'Come on,' Marjorie said, pulling her arm as she paused. 'Come on, we'll be late.' They hurried back past the women, the men, under pipes which dripped hot juice on to their bare arms and hair and Marjorie told her that later they would collect some of the sugar which had formed and she could take some back on her day off.

That night in bed she wrote to Chris, telling him of the sugar, Mr French, Marjorie, the canteen; asking him how he was. And then she slept and dreamt of Heine taking photographs of the beet girls near Hanover, saying he would look after her and make sure she never had to work with beet and he held her with arms that were strong and his skin smelt of the summer. His face was kind when she told him about Ed and how she wondered what his arms would feel like. He smiled but his hold loosened and he drifted from her, fading, and leaving her on the windswept beet fields even though she had called him again and again. She woke up crying.

Mr French told her that the heat in the laboratory was seventy-five degrees but the next day a belt came off one of the machines and because it stopped so too did the fans, as they often did. They all thought they would die and were evacuated down to the nearest windows, breathing in the cold damp air until the maintenance crew arrived. This too Helen wrote to Chris, and the next day told him that she had been the sample carrier, climbing up almost vertical stairs, walking along catwalks between hot sticky pipes to the tank.

She told him how she had been covered from head to foot in hot juice and how she had dropped one sample. When she visited him on Saturday night she explained how, that morning before she left, she had to set an automatic graph way up on the top floor and refill it with purple ink.

She showed him a piece of the sugar, collected by her for the girls' tea at its point of production. It was a yellowish grey colour, but sweet, gloriously sweet. Helen and Laura put some into their drinks at the cottage, sitting in front of a fire which burnt logs collected from the surrounding countryside and for a moment it was almost as though there were not a war on, as though there were luxurious food and warmth, as though men were not dying. At dawn, though, she was woken by the aeroplanes lifting off at thirty-second intervals and wondered if there would ever be something as simple as a dawn chorus of birds again.

After the second week she moved to the two p.m. to ten p.m. shift with Marjorie and was thinner, but then they were all thin and it wasn't just the rationing, it was the sweating, but Chris was even better and was allowed to sit up and hold his own cup, his own knife and fork, to turn the pages of his books. Ed came to see him more often because he was not flying at the moment. His Fortress had sustained a hole in the wing and an engine was shattered and there were no replacements yet, he had told Chris, but not Helen because somehow she did not arrive at the hospital until he had left.

On 15 November Helen was sitting with Chris when they heard the church bells ringing out in the town and Helen clutched at the white sheet, wondering if the German invasion had happened at last but a nurse came in and told them that it was in celebration of Montgomery's victory at El Alamein. At the end of November when the Americans were celebrating Thanksgiving the Russians began to turn the tide against the Germans but Helen sat in her room with the draught blowing past the newspaper and under the door, and read Claus's letter from America before she began her two p.m. shift.

My dear Helen,
I am still unable to fight because of my chest but I have established at last our business. So soon, perhaps, Heine's capital can begin to make your life a little more comfortable. I know it is what he would wish.

I am glad in many ways that he is dead because journalist friends of mine tell me from Geneva that the Nazis are systematically murdering Jews, Slavs and dissidents throughout Europe. Not thousands but millions. Can any of this be true? It would be more than he could bear, more than you can bear.

I shall write again, dear Helen.

My love to you and Christoph.

Claus

Helen worked all that day in the heat of the factory, glad that her head hurt, glad that her hair hung lank, that she was tired all the time, and that night she did not sleep because she remembered so much of her life with Heine, so much of the world outside work, rationing and bombing.

The ten p.m. to six a.m. shift was hard. She could not sleep in the day for more than a few hours and when she did she dreamt that she was searching for Heine but he could not be found and so she cried in her dreams and still heard the sound of his voice in those few first moments between sleep and waking. But at last she knew that Chris was going home to the cottage. The doctor told her that the murmur was so faint that there was no danger as long as Chris continued to rest. He could leave for Greater Mannenham on his birthday. Helen was going to book a taxi but Ed waited outside the hospital ward on 30 November to tell her that he had hired one and would collect her first from the boarding house at ten a.m. tomorrow which should give her a chance of a few hours' sleep.

It was pointless for her to protest, he said, because he and Chris had decided between them and apart from anything else, where else could he spend all this goddamn money?

He came at ten a.m. and Helen wore her best dress and coloured her legs with stain because she had no stockings. There was no snow but a white frost and her feet were cold in her shoes, and red. She sat next to him, listening as he described the Thanksgiving dinner at the base, but watching the back of the taxi driver's head and not Ed's hands which were strong and still. Watching the roads which were still muddy from the lorries, hearing the buzz of the windscreen wipers as they cleaned and smeared, cleaned and smeared the glass. She looked ahead but could still see those hands resting on his thighs. He was so good and strong, so kind, but Heine had faded from her dreams and she couldn't bear him to leave her for ever.

The ride back was full of laughter because Chris sat between them and she did not have to feel the American's thigh against hers and was safe. He opened the present that Ed had brought; it was a baseball mitt and two balls. Ed told him there was a bat waiting at the cottage.

Helen had bought an old cap pistol from Marjorie's brother because there were no longer any new toys in the shops. He had given her two boxes of pre-war caps too and Chris held the pistol with the mitt and rested his head on his mother's shoulder and she felt that he was all she needed.

The suburbs turned to fields and Helen saw partridges sheltering in the stubble and bombs stacked high on the near perimeter of an air base but she also saw Ed's face tighten as he saw them too. So she turned and looked instead at the walled churchyard on the other side, telling the American that the yews had provided the wood for longbows in olden times; that the berries and bark were poisonous and that in the old days the churchyard was the one place where cows had no access. She saw his face relax again.

They talked then about the cattle his family ran on the ranch in Montana, the miles of sage scrub on the foothills, the miles of riding range, the wild hay in the valley, and how his flying crew had laughed when they came to Greater Mannenham because they wondered how Little Mannenham could be any smaller.

'But it is,' Helen laughed.

'It sure is.' Ed leaned forward and helped Chris, who had stirred and woken as they pulled in to let an Army transport lorry pass. He fed the end of the cap spool through the hammer of the gun and Helen watched his hands again.

'Do you miss America?' Chris asked, clicking the hammer down gently, not firing yet; waiting until they reached the cottage when he could pounce on Laura as she opened the door.

'Sure I miss it, Chris, but I guess there are compensations.'

'The flying you mean?' Chris asked.

'No, that's not what I mean.' He looked across at Helen but she was staring back at the yew trees, pretending that those words had not been said.

Before Chris went to bed that night he asked his mother if she had told the village yet about his father.

'No, darling, not yet. Joe has gone so you mustn't worry.'

Chris looked down at the mitt which he had brought up to bed with him. 'But we should tell them. Daddy was brave, wasn't he? We should tell them, Mum.'

But she didn't, not then and not on the following Sunday when she was working in the village hall with Laura after Morning Service, knotting camouflage netting with the other women of the village. Hemp was thick in the air but at least there was no smell of beet, no damp heat. No heat at all in fact. Her fingers were clumsy with cold and Laura passed her some fingerless gloves which helped.

Helen pushed her hand through her hair and pulled a face as Laura whispered, 'The vicar's wife was not pleased that you didn't wear a hat.'

Helen said quietly, 'Well, her very own archbishop has just revoked the rule that insists upon hats. It's all part of the war effort. Perhaps I should tell her that.'

Laura laughed. 'Perhaps you shouldn't, you'll get turned to a pillar of salt with that evil eye turned on you.'

'It's all so silly. There are so many problems and she worries about a hat. Anyway, it's stuck in the hole above the skirting board in my digs, stopping a draught. Perhaps I should tell her that instead.' There was an edge to her voice now. She was too tired, too damn tired. There was too much going round her head, too many thoughts, too many doubts, too many fears. When would it ever end?

Laura laughed again. 'You're right, and next week I shall not wear mine and you can use it to plug a few more holes.'

The woman sitting on the right of Helen turned to her. 'I shall be pleased to do the same,' she said.

Mrs Williams was an elderly woman who lived in a small cottage at the far end of the village. She had lived in India for many years, Laura told Helen as they walked home, and was gracious and kind and had taken two evacuees while the vicar's wife had taken only one even though she had three extra bedrooms. She also told Helen that Joe had overheard the vicar's wife telling her husband about Heine. That was how he had known.

The following week, as they strung the twine together in the village hall again, Helen listened to Mrs Williams talking about the hot sun, the plains which stretched shimmering into the distance, the hill stations where it was cool and beautiful and when hemp dried their throats she fetched tea from the hatch for the three of them, passing the vicar's wife who lifted her voice and said, 'Of course, these Germans are barbarians. They are wicked through and through, all of them. It is no good to say it is just Nazis, look at Kaiser Bill. He wasn't a Nazi, he was a German.'

Helen paused, spilling the tea into the saucers but Laura called to her, 'Don't let it get cold, Helen.' Her voice was loud and determined and so Helen walked on but all that afternoon she knew that she had run away again so she dug out Laura's Christmas tree from the bottom of the garden, thrusting her fork into the frozen ground, picking out the earth little by little, using up her anger with herself, her shame. As she dug she wished there were spare hours in which to think, to clear her head, but at the same time she was grateful that there weren't for what would her thoughts be? She carried the tree into the house, looking at her watch, knowing she had time to decorate it before she left for the bus.

She hung old decorations to Chris's directions and new ones that he and Mary had made, and then Ed came, bringing ginger biscuits which he had always hung on his Christmas tree as a child. He helped Chris light the second Advent candle.

'This is an American custom,' he said to Helen, looking at the Advent candle.

'It's a German one too,' she said. 'Heine's mother introduced us to it. It's part of Heine, that's why we have it. We love him.'

Ed looked at her quietly. 'I know. He was a good man. You were lucky to have him. He was lucky to have you.' He paused, smiled at Chris, then walked out to the kitchen where Laura was sitting at the table, peeling potatoes.

'I'm going to take Helen back now. It's too damn cold for buses,' Helen heard him say as she followed him. He turned. 'Get your coat then.'

They drove in silence all the way but Helen felt calmer now because she had told him that she loved Heine and he had accepted it and so perhaps now the image of her husband would come back to her at night and she would stop crying when she woke.

As she pulled at the handle of the car and stepped out into the cold, waving to one of the girls who was also returning, calling to her to leave the door on the latch, she turned.

'Thank you, Ed.' She smiled.

'That's OK, Helen.' He leaned across, holding the door open with his hand. 'But remember, you can't hide behind your grief for ever, some time you've got to go forward.'

That night she did not sleep but neither did she cry.

During the week Helen received a letter from Chris saying that Mrs Williams and Laura were arranging a party for the villagers and the Americans in the village hall and would she help?

She was on the early morning shift and so arrived in the village on Saturday during the early evening and together the three women talked of the arrangements while Chris lay on the settee and dozed. Ed was practice-flying again he told her when she arrived but not until next week, though he had to stay on duty all this weekend. Helen was glad she would not see him because she needed to push her confusion about him to one side in order to deal with something that had already been too long delayed.

They knotted the netting as usual after church but before they all rose to leave Helen stood up. Her legs were shaking but she could not wait any longer to speak as she knew she must. She felt Laura's hand pat her arm and Mrs Williams murmur, 'It will be all right.'

'I wonder if I could have your attention for a moment, ladies?' Helen began. She looked around, and saw the vicar's wife look up, her face red with irritation.

'As Mrs Vane, the vicar's wife, in her position of billeting officer for the area knows, I am the widow of a German.' She didn't look at the women who turned their heads to one another or listen to the murmuring which broke out, she just looked ahead at the clock which had stopped at ten to one.

'In London we knew great kindness and great prejudice and we survived. My son was the victim of blackmail from a small group of boys when he first arrived here but that has now been solved. Now I see that we must confront the problem again.'

There was silence now and her throat was dry and the hemp made her cough. Mrs Williams passed her a glass of water and she sipped, grateful for its coolness.

'All Germans are not Nazis.' She looked now at Mrs Vane. 'All Germans are not wicked. They are much as we are. They did not protest soon enough. I have not protested soon enough.' Helen reached into her handbag, drawing out Willi's letter.

'I would like to read you this letter.'

Her voice didn't falter as she read the words she knew by heart but she felt the thickening in her throat when she put it back into her handbag, heard the click of the clasp in the silence which still hung amongst the hemp. She walked through the door back to the cottage but did not mention it to Chris because she did not know what would happen.

During the week she received a letter from Chris and Laura explaining the details for the party. Ed had arranged for Earl to sing and a group from the base would be playing but the letter said nothing of Mrs Vane. The village women were providing some food and the men and children were decorating the hall. It was to be held on Thursday, Christmas Eve.

The noise of the factory was a relief all that week because it made her head ache so much that she couldn't think, not of Mrs Vane, not of Ed, not of Heine, and at night she dreamt but the images were confused, vivid and made no sense and she awoke each day tired and anxious.

She arrived in the village in the late afternoon on Thursday. She was to be home for two days and went picking holly and ivy for the hall with Mary who wanted her to climb up for mistletoe but Helen said the Americans wouldn't need it if the street corners in town were anything to go by.

But Mary pleaded and so Helen did and was whistled at by passing jeeps and had to stretch out across a thin branch which whipped up and down beneath her weight. She snatched a small clump from the top of the tree, dropping it down to Mary who cheered. Helen laughed and it was the first time she had done that for weeks.

They dropped it into the village hall and people smiled and nodded at her and so her shoulders relaxed but the vicar's wife was not amongst them. That evening she tied Mary's hair into small curls with pipe cleaners, sitting her by a roaring fire to dry it in time. She wet Chris's hair where it quiffed up, then tied an old stocking of Laura's on to it but he hid in the bedroom until it was dry.

She painted her own legs and Chris told her the seam wobbled and so she licked her finger and rubbed it off and Mary took the pencil and did it for her while Laura laughed. Mary wore her blackout dress and her hair was a mass of curls.

Planes had straggled back in as they walked from the village hall back to the cottage but Helen had made herself not count and besides no one they knew was flying today. So they laughed as they all stood in the hall, looking in the mirror.

Laura and Mary carried the party cakes made with powdered eggs while Helen carried a cardboard box full of bottles of home-made elderberry wine. Chris walked beside them, carrying nothing because he was still too weak but smiling because his hair had stuck down on the top of his head.

There were no lights visible through the blackout of the village hall but they could hear the music tuning up and Helen looked up and down the road. There were olive green bikes slung around the hall and three jeeps parked with more arriving.

Inside the hall it was warm and the decorations glittered. The table was heaped with hamburgers and hot dogs, Boston cream pie and pumpkin pie. There was coke to drink. It was a gift to the villagers from the GIs.

'Pails of ice-cream are coming along later ma'am,' a sergeant told them and Helen and Laura couldn't say thank you because it was inadequate.

The band was playing now and Laura drifted off to talk to Mrs Williams. Helen looked around but Chris said it for her.

'Ed isn't here, Mum.'

'Maybe he will be later,' she answered, wondering why she felt tired suddenly, and irritated with the music, the food, the decorations.

Chris and Mary sat on the chairs spaced out along the walls

while Helen and Laura poured wine into glasses but still he did not come. Mrs Vane did, though, with her husband. They didn't stop and speak but walked down to the stage, through the GIs who stood in groups talking to girls, laughing, flirting, smoking, drinking. Helen watched as they mounted the stage to stand in front of the band. The vicar tapped the microphone; it clicked. He coughed and the hall grew silent. He coughed again, his black suit looking austere against the paper decorations, his clerical collar stark white.

'I would like to welcome our guests tonight. Some sort of a reception was long overdue, and for that we must apologise, but somehow there has been rather a lot to think about during the past year. We are enormously grateful too for the wonderful refreshments. It is as though Father Christmas has come just a few hours early.' He laughed and so did those in the hall.

'Before we begin, though, I have something I wish to say. Mrs Weber spoke to the ladies of our village hall last Sunday and reminded us that we are all human beings, that we all suffer in this war and I am grateful to her for her words.'

Mrs Vane said nothing, just smiled with tight lips.

The vicar continued, looking towards the back of the hall at Helen. 'My wife and I and the other villagers welcome you and your son to our village.'

Helen felt the heat in her face and looked at Chris. He smiled at her; the shadows had gone.

She looked back again at Mrs Vane and knew that there would always be people like her and that nothing on God's earth could change them, but perhaps they could be isolated and contained as she hoped this woman had been.

There was dancing now, gentle, cheek to cheek dancing and Helen sat with Laura watching. Still Ed had not come but Chris was laughing with the boys who gathered round and was not unhappy so it didn't matter, did it?

Earl hadn't come either and so there was no singing yet, just music and the vicar came and talked to Laura who nodded and asked Helen to come down to the stage, telling her quietly as they went:

'The vicar has asked if you will sing. There is a problem.'

Helen stopped. A GI took her arm and said, 'Come and dance, honey.'

'No thank you,' she said and he passed on. 'What do you mean? I've never sung in front of people.'

Laura took her arm. 'Nonsense, Helen, you've sung in the crypt. What about the choir? Now come on, we've worked so hard to make this a success, you can't let us down.'

'But what about Earl? He'll be along.'

Laura stopped. 'No, he won't, not now, not ever. He was on a mission today, taking the place of a sick gunner. He's dead.' Her voice shook.

Helen looked at her, not speaking, not seeing the couples dancing, not seeing the band playing. Earl was too young to die. He was far too young and too nice. He had helped Chris. He was too nice.

She sang then, for fifty minutes without a break, drifting into 'A Nightingale Sang in Berkeley Square', reading the words of 'Boogie Woogie Bugle Boy' before repeating it three times for the GIs who whistled and stamped; but all the time there was a pain in her chest for the young German American. And all the time she sang for him. Ed came in when she was singing 'White Christmas'. She saw him enter, saw him stand and watch, but didn't wave. She just looked and knew that he also grieved and that there was no time in this war to turn aside from love.

Ed watched her on the stage. She was thinner but still beautiful. He watched her and loved her and drank deeply from the glass he had been given. He listened to the words and thought of the snow falling in Montana, clear and white, not like the fog of this morning. Fog which had cleared to visibility of about a mile and so Earl had smiled and gone. Ed took another drink, nodding to Laura but not seeing her, seeing instead the B-17s leaving, one after another, but it had not been clear enough for accurate bombing, or so James Roten had said in his debriefing. Only Earl's ship had made a hit. God damn it, that damn Norden bombsight could drop a bomb into a barrel from Californian skies but how the hell could the bomb-aimer penetrate this damn European mist? What would it be like when the bombing runs really got underway? He drank more wine. He recognised it as Laura's and looked around, finding her, nodding and grinning, but the smile didn't reach his eyes and Helen saw that as she wove her way towards him, standing in front of him, letting him take her in his arms, hold her with those strong hands as they danced.

He talked, his breath soft on her neck. He told of the men in the Nissen hut who had thrown lighter fuel on the meagre coal in the centre stove and how the chimney had got so hot it had kept them warm all night. He did not talk about Earl whom he could not get out of his head.

She talked about the vicar's wife and how she hoped it was all over but not about Heine who she had loved but who, she had now accepted, was dead.

He talked of the interminable mud on the airfield. She talked of the smell of sugar beet which clung to her, although he said it did not.

She asked how Earl had died but instead of telling her of the burning plane which had plummeted, ripped in half, from the sky, emptying the crew into the factories they had just bombed, he told her how strong the Fortresses were, how they were called the battleships of the air, how you could land on one engine. While he said this and held her warm body against his he remembered Earl's grin in the copse with Joe and Chris and held Helen tighter because now his friend would never write his name in candle grease on the ceiling of the pub when he had finished his twenty-five missions.

Helen was called back to the stage during the refreshments and sang 'The White Cliffs of Dover' and 'We'll Meet Again'. Chris came up to the front of the stage then and asked her to sing 'Silent Night' and stood there while she sang the first verse in English and the second in German, his eyes on hers, their thoughts on Heine and Grandpa and Oma.

She left the stage again after that, taking Ed's glass from him, leading him out on to the dance floor, holding him to her, leaning her face against his neck, talking of the pain she saw in his eyes and he spoke now of Earl and how it hurt to know he was gone. Helen knew now that there could be a great love between them, if the war gave them enough time.

CHAPTER 15

In January and February of 1943 Ed flew only training missions and those were only possible when the weather permitted. Dawn take-offs were abandoned and he was still a million years from the twenty-five missions he needed for his ticket home but he didn't want to go home, he told Helen. He wanted to stay with her.

He would drive her from the boarding house to the village on Saturday evenings. Always they stopped halfway at a pub with oak settles. She would only drink a little and so would he, sipping at the weak beer he had bought, his sprinkled with salt to give at least a little flavour, hers without. They would sit together, his shoulder touching hers.

He would kiss her when they returned to the car and his lips were tangy with salt and beer and his hand would stroke her face and then they would drive home to Chris who was now allowed to go to school and into the playground where they played convoys, lining up, waiting for the submarine attack from behind the bike sheds, the toilets, the dustbins.

In February the campaign at the beet factory was over and in March 1943 Helen prepared to begin work at the farm five miles from the village. At the same time Ed was promoted to Major and given the post of Air Executive which meant that, for now, he stayed on the ground.

Laura cooked omelette that night with real eggs to build Helen up for the morning and to celebrate Ed's safety, she said, smiling at them while Mary nudged Chris and winked.

The next morning Helen lay awake, listening to the pre-dawn warm-up at the air base but there was not the familiar knotting in her stomach or the tension in her back because at least now, for a while, she could be sure he was not flying. She stretched, running her hands down her body, wondering what it would be like to feel him close to her, touching her, and suddenly she allowed herself to feel like a girl again, eager and young, because she knew he would not die today, tomorrow or the next day and what came after that was 'the future' and the blitz had taught her not to think of that.

At five-thirty she dressed and sat at the low window, looking out on to the rear garden, seeing the grass of the orchard fresh and pale green in the thin light of the dawn. Mist drifted over the grey meadow beyond. There had been no frost so would that mean deep mud on the farm? But that didn't matter because the air would be fresh, there was no machinery to clang and grind and pipes to drip into her hair, her son was better and the man she loved was close.

She stopped by Chris's door, opening it, seeing his hair, still so blond, and she smiled, walking down the stairs in her woollen airmen's socks which Ed had given her to wear inside her boots. She put the kettle on the stove before feeding the pigs and the hens, feeling the cold on her hands, seeing the layer of heavy dew thick on the cabbage, the grass, the shed, undisturbed yet by the rising of the sun. But later her bike marked a long thin line across the ground as she took it to the road.

She rode to the farm, her dungarees clipped at the ankles, her old jacket buttoned tight against the wind. The farmer had told her last week where to leave her bike, pointing to the old barn.

As she approached the farmyard she dismounted and pushed at the gate, hauling the bike through mud, pushing it to the higher concrete where it was almost clear, then propped it inside the barn against an old mangle. The air was thick with the scent of hay. Already she was tired and it was only seven-thirty but maybe she would see Ed tonight and so what did it matter?

She stood in the entrance looking out on to the yard and then walked through the mud, hearing it squelch beneath her feet and splatter up her legs. There was a smell of manure and steam rose from a heap beyond the yard. Laura would love that for her garden. John met her then, coming round the edge of the long cow-shed which he had built just before the war, he told her as he led the way inside. It was limewashed and bright and he pointed to a Friesian which stood tethered to the manger.

'Just get on and milk that one will you, me old girl, but wash your hands over in that basin first.'

The water was cold and the towel rough and full of holes. John stood watching, his face lined and weatherbeaten, his shoulders hunched from his thirty years on the farm. He had been born here, he had told her, and helped his old dad as long as he could remember.

'Now you come on over and let's get this old girl finished.'

Helen nodded and sat on the stool, waiting for him to leave, but he didn't. The cow's udders were milk-swollen. She closed her eyes and tried to remember what he had told her last week, then took hold of the two front teats, pulling gently together. Nothing happened. She pulled one at a time. Nothing, and John was still standing there, his shadow falling on her hands, his breathing audible.

This is ridiculous, Helen thought. For God's sake, I'm a woman of thirty and I can't even milk a cow. She leaned her head against the animal, feeling its quivering flank against her forehead.

'That's better,' John said. 'You get right in next to her, she likes to get the feel of a person, our Daisy does. You're more than just a pair of hands to her, you know. She's got to like you.'

Helen tried again but still nothing, she pushed her head deeper into the cow's side. Like me, you stupid cow, just like me.

John moved then, bending down and yanking at the teats. 'Naughty old girl's holding back, give her a good pull like that. Don't you go pussyfooting around.'

Helen watched the jets of milk flooding into the pail and then took the warm teats in her hands again and at last some milk shot out, but not much.

'I'll go and start in the other shed then, now you've got the hang of it.'

The evening seemed a long way away as Helen tried again. She had not got the hang of it. She pulled and squeezed, banging her head against the cow, feeling her hand cramping.

'You damned old cow,' she swore. 'Holding back, how could you on my first day? How could you?' She looked into the bucket. There was still very little.

John came back in thirty minutes. He had finished two cows. He laughed and took her place and she watched and listened to the squirting jets, seeing the frothing milk, hating Daisy, hating the farm. All her fingers were red and sore.

She was sent out to help the men chopping out the sugar beets on the four-acre field. It was a long walk before she even reached the field and the hoe was hard against her shoulders and now she knew why John and the others wore folded sacks on their shoulders.

They did not look up as she arrived, but one shouted, 'That row, six inches apart, then single by hand.'

He was pointing and so Helen nodded, ramming the hoe in as they were doing, again and again, hearing it click against stones, feeling her hands growing hot and sore. Row after row was hoed, and lunch was taken at the edge of the field, quietly eating sandwiches which were squashed from being in her dungaree pockets, drinking tea which was lukewarm from the flask which had been banging against her leg all morning. After half an hour they were up again, finishing the hoeing, just doing the last ten rows, and then it was singling the clumps which they had left by hand – a hand which was blistered on the palms by now.

They knelt when their backs felt as though they would break, and then the mud oozed up into her knees and they also became sore, and Helen wondered if this was any bloody way to win the bloody war. She didn't just think it, she said it, again and again, her fingers cold and muddy from picking and then she heard the laughter from the man in the next row and looking up she saw his gap-toothed grin.

'Well, my old girl, I reckon as how it has to be the bloody way to win the bloody war, and soon the blisters will go. You'll toughen up.'

Helen laughed and looked at her hands. She'd bring gloves tomorrow, there was no way she wanted farmworker's hands for the rest of her life. She continued swearing but in her head this time.

John had told her to return at four and so she levered herself up and walked back, feeling the blisters on her heels now, waving to the men, still swearing in her head.

She had to fetch the cows from the pasture.

'Just call, they'll come,' he said.

She did call but they didn't come. She walked up behind and waved her hands but still they continued chewing the cud and now she was angry. Her feet hurt, her hands hurt, her knees hurt and Marian would never believe her when she wrote about this. She walked up to Daisy and shouted at her but she just slapped her tail against her sides and continued chewing without haste. Helen thought she looked like Mrs Vane and so she slapped her across the backside and now she moved and the others followed, walking sedately in single file and Helen shook her head at the feeling of success which coursed through her.

Dear God, she thought, a cow moves and it's as though I've been given the crown jewels.

She had to try and milk Daisy again but it wasn't until a week later that she achieved a frothing pail, stripping the udder, getting all the old milk out and milking slowly enough to draw out the fresh that Daisy was making at that moment. That evening she went home, her blisters drying and healing, and slept as though peace had been declared.

In April the Middle White sow had piglets and she brought Ed and the children up to see their short snouts. They stroked their floppy ears and soft skin, so unlike the mother's. Chris asked when his pig, Helen, would have piglets and Helen laughed and said it depended when Mr Reynolds's boar escaped into the orchard again. In April, the bombing missions began in earnest but Ed was safe. Grounded and safe but the shadows were in his eyes again.

In May he came to the farm and watched while she fed the calves in the small yard. They rushed up to her, pushing, mooing, and by now it seemed as though she had never done anything else but hoe, milk, weed, dig, feed calves. She put beet pulp and crushed oats into the trough, walking in deep straw, pumping up their water. She turned and pushed back her hair which was still curly but longer than it used to be and laughed. She was happy doing this work, loving this man, and she had not thought the war could ever bring anything but torment.

Helen forked hay into the racks, seeing some fall on the calves' heads as they milled about, and then there was just the rustling as they ate. She walked back to Ed who was leaning on the wall, his arms crossed, his cap back, a piece of grass hanging from his smiling mouth and she kissed him, smelling the sun on his skin, feeling strong and fit. He pulled the grass from his mouth and kissed her again and again and she wanted him as she had done for weeks but could never tell him.

That evening he pushed her bike back along the road, his arm around her, pointing out the Nymph and the Tortoiseshell and she was impressed with his knowledge of English nature until he told her that Chris had educated him, last year. She laughed then and he leaned down and kissed her open mouth and the laughter died in her throat and she clung to him.

Ed held her chin in his hand and looked into her face and she knew that her eyes said the same as his and there was no shame or restraint in her. He kissed her gently this time before pushing the bike through a gap in the hedge into the hayfield where cornflowers, daisies and poppies grew, and they lay on the warm grass and kissed, their mouths opening and then they loved, slowly, deeply, and without memories intruding. Afterwards Helen lay and watched the scudding clouds, and smelt the rich hay which had been crushed beneath their bodies. It had been strange to be touched by someone who was not Heine but it had been beautiful. It was as though they had known one another since the beginning of time.

That night as Helen undressed, grass fell to the floor and she thought of his hands, so firm on her body; of his chest, so smooth, so tanned. She remembered the power of him, the pleasure of him, the words which had come from his mouth and from hers. I love you, they had said as they kissed.

He came as often as he could and the summer was warm. They grew to know one another's bodies and to love so much. In the long summer evenings Helen laughed as Chris and Ed pitched and batted in the garden and then let her and Mary try. One day the girls beat the boys and they sulked until Laura brought out the cricket bat and said that they would have to play with this next time if there were any more bad losers.

In June the hay was harvested and Ed brought some men from the base to help with the carting and the raking because, he told John, they needed to be reminded that something existed other than high-altitude bombing, ack-ack, fighters who ripped bullets into their planes, their bodies.

Helen and the farm workers had cut and turned the hay in the early part of the week and now she and Ed and Mario led the carts, each holding four GIs and the farm workers. They moved from the farm across a field of beet and down the long lane leading to the hayfields where Helen had first lain with Ed, and she wondered if he remembered.

Above the clopping of the hoofs she heard him call, 'It sure is a shame to see that grass go. I got kinda fond of it.'

Helen flushed and turned, shaking her head at his grin but laughing back. Rocket was slapping his tail at the flies and nodding his head, and Helen tightened her grip on his harness, leaning back into his shoulder.

'Steady, old man,' she breathed and hoped that Chris and Mary would be able to get out here after school.

They turned sharp left, calling 'Here now' to the horses as Helen had instructed and they were safely into the field, but Mario had to back Satin up and try again and on the third attempt he made it and his crew cheered, yelling that they hoped he was a better flyer than a cart driver, for Christ's sake.

All morning they tossed hay up into the carts with forks while Helen stood in one cart, Mario and John in the others. She loaded from the outside first so that it would not overbalance when she took it back. Ed tossed hay up to her, his bare back glistening in the sun, his shoulders reddening. Her arms were bare and she felt the sun on them, on her head. There was a hay seed in her eye and he leaped up into the cart, pulling her lid down, easing the seed out with his handkerchief. She felt his breath on her face and his lips were so close but they did not need to kiss. They just smiled and he jumped down again and continued to pitch up the hay.

They carted their loads back at lunchtime but brought the wagons straight out again, eating a picnic the Americans brought from the base; chicken legs, hard-boiled eggs, cakes and beer, and John winked at her and said, 'I'm glad you came to us, my old girl. Nice to have this manpower around, not forgetting the chicken legs.'

Helen laughed as the men cheered but she knew that on many farms the Americans were helping, glad to work on the land, glad to be free of the war for a moment. She watched as the GIs eased themselves up from the ground, throwing a baseball to and fro, leaping and falling to catch it. There was laughter and shouting and they were like children but of course they were men, young men who could die tomorrow.

She lay down, her arm under her head, hearing the bees in the hedgerows behind them. The sun was bright on her lids, there was the smell of hay all around and she thought how much she loved England, its beauty, its smallness, its sameness, because she couldn't bear to think of the war.

They worked all that day and the next but there was a different crew this time because the others had gone out on a dawn flight. She had heard them leave but knew each morning that it would not be Ed because the CO had kept his grounding official.

When the hay harvest was finished she limewashed the old cow-shed, now stained green and brown. She scrubbed the walls and then John gave her a bag of dry limewash and pails. She carried a small spray under her arm and mixed the lime with water. It puffed up into her eyes and caught in her throat and as she sprayed one wall her arm felt as though it was on fire from the pumping. But then Ed came and took over and they were both covered in lime, and Chris too when he came with Mary. He only sprayed half the wall because he was still not absolutely strong, and Helen watched him work and smiled.

In August they began the oat harvest and the wheat but Mario was not with them because he had not returned from a mission in July. The men laughed as before but there were deeper lines because the daylight raids were still not escorted deep into Germany and now there were so many and the losses were too great. 'Too damn great,' Ed said as they toiled home from the fields, their faces flecked with chaff.

In late August they went to Cambridge when he had a forty-eight-hour pass. Helen had asked Chris if he would mind but he had shaken his head and laughed.

They stayed in an old inn, climbing up twisting stairs, Ed having to lower his head beneath the beams. Their room had an old marble wash-stand with a rose-painted bowl and jug. There were floral curtains and a big bed and Helen was nervous because this was the first time she had been in a bedroom with Ed.

She watched as he unpacked, hanging his trousers in the wardrobe, his shirts too. She had always put Heine's in the drawer. Helen walked to the window, peering out on to the narrow street. She mustn't think of Heine, not here, not now. Heine had gone.

'What about you, Helen? Are you going to unpack your grip now?'

She turned. It seemed too intimate somehow, to take her clothes out in front of him, to put them into drawers while he watched.

'In a minute,' she said, turning back to the window. She heard him move across the floor, the boards creaking beneath his weight. He put his arms around her from behind.

'It feels kind of strange, doesn't it?' he said. 'I had a girl in college, you know. We lived together for a year. I just thought of her then because she would never take her clothes out in front of me, or undress either.' He kissed her hair. 'I guess maybe you're thinking of Heine.'

She turned and put her arms around him. 'I'm sorry,' she said. 'I was but I'm not now.' It was true, she wasn't, because Ed understood and she smiled as he lifted her up and carried her to the bed.

Later they walked by the river in the cool of late afternoon, talking of Chris and how much fitter he was, of Mary who spent more time at Laura's cottage than in her own billet. Of her sister who never came any more because she had an American GI and so she did not have time.

Ed hired a boat and they punted down the river, under bridges, laughing when he was almost too late dragging up the pole. She trailed her hand in the water, looking up at him as he pushed and pulled, lifting the pole from the water, hearing the water dripping back into the river. His arms were so strong, his body so lithe, his face so tired. The water was cold but she did not feel it, she only felt his arms as he had held her in that small room, his warm lips, and she smiled.

They ate at the hotel and the meal was frugal but it did not matter because they were impatient now, and that night Helen did undress in front of him. Her body was fit from the farm and her hands were not hard because she wore gloves and so she stroked his body and kissed his chest, his arms, his legs and held him to her.

In the morning they looked around the town and Ed took photographs of the colleges, but then handed his camera to Helen because she knew the angles to take. He wanted the sharpness of the shadows on the ground, the age of the buildings etched against the sky. She told him then of Claus and the business in New York and he nodded but said nothing.

They had lunch in a pub and as they walked in the afternoon

along the river they watched other punters, other lovers, but none could love as much as they did, Helen thought, her hand in his. They walked in and out of the shadows, dragging their hands along the weeping willows, not seeing anyone else, only one another, and for a while the world stood still. But then they heard the straggling bombers return over to the east of the town and Ed grew quiet and that night he told her of his guilt at remaining on the ground but he did not tell her of his fear of being sent back into the air because they all had that.

Sunday was overcast but not cold and they walked again but Ed was quiet today and Helen too because tomorrow the war began again. They ate in a small café, watching the people going into the church, some women with hats and very few men, and that afternoon they sat on the bank while a mallard dived in the turgid water. A woman walked past, pushing a young man in a wheelchair. They were pale and thin.

Helen talked as they heard the wheels receding on the path but Ed's answers were short and his shoulders were tense and he counted the planes which flew back over at four, not looking at her, and she felt a distance grow between them. As the last roared over he pulled her to her feet, hugging her, but his mind was not with her. She lifted her face for his kiss but he turned from her, walking to the bank, throwing a pebble and watching it bounce three times. Helen felt cold for the first time that summer and tried to push aside the hurt of his rejection, but could not and walked in silence to the car.

It was a silence which was not broken until they approached Greater Mannenham as the day was drawing to its end. Ed pulled in to the verge by the hayfield and took her hand and asked her to marry him, come back with him to Montana when all this was over. After all, she already had a business set up over there.

Helen sat looking up at him, into his eyes which were still dark. She looked beyond him to the field with the cut grass; she saw the leaves turning on the trees, the clouds thick and full of rain. She looked at him again, his brown eyes, the deep lines. She loved him, so much, so very much, but there had never been thought of a future, the present was enough. Hadn't he learned that yet? The future was too dangerous. She did not dare to challenge the gods, to ask for more than she had. Couldn't he see that?

She looked ahead. There was drizzle on the windscreen now blanking out the road. That is what the future was.

She turned to him then, pointing to the glass.

'That's the future. We have enough. Darling, we have enough.'

She gripped his hand. 'Let's keep what we have, we don't need to talk of tomorrow.' She held his hand to her face. 'Don't ask for too much.'

He pulled his hand away then, looking at her strangely. His eyelid was twitching. He looked so tired, so scared, and she reached for him again but he brushed away her hand, staring out to the fields at the side, talking in their direction, not hers. His voice was tense, taut. 'It's too much, is it? All you want is today, is it? I thought we felt more than that. I thought we loved one another.'

She looked at her hand. 'That's not what I meant. For God's sake, Ed. That's not how I meant it. You know that. Surely you know that. I love you. I love you so much.'

He turned and looked at her now but she couldn't see any feeling in his eyes. She put her hand out to him, smiling because she couldn't understand what was happening; where all this had come from. But he shook her off and reached for the ignition, starting the car, grinding it into gear, skidding the car off the verge on to the road.

'I need you. I need to know you'll always be there,' he said.

Helen caught at his arm. 'I will always be here for you. You know I will, but marriage is different.' How could she tell him she was frightened she would kill him. Heine had died, hadn't he? 'I love you,' she said but he shrugged off her arm.

'Forget it, Helen. Just forget I said anything. Just for Christ's sake forget what I said. Just think of the two nights you've had with a guy with cash in his pocket.'

The car was speeding down the road, swerving past a cyclist, hooting at a jeep and Helen clung to her seat, feeling as though she had been hit. How could this have happened?

'You goddamn Limeys,' he shouted, his hand hard down on the horn as another cyclist came out of a turning, but Helen knew he was shouting at her, not the old man and now she was angry because all this had taken the sun from the weekend and smashed it into darkness.

Helen watched the fields as they drove home, she didn't

watch him, couldn't watch him, because it had all been too quick, all too sudden. Didn't he understand that in the war you lived just for now because you never knew when another bomb would fall, when a telegram would come? Why didn't he understand?

Chris didn't understand either when she told him later that Ed would not be coming to see them again because they had quarrelled.

'But he needs you, Mum.'

She knew that, but one husband had already died. Wasn't that enough? But she didn't say that to her son.

She said instead, 'But it would mean living in a strange country.'

Chris said, 'Dad did.' His face was fierce and he wouldn't look at her.

Helen replied, 'I know.' She didn't say, 'And look what happened to him,' but that night in bed she tossed in the darkness of the blackout and again the next night and the next until two weeks had passed, filled with endless hours, minutes, seconds, and as dawn broke in mid September she knew that she was wrong. That she loved him and had let him down and would marry him rather than live without him or let him be alone. Other people married and did not die. He would not die.

That morning as she listened to the planes taking off, she thought of the war. She thought of the GIs who were working their way up Italy, of the Nazis, who were being beaten in Russia, of Hamburg, which had been flattened, of the Jews who had been taken from Warsaw, the British who were winning the battle of the U-boats. She hurried from her bedroom and cycled quickly to the farm. She must see him, he would come, he had always come on Wednesdays. They had shouted but he would come, he hadn't last Wednesday, but he had been angry. Today she would tell him that she was wrong. That he was right, time could be short and they must take what they could.

But he didn't come. All day he didn't come. The next day he sent comics as usual for Chris but there was nothing for her, no message, nothing. She cried in her room, pacing up and down, but he never came.

The next day she herded the cows, scrubbed the cow-shed floor, always looking and listening for him. That evening she put on nylons that he had given her but they laddered on her chapped hands and so she painted her legs instead and walked down to the village pub because he might be there. He was not.

But Scoot Wheeler was, standing outside leaning on the wall, talking to the landlord's daughter.

'Hi, Helen, how're you doing?'

Helen smiled but she was impatient. Where was he, she wanted to shout, but instead asked, 'Have you seen Ed?'

'He's back on base. He's flying tomorrow.'

'Flying? But he's grounded.'

Scoot laughed and eased himself from the wall, taking a swallow of watered beer and pulling a face. 'I guess he was, Helen, but he ain't now. There was the most humdinger of a row and in the end the CO said OK, he could go. Guess the Major never did like being down here when his boys were up there. Do you want a drink?'

Helen shook her head. No she didn't want a drink, she wanted to see Ed. She started walking then to the base, but she had no pass and the guard wouldn't let her through the wire gate, so she walked back working out the words she would write to him, telling him, begging him to forgive her.

She passed Mrs Vane with the vicar near the church carrying dahlias and chrysanthemums for the altar.

Mrs Vane caught her arm and smiled. 'My dear, I had no idea your little liaison had finished. I'm so sorry.'

Helen stopped and stared. The red dahlias clashed with the purple chrysanths, didn't the woman know that? 'It hasn't,' she said trying to walk on. 'It was all a mistake. A stupid mistake.'

Mrs Vane smiled again, stroking the petals. 'If you say so, my dear, but I've just seen your Major McDonald driving towards the town with Madge Wilcox. They seemed so close you know.'

Helen looked at the woman's face and saw her mother and felt the cupboard, the darkness of the cupboard, and she said nothing, just ran home and up to her room. She did not speak for the next two days, just worked all day and cried throughout the night, and then she came down and told Chris and Laura that she would not try to see Ed again. But the darkness of the cupboard was still there and the scent of chrysanthemums was all around.

*

The controls of the *Emma B* were heavy but honest, Ed thought as he operated the four throttles with palms upwards. She had been cussed to begin with but he had pretty soon got into it again. For God's sake, he hadn't been away for that long, he had said to his co-pilot on that mission back in late August, when Helen had told him she didn't love him enough; or as good as said that anyway. He looked over to the tower, waiting for the green flare. Damn the woman, damn the Limeys, expecting us to come over and win their damn wars for them. Didn't she know he needed her?

Joe, his co-pilot was tapping his knees. Ed ignored him. They were both tense, they were all tense. He had watched the film of the target area last night at the briefing, it was near the ball bearing factory they had got last time, but what they really wanted now were the rest of the factories, the CO said, and then the group navigator had taken over, smoothing back his hair which was grey now, though it had been brown at Christmas. He had explained the route that would be flown before calling on the weather expert who had said the weather would be thick fog in East Anglia, but then it was almost the middle of October. At 2000 feet they could expect to break out of it and it would be clear over Europe.

But not clear of Messerschmitts, Joe had murmured, and Ed had nodded. When would they get long-range fighter cover? It was crazy, the losses were getting close to twenty-five per cent for God's sake. Ed shook his head. He shouldn't think of that now but if he didn't he thought of her. He eased his helmet. He had tried other women but it hadn't worked. He couldn't sleep, he couldn't eat but at least now he was flying he had the fear which stopped him thinking of her every minute of every day – but still, every minute of every night, she was there.

Joe was still drumming his fingers and Ed wished to God he wouldn't. He checked his watch, five-thirty a.m. It had been cold when they had crammed into their jeeps, four in one, the rest of the crew in the other and driven out to the *Emma B* as the dawn was rising over the airfield. He had stood by as they climbed in, checking they were OK, laughing at Patrick who wanted to pee but then he always did.

The engines had spluttered into life all around them, coughing, roaring, until all the propellers were turning except for the *Emma B*'s. He and Joe clambered into the cockpit, hearing the leather seat creak with his weight as his saddle in Montana did. They checked the levers, the dials, compasses, light switches and control yokes. There was a smell of paint and gasoline because the *Emma B* was new.

Still there was no green flare. Ed inched round and checked Joe again. He was still drumming his fingers. He looked back out across the countryside. She had never come to find him, never written and he wished that he no longer loved her as he did.

'There it goes, skip.'

Ed swung back, the flare was hanging in the air and they waited their turn, taxi-ing, lifting off thirty seconds behind the *Mary Rose*, climbing to the assembly point, then flying in formation with more than four hundred bombers from other bases.

Ed spoke into the intercom. 'OK, you guys, keep your eyes on the skies. You don't get a second bite at this cherry. Sam, you keep your eyes swivelling good, OK?'

He knew Sam, his tail gunner, would. His was the most important defensive position in the whole plane. He couldn't afford to foul up; he knew that, everyone knew that.

'Marco, you make sure you've got a fix for getting back,' Ed called and Marco replied, 'Sure, skip.'

The boys would be cold, Ed knew that. It was OK here in the cockpit but Sam's sinuses would give him hell again tonight. He checked with the gunners on the intercom. Steve in the top turret was fine, so too was Ross in the nose. Those in the waist section would be getting back the feel of their guns, bumping into each other, talking of last night's crap game.

They were out over the sea now with the Dutch coast in sight. The P-47s had picked them up now but they were only short-range protection. Ed sighed, easing his back. They would be in the air eight hours at least, and his feet would get cold, his back would ache, and he would get tired, but maybe he would get them back alive and he was hardly thinking of Helen any more.

He looked to either side. The flak was coming up over the coast but they stayed in tight formation because those crapheads at the top of the heap thought that formation was all the real defence that was needed. Ed would have liked one in the pilot's seat now, assing on about having a thousand miles of coastline to choose from so casualties should not be so goddamn high. Try telling that to the men, Ed grunted, looking always to left and right, up and down.

The enemy planes would come, but when? Probably when their short-range fighter cover had run for home. He felt bulky, the bomber jacket, flying helmet, flak vest, Mae West and the oxygen masks were like some pantomime. The radio operator was flicking switches with a gloved hand. They drummed on for hours and Joe talked to Ed of his girl back home and his girl in the town but all the time they looked and suddenly the enemy was there, to the left.

Sam called, 'Hey, skip, we got friends visiting.'

'How many?' Ed's voice was sharp and the sweat of fear burst on his forehead. Jesus Christ.

'Four I think.'

'More up here,' from the top turret.

'Jeeze there's six here.'

The intercom was alive with shouts and Ed said, 'Cut it out. Keep calm, keep looking.' And to himself he said, Keep calm, keep calm. But knots of fear and panic screwed up in his body. He looked ahead, above, to the sides. Where the goddamn hell were they?

The *Emma B*'s guns were firing now and Ed kept on going, drawing up tighter, knowing that if he fell out of formation he'd be picked off sooner. Again and again they came but they'd been in the air nearly four hours, they had to be close to the target. His head was aching from the noise, the flashes, the fear which was still sour in his mouth, and he thought of Chris's raven but then pushed it away because it was black and death was black.

There was a burst of light in front and he jerked his head back, holding the *Emma B* on course as the *Mary Rose* burst into flames in front of them and dropped from the sky and Ed thought of nothing but drawing up into her place; keeping up, for Christ's sake keep up. Push the *Mary Rose* out of your goddamn head, push the flames away and the screams he could not hear, but he couldn't. He could only push it to one side but it kept creeping back and he could see Don's face in the bar last night. Was he screaming now?

The firing and the babbling went on and on and now he spoke, feeling the vibration of the ship beneath his hands.

'Give me a fix, navigator.' His voice was calm. How could it be?

'Five minutes to target. We're at 25,000 feet.'

'We OK for gas, Ed?' Joe asked.

'Look for yourself for Christ's sake. That's your job.' Steady, steady. Don't let it show. Don't let the fear show.

The firing was still going on and now the first of the Fortresses were making their run and Ed wished he had not shouted. He was always shouting now. What the hell was the matter with him?

'OK, you guys, we're going in, then we're going home.'

Ed kept his eyes on his instruments, listening to Marco, the navigator, listening to the gunners, still firing, knowing that their guns would be hot, knowing that so far, none had been hit because he recognised all their voices.

He looked across at Joe and winked and saw him smile in spite of his fear before turning to the front again.

'Keep it up, kid, we're almost there.' Then he heard the crack and the shattered windscreen blew into his lap and across his hands but he held on and saw the fighter go down in flames, hit by shells from the waist gunners, but it was too late for Joe whose blood was splashed all over what remained of his Mae West, all over Ed. It was sticky on his face. Christ, wet and sticky and Joe's, but the bombardier was aiming again so he must keep steady. He held on to the controls, seeing the glass in his gloves, feeling it in his hands.

The bombardier called, 'The beauties have gone, let's get out of here, skip.'

They did but it wasn't over. The ME109s were still waiting for them and stabbed and fired and sent Fortresses spinning from the group, down to the ground in flames, but not them yet, not them, but the blood was still all over his face, and the poor little kid was dead.

'Marco, you make sure you get us home,' Ed said, and laughed when Marco said, 'You're such an old spoilsport, skip. I thought we could drop in on Hitler for a decent glass of beer.'

Ed didn't look at Joe, at the blood which had run from the corner of his mouth, the blood which had spurted from his gaping chest. He mustn't look or he would crack. He knew he would crack, because he had never flown with a dead man before, a man whose blood was on his face, drying on his skin and lips in the wind from the broken screen. But he mustn't think of it, must he? He had to get the boys back so he pushed Joe to the side of his mind with the *Mary Rose* but he too kept sliding back.

They had two hours to go still and his arms ached and his hands hurt but the 109s had gone for now. He spoke into the intercom, checking with them all, but Eric in the waist section had been hurt.

'And he's hurt bad, skip. Got shell fragments in his shoulder but it's too cold to bleed much.'

'Get some pressure on it, Mart, when we finish the run and come in to land. He'll bleed then. And keep a grip of yourself too. Keep your eyes open, we're not home yet.'

The wind was icy in the cabin, streaming in through the broken windscreen, and his face was numb with cold. His hands were bleeding from the glass which had penetrated his gloves. He could feel them sticky against the leather but they didn't hurt now. He rubbed his face on his shoulder, wanting to scrape off Joe's dried blood but he couldn't. Push it back, just push it back.

He spoke into the intercom again. 'How's it going, Martin? Is Eric hanging on?'

'He's still with us, skip.'

The 109s came again then.

'Six above,' called Steve but then his voice choked and stopped and there was no firing from his gun. Ed held the plane steady, sweat on his face in spite of the cold.

'Jesus, where are the escorts?' he murmured. 'Where are the damned escorts?'

He craned his head round, seeing the 109 come down at them, guns firing, before turning away from the waist gunners' fire and then there was another and another and he did not know how the *Emma B* could survive. The men's ammunition was low and their top gunner was out.

He crept up tighter into formation, gripping the controls, holding her steady, hearing the waist guns firing again but then they were hit and the starboard outer engine sparked and flames belched. Christ! Feather, for God's sake feather it, he shouted to himself and his hands shook as he did so. Now there were three engines and his speed dropped and his mind cleared, ice cool in the blasting wind.

He could still get the *Emma B* home if she was a good kind lady but he was dropping back from the formation which was half the size it had been at the start of the mission. He talked to his ship, not listening to the battle which was raging, telling her that it was only one hour, one snitch of an hour she had to hang in, she had to stay up with the others. But she couldn't and he knew she couldn't and that they were as good as dead. The formation was out of sight.

But then the P-47s came and the 109s peeled away with the American fighters firing and hounding and he kept his voice level as he spoke to the crew.

'This is one kind of a cute lady, fellas, she'll get us back.'

They laughed but there was still the flak and he pulled on the controls, weaving, dodging, unable to gain height to rise above it, and they still had the sea to cross.

Ed looked down as the coast eased away. He could see the white foam of the waves but still the *Emma B* held up. His arms were so tired now. His eyes were raw from the cold wind. They churned on until they reached the Norfolk coast and then they were over neat hedged fields and another group of Fortresses was with them now.

'Eric's not looking too good, skip.'

'OK, we're nearly back.'

Marco called, 'Five minutes, skip.'

But Ed knew because he could see the runway lights, gleaming through the mist, and he peeled off from the new group, putting his own lights on, ordering the red flare to be set off to indicate that they had injured on board. He turned in and landed, seeing the ambulance roaring up and heard Marco saying, 'Let's get him to the meat wagon.'

But Joe wouldn't need one, ever again, and neither, they discovered, would Steve.

Ed taxied on to the hard stand when he had counted his men out. He left her with the maintenance crew who would work all night under tarpaulins to get the ship ready again after they had hosed down the top turret and the cockpit.

He debriefed and his voice was level when he told of Joe's death although he had been only twenty-two and he had shouted at him. It was level even when he described the *Mary Rose* which had been piloted by his friend Don from Milwaukee who was thirty with three children. His voice was level when he told them that it was murder to send out bombers without long-range escorts. It was just plain murder.

He had his hands dressed in the infirmary and he didn't shake or moan.

He walked back to his room and took the Scotch bottle down from the locker and tipped back his head, drinking down the harsh liquid because he wanted to go to Helen and feel her arms around him while he cried for his friends but there was no place for him there. She no longer loved him. So instead he drank, and then went to the pub with his crew and laughed and sang as though they didn't care, but they did. Oh yes, they did.

Only half the planes had returned today and more than fifty of their friends had died and it could not go on, for God's sake. They had to have protection or this daylight bombing was just a pointless massacre.

CHAPTER 16

The farm kept Helen on through the winter and so she did no have to sweat beneath the smell of beet but instead milked the cows, leaning her head against their warmth, feeling the twitching of their skin, seeing the steam rise from the bucket because 1944 came in hard and cold.

She wore extra socks inside her boots because the airmen's had worn through and, of course, there would be no more. Chilblains came and in the evening she rubbed on wintergreen, pressing it hard into her swollen toes, preferring the pain to the itching. With Chris each morning she fed Laura's chickens and Helen and Heine, then threw a few logs into the basket before cycling along lanes shiny with ice but happiness had gone with the hot summer days. She did not look up as the planes flew from the base but she ached for him.

In January British and American troops landed at Anzio and the bombing of Berlin and Germany by the Allies continued. They were cold in the village but reserved their fuel for the kitchen only, as the rest of the British were doing as shortages increased. In January the Russians broke through the siege line at Leningrad, and in February the Americans launched the Pacific assault and Claus sent through a parcel of warm clothing for Chris and tins of ham and so they shared their meals with Mrs Williams and Mr Reynolds. In March British troops entered Burma by glider power and the British began to dare to hope that soon it would be over.

But then Germany entered Hungary and Helen knew that Hitler would never give up until the Allies were at Berlin's door, nor the Japanese until Tokyo was reached and the slaughter would continue. In that early spring Mr Reynolds's son died in the Chin Hills and Mrs Williams's nephew was missing in Italy and prayers were said in the church for those in pain.

In April, as the sun broke through and warmed the budding trees, all coastal areas in Britain were banned to visitors, and large military exercises were mounted throughout southern England. Planes flew more often from the Greater Mannenham base and from all those around and Helen rode to work beneath the thunder of their passage and the shadow of their wings.

She worked in fields which had been ploughed, planting cabbages, sowing beetroots, smelling the rich soil, seeing the seagulls whirling in the air, counting the rows she worked, listening to the men, but nothing helped because each minute of each day she ached for the feel of his lips, the strength of his body, the heat of her own response, the words of love, the knowledge of his safety. But he never came.

After Easter they set the potatoes, stooping, pressing in the sprouting tubers, stepping forward, stooping, pressing. Stepping forward, stooping, pressing, and hair straggled beneath her scarf into her eyes, her mouth. The sun was out and it was warm today, warm and clear. Good bombers' weather. Was he flying? Was he safe? She straightened up, pushing back her shoulders, easing her back.

'Nearly time for lunch then, me old girl,' called Ernest and Helen nodded. They finished the rows they were working on, then squatted, eating their sandwiches, drinking their tea, saying little. She looked out across the fields, sprouting and green. Ed had said that England had so many different greens in just one square mile and he was right. Montana would have been beautiful in its way, but it was too late for that.

They worked on throughout the day and in the evening she pitched the ball to Chris, twisting her wrist as he had shown her but it was not the same as Ed. Mary took over and Helen walked into the kitchen. Laura sat by the stove, knitting.

'Sit down, Helen. You should rest while you can. You're getting too thin again. Much too thin.'

But Helen couldn't rest. The evenings were too long, the nights longer still, because then she lay and thought of him stroking someone else's body, moving in rhythm, his mouth on other lips, words of love, words of comfort which had been hers, and she was always glad when the dawn came again.

She walked back into the garden, pruning back the roses, remembering their scent from last year. She touched the tulips, the cool waxy leaves. She pulled couch grass from the soil, picking the earth from its roots, carrying it to the compost, and as dusk fell they heard the noise, the stuttering engines, the tearing, grinding sound and knew that a plane had come down, over to the west, quite close. They heard too the jeeps and the ambulances from the base and looked into the sky, but there was no thick black smoke as there sometimes was and so they knew there was no fire.

Helen took up the ball again and threw hard and fast until the garden sank beneath the night because she had no right to know whether it was Ed.

The next morning the sun was bright but cool as she rode to the farm, the wind flicking at her hair which was too long but what did it matter? Her gloves had holes and she felt the cold of the handlebars through them. The lane was rougher after the frosts of winter and she jolted and weaved then cycled into the yard, but was stopped by John.

'Let's be getting across to Top Field. Those damn spuds you sowed yesterday is in all sorts of a mess.' His face was red as he strode past her. 'Bring Rocket. Elsie's already there.'

Helen leaned her bike against the wall, watching him as he walked, calling to him. 'Why?'

Her breath caught in her throat and she coughed.

'And I hope you're not getting that damn flu. It's enough that one of them damn Yanks puts his plane down in me spuds. Just when they've been sown. It's a bloody liberty.'

He stopped and said, 'For God's sake go and get that damn horse hitched to the cart. I wants them bits out of my old spuds.'

Helen watched as he hurried down the lane, calling, 'Was anybody hurt?'.

'Only the pilot and he's not dead.' John stopped and turned: 'Don't you worry, me old girl. It wasn't your Ed.'

Helen looked again at his bowed back as he continued down the lane, his stick swinging out before him, kicking sideways at stones, at young thistles. John had never said anything to her about Ed before, he had just been kind, talking of the years she had in front of her and how many fish there were in the sea and now she wanted to follow him, take his hand in hers and thank him. Instead she walked back to the yard and harnessed Rocket, pulling herself up on to the seat and taking him out of the yard, down the lane and up into the top field, tying his reins round the brake, leaping down and standing with John and the men as they looked.

The Fortress had crashed through the elm trees and there was freshly splintered wood and bark across the field, bright against the dull metal. There were great furrows gouged into the ground.

'Damn old boys baled out safe, but the pilot was taken away last night. Broke his poor old back,' John said, leaning with both hands on his stick, nodding towards West Field. 'The engines and wings are over there, on the other side of the hedge.'

Helen walked forwards, towards the broken wreck. It was so big and helpless, all its power had fled. She stood looking up at the spines which showed through the jagged fuselage, at the picture of a blonde with the words 'Sarah Jane' written beneath. It made it seem too painful. She turned to John.

'We can't move this,' she said. 'It's too big and they don't like us touching the ones that come down.'

'I know that, but we can move some of these bits.' He waved his stick at the jagged metal scattered all over the field. 'They've never brought one down on me spuds before and I'm not having it.'

Alf was already moving Elsie across nearer the elms. Rooks were cawing in the sky, raven black. Helen moved away, out of the shadow of the plane, picking up twisted metal as she walked back to Rocket, throwing it into the cart, coaxing him closer. He shook his head up and down and backed but she calmed him, crooning softly until he stood steady again. She and John scooped up more, sharing the weight of one bit which looked like part of a door, there was a scarf beneath it, stiff with blood. They tipped the door into the cart and then Helen returned for the scarf, putting it near the front, not in with the wreckage because it had once belonged to one of *Sarah Jane's* crew; somebody's son.

They worked for thirty minutes before the jeep from the base came roaring up the field, lights flashing and horns blazing. Helen ran for Rocket who jerked backwards, snorting. She grabbed for his bridle, gripping it by the bit, talking to him, soothing him but the Americans had leaped from the jeep and were shouting at John.

She shouted to John, 'Tell them to be quiet, Rocket will bolt.'

She hung on to the horse, talking, soothing, hearing John shouting at the men climbing from the jeep who took no notice.

'Leave that plane alone, bud.'

'That's US property. It's not to be moved by anyone but us,' the Colonel shouted.

Helen was using both hands now, pulling Rocket's head down. Another jeep came up the field but she was straining to hold him as he tossed and shook. He was too startled, though, too heavy for her and he knocked her back with his head, smashing into her face. She groaned with pain but the horse was slipping now, his legs kicking and struggling, and she reached out for him again but he went right down in the shafts and she moved forwards as he thrashed, hearing the clink of harness and chains. She caught his mane, and then his head. Her nose was bleeding down on to her dungarees and she cried with the pain but the big horse was snorting with terror and he could break his leg. She threw herself on top of his head, crying out to John, to the men who were running over to her now, knowing that she must press his head down to try and keep him still.

She could hear the shouts, the boots running through the ploughed soil and then she felt hands round her waist, lifting her, but she shouted as blood ran into her mouth, 'No, let me go. He's got to be kept still.'

'Helen, it's OK. Let go.' It was Ed, his voice, his hands and so she let him lift her clear but those hands now stroked another woman and so she pushed herself from him, wiping her face, mixing the tears with the blood.

'Someone must keep him still,' she said looking only at Rocket, but John was there now, pressing himself across the horse's head and Ed moved back to the horse, kneeling in the damp soil, his trousers soaking up the wetness and as he spoke and stroked the horse's muzzle, neck and chest, the thrashing slowed and gradually stopped but his legs were tangled in the straps.

She heard him say, 'Get those cutters from the jeep.'

The Colonel turned, signalling to the driver, who jumped

out, ran to the tool box and brought them across and she watched Ed's hands as he cut through the leather harness and unclipped the chains. Her nose was still bleeding and she undid her scarf which had slipped to her neck and held it against her face, waiting as John shouted at the others to back the cart away from the horse. Now Ed stood back, telling everyone to stand still. They all watched as Rocket scrambled to his feet, waiting as Ed came up, rubbing his hand gently under his chin, holding the bridle, leading the horse from the field.

The Colonel spoke. 'Hey, Ed. What about this mess with the plane?'

Ed didn't turn, he just called 'You can sort that out, sir. This horse needs a bit of peace.' He continued walking and the Colonel shook his head. 'Damn Air Execs, they're all the same. This one reckons he's back in Montana soft-talking his stock, not fighting a goddamn war.' But he was smiling. 'He sure is some kind of guy with a horse, isn't he?'

Helen's scarf was soaked through with blood and her face hurt. Her lip was swelling and she touched it with her tongue. She didn't look at Ed as he left the field with his rolling gait, his strong shoulders, but at John and the Colonel, but now her boss said, 'You get on back to the farm too, lass. Get that nose sorted out. Don't want you frightening any more horses, do we?'

Helen shook her head. 'I'm fine,' she said.

'Do as you're told, me old girl. Get on back.' John's voice was firm now and so she turned and followed on behind Ed, walking slowly so that she did not catch up, so that she would not have to talk to him, see those lips which were kissing someone else.

'And get a move on,' John shouted and so she was forced to quicken her stride, but only until she was out of the field and then she turned towards the farm but Ed was just to the left of the gate, holding Rocket still, waiting for her, leaning into his shoulder as she had so often done.

'You handled him pretty good,' he said, not smiling. His face was even more deeply lined, his eyes sunken with tiredness. 'I guess you'd do pretty good in Montana.'

Helen didn't stop. She bunched her scarf to her face and

hurried on, but he just brought the horse along quicker, rolling his feet, stretching out his legs.

'How're you doing, Helen? You look pretty good.'

She didn't turn.

'Plenty of colour on your cheeks today.'

She stopped, waiting for him to pass, but he didn't, he just leaned back into Rocket's shoulder, pulling on his bit, saying softly, 'Whoa.'

'Leave me alone,' Helen said, hating him for looking so beautiful, tearing apart inside because she loved him so much. She wanted to laugh because he was funny, wanted to cry because, though his words were light, his hands were trembling and so were hers.

Ed narrowed his eyes. 'I dropped in to the cottage this morning because I reckoned maybe you got hurt yesterday when the *Sarah Jane* came down.'

'Well, I didn't. I just got hurt when a crowd of Yanks rushed my horse.'

She walked on, wanting to lean into him, to feel him against her, to hear him say that he loved her, but he never would again.

'I love you, Helen,' Ed said, walking Rocket on again. She heard the stones clicking against the horse's hoofs, heard them slip beneath him, heard the soft snorting of his breath. A finch darted out from the hedge, and Rocket twitched.

She still did not stop; dared not stop.

'I said I love you.' His voice was louder now and he caught at her arm but she shrugged him off.

'No you don't. You love someone else. I've heard. Madge talks about you all the time.' And she did. About the way his moustache tickled when he kissed, about his eagerness in bed, the scar on his left shoulder.

Ed caught her again, his fingers digging into her arm.

'That was over a long time ago. I was hurt and frightened. I love you, you love me. I know you do. Marry me.'

Helen looked into his face now, searching for the truth and saw it in his eyes that were so brown, the face that was thinner, the lines that were etched as though with a chisel, but wondered if it was only there because she wanted it so much. She turned away, and then saw again the scarf as it had lain on the ground. She looked at him.

'Do you love me?' she said, her voice muffled by her scarf.

'Enough to stay over here if you won't come back with me,' he said.

She knew then that his love was as great as hers. She looked at the fields either side of the lane and the finch which was back in the hedge. She drank in the Englishness which surrounded her, the freshness, the smallness, and loved it but loved him more.

'I love you. I love you,' she murmured. He kissed her hand and then her neck, and walked back with his arm around her, knowing that he could not bear life without her again, thinking how glad he was that Mary and Chris had phoned him at the base to see if he was safe and then to tell him that Helen loved him more than ever.

The Colonel had to call at Laura's cottage to go through the formalities of ensuring that Helen was of a good enough character to qualify as an American Serviceman's wife. They drank elderberry wine and laughed to cover their embarrassment and he told them that Ed was the best Air Exec. that he had ever had and that the Major was giving him an easier ride now that they had long-range fighter cover. They laughed again but when he left Helen leaned against the door because Ed would be flying again in five weeks' time unless the war ended; but it wouldn't, it was endless.

They called the banns at the church where the vicar had said that he would be pleased to marry them. Madge looked the other way when Helen passed and Mrs Vane was too angry to be able to speak with civility. Ed completed affidavits confirming that he was in a position to support her financially but Helen had no intention of being dependent. She had her job and her agency in America. They were to be married on 1 May and Helen thought of one day at a time, because tomorrow and the day after were the future.

Helen stood with Ed inside the Parish Church, in a suit made of damaged parachute silk. Chris watched with Laura and Marian on the bride's side which was filled with villagers – but not Madge – whilst the Americans filled the right. Mary was the bridesmaid, also in parachute silk, and Chris found her lovely. She was not so fat and her hair was curled again with pipe cleaners and now she was looking round and smiling at him. He wondered how he could leave England without her because she was his friend, but also somehow more than that.

He listened to his mother as she spoke her words in a voice which was clear and true. He listened to Ed as he promised to love and to cherish, till death do us part, and hoped that his new father would never have to fly the Purple Heart Corner as Earl had done. That bottom rear corner was the most vulnerable position and won too many wounded-in-action medals for the crews that flew in it. Later they walked from the church to the lounge bar of the Royal Oak and talked to the guests, who ate and drank refreshments provided by the base and as the knife sank into the cake which the Master-Sergeant cook had sent, he whispered to Mary, 'Will you come to America too?'

She didn't answer, just looked at him, and then turned back to Helen and Ed as they kissed, then threw homemade confetti as they left, laughing as Mrs Vane caught the bouquet.

Helen and Ed took a taxi to Norwich. They sat close and he felt warm against her. His hands clasped hers and they did not speak. They climbed the stairs of the inn past peeling paper and beneath dimmed lights, but did not notice. The bedroom was warm, a fire burned and Ed said that this was his CO's present to them. His voice was low and he didn't smile as he took her coat from her shoulders and dropped it to the floor. He didn't smile as he slipped her clothes from her body and then his own. Helen didn't speak, just stood as he held her, kissed her, ran his hands down her body and now she trembled and lifted her arms to him, pulling his head down to hers, kissing his mouth, saying his name again and again because he was so beautiful and she was so full of love.

They did not sleep that night but lay together on the bed, feeling the heat from the fire, seeing the flickering shadows which licked at the ceiling. They clung together and then away, loose and easy and full. Tonight there was no war, no world outside this room. They talked of their love, their passion, their fears, and then they kissed again and felt the weight of one another and breathed in the scent. They talked of the blossom on the trees, the skies which were starlit tonight and then they merged again, lying together as the dawn rose, pink and clear and fine. They did not speak of the future because there might not be one for them both.

Ed flew the day after they returned and Helen counted the planes as she hoed the beet in the fields. Only seventeen Fortresses returned; twenty had flown out. Chris counted in Laura's kitchen and waited for the phone to ring but it did not and Ed came back that night to the cottage, tired and trembling but safe. Again and again he came back until, at the beginning of June, no more leave was granted. Helen lay in bed that night alone, missing him, wanting him, and full of fear because there were no Americans in the villages, in the towns. Something was happening in England.

As the fifth of June became the sixth the village and the country did not sleep because, wing-tip to wing-tip, British and American planes roared, circled and assembled: Mustangs, Thunderbolts, Flying Fortresses, twin-engined Marauders, Dakotas with wings swept back, Mosquitoes, Spitfires and Hurricanes, Halifaxes and Stirlings. In the cottage Chris and Laura wondered if now, at last, Hitler would stop fighting, but Helen knew he wouldn't because she had seen his image in the eyes of the black-booted torch-carrying soldiers.

All that long night preceding the sixth dawn in June the weather was not good, a strong north-westerly blew offshore from Europe but the German batteries were pounded along the French coast as night turned to day. At five a.m. while battleships pounded the German defences, a seaborne force of Allied soldiers landed on the coast of Normandy. British and Canadian troops took Gold, Juno and Sword beaches. American troops took Utah and Omaha. Omaha was steeper and there were many German soldiers behind quick-firing guns. Too many died.

At eight p.m. that night, while Ed was at the air base, safe, thank God, safe for now, Helen listened to the King calling for his people's prayers 'as the great crusade sets forth'.

She sat before the fire with Laura, Chris and Mary and listened as they talked of peace, and the children said they could not remember what that was like and she cried.

The next week the Allied advance continued and there was hope and satisfaction in the faces of the people she met. The next week Marian rang the air base. Their friend Roger, the vicar of St Bede's and the crypt, was ill, and Ed was given a thirty-six-hour pass to accompany Helen to London because his station was being stood down now that the initial invasion force was working its way inland. He drove her to the station and travelled in a crowded train to London, walking to the Underground, then passing through a capital which was bare of troops though there were children. Again there were children but Helen watched them as they played and looked up to the skies. They walked to her flat through streets broken like rotten teeth. Rosebay grew in the bomb craters and over the ruins and all the time Ed looked around but said nothing.

The flat was untouched and the vicar pale.

'You've been overdoing it, my dear,' Helen said, sitting in the room holding his hand, looking round and remembering the telegram and her despair but she no longer had to remember Heine because he was always with her.

'Dear Roger, you really have been overdoing it,' she said, leaning over and kissing his thin forehead.

They had brought ham from the base and eggs from Laura's hens and together with Marian she cooked in her own kitchen again, looking out on the shelter, talking of the crypt members who, Marian had told her, still met each night but only because they wanted to.

As the afternoon drew on Helen watched Ed, who stood at the sitting-room window, looking, just looking. Then he reached for his hat.

'Guess I'll take a walk, honey, just a walk.'

His eyes were shadowed and his hands trembled and so she grabbed her jacket and went after him, walking down the street, holding his hand, which was warm and strong, hearing her shoes but not his, because of his rubber soles.

He looked at the streets, the buildings, the fronts of stores which had no backs, the wooden crosses which were hammered into rubble where a daughter, a son, a husband, a wife had died. There were flowers on some, wilted and sad.

That night he did not make love as they slept in the spare room but he held her all night, feeling not her soft flesh but the vibrations of the *Emma B* as he delivered her bombs. But buildings had no shape from 25,000 feet when flak was all around and fighters were diving. No human was ever visible beneath the falling bombs. No screams were audible, only those of his gunners as they bled for a second before their blood froze. He must think of them, not of the people beneath the ruins, the families he destroyed. He must not think of them because it was not his job to think. His job was to help to win the war. He knew that, it was what he told his nineteen-year-olds when they flew their first mission. It was what he told them when they were sick in the latrines after they landed.

He tightened his grip on Helen. But did the Germans put wooden crosses in their ruins too?

He wished that he had not come today. He wished there had never been a war.

He travelled back the next day but Helen stayed for two more days and it was while she was there that the doodlebugs hit London. Droning, revving, the searchlights tracing the streaking tail and the shells bursting to either side but without effect. On they came, buzzing, until, suddenly, there was silence and it was then that they fell to the ground and exploded. Helen insisted that Roger should move to the crypt and they took him in the afternoon, returning for tea and provisions and it was in the evening as they returned to the church that one came buzzing through the air and cut out. She and Marian threw themselves to the ground screaming, both of them screaming, because they had been through this too many times before.

The explosion rocked the street, showering dust, so much dust, and then they heard the roar and saw the flames but turned away, hurrying to the crypt, because the ambulances were already coming and they were not needed. Hurrying away from the shrieks and the groans, knowing that this pilotless plane which catapulted from the Continent in the direction of southern England was going to wreak every last inch of havoc that Hitler could manage.

Helen ran down the steps of the crypt, checking that Roger was all right, listening as Ruth knitted and cursed 'itler for not knowing when he was beaten. She drank tea already strained twice through a sieve and felt as though she was running away as she took the train back to the village.

Helen drove the cart out to the field for the hay harvest and this time there was no help from the young American boys, most of whom were now dead, but neither was there help from the new intake because they were too busy in the skies, too busy trying not to die.

She heaved at the hay, smiling at John as he told her to work harder and build up those muscles because the war would be over soon and Montana would want to know what little British girls were made of. They carted loads back and then forked again. They raked the next day and Chris came, drinking cold tea at lunchtime, picking up the grass beneath the hedge and tying it into knots before throwing it up to the wind and watching it as it fell.

'Will the war be over soon, Mum?'

'I don't know, I really don't know,' she said but she did know that it wouldn't. But John nodded because the Allies were advancing across France and the Americans were attacking Japanese strongholds in the Marianas Islands.

Hitler did not give up and bombed England with more doodlebugs and the crypt was busy every night. In July children who had returned to London were evacuated again and so too were those in the bomb alley in Sussex, Surrey and Kent because Hitler's doodlebugs were intensifying. Mrs Vane now glared at Helen but Mrs Williams patted her and told her not to take 'the merest bit of notice'.

Ed flew only when there were no other crews because he was too busy on base, but each night when he could he came for a few hours and laughed as Helen dropped grass on the bedroom floor and held her tight as she slept, knowing that when he was with her he was safe from the fear of dying, safe from the knowledge of his destructive load, though he did not tell her that. But Helen knew, each night she knew, because she did not really sleep and heard his whispered words which he spoke aloud to himself.

In August Russia captured Bucharest and its oil, and Nazi death camps were found in Poland, at Maidenek where one and a half million people of every race and creed had been murdered with great efficiency. Helen cried that night and was glad that Heine was dead. She cried too for his parents because they might still be alive. And still Hitler did not give up.

As they harvested the wheat, Chris asked if the war would be over by Christmas and Helen said again that she didn't know; but she did because the Allies had not reached Berlin yet and that madman would claw and bite every drop of blood from everybody before he laid down his arms, and so would the Japanese.

In September the British and American attack on Arnhem failed and now other people also knew that there would not be an early peace. Now also the V2 rockets fell on England.

In October MacArthur landed in the Philippines and Helen harvested the beet, driving Rocket forward for the men to heave and empty their baskets up into the cart, then changing over so that John led the horse while she picked up beet, working in a steady rhythm, so much stronger than when she had arrived from the beet factory with the smell still in her hair.

There were prisoners-of-war to help now: Germans and Italians. And the villagers gave them fruit from their stores and knew that they did not suck blood from small children, but drew out photographs of their own, showing them and smiling, their faces gaunt from the war and memories which only they knew.

There were not as many missions from the airbase now. The Allies were gaining air superiority as the German bases in occupied countries were overrun and industries fell into the hands of the advancing Allies.

'Soon,' Ed said as he drank warm cocoa in front of the small fire in the sitting-room that they had lit for Chris's birthday on 1 December, 'soon we shall not need to go up at all.'

Helen did not reply because the Allies had not yet reached Berlin, though the Home Guard had been 'stood down' and Mr Reynolds had let his boar into the orchard because he was so angry.

But, she thought again, Berlin had not been reached and so the war had months to run.

That night Chris lay in bed, thinking of Mary because he had asked her again if she would come to America when the war was over, and again she had said she didn't know.

In the morning he asked Helen if they could take his friend when they moved to Montana and she nodded, pulling on her boots, wrapping her long woollen socks over the top, and her scarf around her neck because snow had fallen in the night and the cold almost crackled in the air. 'Only if she wants to and then we would have to sort something out with her sister. Mark you, darling, if we adopted her she would be your sister, had you thought of that? You could never be anything else.'

She opened the door, just a crack before saying again, 'You must think of that.'

Chris flushed, he felt the heat in his face. 'Oh Mum, don't be so stupid.'

But Helen thought about it all the way to the farm because Chris was twelve now and he and Mary fitted like a hand in a glove.

On 19 December, on a day of fog and cloud when Ed had been due to fly, the Germans attacked the Allied front in Belgium, following the same route through the Ardennes that they had used in 1940. England reeled from the shock because they had thought Hitler was finished, but Helen had not. The Germans held up the Allied advance in Belgium and the casualty lists of the Battle of the Bulge grew longer as the days passed. The skies stayed cloudy and no aerial help could be given. Ed's nails were chewed by Friday and two of his crew had learned that their brothers were dead. The skies didn't clear until the last week in December but it was still snowing on the twenty-third when Ed climbed the tree which was slippery with ice and nearly fell reaching for the mistletoe and as Mary shrieked, Helen called, 'You bomber pilots! You can't even cope fifteen feet from the ground!'

He threw the mistletoe down on her and clambered to the ground, chasing her, calling to Chris to bring the sledge, scooping up snow and throwing it so that it sank down beneath her collar and on to her neck, laughing as he heard her scream. She ran faster, feeling the snow crunch beneath her feet but he caught her, swinging her off the ground and kissing her. Chris threw a snowball and it hit their faces and the snow found their mouths and they tasted it together.

They roasted chestnuts on an old shovel that night, seeing the skins crack and grow black, smelling the sweetness in the air, and they talked of the midnight service on Christmas Eve when they would be allowed to show light from the stained glass windows for the first time since war began.

'So it really will be over soon,' Chris said as he sorted the straight pieces of the puzzle which he had done three times before but Mary hadn't.

'I guess it might,' Ed said, smiling at Helen who said

nothing, just looked into the fire as she reknitted a pulled out sweater. Ed picked out a chestnut, throwing it from hand to hand and blowing on it but in the end he flicked it back on to the shovel while the others laughed.

'Don't be so impatient,' Laura said.

Ed nodded, rubbing his hands together and grimacing, watching as Helen knitted, the needles clicking softly.

'It's kind of nice to see you doing that. In the States they don't, or in Little Fork they don't anyway, not much. My mom has some pins somewhere.'

Chris looked at Mary. 'Will you come with us?' he asked her.

Helen looked up at Ed and they both listened as Mary said, 'I don't know. I think Laura will be lonely and I've got me sister too. I don't know what to do.'

Helen said softly. 'What's happened with Irene's GI then, Mary, do you know? Has she heard?'

Mary shook her head. 'No, he's never written, not after she told him she was having the baby.'

Ed took the shovel off the logs. It had burnt black from the smoke.

'Maybe the guy just got busy. He'll get in touch, Mary.'

Mary shrugged. 'I like it here so much,' she murmured and Chris looked up at Helen who smiled gently, and that night, as she said goodnight, she told him that he must let Mary make up her own mind because Laura had said she could live with her and come across to America in the holidays.

'I like England too,' Chris said, 'but I want to go to America.'

'I know, darling, but it's different for us. We love Ed so much.'

She walked down the stairs, running her hands down the vertical beams, hearing the creak of the cottage which had been home for so long and which she loved as much as she loved the fields and the towns of England. But she loved Ed more, she knew that now.

She told him as he left that night, called back to the base early by the Colonel, and she watched as the jeep drove away. Its lights were still dimmed but they would not be for much longer if the rumour was correct, but Helen knew that this did not mean that the war was almost over.

She looked down the road, following the path of the jeep,

knowing that the recall meant he.was flying and that night she lay and cursed the clearing skies.

CHAPTER 17

The Sergeant woke Ed with a 04.00 call. He had slept and dreamt of Helen laughing up at him from the snow and he swallowed hot coffee quickly before walking through to the briefing room. He wouldn't think of Chris lighting the Advent candle tonight, he wouldn't think of the stockings on the bottom of his bed because there was a whole goddamn day to get through first and many miles to fly.

The Colonel told them that the weather had at last improved enough for air support in the Ardennes. That there was to be a combined attack on enemy airfields along the Rhine and other targets in support of the troops being pounded and pressed by von Rundstedt's offensive. They were given their route and the weather report and Ed lounged back as the others were doing because losses were light now and they should act relaxed.

He drove with two other officers on to the airfield, the wheels spinning on the hard packed snow of the verge.

'For Christ's sake, driver, let's get to the ships at least before we take a fall,' Bob Tucker said, chewing gum, rubbing his fingers together as he always did before a mission.

Ed grinned. 'Take it easy, Bob, you might end up with a sprained wrist and have the day on base.'

Bob laughed, throwing his head back and slapping his leg. He was over-reacting, too nervous, but then weren't they all? It helped them stay alive.

Ed was dropped at the *Emma Lou*. He felt the sweat start on his hands as he walked beneath her wing. The *Emma B* had blown up over Hanover with a new crew. The pilot of the *Emma Lou* had completed his twenty-five missions and, except for Marco from the *Emma B* who had been grounded for months, this was a new crew fresh from the States he was taking up, poor buggers. Poor damn buggers, Ed thought as he smiled at them, tipping his hand to his cap, thinking how alike they looked in their heavy cumbersome sheepskin jackets with gum rolling from one cheek to the other, helmets dangling from their hands. He wouldn't tell them until they were airborne that they had been assigned the Purple Heart Corner.

He handed out their packets of money, maps, survival rations. Joking, chatting, not remarking on the shaking hands which took them from him, hoping that his own weren't trembling. He took a look around the airfield, the ground crew in coveralls and fatigue caps were hanging around; the sky was pink where the sun was rising. Helen would be up by now, stirring meal and potato peelings for the hens.

He looked at the other bombers lined up, enormous, powerful, and then up at the sky again. Just get these kids back, he ground out to the Fortress, then grinned at his men.

'OK. Let's get in.'

Ed checked the instruments with Barney, his co-pilot, then used his hands palm up on the throttles. This old lady was heavy like the *Emma B*, but balanced. Yeah, she was pretty well balanced. The sound was deafening as the engines turned over then caught and held, and he saw the ground crew clutch their caps as winds swept across the deck. He tipped his fingers to them through the cockpit window knowing that as the *Emma Lou* took off these men would drift back to the Nissen huts whose walls were covered with pictures of half naked women. Here they would play cards and shoot crap with only half their minds because the other half would be up here with the *Emma Lou* until she came back – or didn't.

The flare had gone up and they were taxi-ing now. He adjusted his helmet, the throat speaker and earphones, taking off half a minute after *Juliet*; tucking in behind and climbing as she did, following in position to the assembly point, then on to rendezvous with the squadrons from other fields until turning back on themselves in tight formation, safe in their own airspace for now, then out and over the Channel.

'Let's keep looking, guys.' Ed spoke over the intercom. 'The Mustangs are with us so that's a help but we need your eyes, always, every minute. I want to get you home to your hearths, remember, and I'm kinda old myself and need my pipe and slippers at the end of the day, not a dose of cold hard snow.'

He listened to the laughter, then checked the tail turret, and young Eriksson who looked as though he should still be in high school. The waist gunners checked out well, they were running through their guns. Ted in the top turret was fine and the nose too.

'You OK, Marco?' He smiled to hear the familiar voice reply, 'Great, skip. Fancy a little outing today but get us back, this is my twenty-fifth.'

Ed heard groans from the others and laughed, always looking to left and right but he'd picked up the escorts now, Mustangs who could fly at 440 mph and make Berlin and back. He did not think of the men who would still be here if they'd only had those little beauties earlier.

'OK, you guys, you'll get there one day,' he laughed into the intercom but knew that the life expectancy of a bomber was only twenty-one missions, so where did that put its crew? Maybe the war would be over by then. Maybe. His hands were steady on the controls and he could feel the vibration, smell the leather, the gasoline. The formation hadn't lifted to a higher altitude over the coast because there was no flak any more now that it was in Allied hands.

Ed relaxed his shoulders and glanced at Barney who said, 'Kinda quiet, eh, skip?'

Ed smiled. 'Sure is.' He wouldn't tell the kids the position they were flying in. What was the point?

He said again into the throat speaker, 'Just keep your eyes busy. Remember that.'

The formation was rising now, up to 25,000 feet, out of range of enemy guns because they were getting pretty close to the drop zone, Ed reckoned. It would be cold for the guys in the rest of the ship.

'Get your oxygen masks on,' he ordered. 'We're going up. Give me a post, Marco.'

'I reckon on another thirty minutes to target, skip.'

They flew on and he knew the crew would be huddled into their jackets and flexing their hands in gloves which made their fingers clumsy but stopped frost-bite. Did they know that if they were hit their blood would freeze as it hit the air? But Ed jerked his head, concentrating on the sky, the instruments, anything rather than staying inside his head because he was being crazy. They had been told losses would be light, hadn't they?

'So how many more missions have you got to do?' Barney asked, his eyes to the left and right, up and down. His voice was high with tension.

Ed shrugged. 'A few.'

'Yeah, but how many?'

'This guy's done thirty-two.' Marco's voice came in over the earphones.

Barney turned and stared. 'Thirty-two, but you could be home.' There was disbelief in his voice.

'Couldn't bear to leave us could you, skip?' Marco called.

'Something like that. Now keep on looking.'

It had been Helen he hadn't been able to leave, but she would never know he had volunteered for a second tour.

'Give us a post then, Marco.'

'Five minutes to target, skip.' Marco's voice was sharper now.

'Bombardier, you with us?' Ed's voice was crisp. He followed the squadron in tight formation.

'Right there, skip. Hold her steady.' But there was gunfire now from the ground and the ship lurched as a shell exploded nearby.

'Jesus,' Eriksson shouted. 'Jesus.' He was frightened, Ed could hear it in his voice.

He held on to the controls, feeling the sweat break out as it always did.

'OK, Eriksson. It's OK. Just keep looking.'

He was over the target, dropping the bombs, and there had been no air attack and the ground fire had been light. So far, no Focke-Wulfs swarming, no ME109s.

He pulled out and away, keeping in tight. 'OK, guys, we're on our way home. I guess maybe this is going to turn into a milk-run.' He was still looking and listening, up, down, left, right because they could still come, and they did, ten minutes later, roaring down on them, breaking away so close Ed could see the German in the cockpit.

The Mustangs were fighting too, but the Germans were getting through, again and again stabbing at his corner.

'Jesus, skip. I got one.' Eriksson was screaming. 'I got one.'

Ed cut in sharply. 'Keep looking, Eriksson. There'll be others.'

The Focke-Wulfs kept coming in on a pursuit curve, but this

time Ted in the top turret sent one spinning down in flames but still they kept coming from three thousand feet ahead and one thousand above, coming in fast before rolling and firing.

One passed, streaming thick dark smoke. Was he hit or was it just the synthetic fuel made out of coal and God knows what that the Germans were using? Ed didn't know, didn't have time to think because the guns were started up from below and he was falling back from formation.

'Come on, you bitch,' he ground out, pushing at the throttles, the controls, pulling up again and so far she wasn't hit but Eriksson was screaming, always screaming, and it wasn't because he had scored a hit, it was because he had just screamed that his arm had been torn off, for Christ's sake.

Ed shook his head. For God's sake, how could you think? He had a plane to get back but there was the screaming and the black smoke to fly through, the fighters to avoid and the fear to push away.

He hauled on the controls as another 109 flashed across in front, firing, and he felt the *Emma Lou* judder. She was hit but would she burn?

Barney called out. 'Number one engine's been hit, Ed.'

Christ! 'It's OK. I got her,' Ed said, still hearing Eriksson's screams, but there was no fire.

'Where are the Mustangs for Pete's sake?' Marco called out.

But they were there, fighting, turning, firing, but there were so many Germans. Didn't they know they'd lost the goddamn war? Now Eriksson was no longer screaming but voices were babbling and shouting and Ed called, 'Get off the intercom.' He must hear the orders coming through from the group. An ME109 was coming straight in, his nose cone pointing straight at him, his guns firing and the *Emma Lou* juddered again and now number two engine was windmilling and burning.

'Feather it,' Ed snapped to Barney and he did.

The *Emma Lou* was heavy now and he was fighting to hold her even, fighting to close the gap between him and the Shark in front but he was losing speed and altitude.

Frank, the radio operator called through. 'I got Ted here, upper turret empty now, he's hurt but not bad, the blood's frozen.'

'OK. Throw a spare jacket over him.' Ed's voice was firm, though his hands were trembling, and all he could see and hear were ravens coming, again and again, but they weren't ravens, they were planes, so for Christ's sake, snap out of it.

He did. Barney was swearing, long streams of words which he repeated again and again. There was an explosion amidships and the *Emma Lou* hesitated, shuddered, hit by cannon fire, but then carried on. The waist gunners were still firing, he could feel their vibration, see the tracers spitting into fighters but it was not enough, and now bits of his wing had been shot away and the ship was careening from side to side as another fighter streaked past.

'Give me a post, Marco. Give me a post,' Ed shouted.

There was no answer.

'For Christ's sake give me a post.'

Marco spoke then, his voice was weak. 'Four minutes to the sea, skip.' He gave him the course.

'You OK?'

Marco laughed but it was faint. 'That shell got a bit familiar, the bitch.'

Ed gripped the throttle. 'Hang on, kid. I'm getting you back. It's your last one. Trust me.'

Number three engine was spluttering and the *Emma Lou* was fighting him, swaying, but he held her firm, talking to her as though she were a mare, and now they were over the sea at last and the Focke-Wulfs and the ME109s were gone but the Mustangs stayed with them, waggling their wings to indicate that they would stay with *Emma Lou* until she made it, or didn't. She was losing height and her speed was still decreasing.

But land was in sight and Barney did a count of dead and injured and Ed listened on the intercom. Maybe Eriksson was dead, there was no answer. Marco, Frank injured.

The *Emma Lou* was lower now and he didn't know if he could get her back. Some of them must be saved at least.

'You guys that can, bale out.' He nodded at Barney. 'You too. Get out. Now.'

He didn't look as Barney left, but fought to keep the ship up because he still had Marco and Frank. Maybe he could do it but the fighters were still with them and they were indicating that he had no undercarriage and he waved as they flew past, not showing what he felt. He was cool and calm because he had to be. For Christ's sake, he had to be. Number three engine was struggling but the prop was still turning. The ship was yawing and he corrected her, just. Swearing, he kept her on course, checking the compass, seeing the fields too close, too goddamn low. He eased her up, feeling the drag pulling the wing round, but he fought back, careful not to stall. The airfield was ahead now.

The bombers were all down, all on their hard standing but the crews would not be debriefing, they would be there, waiting, watching, but he didn't think he was going to make it and he hoped to God there was no fuel left because he didn't want to burn.

The Mustangs were above him now.

'You OK, Marco, Frank?'

'Just fine and dandy, boss,' Marco said but his voice was very faint.

'We've no undercarriage. Just hang on, and I'll bring you in safe.' But would he? He was so tired and his arms were shaking. His mouth was dry, so dry.

The ship was yawing again and he had to bring her straight. She was low and slow, the engine still spluttering, and now he could see the ambulances hurtling from behind the tower, out to the end of the runway but he couldn't hear the siren because of the wind in the plane, the cracking of the fuselage, the spluttering of number three engine. She was lurching in over the tree tops, and he reached to put down the landing gear, but then stopped, because there was none there.

He brought her down on the runway then and he felt the drag on that goddamn wing, saw it tip then right itself, and then tip again, catching, tearing. He heard such noise, such noise as he had never thought existed, and then the plane flipped over and he saw the ground come up to crush the cockpit and for a moment he felt the pain, but only for a moment.

Helen was home, standing by the sink unable to work because she was so cold, suddenly so cold. She put the potatoes back into the water, then turned and stood quite still. She stood like that, just looking at the Advent candles, the tree which stood surrounded by presents, watching as Laura and Chris laid the table and looked at her, their eyes masked, uncertain. Then the jeep came.

They all heard the knocking at the door but Helen insisted

on answering because she knew who it would be and in a quiet voice the Colonel told her that the *Emma Lou* had crash-landed, that Marco and Frank were injured but that Ed had been hurt too, so badly hurt that the medics did not know how long he would survive.

Helen reached for her coat and looked at Laura, telling her to stay with Chris, and then she left, out into the starlit night. She felt the air harsh in her lungs and breathed it in and out, in and out, but then it changed into the thick leather warmth of the car. She sat back and breathed and counted and looked up at the stars and the moon and knew that she and Ed should not have thought of the future.

She didn't cry, she couldn't cry because he wasn't going to die. He was her husband and he couldn't die. But he might if she cried.

She sat, holding one hand with the other, squeezing, hurting, but not allowing the tears to come, or the hoarse voice to be heard. It must stay inside to tear jagged into her mind but it must not escape because the raven of the gods might hear, and lead them to him. No she must not cry or call because then he might be found.

They drove up to the largest Nissen hut at the field hospital at Little Odbury air base. The roadways were filled with jeeps, command cars, ambulances, MPs and a plane flew in low overhead to land. Men were rushing but not running and Helen wondered if she was going mad.

The Colonel pushed his way through the men and soldiers who stood in lines or wandered about, looking shocked, tired. He spoke to a corpsman who pointed to the far door, giving directions. They hurried from one hut to another but could not find him. In and out, from darkness to light, from cold to warmth and he could be dead while they walked like this.

'He could be dead,' she shouted at another corpsman who had shaken his head when McDonald was mentioned, pointing to yet another hut.

The Colonel took her arm. 'It's going to be OK. He's in the next one, I'll bet you.' But he wasn't and neither could they find Marco or Frank.

They pushed back to the clerk behind the main desk who told them that all three had been transferred to the Winton Hospital near Norwich.

They drove for what seemed like hours, picking out the white line along the side of the road when it existed and now the darkness inside her head was lifting and just despair remained. They passed through a village and saw the lighted church, the stained glass windows illuminated for the first time since war began but it meant nothing to her, not now.

It was two a.m. before they arrived and then they followed the nurse down a long ward, hearing her shoes squeaking on the waxed floor and the groans and breathing of the shapes behind the white screens which surrounded each bed. A nurse came out from one and a doctor from another and others were busy too. Ed was in the end bed, near the double doors and the sister's desk so that he was never beyond her hearing.

Helen stopped and looked as the nurse eased back the screens and she was counting again, breathing in and out; one, two, three, four. His head and body were bandaged but his hands were the same, lying still, so still on the sheets. She sat on the chair, holding his fingers.

'Falling from more trees, my darling,' she said and though her voice was steady tears were coursing down her face. His fingers squeezed hers but his eyes did not open.

She stayed all night and the next day and the next, refusing to be moved until the X-rays showed no broken spine but two cracked vertebrae and a broken leg. And head injuries.

She didn't know for another week whether he was going to be brain damaged, blind or crippled and so she could only sit by his bed, holding his hand, talking of Greater Mannenham, of the snow which was deep and cold, of the hoar frosts, and all the time she did not know if he heard her. She didn't think of the gods they had challenged, or the man in the wheelchair by the Cambridge river. She thought of Ed tossing hay, playing baseball, and gripped the sheet but not his hands. These she stroked calmly and never cried when she sat with him.

The doctor came to her as she left the room at the end of the first week in January, taking her into the office, sitting down behind the desk, steepling his hands as he smiled and told her that there would be no lasting physical damage but perhaps there would be trauma, though war had a habit of producing that anyway.

Helen went to the room she had taken in the local inn, climbed the stairs and sat by the window, not drawing the curtains across because she wanted to see the snow, so clean and white like his bandages were. She wanted to feel the cold air and opened the window. Her breath puffed out in the crisp night. He was not going to die. She wanted to shout it out for the world to hear because this time the man she loved was not going to die.

On 9 January the Battle of the Bulge was over and the Germans were being squeezed out of their Ardennes salient and Helen had to sit by his bed, holding his hand tightly, and tell him that Marco had died of his injuries.

He cried and she stayed until he slept but then had to return home because she had to be up as usual at five-thirty to begin work at the farm.

Ed lay in the dark when she had gone, still unable to feel his feet or move them, but it was of Marco he thought, killed on his twenty-fifth mission and that night he had a dream of blood on his face, dried blood which would not scrape off even though he rubbed it against his shoulder. The nurse came and soothed him, asking who Joe was. He had almost forgotten but he dreamt the same dream the next night and this time the blood was all over him and it wasn't Joe's blood, it was all those people who had been beneath his bombs and the nurse came again, but he only wanted Helen and she came when the hospital called her.

In February he was transferred to a recuperation hospital in Scotland and was able to write to his father that at last he had seen the country where their ancestors came from and it was very like the valley in Montana where they lived.

From 13 to 15 February Dresden was bombed by the Allies when it was full of refugees. Hundreds of thousands died and Ed lay listening to the news of the raid, glad that he was lying here with pain coursing through his body because at least that particular guilt was not added to the load he already bore and which was heavier than anything else had ever been.

Helen wrote every day to Ed before cycling to work through a winter which was harder than any she remembered. Her hands were numb before she had left the village, her breath was frozen in the scarf which she wound round her nose and mouth. In March the Allies crossed the Rhine and now, when Chris asked if the war was nearly over she said, 'Yes, my darling.'

In the middle of March Ed was shipped back to the United States to convalesce and she travelled to Liverpool to catch a glimpse before he sailed, but the train was held up for troop movements and so she missed him and had to stand, watching the stern of the ship and its wake, feeling the cold, remembering Heine who had left from here too. She was alone again.

CHAPTER 18

The trip back on the troop ship would take ten long days, Ed had been told as he hauled himself up the gangway, a corpsman following close behind, but he would not go on a stretcher. He was going to walk out of England as he had walked into it.

He looked over his shoulder all the time but she didn't come. Helen didn't come. He eased himself down into the bowels of the ship, feeling the heat, the stench of illness and lay on a bunk in a converted hospital ward filled with bunks. Men lay groaning, swearing or were silent and Ed looked up at the base of the bunk above him. She hadn't come.

He felt the heave of the ship as they met open water and the pain in his back from his cracked vertebrae grew worse and his leg throbbed though it was out of plaster. A corpsman came round to each bunk checking pulse and blood pressure and it was good to feel fingers on his wrist and a voice saying, 'You're doing just fine, Major. Be home real soon.'

But he didn't want to go Stateside. He wanted to be with her.

Doctors were on call all day and all night and as the pain grew worse and the throbbing of his leg drowned out the vibration of the engines and the roll of the dice as three men shot crap, they gave him morphine.

'But not much, Major. Just enough. Don't want you getting too fixed on this.' The doctor smiled, holding the syringe to the lights, easing up the plunger, expelling the air.

'I seemed to be getting better, Doc,' Ed said, his voice tight from pain. 'So what the hell is happening?'

The doctor swabbed his arm, inserting the needle. 'Everything's going just swell, Major. It's those roads you had to use to get to the docks in Liverpool.' He grinned, pressing in the plunger. 'Got themselves a few pot-holes I guess, knocked everything about a bit. It'll settle, don't you worry.'

'Hey, Doc, there's a man here bleeding from his goddamn nose.' The voice was urgent, frightened, and the doctor moved quickly, dropping the empty syringe into the enamel kidney bowl the corpsman held. Ed heard voices, murmurs and always the groans, and then there was nothing.

When he woke the pain was better even though the ship was lurching and bucking and as the days passed he was able to ease himself from the bunk and, with a Captain who had lost a hand flying a bitch of a Fortress, he inched along the deck, feeling the lash of the wind, watching the other ships steaming with them, noting the zig-zag course.

The Captain handed him a Lucky Strike and put one in his own mouth but Ed lit the match because Captain John Bryan still held the pack and he only had one goddamn hand, hadn't he? It was good to be with a flyer, to ease into chairs and look out on to big seas which broke and sprayed the deck; to look out and see no planes, no wind socks, no bombed houses, to hear no dawn roar of departing planes.

He sucked on his cigarette, drawing the nicotine deep into his lungs, feeling its heat. He expelled his breath, seeing it whipped away. There was no reason for them to talk much because they had both felt the same fear and pain as their Fortresses were hit. They both remembered the judder and the stagger and understood the darkness in one another's eyes.

They ate a plateful of food in the canteen which would fill six stomachs in the villages they had flown over and John told him of the girl he had met but would not marry because his high school sweetheart was waiting in Arizona.

Ed told him of Helen, whom he had married. He cut up John's steak, grinning when his buddy said they would make a good team.

'I'll be your legs, cling on to that mare back in Montana, you can hold the reins,' John said, eating relish on its own. 'Gee, it's going to be good to get back.'

Ed shook salt on his meat, seeing the blood ooze from the rare steak. 'But do you reckon they'll understand?'

It was hours later that John replied. They were sitting in on a poker game, the two of them playing one hand; John holding the cards, Ed slapping them down.

'I guess Ruby won't know what the last two years have been

like. I've changed. I don't know if we'll make it. Maybe I should have brought my village girl back, she knows what it's all about I guess,' John said.

He said nothing more and the smoke was heavy in the room off the end of the ward. It stung Ed's eyes and he narrowed them, checking the cards, raising the stakes until they lost and then they walked around the deck, slowly because he was still limited in his movement.

They knew there were clouds above them because they could see no stars and there was only darkness around them because the blackout was still in force on this sea crossing.

John lifted his head, pushing back his hair with his stump. 'You see, I get these dreams. Ruby won't know why.'

Ed flicked his cigarette over the side, leaning on the rail, feeling it digging into his flesh. The Captain had told them they would be passing the Statue of Liberty at 07.00 hours but he didn't want to arrive and be in a country where no one would know how he felt, how John felt, how the thousands of draftees were going to feel.

But he did arrive and was flown by transport plane which rattled and bucked, bouncing into the nearest airfield in a way that Ed would never have allowed from any of his young flyers. And his pop was there, grey and strong, his stetson pulled down, his eyes the same clear blue. But his mom had been crying, her face was puffed and her lips swollen. They hadn't changed, but he had. Jesus Christ, he had. He wanted Helen, he thought, as he felt his mother's arms around his neck.

They drove through the dry cold air of late March. He sat near the window of the pick-up looking out across the space which England did not possess. Seeing the mountains which were his home but not really his home because Helen wasn't here. He looked up at the peaks and missed the flatness which was East Anglia. He didn't speak because he didn't know what to say to these people who were his parents but whom he hadn't seen for three years, three long strange years. They drove into Little Fork, driving past the wood-fronted stores which looked like something from the cowboy westerns which Chris sat and watched at the cinema. He missed the boy, he missed his wife.

Ma Benson was on the corner of the drug store, Ma Benson who had bounced him on her knee and who was now waving the Stars and Stripes as the pick-up approached. His pop slowed, then stopped and Ed wound down the window.

'Gee, it's great to have you home, boy,' Ma Benson said, kissing his cheek. She still smelt of lavender water. Some things never change and now Ed smiled.

'It's kind of good to be back, Ma,' he said.

The ranch was the same, just the same, and Ed lay in bed, looking at his curtains which still had the ink mark he had splashed across when he was sixteen and trying out his new pen.

The stars were bright and the moon too, throwing its light down on to the snow which Helen would not be able to believe was so deep, so hard, so cold. His leg and his back were hurting and it kept him awake all night and he was glad because he did not want to sleep.

That week he received her letter.

Greater Mannenham

My darling Ed,

I missed you. I travelled all the way but I missed you. The journey back was so bleak without a last look at your face, a last feel of your hand in mine.

It won't be long before I come. Let's just see this war out first. You will be home and in your own bed by now with your own people around you. I hope that you are feeling better and that you can relax but I fear there will be a gulf between you all, at least for a while. Be patient. You've come from a strange war world and you go back to something which has not been touched like Europe. Remember, though, that they will have had their changes. Boys will have gone, hearts will have been broken, even if buildings are not crushed and rations reduced as ours have been.

Get well, my love. That is all that is important. And try to forget all that has passed.

I love you, I love you.

Helen.

For the first two weeks Ed sat in a chair in his bedroom,

wanting the small room around him because it made him feel safe but now at last he was sleeping at night though his dreams woke his mom. He knew that they did because she came in and sat with him, but he wanted Helen because she knew where he had been.

In the third week he walked downstairs and sat by the lounge stove, listening to the crackle of the wood and the sound of the wind. The generator was cranking up, his father said on Friday evening, and Ed nodded but what did it matter? It always cranked up.

By the middle of April the pain was easing enough to push to one side and he walked around the ranch, but he was still so goddamn stiff, he murmured to his mother.

'I know, Ed. It's a plain nuisance and you must be plumb tired out. Shall I get you something from Doc Mathers for the dreams?'

He looked at her as she walked along the path to the creamery. There was mud everywhere, it had come with the spring thaw as it did every year. Did nothing change over here?

'There's nothing he can give me that would help. It was different over there, Mother, you see. We killed people, not cattle. People.' His voice was hard. 'And they tried to kill us.'

Her eyes were shocked and she moved ahead and he was sorry and caught at her hand. 'I'm sorry, Mom. I guess I can't quite get used to being back. It'll take a bit of time.'

'I know. I try to understand,' she said, taking some butter from the wooden ledge inside the damp building which his father had built when Ed was only ten.

'Business could be a whole lot bigger, you know, boy,' His father said as they ate turkey in the well heated kitchen that night. 'It's shipment that's the problem. That train takes so damn long, winding through the country, changing at Chicago. Anyone would think we hadn't got a living to make.'

There was half a turkey left on the platter and bacon too. It was too much, too damned much. Ed looked at the stove and there was too much damned heat. He looked out of the window at the buildings which were the same as the ones he had left before the war. There were no smouldering ruins, no wrecked Fortresses or Spitfires in the fields.

Ed couldn't eat any more. 'Some people over in England

aren't concerned with making a living, they just have a lot of dying to do. Don't you folks ever think of that?'

He got up, knocking his chair to one side. His back was painful tonight. He pushed from the room, climbing the stairs. He stood by his bedroom window, looking up to the mountains. It would be peaceful up there. Helen would like it. He gripped the curtains, the ink mark was dark against his hand and he wished he was sixteen again and not the old man he now was. He gripped the material so tightly that it ripped and he didn't care, he tore again and again, shredding it, wanting to wipe out the months and the years which had made him old and frightened.

His father knocked on the door but he didn't answer, just leaned his head against the window, feeling the cold, seeing the strips of curtain in his hands.

His father knocked again and came in and stood next to his son and now Ed turned to him and saw the face which had always been good and kind, the body which had always been bigger than his and still was and he moved and pressed his head against his pop's shoulder and cried as he had not done since he was twelve years old.

His father held him, rocking him backwards and forwards as he had done years ago, stroking the back of his son's neck which was still the same as that young child's and he didn't let him see the tears in his own eyes for the boy who would never be the same again.

They sat and talked into the night because Pop had heard the screams and had lain awake alongside his wife, holding her hand until the morning, grieving but impotent. Arthur McDonald told Ed how grey paint had been painted over the gold leaf dome of the Massachusetts State House on Beacon Hill in Boston three months after Pearl Harbor so that it was less conspicuous in the event of enemy bombardment. He told him how black paint was painted over the gold leaf roof of the Federal Building so it would not gleam beneath the moon and attract enemy submarines in American waters and they both laughed, gently.

He put his hand on his son's shoulder as they sat side by side on the bed, filling the ashtray with half smoked stubs, drinking Scotch from the flask which Arthur had filled and brought up with him.

'So forgive us for not understanding. We are trying,' he said.

He went on to say how German U-boats had prowled up and down the East Coast from Canada to the Gulf of Mexico and the Caribbean sinking tankers and freighters sailing for Britain with guns, tanks and planes. Many were sunk. Ma Benson's neighbour's son was drowned that way. There was no longer a star in her window.

Ed nodded, knowing that his mother had removed the one which had been in theirs when he returned home.

'The war has touched us in that way and in others. We have interned the Japanese. Their houses have been vandalised or sold for a pittance but we have allowed their sons to be drafted to die and fight for America.'

Arthur stubbed out his cigarette, grinding it down until the remaining shreds of tobacco stood out stark against the black.

'You see, Ed. War does strange things to people. On the one hand it gives them opportunities. Gee. Just think of the women who have been taking over the factory jobs, working alongside men, showing their worth. On the other hand war also brings despair. Think of the Little Fork families whose boys died on D-Day on Omaha. It does touch us but not as it has touched you. We feel for you. We love you but we cannot understand because your fear hasn't been ours.'

He rose then, leaving the flask with his son, hoping that tonight he would sleep. But he didn't, he lay away loving his father, his mother too, but it wasn't just fear. It was guilt, and how could they understand that, because they had never had to kill.

He was in town when the latest draftees left Little Fork. He stood on the sidewalk watching the crowd gathering outside the hotel where the kids ate breakfast – their last small town breakfast. He leaned on his stick watching the High School band falling into position and then the colour guard from the American Legion. As the boys, for that is what they were, he thought bitterly, came out of the hotel they lined up and the head of the draft board called, 'Forward march.'

Ed stood still as the kids marched down the street heading for the railroad station where the crowd gathered again. Ed walked along now, stiffly and silently, watching the parents forming tightly round their sons. Hugs were given, long strong hugs, and then the train came in and as they boarded the band played the Marine Hymn, as though it was a game, for God's sake.

Ed walked back to the pick-up, forgetting the stores his mom had asked him to buy from the grocery store, thinking only of the kids leaving, so young and fresh. Some would die, some would survive and not be scarred. Some would survive and have to fight to try to come to terms with the things they had done and seen. Would they make it? Would he?

He wrote to Helen that night, knowing that it would be a long wait until she came because he had heard from John in Arizona that he was going to marry this English girl instead and there would be no official ships until months after the war had finished and who knew when that would be? It was now March 1945 and even if there was victory in Europe, what about Japan? Would he have to fight again in the Pacific?

He put his pen down and reached for the flask he had filled in Little Fork and longed for Helen and for peace.

CHAPTER 19

Helen was planting beet when Hitler shot himself in a bunker at the end of April as the Allies swept through Berlin. The Germans in Italy had surrendered the day before. She sat in the garden that evening, seeing the hedge in bud and the apple trees in the orchard, watching her son and Mary practising pitching and batting, hearing the thud of the ball on the bat, their shrieks. They were slim – everyone was slim – because food had not been plentiful for the last six years but what there was had been equally shared and that was good.

She turned as Laura came out, wiping her hands on her apron.

'I shall miss you so, when you go, my dear,' Laura said.

'I can't imagine what it is going to be like to leave and so I just think of today,' Helen replied, looking out over the fields at the back.

'It'll be great,' Chris tossed back at them over his shoulder. 'It'll be just great.'

Mary pulled a face. 'Huh, when I come out to see you you'll be all American and sit there chewing gum.'

'Over my dead body,' Helen called and they laughed and so, for another day, Helen pushed the thought of leaving from her head though she could hardly bear to live without Ed for much longer.

The next week they heard of Belsen and Buchenwald and the millions of dead and the village was loud in its hatred of Germany again and Helen was quiet but wondered where Frau and Herr Weber were but Chris did not want to talk of them, or think of them now, he said, or ever again. Helen spoke to him, saying he was half German, saying that not all Germans had done this but he turned to her.

'I'm going to be American. I'm Ed's son.'

Helen knew that one day, she would have to bring Heine's son back to him but for the moment she did not know how.

On 1 May she received a letter from Montana.

> My darling,
>
> You would be pleased if you could see me. I'm getting about great. My folks send the enclosed affidavit saying that they are prepared to take financial responsibility for you if necessary. I guess I can see your face getting red and sassy but don't let it, this is just to support your application. I know you have my own affidavit and your money over here, and they do too, but I don't want anything going wrong at the last minute.
>
> I'm getting real impatient to see you but it's not over yet and there's Japan still. I guess too that you'll have to wait for a while for passage. We were all shocked when Roosevelt died. It seemed wrong somehow for him not to see the end of this great mess and not even to know that Hitler killed himself. I long for you, so much. I need you. You just don't know how much I need you.
>
> Ed.

On 8 May an announcement was given out on the wireless that on VE-Day all work would cease for two days and a party was held in the village when people danced and wept and could not believe that it was over.

There had been no blackout since April and at the air base searchlights swept the sky and fireworks soared up into the air as they stood on the green and watched. GIs then came into the village, screaming their jeeps to a halt, whirling the women off their feet and kissing them.

The Colonel shared his brandy with Helen, sitting on the benches which had been put up that afternoon, laughing and joking until she asked about Japan and then he said, nodding at the young Americans, 'They are happy tonight but they're scared they'll be sent to the Pacific. I hope your Ed will be spared that.'

Helen, Chris and Laura didn't leave the party until dawn was breaking and then they strolled back, streamers hanging round their necks, and as Helen fell into bed she thought of Ed, of Heine, of Roger the vicar who had died in March, of Marian whose Rob was home, and it all seemed much longer than six years.

On 6 and 9 August atomic bombs were dropped on Hiroshima and Nagasaki. On 14 August Japan surrendered and Helen knew that Ed would never have to fight again but she also knew that those who had survived would never be the same as they were before.

It was not until 1 March 1946 that she received notification from the United States Army that she would need to produce a British passport, two copies of her birth certificate, two copies of any police record, her original marriage certificate, three photographs on thin paper with light background, evidence showing that on arrival in the United States she would have a railroad ticket or enough money to buy one and finally two pounds or ten dollars to cover her visa fee. It told her that she would be notified any day now of her passage to the United States and would be expected to proceed to a collecting camp at Tidworth because the hotel in Bournemouth where mothers with older children normally stayed was full.

Helen went with Laura and Chris to Norwich, thinking only of today, not thinking of the collecting camp at Tidworth, not thinking of the North Atlantic or the land it led to. She bunched her fists and blinked at the flashlight, knowing the photographer had the lighting set up badly. She withdrew ten pounds cash for America and transferred her bank account to the one Claus used in America. On the train home she looked out at England and could hardly bear it, but Ed was over there and she loved him.

In the middle of March she and Chris received luggage labels for their ship and were asked to proceed to Tidworth for processing on 18 March. They were allowed to take one small suitcase each and one trunk which could be sent separately. She fingered the paper, folding it again and again while Chris whooped and ran down the road to tell Mary.

All that day Helen packed, her head down, folding, wrapping, not stopping to eat because she was not hungry.

She sat on the bed when she had finished, looking out of the window, and she cried for the country she was leaving, for Laura, for the years that had gone. She cried for Heine and for her mother, for the things that might have been, and slept then, until dawn.

On 18 March they travelled to London to meet a special train at Waterloo which would take them to Tidworth. As the train drew out of Norwich they leaned from the window and waved and waved until they could no longer see Laura and Mary and then she held Chris because he was thirteen now and felt he shouldn't cry but he couldn't help it and neither could he stop. Helen talked to him of the life they would have, of Mary who would come and of Laura, and at last he was silent and together they watched the countryside pass and Helen felt her heart breaking.

Lorries took the women and what children there were to the Wiltshire camp; it was late evening by the time they arrived. They were shown into huts which slept four to a room though Chris went to the service personnel barracks. He took his baseball mitt and ball and waved to Helen, then hid his face from her because he was crying again.

He looked round at the trees surrounding the camp, hemming him in, and dragged his sleeve across his eyes. The wool was coarse and scratched his skin. He wanted to stay with his mother but he was almost a man.

A GI showed him his bed and locker and asked about his girlfriend. He winked when Chris told him of Mary, pretending that he had kissed her, and now he put his shoulders back and rolled his feet like Ed as the Corporal took him back to the mess hut where a meal of pot roast and noodles was being served by German prisoners-of-war.

His mother waved and beckoned to the seat next to hers and they talked to the women either side, one of whom was trying to spoon-feed a toddler who pushed the food on to the floor. The mother cried and Chris watched as his mother took the spoon from her, gently pushing it into the child's mouth while a Red Cross helper led the woman from the room.

Talking and crying filled the hut, together with the scrape of cutlery on plates as people ate food they had forgotten existed because they were under the jurisdiction of the United States.

There were too many people here, Chris thought, that he di
not know, and Germans, those damned Germans, brushing hi
shoulder as they reached past him with food. Outside wer
great sweeps of chalk hills and he missed his home.

All night, in Helen's room, the babies cried in the cots whicl
had been constructed out of steel filing cabinet drawers, bu
she would not have slept anyway because her journey ha
begun and now there was no going back. Two of the womer
cried throughout the night and in the morning one left to g
home to her mother.

All day Helen was interrogated along with everyone els
after she had surrendered her identity card, her ration book
and her clothing coupons and she felt that they were taking the
last of her country from her. She filled in a form nearly two feet
long and wanted to tear it up as she was required to answer
questions no one had any right to ask. Against the one asking
whether she intended to overthrow 'by force or violence' the
Government of the United States she nearly replied yes.

She was given a medical and had to stand in line with other
girls, waiting until it was her turn to have a torch shone
between her legs to check for venereal disease. Like the other
women she tried to ignore the American Army officers who
were standing along the walls watching and laughing.

Anger coursed through her but she said nothing because all
this was for Ed. She was given a smallpox vaccination and the
corpsman said that Chris would be given one too. She was
finger-printed in another room, as were the others, and the
smell of petrol was strong as the ink was wiped off with cotton
wool pads. She was leaving with Susan, another bride who was
married to a Naval Officer, when she was called back.

'Please return to the interrogation room, Mrs McDonald.'

Helen walked across the fresh spring grass, seeing the
moisture on her shoes, keeping her mind clear, knowing what
would be said.

'We would like to ask you some questions about your first
husband. It appears he was in prison over here.'

The officer's face was bland but his eyes were hard and
Helen sat down again, not letting him see the tension she felt,
but fearing that it was all going to start again and wondering if
there would ever be any peace.

For two days she was questioned and enquiries were made.

Those in her hut embarked on their ships on the fourth day, but she and Chris did not and she was told that there could be no guarantee that she would ever be allowed entry to the United States.

Helen insisted on an interview, and sat and talked reasonably for one hour to the bland-faced man but still he would not make any commitment and his voice was terse and dismissive when he spoke to her. It was then that she grew angry, standing up, banging the desk.

'My husband flew too many bloody missions. He is in Montana injured. I have a business in the States, pouring money into your Government's coffers. Heine Weber did nothing that was dishonourable and I was cleared by the tribunal. How dare you! How bloody dare you!'

He sat and looked at her, the colour rising in his cheeks. 'I suggest you calm yourself down, lady.'

'I suggest you pull your damn finger out. I didn't sit in a crypt while bombs fell or pull tops off beet to sit here while you shine your backside on that chair. Get on that telephone and sort it out.'

She stormed from the room, out into the March sun, then across to the recreation hut where the Red Cross were teaching seventeen-year-old mothers how to cope with babies they had not been alone with before. For the next three days she talked to the girls, helping them to change and feed, babysitting while they went to the movie house, listening while they talked of the men they had married and of whom they really knew nothing. She bought chocolate for Chris from the PX and he ate too much and was sick.

She didn't sleep because each day her clearance did not come. She hadn't told Chris because he hated the Germans too much already. She talked to the prisoners-of-war, hearing the guttural tongue, listening to the voices of worry and defeat from these draftees who were not Nazis. No news had reached them either from that broken, devastated land.

On Thursday when the sun was hot and long shadows sliced across the grass where Chris was playing baseball, a letter arrived from Ed, forwarded by Laura, and it was good to see his handwriting, to feel him close as she read his words.

February 1946

My dearest Helen,

The winter will be over by the time you get this. Our spring is so quick you would miss it if you blinked. But you will be here for the summer, thank God. It is so hot here, you won't believe it after little England. I had forgotten myself. It's so dry you see. You Britishers are going to have a shock when you finally come. I've been sorting the room and I hope you like it; honey. Maybe next year the new house will be finished.

Say, I've been hearing of this 'flying windmill' that's been developed over here. It's called a helicopter and looks quite something.

Mom tells me we had a bit of rationing Stateside, but I guess it's a tiny pimple, though not to her. She's been a mite short of sugar and you'd think the world had come to an end.

I do miss you so, your laughter, your anger, your Englishness, your soft skin. I'd better get on to something else quick, hey? How about a bit of American news? Did you know that we nearly lost our chewing gum in the war? Would we have won if we had, do you think?

Apparently the Wrigley guy had to put forward a case that chewing gum was essential to win the war if he wanted to continue in production, and he did, saying that it relieved the tension. So he was allowed to get his chicle from South American trees and ship it back on a war effort ticket. So, what do you think of that, Chris?

I just hope and pray you're here soon but you must be so sad at leaving, Helen. I love you for doing it. I need you. You don't know how much. I'm better but there are still bad times.

Ed.

Chris laughed when she read him the letter and so did Helen but inside she was knotted, and a headache never left the left-hand side of her forehead. Would clearance ever come through and were his dreams still bad or was it just his injuries? If so, it didn't matter so much because those would mend.

Helen's clearance came through quite suddenly. The bland-faced man wouldn't look at her as he gave it, just threw the paper on to the desk. She didn't say thank you because she hadn't survived a war to be grateful to people like him.

They boarded the ship in Southampton in the evening of 27 March hearing the gulls wheeling above them and all they could smell was engine oil, not salt. Helen and Chris carried a case each and took bags for the mothers with babies. They inched up the gangplank, seeing the oily water beneath them, setting their feet above the raised slat which was placed just too far to be taken in one stride and Helen did not look back because she was afraid that if she did she would leave the ship.

The chaplain waited on deck shaking each hand, and his smile was warm, his American accent familiar, and suddenly Helen wanted Ed, the slow smile, the arm about her. She wanted him to stand on the rail and help her leave England but there were others behind her and more in front and there was no time to think, only time to put one foot in front of the other, feeling her case dragging at her arm as she followed the other women who also did not look back.

The *Queen Elizabeth* was berthed alongside, large and splendid, casting shade across their smaller liner. A steward took Chris to the men's quarters and Helen followed a smiling Red Cross helper down the companionway into a room with thirty bunks, three high, and all were taken except for two on the top. The room was dense with the sound of nervous laughter, and stilted conversation as she unpacked, smiling at the girls around her, joining in with the ebb and flow of awkward sentences, pausing in the silences until she was shown the showers; semi-private stalls with the toilets further along the passageway. She returned in time to hear the message on the loudspeakers asking all brides to meet on the upper deck where dinner would be provided and informing them that they would sail at seven a.m. the next morning. She felt too old to be called a bride at thirty-three.

Chris was waiting by the door, talking of the steward who knew the knuckleball throw and was going to coach him and another boy, Tom, was going to Arizona. He was only twelve, and may he sit with him? And he was off before Helen could say yes or no. She laughed, looking at a woman who was in her room and whose eyes were red from crying; her blonde hair was swept back in a bun and her fragile face was beautiful.

They walked into the dining-room together, Helen grasped at anything to talk about while the other woman swallowed and fought her tears. She looked up at the painted ceilings evoking memories of past peacetime voyages and spoke of the history of the ship which she had read on the distributed printed sheet. She told Yvonne that when the *Nicholas* was a peacetime liner the passenger capacity was one hundred; when it was a troop ship it carried 2,200 and now it transported 530 brides and children.

Yvonne smiled and queued with her but neither was able to speak when they were handed a plate full of roast pork, mashed potatoes and succotash. They carried it to a table and ate the food too quickly because it was so good and there was so much. Frozen blackberries and cake made with sugar and fat followed. It was a luxury after rationing and their stomachs would only allow them a little. Helen hoped that Chris would remember the chocolate and be cautious. She looked around but he had already gone. Then there was bread and butter, jam, mustard, pickle, strong tea or coffee or cocoa.

Helen looked at the dark brown liquid, thinking of Laura straining the tea again and again and suddenly her tears came and now Yvonne talked to her, telling her that the trip should only take ten days or so an officer had said because the Captain would be following the shortest route. And so it went on all the night in the large room with thirty bunks full of women who doubted and wept but determined that they would go on.

In the morning the women lined the rails to see the ship leave, but Yvonne and Helen could not watch as England faded out of sight. Instead they stood with their faces into the wind, letting their hair whip back from their eyes, at last breathing in the fresh sea air as the ship steamed towards America.

At nine-thirty the brides were invited to a talk in the lounge about the ship and the voyage. They sat in chairs which were bolted to the floor in case of bad weather and here too the ceilings were ornate and there were gaps where chandeliers had once hung. The years of the war had soiled the walls and

Helen thought of the passengers who must have sat over cocktails, listening to music, playing cards, thinking their tomorrows would be the same forever. Where were they now? Were they the parents of the troops who had sailed across throughout the war? Where were those boys?

Seated later in the dining-room, looking through salt-streaked windows which showed a blue and balmy sea, they ate a lunch which Helen had dreamt of during the long years of rationing, and she wanted to be able to send some back to the village. Chris came running up to her afterwards, showing her the ball held between the thumb and first two joints of two fingers, telling her that it would not spin but turn, and that Ed would have to be sharp to hit that and then he was off again, his face red from the sun and the wind, his eyes bright.

Yvonne talked then of her husband who had been injured in the Ardennes offensive and was now at home in the Bronx. He had told her he lived in a mansion and Helen said nothing but later heard an officer telling her friend where the Bronx was. There were no mansions.

They were out into the Channel now and the feel of the sea was different; it moved the ship. Helen walked around the deck, unused to leisure, missing the feel of the ploughed earth beneath her feet, missing the sound of the birds and the snort of Rocket and the pony she and Chris had learned to ride in the past year in preparation for Montana.

She leaned on the rail, rising and falling with the ship, changing her weight from one foot to another, watching the sea running up against the sides and down. The waves chopped and broke, white froth breaking from their peaks. She looked up at the sky, feeling the weak March sun through the breeze, missing Ed, wanting him, wondering if the darkness inside his head was gone.

That evening they watched a film in the lounge after an early supper and then they slept for some of the night but girls were ill, clinging to their bunks though the sea was not rough, calling for their mothers because some were no more than seventeen and eighteen. Helen and Yvonne padded up and down, soothing, talking, bathing foreheads but the girls were still ill the next day. Sick call was extended and they were told to suck lemons. It didn't work, and Helen alternated between the girls and the deck, and Yvonne did too. They soothed the sick and then walked, then sat in deckchairs, talking of the blitz, the rationing, their families, but not yet of the future.

The girls in the bunks had no spare clothes left and so in the afternoon Helen washed and ironed and laughed with Yvonne over the thought that maybe it was better to be seasick. That afternoon the Red Cross gave out long-sleeved sweaters to supplement the meagre clothes that rationing and one suitcase had allowed them all, including the girls who lay on the bunks and who only wanted to die.

Helen wore slacks which Laura had made and pitched balls at Chris and Tom, the twelve-year-old and that night the clocks were put back one hour and they had 2,636 miles to go.

The next day the ship was rolling and the waves were fifteen feet high and no one was allowed on the open decks. The ship stopped for an hour for some repairs and they were told over the loudspeakers that they would be on the water for about twelve days, two more than expected. Helen groaned and so did Yvonne and soon they too were on their bunks wondering why they had ever come as the ship pitched and tossed. The lemons did not work for them either.

The storm eased in the night and the sun shone the next day, bouncing off the water into their eyes. They tap-danced in the lounge that afternoon in a class arranged by the Red Cross and Helen realised she hadn't laughed as she was doing for a very long time. She sang in the shower which was hot every night and a luxury she had forgotten existed and brewed tea for their room because they were allowed to do so now, after a general complaint that it was too long to last from five-thirty p.m. to seven a.m. without a drink. Bedtime was still eight-thirty, however, and surprisingly they slept.

On Sunday there was a church service in the lounge and there was turkey, asparagus and ice-cream for dinner but that afternoon there was another storm and the waves were eighteen feet high and grew worse during the night so that Yvonne was thrown from her bunk and landed on the floor, torn between laughing and crying. The clocks were put back again one hour and they now had 1,636 miles to go.

There was an orientation talk on food and clothing the next day and an emergency fire and lifeboat drill in the afternoon and one girl appeared in her towel straight from the shower and she danced in time to the slow hand clap.

On Monday fresh water was rationed because the journey was taking so long and purified water introduced. It tasted strange and Helen found it difficult to swallow.

They tap-danced again and now it was easier, though their next session and the movie had to be cancelled while the crew bored a hole through the lounge wall so that they could pump oil from one part of the ship to another because they were short of fuel due to the delays. They took the hose through the lounge and momentarily Helen saw the fire hoses again and heard the screams beneath the rubble, smelt the smoke and the darkness of the cellar beneath the shop, the arm into which she plunged the painkiller, the dark cupboard in her mother's house. She wanted Ed and went to her bunk so that she could lie in peace and remember him.

That evening it was announced the ship would travel at half speed to try and eke out the fuel or they would need to put in to Nova Scotia which would delay them even more. As it was, the arrival date was put back another day but there were only another 784 miles remaining. Now the girls were all up and some were visiting the hairdresser, pressing their good suits and dresses as the excitement rose.

Helen and Yvonne performed in a concert the next night, tap-dancing in the back row because they had only had two lessons. Helen did not sing but laughed and listened, eating mince pies after the show.

The next day there were only 523 miles to go and now Yvonne was quieter, twisting her ring and she spoke in a low voice to Helen of the lies Danny must have told, looking out on to the sea which was grey today, reflecting the sky and their mood.

At lunchtime the Red Cross gave out khaki towels for the showers because the women had only been able to pack one in the hand luggage they were allowed. There was a birthday party in the lounge for a bride who was twenty-one. Afterwards Helen sat in a deckchair listening to Chris talking of his friend, his batting action and Mary. She lay her head back and wondered what she would find in Montana, who she would find. Would it be the Ed she knew?

By Saturday there were only 200 miles to go and they were

all given a medical examination and the names of others going to their states. Helen and Chris were the only ones travelling to Montana. Excitement grew even higher on board. Women with babies carried them around the decks, hugging them tightly, talking into their necks, telling them of their daddies their grandmothers. Helen listened and watched as joy, then anxiety, crossed their faces as they hugged their children to them. She found Yvonne crying in her bunk, looking at the photograph of her husband; so young, so handsome, and held her but could offer no words of comfort because what could she say? She felt so old suddenly, and when Yvonne slept she walked the deck herself, calling in on Chris in his berth, staying with him, watching his face, his hands, listening to his laugh She reached across and touched his cheek and he did not draw away but leaned his head against her hand looking at her, and in his eyes too was joy and then anxiety. It was the same in hers.

That night they went to bed, knowing that they were due to pass the Statue of Liberty at six the next morning. The girls whose husbands were meeting them at New York would leave the ship first and Yvonne was quiet and said nothing, not even to Helen.

At twelve-thirty that night it was announced over the loudspeaker that they would be in sight of the Statue of Liberty in half an hour. It woke no one because that night their thoughts were too active to allow sleep. They threw on clothing and rushed up on deck, seeing the lights in the distance, the cars going along the road on Long Island. The Statue of Liberty was floodlit and it seemed strange to Helen to see so much light. The water was calm and oily black in the darkness and all she could feel was the vibration of the ship and her own uncertainty.

At four-thirty names were given out over the loudspeakers of those whose husbands were waiting for them at New York and although everybody had returned to their bunks they were not disturbed because sleep had never been so far away. Those leaving in the morning had red labels given to them and Yvonne looked at hers, turning it again and again in her hand and hardly ate her breakfast. Helen touched her hand but she didn't look up and so she went on to the deck and stood at the rails, watching the tugs coming to tow them in, staying there as they berthed. She could see the Empire State Building immediately ahead and young men waiting behind a cordon, cheering and waving and she wondered which was Danny, with the smiling face and the black heart.

Chris joined her at the rail.

'It's all so big,' he said. 'I hadn't thought it would be so big.'

Helen nodded. 'It's a different world,' she replied, her voice quiet, still looking for Danny, but the faces were too indistinct, too far away. The clothes were a shock; no uniforms, just vivid shirts, warm jackets and trousers.

Only those who were being met in New York were allowed off the ship, the others had to stay until train reservations had been made but a tour of New York was organised for the next day. Helen nodded as Mrs Senton of the Red Cross told them this, but she was looking past her, at Yvonne who was waving to her from the head of the gangplank, her face white.

Helen ran through the other women and held her friend, pressing her address into her hand, telling her to come to her, to write if she needed help, and then she watched her walk down the gangplank, seeing her look over to the men and hesitate, try to turn, but another girl pushed her on. Helen watched as the other girls ran towards the cordon. There was only one woman walking and that was Yvonne and now Helen could see nothing more because her eyes were blurring and it was more than she could bear. And so she turned away, back to Mrs Senton. At least all the brides were entitled to a free return ticket.

It was quiet on board that night and she sat watching the movie flicker in the lounge, hearing the click of the projector and the laughter of the audience, but she was wondering how the Bronx would feel on a hot summer night with a man you had thought was someone else. Would Ed be someone else?

The next day they left the dockside in a coach to see the sights and drove through streets towering with skyscrapers which seemed to block out the light and would trap the heat. They drove round Radio City and wherever they went, Helen felt she had been there before, knowing that it was because of the movies she had watched on the ship.

They stopped outside a diner and she saw a road worker in unbuttoned shirt sitting next to a man in a business suit eating salami on rye, and knew that this mingling would not happen in Britain and it was good to see it. Trucks hooted, whistles were blowing and buildings were being knocked down. There were police sirens, yellow cabs and cars, so many cars in the wide multi-laned streets and through the windows of the bus came the smell of gasoline, cigars, steam and restaurants. Helen leaned her chin on her hand, seeing people running down subways or clambering on to buses, so many people, so many different races and colours. She felt homesick for small streets, short buildings, trees and felt angry that here there were no gaps in the streets like rotten teeth. How could these people she had come to live amongst understand those who had survived? She wiped away her condensed breath from the window. How were Ed's parents understanding him?

When the coach returned to the ship, Claus, dear Claus, was there, flashing his press badge, coming on board, taking photographs, hugging her, hugging Chris who stood stiff because this man was a German.

'So, how are you?' Claus said, looking at Helen. He touched his nose when she asked how he had known, saying that the press had access to all sorts of information.

'A bit older,' she said, wanting to cry because he was from her past and he was here, the first person to meet her in her future land. He knew Heine, he knew her mother, her flat, so much that had made her. But he did not know Ed, or did he?

They talked of him and he had remembered the picture she had drawn in her letters.

'The dreams?' he asked. 'What about the dreams?'

But she didn't know and then he held her hand and told her that this is what must be solved, and she knew from his deep-set eyes that his mind had its darkness too because the shadows were there. His dark face was as thin as always, as handsome as always.

He told her of the business, which was thriving, of his wife, who was having a baby, of his parents, whom he had not heard from, but who he thought had been in Buchenwald. She asked of Herr and Frau Weber but he shook his head.

'There is no news,' he said, and for a moment they were both quiet and she knew that he had not yet solved his own darkness, his own dreams.

Chris moved from them, over to the rail, looking out towards New York.

Claus raised an eyebrow at Helen, his dark hair grey now. 'So like his father.'

Helen shook her head. 'He would deny that, my dear Claus. He doesn't like the Germans.'

Claus nodded, his face sad. 'But one day he will have to face that he is partly of that race.' He eased himself down into a deckchair, beckoning her to do the same. 'One day, my dear, he will have to be made to face it, be proud of it.'

Helen nodded, looking at her son who was so torn again.

'And now, the future for you?' Claus asked, looking through his camera, sizing up an angle.

'Who knows? Getting used to peace, I suppose, getting used to all this.' She watched Claus as he focused.

'Will you stay in Montana or can I persuade you back to photography? We need you. They remember you over here.'

Helen smiled, surprised. 'Really?' She leaned forward, her arms on her knees, seeing the wind lifting Chris's hair, the brides walking past talking quietly. 'It's tempting but Ed's home is in Montana. It's what he needs. At least, I think it's what he needs.'

She held her hands loosely together, enjoying his familiar voice, talking of little things, brushing against the larger ones, reaching out and bringing England close, Germany close, and now the future did not seem so vast. Then he left, called away by the First Officer because his time was up but before he went he left his camera with her, laughing at her face.

'Yes, why not, my dear? You own half the business. Who knows, you might decide to take on a project in those mountains. I could sell your work, you know.' He bent to kiss her. 'It might be something to hang on to, Helen, if the darkness comes between Ed and his life, as it did once with me. Call me, if you ever need me. I loved Heine, he saved my life. You saved my life too.'

He shook hands with Chris, his face solemn.

'You must not deny your roots. You are from good Germans. Remember that.'

Chris turned and ran off along the deck and Helen did not go after him but watched Claus walk down the gangplank waving, waving until she could no longer see him.

The next morning they ate a breakfast that was too large or was it just that none of the women were hungry? Names were called over the loudspeakers, requesting that the following brides report to the Immigration Officer in the lounge and have their landing cards stamped before proceeding to the library for their luggage tags. Chris sat with Helen, waiting, but so far they had only reached the Ds. Neither mentioned Claus and there was a barrier between them; it was slight but it was there and Helen wanted to push it aside but did not know how.

At noon they heard McDonald and joined the queue for Immigration and then for luggage tags. Helen told Chris to fetch his case while she collected hers from her berth. She tied the tags on, knowing that in a moment she would be starting on the final stage of the journey which would take her to Ed. They had also been given identity labels which they had to pin to their coats but Helen refused because she had not come all this way to be labelled. No one insisted when they saw her face.

Together with thirty other brides they were bused through the Holland Tunnel to New Jersey accompanied by two Red Cross personnel and there they boarded a Pullman which was larger than any train in Britain. The station was so large, the train too, and the suitcase was heavy in Chris's hand and cut into his fingers. He thought of the string bag he had taken from London to Greater Mannenham but he pushed that from him, because now he was going to a new life and, therefore, he had no use for his old.

He looked at his mother. Couldn't she understand that all he wanted to do was forget? That he could not bear to be from the same people who had made the village hate the Germans again because they had murdered so many people in camps? He couldn't bear always to be on the outside because of who he was. It was easier just to push it away.

They travelled for forty-eight hours, sleeping in bunks, then sitting for hours, and the rattle of the train drummed through their heads as they lurched through cities and great open spaces. They walked in the corridors, stretching cramped limbs, and Helen wondered how long she could stand it, but there were other brides and so they could still laugh together, and listen to familiar English accents.

When they reached Chicago she and Chris were met by the Red Cross, driven to another station and put on to another train, this time alone. The conductor was told that he must hand Chris and Helen over to relatives or take them on to the next town where the sheriff must take custody of them. They must not be allowed free access to the country in case they became a drain on the economy. Helen listened to the poignant hoot of the train as it drew out of the vast town and she knew now how Heine must have felt, arriving as an alien in a strange land.

They travelled for another twenty-four hours and all the time her head was throbbing in time with the rattle of the train over the sleepers. The last four hours were covered in darkness. Chris and she had talked as the country unfolded, staring at the space, the mountains, the plains, the valleys, the rivers which seemed endless. They had talked of Ed, of the food, of the language, of Mary and Laura, but not of Heine because Helen knew that she must be careful or lose her son.

They drew up at last into Little Fork station which was small, like so many others they had passed through, but Helen could not see Ed as she peered through the window, holding her hand to her face to shield it from the light. The conductor came through, taking them to the door, helping them down on to the platform.

The Red Cross had sent a telegram informing Ed of her arrival. He should be here. She looked, then took Chris's hand and he let her because he was uncertain too. They walked through the booking hall with the conductor, then out on to the yard where cars and trucks were drawn up but he was not there and the sky was so vast, this land was too large and she was frightened of being adrift in it.

She turned back, walking towards the train and Chris but then she heard feet running behind her, his hands turning her, holding her, his breath gasping in his chest.

'You're early, for Christ's sake, you're early, darling.' He was kissing her, holding her and pulling Chris to him, clutching them both and he felt the same. Just the same as Helen leaned into him, so tired, so glad to be with him, so glad that, for a moment, it almost felt as though she were coming home. But only for a moment.

CHAPTER 20

Helen lay in bed that first night, feeling Ed beside her, his arms round her and neither of them slept and they did not speak, just touched and kissed, and as dawn rose she looked out through the window at the leaning jackpines on the ridges which seemed to surround the valley, holding them gently within the mountain range. The journey was at an end.

She stretched, counting the roses which climbed the wall-paper trellis, seeing their colour picked up in the new curtains. The chest of drawers was rough pine, made from the trees she could see from the window. A mirror stood on the top and Ed's hairbrush was there, silver backed; his graduation present. His photographs were on the wall, his face smiling down as a young man without lines, without fear.

She could hear the sound of pans in the kitchen and smell cooking and as Ed looked at her through lids half open she bent to kiss him, wanting to stay within the scent of his skin all day.

'I love you, I love you,' he said, reaching for her and as she sank beneath his kiss she thought of Yvonne and wondered how her mornings were.

She dressed at last, knocking on Chris's door but he was up, and as she ran down the stairs she heard him talking in the kitchen to the woman who had welcomed them to Little Fork last night; the woman who had taken her in her arms and held her close, saying that her son loved her and she did too. Ed's father had kissed her cheek and smiled, then picked up his pipe again and puffed before looking at Chris and saying that he needed a few more vittals inside him and then he'd pretty soon lick the hired hands into shape.

Mom, as she insisted on being called, cooked waffles and passed them thick corn syrup, followed by steak for breakfast and Chris looked at his mother and then ate until it was finished, drinking coffee while Ed laughed.

The black stove threw out heat though the spring morning was not cold, but fresh, the frost and snow all gone as April drew towards its end.

'So,' Ed's mother said, sitting down with them, pouring more coffee, her plump face pink from the heat of the stove, her grey hair caught up in a bun. Ed's eyes were the same as his mother's, Helen thought, looking from one to another and she felt good to be here amongst his people, but so far, it was not her home.

'So, there's no work for you today, Ed, your pop says. You're to look after this little family of yours, and look after them good.' She was shaking her finger at her son who dodged and grinned at Chris.

'We're going into town,' he said, levering himself up from his chair stiffly since his back and his left thigh were still not fully mobile. 'Thought I'd show Helen the place, get a few clothes for them both because there's this hotpot supper at the house behind the drug store on Friday.' He smiled at Helen. 'It's kind of a welcome shower.'

Helen looked up as she stacked the plates. 'A shower?'

'That great kid of mine means a party I guess you'd call it. It's just that a few folks said they'd like to meet "this girl from England" and I thought it would get it all over and done with and then you can get on with your life.' His mother wiped her hands on her apron smiling at Helen. 'That's what you all need, you, Ed and Chris. Just to be allowed to get on with your lives the best you can.' She turned and walked to the sink with the dishes, waving Helen away and calling to Ed.

'Just get your new wife downtown to the store to pick up some books for her to read when she's feeling kind of lonesome for England and then on to Joanie's for some clothes. But before that, maybe you should show her the house.'

Ed put his hands around Helen's waist, pulling her down on to his lap. His laugh was the same and his body too. His lips as he touched her neck were gentle and she smiled at Chris who was lifting his eyes to the ceiling and drumming his fingers on the table.

'Shall we get into town first, Ed?' he said. 'And then, when we get back can you show me the horse you said I could have?

Mum and I have been learning to ride on John's old mare for the last year you know.'

'Is that so? Well, you kept that kind of quiet in your letters, didn't you, Mrs McDonald?'

He laughed and kissed her forehead and Helen remembered the falls she had taken as old Betsy had trotted up and down, up and down, and how she thought the world had taken a tumble when she had been lurched into her first canter.

Ed squeezed Helen and let her rise, holding her hand as they walked to the door, slapping Chris on the shoulder.

'Come on, cowboy.'

They drove down the narrow road which ran alongside the creek edged by muddy banks and interrupted by clumps of willow. Helen looked out either side of the truck towards the mountains. Those to the west had snow on them which, Ed told her, remained throughout the year. Those to the east had been whipped into towers and turrets by the winds which swirled around the range day after day without respite.

'We get our ravens here too,' he told Chris. 'Some real mean storms blow in but towards the end of the summer I guess.'

There was mud on the road and tracks leading to fields where hay was beginning to grow and he looked at Helen as they passed and both were remembering the first time they discovered one another's bodies. Ed told Helen that the roads were always like this in the spring because there was so much snow.

'When it thaws it makes one hell of a mess,' he said. 'And it makes it kind of slippy to drive. Now, you must remember that when I teach you because you'll need to learn out here. It's not like England with buses and trams.'

He drove on, showing them where he had skidded off the road when the first snows had come after he had just learned to drive. He pulled in to show them where his pop said his great-grandfather had first pitched his tent, down on the bank of the creek.

'My great-grandfather settled here because it looked so like his home. He had come from the lowlands of Scotland and ran sheep here because it was all he knew about. He kind of bought up the other homesteads.'

They sat quietly for a moment and Helen thought of these people coming so far and staying to build a farm and a family and felt less alone.

He started the engine again, slipping it into gear, showing her what he was doing and it was not so very different to the old van which John had insisted she drove round with the hay in the hard winter of forty-five.

In the town he drew up and pointed to the railroad shipping pens to the left of the station where they would bring the sheep in the autumn.

'Who was here before the settlers?' Chris asked, peering through the window at the swallows' nests which hung beneath the eaves of the few stores in the street.

Ed drew into the side of the road, checking his mirrors, pulling the steering wheel over before stopping. 'The Crow Indians. They hunted across here in the early days. There was wild turkey, all manner of things then, or so pop says.'

'Where did they go?' Helen asked climbing down from the truck behind Chris, looking up and down the street, wondering if this really was all there was to Little Fork

'Across to the long-grass prairies over the Missouri River,' Ed replied, touching his hat to the two old men who had chairs at the open hotel door. 'Hi, Jack, Tim. This is my wife straight out from England. And her boy, Chris.'

'Hello,' Helen said and smiled. The men nodded and sucked on their pipes, their faces wrinkled and their hands gnarled.

'Couldn't find no nice clean girl over here then, Ed?' Jack said and Helen felt cold and turned, walking on, hearing Chris come up behind and then Ed who took her arm, his lips thin. 'Ignore 'em, honey. They are the only two likely to be sour. Nothing's ever right for them.'

But it had been said and Heine had had to live with that all the time, hadn't he? Even the dress which Ed bought her with a long zip instead of buttons which she had never seen before and the shirt and thick trousers for riding could not brush the words aside. She watched him walk ahead of her into the grocery store, leading her to the books beyond the shelves which were stocked to bursting in a way that Helen had not seen for so long. She longed to see his rolling walk back again but for now it was pushed away by the stiffness of his injuries. Oh God, there was so much that was different, but last night in bed it had been the same. She must hang on to that; and there had been no dreams for him. But then, they had not slept.

That afternoon they saddled up three horses and rode out to

the house which was being repaired for them. It had been built by his grandfather, Ed told them, out of pine logs from the slope above them and had two bedrooms but would be big enough for now though it would not be finished until next spring. They stood and looked but somehow it wasn't her house, though it had windows and a door. There was no roof, just bare rafters which looked pale against the seasoned pine of the old walls. She smiled at Ed.

'It's going to be splendid, isn't it, Chris?'

Chris nodded and then urged his horse on up the rutted track and his hoofs sucked and slurped at the mud.

The horse was gentle beneath Helen and she felt confident while Ed pointed out the cabin hundreds of feet up the slope where the sheep herders based themselves in the summer and where you could hide from the world in the winter. She watched his hands as he pointed, his face which she loved, and she pushed the words of the old man and Heine's pain away because her husband was here and therefore Little Fork must become her home.

The next day she sat in a chair in the lounge looking through the window at the men hurrying from the bunk-house to the lambing sheds. She saw Ed walking stiffly to meet them, his hat sat back on his head as he nodded to his father and sent one of the men into town. He had taken Chris with him, saying that Helen had done too much for too long but she was restless and walked around the room, smoothing the settee covers, flicking open books and then shutting them. The newspapers were there but held no news of England, only of America.

She walked into the kitchen and baked alongside Mrs McDonald who told her how ill Ed had been, how bad the nightmares were until he knew that Helen was coming.

'That's when I knew I loved you, my dear. I feared for him you see. I didn't know what was in his head, why he screamed out like he did. We haven't been in the war, out here. How can we know? But you know. You've been through it.'

Helen put her arm round her shoulder. 'Don't worry, he'll be fine. He's such a good man.' She mixed the flour with the butter, squeezing it through her fingers, wondering how long she could keep the darkness out of Ed's eyes. She rolled out the pastry, shaking flour on to the board, wanting to be busy, but using her body, not just her hands because there was too much time to think about how little she really knew of the horrors, the reasons for the dreams. And how could she help unless she knew?

'I guess you might like to come down and take a look at the creamery, honey,' Mom said.

They went after lunch, a large meal which was served in the kitchen to the men and the family. No one spoke very much as they crammed food into mouths then left, busy, purposeful, and Helen wanted to be with them, but instead walked with Mom down across the red shale track towards the bunkhouse and beyond. There were no flowers, no colour and Helen thought of the daffodils and tulips at Laura's but then she must not think of things that were English.

It was damp in the creamery and her hair hung limp as she asked questions, shouting to be heard above the clatter of the churns and machinery. She saddled up her horse at four and rode out across the edge of the hayfields, missing John and the horses, missing the hoeing, the weeding, the feeding, and so the next morning she rose with Ed, pulling on her riding trousers and shirt and going with him to the lambing sheds because, she told him, she had come to America to be with him, not to get in his mother's way.

He looked at her, then stooped and kissed her hard, calling to Chris to come too and roll his goddamn sleeves up or his mother would beat them both to it.

All day they worked because the lambs were coming thick and fast. In the lambing shed board pens about four feet square stretched row upon row and the bleating and curses of the men mingled with the smell of iodine, manure, wool and alfalfa. Helen's hair hung in her eyes and Ed threw her his bandana to tie up around her head. Chris stayed with her, watching the lambs nuzzle the sheep, pointing out ones which were not suckling, then climbing into the pen with his mother to work the teats to make sure that the milk was flowing before putting the lambs on to suckle.

Again and again Helen did this and the heat in the shed built up until sweat poured down her body but this was work she understood and for the first time since she had left England she felt at ease. Ed called to Chris and showed him how to stamp the ewe and lamb with the same number to show that they belonged to each other.

After a lunch eaten in haste and with little conversation as they had done in the English fields they were out again, though this time Helen went with Ed to the pasture where they had to wrestle the ewes into the jugpen pulled by horses and then take them back to the shed. The sheep fought and Helen tussled them, holding them firm or snaring them by the hind leg with a sheep hook to snake them in backwards.

That night Chris and Ed tallied the numbers. It was mid April and now they had numbered over a thousand head of sheep and his father laughed and winked at Mom.

'I guess we got a good bargain, didn't we, Momma?'

That night Ed made love to Helen and it was not gentle but filled with passion as hers was and later she whispered, 'I need to work alongside you, my love. We have had too many hours taken from us.'

He kissed her and said, 'I love you and hate every second away from you.'

The next day a lamb died and Ed showed Helen and Chris how to skin the dead lamb, snipping four small leg holes and a head hole. Then he took a twin from another ewe, fitting the skin to the lamb.

His hands were smeared with blood and Chris looked away. 'Now you have to present this to that ewe over there. The one whose lamb has died. She'll accept it in a coupla days because she'll recognise the smell as her own.' He nodded at Chris and Helen. 'You got that?'

Helen nodded and Chris too but he was pale. Later Helen found a dead lamb and called Chris to grab one of triplets from a pen higher up. He did and then watched his mother do a job he felt he could not attempt and later that evening he went and put his arms around her and said, 'I love you, Mum.' But what he wanted to say was, I respect you. You are so brave and so strong and I don't know what I would do without you and I wish I could accept my German part but I can't.

On Friday they went in the car to the house behind the drug store taking two casseroles with them to place on the table as Ed's mom said they must. Mrs McDonald introduced Helen to the younger women first and they were kind and friendly and kissed her when the British would just have shaken hands. They also heaped presents on them for the new house.

They talked of Ed as a child, how he had fired arrows at targets and missed, breaking the drugstore window. How he had ridden his horse down the main street on Independence Day, firing his pop's old gun. Helen looked across at him as he talked to a ring of men, throwing his head back and laughing, his arm on Chris's shoulders and she loved him more than ever.

Two of the women talked of working in factories during the war, of leaving home while their men served in the forces. They spoke of how small the town seemed now. Of how they had been hated by the men in the factories and feared by them because of their abilities. They put their hands on Helen's arms.

'I guess it must be the hardest thing in the world, to come over to another country. It was sure bad just moving to a bigger town,' Susie said, her blonde hair swept back in a pony-tail, her blue eyes sympathetic. 'Come see me sometime, anytime.'

Though their heads ached the next day from too much to drink they were up at daybreak as usual because lambs did not stop being born to accommodate a hangover, Helen groaned, as she pulled on her trousers. But now she felt as though she had a friend in the small town and that made her feel safer somehow.

In the evening she wrote to Germany to try and find Frau and Herr Weber and Chris watched her but said nothing. They packed up a parcel of tins to send to Laura and Mary and next year Mary was coming, they decided, even if they had to go and fetch her, because Helen was looking forward now.

In June the mosquitoes were rising from the creek and the sheep had to go through the gate and be counted but Chris was not here during the day now because he had gone into the town along from Little Fork where the High School stood and he talked of pitching and batting, chewing gum as he did so. He handled the work well and liked the kids, he said, and Ed and his father chuckled when Helen told him to take that disgusting stuff out at once.

Chris lay in bed feeling the heat of the summer which he had never before experienced. Life was good but he missed Mary. He had not thought he would quite so much, but there was a difference between these kids and those back home. These ones were fresh and bright-eyed and knew nothing of bombs and death. He was thirteen and he did. He knew its sounds and smells.

He lay with his hands behind his head. Mary had written to say she would come next year, definitely, and Laura too, and he wanted to show her the jackpines, the creek and his horse, Sorrel. He wanted to show how he could lasso a calf, hauling back on the rope. He wanted to show her the calluses on his hands.

Would she like his friends? Roy with the broken tooth because he was a fighter; Ted with his red hair. And what about the coach who said he'd make a great batter one day? He turned over in the bed. Gee, it was hot. He lifted the sheet, waving it up and down.

The coach was German but nobody minded. He should tell them he was too, but he couldn't and he didn't know why. Chris turned over towards the window. He needed to tell. He knew he did but he couldn't because he hated the Germans. He still hated them.

In mid June Helen and Ed drove with Mom and Pop to the High School game because Chris was playing. Helen sat in the stand and watched the girls dancing at the edge of the pitch, heard the school band and ate popcorn which Ed handed to her in a cardboard carton. She wanted to wave to Chris when he ran on to the field and the supporters stood and cheered their team but she did not. She just watched and wondered at how American he had so easily become and how English she still was.

She watched the battle between the pitcher and the batter, heard the screams and cheers as runs were scored and home base was reached. She listened as Ed explained that each team had nine innings and that each team's inning lasted until three men had been put out.

'The visiting team is always the first to bat,' Ed's father told her, roaring as another run was scored then groaning as a batter hit an infield fly.

Helen didn't understand but shouted when Chris hit a homer and scored a run and the rest of the team went wild.

'I showed him how to hit that, Christ almighty. I told him,' Ed said, grabbing her and kissing her and she laughed, feeling free tonight, and happy. She looked along the rows of people watching, seeing their faces, hearing their voices drawling and

American, but not seeming as strange as they had two months ago and she settled back for the rest of the evening. She would write her monthly letter to Claus tomorrow and he would laugh at all this.

On 15 June, while Chris was off on a baseball tour, Helen and Ed went into the timbered slopes to herd sheep for two weeks with a wagon full of groceries, opening fence line gates on the rutted tracks leading up into the mountains, feeling the coolness of shade which could not be found in the valley.

The wagon sat high on the spoked wheels and the leather reins were soft in Helen's hand from years of use. She propped her foot up on the weatherboard and smiled at Ed, feeling the lurch of the wagon over roots and stones, hearing the yap of the herd dogs as they ran round and round the wagon as it moved along, so slowly.

'I'm looking forward to this sheep herding your mom's been talking about.'

He smiled and his mouth was lazy. 'I guess I am too.'

They looked back down into the valley. Smoke rose from the farmhouse chimney and the creek moved sluggishly through dried banks. They could see the shimmer of the heat and Helen relaxed in their shaded cool, bringing out her camera, taking shots of the valley, the mountains, the darkness of the pines.

'It's a bit more like England up here,' she murmured, leaning over and kissing him.

'I guess so, honey. Do you miss it so much?' His hands caught at hers and held them loosely and he watched the horse as it picked its way along the track.

'No, not at all,' Helen said but she did. She still did, though not with the sharp pain of the first days of strangeness. She looked up picking out the sky through the branches. It was a dull ache which never left her. But she loved him so much that it filled every other part of her and it was this that she tried to think of each day.

They stopped beneath sun-splashed pine boughs before the day ended, knowing that the sheep were all around, hearing their bleats and the whine of the dogs. They unhitched their horses from the tailboard and rode out; checking, laughing, listening and just sitting with their hands on the saddle, looking together up at the mountains, breathing in the pure air, hearing nothing of the world beyond the timber and it was a touch of heaven. A soundless time which they each sucked in after the screams of the last few years.

That night they lay together on the soft pine needles and loved beneath a sky filled with the smell of jackpines and clear mountain air, and Helen felt that this was what she had been waiting for all her life and the ache for England would subside with each day that passed for this was her home, here in the cool of the mountains, in the silence of its skies.

She kissed his mouth and told him this; that here they were together and there was no past and no future, just their love and he held her then and told her of the dreams he had when the war still roared and crashed across the world. He told of the blood on his face, on his body, of Joe, and she held him as he told her it was not his guilt for Joe that made him scream but his guilt for those beneath his bombs. He told her of London that day, of the crosses in the rubble and she kissed him and said that war asked strange things of people and that it was all over now. He held her.

'Dear God, I hope so,' he murmured.

They followed the sheep along the range for the next two weeks and Helen grew to love the wagon, its storage bins which doubled as seats, a table which hinged down from the wall. There was a bunk bed which fitted across the end of the wagon but they lay beneath the stars or used a canvas tent which they folded each morning and set up again at a new site every evening.

They sat in the wagon with the Dutch door half open watching the sheep, listening to coyotes and Helen thought of Ed as a child, coming up here with his father, shooting grouse as big as hen turkeys, eating half at night, putting the other half in a jar, dangling it in the stream and having it for breakfast.

He told her of the small cabin which he loved to camp in, the winter he had spent guarding the sheep and just existing and how it had honed him as a man.

They talked of the child they would have when their own house was finished and Helen called it their home and said that maybe they'd have to divide the larger bedroom into two.

She learned to balance a cup of water on the table at each night stop to check that the wagon was level and to dig beneath the wheels if it wasn't, and for those two weeks there was nothing and no one in the world but them, and there were no words left unsaid, no thoughts and fears left unspoken, and Helen prayed that the darkness had left Ed for ever. But sometimes his hands still trembled and tightness gathered round his eyes.

CHAPTER 21

In late June they were back in the valley, joining in the heaving and raking of the late wild hay after Helen had fed the chickens and checked the seed potatoes which she had bought from the store and set behind the unfinished house, digging in the cool of the evening, and after Ed had ridden round the cattle, checking the fences, repairing wire where it had sagged and posts which had loosened.

They set half the bunkhouse on one of the fields and took two other men, sending the others out to the pasture to guard and move the cattle. Helen laughed because Pop wouldn't use 'new fangled machinery' for harvesting when he had good horses and idle men. She tossed loads up to Ed who pulled his hat down hard and worked to keep up. His back and leg were looser now and his stride was almost easy.

The smell of the hay filled the air and midges danced along with the seeds which scattered and blew on the wind, and as Helen drove the wagon through the field she thought of all the young men who had helped in East Anglia and whose parents would never again see the sun on their backs as she was seeing it on Ed's. They worked with the men for two days transporting the hay to stacks which looked like loaves and on the third she dragged the stetson which had been Ed's when he was young well down, grateful for the shade across her face, feeling the heat beating down on to the ground and then rising in waves from the parched earth. The creek was almost dried out and the willows rattled in the slight breeze which gave no relief because it too was dry and hot. The dampness of England seemed a miracle, one which she could almost no longer imagine.

Helen wiped her parched mouth. Ed threw down a leather flask from the wagon where he was stacking the hay, outside first moving inwards as John had shown her.

'Drink this, honey, you'll be losing a heap of moisture.'

She lifted it to her mouth. The water was warm but she needed it. God, how she needed it. She looked across to the other field seeing it fragmented by the blazing heat. She drew up her leather gloves so that they met her cuffs, unbuttoned to allow a draught. Her arms had burnt on the first day and now she kept them covered and her hands too.

The letter from Claus crackled in her pocket. He had sent bulbs for the fall and three rose bushes which he said she must bury deep down beneath the earth for the winter and then dig up for next spring. A little bit of England, he had said, and Ed had promised that he would help. They would plant them round the new house and even if they were still not in by then, at least it was as though their souls were there.

She smiled up at him. His hair had bleached under the searing heat and his moustache too. His skin was burnt dark brown and he was beautiful. They sent the two men back to the range in the afternoon for they were almost through with the field and they wanted to be alone, lifting, heaving, throwing, hearing the breaths they each drew, speaking words which only they should hear. Helen leaned on her rake as Ed stretched back his shoulders, standing above her on the wagon, ankle deep in hay, balancing, then falling, sinking into the green grass and laughing deep down in his body.

It was darker now, though it was only four o'clock and Helen raised her arm, shading her eyes as she looked towards the mountains to the west. Dark clouds were forming, tumbling on top of one another, grey, then black, and she shouted to Ed to look. He did, then stopped, his head lifted. He jumped down, picking up the tools throwing them on top of the load, calling to her to do likewise.

'There's a storm coming.' His voice was tight and his movements quick. 'Get up on the wagon, Helen, let's get this load back.' He took the reins and shook them out and now it was humid, heavy and wet, and just as hot as before.

Helen saw his hands trembling as the thunder rumbled in over the mountains, coming before the rain, before any lightning that they could see.

He shouted at the horse now. 'Get your goddamn butt moving.'

She looked at him and then back at the storm, swirling in,

filling the valley with darkness and noise and now the lightning flashed, tearing jagged through the clouds and the thunder clapped above them, rolling round and round, trapped within the mountain range, and then the rain, heavy and hot. So hot.

The horse was nervous, edgy, side-stepping within the traces. Ed clutched the reins with white-knuckled hands, shouting above the storm.

Helen gripped the sides of the seat, water running off her stetson, crouching as the lightning sliced through the air again and the thunder rolled and banged.

'For Christ's sake,' she heard Ed say as the roan staggered and side-stepped. 'For Christ's sake.'

Helen looked ahead, knowing the farm was along the road, but she could not see through the steam and the rain and the darkness. The noise went on and on and the lightning was like the searchlights seeking and the gunfire probing and the noise was the noise of bombs.

The lightning ripped the skies apart again and Helen gripped Ed's arm, rising as he was doing as he slapped his reins on the horse, shouting at him. She felt the roughness of his shirt, it was full of water. There was water everywhere, in her face, her mouth and in his too.

'For Christ's sake,' he said again tightening the reins as the horse moved faster, balancing as the wagon shifted from side to side.

'Hang on to these,' he shouted, passing them to her, leaping down from the wagon, running to the horse's head, dragging him forward as he side-stepped again and Helen could hardly see him through the torrent and was afraid.

'Don't leave me,' she cried and he looked up at her, his arms pulling at the horse, effort stretched across his face and then the lightning seared again, close, too close, and thunder crashed, cruel and consuming, and she screamed as the horse reared in the traces, striking out at Ed who was knocked to the side. Helen saw the roan's ears flatten as lightning again and again stabbed across the blackness and then he ran; his legs fully stretched, his head wrenching at his bit and she heard Ed's cry.

'Helen. Helen.'

But she could hear nothing but the rain and the thunder and she thought of the raven and the gods and knew that the wagon was tipping, lurching, straightening and rushing forward again. And then it hit the boulder and flew high and sideways. She heard the wood tearing and the thunder and it was as though bombs were coming down and crushing her into the ground and there would be dust and bricks and death and she screamed into the darkness of the cupboard.

She wasn't hurt, she kept telling him. Not hurt, as he pushed the broken wagon from her legs but he was crying and holding her and that night, after they struggled home he went into the bedroom and drank whisky until he passed out and then he screamed all night as the darkness closed in on him because he had nearly killed Helen as he had killed so many others.

As summer turned to fall and the leaves shone orange, red and gold, he saw none of it, only the shadows of his mind and at night he could not scrape off the dried blood which belonged to Joe and the rest of the people he had killed. Helen lay and listened and wept because she could not reach him, could not help him any more. But could the whisky either?

He would not let Helen drive the wagon again and so she rode her horse out across the valley, taking photographs of the trees, the creek, and the men as they cut out the calves from the mothers, and stooped and wrestled in the bright air, their chaps dust covered, their hats sodden with sweat. She used black and white, and created clear true images and sent them off to Claus who sold them, ploughing the money back into the agency for her and sending her the half-yearly statement of accounts. Business was good.

And then Ed slapped her one night with a drink-clumsy hand because he said she was going to leave him here while she ran away to New York. She put her camera away and held him and said she would never go. Never ever go. But it did not stop her from viewing her world with a photographer's eye because, when all this was past, she would work again.

She told Chris that Ed was not well but he knew that already. He had heard the words which tracked from Helen to Ed's parents as evening followed evening and seen the strength which had been Ed become sodden and fumbling. But sometimes Ed laughed for a moment like he used to, and Chris would sit with him then because he loved him and he had saved him from the bullies all that time ago.

But as October became November there were no more

smiles, just shouts. No kindness, just tension and he knew that somehow the war was not going to leave Ed again as it had done, briefly, for the summer. Each night he would listen for the stumbling feet on the stairs and grieve for the man who had pitched at him and his hate for the Germans was fuelled.

Mr McDonald sold a hundred head of cattle in the first week of November, and Helen worked with him and the men, driving them to the shipping pastures where they milled and worried until the train came in, and then she and the hands pushed the shoulders of their horses at the cattle, moving them forward, feeling their heat, breathing in their dust until finally they were on board. Ed did not come. She did not look at Wilton's Bar as they passed and neither did Pop but all the way back they talked about the man she loved. But their words did no good. Pop's son, her husband, did not want a clear mind.

At the ranch she manhandled the sheep up the chutes into the trucks, gripping their fleeces; her fingers thick with their oil, not feeling the chill of the autumn until she stood back and watched the truck leave. She drove the pick-up into town, following on, Mr McDonald at her side guiding her with the gear shift, praising her until they reached the railroad shipping pens, and she wondered if her husband would ever be sixty with hands as calm and eyes as clear as this dear old man's for he was becoming the father she had hoped for.

Again she wrangled the sheep up into the boxcars when the train came in, cursing as the men did, but not loudly, coughing too and falling, grazing her arm but rising and smiling, bearing Ed's share of the family labour. The days passed, busy, empty, because Ed was not with her but a million years away, fighting the war again, drinking until he could no longer stand and somehow she must stop it, but did not know how.

Mr McDonald told her as the chill wind blew across the valley that soon she must take her driving test and she nodded but said to Ed the next morning as he lay in bed, his breath sour and his skin too, that she must dig a trench for the roses before the winter froze the ground.

'You promised to help, my darling,' she said.

He looked at her with eyes grown dull and dark, then turned away and so she bent and kissed his head, his cheek, and thought of his hands which never stroked her now.

'It will pass,' she whispered. 'This is just a fragment of time.'

She rode her mare to the house which would one day be theirs and dug the trench, wrapping the rose roots in sacking, covering the plants with layers of newspaper and earth. She then sliced the spade into the ground around the house, digging once, twice. Counting as she struck stones, rocks and thick clay but never stopping until the sun was low and the beds were finished.

She looked up as Chris rode along the track towards her, halting, his arms folded on the saddle horn.

'Why, Mum?' he said pointing to the ground.

Helen looked up at him, seeing the man he was becoming, hearing the voice beginning to crack and deepen.

'Because it's going to be our home and I'm staking my claim.' She straightened her shoulders, passing the spade up to her son. I'm staking my claim to my husband's life, she thought, staring up into the sky, seeing ravens where there were none. The gods are not going to get him, somehow I shall make sure of that, but she couldn't speak the words because if she did, the pain would flow from her in a torrent which would drown them all.

On 1 December Chris was fourteen and Mr McDonald drove him and his friends to a movie in Rider's Halt, the first big town, and she sat and joked beside him, listening to Ed's father laugh with his son's laugh.

They ate hamburgers thick with a relish which could still not wipe out the memory of the English sauces and the boys were happy and whistled 'Little Brown Jug' all the way home.

Helen and Mr McDonald checked the sheep in the lower pastures in the early evening and Pop said that there would be snow that night, he could smell it on the air, and Helen remembered all that Ed had said of the Montana winters and pulled her padded jacket closer around her body.

When they returned to the house Mom sat by the stove, her face worn into deeper lines.

'Ed took Chris into town,' she said. 'Because it's his birthday.'

Helen stood with her hand on the door, listening to the wind rising, seeing the first big flakes come down beyond the window, thickening until there was almost no darkness between them. He couldn't have taken her son there, Heine's son there? Surely not. But he had. For God's sake, he had. She made herself smile at Mom and Pop who did not smile back, their shoulders tense as they sat, legs crossed before the stove. There was only the crackle of burning wood, the wailing of the wind to fill each minute until the clock on the shelf struck eleven and then she could bear it no longer.

She took the truck, driving in along a whitened road which was indistinguishable from the meadows, the headlights probing the falling snow. There was nothing to hear but the straining of the wipers, silting up with snow and then free again. The only thing which indicated her path was the fence, snowed up four inches and it was like the German winter with the trees and shrubs foreshortened and she felt Heine with her again. She drove into the skids as Pop had said she must, not afraid though he had been, as he watched her from the door, wanting to come. But this was her job.

Ed's pick-up was there, slewed in at an angle to the sidewalk as she had known that it would be. She drew up her hood, stepping out into cold which dug long-fingered into her lungs. She shouldered her way up the steps, across the sidewalk where snow had drifted against the walls and in through the wooden slatted swing doors like some mockery of an old western.

Cigarette smoke was thick and heavy in the room and the colours of the juke box which played 'Chattanooga Choo Choo' spun across the ceiling: blue, red, green. Blue, red, green. She walked into the room and the men stopped talking. Chris was there sitting on a stool at the mahogany bar. She watched herself in the mirror which stretched behind the bar, walking so slowly towards the man she loved whose face sagged in the dim light and her son who held a glass of Scotch to his mouth. She looked old.

She saw the labels on the bottles of whisky ranged in front of the looking-glass and the glasses which rested mouth down on the shelf.

She looked at the nuts in neat packets and the naked woman on the calendar which hung from a rusty nail. She watched the barman pulling the spigot, steadily, carefully, and now she had reached them and took the glass from her son's hand, took it away from his mouth. The saxophones were playing in perfect time as she put her sodden son's arms around her neck and heaved him from the stool. He was coming home.

She saw her husband turn now and look at her, his eyes narrowed, his glass to his mouth. She passed by, saying nothing, dragging her son back out to the truck, pushing him in, propping him in the corner. She used the clutch with the gearshift, crouching behind the wheel, hearing the wipers, seeing the snow which had stopped falling but now drifted in waves like the sea and ripples like the shore. She drove back carefully, saying nothing to Mom and Pop as she dragged her son to his room, lying him on his stomach.

In the lounge their faces were grey with shock and shame but Helen came up to Mom and hugged her. 'Don't worry, it will be all right. Now go to bed and don't get up, whatever you hear.' Remembering that she had once said this before, long ago.

They did go, and alone, in front of a stove that she replenished with logs every hour, she waited. He came home at two in the morning and stood in the doorway, bourbon spilt down his shirt, his eyes sunken, his lips loose.

'You are coming to the mountains with me tomorrow,' Helen said, full of love for him, wanting to take him in her arms because he was in so much pain, but she did not. She kept a hardness in her voice, a command.

'For goddamn why?' he said, still slumping against the doorframe.

'Because I say so,' Helen replied, not standing, just sitting up straight, her hands on her knees. 'Now go to bed.'

He didn't move to the stairs but walked towards her, standing in front of her. 'Don't you go giving me orders, you little bitch. You little English bitch. We came and saved your little two-bit country.' He was shouting and the smell of alcohol reached her. 'We came and saved you and now you take your boy away and he was only having a drink, a little friendly drink.'

'I know you came and saved us. But you've lost something of yourself and I won't let you go on without finding it. We are going to the mountains.' Her voice was level and she never took her eyes from his face even when he reached down for her, gripping her arm, pulling her up to him. She felt his spittle as he shouted.

'I don't need you.' He shook her then and her head rocked back. He slapped her and her lip cracked.

Again she said, 'We are going to the mountains, to the cabin where you once found peace, because I love you more than life itself.' Her voice was still level. 'And I don't care how many times you say no, you are coming with me. I won't leave you to fight this alone.'

She tasted the blood from her lip, felt it run from the corner of her mouth, felt the pain.

Ed stumbled back, looking at the red on her chin and reached out his hand. He touched it, then started to wipe it on his shirt, again and again and again, and now he was crying and Helen held him, rocking him as though he were a child. Listening as he choked out words, sentences, curses. She pulled him down on to the settee, feeling his tears, until at last he slept. She stayed with him, sitting before the stove, listening as he dreamt and mumbled and groaned but tonight he did not scream and she dared to hope that the cold hardship of the winter would bring release.

At seven they left, Helen and Pop harnessing the workhorses to the hay-sled, working the stiff webs of leather across each wide back, fastening the ice-cold buckles with numb fingers before passing the reins to Ed who sat bowed and limp on the driving seat. They drove off into the white shadowless snow, heading up for the homestead which was hidden behind the frozen jackpines.

She had left him at five to stock up the stores, to wake Chris and explain and ask him to come, if he wanted to. He was pale. His head ached, his mouth was sour, and anyway, he said, he did not want to come because Ed must get better. Besides, he had things to do. She had kissed him, holding him, telling him she loved him and that it would only be for three months and she could come back at any time, or he could come to her. That there were no bombs keeping them apart, no bullies hurting him. He had smiled and so had she, but the guilt at leaving him was great because he too needed to be freed from the hate which he carried like a torch.

She had taken pen and paper and written once more to Germany before she left.

Chris took the schoolbus the next day, carrying his lunch in his bag, lugging it over his shoulder, his earflaps down, his hat low. It was cold and the air was sharp in his chest and on the bus he waved to his buddies but did not talk because he had something to do.

All morning he listened in class, answering questions, chewing gum until the sugar was gone, then he unwrapped another strip and chewed again. At lunchbreak he ate in the dining-hall, eating peanut butter and jam sandwiches and cakes.

'Which you guys call biscuits. Crazy Americans,' he said to his friends and then threw the ball in the sports hall but he didn't talk to the coach; not yet.

At recess he listened to the talk all around; the ball game scores, the high school prom, but he was thinking of his mother and Ed. Her face had been swollen this morning when they left and he had heard the shouting last night, though his head was swimming from the bourbon.

How far had they gone? Up beyond the timber line? Why should they have to go? It wasn't fair. Ed had fought his war but it wouldn't leave him. He knew that now because Ed had cried last night after he had shaken his mother. He had wept and said, I can't wipe it out. I can't forget the missions, the blood. It's all over my body, my face and I can't wipe it off. And now I have yours.

Chris sucked on his straw. His Coke was almost finished. He put it to one side and walked down corridors lined with lockers to the sports hall. His coach was there, bouncing a football, up and down, up and down. Chris walked up to him. He wasn't a very big man really, he thought, as he hit him where his abdomen was soft and unprepared. It was the same punch that Ed had shown him when the war was raging and the gang was taunting. He hit him again and chopped his legs from under him.

The coach lay on the floor and Chris turned and walked away, but before he did so he said, 'You're a German bastard. You people killed my real dad and now you're trying to kill Ed.'

He spent the afternoon in the Head Teacher's office waiting until old Mr McDonald came. He didn't mind. He sat on the chair thinking of the air raid sirens, his father's face when he had kissed him goodbye. The letter from Willi. He thought of Mary and Laura and it all seemed so long ago and far away. His head hurt and he missed his mother and somehow life had gone wrong again.

He sat nursing his sore hand as Mr McDonald explained to the Head Teacher about Heine and Ed. Chris looked at the picture on the wall. It was of the school's winning ball game last season. He would never play for the team now but he'd had to do it, whatever they said or did, he could have done nothing else.

The snow was falling again outside the window, great thick flakes as the talk flowed to and fro between the old man and the younger one and Chris felt older than fourteen. How far had his mother got, he wondered. Were they there yet?

The Head was talking to him now, his voice dry and angry, his fingers picking up and putting down a wooden rule.

'Well, Chris. I guess that you've been through some things in England that we must make allowances for. I shall delay all action until your mom returns and then we shall decide what to do with you. You have until the spring to settle in again. No one knows about this but you and the coach. It shall remain this way. You may not practise for the team. You will take sport under another teacher. So. We shall wait until the spring.'

Chris nodded. It didn't matter, it wasn't as though bombs were falling, as though anyone was getting killed. He looked out of the window again. Would his mum save this dad? Would she save him from the Germans? He knew he had to wait for the coming of the spring.

He looked out of the window again. How far had they got?

CHAPTER 22

Helen slapped the reins against the horse's back with numbed hands. She sat next to Ed on the planks which Pop had lashed on to the front pair of sled runners and there were blankets heaped beneath and around them. She pulled her hat, tugging it down and her collar up. There was more snow now but at last she could see the cabin in the distance, though all she could hear was the sliding of the tracks, clean and clinical, and the jangle of harness.

Ed sat with his head down on his chest saying nothing. They had travelled all morning with the dog leaping in and out of the deeper drifts, then jumping up on to the seat, its hot breath on Helen's face. The provision boxes were heaped with snow, their weathered rawhide a stark contrast where they speared through settled flakes at the corners. They didn't stop to eat but swished along behind the horse which heaved and leaned against the harness, pulling steadily uphill towards the pines which were laden with frosted snow. There had not been one word between them.

It was three in the afternoon before they reached the cabin, its varnished logs coated with blown snow on the east side, its roof hung with icicles as they would hang on the roofs in Hanover – if there were any roofs left. Helen dug her chin deeper into her coat as she tied the reins around the brake. Would Frau Weber receive her latest letter?

She pushed aside the blankets. The temperatures were lower than any she had imagined. The blanket was encrusted with iced snow and it cracked and fell in large clumps on to the sled.

'Come on, my love,' Helen said, touching his arm. 'Let's get the things inside.'

She moved towards the unlocked door, opening it, hearing the creak of the hinges. It was dark inside but not as cold and the wind could not pierce her body as it had been doing. The stove was where Pop had said it would be, the logs too and coal and kerosene. She pulled her mitts with her teeth, shaking the snow to the wooden floor, letting them fall at her feet. She turned and kicked the snow from her boots on to the step and then walked, hearing each step, and then there were his behind her. She did not look but opened the black stove door, soaking the coal with kerosene, throwing in a lighted match, hearing the burst of flame through the closed iron door.

She turned and watched as Ed put the rawhide boxes down and went out into the cold for more. Still they had not spoken. She picked up logs and threw them into the stove, lifting the metal jug from the first of the boxes, walking back out into the cold, heaping snow into its mouth with her bare hands and then she felt his around her waist.

'Let me, honey. And get those mitts back on. I don't want you to lose your fingers.' He didn't look into her face, just crouched where she had been and rammed in more snow.

He carried the jug on to the stove and she heard the hiss as the snow which clung to the base melted and was then heated into steam. She fought her way back out to the sled through the wind, bringing back the saws and wedging them in the corner. One fell and the noise was loud, though the wind was wailing as he left again to rub down and stable the horse. The dog was in front of the stove and its smell rose dankly from its coat.

The sky was darkening now, sucking the daylight from the room. She lit the kerosene lamp and put it near the window. Its yellow glow would reach the valley and Pop and Mom would sigh and so would Chris. She moved heaped dry blankets from one of the boxes on to the bed, and sheets too because for the next three months they would live and eat and sleep in here.

He came in then, his moustache ice-encrusted, his hat thick and white. He knocked it against the doorpost, kicking his boots off and then coming to her, taking her hands in his, breathing on them, rubbing until the feeling burned in her fingers and in her heart because he had touched her. After so long he had touched her.

That night they lay together though passion did not rise. He dreamt and cried and called but there was no bourbon and so he did not breathe sourness into her face.

As dawn settled into the day they used a pick to cleave an

earth closet behind the cabin and ate oatmeal cooked on the stove. His hands were shaking and his face was pale but they took the saws and the sled and worked on the pines one hundred yards beyond the cabin. They chose one that was long and straight and nicked one side of the trunk, then sawed the other, one on either end, pulling and pushing, hearing the teeth driving and tearing, feeling the snow drop around them and on them from the tree's branches. When the saw stuck they eased in a wedge. Her breath was cold in her chest and her back ached and so did his, but they didn't speak, just worked.

The tree fell where he had intended it should and then they lopped the branches; neatly, efficiently, while the dog ran around, yapping and barking and chasing his tail. Helen laughed but Ed did not.

He tramped back to the cabin and she could see his breath billowing in great gasps as he brought the chains and the ropes. Together they pushed the chains through the packed snow beneath the tree, wetting their sleeves but not noticing. Round and round they wound it and now Helen went back for the horse, into the warmth of the dark stable, harnessing her, easing her out into the dazzling white silence of the day, hearing the crunch of the snow packing beneath her hoof. She steadied her up as Ed hitched the rope to the harness and then they led her as she dragged the tree to the skidway, plodding down the slope, leaving great sliced marks in their wake. Down they inched to the flatness of the ledge and the saw bench where they released the tree, slipping off the chains, sawing it into sections, heaving them on to the bench, then sawing again. One two, one two, one two, while the horse waited for the hour it took and the sawdust mounted, the logs too.

Then back up to the stable and another tree and so each day they worked and the logs grew and Helen slept with the smell of pine in her clothes and her skin and her hair and it was the same smell as the pines in Heine's forest so long ago.

Each day too they checked the bawling cattle which drifted on the lower slopes amongst a whirling mass of whiteness, searching for buried sage. As mornings turned to afternoons they carted hay from the barn behind the cabin, carrying it between them to the hay sled, tossing it with pitchforks towards the cattle before returning to the saw which became hot to the touch as they pulled backwards and forwards.

*

Christmas came and went but they did not stop and each night Helen looked down into the valley, seeing the lights where Chris slept and woke and played, and missed her son and longed for him, but Ed would have been lost if they had not come. She could not have allowed that to happen as it had happened to Heine. And so she worked and watched and hoped, but the days went by and the dreams continued and no contact was made between this man and herself.

In January the sun was bright on the last day of the first week and they tossed out to the cattle hay which they had harvested in the valley, in the long hot summer and Helen talked as she always did; this time of the harvest in East Anglia. He looked at her and she saw him smile and he replied in a voice ragged and unused.

'I love this kind of a day,' he said. 'Nothing bad can ever happen when there's this feeling in the air.'

He told her then of the winter when the cattle had eaten the willows by the creek and died of starvation, lying in dark heaps, like mole-hills on an English lawn and she hardly dared to breathe as, slowly, he came alive.

'We brought in hay and saved them but it damn near broke us,' he said, wiping the breath which had frozen to ice on his scarf.

That night he did not dream but held her and in the morning he touched her face and kissed her.

As they worked that day he told her of the square dances they had held in the town with his pop calling, 'Now swing your corners, twirl your partners and mosey on down.' And then his mom had dished up the punch.

'They were good days,' he said. 'Good clean days.'

The next week, as they slid a long tree down the slope he slipped and gashed his knee and the blood was vivid against the snow. The cut was deep and clean, Helen saw, as she cut the trouser from his leg in the warmth of the cabin.

'In the Fortress the blood froze before it spouted,' he said, as he sat on the chair and looked into the open stove. 'Except in the cockpit where it was warm, and then it flowed like Joe's all over him, all over me.'

Helen laid the scissors quietly on the table, taking the cotton wool, bathing the cut gently, listening as he told her again of the blood and of the guilt.

'The bloody, bloody guilt and the cross stuck so goddamn crooked in the rubble,' he said, looking at her as she took his hand. 'Help me, Helen. I'm going kind of mad. I can't get it out of my head.'

She came to him, holding his head against her breast. 'I'm here. I'm always here. You did the job you had to do. What else could you have done?' She was stroking his hair, wiping the tears from his cheeks, feeling them soaking through her blouse. And then he pulled away, jerking his finger at the lint on the table.

'Come on then, Helen. For Christ's sake, we've got work to do.'

He wouldn't look at her again, wouldn't listen to her voice and so she knelt and dressed his knee, sewing up his trousers again, knowing he would go out again into the cold because his face had closed. He would not talk any more of the darkness today, but perhaps tomorrow? Oh God, she hoped it would be tomorrow and that the darkness would escape for good.

It did not. Instead he talked of the tadpoles he had scooped into his hands in the pools of the creek when he was barely six and the summers were long and hot. The water had run through his fingers and dripped back into the pool and it had been so cool and so clear.

He talked of the igloo he and Pop had built, hacking out February snow which had frozen so hard it was ice. How white and cold it had been to build but so warm inside, and silent.

All day they sawed but then the dog barked and called and they found a cow by the barn toiling with a breech birth. They moved her into the barn. Ed heaved and pulled until the calf slipped into the straw, slippery but warm and alive and then he turned to her, his face gleaming with sweat.

'I would like a child, Helen, a daughter that looks like you.'

She stood still as the cow nuzzled the calf and Ed rubbed it with straw, and they shared the cry of the newly born.

He came to her then and they walked back to the cabin, to the bed, and he held her but did not love her, not then, but that night he held her and stroked her.

'I love you, I love you,' he said, his mouth finding hers and every touch of his body against hers was tender and all that night he loved her and then he talked of the raids, the bombs, the people, and again the next night and the next. Each day the lines grew less and the trembling left his hands and Helen knew the taste of happiness again.

In February the cold was at its most intense, deep and bitter, and now they sat before the stove, talking and listening, and she told him of the cupboard and her own fears, her own guilts. He told her of his first loves, his first kisses. They checked the cattle in short bursts, pinching their own cheeks to make sure that there was no frost-bite. She drank coffee, her hands around the tin mug as he took the hay sled to the cattle by the lower pasture, hearing the wind whipping round the cabin. It grew worse as the day got older and then she blocked out the draughts with old sheets, newspaper, anything, and the smell of beet came back to her; over the miles, over the years.

He came back as the afternoon ended and she rubbed his hands and feet, listening as he told her of the horses he had broken, how he had worked them gently until they understood, how he had been tossed and hurt but had come back again, gripping with his knees, never shouting, never hitting, as his father had shown him. She learned of the hill horses who were not mongrel mustangs but pastured and forgotten ranch horses who had grown stronger from their wildness. And these were his first love. They looked gentle and kind but were too proud for a saddle, too proud for a man.

'Until they understood that you weren't about to own them, just use their greatness,' he said, his face ruddy from the stove, his voice gentle as it should always be. Each night they lay in bed, loose limbed and free from the shadows.

'For now, free from the shadows,' Helen whispered against his skin while he slept. But would it last? She looked round the one-roomed cabin in the yellow warmth of the kerosene lamp, smelling its scent, hearing the breathing of the dog. Snow had built up at the windows and the wind was blowing drifts whichever way they looked but in here was warmth and love. For now there was love which reached out and held them both. She looked at the rawhide boxes which held two more weeks' provisions.

It was the next week that the calf drowned, down by the great pine where in the summer the mountain stream turned and followed the boulder path. They were laughing, holding the horse by its harness as the sky rose, clear blue above them when they heard its mother's bellows across by the stream.

They ran then, across the skidway's packed solid snow, slipping, falling, rising, then plunging through the drifts up to their knees and out again until they reached the snow path the calf had taken.

He was gone when they reached the broken ice, and there was just jagged blackness scythed out of the frosted ice where he had jumped and broken, then died. They followed the stream down but never found him and Ed remembered that he had left the barn door open. There was no laughter again, no loving, just the dreams and the calling of the cow, night after night after night as he slipped relentlessly from her grasp.

On the first of March they came back down through the forest because there was no point in staying any longer. She steered the horse through the lower pastures, seeing the road from the ranch to the town stretching away like a dirty ribbon. It had been cleared by ploughs and the snow heaped like swollen waves on either side.

She drew up the horse before they reached the ranch, holding his hand and kissing it where the mitt ended and his sleeve began, smelling his skin.

'I love you,' she said. 'But I am not enough. You need something else. You need absolution and I don't know how I can give it to you.'

He kissed her lips and looked towards the house where his parents waited. He loved her so much but she was right and he despaired, because how could anyone here give him that?

Chris hugged his mother and then Ed, knowing his new father was not better. He could tell it from the tension in their bodies, their faces which were drawn and tired. He stood as they pulled off their clothes and hung them in the laundry. He stood as they sat and drank coffee and talked of the cattle, the calf, the logs but not of themselves. He stood as Mrs McDonald told Ed and Helen of Chris and the coach and in his mother's face he saw despair and anguish.

She took him into the lounge, holding his hand, listening as he told her that he had to do it, and he couldn't understand why she ran to her bedroom and wept until the next morning;

not eating, not speaking, but howling as a dog would do when there was nothing but horror all around. She didn't see the rose wallpaper, the new curtains. She didn't think of the bulbs she had planted, the rose bushes she had buried because the darkness of the cupboard was in her and outside her.

It was then that Chris took her up the letter which had come in February. It was from Germany, from his father's father and he read it to her, loudly above her tears, shouting it into her face.

Hanover
December 1946

My dearest Helen,
It is with such relief that we receive your letter and forgive my language. I do not use English since you left but now I must begin again to practise and I shall.

We have not received others of your letters and thought that war had taken you also, as well as Heine.

Yes, we survive. Oma is thin but lives. That is all we can do, is it not? There is hunger here and nothing, not even a bird sings but we deserve nothing more.

It is glad news that you have another man you love. Perhaps it is a time for new beginnings.

I cannot ask you to come to see us because our shame is too great, such terrible things have been discovered. Did we know? No, but perhaps we guessed and did not wish to know? But I wish you peace, my dear. Peace for you and your husband and your child.

With loving thoughts from your father.
Wilhelm Weber

Helen stayed in her room all day, holding the letter, listening to the sounds of the farm, seeing the sun reflected off the snow lightening the room, and then she rose, sitting on the bed, feeling old now, hearing again the news of her son and his hatred, his confusion. She grieved for his lost youth. She heard again the screams of her husband and the years which had gone from his life and which perhaps would never be regained and then she read the letter again.

CHAPTER 23

Helen drove into town that sunless day, down the sanded and salted road, between high drifts where no shadows carved and cut. She rang Claus from the old hotel lobby, talking in a low voice, listening as he agreed. She drove back then and into the yard, through the kitchen, past Ed and Chris who looked at her, but she did not stop.

She walked up the stairs, going into Chris's room, throwing open his cupboard, heaping clothes on to the bed, hauling out the case they had brought with them from England, because Chris was going home. She folded the clothes, knowing that now her son and husband were at the door, watching, but still she said nothing. She put in his baseball mitt, his ball and then looked at Chris.

'Do the case up.' It was an order but she did not wait to see him force it down and click the locks. She marched instead to her own room and took Ed's clothes and hers, folding them, pushing them into her case and his, then she looked at him as he stood silent in the doorway.

'Do the cases up.' It too was an order and again she did not wait to see him zip his own and lock hers but went down into the kitchen, sorting through cupboards as Mom watched, bringing out elastic which she knew would be needed where they were going. She put toothpaste, soap, cotton, needles, cigarettes, cans of ham, sugar, coffee and flour into a rucksack which she pulled out from the drawer in the laundry room. She told Mom and Pop where they were going then and they nodded, for what else could help?

Helen showered then, raising her face to the jetting water, letting it drench her hair and her skin, letting it take her breath and her thoughts away, just for those few moments. She felt it sting her skin and ease heat into her body. The towel was rough and the mountains clean and snow-laden as she rubbed the condensation from the window with her hand, her tiredness gone now because she knew now where they were all going.

She told them that it was to Germany that they were travelling as they stood on the platform, stepping backwards as the Pullman roared in, so loud and large. She and Claus had arranged that her share of this year's profits from the agency would pay, but she didn't tell them and no one asked. She took Chris's arm as he spun round away from her, from the train.

'You will come because you need to, and I insist.' That was all, and her voice was hard and angry, but there was love in it too. She looked at Ed and there was shock in his face.

'You will come because I can think of no other way of clawing back your life and if you don't then I will go alone and never return.'

They both boarded the train with her, heaving up the cases, then sitting, watching the white valleys and mountains merge into night. They slept and woke and ate and slept again but did not speak. The train rattled and jerked and Helen felt Ed's arm against hers but it was stiff and afraid. Chris watched America, not her. He read comics which they bought from the stations they halted at, flicking the pages, his head down. Helen did not try to reach him. She could wait.

They reached Chicago and changed trains and travelled again and slept again until New York loomed, cutting out the light, its tall skyline one of the few left in the world which was untouched by the war.

They caught a cab to the docks where Claus met them in the shadow of the liner. He held her and his body was warm, and she wanted to lean into him, rest on him, but she could not. There was no time. Until they had been home, there was no time.

'So, my dear Helen. You have heard at last.' His smile was kind and his face no thinner than it had been last year.

She nodded. 'And you?'

He shook his head. 'There is nothing. I never will, I think. But you, at least you have heard.' His eyes were deep with distress but there was a certain acceptance. 'It comes in the end, a sort of acceptance,' he said. 'It has to.'

He looked at Ed and Chris. Chris looked away but Ed put out his hand.

'I'm grateful,' he said. 'It's good of you to do this for us.' His hand trembled and there was stiffness in his every movement.

Claus smiled and shrugged. 'My friend, it is so little. You did so much for us. Do not forget that as you travel back.' He turned now to Helen. 'I have the press pass. You have your camera? Good. Present it if you need to bypass the occupying regularities.'

Helen took the pass, stepping to one side as a passenger pushed past them up the gangplank. There was movement all around and the noise of traffic and ships and tugs. Their liner hooted, long and low, and she looked at the ship and then back at Claus.

'I will try to find out what I can, my dear friend,' she said, holding his arm and kissing his cheek. 'Really I will.' A steward was beckoning to them, his face red as he gestured from the deck.

'*Auf wiedersehen*, my friends,' Claus called as they started up the gangplank and Helen turned, her eyes meeting his, both wondering what she would find in the Germany they had once known.

The voyage to Liverpool lasted ten days and the weather was rough. They lay in their bunks for the first three days and then walked the decks and still Chris would not speak, though Ed held her arm and they breathed in the air together, feeling the cold on their skins; the wind whipping their salt heavy hair. As the days went by she felt him loosen and his walk became his roll. He bought more cigarettes to take as currency but smoked some too. They sat in deckchairs and talked a little and his hands grew still as his face took on the look of someone who could not turn back now. His cigarette glowed in the wind and the smoke was brushed away before it became visible, and its smell with it. He did not drink. But he did dream.

They docked in Liverpool and drove by taxi to the airport through drizzle-drenched streets, passing women in head-scarves and streets gouged by bombs, the ruins laced with rosebay. There were queues outside shops and now Chris turned to her.

'Remember what they did,' he said. 'And you are making me go back.' His face was set and his lips were thin.

'I am making you go home,' Helen said. 'Because you have to face yourself, you and Ed have to face yourselves.' She reached for her son's hand and held it, though he tried to pull away.

'Listen to your mom,' Ed said. 'She loves you. Listen to her. She's right. We've got to face it.'

But Chris would not listen and so Helen looked from him out to her homeland, its smallness, its hardship. It looked broken, like Ed, but it wasn't, she knew England better than that. But what about Ed? Was he broken?

She sat back, feeling the streets and rubble pressing in on her as they followed behind small cars driving on the left-hand side. She had forgotten how comforting such closeness was, how England clustered, keeping the great vast spaces out of view. She loved it, but she loved Ed too.

She reached for his hand and he squeezed hers and smiled but there was a distance between them which would always remain until he had come to terms with the past. Would Germany do that for him? Would there be absolution?

'Anyway, I want to see Laura and Mary,' Chris said, looking out at a park with no railings, his breath misting the window. The drizzle had turned to rain and it jerked down the window as the taxi rattled along the pot-holed road.

'We shall see them, on the way back,' Helen replied, looking at her watch. Claus had arranged for a flight at four and it was now two o'clock. She looked up into the grey sky. We shall also visit Heine's grave, she said to herself. This was something they must both do at last.

The arrived at the airport at three-thirty and as Helen strapped herself into the small Dakota she looked at Ed who was at the front talking to the Captain. He was investigating the controls, sitting in the pilot's seat, getting the feel again, and she saw life in his face, in his hands which moved quickly, competently and knew that she was frightened. She had never flown before.

Chris sat next to her with Ed in front and Helen couldn't speak as they took off, rearing up into the air, the bucket seats hard, the air pockets bumping her so that she was lifted from the seat. She gripped at Chris and screamed.

Chris and Ed turned and saw her face, so pale and fraught, and they laughed, looking at one another and then at her, and Chris put his hand on hers while Ed explained the rudiments of flight, though she heard not a word. She did feel her son's hand, though, and feigned fear long after it had gone.

There was a steady drumming of sound in the plane and they looked down through the narrow window as they skimmed over the North Sea, seeing the waves rippling and breaking.

'Just like the snow, Mum,' Chris said, leaning across her to see more easily and she liked his closeness and touched his hair where it stuck up at the back. He didn't feel it and so did not pull away. She looked up and Ed was watching. He smiled and for a moment there was no distance at all between them.

The plane bumped its way through the overcast sky and the sea seemed to last for hours. Helen looked around at the plane. It was small and cramped and seemed to be held together by wire, but it was quick because she could see a sandbank ahead already.

'This is the coast of the Netherlands,' the pilot called.

They flew over the island of Walcheren, most of which had been under water, though the floods had now receded, the pilot told them, as the gaps made in the dykes by the RAF had been closed.

'The fields will be barren though because of the salt,' he added and Helen looked at Ed but couldn't see his face because he had turned towards the window.

They flew over bomb-damaged woods, in one of which a wrecked plane still lay. There were bridges and railways sprawled beneath them, some still useless and in disarray. Long stretches of electric railway lay grass-covered and unused. The pilot brought the plane down lower so that they could see.

'The Nazis looted miles of copper wire which was needed for the cables,' the pilot explained and now Helen looked at Chris who just stared at her.

They landed and drove through the once flood-ravaged streets of Holland, sometimes breathing in the smell of sea-saturated earth and there was magenta rosebay here too on the ruins, though clearing and rebuilding had begun. They stopped to buy milk and the Dutch pastor told them how the Dutch had eaten tulip bulbs to survive but that Canadian rations had entered and the children were beginning to put on weight.

Helen looked around at the scabied legs and the hand-made shoes that the thin children wore.

Ed said, 'In Little Fork they grouse because they had to pay heavy taxes for the war. They don't understand.'

Helen took his arm. 'How can they? It is only those who've seen and been amongst it all, like us. We are the only ones who can understand.' He looked at home now, relaxed as though there was no conflict, no battle. Would he still dream tonight?

They stayed in an old inn and he did dream.

They drove the next day along roads which were full of Allied vehicles. They reached the border and this time there were no Nazis holding them up, no red and black flags, and no hidden camera. Helen looked at Chris as they were waved through and his face was tight and cold.

'We brought in a camera for your grandfather. Do you remember? We brought it in so that he could blackmail the Nazis and save some people. He is a man to be proud of.'

But Chris turned away and did not reply.

They drove through the west German countryside, along roads carved through heathland, dotted with pines. Some snow remained where clumps shadowed it from the sun. They passed through decimated towns where hardly a building remained and the people pushed prams from ruin to ruin, searching for fuel. Rosebay grew here too, though clearance had begun.

Helen watched Ed's face as he looked at the crosses which were still planted in the rubble so long after the war. He stopped the car and walked across and stood near one and she joined him and could smell the dust. It was the same dust as in England.

They travelled along the great Nazi *Autobahn* from then on which bypassed all the big cities, and now the three of them were quiet, filled with their own thoughts.

Helen counted the steel-helmeted military motor-cyclists which wove in and out of the Army lorries, the small military cars, the German farm carts pulled by thin horses. They passed the flat beet fields and there were women bending and walking, bending and walking. Helen asked Ed to stop and she stood by the car, taking photographs because Heine had done this once.

She told Chris to come and see. He stood next to her and was almost as tall. She told him of his father; how he had taken photographs and exhibited them, how he had thought life would be simpler if he lived as one of these workers, hoeing and weeding and harvesting.

They stood in silence and then he turned to her.

'I guess maybe he was right.' There was not the earlier hardness in his face, there was doubt and this is what Helen had wanted to see.

At last they drove into what remained of Hanover. The Kröpcke was destroyed, its glass dome gone and cleared away along with the smart women and their cigarette holders, along with a world which had once glistened and glittered. In its place there was ruin and devastation, and rosebay too.

They parked and watched labourers, thin and with sacking tied to their backs for warmth, clearing piles of melted lead and stonework. There were people here too who pushed prams and sorted in the rubbish and Helen wondered where the old Jew dressed in black was now. Had he survived? Had Claus's family survived? They were also Jews.

They passed broken bridges and bomb-proof shelters which had saved thousands of people, but not enough, because thousands had also died. Now a policeman told Helen they housed the homeless. She took photographs and Chris stood with her, while Ed walked to the ruins, picking up rubble, turning it over and over in his hand.

They drove to the Headquarters of the British Occupying Army and Helen presented her press pass to the commanding officer, explaining why she was here, the real reason why she was here and the officer nodded and turned away, saying he had not seen her, because fraternisation was not allowed.

Helen smiled. 'Thank you,' she said and left the room which was solid and full of photographs of his wife and children and very English.

Her footsteps sounded on the steps and on the road and an old woman glared at her.

'*Engländerin*,' she hissed but Helen did not mind because she would feel the same if the Germans were marching all over her ruined land.

They reached the village as dusk was falling and now there were no Nazi flags, no blonde girls with coiled hair, no windowboxes, and only six houses left standing in this main street. The church was still there and Herr Weber's house, or part of it. Helen walked up to the front door. There was ash on the path, left over from the snow which only lay now beneath the stumps of the limes which was all that remained of the trees that Heine had loved, and for a moment she thought she could smell their summer scent.

She knocked, knowing that Claus had telegraphed ahead for her but she was nervous. Perhaps Oma would hiss at her too. She knocked again, feeling the hardness of the wood on her knuckle. She did not recognise the woman who opened the door until she spoke, and then she knew it was Oma, and she held the small thin body in her arms, hugging her, crying because this was Heine's beautiful mother, and she had no teeth and her once thick hair was thin and white and limp.

She held her saying, 'I'm so glad to see you. So sorry that Heine died,' and together they wept for the man they had both loved and then Chris was there, standing and looking, until Helen turned, her arm around Oma.

'This is your grandmother, Chris. This is Oma. You have come home.'

He didn't move or speak, just stood with his face closed and then Herr Weber came, walking slowly on two sticks out from the darkness of the hallway. His hands were gnarled and his fingers crooked. Oma told them the Nazis had beaten him when he had been betrayed; all over his body, including his hands and fingers. Still Chris just stood with Ed behind but Oma and her husband smiled.

'Come, my child,' they said to Helen, drawing her into the house, drawing them all in. 'Come. It is hard for him. It is hard for us to forgive ourselves.'

That night Helen lay in the room that had been Heine's. The lead soldiers were still on the shelf but the blue tiles of the stove were cracked from the blast of the bomb which had taken off the corner of the house. The brass knobs of the stove no longer gleamed and the body beside her was not Heine but Ed, and she loved them both.

They slept in their clothes because it was so cold and there was no fuel for the stove and only one blanket. She lay looking at the ceiling lit by the moon; a bomber's moon and she wondered if there would ever be a time when they stopped using the language of war.

She tucked her arm beneath her head turning to look at the clouds scudding across the sky.

'Will you lay your ghosts too?' Ed said.

She turned to him, not knowing until he spoke that he was awake.

'My ghosts? she queried.

'Sure, Helen. You have Heine to set down quietly in your life. He died alone. That's why you are trying so hard with me.'

His voice was gentle and he reached out and wound her curling hair round his finger.

Helen grasped his hand, loving it, loving him. He was right, she needed to lay her ghost, but she was fighting because she loved him, not just because Heine had been alone. She told him this, pulling his head down, kissing his lips, his eyes, his cheeks.

'I love you, I love you and I always will.'

He put his arm around her and pulled her to him and she felt the buttons of his overcoat against her throat.

'Even if I don't stop this goddamn war inside me?' His breath lifted her hair and it was warm on her skin.

'We'll stop it. It might take a while but one day it will all end.' But it did not end that night because the dreams were there as usual.

Chris lay in his room with his Oma's old duvet over him, dragged down from the attic which he had remembered as smelling of apples, but which was now open to the sky, the roof sliced open by a bomb; a British or American bomb. He was warm, though the stove was unlit, and he remembered now how his father had carried him from the dining-room when they had arrived that last time. There had been the scent of honey candles and heat from the stove. There had been the taste of venison in his mouth and the feel of his father's arms about him as they came upstairs into this bedroom where the stove was unlit. There was frost on the window and he could remember the mark his mother's nail had made where she had run it down, scraping at the ice.

He lay in bed and smiled and thought he heard his mother's voice. 'In my family, children sleep in warm rooms even if it means the adults go into the cold one.'

His father had laughed and said, 'My darling girl, do not prepare to do battle.' Chris looked round because the voice had been so clear but there was no one there. His mother had always been prepared to do battle for him. She was doing it now and he knew that she was winning because he had seen the ruins, the despair, his Oma and his grandfather. The Germans were just people like him and their houses had been ruined and their children killed and he knew now that all Germans were not monsters, only some had gone mad. He knew that he was not from a family which had done that.

The next morning they ate ham from the cans and a few potatoes but not many and Helen was hungry as she had not been for over a year.

They sat in Wilhelm Weber's study because it was smaller to heat, Oma said, her voice tired. There were still old shirts laid against the gap in the bottom of the door but it was not against the prying ears of Hans but against the draught which whistled through the damaged house. There was the same lamp on a cupboard which had lit the room when she and Heine had come before and the same chairs, but they were ripped and torn and the horsehair protruded.

All morning they talked and Chris listened. Herr Weber told them how Hans had betrayed him but that they had never found the camera. They had taken him, the local *Blockwart*, to the cells and beaten him.

He told Chris and Ed how the Americans had come before the Nazis could kill him. The Americans had destroyed every house not flying a white flag and any resistance near a village meant retribution by United States artillery fire and the people knew this.

'Soon,' he said, 'there was a forest of white flags. Some still died though because the Nazi guerrilla fighters shot the first to put up the white flag. In our village it was the pastor who died. The madness, you see, lingered even until the last moments of the war. Perhaps it still exists.'

Helen watched Chris who sat, his head on his hands.

Wilhelm Weber looked at Ed. 'You were a bomber pilot. Well let me thank you. During the last months the Allied bombing smashed the transport systems faster than they could be repaired. Aircraft parts could not be moved from the factories.'

Now he tapped Ed's knee. 'So you see, my dear young man, in this war you served a purpose.'

Herr Weber nodded then to Helen because she had told him of her husband and the nightmare he lived through each day.

Ed shrugged. 'I guess maybe that's good of you to say bu there's still an awful lot of death beneath the bombs I dropped. His voice was unsteady and he clasped his hands together Helen heard the creak of his chair as he hunched his shoulders.

The old man nodded. 'Yes, that is true. There was so much death everywhere and mistakes were made. Of course they were made. We played a game which was so big, so ugly that no one knew what the results would be.' He sighed. 'Did you ask for the war?'

It was a question he wanted answered and Ed shook his head.

'No, I guess I never really gave it a thought.'

'Of course, my boy, no one really knew that any of this would happen, even we Germans. In the early days the Third Reich was going to bring us, oh, how do you say . . . I know, employment, stability, grandeur. Your wife will have told you that Heine saw other things. I did not. I supported Hitler.'

He coughed and Oma went to him, patting her own mouth and sucking in her lips. Helen went to the kitchen and brought back aspirin for him, glad that she had packed three bottles.

'The Nazis gave us work though it became work in support of war. They improved housing, promised equal pay for women, gave marriage loans, increased family allowances, built roads. Things we had thought we would not see again after the First World War, the poverty of the twenties, the street fighting of those years. He gave all this to us, he gave us order and we looked away from the sickness we should have seen.'

Helen watched Chris. He was still resting his chin in his hands and Ed put his hand on his shoulder and together they learned about another side of the war. Oma left to brew real coffee brought from America and the smell invaded the house, bringing a smile to the old man's face.

'Ah, that is good. We have used acorns for so many years I had forgotten that there is such a thing as a coffee bean.' He laughed but there was still a deep sadness in his eyes.

She looked around the room. Two prints remained on the walls. The glass was cracked. The telephone had gone.

'Willingly we turned aside, you understand? At that stage, no black boots kicked at us. That, my fine young pilot, is our guilt. We allowed this to happen, all this.' He swept his stick towards the village, then sucked at his lips, rubbing his age-spotted hand over his mouth.

'It was only later I realised the truth and then I did something, but it was so little.'

Helen began to speak but Chris interrupted. 'You did not do little. You risked your life day after day like Ed did. That is more than I've ever been asked to do. Perhaps more than I ever will be asked to do.'

His voice was adult, his words too, and now he looked at Helen and smiled and she knew that he had seen, and was on the way to accepting, his heritage.

Herr Weber tapped Chris's leg lightly with his stick. 'You are very like your father, and your mother too. My son would be proud of you.'

He turned to the door as Oma brought in the coffee and they curved their hands round the mug because the stove was burning small bits of the dining-room furniture and there was very little heat.

'Before the war Hitler talked to his people. He travelled amongst them. But afterwards it was different. No. Seldom did he go to his soldiers. Never did he go to the bombed cities to talk to his people. But, my dears, the people still trusted him to win the war.' He threw up his hand, spilling some coffee on to his patched trousers but he didn't notice. 'And do you know why? Because they had so much suffering they had to have victory to justify it all.'

Helen thought of Churchill and the King and Queen, stepping over rubble, their faces compassionate, sharing the danger.

'I guess victory makes it better,' Ed said, sipping his coffee. Helen could see the steam rising from his mug.

'Defeat makes it all a mockery. But it is a mockery anyway. It was a game of the Nazis that went so wrong and we did not oppose it in time. That is our crime. That is the crime of the people, and your task for the future is to make sure you never let that happen in your lives. That must be your expiation. You must make every day of your life count for something good.'

There was silence and then Chris said, 'But what about the camps? That is what is so terrible.'

Oma wept now and Wilhelm Weber looked at her and then at Helen, Ed and Chris.

'And do you imagine we can forgive ourselves?' He looked at Ed. 'You dream at night because of the job you did.' His face was fierce now and his voice that of a younger man.

Ed looked at him, listening intently, his eyes fixed on the old man as he continued. 'We have to live with the knowledge that, as Germans, we allowed this murder of innocents to happen. We read *Mein Kampf* but we thought it too outrageous.' He was talking quickly now. 'But it happened. It was a state secret and knowledge of that secret was punishable by death. The secret was preserved.' He stopped now and looked at them all; one by one.

'But each night and every minute of every day I ask myself the question. Did I know? Had I guessed and turned from the truth?'

He sat back now, his coffee forgotten, his old damaged hands limp on his thighs.

Oma took one and held it, sitting on the arm of his chair. She said, 'You see, it makes anything that we did seem so little. Can you understand that?'

Again there was silence which was not broken by anyone until Helen touched Ed's hand and they left the room, walking out to the car, hearing Chris behind them.

They drove to the forest, walking amongst the trees, away from the paths, picking up kindling and carrying it back to the car, loading the boot, then the back seat. They drove and emptied it into the corner of the kitchen where newspaper was laid on the floor and chairs were dumped, waiting to be burnt.

They went back again, but only Ed and Helen now because Chris wanted to stay with his grandparents. They walked amongst the oaks, the beech, past the woodsman's cottage where there were no tables any more. She showed him where once logs had been stacked. They gathered what they could find but many had been here before them. It was grey and the cold seeped through their clothes and into their bones but there were too many thoughts for them to speak.

That night there were no dreams but they were there again the night after that, though not so vivid nor so loud and he woke when Helen touched him and wept in her arms and it was the first time he had been able to leave the blood and climb out of the darkness. She stroked his hair and kissed his eyes and they talked, slowly and carefully until the sun began to rise.

In the fresh dawn Helen took him to the woods, making him walk on the soft pine needles which had eased the ache in Heine's leg and would help his too. The sun was filtering through this time and now Helen remembered that soon there would be wild anemones and violets beneath the spreading branches. There were buds on the trees which must have been there before but they had not noticed.

'I kind of forgot for a while that the sun comes out and trees bud,' Ed said, reaching for her hand. 'I guess I've forgotten a lot of things.' He stopped and pulled her to him. 'Maybe your bulbs will be out around our house, and we should dig up your roses when we get back.' He kissed her with lips as soft as she remembered.

'Our bulbs and our roses,' she said against his mouth.

They walked again, mud clinging to their shoes as they walked on paths which had become overgrown and unkempt beneath the trees, and looked up through the branches at the sky.

The next day Ed began to seal up the roof, taking the asbestos off the sheds in the garden, dismantling their wooden joists and resettling them across the damaged corner of that attic, wrenching rusty nails out, sawing, chiselling, using Heine's old tools. He did not use those of Herr Weber because it was the son who had been denied the right to live long enough to do this for his parents and so Ed would do it for him.

He dug out slates from the nearby ruins, knocking and tearing his hands, seeing his blood in German dust, sifting where others had been before but always finding more as the days wore on, until at last there was a shape to the roof and that night he did not dream nor the next nor the next until he no longer dreaded the end of the day.

Helen drove round, taking photographs, asking questions about Claus's family. She took Wilhelm and Chris with her and together they worried and urged the authorities and saw the poverty all around, the children without shoes and little flesh. The meagre rations which were dependent on employment.

In the third week the old man took Chris to the end of the garden and asked him to dig three feet down, and there in an oilskin was the camera that they had brought through the border just before the war. He gave it to Chris and there was still film left and so Heine's son asked his mother to drive him to the beet fields and stood where his father had been, and took the same photographs.

In bed, two nights before they left the village, Ed held Helen and they talked about America and whether the dreams would come again when they were back where people could not understand.

'I guess not,' Ed said. 'I've got too much to do. I'm thirty-six, Helen, and Wilhelm said that we were the ones who have time. We do. I don't want to go back and just farm. I want a plane. I want to start an airline and Little Fork is as good a place as any.' His voice was eager and he pulled himself up on his elbow and looked down at her. 'There's more business setting up there all the time and the train's so goddamn slow. That war taught me too much and I reckon I'm going to take something out of it other than dreams that keep us both from our beauty sleep. We both need that too much.' He grinned. 'You want to learn to fly a plane or are you going to play around with your camera like I kind of think you are?'

Helen lay back in his arms, looking at his face which was so beautiful even though the lines remained and the scars from the crash were there beneath his hair. 'Why can't I do both? And while you're about it, you can teach Chris too.' She kissed him, feeling that now there was the hope that he would push the images to one side if they returned; when they returned.

The curtains were wide open because there had been too many years with the light blacked out, too many years of restrictions. She lit the candle by the bed, then carried it to the window, leaving it on the sill wanting to see its frail light seeping out into the sky.

The next night she did the same, and Ed laughed and kissed her as they watched the flame flickering in the draught.

Helen said, 'You can't just let your parents down, Ed,' because the thought had played in and out of her mind all day as she scrubbed the floors, washed windows, beat rugs. 'They have the ranch and farm to run and expect you to share in it.'

He sat up, taking a cigarette from the pack by the bed, lighting up, blowing the smoke up to the ceiling. 'I don't intend to leave them stone cold. It'll take a while to get set up, won't it? We'll be living in the house and we can amalgamate the ranch and the airline. It'll all work out, honey.'

And now, tonight, Helen began to believe that it would, and felt the darkness released from deep inside at last. And later, while Ed slept, she finally allowed herself to listen to the sounds of the house which had been Heine's home and grieved gently for the plans he would never make, the dreams he would never dream, and said goodbye.

As night became day and Ed woke they talked gently, deeply, about what could be done over here in the village, and Ed said they would send goods – food and clothing – and come back and finish the house. It was something that he owed these people.

Wilhelm and Oma did not want them to go; it was in their eyes as they stood on the doorstep with the scent of spring all around and the tips of bulbs green against the earth, and as Oma held Helen's hands they promised to go on searching for Claus's parents; it was something they wished to do, they said.

Helen asked if they would try and locate others that Claus knew and they nodded, knowing that she knew it would give them peace. She left the cigarettes for them to use as currency for information and she would bring more when she came again, she said. They would all come. She kissed them both then walked down the steps from the front door. The sky was deep blue today and at last there were violets in the shelter of the garden wall.

She waited while Chris stood before his grandfather.

'I shall see you again soon, Grandfather. Will you come to us too? There's someone I would like you to meet. He's my coach.'

Helen turned then and walked towards the car where Ed waited, smelling the violets, feeling the sun on her skin. When they came in the summer they would bring lime trees.

MARGARET GRAHAM

The Future is Ours

For Mum and Dad

I would like to thank
Sheila Doering of the United States,
Helen and Danny Buckley of Dorset,
Jackie Gaines, Marian Farrow,
Miss E. M. Glass of Somerset and
of course Sue Bramble and her library team
for their invaluable help with
the research for this book.

CHAPTER 1

Rosie gripped the ship's rail, feeling the throb of the engines, feeling the surge of the ship through the sea, seeing Frank and Nancy standing so far away on the quay, so far away and so small. The wind was harsh and hot but it didn't matter. It was 1946 and she was leaving America. That's what mattered. She was leaving to return to a family and a country she had almost forgotten after six years as an evacuee and it was unbearable.

The wind carried spray into her face but still she stood there; there was nothing else she could do. Just stand and watch the two people she had grown to love become smaller. Just stand and wonder whether she would ever see them again, whether she would ever see the bedroom where she had read Grandpa's letter three weeks ago and heard the jazz sweeping out from the gramophone, as always, across the sloping Pennsylvanian lawn.

No breeze had ruffled the maples, the sycamores or the chestnuts that day as she stood at the window. There were skis in the corner of the room, Cougar pennants on the wall. She had wanted to be a cheerleader but that wouldn't happen now. The letter had said it was time she came home – there was a job waiting for her at Woolworths – it was only fair on Norah – the war was over and the two sisters should be together again.

From the ship, Rosie had to strain to see the two small figures. How could they be so small? Frank was big, with arms that had held her when she had finished reading the letter out to them in the kitchen. Nancy was large too, and had put her arms around them both and said, 'We'll write to your grandfather in London, Rosie. We'll ask him to let you stay and complete your education, and become the journalist you want to be. We'll tell him how much we have grown to love you.'

'Woolworths, goddamn it,' Nancy had said while 'Rinso

White, Rinso Blue' filtered out from the wireless. 'Woolworths for Christ's sake.' They had all had tears in their eyes which Frank blamed on the onions sliced up on the side for the evening's barbecue. 'Goddamn onions,' he said and then stamped into his study, his pipe clenched between his teeth, and Nancy had laughed gently.

'This'll be the third he's broken this year if he's not careful,' she said, 'and the Sub-Editor will just love that. They've got a bet on that this year it'll be three within six months.'

But Rosie hadn't laughed. She had stood with Nancy's arms around her, wanting to cling to this plump, grey-haired, blue-eyed woman who had become her mother, who had watched her grow from a ten-year-old English girl into a sixteen-year-old American. But she didn't, because Nancy wasn't her mother, was she? She had no mother. She had a grandfather whom she knew she had once loved, and a sister whom she had never known whether she loved or even liked, a sister who had never written.

The wind on the ship was steady, no longer snatching at her cotton jacket, just streaming past her, through her, and now she looked out to the yawning emptiness of the sea and the sky, beyond which lay England. But she wouldn't think of that, or of Manhattan which was fading behind her. She would think instead of the lake, where they had gone the day after Frank had written the letter.

They went upstate each summer but this time it was different. This time they were waiting.

They had driven down through small towns which smelt of diesel as they passed the petrol stations. Her tanned legs had stuck to the seat in the heat. She could still feel the stubbled kiss from Uncle Bob who had wrapped his arms around her before she climbed into the car. His new jazz band had played at the barbecue the evening before.

He had hugged her and said, 'If you go back, Rosie, don't forget that it's the half valving that sets jazz apart, gives it the variation in pitch, oh hell, which sets it above other music. You remember us, you remember jazz, you remember that we love you. You hear me now. And you scout out for bands to send me. I want one with a middle tone, hear me? I love you, hear me? I'm glad you came. You made me glad we fought with Europe.'

She heard him. She had heard him on a dark evening five years ago too when he had been an isolationist shouting at Frank in the living-room that there was no way the States should be drawn into a war. There was no way they should supply the Britishers. For Christ's sake they wouldn't even pay their debts. She had stood then, gripping the banister, shouting at him, 'You silly old bugger. Over there the 'ouses are being bloody bombed. Me grandma's been killed and there ain't no kids in London any more. Even me best friend Jack's 'ad to go to bloody Somerset and you carry on about bleedin' money.'

The banister had been hard, but warm, unlike the ship's rail she was still clutching.

Bob had called up, 'Why did you run away then?'

And now she heard her voice as it had been then; so young, so different.

'I didn't. I was bloody sent. No one asked me. I was just sent.'

Rosie said those words again now, into the wind which stretched them out then scattered them. 'No one asked me.' And her voice was now an American drawl and there was the same anger in it that there had been then. 'No one asked me, did they, Grandpa?'

They had stopped to eat at a roadside diner surrounded by walnut and ash trees and the earth had oozed out the last of its heat as they drove the last leg towards their wooden lake house. Rosie had stood in the hall. It had smelt the same, dry and warm, filled with the scent of pine. Frank's rods were there, the old clock. But this time there was the dark sense of waiting.

She barely slept and rose with the dawn, not allowing herself to look out at the lake. She never did. She liked to feel the cool of the polished floors as she walked silently, barefoot, through the house, and then across the grass, and then the mulch of the woods before she saw the water. It was a ritual. It would keep her safe. But it hadn't this time, had it?

Still beneath the trees she had heard the lake, rippling in across the stones and on up to the sand which might still be cool. Then she was out into the light and at last the lake was there, glinting, easing in across the shore. And yes, the sand was still cool and loose and fine-grained. There had been no storms recently then. No storms to force the water into three-foot waves, to smash down beyond the pebbles, soaking the sand.

Rosie looked out on to the grey sea now. The prow of the ship was slicing through the waves, her hair was thick with salt and still she could see the skyline of Manhattan and she knew that Frank and Nancy would remain there, waiting until she disappeared.

And so too they had waited at the lake, day after day, swimming, sitting, beating time to jazz; Erroll Garner, Billie Holiday, Bix Beiderbecke, always Bix, and Grandpa's reply to Frank's letter had not come.

On Nancy's birthday, towards the end of June, they had driven to the Club, taking their costumes, swimming in the pool. She hailed her friend Sandra who was up here from town too. They sat on white wrought-iron chairs which dug into the grass at the edge of the terrace overlooking the pool. They slid ice-crowded glasses to the table's edge to break the vacuum the condensation had produced. They sipped their Cokes, slowly. Behind them was the lawn which stretched back to the Clubhouse.

Frank passed them bourbon-soaked cherries from his and Nancy's cocktails and the talk was of the latest jazz band Uncle Bob was promoting, or the parched grass back home behind the rhododendrons where the hose did not reach; anything but England. Anything but Grandpa. Anything but the waiting.

And then Joe came towards them from the Clubhouse – Joe who had been here last year, who had been a Senior at their school, who was now at College. Joe who she had thought was beautiful since she had arrived in Pennsylvania, who was even more beautiful now that she might be leaving. But no, she wouldn't think of that. If she didn't think of it, it might not happen.

He was nodding at the girls, holding his hand out to Frank.

'Hi, Mr Wallen.' His voice was deeper than last year. He was taller, more blond. The hairs on his arms were bleached by the sun. Sandra nudged her and grinned. Joe didn't look, not then. But then he hadn't looked last year either. He did after dinner, though, when he smiled, his teeth white against his tan, his watch gold against his skin, and he asked her to the Subscription Dance which was being organised to raise funds for a new tennis court.

That night she had dreamed that she was on a ship, like this ship, being pulled in half by Grandpa and Norah at the prow and Frank, Nancy and Joe aft.

But she'd gone to the dance, goddamn it, she thought as she pulled her jacket round her throat and let the wind tear more strongly at her clothes. Yes, I went to the dance.

She shut her eyes because the wind was dragging tears across her cheeks. That was all. Only the wind.

She had gone to the dance because the letter had not yet come, and therefore there was still time. And now she laughed, but it was not a proper laugh as she thought of Joe's arms around her, the taste of vermouth and lemonade, the talk of College, of majoring in Politics, of his wish to enter journalism, his hopes that he might work on Frank Wallen's newspaper.

She had listened to his ambitions, which were also hers, and pushed away the thought of England. Later she watched the lake as they drove back to the house in his Buick, and then smelt his skin as he leaned down, his lips touching hers, but then his tongue pushed into her mouth and she drew back, uncertain. She had never kissed like this before.

Her feet crunched on the gravel as she walked towards the porch. 'I'll see you, Rosie,' he called as he drove away, his wheels spinning.

'Sure,' she said and had hoped that she would, in spite of drawing back, because he made her heart beat faster and her lips feel full, her skin feel as though it needed to be touched, and if she felt like this, she thought, it couldn't all end. Could it? Grandpa? Could it?

She did see him again, within two days, because Sandra had rung and asked her to a barbecue on the beach, where Joe would also be. She had answered the phone then grinned at Nancy as, later, they both strolled down to the lake and Nancy sat while Rosie swam in the cool clear water out to the raft. She lay on the wet wood, then dived into the water again, swimming back to shore, to the beach house.

She had rolled down her costume, running her hands down her body, brushing at the wet sand which had caught between her breasts and along the top of her cold buttocks, and between her thighs. Should she let his tongue search her mouth? What did she do with her own? What did other girls do?

She returned to Nancy, and sat against her chair, taking handfuls of sand and letting it run through her fingers on to the ground.

'So why don't you ask that Joe over for a swim?' Nancy had said, handing her a salad roll.

The tomato was warm and the lettuce limp. It was the taste of summer by the lake for her.

'I don't know really, Nancy. I guess I just don't want to somehow.' She had bent her head down, resting it on her knees.

'You know, when you've just come out of the water and your hair's wet it's just the same as when I used to wash it back in 1940 when you first came,' Nancy said, her voice lazy. 'I remember my first date. I didn't want him to see my body, even in a costume. Too kind of personal if you know what I mean?'

Yes, she'd known what Nancy meant and now she remembered the feel of Nancy's hand stroking her head, her voice as she said, 'You've really grown, Rosie, and I guess Joe has too. I remember it was difficult to know what to do with a new date at your age. Sometimes things that you've read in books become real and you don't know what you think about it.'

Rosie remembered now how the lake had lapped at the shore while Nancy continued.

'I guess my mom was right, Rosie, when she said that you do what seems right at the time but don't let yourself get hustled, if you know what I mean, my dear. Letting a boy go too far is wrong at your age. Kissing is enough, I think.'

And Rosie remembered saying, 'But Grandpa is hustling us. Can't we just say I'm going to stay here?' She had gripped Nancy's hand, looking up at the woman who had come to her in the night when she had been ill, the woman who had smiled from the front row when she collected her literature prize. The woman who now said that Grandpa had the right to make the decision for them all. Rosie was sixteen, not twenty-one. It was only right, but Nancy had turned away as she said this.

At the barbecue they had all jitterbugged in the humid heat which was heavy with the smell of hamburgers and onions. Joe was good, very good, but so was she and they picked up the rhythm and didn't talk, didn't laugh, just danced as a breeze at last began to ease in from the lake. Dave, Sandra's date, tapped Joe on the shoulder and they swapped partners and danced again, but though the rhythm was the same it wasn't Joe's hand which caught her and turned her and threw her up and then to one side, and so it was good to be called to eat, over by the glowing barbecue.

She didn't eat the onions but sat with Sandra on blankets out where the woods met the sand and they laughed while the boys fetched root beer which Sandra's mother had brought from the ice-box. The parents smoked cigarettes which glowed in the dark and Rosie watched the lanterns blowing near the barbecue. Frank and Nancy hung up lanterns in their garden when they had a barbecue and people danced and ate. Did Grandpa? Of course not. But it hurt too much to think of that, so she watched as the moths beat against the lights.

'Don't they know it's hopeless?' she murmured.

'D'you remember that darn great Polyphemus the old coach stopped the game for in ninth grade?' Joe called across to Dave. 'He stopped play and we watched it crawl out all wet. We had to wait until it dried and the wings got as tough as Flying Fortress wings. Jeez, those moths are more like birds. Six inches from wing-tip to wing-tip. We swatted it.'

The breeze had become a wind as the music played again and Joe pushed his fingers between hers, pulling her up, dancing so close. Her head had lain against his shoulder. The humidity remained and they were drenched with sweat and Rosie had thought of the wings beating about her face. She hated moths. She always had done and she remembered Grandpa swatting at a hard-bodied one which had banged into the kitchen light but it was Jack who had come in, cupped it in his hands, taken it into the yard, set it free. Grandpa, let me stay.

She shivered and Joe held her, looking into her face, but it wasn't the moth, it was the thought of England. Joe kissed her and she felt his lips on her forehead, in her hair, his breath on her skin, and it was what she had wanted all evening.

The music was slow and she felt his chest against hers, his hips, his legs. She wasn't going to think about moths any more, about anything any more. Not about school, not about ninth grade – only kids were in ninth grade. She was sixteen, Joe was eighteen. They were no longer kids.

Her breath made a wet patch on his shirt and she concentrated on this, not on the mailbox which would one day soon hold the letter.

Then they were dancing in the darkness beyond the lanterns, and all she could smell was him, all she could feel was him, as he moved his hand all over her back and kissed her, again and again, and her mouth opened under his, but this time his tongue didn't flick into hers.

The hand which led her off to the shelter of the wood was soft and sure and kind. The ground was dry, his kisses were on her face, her neck, and hers were on his, but then he unbuttoned her dress, slipping his hand across her shoulders, her neck. Her breathing felt strange.

She put her hands either side of his head, holding his face so that she could kiss his mouth, see his eyes which looked at her, then through her, heavy-lidded. At his lips which were as full as hers felt. Now she let his hands stroke her breasts and she knew the adults would not approve and she thought they could go to hell.

She closed her eyes as he pushed her dress back off her shoulders and it was now that he kissed her breast with his open mouth, with his tongue. She felt it, soft and warm, and allowed him to do all this because the adults were making decisions, had always made decisions, and this was hers. And they wouldn't like it.

But then she opened her eyes. The wind was howling now and she saw his head down against her skin, her body felt his hands along her thighs and his mouth was no longer soft and neither were the sounds which came from him. She was frightened, wanted Nancy. Everything was so quick. After six years everything was rushing, too fast, too goddamn fast, even this, and she didn't know how to stop Joe, how to stop anything, anything at all.

But then the rain came and Joe lifted his head, pulled back her dress, took her hand, helping her from the ground, laughing, running, and that night the waves on the lake were three feet high as they drove along the surface of the water. Tomorrow the sand would be solid and wet as she walked on it and she knew now it would be all right because the rain had fallen tonight when she needed it. So that meant everything would be fine, wouldn't it? And she and Joe would have the time they needed to take everything so much more slowly.

But she did not walk on the sand the next day and everything was not all right, because there was a letter from England in the mailbox. Norah insisted that she came home and Grandpa agreed. The waiting was over. There was only grief and anger to take its place.

Rosie lifted her hands now, leaning against the rail, standing on her toes, looking back, and, yes, Manhattan was still visible, she hadn't quite left, not yet.

She hadn't said goodbye to Joe, or to Sandra. Frank had driven them back to the house on the last day of June and there had been an ache inside her which seemed to reach into the air, taking the colour from the maples, the sky, the whole world. The ache hadn't left her still. She wondered if it ever would.

She had packed her trunk, listening to Louis Armstrong, ignoring the visitor from the Children's Aid Society who called to speak to Frank and Nancy. She folded her clothes neatly but left her baseball bat, skis, her pennants on the shelves and on the walls, because there would be no place for them in London.

She looked out at the baseball target set up by Frank on the back of the garage, then took the ball from the shelf, feeling its stitches, its leather-covered hardness, the slap as she whacked it into her other hand. The mitt was there on the shelf. She put the ball with it. It was all over and the tears would not stop running down her face.

They took a cab from the house the next day and she waved at Mary, the domestic help, who cried, but Rosie did not, she seemed too empty, too grey, too tired. But she had cried all night. Had Frank and Nancy?

They talked on the train to New York but the words were dry and flickered from her mind and it was as though everything were happening two feet above the ground and there were no shadows.

At Grand Central Frank showed her the bulbous clock above the information desk.

'This is a good meeting place,' he said, taking his pipe from his mouth. 'You just remember that when you come back.'

For a moment she had seen the colours and shapes of Grand Central Station and then it slipped back to the flatness and to the noise which whirled around her, sweeping in and out of her head but never staying, and she turned away but Frank pulled her back, put his arm around her. His brown eyes close to her brown eyes.

'You've got to fight a good corner. Make something positive out of the next three days before you get on that boat. We want you to soak it in, remember it. Remember America. That's why we're filling in the time here, not back home. The future is yours, Rosie. You must make something positive out of the rest of your life. Have we got a deal?'

Rosie looked at Nancy and then back to Frank and wanted to shout, But there's this pain, deep inside and it's because I'm leaving you, the lake, Sandra, America; and Joe. And I'm angry with Grandpa and Norah and you, for letting this happen. And I'm frightened because I'm going to a place which used to be home but which isn't any more.

Nancy touched her face as the people parted around them. 'None of this is the end of the world, you know. We can write. You'll come and stay, or we'll come over.' Her voice was heavy with sadness, her eyes shadowed as Frank's were, and Rosie knew that these two people were hurting too. That they loved her, that they didn't want her to go, any more than she wanted to leave.

They walked on through the pillared hall and the noise was greater. People clustered at the ticket booths. Were they going home? Were they laughing and smiling because they were going to people they knew and loved?

Frank had gripped her then, as Rosie now gripped the rail again, her hands down from her face, Manhattan all but gone, though not quite.

He had gripped her, pulling her back to him. His hands had

been the same as they had always been, short-nailed, strong. Would they be old when she saw him again?

He had said, 'Nearly sixty cleaners come in the early hours, just so you can put your toots down on the great big shine. Now isn't that something?'

She had nodded, but it was nothing in amongst the pain. She had leaned her head back at Nancy's command and looked at the picture of the zodiac on the towering ceiling.

'There's something wrong with it, so people say. Maybe Orion is back to front or something. But it looks pretty good to me.' But it was nothing.

They called in to the Oyster Bar, then passed the movie house and stood and looked at the bronze doors behind which the trains waited at their platforms. There would be one taking Nancy and Frank back to Pennsylvania on the fourth, but not her. No, she would take a ship and a train and then a cab, each one taking her further from them, from Joe, from them all.

'These trains leave at one minute past the scheduled time. Always one minute past. Remember that when you come back,' Nancy said.

They took a cab to the Plaza Hotel but Rosie turned before they left the station and saw 89 East 42nd Street in gold lettering above the main doorway. Did Euston have its address written up? She couldn't remember. She didn't care.

She still didn't care, standing here, surging away from America, remembering the avenues they had driven along and across, the streets they had turned down which were plunged into darkness by the shadows of the skyscrapers. They had driven beneath bridges, slicing in and out of the shadows of the girders.

'In winter the tops of these skyscrapers are sometimes in the clouds,' Frank had said, his hand clasped over the bowl of his pipe because Nancy would not tolerate that goddamn smell in the car.

The buildings reared up, jagged against the blue of the sky. They were complete, untouched. But the place she was going to wasn't. The bombs had made sure of that.

In the Plaza lobby there were plants with rich green waxy leaves. They looked so cool in the heat, like the lake. She touched one. It was plastic and warm.

Her bedroom was silent, empty. She had no energy to draw the drapes across the full-length window, she just let her clothes drop to the floor in the bathroom and stood beneath the cold water, wanting the sharpness, the intake of breath, the soothing of the pain which could not be soothed.

They walked in Central Park. There were tennis courts.

'Will the Lake Club raise the money for another one?' she asked and Frank nodded.

'They usually do.'

Would Joe take someone else to the next Subscription Dance? Would he kiss her breasts too? If she had stayed, would they have been able to take it all more slowly? Would she have been able to ask him to kiss her gently, to hold her in his arms, not press his lips against her nipples, not yet. Not until she was less of a child. Not until they really knew one another.

Would Frank and Nancy still sit around the pool, would the glasses still stick to the table? Would the world go on?

Frank had stopped and was pointing his pipe towards the grey rocks, the drying grass.

'This was covered with squatters' shacks in the Depression but wars are good for us. We make money, we save money. Now we need something to spend it on, so we'll have a boom. Poor old Europe won't. It's been drained white. It'll be tight back home, Rosie.'

But London wasn't home, and neither was Pennsylvania any more. She was in no man's land. Didn't anybody see that but her?

That night when midnight had been and gone she stood at the window of her room, a strange room in a strange city. She listened to the garbage trucks wheezing and clanking, the air-conditioning humming, the police sirens wailing, and knew that she had felt this lonely before. She recognised the panic which surged and tore into her, gripping her hands into fists, squeezing the breath from her throat. She recognised the pain which tumbled along with it.

It was the pain Grandpa had tried to hug and kiss away so long ago on the wharf at Liverpool but he had not been able to touch the rawness inside her because he was the one saying she couldn't stay.

He was the one saying those words again.

Rosie held the drape tightly, screwing it up, holding it to her mouth, leaning her head against the glass. All around her was the humming, the wailing, the clanking, and now there were tears too. Tears which turned to sobs and the drape was creased and damp when she turned to her bed, but even then there was no peace because the waves of the lake lapped and rippled and its glare hurt her eyes as she dipped in and out of sleep. In and out. In and out, until she woke, sweat-drenched, the sheets twisted about her limbs.

But it was still night, and the water was cold from the shower as she let it run over her face, her body. She was almost a woman now and had been a child when Grandpa had held her with the cold September wind whirling around them on that Liverpool dock.

'My little Rosie,' he had said. 'My darling little Rosie. It won't be long, my love. I promise you that. It really won't be long but I want you safe.' And he had cried. Tears had smeared – not trickled – just smeared all over his face which had been old even then.

Rosie turned the shower on harder. 'It's been too long, Grandpa. It's been such a very long time and I don't remember you any more. I don't belong any more. You are tearing me away from my home again and I think I hate you.'

In the morning they watched the riders exercising their horses in Central Park, then took a steamer which smelt of diesel. They looked at Staten Island, Ellis Island, the ancient ferries which plied to and fro, one with funnels, and it had meant nothing because she was leaving.

They took a cab up to Fifth Avenue, driving past the steam that drifted from manhole covers and came from the cracks in the hot water system carried in underground piping.

They shopped in stores for a crêpe de Chine nightdress for Norah which Nancy chose and Rosie knew should have been flannelette, but then, Norah might have changed. But what did it matter?

She looked up. Behind her, captured by the mirror tilted on the counter, was a red-haired girl, and for a moment she thought it was Sandra. But of course it wasn't.

They moved on to the candy department and bought maple candies, butterscotch and toffee because, Nancy said, the neighbours would like sweets especially now that the rationing was so intense.

She bought gum and fruit-flavoured envelopes. And stockings for herself, for Norah, for Jack's mum – and Camel cigarettes, too, because Maisie was a twenty a day girl. She bought a toy car for Lee, Jack's new brother, but she didn't mind whether it was a Buick or a Cadillac. None of it mattered. She bought a sweater for Grandpa and another for Jack, another for Jack's dad, Ollie.

For lunch they put nickels in a slot in a diner and she saw a boy who she thought was Joe. But of course it wasn't and by this time tomorrow she would be drawing away from Manhattan, hearing the gulls, losing Frank and Nancy, losing them all.

Now Rosie, standing by the rail, looked up at the sky. She hadn't noticed the gulls before.

They hadn't been able to eat their meal and had taken a bus to the Rockefeller Center and Rosie had watched the coins clink through the driver's change machine, like the hours and minutes of these last few days. They had stood on the sidewalks as Nancy told them of the cleaner employed full-time to keep the Center floor clear of gum and she had thought of her Grandma who had worked as a cleaner at the bank. It was there that she had died when the bomb had fallen just before Rosie left for America.

That evening they went to Chinatown and she bought a jar of spice from a shop which had varnished ducks hanging in the open shop-front. An old woman passed with shoes that slopped as she walked.

They sat and drank cold tea at an outdoor café and Rosie bought a book of Chinese art from an old street vendor. Maybe Jack would like that. And still the minutes clicked away.

The cloud layer had not dispersed with the coming of night and reflected the Manhattan lights. The London skies had been aglow on the nights before she left. Not with light but with flames.

It was nine o'clock now. It would soon be the fourth. They flagged down a cab and drank Manhattans in a restaurant which spilled seats out on to the pavement.

They sat and watched the women in hats, the men in smart

grey suits, the boys in shirtsleeves, the girls in cotton dresses. Each girl looked like Sandra, each boy like Joe. She picked out the ice-cube from her drink. It numbed her tongue, but not her pain.

'I'm saving the best for tomorrow,' Frank said, taking her hand in his. 'It's somewhere you'll never forget, somewhere that'll warm you on the long trip home, on the nights when maybe you can't sleep.'

Nancy touched her shoulder and smiled.

Frank continued. 'It's a place I always think of when times are tough. It's the street where Bob and I used to visit to soak in jazz. Real original jazz.'

Rosie looked at him and saw that his eyes had lost the shadow of pain which he had carried over these last days.

She stood at the window again that night listening to the lorries, the garbage truck, the sirens. She showered, she cried and drifted in and out of sleep and there was Joe, his wristwatch glinting, his hand on her skin, his mouth too. There was Grandma, lying beneath the rubble. Jack reaching out to her. Then Frank and Nancy holding her, sure and strong, then Grandpa calling her from their arms but she couldn't see his face.

They didn't talk over breakfast. The pecan waffle looked good, the celebrations in the street outside were loud for the fourth of July but it didn't matter. Nothing mattered.

It was hot again, so hot. They took a cab to Frank's favourite place. She stretched out her arm along the window, loosening her fingers, breathing slowly, keeping the panic in, mixing it up with the pain. They passed in and out of shadows and the noise of the streets was loud. Life was all around them but not in her. Not with her.

Frank was clenching his unlit pipe between his teeth, his fingers tapping on the armrest of the door.

'Charlie Parker and Dizzy Gillespie played in clubs next door to one another down fifty-second Street, this goddamn great street. I heard them. Billie Holiday sang too. Dixieland and New Orleans just roared out across the street all day and into the night.' He was stabbing the air with his pipe now. 'There was nothing to pay, just the price of a beer and the love of the music. It's stayed with me. It'll stay with you, keep you warm.

It's special for me, and for Nancy, and Bob. Now it'll be special for you.'

The cab slowed, turned into the street and Rosie watched as Frank leaned forward, his face eager, and then she saw the bleakness begin in his eyes and his mouth set into a tense line. She had looked then, out of the window, at the clubs which would warm her, remind her, and she saw what Frank had seen.

She saw the smoky brownstone buildings which were still there, but without the clubs. There was just paper which scudded about the street and paint which was peeling off doors and window glass which was cracked or gone. Dented cars lined the street, a trash can rolled on the sidewalk.

They drove down slowly and where there had once been jazz sweeping out of the windows were groups of men lounging, staring. There were more standing in dingy doorways, buying drugs, selling drugs, taking drugs, and Rosie held Frank's hand and told him that it was jazz sweeping across the sloping lawn that she would remember. It was Uncle Bob's groups, the barbecues, the baseball target, the maple syrup on pancakes at breakfast – those were the things that would warm her.

'This is nothing. This doesn't matter.' But then she could speak no more and her pain was gone as she saw his in the tears which were smeared across his face, as Grandpa's had been. Frank looked old too.

And now, standing on her toes again at the rail, she could no longer see Manhattan. They were gone and she finally turned from the wind and wept. It was over. All over.

Frank and Nancy stood hand in hand now that the ship had quite gone and Frank didn't look at Nancy as he said, 'When I saw those clubs had gone and everything had changed I felt my heart break. It looked like us with her gone.'

Nancy put her arms around him, holding him.

'It's over,' he said. 'Those six years are gone and I love that girl more than I ever thought I could love anyone, other than you.'

Nancy said into his jacket, 'We knew she had to go back. We chose to forget. That wasn't fair on her. We let her down, but maybe we could go visit in a few months, make sure she's OK?'

They were both crying and the sun was too hot.

Frank said as he looked back to the ocean again, 'No, she must settle back with her family and only come when it's right for her. She's had a safe war and it's over now. We all just have to get on with the rest of our lives.'

Neither could speak any more and they caught a cab, and then a train and then drove back to the lake, but Frank did no more fishing that summer. He and Nancy just sat and listened to the waves on the shore.

CHAPTER 2

For the first three days of the voyage to England, Rosie lay on her bunk, not eating, not sleeping, just pushing the sheet into her mouth to smother her tears. The other three girls thought she was seasick.

On the fourth day she dressed, showered and walked the deck, feeling the rise and fall of the ship. There were loungers lined up near the rail, quoits to play, music in the evening, and space. She leaned against the rail, the sun was hot, the wind fierce. It tore at her hair. She was going back to England because she had been told to and that was that.

But there was all this anger and pain which seemed trapped inside her body, inside her mind, and she wished it would break free and be swept into nothing by the wind. Hadn't Grandpa realised that she'd grow to love her new life? Didn't he know how she would feel being dragged away again? But then he didn't know her any more. She didn't know him.

She walked on, holding the hair back from her face, watching as a child threw a bean bag to his mother, and then to the father. Some others were playing French cricket. There was room for that on the upper deck.

On the trip six years ago there had been no room, no parents. Just children with labels pinned to their lapels, wearing plimsolls, gumboots, their faces grown wary and tired. There were destroyers and other ships ploughing through the grey waters, not the space about the ship that there was now.

One morning Rosie had come with the others to the rails to wave but the destroyers were gone and each ship had to make its own way. It was that dull grey expanse of sea that Rosie remembered because that was when she realised that she and all the other children really had left their homes. They had to make their own way too. There had been a bleakness in her then, deeper than tears, and anger too.

But that night some of the boys had rolled marbles across the dance floor and the children's escorts had fallen, in mid foxtrot, on to great fat bums. Rosie and the boy who reminded her of Jack had laughed, along with so many others. The escorts hadn't laughed, they had gripped the children's collars and with red angry faces had told them of the dangers of a cracked coccyx. One lad had said that he didn't know you could break your flaming arse on a marble and they had laughed again.

Rosie stopped now, near the stern, watching the flag streaming out and the wake frothing and boiling. Yes, they had laughed a lot, and cried with despair and anger, but in the end it had been all right, hadn't it? She looked down at her shoes – open-toed, leather – and the tanned foot, and remembered the plimsolls, the child that she had been.

Yes, that had turned out all right, and so would this. Wouldn't it? But the child was almost a woman, and the pain seemed deeper, more sharply etched, and she wondered who would be there to meet her when the ship docked.

There was no one to meet her at Liverpool. She took a cab to Lime Street. The streets were so small, the sky so grey, the rain so heavy and no one had come to meet her.

There were no gold letters above this station, no drawling men in short-sleeved shirts, no women in slacks and dark glasses. No one who called her honey and showed her a bulbous clock under which they would meet when she came back. No one to meet her here at all. She wouldn't cry, not here, in this strange land. Later she would though – in Grandpa's house in Middle Street, but only when it was dark and everyone else asleep.

She bought tea from a trolley and handed over a sixpence.

'That's swell,' she said, picking up her case, shrugging so that her bag wouldn't slip from her shoulder, moving to one side to let the man with the cap buy his.

'Yank, eh?' said the woman, passing the man his cup without looking. Her headscarf was knotted at the front and her hair hung down her forehead. She looked tired and thin.

Rosie sipped the thick stewed tea and looked at the woman,

the man, all these people who spoke in a thick scouse that she could barely understand.

'I don't know,' she replied, putting the cup back down on the trolley and moving towards her platform, tears stinging the back of her throat. I don't know goddamn anything. I only know I'm hurting. I only know I shouldn't be here. And nobody has come to meet me.

The train shuddered out along the tracks, through suburbs which were torn and jagged, splashed with purple from the rosebay willowherb. There were great gaps in the streets and bomb-damaged houses with rooms hanging open to the air, their damp and peeling wallpaper still clinging to the plaster. She had seen photographs in the newspapers but nothing had prepared her for this.

The train was taking her further from the sloping lawns, making her see what she had escaped. But that wasn't her fault, was it? Grandpa had made her come back and he hadn't even come to meet her, and neither had Jack.

She wiped the train window clear of condensation, felt the wet on her skin as she made herself count the telegraph poles, made herself smell the train, taste the tea thick on her tongue and teeth, watch the rain, because all this was England. The raindrops jerked down the pane as the train rattled slowly over the points.

Poor little country. Poor goddamn little country – and she saw tired brownstone buildings where no jazz played.

Guilt came then and it was shocking in its forgotten strength. It was the same guilt which had come on heavy heat-laden nights when she was safe and thousands of miles away from the bombs, the rationing, the grind. But the feeling had faded with the years and she had forgotten it until today. And now there was so much pain, so much anger, so much guilt that she thought her head would burst, but then this too faded. All of it faded. Nothing stayed. She was too tired. Right now she was too tired but it would all come again, along with the panic. She knew. It had been the same six years ago.

She wiped at the window again then sat with her hands clenched. She watched as the man opposite took out a packet of Woodbines, and struck a match. The smell of sulphur filled the carriage before being swept away in a rush of noise and wind as he hauled on the window strap, flicked out the match, then snapped it up again.

She watched as he drew deeply and read his paper again. She watched as the woman opposite took out sandwiches wrapped in greaseproof paper. The tomato was warm and had stained the bread. The child in the corner was kicking his leg against the opposite seat. He had soft brown eyes like Jack's. She looked away quickly.

Why hadn't Jack met her? She pressed her hands together tightly in her lap. Why? He had written all through the years and had said he would come. Frank had cabled Grandpa telling him the time and date. Why hadn't one of them come?

She looked at the boy in the corner again and then out at the fields, so green, so lush, even in the greyness, even in the rain. She had forgotten how green it was, how small the fields were. They passed old houses made of deep red Cheshire stone, and copses. She'd forgotten there were copses.

Yes, why hadn't either of them come? She had known Norah would not. 'Norah's walking around like a flaming great purple bloodhound,' Jack had written in his first letter to her. 'She'll not forgive you for going, leaving her here with iodine and impetigo. It'll be your fault that the programme was scrapped before she could come too. Just shrug her off.'

Rosie had, she'd forgotten about the older girl who had increasingly pushed, shoved and scowled her way through life the older she became, but now they would be meeting again. Would it be any better?

The man opposite stubbed out his cigarette on the floor, grinding his heel down, squashing it, mixing it with the dirt from the floor.

Rosie remembered salvaging dog-ends with Jack before the war then rolling them into new fags and selling them for twopence a pack. She and Jack had done that together and his mum had laughed but Grandma had never known. She would not have laughed and now so much of the past was coming back. Grandma would have told Grandpa he was a fool not to tan 'that girl's backside'. He had always loved Rosie so much, but he hadn't come to meet her, had he? He had just issued the order.

Rosie hadn't cried when Grandma died beneath the rubble

of the bank. Norah had cried while the funeral guests were there and then she had gone up and sorted through Grandma's mothballed clothes trying on the coat with the fox fur and the paws and the head with eyes which followed you around. It hadn't suited her purple face, Rosie thought.

Norah had kept that and the cardigans and given the jumpers to Rosie to cut the arms off and sew into blankets. They had smelt of sweat until Rosie had washed them. Norah had sold the rest to the rag and bone man and kept the money.

Rosie shifted in her seat. Surely she had changed? They were grown up now, things were different. The seat prickled and the view of Arundel Castle on the wall above the man's head was faded.

Jack had unscrewed the one of Weymouth on the evacuee train carrying their school down to Somerset when war first began. He had sold it to the owner of the village pub to get them enough money to travel back at Christmas when the bombers still hadn't come.

His mum had sent him again though, after Rosie had gone and the bombs were falling night after night and after old Meiner's house down the road was crushed. Rosie had liked Mr Meiner. Jack had fiddled them both a job lighting fires at his house on the Sabbath by saying they were older than they were. 'Meiner left Germany but the buggers killed him anyway,' Jack had written and his mum and dad had sent him back to Somerset then. But it was to a different area. Norah had gone too.

Rosie watched the woman next to her peeling off the crust of her last sandwich, eating it piece by piece, licking her finger and stabbing up the crumbs. Then she folded up the paper and put it away again in her bag.

Rationing was still on in England. They had debts to repay, the country to rebuild, and Rosie couldn't take out her great slab of cheese, or the fruit, and the biscuits prepared on the ship. Instead she put her hand into her bag and pulled out a bread roll she had saved from breakfast.

They were passing through towns now and these were damaged too. They pulled into stations; doors slammed, whistles blew, and there was never the long mournful hoot of the American trains.

The man smoked another cigarette and this time the sulphur filled the carriage, and Rosie remembered the oast-houses and the hops, and smiled. Then there were the candles which the fumigation man lit when she and Norah had scarlet fever. How ill they had been, how the bed bugs had bitten, how they had tossed, turned, sweated, ached.

Rosie threw the little boy a sweet and his mother smiled.

'How old is he?'

'Seven.'

Their father and mother had died in the year of Rosie's seventh birthday. She knew she was that age because her grandpa had said Martha, his daughter, her mother, 'had seven years of sunshine with you, my little Rosie'.

Grandpa had bought the house then, because the landlord wouldn't improve it. How he had managed she didn't know. He wouldn't tell, he had only muttered that his daughter hadn't worked herself to death in that laundry and he hadn't worked two shifts twice a week to see it all slip through his hands. So he had bought it off the landlord and together he and Ollie, Jack's dad, had chipped at the plaster, stripping it down, disinfecting the bricks, replastering, reflooring both houses, because Ollie had bought his too.

Since then there had been no cockroaches to scuttle from beneath the wallpaper and no bed bugs. No tins of paraffin at the foot of each bed leg. Rosie scratched herself as the train gushed into the blackness of a tunnel.

There had been no more bed stripping, mattress scrubbing, but there had been . . . what was it? Oh yes, roses. Roses whose fragrance filled the yard. She had forgotten those until this moment.

The train slapped out into the light and Rosie put up her hand to shield her eyes. The rain had stopped. It was four p.m. and they would be in London in an hour.

She leaned her head back, letting it roll with the train, watching the man opposite tap his knee with his newspaper. The child was asleep, his head against his mother's arm, and she missed Nancy and felt the pain again, raw, savage, and the sky seemed darker.

There was no one to meet her at Euston either and she gripped her case more tightly as she queued for a cab. 'Putney, please,' she told the driver, leaning forward, easing her case into the taxi. The trunk was tipped on end by the porters and juggled upright in the front. She tipped them half a crown.

'Bloody Yanks,' she heard a man say behind her, and his voice burst through her pain.

She turned as she got into the cab. 'Bloody Britishers,' she said. But she wished she hadn't as they drove through a ruined London. The skyline was different and there was uncleared wasteland where there had once been streets.

She pulled herself forward, looking out. It was drizzling now. It would be hot at home in Pennsylvania. But no, that wasn't home. This was home. She pushed the strap of her bag from her aching shoulder, remembering the same ache from her journey to Liverpool so long ago. But then it had been her gas mask which was heavy, filled with sandwiches and fruitcake.

A man with a long nose and dark suit had taken the gas mask away from her. He had given it to Grandpa to take home because she wouldn't be needing it where she was going. Had Grandpa given it back to the Town Hall?

They were getting closer now. The streets were clustering. The lampposts had cracked bulbs. There was rope on one of them. So children still swung on them as she and Jack had done. Why hadn't he or Grandpa come?

She sat back, pressing herself deep into the leather seat. She didn't want to go on. She didn't want to reach Middle Street, leave the cab, see Norah, see Grandpa. She wanted to go home.

But they were there now, turning into Middle Street, and the taxi slowed.

'Which one, miss?'

She didn't know. It was all so small, so narrow, and the far end had gone; flattened into piles of bricks, tiles, rosebay willowherb. Grass spurted out of the hard-packed earth and there was a surge of sadness within her for the people who had once lived and laughed here where children were now scrambling, shooting guns made out of wood, cowboys shooting Indians.

'Your grandpa's been watching too many bloody Hopalong Cassidy films at the flicks,' Jack had said when she had told him she was leaving for America.

'Will you write?' she had asked, sitting on the kerb rolling marbles, trying to get his tenner, and he had, though he hadn't come to meet her. But she mustn't keep saying this, she must try and remember which house had been her home. She must try and stop the panic.

'Which one, miss?' the cabbie asked again, almost coming to a halt, and then she saw it. Number 15, with a front door which had once been bright red and was now dark, dirty, almost colourless. It was only now, with the taxi halted and the meter still clicking over, that she remembered the colour it should have been. It was all so small.

The panic was gone. There was nothing in its place, just an emptiness.

She couldn't leave the cab. She couldn't move. She fumbled in her bag, looking for money. But it wasn't money she was looking for, it was just time, and then Norah came out, standing by the open dirty door, leaning back against the wall, staring at her, her face just the same but her hair frizzed up into a perm, tight like her face. She looked more than her eighteen years and Rosie felt a rush of pity for the sister who had been left behind.

She pulled on the handle, pushed open the door and walked towards her.

'Hi, Norah,' she said, leaning forward, but Norah stiffened and so Rosie pulled back without kissing her cheek and the emptiness was filled again.

'You're back then,' Norah said, and her voice was the same too. Sharp and hard. 'Grandpa's asleep, don't disturb him.'

Rosie could hear the children playing on the rubble at the end, where Mr Sims and Mr Elton had lived, Mr Meiner too. She looked down there, not at Norah. She had come back as she had been told to, and Grandpa was asleep, Jack was nowhere and Norah had not changed. So this was it, was it? This was goddamn it. But she wouldn't cry. Not yet. She had no right to in this ruined street.

'Mr Sims died then, did he?' she asked. 'It seems kind of sad. He used to give us toffee, do you remember?' It was better to talk, to drawl out the words slowly and make sure her voice did not shake. It was better to do that than stand here making no attempt to reach out and touch this girl she had not seen for over six years.

Norah moved back into the house. 'That trunk will have to go into the yard. There's no room in the house,' was all she said.

Rosie knew there was no room. The small hall ran into the only downstairs room and upstairs there was just a bedroom and a large boxroom which she and Norah had shared, head to toe. Would that be the case again?

'Hey, miss, how're we going to get this lot in?'

The cabbie was out now, heaving at the trunk, and Rosie called after Norah, but there was no answer and so she dumped her bags on the sidewalk and tried to help him edge it out and lower it to the road, but it was too heavy for the two of them.

'I'll see if those kids will help,' she said, running on down the road, calling to them, wishing that she was running back to Liverpool, back to Frank and Nancy. But then she heard her name, and then again, and footsteps sounded behind her, closer, catching her. Then a hand caught her arm, slowing her, stopping her, and it was Jack. At last it was Jack, turning her to him, gripping her shoulders, shouting, 'Where the hell have you come from?'

'I'm back from the cowboys, didn't you know?' she whispered. 'Didn't you know? Why didn't you meet me?' His eyes were brown as they had always been, his smile the same.

He picked her up now, swung her round.

'Where are your plaits? I've always thought of you with your plaits. Where are you going to bung your rubber bands now?'

It was so good to feel his arms, hear his voice, see the hair which still fell across his forehead, because he was her friend. He had always been her friend. She laughed and cried and held him close and he put his arms round her.

'God, I've missed you,' he said and it was almost more than she could bear.

He pulled her back towards the cab. 'I didn't know you were coming back.' He squeezed her hand then dropped it as they reached the cab.

'But Frank cabled Norah to tell you.'

'Then it's your own bloody fault I never got the message. You should have known better.' He was heaving at one end of the trunk and they had it up, and he and the driver went down the alley between the houses, through the alley at the back where the gutter was damp from the drizzle which had now stopped.

Jack was so tall, his shoulders were wide and his body was thick. He looked more than sixteen. He sounded more. His voice was deep like Joe's but there wasn't the tan, there wasn't the soft quality of the clothes, of her clothes. He was like England, worn and tired. Norah was right. It hadn't been fair that she had missed all this. She turned and looked at the crumpled skyline of the houses backing on to the alley.

They were at the back gate and she didn't want to go in, she held it for them because the yard was home and she couldn't go in, not yet, because Grandpa was in there, and he hadn't come to meet her, he hadn't even stayed awake. He had just dragged her home and she thought she hated him even though he had once loved her so much and she had loved him.

They walked back to the taxi. She paid the fare, tipped half a crown and didn't care what Jack thought, even if it was 'bloody Yank'. He said nothing, though, and she watched the taxi drive away, leaving her here. Her journey was over. She turned to Jack, to his warmth and his smile, and looked at the hands which had written her letters when others hadn't.

'So where *are* you going to put your rubber bands then?' He was leaning back against the wall, putting his hands in his pockets, sloping one leg over the other.

'Round my little finger, I guess,' Rosie said, leaning back on the lamppost which threw light into Grandpa's bedroom.

'Will Woolworths like that, I ask myself?'

'Woolworths will have to get stuffed if they don't,' Rosie answered, looking up into the sky where a weak sun was filtering through.

The sun would throw sloping shadows across the lawn tomorrow. It would glitter on the lake. Nancy would wear goggles to sunbathe. Frank would fish.

'Are you glad you're back?' Jack asked.

'Now you're here,' Rosie said, and flushed because the boy she had known was gone and this half-stranger was in his place. 'Can I come and see your mum?'

She said this because he had blushed too and she felt awkward and wanted to include his family in her feelings, in her words. She loved his mum anyway. She was full-breasted like Nancy, and kind too.

Jack took out his cigarettes, ducking his head down to catch the flame of the match. Something was different between them. Had there been too many years? Too many miles? Had they grown too far apart to be friends? But that could never happen, not for her anyway. This was the boy who had swung her at the rec, who had beaten her at flicksies, helped her tie string to all the knockers in the street, then pulled them with her, heard the knocks. This was the boy who had run whooping through the streets with her when their neighbours had come to their doors, shouting and swearing at them. Who had written.

'Make it tomorrow,' Jack said, pushing himself up from the wall. 'Come and see me on the stall first, down Malvern Lane. We'll talk, catch up. Things aren't the same in there.' He nodded to his house, his face angry, and then he smiled. 'Get in there and see your grandpa. He's been waiting. He's missed you.'

He sauntered off, nodding at her, not going into his house but on down the street. Then he stopped and called back, 'Got any gum, chum?'

'Sure, a goddamn trunkful,' she called back.

He walked on. Then turned again. 'Glad you're back, Rosie. I would've met you. We've only grown, we ain't changed, you know. Not really. Tomorrow then.'

The hallway was dark and so small and there was no sound in the house. No Bix Beiderbecke, no Erroll Garner, no New Orleans with the banjo cutting through the jumble of sounds, keeping the rhythm going. Rosie stood still, her hands on the wallpaper. It was the same; she could feel the pattern running on down beneath her fingers. She had done this when she left. She remembered now.

She thought of the houses she had passed on the train, with their rooms hanging open to the world, wallpaper torn and flapping. That could have been this house. Her grandpa could have been one of those who died, and she pushed open the door into the room where they cooked and washed and lived because she couldn't bear the thought of that and knew now that she still loved him.

There he was, sitting at the table with the brown chipped teapot in front of him. It was the one Grandma had bought. So that hadn't changed. But, dear God, he had. He turned as she entered.

'Rosie, you're here. I didn't know when you were coming, if you were coming. I couldn't rest. I've waited all week for you.'

Somehow she smiled, put down her bags, her jacket and walked towards him, her hands held out. He stood and pulled her to him, holding her close. Her arms were round this man who had once been strong and firm, who had held her with nailmaker's arms and told her he loved her. He was thin, and so small, so old with an old man's smell and he had always been so clean.

She looked past him to Norah. You bitch, she thought, you've just lied to me, you lied to him, kept my cable from him. You black-hearted bitch.

'I'm sorry, my Rosie.' His voice was cracked, stumbling, and his words were loose, clumsy, as he whispered, 'I'm sorry for bringing you back. Norah wanted you here and I promised your grandma you'd come home. I thought you'd want to. Norah said you'd think we didn't want you back, if we let you stay. Sometimes I can't think straight, like I used to.'

She held him, remembering how much she had loved him, knowing how much she still did.

Norah was washing dishes in soda, her head up, listening for the words Rosie knew Grandpa did not want her to hear.

'I love you, Rosie. I couldn't have you thinking we didn't want you back,' he repeated.

'I know, I know,' she soothed because the man was now the child and that hurt more than all the pain so far. 'I love you too.'

Rosie moved back, holding his hand, guiding him on to the chair again, pulling another round to sit at the table with him. He wouldn't release her hand. His joints were loose, his face long, his jaw slack and he had no bottom teeth.

'I've sure missed you, Grandpa. Every day. I guess I couldn't wait to get home, to you.' A lie, but what did it matter.

Norah banged down a cup she was washing on the draining board. 'Took your time, then. Planning to stay for more school. That wasn't fair. I told him so.'

You talk too goddamn much, Rosie wanted to say, but she didn't because Grandpa didn't move, didn't say anything, just dropped his head and Rosie rubbed the back of his big veined hands, touching the swollen knuckles with her fingers.

'Woolworths not good enough for you, then? It suits me.' Norah was wiping the cup with a teatowel.

Rosie sat back. 'Woolworths will be fine. Just fine. I can't think of anything I would rather do, Norah.' But she wanted to say, You still got that dandy fox fur? You must think you're the tops waltzing in wearing that, but she didn't because Norah had been left behind and no matter what she'd said or done since, it wasn't fair. And that was that.

Norah turned back, tucking the edge of the towel into the cutlery drawer beneath the drainer.

'You'd better get down to the Food Office tomorrow to get your ration book. You're eating our points.' She gestured to the pan on the old gas oven. 'Put that on the table.'

Rosie wanted to tip the pan upside-down on that prissy perm but instead she smiled at Grandpa, who brought out a handkerchief with a trembling hand and raised it to his mouth, wiping the corners, putting it away again carefully. So careful, so slow; like his writing had looked, but she hadn't noticed.

Too many years had passed and Rosie saw the old brownstones as she fetched the pan full of mashed potatoes. She looked for a bowl.

'Put it on the table in the pan. Or have you forgotten how we live?'

Rosie flushed. There was nothing she could say because she had.

'I've got tins of ham in the trunk. Shall I go get them?' She moved towards the door.

'No, the Spam's cut. We'll save the ham for something special.'

So there we are, Rosie thought as she sat down. I'm home. I sure am home. But she wouldn't cry, not here, and she reached again for Grandpa's hand. Now she was here she remembered the room and it hadn't changed. Along one wall were all Grandpa's books. He'd read each one and had wanted her and Jack to do the same, but she'd run out of time, and so had Jack. Norah had refused to read them.

She looked round as she cut the pink Spam, eating it with mashed potatoes but no salad. The dresser was the same, the bread board, the bread knife with the burned handle, the worn lino, and there were no cockroaches, maybe no bed bugs. There was a bed in the room though, the folding one that her mother had slept on whilst her father used the chair.

She turned to Norah. 'Is that my bed?'

Norah pointed her knife at Grandpa. 'No, it's his. He has accidents. It's not worth soiling a proper bed and he can reach the privy quicker.'

Grandpa continued to chew but flicked a glance at Rosie, then reached for his handkerchief and wiped his lips, again.

Rosie talked then about the trip over, the train, the damage, the bombs. She talked of anything and everything because she couldn't bear to see the shame in Grandpa's eyes, to hear that voice slashing and wounding as it had always done. The war had changed nothing in Norah.

Norah ate on, chewing, drinking her water, not listening. Rosie knew she wasn't listening but at least she wasn't speaking.

Grandpa rose and walked to the back door, out to the privy. 'Won't be a moment,' he said.

Norah continued to eat. Rosie talked then of New York's rundown East Side, the 'lung blocks', those tenements which gave their people TB.

'Like Mum and Dad,' she said. 'If we hadn't had Grandma and Grandpa, what would we have done? He was just great to us.'

'They wouldn't have been working in the laundry anyway if he'd stayed in Bromsgrove.' Norah pointed her knife at the yard. 'What was wrong with being a nailer? He goes on about it enough. Grandma didn't want to come down. She told me.'

Rosie said, 'Grandma was always complaining. You couldn't take anything she said seriously and you've got awful like her. You've got a tongue like a . . .' but Grandpa came back and so she hurried on and spoke of the hop-picking they'd done in the years before the war. The sun, the smell, the fun.

'Couldn't go to Kent like the rest though, could we? Had to be up in Malvern because that's where the Midlanders used to go.' Norah didn't look up as she spoke, just hooked a piece of mash at the corner of her mouth with her tongue. 'Why couldn't we be the same as everyone else? That's what I want to know.'

Rosie cut in. 'So, how was Somerset then, Norah? Did you settle in?' She wanted to draw that sour tongue away from the old man who had sent her away and then brought her back, but only because he thought it best for her. She knew that now. She had always known it really, but the anger was still there, inside her, mingled with the pain.

'Not as good as America. Country life is hard. I skivvied, worked my fingers to the bone.'

Rosie looked at her. 'Got enough flesh on you now then, Norah, you could slip on a marble any day and not break that goddamn backside.'

No one was eating now. Norah sat back, her eyes dark with rage, her mouth closed into a thin line. Then she finished her potatoes, stabbing them with the fork. Rosie took the plates, washed them in the kettle water. It was nearly dark now and the cracked clock above Grandpa's bed said nine o'clock.

'I've got presents in the trunk,' Rosie said, turning, leaning back on the sink. 'A great nightdress and stockings for you, Norah, a sweater for you, Grandpa.' Her voice was conciliatory. She must try again if they were to live together. She must keep telling herself that, because Norah had suffered, while she hadn't.

Norah was reading a magazine at the table but she looked up now.

'You're sleeping in the boxroom. I've got the front bedroom.'

Of course you've got the goddamn front room, Rosie thought, and I bet that goddamn fox fur is hanging on the back of the door, his goddamn eyes glinting, but she said nothing.

She pushed open the door into the yard and took Grandpa's arm, feeling him lean on her as she helped him to the bench under the kitchen window. The air was full of the fragrance of his roses.

She put the newspaper on the bench which was still damp and then they sat, neither speaking, for what was there to say? So much, too little.

'Of course he wouldn't dig up his precious yard to put in a

shelter. It would have disturbed the roses,' Norah called through the door.

Rosie put her hand on Grandpa's. 'Quite right too,' she said quietly.

'Wouldn't go down to the shelter in Albany Street either. He wouldn't sleep with strange people. Got to be different.'

'I like my privacy,' Grandpa said loudly now.

'I guess we all do,' Rosie nodded, patting his hand, glad that he was answering Norah, jerking his head up, sticking his chin out. Glad too that she need not sleep in the same bed with that girl ever again.

She leaned forward, smelling the dark red cottage rose which was growing well in the raised bed which Grandpa had built years ago. There was a trailing pink clambering up the privy.

Rosie walked round the plants now, looking closely. There was no greenfly. She drew near the shed which still smelt of creosote but only faintly.

'I guess we need to do this again,' she called to her grandfather.

'If you can find any, go on and do it. Don't forget we're rationed even if you haven't been,' Norah shouted. Rosie didn't bother to tell her that America had in fact been rationed. She knew it couldn't compare with British measures.

In the shed the trunk was laid down flat and behind it was an old upended pram turned into a cart. Rosie edged past the trunk. She had forgotten all about the cart. Ollie and Grandpa had made it and she and Jack had raced it against First Street. Norah wouldn't race with them. She might get hurt, she might get dirty. Rosie leaned down and smelt the old leather, spun the wheels.

'I told him to get rid of it but he wouldn't.' Norah was there behind her now. She was waiting for her present. Well, she'd have to wait a little longer.

Later, when it was quite dark and the curtain had been drawn round Grandpa's bed, Rosie called good night.

'I couldn't let the pram go,' he replied softly. 'It reminded me of you, see.'

Rosie did see and she called, 'I love you, Grandpa. I've missed you so much.' And to begin with she had.

That night Rosie didn't shut the door of her bedroom. She

hadn't shut the door on her first night at Nancy and Frank's either. She had felt too lonely, too homesick and had cried silently. She cried now, silently too, thinking of Frank and Nancy, of Sandra, of Joe, of the lake. Crying more as she thought of this house where she'd been born and which wasn't home any more, of this country which was strange to her, of the anger, the pain, the confusion which swept over her in waves. And the despair.

She clenched the woollen knitted blanket she had made before she left and sleep would not come as she tried to cling to Frank's words. 'The future is yours. Make something positive out of the rest of your life.'

Downstairs, Albert lay back on his bed. He could see the table, the cooker, the sink in the dull moonlight. She was back, his Rosie was back. She had looked like her mother when she came in, her hair short, her plaits gone, but the same love in her face that Martha had always had for him.

He coughed, his chest was bad. He was old. The rubber square beneath his sheet made him sweat and it smelt, but then, he smelt too. He turned from the room, lying with his face to the wall. Perhaps he shouldn't have brought her back.

He turned again, back into the room. It was hot now and he was tired but he didn't want to sleep. He sometimes had accidents when he slept.

Perhaps it had been too long, he thought, for he had seen that behind the love there was despair. But he had to believe he had done the right thing as he had had to when he waved her off from Liverpool. It had broken his heart to see the ship becoming smaller and then the loneliness of the war had broken him somehow.

He struggled now, pushing himself up, looking at his books. Maybe Norah had been wrong to think that Rosie would feel deserted if they left her there. And there again she was right, it wouldn't have been fair if one sister had advantages denied to the other. It was all so confusing. He just didn't know. Norah was wrong too, about Nellie not wanting to come to London.

Nailing was dying in Bromsgrove, there was nothing to be made from it any more. His wife had wanted to come south and he remembered with bitterness her face that day when she had insisted they move. But then he pushed the memory from him and thought instead of the land of his roots and Herefordshire too; the sweeping hills, the lush green of the fields, the hops strung so high – and he smiled at the comfort the memory brought.

Yes, there had been despair behind Rosie's love, and he knew it was because she'd left a land and people she'd grown to care for and there was an ache in his chest at her pain. He eased himself back down, pulling the sheet up round his shoulders. He understood that and he would try and take her back to those hills where the scent of the past would ease the present, perhaps for them all, even Maisie and Ollie.

CHAPTER 3

The night had been long, and as Rosie washed in the sink she longed for her own shower and scented soap back in Lower Falls, but there was only the tin bath which hung on the yard wall. Tonight, she thought, she would drag it in when Grandpa was asleep and Norah in bed. Tonight and every night, not just once a week like before she went away.

Grandpa was sitting at the table. Rosie had washed through his drenched sheets and his pyjamas and they were hung on the line, along with his rubber square. She had hoisted them high with the pole but not too high, because he had said that he did not like the neighbours to know.

'Even Jack's mum and dad?' she had asked gently as he dipped his bread in some warm milk after he had sponged himself down standing on newspaper behind the curtain.

'Even Ollie and Maisie,' he had said.

She carried her tea out into the yard, standing by the shed in the spot the sun reached at this hour of the morning. She listened to the sounds of the street, the dogs, the children, the whistling bike-riders, the rag and bone cry. She looked up at Jack's house. The windows were blank and there was no sound. Before she left there had always been laughter and music and shouting.

Her grandfather walked out now and sat on the bench, his back against the wall. He had a walking stick which he propped between his knees. When she was young he would bring peas home on a Saturday wrapped in newspaper and on Sunday they would shell them, sitting on the back step, eating some, putting the rest into Grandma's pan.

Jack would come in and pinch five, always five, throwing them up and catching them in his mouth. Then Maisie would shout across the wall that there was bread and hot dripping from around the piece of scrag-end. She, Jack, and sometimes Norah would go while Ollie and Grandpa went to the pub on the corner for a pint.

The pub had gone too, she realised now. She had forgotten that it had existed, down next to Mr Meiner. She fingered the peach rose, The Reverend Ashe, which grew up against the shed. It had taken a fancy to the creosote, Grandpa had laughed in the year before the war. She had made perfume with its petals. The water had gone brown but there had been a weak scent.

She had given a bottle to Grandma, Norah and Maisie. Maisie had laughed and dabbed some on behind her ears, heavy with earrings, throwing back her head, patting her hair, telling them it made her feel like a ruddy duchess. Ollie roared and slapped her on the backside. Grandma and Norah had thrown theirs down the sink.

As Norah grew older she had always copied Grandma, though Rosie could remember that when they were small sometimes they had laughed together. But as Grandma grew more bitter, more angry, Norah copied her. They froze Rosie out. They formed a team. A team 'who knew better', who were older, wiser. Just more crabby, Jack had always said.

Rosie drank her tea, which was too cold now, then threw the dregs around the roots.

'You remembered then, Rosie,' Grandpa called.

Rosie smiled. 'Yes, I've never forgotten.' But she had until this moment. She had forgotten that the tea leaves nourished the roots.

She moved into the shadow, sitting with him, tucking her hand in his arm. It was thin and his armbands sagged above the elbows. His cuffs were drooping on his wrists. 'I'll sew a tuck in those sleeves for you, shall I?'

She smiled as he nodded and patted her hand. His joints were swollen, his skin was dry and thin, stretched too tight. They sat in silence now and still there was no movement from Jack's house. At home there would be the smell of waffles cooking and the sound of jazz playing, and she had to talk to muffle the memory.

'Do you remember the peas, Grandpa?' Rosie asked as she watched a bee weave in and out of the rose bushes.

He chuckled. 'They were good times.'

Rosie nodded, looking up into the sky, which was pale blue with small white clouds that seemed to fit the size of England. Yes, perhaps they were but she had seen another world and she couldn't leave it behind yet. Would she ever be able to? She looked at Jack's house again.

'What's wrong next door? Jack seemed strange. He told me not to go in. There was something in his eyes.'

Grandpa leaned forward, poking the ground with his stick, rubbing it backwards and forwards across the cracks in the concrete. 'You'll have to ask Jack. People have a right to their privacy. He'll tell you what he wants you to know, if there is anything. It's maybe just the war.'

He brought out his handkerchief and wiped the corners of his mouth. 'It's maybe just the war, Rosie. It changes so much.'

'Yes, Grandpa. But you haven't changed and neither have I.' Did he know she was lying?

Rosie left him in the yard then because she was thinking too clearly of Frank and Nancy, of Sandra and Joe, and there was no place for them here where there was no shower, just a tin bath. Where her grandpa's skin was tight and old, where there was no laughter from Maisie.

She was glad she had to sort out ration cards, jobs, shopping. That would do for now. Later, when the sun was past its height she would talk to Jack. Later still she would write to Frank to refuse his offer of money to finance further education. All that was over. They were no longer responsible for her. She was back in her old world. She looked at the list Norah had written, this was her reality now.

Rosie spent an hour at the Food Office waiting for a ration card, then joined a queue forming outside a small shop and waited for half an hour shuffling forward slowly while the sun beat down. Norah had said, join any queue you see, there'll be something at the end of it, but today it was dog food and they didn't have a dog. She bought a pound anyway and gave it to the woman at the end of the queue with two crying children. She knew Jack would have sold it to a man without a dog for twice as much and she smiled at the thought.

She registered with Norah's grocer round the corner whom

she had known as a child, collecting tea and cheese at the same time. The shop seemed so dark, so small. The goods on the shelves were dull, meagre. He nodded to her. 'Back then. Norah told us you'd had it easy.'

'I guess I did,' she replied and watched his tight withdrawn face, wanting to apologise, wanting to take the years back, stay here, be one of them again. But at the same time, wanting to shout her anger at him.

'Next please,' he called, hurrying her, looking past her.

'I'd like some Players, please,' she said, resisting the push from behind.

'Only available to our regulars.' He was reaching forward for the next customer's ration card.

'They're for Grandpa,' Rosie insisted, not moving over. She had just enough for a packet and then her money from Frank was gone.

The man sighed. His brows met across the bridge of his nose and his eyes were tired. He bent below the counter and passed her one pack.

'Thanks.' She paid and walked past the queue which was jostling behind her.

'These Americans think they can come here and throw their money about. Isn't right, it isn't,' one old lady said to the woman next to her. Rosie didn't look at them, she didn't look anywhere but in front, thinking of the lake, of the sloping lawns and the soaring music. I didn't choose to go, she wanted to scream at their shadowed faces and resentful backs.

She walked back down the street towards the Woolworths in Albany Street. She wouldn't cry, she mustn't. Whatever she did, she mustn't let these Britishers see her pain, or even her anger because she had no right to that. They had stayed and endured. She had fled.

Outside Woolworths she stopped, looking in through the glass doors, seeing the lights, the long alleys of counters. She and Jack had pinched a 6*d* car from here when they were eight. She'd longed to work in amongst it all. But that was then.

At eleven she stood in an office before a white-haired supervisor, her hair permed like Norah's.

'So, you're Norah's sister. Good worker, that girl.'

The woman had run her lipstick outside her top lip to

thicken it. Her breath smelt of tea as she moved behind Rosie to take out a file from the cabinet and then returned to her seat.

'Sit down then.' There was a cup half full on the desk with a cigarette stub floating in it.

'Thanks,' Rosie said, smoothing her skirt, not looking into the cup.

The woman brushed at the corners of her mouth with her little finger. There was a brass ring with a bright red glass stone on her wedding finger. 'Well, you'll have to do something about your voice, if you know what I mean.'

Rosie looked at her. 'No, I guess I don't.'

'Well, listen to that. You sound like a Yank. I don't know what our customers would think, I really don't. This is Albany Street, not Hollywood.' The woman frowned. 'But Norah did put in a good word for you. You've got that old man at home to support, haven't you? Need all the help you can get, I should think.'

'My grandfather, you mean. He has his own money. He doesn't need ours. Norah and I have to work to keep ourselves, not him. It's his house, you know. He gives us a home.' She was tired now, so goddamn tired of it all, so sick of Norah. 'He's a real nice man. Kind of quiet but nice.'

She looked out across the store with its counters glistening with goods. Norah was on jewellery, leaning back talking to the girl at the other end. She was smiling, her mouth a slash of red.

'Oh well, we need someone on records anyway though the stock is very limited these days. Maybe the voice will fit in there. All American anyway, aren't they, these singers?' The woman's voice was slower, kinder. When she smiled the lines cut deep. 'My dad was a nice man too.'

Rosie looked at her closely now and felt her face begin to relax.

'We had a lot of Americans here in the war. They'd come and talk. My friend married one. She's in California now.' The woman was pulling her overalls across her breast. 'Yes, proper little meeting-place in here. It's very dull now. England is very dull. I expect you've found that.'

Rosie looked out again, across the aisles. 'I only got in yesterday and I guess it's real good to be here.' If she said it often enough it might help it to be the truth.

'Oh well, that's nice.' The woman was moving towards the door. 'Perhaps we can move you into the snack bar when we get one. You seem like a good girl. Start tomorrow, why don't you.'

Rosie walked out of the office into the hub of the store. The Andrews Sisters were singing 'The Three Caballeros' and she wondered how Albany Street would take to Bix Beiderbecke. She walked past Norah and smiled – after all they were not children feuding any longer. Norah had been unfairly treated and Rosie must damp down the anger.

'I'm on records,' she said.

'Well, don't be late. Grandpa needs his lunch. There's a nice bit of Spam in the meat-safe.' Norah turned away, then back again.

'I suppose you're meeting that Jack. Well, not until you've done the chores, you're not.'

'One day, you'll find yourself being pleasant and it will be as much of a goddamn shock to yourself as it will be to the rest of the world.' Rosie walked away, leaving Norah to close her open mouth, and all the way home she was glad she had let the anger out. It helped her to lift her head, but from now on she must rein back in.

She opened a tin of American ham for Grandpa instead.

'This is our celebration,' she told him. There was no ice-box so Rosie drank lukewarm milk, then sank the bottle into the pail of water again. She stood a bowl in water and left half the ham in it for Norah's meal that evening. It was only fair.

She and Grandpa ate tinned peaches which slipped on the spoon and were easy to eat. Juice trickled down both their chins and they laughed as they had done before she left.

It was only when he was asleep and the floor was washed, the dishes too, when the cooker was cleaned and her arms were black from the grime, when the beds were made, that she left, wondering how Norah could sleep with those fox's eyes glinting on the back of the door. But what did it matter? She was going to see Jack, but then she heard her grandfather calling. She turned. He was in the doorway, waving to her, leaning on his stick with the other hand.

'You forgot your matchbox.'

For a moment Rosie paused and then she remembered the ladybirds which she used to catch in a matchbox she always carried when she went out. She called, 'No I didn't, I've got one in my pocket. Don't worry, we'll keep the roses clear of greenfly.'

He smiled and waved again and turned back into the house. Rosie stopped at a tobacconist, bought a matchbox and tipped the matches out into the bin. He mustn't know that she had forgotten.

Malvern Lane was too narrow to receive much sun and Rosie watched as Jack moved backwards and forwards in front of his stall, holding a flowered teapot high above his head, laughing with one woman, nodding to another who picked up a saucer and turned it over in her hands. She dropped money into his left hand and pushed the saucer deep into her shopping bag.

'Come on then, ladies. Don't let the rationing get to you. Look, it's a lovely day up there above the clouds, let's have a smile, shall we?' He was laughing now and the crowd laughed with him, Rosie too, but he hadn't seen her yet and she was glad. She wanted to stand here, listening, watching, trying to ease into London just for a moment. Trying to push away the thought of the intersections, the streetcars, the ice-cream parlors.

'Just look at this.' Jack pointed to the teapot which he still held high. 'When did you last see a splash of colour like this then, eh? Can't buy it now, can you? Certainly not. Only white can be made the chiefs have said.' He looked round at them all. 'Well, that's as may be, but today is your lucky day. Here – ' Jack turned and gestured to the back of the stall – 'I have just a few little treasures so who's going to give me five bob for this then?'

It went on like that for half an hour and by that time all the coloured china had gone, as Rosie knew it would, and as the crowds thinned he saw her and called across.

'Did you remember your matchbox, then?'

The woman in front of Rosie turned. Her cheeks were red and her smile broad. 'He's a one, that lad. Could charm the bleeding birds out of the trees.'

Rosie laughed and held up the box. She didn't want to speak, to drawl. She didn't know if the woman would stop smiling.

'Be with you in half an hour. The gang's coming,' Jack called again, then he laughed as a woman came and slapped his arm, giving him money for two plates and telling him she'd take another if he threw in a kiss with it. He looked at Rosie again and pointed to his watch. It wasn't gold, his skin wasn't tanned. Was Joe playing tennis now? Was Sandra?

She wandered off, down the lane, moving out round a heap of yellowed cabbage leaves whose smell followed her on down past the potatoes, the lettuce, and drowned the scent of the pinks tied in small bunches and left to stand in a tin jug.

There was a tea stall and she bought a cup, sipping it, hearing the past all around her, the noises, the voices, breathing in the smells which had faded and vanished with the years. But they were here again, all here.

So, the gang was coming too. She didn't remember them, not their names or their faces. It was only Jack she had pictured over the years and the miles. Would Joe and Sandra forget her too?

When she returned Jack was waiting, his old leather money apron now tied around the waist of his father, Ollie, who had run the stall for as long as Rosie could remember. She started to walk towards Ollie but Jack caught at her arm.

'Leave it for now.'

They walked to the rec where they had scuffed the ground with worn plimsolls on hot days as they pumped themselves higher and higher on swings already raised by being thrown over the bar. They didn't talk as they walked through the streets, and Jack had to lead the way because she had forgotten. He sauntered, hands in pockets, his two-tone shoes worn, his hair hanging down over his forehead.

She remembered her shoes, and the sweater she had worn back to front as all Lower Falls girls did, but they were in her room, on the shelf below the Cougar pennant and she mustn't think of that.

They crossed wasteground which had once been three houses. The rec was across the road from Oundle Street where there were houses with black-tarred casement sheets instead of glass. They were all deserted and two were ripped apart; just as she felt.

She remembered the park with railings but they were gone and now Jack told her how his mum had written to say that they had been taken away by men with oxyacetylene cutters to build Spitfires.

'How's your mum?' she asked. 'It was so quiet today.'

His eyes were dark as he turned, then looked past her. 'Race you to the swings.'

He ran, catching her arm, running with her across worn asphalt where weeds were breaking through, running faster than her, goddamn it, and so now she spurted but he was still ahead and the breath was leaping in her throat as the swings drew nearer. But he was first, throwing himself on to one, pushing back with his feet, lifting them high and then surging forward, up into the air.

She sat on hers and looked at the sign that said, '12 YEARS AND UNDER ONLY.'

'Hey, we'll be done.'

She heard his laugh. 'Come on, Yank. We've just been through a war. No one's going to stop me swinging if I want to.'

She pushed off now, feeling the air slicing through her, half pain, half pleasure. The links were rusty and stained her hands and then there was only the squealing of the chain and their laughter. She leaned back, the sky was blue. It was the same sky over America. Maybe it wasn't so far after all, but she knew that it was.

Afterwards they talked, still sitting on the swings, Jack's legs gently moving his, his shoulders leaning hard into the chain, his hands between his knees.

He told her then that Ollie was drinking, snarling. Sleeping a little. Working a little. That Maisie seldom laughed now.

'But they were so different. Was it the war? What about Lee? Hasn't he helped?'

There were two small children standing by the swings now and Jack winked at them, standing, nodding to them.

'It's all yours,' he called and they ran past him and Rosie, who stood too and watched as they scrambled on to the swings.

'Give us push, mister,' the boy with red hair said.

Jack did and Rosie watched as his broad hands pushed and caught, pushed and caught the swing.

'I'm OK now,' the boy said and they walked over to the bench. The dark green paint was flaking. Rosie brushed the seat with her hand, rubbing the paint off as she sat.

'Didn't Lee help?' Rosie insisted, watching the two children, hearing their yells clearly across the intervening space. She didn't want to hear of Ollie snarling, of Maisie silent. She wanted to hear of laughter, of bread and dripping, of earrings jangling.

Jack shrugged. He reached down, pulling at a dandelion which had lifted the asphalt. 'He seems to have made it worse and he's a lovely kid. It can't have been the war either. Dad didn't get called up. It's his chest you see, collapsed lung. He built the new airfields, that sort of thing. Did a bit of dealing.' He smiled slightly but his eyes were so angry.

Rosie smiled, looking away. 'I just bet he did.'

'I wasn't there, you see. The kids that came back after the first evacuation went away again with the Blitz, like you did.' He flicked the shredded dandelion at her. 'She was good to me though, Mum was. She came down visiting, you know. All the time. It was good fun.'

'Was your dad jealous of that?'

'No, I don't think so. He didn't change until later. When he came to see me first he was fine. Took back a few hams, sold them well. Even did a bit of dealing with the GIs who were camped in the village.' He paused and looked up at the sky, and his voice became angry. 'But then, all of a sudden like, he stopped coming. Didn't see Mum much come to that after D-Day. Busy, I expect, and then there was Lee. He's got red hair too.' Jack flicked a piece of grass off his trousers, nodding towards the boy he had pushed on the swing. 'I don't know what's wrong. It's just wrong. I wanted to tell you before you came. I didn't want you upset.'

His face was red now and he didn't look at her. She wanted to reach across and hold him as he had once held her when she cut her knee and needed stitches. But they were children then. They were grown now and there was a difference somehow.

He looked at her now and the anger had gone, there was just tiredness, like hers. 'Come anyway. They want to see you but it's funny, me dad doesn't like Yanks.'

Rosie looked at her hands. 'He's not the only one.'

'Oh, I reckon it's this rationing, you know. Makes people crabby.'

There were voices behind them now, calling, shouting, and a

football bounced behind them and over them and Jack looked at Rosie. 'Remember the gang? I thought it would help you settle back in.'

She did remember when they were all around, touching her clothes, laughing at her tan, at her voice, asking about Lower Falls and New York and the skiing. Telling her about Somerset, where they had all been evacuated. She looked away, wishing she had been with them, wishing that she belonged as she had once done.

It was Sam, the old second-in-command, his hair in a crew cut, who showed her that for him at least she no longer did.

'So you came back. Slumming, eh?' he said, not looking away when Jack told him to shut his mouth. His pale eyes held hers as he bounced the ball, then threw it to Ted, then Jack. Then bounced it again.

Her eyes were blurred but it was tiredness, she mustn't think it was tears. She remembered Sam all too clearly now. He had tied her to a lamppost when they were nine and fired arrows at a potato he stuck on her head. She hadn't cried then and she wouldn't now.

There were laughs and jokes, and always the ball was on the move. She watched, listened, smiled, waited and then Sam threw the ball to her, hard. She had known that he would and batted it straight back at him with a clenched fist as Frank had taught her. He caught it and threw it again, talking to Ted as he did so, but looking at her all the time.

She threw the ball to Jack. He looked at Sam, then back at her. There was a question in his eyes and she knew he had brought them together deliberately, to face up and get it over with. She shook her head. She was angry now and she would deal with this herself. This was her rec too, her gang, and nobody was going to take it away from her. They'd taken enough already.

She hurled the ball hard at Sam, and nothing more was said as they caught and threw, caught and threw, just the two of them. Her arm was tired and she was hot, but it didn't matter. Frank had trained her well.

It was Ted who broke the silence. 'So, how's po-face taken to you coming back?' he asked.

Rosie kept her eye on the ball, waiting for it to come again, feeling the stinging in her hands, seeing the two small boys running over from the swings, leaving a space beside her for them to join in. Waiting, too, for Sam. The ball came. She hurled it back. He caught it; she heard the slap of skin against leather. She needed her leather mitt.

'You can't blame Norah, she had a lousy time, like the rest of you,' she panted.

She caught the ball again, then batted it back but Jack intercepted and passed it on to the small red-haired boy. Rosie felt the throbbing in her hands, but she wouldn't look at them. She looked instead at Sam. What would he do now?

'No way that old bag had a bad time. Come on, let's sit down,' Dave called.

Sparrows were sitting in the clubbed trees around the rec, singing and flying. Jack walked to the bench and the others followed. Sam took Woodbines from his pocket, shaking his head, looking at Rosie, his eyes still cold. His hands were red, like hers. Did they throb like hers too?

'Your Norah should have gone too. Bloody unfair, I call it.'

Jack looked up at Sam, then at Rosie and she shook her head again.

Ted said, 'That's a load of rubbish. She was billeted with the doctor over in the next village. Had a life of old Reilly, never even had to flick a bleeding duster.'

They were sitting and leaning on the bench now, cigarette smoke drifting up into the air, watching the two small boys kicking the ball from one to another, hearing the thuds. Rosie said nothing, not yet.

Sam flicked his ash on to the ground, rubbing it in with his shoe. 'I bet Rosie never had to flick a duster either. Bet she never had to queue for food. Bet she stuffed herself with ice-cream, steak, got taken out by flash American boys, the brothers of those GIs who swanked over here.' Sam laughed but it was a hard sound. 'Well, go on. Did you?'

Rosie flushed, looking across at the two boys, then back at Sam again. 'What's wrong, bud, did a GI steal your girl?'

Ted laughed, clapped Sam on the shoulder. 'She got you there.' They were all laughing now, Jack too, but his eyes were still watchful. Sam did not laugh.

He stubbed out his cigarette carefully on the sole of his shoe and put it back in his cigarette packet. Rosie watched. She had forgotten people did that. She had forgotten that they needed to and she wanted to say she was sorry, but no, she had to fight Sam. That's all there was to it, or there was no place for her here, with them.

'No,' Sam said, 'nobody stole my girl. I just don't like freeloaders who come back home and lord it about in their new clothes, expecting everyone to bow and scrape because they're back. This is the real world here.'

They were all standing now and Rosie looked at all their faces. They were uncertain, all except Jack, who was looking at her, waiting to see if she could make it on her own. It was only if she couldn't that he would come in. He had always been like that. He had always been there behind her.

Sam turned to her. 'You've had it on a plate. No rationing, no bombs, just bloody everything you want. So just don't come back here, Rosie Norton, and drawl all over the rest of us.'

There was silence. Jack was still watching her. 'There *was* rationing,' she said but that was all because they were never really short of anything, and there was no danger for her.

'Oh yeah, when did you last have a banana?' Sam said, his eyes narrow. Jack's were, too, but they were looking at Sam.

Rosie couldn't answer because Frank had exchanged a piece of pork for a hand of bananas last year and the year before. She looked at them all, at their pale skins, their tired faces, and said, 'You're right. I had it cushy, I have a drawl. I had bananas last year and I'm sorry. It's not fair. Do you think I don't know that? But I'm back. I haven't changed.'

There was silence as they stood around her. Sam's lips were still thin. Jack's eyes were steady. The others were nodding, smiling, all uncertainty gone.

Sam still didn't smile though. He said, 'OK, you say you haven't changed.' He looked at Jack. 'You tell her about tonight, then bring her along. We'll see if she's changed. We'll see if she's got too good for us all.'

Jack's face set, he took Sam by the arm, moving him along towards the pavement. Ted followed. Dave and Paul too. Rosie didn't. She watched them, then the delivery boy cycling past. He rode 'no hands' and sat with his arms folded, whistling. She looked back at the gang. What was happening tonight? Whatever it was, she'd do it.

Ted turned towards her, then nodded to Jack, so did the others. Sam just stared and then called to her, 'Be there.'

The delivery boy had reached the corner. Rosie called back, 'Bank on it, Sam.' But what was it?

As they walked back without Sam and the others, Jack told her about the bomb which had killed Sam's mother, the GI jeep that had killed his sister. But he wouldn't tell her about tonight. 'Not yet,' he said. 'I didn't want you involved. I have to explain some things first.'

They passed the black-tarred replacement windows in a damaged house and he told her how in this time of shortages he, Ollie, Sam and the gang had bought demob suits off the men coming home and resold them at a profit, and that didn't hurt anybody because the soldiers didn't want them anyway.

He told her about the drivers who would deliver twenty-one pigs to the wholesalers and be given a receipt for twenty. How the odd one would be sold, piece by piece. For a lot of money. It was big business. Nasty business.

'But what about tonight?'

He told her about the police swoop on marketeers in March designed to end the racketeering. About the major roadblocks around London and other cities. About the lorries and vans the police searched for eggs, meat, poultry. He told her about the market stalls being raided. He told her that the police were still stopping and searching anyone who seemed suspicious. That it was a dangerous time to be out and about if it looked as though you were up to anything shady.

'But what about tonight?'

He asked her if she remembered Jones who had owned their houses. Jones was getting very flash, he said, because he took people's money for black-market produce like that extra piece of pork – and only sometimes delivered the goods. He also pinched produce from the local allotments, but they could find no proof. Last of all, he had taken two cheeses from a farm where the neighbourhood owned two cows and had a cheese club.

'Sure I remember him, now what about tonight?' She

grabbed him now, turning him to her, laughing, and it was the first time she had done that for so long.

'Tonight we are not banging door knockers, we are not cutting up sleepers for fuel and selling it, we are not making cigarettes out of dog-ends. Tonight we are breaking into a warehouse owned by Jones and taking two of his cheeses. You, me, Sam and Ted. All the gang. We're taking back what's ours. Are you coming?'

He was still facing her, his eyes serious, though his mouth was smiling. She thought of the lake, but all that was slipping away from her. Just for now, it was more distant.

She thought of Grandpa, the police action Jack had just explained. 'We could get caught?' He voice was serious.

'Yes.' He didn't hesitate. 'Yes, we could. It might be big trouble.'

'Does this cheese really belong to the street or is it all for money?'

'No. The cheese is ours. We're sick of getting taken for a ride, and being pushed around.'

She smiled, walking on now, hearing him catch her up.

'When do we start?' she said because she knew all about being pushed around.

It was dark when she left the house. She had bathed in the tin bath as she said she would and felt better. She wore a loose dress, it was so hot.

They met outside Jack's and walked quietly, neither speaking until they reached the end of Middle Street, then cut across to Vernon Terrace, up the alley, down to Futcher's Walk, picking up the others, picking up Sam. Nothing was said as they approached the wall which ran round the warehouse.

There were dogs but Jack knew them and called to them quietly. Then he was bunked up and over by Sam who shot Ted up too. Sam went next, the others after. She was to be look-out. Sam would wait the other side of the wall to relay any warning.

A cyclist approached and Rosie walked slowly on, then back again when he had overtaken. She listened and looked and wished they would goddamn hurry. She thought of Grandpa asleep, of Norah too. She thought of Joe and Sandra, Frank and

Nancy, but still she looked and listened for over half an hour and again wished they'd hurry because she was out here on her own.

There were sounds now, the soft bark of a dog, voices, and Jack called, 'All clear?'

It was, and so he threw one cheese, then the other, then scrabbled over himself. It had all been so easy. She had proved herself to Sam, to them all.

But then they saw the police, walking towards them, dipping in and out of the lamplight, and Jack grabbed her, told her to run, told the others to stay – for Christ's sake stay behind the wall.

She felt her fear and his. She thought of Grandpa, and then of Sam, and now the fear was gone. She turned to Jack.

'No, put your arm round me, kiss me.'

He looked at her, then at the police. He ducked his head and kissed her with soft lips and she hugged him, turning her back, pushing the cheeses up inside her dress, and then they walked towards the police. Everything was quiet, all they could hear were the footsteps walking in time towards them. She didn't know if they had seen. She didn't know if a hand would grip her shoulder and her Grandpa would know what she had been doing.

She held her stomach, walking with legs slightly apart, feeling Jack's arm around her. It too was tense, trembling, and then she started to cry, asking him why they couldn't marry, especially with the baby due so soon. She clutched the cheeses to her.

They were level with the police now and Rosie turned her face into his shoulder. It was warm, as Joe's had been.

'Just don't leave me, that's all. If you won't marry, don't leave me.'

The police looked away, embarrassed, and Jack held her closer, his breath warm in her hair, and his arm was relaxed, warm now because they hadn't been stopped yet, and maybe they wouldn't be. He held her close and said that he would stay for ever, but she must eat more calcium, more cheese. Then they were well past the police and near the corner.

'Oh Jack,' she said, 'I know the baby will look just like you.' And now they were round the corner and running, laughing.

That night she lay in bed, hearing Jack's voice, feeling his lips on hers. Sam had bought her a ginger beer. Ted had said it would be bad for the baby. She had laughed with them. The anger in them had eased because they had taken what was theirs and she knew she could do that too. She could take back the future which had seemed to be hers until last month. She would have her journalism, somehow, and she would start tomorrow.

Welcome back, Jack had said when she told him.

CHAPTER 4

The next day Rosie enrolled at evening secretarial classes which would begin in late September. Frank had joined his paper as a cub reporter after teaching himself shorthand and typing. If college hadn't been necessary for him, it wouldn't be for her.

September was too long to wait, though, so she brought home a shorthand book from the library because she was working towards her future now, this very day. It was the only way she would survive the loss, the separation from that other world, those other people she still loved, still grieved for even though she had Grandpa, the gang, and Jack.

July turned to August which was heavy with heat and with rain too, but by then Rosie had learned the rudiments of shorthand on her own late at night in her room, though she still had no speed. But it would come. Goddamn it, it would come. She would make sure it did.

The weather didn't matter during the day either because she had coaxed Mrs Eaves into letting her play Bix Beiderbecke through the speakers so that his mellifluous cornet-playing filled the store. But only once a day, Mrs Eaves, the supervisor, had said, jangling the keys on the belt of her overalls, leaning across the mahogany counter, because the public prefer the Andrews Sisters, Glenn Miller – the romantic, the slick.

So too did Norah, but Rosie didn't care so much about that now that she knew. Norah had not had such a bad war. She had pranced around, showing off, drinking tea with a cocked little finger, putting the milk in last.

'So why lie?' Rosie had asked Jack.

He had shrugged and so she had asked Norah that same day, leaning on the rectangular counter, talking quietly so that the other assistants could not hear.

Norah had flared with anger. 'I'm not lying,' she said, 'not really. You had a much better time. It should have been me. I'm older.'

Perhaps, Rosie thought now as she ticked records off against the stocklist, Norah was still trying to adjust, to come to terms with leaving Somerset. Perhaps she yearned for the people who had been her family for that time. If so, she understood and so she played the Andrews Sisters and smiled at Norah, who didn't smile back.

Rosie turned as a customer, a woman in a felt hat, asked for 'Chattanooga Choo Choo'.

'It's sure nice. I really like Glenn Miller,' Rosie said as she wrapped it. Grandpa did too. He had heard it on the wireless and tapped his foot as he read *Silas Marner*. Rosie had laughed and told him that she would try to buy a gramophone and he could bop to Duke Ellington. He had stopped having accidents now. There had been no soiled sheets, no embarrassed lowering of the eyes, and he even wanted to hear of her evenings at the Palais with the gang.

She told him how she and Jack jitterbugged around the floor, feet moving fast, swirling in and then out, up and over his hip, his shoulder, while the MC shook his head, tapped them on the shoulders and pointed to the sign on the wall: ABSOLUTELY NO JITTERBUGGING ALLOWED.

They didn't stop. No one stopped. They all danced. The war was over. They had all fought it, Rosie too, Jack said. They all bore the scars. He could see hers, he had told her, in her eyes, and they were still fresh, but they would go. One day they would go. And we're alive so we'll jitterbug like the others and no one will tell us we can't. So they jitterbugged and it kept the shadows and the pain away.

But there were nights when Ollie lurched home drunk and there was shouting and banging to be heard through the walls. On these nights Jack didn't come dancing, he stayed behind to stand between Maisie, Lee and Ollie. It wasn't the same without him. Dancing with Sam and Ted, Dave and Paul didn't stop her wanting Frank and Nancy. It didn't stop her wanting Maisie and Ollie as they had been before the war. It didn't stop her wanting a much earlier time when there had been no pain or anger in Jack's eyes. And it made her think of Joe.

Rosie tipped the Beiderbecke record back into its sleeve. Her legs ached. There was no air in the shop and the heat was thick about her. She longed for a draught or the cool of the evening. She pulled her burgundy overall away from her back and then stood still. Nancy had said it was the best way of cooling down. It did no good to fret. Maisie had said that too last night when at last she had come round and Rosie stood still now, thinking of Maisie's plump arms, so like Nancy's.

For a moment it had been like Pennsylvania again but then Nancy had never smelt of lavender. Maisie did, always had done, Rosie realised as she was pulled against that warm, plump woman who had pushed open the yard gate as she and Grandpa were hugging mugs of tea between their hands and breathing in the roses.

What were they talking about? Rosie served another customer, smiling, giving change, settling back against the counter. She couldn't remember, but she smiled again at the thought of the pushchair coming through the gate, the child wide-eyed and unsure. Then Maisie, her red hair brown at the roots, her earrings jangling and her face bright with a smile.

Rosie had stood her mug in the earth of a rose bush and run to Maisie, flinging her arms round her, smelling the older woman's lavender scent. She had looked at Maisie, taking in the circles beneath her eyes and the lines from her nose to her mouth. But the smile was the same and the voice too.

'You took your time coming home. We've missed you,' Maisie said, pulling her close again. 'We've really missed you.' Rosie hadn't spoken. She knew she would have cried, for these arms were Nancy's too and she could hardly bear the pain.

She squeezed Maisie, then turned, her head lowered, to Lee. He was squirming round, his eyes watching her; his smile was Jack's but his skin was pale, freckled. Not like any of the others.

He reached up his hand and gripped her finger and she said how cute he was, and lifted him from the pushchair, taking him to Grandpa, sitting with him on her knee. Maisie poured tea from the pot for herself, fetched Rosie's from the rosebed, dusted the earth off the bottom with her hand, and called Rosie the same mucky devil she'd always been. They laughed together, as they used to do, and then just looked at one another.

'You look tired,' Rosie said, rubbing her cheek against Lee's head. He pulled away and looked at her, his smile there, his eyes watching hers.

'Don't fret at what you hear,' Maisie said, her face drawn. 'It sounds worse than it is.'

Would she come again tonight? Rosie wondered. She'd said she would.

Maisie did come, with Lee again, while Rosie washed clothes in the sink. 'Sit with Grandpa,' she called through to the yard. 'I'll bring the tea out in a minute.'

Norah slammed through from the hall. 'I'm going out, especially now that kid's here. There's no bloody peace.'

'Why don't you stay?' Rosie said as she wrung out the blouse and dress. 'We should try to get on.'

She had decided to be pleasant again, to try and build some sort of a bridge between them this summer because they needed one another. Couldn't Norah see that? Families were important, but then it seemed that Norah preferred her friends.

Norah pulled her cardigan over her shoulders and checked her make-up in the mirror, tucking the lipstick she had melted down last night into her bag.

'I've got better things to do,' she said. 'We're going dancing. Not at the crummy Palais but up West.'

Rosie smiled, wanting to wring her neck instead of the blouse. She shook her hands over the sink, dried them, then picked up the tea tray. Norah's dress didn't fit. It was too tight over the hips.

'Have a good time,' was all Rosie said.

Lee put out his arms to Rosie as she sat down between Maisie and Grandpa.

'Go on, pick him up then,' Maisie said. 'He gets nothing but spoiling from Jack too.'

She was smiling as she pulled out the Camel cigarettes from her bag. 'Thanks for these, Rosie. I should have been in sooner to say thanks – and to say hello. Here you are, Albert.' She leaned past Rosie, handing him one. 'Got your own matches, have you?'

He nodded.

Rosie let Lee walk up her legs and body, holding on to his hands while he arched away, and then she put him down, watching his unsteady walk. He reached into the raised beds, picking up soil, looking at it, dropping it.

Grandpa laughed. 'It's good to have you here, Maisie. A bit like old times. Can't believe this little nipper is one and a half. Seems only yesterday it was Jack and Rosie digging up me roses.'

They flicked their ash into their hands and Rosie leaned back, her face to the sun, watching the smoke spiralling, disappearing. She didn't like the smell and moved to the upturned pail, hugging her knees, laughing as Lee tottered towards her.

'Yes,' Maisie said. 'Just like old times.'

There was silence except for the grunts from Lee.

'Can you put back the clock then, Albert?' Maisie said.

'Yes, can you, Grandpa?' Rosie echoed.

That night Rosie replied to the letters she had received from the previous week. She was glad the lake was so warm, and the swimming good, that the Club tennis court was already being built. But, she wanted to say, how can it all continue as though I've never existed? How can all these things go on when I hurt so much inside?

How many Subscription Dances had gone into the court? she wondered. How many girls had danced with Joe? Had Frank leaned back in his chair and said, 'You make sure you don't drink when you drive that girl.' Of course he hadn't. He only said that about her. But not any more.

She told them of the evening classes to begin at the end of September with Miss Paul over the piano shop – shorthand, typing, book-keeping. She told them of the rationing, of the cheeses; of the roses which were still free of greenfly. She did not tell them about Woolworths, nor about Norah or Maisie. She cried all night and she thought her sobs were silent but they weren't. Grandpa heard them and it was more than he could bear.

The next day, which was a Sunday, he held her hand and said that they would go to Herefordshire again this year. They would go hop-picking as they used to, before the war, before things changed. All of them, Maisie, Ollie, Jack and Lee, just like they used to, and perhaps there she would learn to laugh again deep down inside, and the others would too, and they would cast the war from their lives.

They did go, even Ollie. Even Norah. They took a train on 1 September and then a bus along the roads which wound round and along the rolling green hills because here no one had sliced through nature, but had fitted in with it. Or so Grandpa had always told them when he brought them here each year before the war. Rosie remembered the American street grids, slicing up the towns, and the long straight roads of Pennsylvania, thinking of Frank and Nancy returning to Lower Falls without her now that it was September.

She pushed that from her. She looked out at the fields. There were cider apple orchards. There was space, sky, air. It was green in the distance, not grey and cramped, and slowly she began to remember what had once been, so long ago.

Close by, the barley had been harvested and the ground re-ploughed and that was still the same. Though not each field, not yet, and now those that were left unploughed must wait until the hops were in because for those few short weeks of the harvest all else was put to one side. Would her pain be put to one side too, and everyone else's?

Jones's farm with its large spacious pigsties was the same too. Swept, scrubbed, white-washed, for this was where they always slept. Jack laughed as they stuffed straw into the palliasses, chasing Lee with a handful, pushing some down Maisie's back, then Rosie's. Maisie crept up behind him and they pushed him on to the heaped pile, sitting on him, stuffing straw up his trousers and down his shirt until he begged for mercy, and even then they stopped only when he had gone down on his knees.

Grandpa, Ollie and Jack slept in the end partition. Rosie, Norah, Maisie and Lee were in the next. The rest of the sties were taken by Black Country people and a few from Bromsgrove, and this was why Grandpa came here, and not to Kent. It was here that he heard his Bromsgrove dialect, his roots. Where were hers? Rosie thought.

'Just you wait, he'll be calling us "me dooks" before the day is out,' Maisie said as she gave Lee a biscuit to chew. As they ate supper heated over the primus in the end building he did and they all laughed, even Norah, even Ollie, even Rosie, and it was from deep inside.

Jack and Rosie walked down the lane to the road, watching for the caravans that they knew would come bringing gypsies on from the plum-picking at Evesham, the cherries at Shropshire and the peas at Worcester. The gate was warm from the sun, deep cracked, chipped with the initials they had carved in 1938. Jack covered it over.

'Your Grandpa would catch us with his stick,' he laughed.

Rosie nodded, looking down the lane, hearing the caravans, the barking of the long dogs and lurchers, the ponies which plodded, the brasses which jingled. She felt the wind in her hair and was happy because for the four weeks they were here, this place belonged to her, just as much or as little as it belonged to the others.

The gypsies came now, the women walking at the pony's head, one smoking a clay pipe. The men sat, the reins in their hands. The children sat too, looking ahead, not at Rosie or Jack.

'Never changes, does it?' Jack murmured, watching as they rolled past.

They walked then, up to the hop-fields, neither speaking, taking the path which ran along the top of the kale field. She remembered where to go, she realised. Somehow she knew where to go.

She walked ahead now, confident, hearing Jack close behind. On round the kale which looked like small trees, then further to the ragwort-spotted meadows. At the bottom of these, past clumps of purple-crested thistles, lay the stream. They used to picnic there at the end of the day. She turned.

'Do you remember . . . ?' she began, but stopped for Jack was nodding.

'Yes, I remember. Tinned salmon sandwiches.' He was smiling and there were no shadows in his eyes today. Rosie hoped that there would be none as the four weeks went by. Would Ollie and Maisie be able to go back in time, enough for a fresh start? Would she?

In the distance rooks clawed up into the sky from the copse planted on Trafalgar Day. She turned further up the hill and they were on to the worn top path and into the hop-fields where the bines swung fifteen feet above them in the wind and Rosie stood still, looking about her, remembering.

Her mother had come every year before she died. They had picked all September and her mother had said it made her feel safe, standing here, as Rosie was doing now. Safe from the world. She had died though, her father too. They hadn't been safe. Was there such a thing as safety? Everything changed. It always changed.

'It's like being under the sea,' Jack said, standing close to her, looking up.

It seemed so quiet, no dogs barking, no cyclists whistling, no children playing. She loved this first evening before the picking began and the hops were stripped.

'I love this first evening,' Jack said.

When they returned to the sties the Welsh had arrived and were in the barn, singing, shouting, laughing. One child was crying but Lee was sound asleep and Maisie too. Norah lay on the straw mattress. It always itched the first night, Rosie thought as she settled on hers, but she could see the sky through the window, the clouds scudding over the moon, and then she slept and dreamed of nothing.

In the morning she was up early, walking along the lane again. The mist lay still over the land and there were blackberries on the bushes as she passed. She picked two and they stained her fingers. They were sweet and cool.

The oasts were shrouded by the mist, the farm buildings too. A cockerel crowed. She was at the kale now and there was dew on the leaves. She reached down, rolling the drops off into her hand. There were ferns at the edge of the field and everywhere the earth was red and smelt of a long warm summer.

There were partridges flying up before her, and a lurcher dog over from the caravans was leaping and bounding in the kale, making more birds rise. There was smoke from the gypsy caravans and washing strung across the bushes. The hedges nearby were stripped of branches for their fires. Rosie turned now, back to the farm, to the white-washed, partitioned sties, because the sun was breaking through, the mist was rising and soon the picking would begin.

As they left for the hop-fields, the sun was casting sharp shadows from the two oasts and the distant Welsh hills were black. Rosie tightened the hessian sacking around her waist and took Maisie's bag from her, passing it on to Jack when he nodded. It left both Maisie's hands free for the pushchair.

'That's better,' said Maisie, pushing the chair and laughing.

The hop strands had been strung in the spring by men on stilts and now the pickers pulled at the bines, flip-flipping the hops into the wattle bins. The Welsh were ahead of them, the Black Country people with them, and Grandpa was laughing and talking, his voice soft, almost young again. The gypsies were further back, the children silent as they worked. One had a ferret and carried dock leaves in his pocket as a cure for its bites. Rosie looked at Jack and they laughed.

The hop-leaves hung down from the strings, deep etched by the sun filtering through. The sprays of hops were a delicate green, the pollen-like powder was yellow on her fingers. It made the beer bitter.

Her fingers grew sore but soon she was picking without looking, flipping the hops into the bins, smelling them on her hands as she pinned back her hair. Norah wore grips in hers.

'Sensible,' Maisie whispered, 'but not going to set anyone's heart on fire.'

They worked until lunch, then sat in the shade eating sandwiches, drinking water that was warm from the heat of the day. Grandpa went back to the sty to lie down but he returned at four looking rested and happy. Rosie lost count of the hours, measuring time by the level of hops in the bin, watching the pale green piles rise. The hoverflies were all around, humming, buzzing. Butterflies too. There were moths at night, she remembered now.

The busheller came round again and again, dipping his bushel basket into the bin, counting aloud each time as he filled it. He tipped the hops out into one of the big sacks, giving them a card with the number written on, and Ollie initialled it each time. They heard him counting as he went down the next aisle and the next.

So it went on from day to day and the sun never faltered and in the evening they sat around the fire and never raised their voices, even Ollie, even Norah.

Rosie told them of the moth as big as a wren and shrank back as smaller ones came, attracted by the kerosene lamps. She watched as Jack gently brushed them away. Joe would have crushed them.

On Sunday this hop-farm did no picking and there was a stillness in the hop-yard, but the kiln was still in use, drying off the hops picked late yesterday afternoon. She and Jack walked into the oast-house and below the hop-floor was row upon row of long white sacks waiting for collection by the brewers who would come when all the hops were in.

'Tidy little sum,' Rosie said, breathing in the scent of the sulphur, the sweetness of the baking hops.

'Yes, I'd like to live here amongst these hills,' Jack said, fingering a sack. 'I like the country.'

'What about Somerset?'

'Yes, I like that too, but this is more like home, somehow, if you know what I mean.'

She did know what he meant. The lake was fading from her dreams, the baseball target too.

They packed a picnic and went to the stream where the cattle came down to drink. They laid blankets on the dry warm grass and lay back, listening while Maisie and Ollie laughed together and Grandpa took Lee down to the water and Jack told Rosie about Somerset.

He told her about the cart he had driven through a stream like this to soak and tighten the wheels. About Elsie, the farmer's wife, who wore cord trousers, and Tim the farmer, who gave him books to read because they only had a morning of lessons in the school below the big hill where the locals had quarried for hamstone before the war.

The quarry was fenced off in the war, Jack said, used for 'something 'ush 'ush' the old men had said. He told her about the cows he had to milk, the udders he had to wash, the apples he had to pick. How he had stayed down there to work on the farm when he was fourteen, rather than come back to the V1 and V2 raids, but really because he didn't want to leave the country.

He told her about the hams that had hung from the ceiling, the blackberries he and the other lads picked down by the fields which were joined to the next village by a long path.

He told her how Maisie had come down and how they had laughed with the farmer and his wife over thick fat bacon and pints of cider. How Ollie had come too, released from his job building airforce huts for a weekend. How they had herded in the cows for milking. How he had shown his dad the pigs he was rearing, how Ollie had kissed him when he left, and Maisie too. They had been happy then.

He told her about the Blitz and how he had worried, though he had never written about this in his letters to her. How he had thought of his mum and dad beneath rubble, burned, suffocated, but they had never been hurt, not so you could see anyway, he said.

He rolled over then, pulled at a shoot of grass, chewed the end, spat it out. He told her of the GIs who had come and pitched their tents opposite one of the village pubs and further up too, opposite the blackberry bushes. How they had danced each week at the social club, how they had made friends. And he told her of big Ed who reminded him of his mother because of his laugh and his hair.

'He gave me candy,' he said to Rosie, lying on his back now, his arm over his eyes. 'He sort of adopted me. He was good, and kind, and clumsy. He'd meet me on the green. I'd lend him me bike to go to the village across the main road for the bigger dances. That was where Norah lived.'

'Do you miss him?'

'Yes I do. We laughed a lot. Those GIs were good to us kids. Really good, they took us under their wings a bit, one to one. They were warm and friendly, not like us. D'you know what I mean?'

Yes, she thought. She did know, because that is what her American family were like. Then Rosie told him about Frank and Nancy because they, too, had taken *her* under their wing. She had not seen her real family for six years and so they had become unreal, too distant, too different. She told him about her pain, but he already knew, he said. She told him about the lake, and about Sandra. But she did not tell him about Joe.

She told him how she would not pledge allegiance to the flag as she was supposed to each morning before the start of school. She told him about the barbecues, and about Uncle Bob – of the jazz and the long shadows across the sloping lawn.

Then Grandpa called from the stream and she took Lee,

dipping him in and out of the water because Ollie and Maisie were talking to one another at last.

Jack felt the sun on his face and he thought of his own pain. He remembered how Maisie had come again and again to Somerset, how she had laughed when she met Ed, how she had popped out when Jack was asleep and he was glad that she did because the war was long and dirty for her in London.

He looked across at Rosie, at her legs, which were tanned as his were not. Tanned and strong, she lifted her skirts higher as the water rippled around her. She was pretty, not really changed. She reminded him of Ed, the way she spoke, and it warmed him. He had trusted Ed, liked him.

He looked across at his father. He loved him, too, he knew he did, but he didn't know this dark, fierce man that Ollie had become. He didn't know this father who wouldn't throw Lee up in the air, or blow on his stomach to make him laugh as he had made Jack laugh. No, he didn't know him at all and he didn't like him. Jack sank back on the blanket. His father had taken the laugh from his mother's face and didn't love their baby. Is that what the war did to you?

Rosie was calling him now and he pushed himself to his feet.

'Go on, son,' called his dad. 'I bet she splashes you.'

Jack laughed then because his dad looked like he used to and sounded like he used to and he hoped it would last so that the anger, confusion and pain which swept through him and frightened him would go.

The sun kept shining and the hops were brought in and neither Jack nor Rosie wanted the weeks to end. They walked to the shop pushing Lee and bought him liquorice shoelaces. They all sat outside the pub with the Welsh and the Black Country people and watched the gypsies running their ponies up and down. They drank ginger beer and cider while one old gypsy bought a pony 'With All Faults'.

They paid the sixpence deposit on the glasses just to sit outside in the last of the sun, and talked again of Somerset and America and watched as Ollie and Maisie sang 'Roll Out the Barrel' after three glasses of beer and Grandpa asked, 'Will you have another drink, me dooks?'

They sat round the fire on the third Sunday night and

listened as Grandpa told them, as he always used to, how the nailers would put their babies on the bellows to rock them to sleep. How he had been bellow-rocked by his parents, and had then pumped the bellows when he was a bit older than Lee, standing on a box. How he had learned to have the irons in the fire ready for his father as he finished one batch of nails, so that a few seconds could be saved on each nail and a few more pennies earned from the middleman.

He told them how some children had stood in the roof with their backs against a beam and pumped the bellows with their feet. He looked at his hands as Jack put more wood on the fire and told how he had grown tall enough to work at the nail bench. How he had made his first good nail. How he was given a penny dated for that year.

He told them how one boy had not wanted to work. How he had been nailed by the ear to the doorpost and left until he promised he would work.

Rosie held his hands but Norah just looked bored.

That night Rosie wrote to Frank and Nancy, telling them that she was living in a pigsty, and about the smell of hops on her hands, and the feel of the water about her legs in the stream, telling them that she was happy. And she was. She still missed them, but she was happy. She had been taken back to her childhood, reminded of so much, and, yes, now she had found her English family again.

As the last week drew to a close, all the pickers dragged down the longest bines from the end of the rows and Rosie picked up the hop-dog caterpillars which fell out and carefully laid them to one side.

'They'll turn into moths, you know,' Jack teased.

'I know but I guess I can handle it.'

They carted the bines to the oast-houses, the largest of which had been scrubbed and swept that afternoon. Jack and the rest of the boys stood on ladders and draped the bines, because tonight there would be a dance. There was always a dance.

Everyone came, and the band played jazz for half an hour and Jack told Rosie how much he liked it too, but his favourite was Duke Ellington, not Bix Beiderbecke, and then the band played swing and jive and they danced in the heat, their bodies touching and then away again. And always there was the smell of the hops. Norah danced with a Welsh boy. Their bodies did not touch but she smiled, and that was good.

Rosie went outside, sat with Grandpa and drank cider while he had a beer. Maisie and Ollie drank too, and laughed and then Maisie pulled out her cigarettes and Grandpa took one, and Ollie too. Then he stopped, his hand too tight on her arm. His face was hard and Rosie looked at Maisie, at the tension on her face. Now Jack was there, leaning over, trying to take his father's hand from his mother's arm.

'Where did you get those bloody Yank fags?' Ollie shouted and those about them looked. Lee was in his chair and he was crying now.

Maisie winced at the tightening grip. People closed in and now the band were playing 'I'm Dreaming of a White Christmas'. In goddamn September, Rosie thought, even as she moved closer to Maisie, pulling at Ollie's arm, wanting them all to be safe again, as they had been just a moment ago.

'I gave them to her,' Rosie said. 'I brought them back from America, don't you remember?'

It was over then, over as though it had never been, and Jack took her back into the dance and the heat. The music was slow as Jack took her in his arms.

It was too hot but it didn't matter, he was with her, touching her, and she almost felt safe again but she could still see Ollie's anger and Maisie's fear. She didn't tell Jack that she had given Maisie Camels, not Lucky Strikes.

Jack was leading her out now, into the dark cool air, away from the music and the people, and they stood down at the gate again, feeling their carved initials with their fingers, seeing the wild hops winding round the hedge and the telegraph pole, seeing the lights from the farm, hearing the owl in the distance, the music from the oast-house. It was now that he kissed her, with soft, gentle lips, and it was as though she had known this feeling of warmth and safety all her life because his tongue did not intrude into her mouth, nor his hands move to her breast, and his skin had the smell of the boy she had grown up with.

She kissed him back, holding his head in her hands, wondering at the children they had once been, and the people they had become, and it seemed that their friendship had become something stronger. Something good. Yes, she was home at last, safe at last, and the cigarettes meant nothing.

CHAPTER 5

On their return Mrs Eaves had assigned them to different counters. Rosie didn't mind. She stacked the notebooks, laid out the pencils, the few sharpeners clutched inside the tiny globes. She looked at America. So large. And at Britain. So small. And as Glenn Miller played 'The Boogie Woogie Bugle Boy of Company B' she thought of Nancy and Frank, of Sandra and Joe, and it didn't hurt so much, because she had spent September in the soft warm hills with Jack and was at her evening classes twice a week.

Norah minded though. She had been put on haberdashery and measured out quarter-inch baby ribbon, cord, and tape and added up on a pad, her face set, her voice sharp.

At home she sat nearest to the fire, her stockings rolled down round her ankles, her slippers trodden down beneath her heels, and would not talk of hop-picking, or the sun which had turned their skin brown, or the stream which had lapped at their legs, because if they hadn't been there she would still be on jewellery.

Rosie and Grandpa talked though, long into the night, and his skin was tanned too, his eyes bright again. They talked of the bines which floated like seaweed in the evening breeze, of the gypsies who danced on that last night as though they were part of the earth and sky. They talked of Maisie and Ollie whom they often heard laughing in the yard now, of Lee who was tossed into the air, Ollie's hands strong around his waist. They talked and they laughed but Grandpa did not discuss Jack, he just took her hand one night, and said, 'I'm glad you've found your friend again. Sixteen is difficult, it's half child, half adult. You need someone you can trust.'

Rosie told Jack as they walked to the Palais, Sam and Ted behind them, and Jack nodded. 'Yes, that's it. It's the trust.'

Jack came dancing with them every night now, because Ollie wasn't drinking and shouting and sleeping. He was working on the stall, selling nylons out of a suitcase, his finger to his nose if he was asked what else.

On Mondays, Wednesdays and Fridays the gang went dancing, slipping 1/6*d* on to the pay desk, making for a table at the edge of the floor. Sam and Ted looked at the girls who clustered down one side, deciding, choosing. Then they danced beneath a great glass revolving chandelier while the band played swing and jive, but never jazz. They coasted around the MC who stood in the middle of the dance floor, checking that no one kissed, that they all danced in the same direction, that they did not jitterbug.

Few kissed. All went in the right direction. All of them jitterbugged and her hand didn't sweat in Jack's and she could smell his skin as he swung her close, and then away.

They drank warm ginger beer mixed with cider and it brought back the buzz of the hoverflies in amongst the bines, the smell of the hops on her hands, the sun which washed her past back into her bones.

They walked home, dropping Sam and Ted, standing in the alley at the bottom of their yards. They stood looking at the light thrown out across the roses, looking at the shed rotting in the left-hand corner, looking at one another.

He would kiss her, gently, lightly, squeeze her hand and then leave her, walking in through his gate, she through hers. She would hear his steps in time with hers, and it was only with the closing of the door that the sound of him left her, but the knowledge of his presence in the bedroom next to her wall kept him close.

Tuesdays and Thursdays she went to Miss Paul's above the piano shop and typed to Chopin, chasing the notes, rubbing out the errors, blowing the rubber dust from the keys, cursing inside her head because Jack was watching Jane Russell at the Odeon whilst she was here.

But each week she was faster and her shorthand was better, and she wrote to Frank and Nancy that next spring she would find a job in Fleet Street. Just you wait and see, she wrote, and she knew that her letter was strong and positive, and that they would be glad.

By the middle of October she was moved back to records and played Duke Ellington for Jack and he touched her face when he walked in and heard. He stood still, listening to the piano as it beat its rhythm.

Norah was on spectacles and would stand waiting while customers read the printed card with the letters that diminished in size. Her nails clicked on the metal frames that she held in her hand while she waited, her face long as she fitted them around strange ears.

Rosie played 'I'll Be Seeing You', and smiled across as Norah scowled, but then regretted that she had done it, because the bridge between them had not yet been rebuilt.

October became November, and though there was still grief in the quiet hours of the night, she no longer kept her bedroom door open. There was hope, there was fun, there was Jack.

They danced and they kissed but still lightly, gently, and his hands didn't slide beneath her blouse nor his tongue probe her mouth and she was glad. She didn't tell him about Joe though, even when he told her of the girlfriend he had had in Somerset, the one he had kissed in the apple orchard. She said instead that it was only another five months until her exams and that she must work until midnight again.

She said this too when she wrote to Frank and Nancy but she also told them of the rationing, and the wind which grew ever more cold. She told them how Maisie called over the fence every Sunday and passed bread and hot dripping and how she and Grandpa ate it on the bench, wrapped in scarves and coats.

She told them how she, Jack and Ollie had helped Mrs Eaves's sister move into an old Army barracks north of London along with two hundred other squatters. They had pushed an old barrow with some furniture down the road from the flat she shared with her son and his wife and three children – a flat which had only one bedroom.

She told them how the people were taking over these empty buildings because there was nowhere else for them to live. How the Local Authorities were accepting them and connecting water and electricity, for what else could they do? There were no houses available. She told them that these were the things that she would write about when she started her proper job in the summer.

Frank wrote back asking why Mrs Eaves's sister hadn't moved into one of the prefabs they had been hearing about. If she didn't know, she should find out, get the complete picture, start thinking like a journalist.

Rosie asked Grandpa as they sat in front of the coal fire while the rain teemed down as it had done for the last seven days. Jack had collected some wood from a flooded bomb site and this was stacked on its end to one side. There was a smell of wet dust from it which crept through the whole house, but it would make the coal last longer.

'There aren't enough. They're having lotteries in some Local Authorities, though why anyone would queue to live in one of those I don't know,' said Grandpa, flicking the ash of a Woodbine into the fire. He coughed. The damp November air was making his chest thick again and his tan was fading, but he had had no accidents for months.

'Well, I can,' ground out Norah. 'A nice clean bungalow with a neat garden, a nice sort of neighbour. A nice new town away from London's mess. I'd want it.'

Rosie looked round the room, at the books either side of the fireplace, the American oilcloth on the table, bought from Woolworths. She thought of the house by the lake, the house in Lower Falls, and knew now that all three were home. At last all three were home.

As Christmas drew near she sewed cotton sheeting into two small pillowcases and filled them with hops, sending one to Frank and Nancy, hiding one for Grandpa. She bought a Duke Ellington record for Jack and Evening in Paris perfume for Maisie, Californian Poppy for Norah (because Norah needed all the sweetness she could get, she told Jack).

She bought Ollie paint brushes because he was always talking of doing up the house, but there were so few materials available. She bought Nancy a Union Jack brooch which was left over from the war. It was luminous 'so Frank will be able to track you down wherever you are', she wrote as she put their card in with the parcel.

She told them that her typing was still improving, the Palais was still fun. She did not tell them how Jack kissed her good night or that, as she crossed off the days to Christmas, her grief was deep and dark again because she remembered Lower Falls and the times they had spent together.

Instead she sat by the fire with Grandpa on 20 December until ten p.m. colouring, cutting and sticking paper chains together as they had always done.

'I've missed this,' he said, his hands folding the strips slowly, holding the ends between thumb and finger while they stuck together. 'I've missed our Christmases.'

'So have I, Grandpa,' she said. But she was not thinking of paper chains. She was thinking of the thick snow where here there was rain. Thick snow which had turned the world into a Christmas card as they had travelled by tram on her first American Christmas to the main shopping centres which were decorated with lights, and with streamers and garlands, snowmen and Father Christmas. The air had rung out with carols and there had been a Father Christmas on each floor, wilting in the central heating.

That night she didn't sleep at all. The next day when she walked home from work, there were no lighted trees in the windows, no people on skis and horse-drawn sleighs, no sparkling snow. There was nothing of the excitement she had known in Lower Falls for Lee, who was looking out into the street, his face pressed against the window. It wouldn't goddamn do.

At home there was a small piece of fatty bacon to boil along with carrots and potatoes. She did this but didn't talk. She poured Grandpa's tea, smiled at Norah and then went in to Maisie, wrapping Lee up warmly, taking the pushchair, going to the market, talking to Jack who nodded and asked Ollie to mind the stall.

They went by bus up West, and walked down the streets where there were some decorations, but not many and no Christmas lights. They saw the tree in Trafalgar Square, a gift from the Norwegians, then went into an Oxford Street store, up in the lift, Lee looking, laughing, touching, until they reached the grotto.

They queued, Jack's arm about her waist, holding the folded pushchair with his free hand. She held Lee, kissing his face. His skin was soft and warmer now than it had been in the street. He pulled her hair and she laughed.

'You should have kept your plaits,' Jack said. 'He could have swung on those.'

He leaned the pushchair against his leg, and took Lee from her, holding him up, turning him round in the air, laughing as he laughed, dropping him down against his chest, blowing on his neck.

'I love him,' he said, looking at Rosie.

She nodded. 'Silent Night' was playing on the gramophone. The record was scratched but it didn't matter. She wanted Lee to see and feel the magic as she had done because it would help her own grief this Christmas; her first away from Frank and Nancy.

She told Jack of the sleighs, the Christmas tree they had put up in the front garden, the garlands that hung on every wall and from every ceiling. She told him of the trams which had flattened the nickels she and Sandra had laid on the tracks when they were eleven. Jack blew again on Lee's neck, then bent and kissed her cheek.

Lee cried when Father Christmas took him on his knee in the dimly lit grotto, but Jack dropped down beside him and the crying stopped. The present was wrapped in red paper and Lee tore at it as they left. It was a wooden car. Blue and red, with wheels which spun.

Rosie remembered the bald tyres which Frank had heaped into the boot of the car during the war in case the worn ones he was using punctured. There were no new ones available.

There were plenty now, though, and new cars too, but here, in England, new cars were to be sold abroad to help the national debt and people patched up their old ones and made do. In America they were pitching into a boom, Frank said. Over here they were trying to pay for the war which had bled them dry.

'I don't mind queuing. I don't mind being rationed, or being cold,' Rosie said as they walked back down Oxford Street. 'It's time I had my share of that. But I wanted Lee to see another world, just for tonight.'

That night she slept, at least for a while.

On 23 December Jack called as she was settling Grandpa by the fire, his newspaper on his lap, his Woolworths glasses catching the light from the flames. The coal was wet, hissing and smoking. As Jack came in she put a sheet of newspaper to the fireplace.

'Leave the door open for a moment, Jack. Let's get a bit of a draught.' She held the paper with her fingertips as the fire roared suddenly, blazing red, browning the paper, which she snatched away, the heat hurting her face.

'That's great.'

She dug into the coals with the poker.

'There you are, Grandpa, that's a bit better.' She turned to Jack. 'Are we going up the Palais?'

She was reaching for her gloves, catching the coat which Jack tossed to her from the back of the chair.

Jack looked at Grandpa and winked. 'What d'you think, Grandpa? Shall we go up the Palais? D'you reckon this girl could take a change?'

Grandpa looked at Rosie. He rubbed his hands together, then picked up the paper. 'I expect she can. It sounded a good idea when Maisie told me.' He looked over the top at Rosie. 'Just put the guard up, there's a good girl, and don't hurry back.'

Rosie looked from one to the other. The guard was warm, she pushed it up against the fireplace, pulling the hearth rug well back.

'What are you two goons talking about? What's wrong with the Palais? It's the special Christmas night.'

She was pulling her coat on now. The buckle was cold as she threaded the belt through. Jack pulled up her collar.

'Keep that up, it's cold enough to freeze the balls off that monkey in Elm Street.' He pushed her towards the front door. 'Bye, Grandpa,' he called. 'Be good. And if you can't be good be careful.'

Rosie heard Grandpa laugh and said, 'If I'd said that he'd have lathered me.'

Jack marched through the yard, past the hard-pruned roses, out down the alley to the Tube station where people were rushing, their faces pinched. Rosie was tired, cold. Presents had arrived from Frank and Nancy for them all this morning. She had asked Norah what she had sent to the doctor and his wife in Somerset. What had they sent her?

Nothing, Norah had replied. They have their own children. There was nothing in it for me. Everything will go to the kids. All they offered was college, like yours did. I don't want that, too much hard work. Why keep in touch?

Rosie told Jack now what her sister had said.

'I don't know why she can't love or why she's so bitter,' she added.

Jack shrugged. 'She always has been. When will you realise that? Nothing will change her. It's in her bones. She's just getting more like your grandma every day. Nothing is ever enough. Nothing is ever right, but I think she misses your grandma too. It was always the two of them against you and your grandpa.' He shrugged. 'It's made her more spiteful. Maybe she'll change when she gets a boyfriend, someone of her own.'

The Tube train lurched and swayed through the tunnels and Jack held her hand. He never wore gloves.

'I'm hot,' she said, removing her own, because she wanted to feel his skin against hers.

'Nearly there,' Jack said, standing up as the train stopped in Bond Street station.

'Nearly where?' she asked as she was pulled along behind him, still holding his hand but jostled now by the crowds surging up from the train into the evening air.

'Nearly reached your Christmas treat,' Jack said, turning and grinning at her as they reached the pavement, slowing until she was up with him. 'You've been looking as though you've been hurting, deep inside. Can't have that, can we?'

He wasn't looking at her as he said this. His cheeks had flushed. 'Thought this might help. You gave Lee a treat. This is yours.'

They were south of Oxford Street now, in Soho. They were strolling along with many others and Jack told her that Soho had been the hunting cry of the Duke of Monmouth and that he had built a rather 'super' house on one side of Soho Square.

Rosie laughed. 'This is my treat, is it? A guided tour of Soho?' She dug him in the ribs.

'That's right, but there's more, my dear girl. Just you wait and see.'

They were walking past an accordionist who held his cap

between his teeth. There were two sixpences in it. Jack gave him another and then they turned into a pub, past two tarts who stood either side of the door.

'Not tonight, ladies,' Jack said.

'Too young anyway, ducks,' the blonde with black roots called back. Rosie flushed but Jack laughed.

Inside it was dimly lit but warm . . . There were sailors at the far end, sitting with civilians, all men.

Jack ordered a beer and a ginger beer for Rosie. Rosie stood back in case they were thrown out because they were too young. Jack was grinning, chatting, and he was served with a beer after all. Charm the bloody birds out of the trees, Rosie echoed the woman in the market.

She moved towards the end where the sailors sat, and Jack pulled her back as he sipped the froth and edged her towards a table nearer the other end.

'That's a pick-up,' he said, nodding towards the sailors.

Rosie looked again. 'But they're all men.'

Jack smiled and leaned his head back against the dark wood panelling.

Rosie looked at her own drink. 'I haven't seen this in the States,' was all she said.

'Or this.' Jack nudged her, pointing to the onion seller who wore his strings of onions over his shoulder. One woman sneaked up behind and cut a single one off, disappearing into the crowd. No one said anything.

Rosie remembered the cherries she had put over her ears in Frank's back garden. Rich red shiny earrings and they would be having Christmas over there without her.

They finished their drinks and moved out past the tarts again.

'A little older but not enough,' the blonde said again, rubbing her shoe up the back of her leg. 'It's a bit bloody cold.'

'You're right there,' Jack said, steering Rosie past them, strolling with her along the street. The restaurants were busy, holly hung from the ceilings and the white-bibbed waiters looked like the dippers which flew in bursts around the hop-yards. Rosie felt the tears gather in her throat because it was dark and cold and she was a long way from Lower Falls, a long way from Herefordshire.

It was further on that she heard the cornet, wailing up from the basement of a house just ahead of them, and then another and another and it was like the brownstones, though here, this time, the buildings weren't empty and dead. Here, close to her home, there was jazz.

She said nothing, just clutched at Jack's arm as they stood on the pavement, hearing Dixieland, New Orleans, hearing the drums. It was 'Take Your Tomorrow'. Pure Bix, pure gold breathing life into the streets, and into her mind. She looked at Jack, his head bent towards her, watching her face carefully.

'Does it make it better, little Rosie?' he asked, his voice quiet.

She reached up and kissed his cheek because she couldn't speak. He drew her towards him and this time their kiss was not soft and gentle, but filled with an excitement which left them both breathless, both awkward, until Jack turned towards the steps leading down to the door.

'You coming then?'

Inside it was dim and smoky. Rosie sat at a table near an opening which led to a counter where Jack bought coffee and rolls. Rosie watched as he put sugar in using the spoon which was chained to the counter. She wanted to hold the kiss in her mind but the music was surging and as Jack joined her she sat back and listened, feeling the heat of summer, hearing the jazz across the lawn. Seeing the faded, empty New York brownstones. But here, in England, they were not empty, and she was sitting with Jack, breathing in the rhythm once again.

All evening they sat as the trumpet played that deliberately impure tone which distinguishes jazz from straight playing.

'He's using his lips,' Jack said quietly.

'No he's not, he's half-valving.' But then she saw that he wasn't. 'OK,' she said. 'You win.'

'I like the banjo, it's cleaner than the guitar.'

'No, it's not. Charlie Christian showed us that.' Rosie pointed towards the guitar player. 'See, that guy's using his fingertips to strike the strings as well as stop them. How about that for a clean note.'

'How about that for a know-it-all.' Jack was leaning towards her and they laughed together quietly while the music played and all pain ebbed away. They kissed, lightly, but they were older tonight, closer tonight.

They listened to the trumpet's break, tapping the table with their hands as the player improvised and the others in the band fell silent. He was good, a young man with long hair, and then the rest came in. Jack picked at the wax which had clumped around the candle which stood in a jam jar. 'Duke Ellington is right not to like improvisation. He plans everything, you know.'

Rosie looked at the candle. They had used candles to burn the bed bugs from creases in the mattresses when they were young. They had used candles for the Christmas table in Lower Falls but it didn't hurt to think of that here. She picked at some wax herself. It was slightly warm. She rolled it into a ball. Looked at the band again. Did they play to a written arrangement or to one made familiar by use?

'Their improvisation works though,' she said as the band broke for a coffee.

'Yes, you're right, but it can turn into a right mess. Like your shorthand when I read to you too fast.'

Rosie sipped her coffee. It was cold but it didn't matter. 'What about you?' she said. 'What about your plans. Will it always be the stall? Once you were going to be an artist.'

Jack sat back, tipping the chair, resting it against the wall. 'Don't know. Me art's not good enough. Not much point sorting anything out. Not yet anyway.' He turned round to look at the band. The trumpet player was standing near them, talking to a girl with long black hair.

Rosie drank the last of her coffee. It was bitter at the bottom. 'Why not? What's stopping you?'

Jack turned and smiled. 'Look, you had a good schooling. We had very little. Just mornings and then it was bloody chaos. All the evacuees in the one large school hall.' He leaned forward taking her hand. 'It's not that though. Got to do me National Service, haven't I? Not worth starting anything until then.'

She had forgotten about that. Forgotten that he would be going away for eighteen months. It was too long. She couldn't bear to be without him. She squeezed the wax, looking at that, not at him. 'When?'

'Not until I'm eighteen. There's loads of time. Bit more than a year when you work it out.'

The band were playing again and she looked at him as he sat four-square on his chair again, his hands slapping on his thighs in time to the beat, and then he turned to her.

'I'll fix something up afterwards, like everyone does.'

They didn't leave the club until eleven p.m. and then travelled home, talking and laughing because tonight had been filled with music, with talk, with gently held hands. The kiss he gave her at the back yard gate was soft again but as he held her there was excitement too.

She slept that night with scarcely any dreams, only one about a silent brownstone house that turned into a noisy jazz-filled Soho basement. She woke in the morning and scratched the frost from the window. The cold didn't matter because they were young and the war was over. Their lives were just beginning and they had a year before he had to go and that was a long time. Besides it was Christmas Eve.

Maisie cooked the turkey in her kitchen on Christmas morning and Rosie helped Jack to carry the table from Grandpa's house and they all ate together, pulling home-made crackers, drinking beer that Ollie had 'found'. They ate tinned peaches and tinned ham for tea and Grandpa raised his cup of tea.

'To Frank and Nancy, God bless them.'

Yes, God bless them, Rosie thought, thinking of the stockings which had hung at the mantelpiece last year, the turkey, the Christmas lights, the smell of spruce throughout the house. The wine, the liqueurs, the guests, the warmth, the skiing in the afternoon, and the ache wasn't as sharp, and she knew it was because of the jazz, and Jack.

She fingered the light woollen scarf which Nancy had sent. It was warm draped around her shoulders and she barely felt the draught coming from the ill-fitting windows and the gaps in the doors. All the houses were the same after the blast of the bombs which had rocked and cracked the buildings.

She looked across the table which she had helped Maisie to set for tea and smiled at Jack. His bed was down here now, moved from the boxroom to make room for Lee. Rosie wished he hadn't moved, she wished she could still hear him shut the door, sink into bed, cough. Lee climbed on to her knee now and she hugged him, rubbing her face into his neck, making him laugh, making herself laugh.

'That's a nice scent,' she said as Maisie leaned over her shoulder to put a toast soldier into Lee's mouth. 'What is it?'

'You should know, you gave it to me,' Maisie said, turning from the table quickly, moving towards the sink. Ollie stopped eating his Christmas cake, looked at Rosie and then his wife. He dropped his knife and the noise was sharp in the sudden silence. Maisie's back was still and Ollie's face was dark again as it had been before the hops were picked.

Rosie looked at Jack. His face was tense, his eyes wary, pained.

She turned to Maisie and laughed. 'I'd forgotten. It's Evening in Paris. It's nice, isn't it? I've got some myself at home.' She poured another cup of tea for Ollie. 'Drink up, Ollie, that cake of Nancy's is pretty dry.'

He looked from her to Maisie, his eyes guarded, his thoughts elsewhere.

'Don't make those bloody crumbs,' he said to Lee.

Rosie looked at Norah. 'Did you like your Californian Poppy? Maybe I should have bought you the French one too.' Norah wasn't listening, she was reading the book of women's love stories which Maisie had given her.

Ollie was relaxing again now with his cake and tea and Maisie brought Lee another toast finger, smiling at him, at Jack, at Ollie, at Rosie. But Rosie looked into the fire instead because she knew the perfume was not Evening in Paris. But she saw that her words had taken the anxiety from Jack's face.

CHAPTER 6

January 1947 brought bitter cold and a letter from Nancy.

Lower Falls
January 1st

My dearest Rosie,

We were so very pleased with your presents and the good wishes from your Grandpop. Please give ours to your family for a happy and safe New Year.

I say safe because Frank is getting real uptight. He's been seeing bogeymen in the woodpile ever since Churchill's Iron Curtain speech at Fulton, Missouri. He sees East Europe falling under the Communists and Truman's Government getting real upset about it. Thinks they'll have bad dreams about the Reds sweeping over here too.

Already that goddamn busybody, Gallagher, in Local Administration, is getting busy sharpening his knife, asking questions about Art, our friend in planning. Do you remember him? Had some kind of a soft spot for those revolutionaries in Russia in the thirties. He's got a wife and kids now. Doesn't think of politics any more but this LA is really sniffing. Does he think that there are Reds under every bed or something crazy like that? Even came round to the newspaper offices asking how long Frank had known him.

But, let's not go on about that now. I guess Christmas without you has made me mope. I can't tell you how we miss you. We took a ride into town. It wasn't the same.

We're off skiing for a week at the end of January but that won't be the same either, without you. Sandra is busy, having a good time as always. Talking without drawing breath. We see Joe from time to time. He'd like a job on the paper. Maybe he will, but we'd rather it was you.

How are things with you, Rosie?

All our love,
Nancy

Rosie read the letter standing in a queue during her lunch-hour hoping that at the end of it there would be some sort of meat. But there wasn't and she walked back to Woolworths, her feet cold in her Wellingtons even through the thick socks she had knitted from a pulled out jumper.

It hadn't mattered until she read the letter, saw the round handwriting, remembered the feeling of Nancy's arms, the smell of Frank's pipe. Perhaps it would be better if they didn't write, didn't stir up memories, but then she shook her head. No, her feet would still freeze and she wanted to feel Nancy reaching out to her.

She shook her head at Norah and Mrs Eaves as she went in.

'The soldiers couldn't get through with it. They're slower than the lorry drivers. Maybe tomorrow.' She shrugged and pushed her numb feet into her shoes before taking her place behind the counter, feeling the letter in her pocket.

She wrote back to Nancy that night telling her that the road haulage workers were on strike, the meat was rotting in the warehouses, the soldiers were slowly getting it through. She told her how they thought they'd bought some from a guy called Jones at the pub who had meat which would otherwise rot, but he took their money and ran. We never seem to learn, she wrote.

She told Nancy how the greengrocer was rationing potatoes to two pounds a head a week. But there *was* corned beef – 'So we party every night, Nancy. You'd love it.'

She switched out the light and lay back in her bed. Did her letter sound angry or just plain tired? She felt both as she lay here listening to Grandpa moving about beneath her. She sat up, read the leader column of *The Times*, and analysed a report which Frank had enclosed for her as practice. Wrote it up. Transcribed her shorthand because there was no time to waste. It was 1947. She was moving forward. She had to keep telling herself that.

She had said it as she heaped the fire with ash before she came upstairs, banking it up, hoping it would stay in until the morning. They were wrapping coal in soaked newspaper to make it last longer and Jack's wood from the bomb site helped.

She lay down and pulled the blankets up round her ears not thinking of the food in the American shops, not thinking of the skiing slopes. Beating back the anger at the ease of the world which she had left behind.

Maisie hadn't been any luckier with her meat queue either. Lee had been so cold after two hours she had come home and Rosie had rubbed his hands between hers to warm them up. She listened to his crying and coughing through the wall.

He was ill, his temperature was high. She put on the light again and added to her letter, telling Nancy that on New Year's Day flags had been raised at all Britain's collieries as they were nationalised. It hadn't meant more coal though, not yet. A fuel crisis was threatening.

Here Rosie put down her pen. Lee was still crying and now she could hear Jack's voice, soft and gentle, and Maisie's too. She listened, wanting to speak through the wall to Lee, to reach out to him, but she didn't, she just waited until there was no more sound and then she wrote again, wondering how long it would be before the new National Health Service took effect. She did not mention the Local Administrator or Eastern Europe and the Iron Curtain. It was too far away, too trivial against Lee's cough and the bitter cold.

The next day Jack came round. It was Sunday and Lee was a bit better, he told her, his muffler up round his mouth, his dad's old coat worn at the cuffs, the belt missing. Rosie nodded, heaping Grandpa's sheet from the sink into a bowl, drying her hands, pulling down her sleeves, throwing her coat around her. The accidents had begun again, but Jack was here and nothing else mattered.

Jack carried the sheet into the yard and they each took an end, twisting it, hearing the water pouring on to the yard, seeing it begin to freeze even as it hit the concrete. Again they twisted. The water splashed on his coat.

'Why are you wearing that thing?' Rosie asked. 'It's so darn big.'

Jack just shrugged and grinned. 'Makes me look older. Maybe those tarts up West would take me on now.'

Rosie looked at his face, then flicked a corner of the sheet, splashing him. 'There'd have to be a pretty thick fog, and a Derby win to make it worth their while.'

She carried the sheet in and Jack hung it over the airer which hung from the ceiling above the fire while Rosie lifted out the other sheet from the sink. They did the same a second time and Jack asked how Nancy was, and Frank. As the cold sliced into her wet hands she would not let herself think of the skis which would be propped up in her old bedroom. She would not let herself think of the central heating, the washing machine, the hamburgers oozing out of toasted buns. Nor would she think of the Local Administrator, or Art, or Frank, because as dawn had come she had realised it wasn't trivial, or Frank would have written himself. Nor would she think of the big coat that Jack was wearing because she thought she knew what it meant.

She made mugs of tea with twice-used leaves and they cupped them in their hands, Grandpa too, his eyes not meeting theirs because he was ashamed. Jack pulled a newspaper out of his pocket.

'Ollie sent it round. He's stuck on the crossword. Wants you to finish it, if you've got the time.'

Rosie smiled as Grandpa took it, concentrating on this, not that land across the sea.

'Number five down. Can't get that at all. None of us can.'

Grandpa took the stub of pencil from Jack, read the clues, knew the word and they all smiled as his eyes met theirs.

'Hypothermia, that's what it is,' he said.

Rosie looked at Jack. He had known all along, she could tell from his eyes.

'Where are we going?' she asked, blowing on the pale tea, feeling the steam damp on her face. The room was damp from the sheets too.

Jack drank his tea, wiping his mouth with the back of his hand. 'Nowhere today, Rosie. I'm a bit busy.' He reached forward, giving her his mug. 'Thanks for the tea.'

She had known he would say that. Ever since Jones had taken the money and not brought back the meat, she'd been waiting for this because she had seen the anger in his eyes, and knew it was reflected in hers. And today he was wearing that coat which would cover any amount of meat.

'I'll come.' Rosie was up again but Jack was at the door now.

'No, you won't come. Stay here. I've just got a bit of work to do.'

He didn't turn back as he moved quickly through the yard, stepping over the ice from the sheets, slamming the gate behind him. But then he heard the latch lift and she was there, shaking in the cold, her coat slung over her shoulders. There was a freezing fog coming down now, its droplets were on her hair.

'Rosie, get the hell back in the house. Do as I ask, just for bloody once.' His voice was angry but she looked so small, so cold, and so he came to her, taking her in his arms. 'Go on now, get back in. It's nothing. Nothing, just a job.'

'Like the cheeses?' Her voice was indistinct, muffled by his coat.

He laughed. 'Yes, a bit like the cheeses.'

She stood back from him now. 'Well, I'm coming. He owes my grandpa too. And we should do this together.'

Jack looked at her. 'You're crazy. You won't give up. I'm getting it for all of us. Let me and Dad do it. You don't have to be involved. Just go back in and wait.'

But Rosie was walking into his yard now. Didn't he know that waiting was too hard?

Ollie drove out of London, grinding the gears of his friend's car but using kosher petrol. 'Don't want to be stopped before we start, do we?' he said as he wiped the windscreen again, scraping his frozen breath from the screen, passing Jack the rag. 'Here, you keep at it. Make sure I can see my way. And you keep quiet in the back, Rosie. You shouldn't be here anyway.'

Jack looked out through the small patch he had cleared for himself, scrubbing the windscreen in front of Ollie. The fog was freezing on the screen, the wipers were scraping some of it away. His dad was peering down at the map then out again at the road signs. Fog was seeping thickly around them now.

'Don't matter. It could help,' his father murmured, pointing to a turning on the pencil-drawn map. His nails were thick with dirt from the tyre they'd had to change ten miles back. They turned at the next crossroads. There were factories either side, flat-roofed. Two in ruins, burnt out by incendiaries. There was another old three-storey building with blackened bricks. The edges were indistinct, the fog was thicker now.

'Bert said it's along at the end. Might be guards though. Do you want to go through with it?' Ollie was looking at Jack now.

No, I don't want to go through with it. I'm frightened. I

want to go home. I want me mum, I want to turn round and take Rosie back with me. I don't want the bloody meat. But all he said was, 'Course. Why not? That old bugger should have let us have it. He took our money.'

He wiped at the windscreen again. Lee needed it. He needed some good red meat inside him. He was pale, his cough was bad. It was crazy to let the meat stay in there – and besides Rosie was here. She had made him bring her. She wouldn't give up. It warmed him, made him smile, gave him courage.

They were close now and it was quiet as Ollie turned off the engine and drifted into the side of the road. Had old Jones posted guards? Jack wondered. He must have known that if he cheated them they'd come after him. He knew Ollie too well, didn't he?

'He did the same with the Wind and Flute regulars. Took their money, said they could come and transport their own meat, then said the meat had gone off. They'd paid their money, it was their loss, the old devil said.'

Ollie was tapping the dashboard, peering through the fog. Jack wound down his window. He could hear nothing but church bells. He looked at his watch.

'What time are the others supposed to be here?'

'By now,' Ollie said. His voice was short. His eyes darting to the mirror and then to the front again.

'What if the meat has gone off?' Jack asked.

'Then we've done all this for nothing but at least we've tried. You see, he stamps on us, that bugger, always has. Runs the Pawn, runs the betting shop, thinks he runs us. Someone pinched two of his cheeses, you know. Upset him for weeks that did.'

Jack nodded, remembering Rosie walking beside him with a swollen stomach and now, as he leaned his head out of the car, he grinned, banging lightly with his hand on the side of the van, hearing her knock back.

She was his past and his present. She was everything and she was tired and hungry because Grandpa had all that she could spare. Rosie had never told him that, but she didn't need to, he had seen it for himself.

Ollie pressed his mouth to the grille between the cabin and the back.

'We can't wait any longer. You come through to the cabin,' he called softly to Rosie. 'Keep a look-out for the cops, for anyone. If you see them, come and get us, don't hoot the horn.'

Jack followed Ollie from the van, walking on the grass to deaden the sound of his footsteps. They could see the fence ahead. There was barbed wire on the top. Ollie gestured and Jack crept round to one side, Ollie to the other. There was a gap, but it was too small for Ollie so it was Jack who went through alone, carrying cutters for the padlock, carrying his fear.

The fog was thicker now, he could taste the sulphur in his mouth. It stung his eyes and was thick in his throat. His feet were frozen in his plimsolls but they were quieter, like the GIs' rubber-soled shoes had been, like Ed's had been in the Somerset village. Had they worn them in the Ardennes? Had Ed been frightened? Had he shown it? He'd always said there was nothing wrong with fear. It kept you alive. Why had he never written? Why do I think of him so much? Why do I lie awake at night and think of him?

He stopped, gripped the cutters. Keep your mind on the job, you bloody fool. He listened again. Had there been a noise? He waited. No, nothing. Fear kept you alive, Ed said. He repeated it to himself. There was nothing wrong with it. The door was ahead, the padlock dripping in the fog.

He eased the cutters round the chain, bending his elbows, putting his weight behind it but it was no good. He tried again and they slipped and fell. He froze, his breath loud. He couldn't hear. He breathed through his mouth. That was better. There was nothing. No one.

He stooped and picked up the cutters, tried again, and this time fear had put strength into his arms and he ground the cutters through, catching the chain before it fell, laying it gently on the ground. Ed was right, it helped. He took the sack from beneath his coat, opened the door, and crept on, into the cold store. Looking. Listening. Breathing. Christ, why was he so loud? He could see his breath. He had seen Rosie's in the yard. Shut up, concentrate. Listen. Look. Breathe.

There were carcasses hanging on hooks, others cut into joints. He took only what they had paid for. There was no rancid smell. This meat was good. He turned, easing his way back out, shutting the door, running now, back to the fence, but where was the gap? He edged along. The fog was thicker now. He couldn't see. The meat was heavy in the large pockets inside the coat. His hands were numb, his feet too.

'Dad,' he whispered. 'Dad.' But there was no answer, there was just a noise behind him, an arm round his throat, a fist hard into the side of his head and pain which for a moment crushed him but he didn't drop the cutters because he knew they could be traced back to Ollie.

There was another punch and he felt his lip burst. He spun round, out of the grip because he didn't want to be locked up, he didn't want to be kept from Rosie, from Lee, from his mum, from Dad.

No, he didn't want to be kept from his dad and he swung his fist at the large dark man whose face he couldn't see in the fog. He felt the shock of contact up into his shoulder, saw him fall, begin to rise. He swung at him again. Rosie needed her meat. Lee needed his.

'Dad,' he shouted. 'Dad.'

But his father was already there, the fence planks that he had torn away thrown across the yard.

'Get out now, son.' Ollie was struggling with the guard, his breath coming in grunts, warding off the blows, parrying, grabbing an arm, twisting it up behind the guard's back now, bringing him to a standstill.

'Quick. I'll cover you. Get to the van. If I don't come, drive off. There might be more than one.' He was tying the guard's arms together.

Jack ran off through the gap, the meat heavy in the coat, but then he stopped and waited by the fence. His dad had come for him. His father was putting the guard into a hut.

'Out of the cold,' he told him as he ran back. Together they went to the van, pushing the meat beneath sacks, keeping Rosie in the cabin. Together they drove until they found a phone box. Then Ollie rang the police, telling them that there was a guard tied up in a shed in Jones's warehouse, nothing more. They drove back, neither speaking, scared the police might see them, might stop them, but they didn't.

They threw the sack into the back yard, then drove the van back to Bert. They were stopped and searched but Rosie had wiped the blood from Jack's face with her handkerchief moistened from the yard rainbutt and there was nothing to be seen but the sweat on the palms of their hands, the fear in their eyes.

That night those who had paid Jones received their meat and Jack held Rosie and told her that he hated the cold, he hated to feel such fear, but Ollie had been like he was before the war – strong and reliable – and it had been worth it for that. She kissed his bruised cheek, his swollen lips and remembered that she had never been able to see him hurt, even when they were children.

That night she wrote again to Nancy, asking about the Americans' fear about Russia. Asking about Frank and the Local Administrator because she couldn't bear to think of Frank being hurt either.

As January turned to February the cold was like nothing anyone could remember. The snow heaped itself in drifts over the roses and up against the windows. They dug paths through to the road and walked in the gutter. They slipped and fell but went on and heard in the grocer's queue that Mr Philips's son, a conscript, had been killed in Palestine.

Nancy wrote that it was suspected that the Polish elections had been rigged to allow in the Communists and that the United States Government feared that the Soviets had atomic secrets. Would they too build a bomb? Would the Government feel forced to stand out against the Communists?

Rosie didn't want to read this. She wanted to read words of love that she could hug to herself at night, keeping out the darkness of the winter, the worry that the world was going crazy again. That there might be war. Is that what they were saying? Hadn't they all gone through enough in the last one? Weren't they still going through it?

Wasn't it enough that there was snow *and* that there was a fuel shortage? That there was no power during the morning and afternoon at home, so Grandpa had to go to Maisie's to huddle round one fire, and one set of candles? For Christ's sake, wasn't that enough?

She was standing in her room, tearing up the letter, talking aloud, going mad. Is that it? Am I going mad? She took down her books and her pencil and transcribed long into the night because none of this mattered. She must keep saying that. All she had to do was get through to the summer, because then her career would begin.

In March the snow turned to floods and drowned sheep that would have been part of the meat ration. Violence continued in India, terrorist attacks continued in Palestine, and President Truman told Congress that America must be prepared to intervene throughout the world to oppose Communism.

There was another letter from Nancy.

Lower Falls

My dear Rosie,

The snow sounded like fun. Are you getting in any skiing? How is the rationing? That doesn't sound fun.

Here it's pretty mopey. The Local Administrator has interviewed Frank again. His friend Art lost his job. He was once a Communist. He'll never work again unless Frank can take him on. He's looking at it. The LA asked Frank if he is, or ever has been, a Communist. Of course he threw the goddamn man out.

It'll all settle. A few people are getting a bit uptight but it'll pass. Your exams are soon. Keep working but have fun too.

Sandra says she'll write but you know her. Too much partying, too much talking. She means well though. Mary sends her love. Wonders if you're missing her hamburgers.

Will write again soon.
Nancy

That night Rosie danced with Jack at the Palais, she swung, danced, smiled and clung to him. That night she couldn't sleep. Hamburgers – what the hell were they? All she knew about were the sheets from Grandpa's bed to be washed in the morning, the coal to wrap in newspaper, records all morning, queuing all lunchtime, like the rest of this country.

March turned to April and the blossom came, filling the parks with colour, the daffodils too and hyacinths which scented the paths. While Rosie queued she read her shorthand book, testing, thinking, transcribing in her head. She had no time to dance in the evenings because she was practising on an old typewriter of Maisie's.

'It's the exam in two months. It's so important,' she told Jack, and he understood and read to her from a book. She took it down in shorthand, typed it up while he timed her, sitting at the kitchen table, his feet up on another chair, chatting with Grandpa. Norah wouldn't help.

In June she took her exams and they danced that night and kissed in the yard because she dared to believe she had done well. Ollie brought round bottles of beer and Grandpa had some too, and Norah. Jack winked at Rosie.

In July, the results came through and that night they celebrated again and then danced at the Palais until midnight because there was no more shorthand, no more typing to be learned.

'We've done it,' she told Jack, kissing him on the mouth, tasting the beer on his lips, knowing that he could taste it on hers. 'We've goddamn done it.'

Tomorrow she would walk up and down Fleet Street and find a cub reporter's job and she ignored Norah's scowl as they danced in through the yard, because now she was really on her way and Jack had said that he was proud of her, and so too had Grandpa.

CHAPTER 7

The newspapers would not take a girl of seventeen. They wouldn't take her if she was older either. She was not sufficiently well educated. She was a girl. There were too many men back from the war. They wouldn't even take her as a messenger. It wasn't suitable work for a girl.

She thought of the baseball she had thrown, the bike she had ridden, chasing down other kids on the block, down the street, in and out of cars, trams, hunting for Indians when she was the cowboy. The nickels she had pushed on to the tram lines for the trams to flatten. That wasn't suitable play for a girl either. This was the end. Somehow it brought everything to an end.

She didn't go back to Woolworths for two days because she couldn't stop the tears. She lay on her bed, the curtain drawn across the small window, but there was no light anywhere, anyway, any more. Everything had gone, nothing was worth getting up for, going on for. It was not only that her plans had failed but her protection had been stripped away and now she faced again the pain of her separation from the two adults she had loved with all her heart and it was all too much.

Jack came. He sat on her bed, held her hand but she couldn't feel him, she couldn't hear him as he told her she must not give up. She must get angry again, he said. She must fight. Remember the cheese, and the meat. Remember the rec, the hop-yards where it had been warm, where things had changed for them all.

'Don't let yourself lose, Rosie, not now, not ever. Don't let yourself despair. You'll see Frank and Nancy again.'

She turned from him. She was too tired, couldn't he see that? And she hurt too much. She wanted Nancy's arms to make it better. To take the ache away and to wipe out the hours of work which had all been for nothing. It had all been taken from her, as she had been taken from America. She felt dead and to tell him would be to hurt him. How could she do that?

Maisie came too, and Grandpa sat with her, but how could she tell any of them about the emptiness, the pain? How could she hurt them like that?

On the third day she returned to work because there was nothing else to do. She must live every day, Frank and Nancy had said. What would they say now, when she had failed to use all that they had given her? How could she hurt them like that?

Mrs Eaves gave her Erroll Garner, Louis Armstrong, Duke Ellington, Charlie Parker to play because Jack had been in to explain her absence. She took her by the arm, and led her to the office.

They sat and drank Camp coffee while Mrs Eaves talked of the Americans she had known, the GI, Stan, she had loved, although she was married.

'My husband came home in the winter of forty-five. Desert Rat he was. I was white haired by then and he thought it was the Blitz that had done it. It wasn't though. Stan had been killed in the Ardennes. It broke my heart and turned me white nearly overnight.' Mrs Eaves was holding Rosie's hand tightly.

'It's all right,' Rosie said. 'Don't talk. Don't say any more. Don't hurt yourself like this.'

Mrs Eaves swallowed but then continued. 'War breaks hearts. It breaks lives too. There's so much love that can never be spoken about; so much pain. There's so much death. So much injury which takes away futures. Really takes them away, Rosie.'

Mrs Eaves leaned back and lit a cigarette with trembling hands, letting the match drop into the ashtray. They both watched the flame die.

'Life's not a bowl of bloody cherries you know, Rosie.' Mrs Eaves's voice was tired, quiet. 'You're growing up. Frank and Nancy aren't here. Your Grandpa's old. You're on your own, my dear. Everyone is.' She flicked her ash into the ashtray, picking a shred of tobacco from her lip.

'But . . .'

'No buts. You can either sit down and give up or get out there, find a job as a secretary on a magazine, a paper. Get into it that way. Then maybe go back to America if you want to.

You're lucky, you have people who love you. You have a life and a future. So many haven't any more.' Mrs Eaves was crying now and Rosie held her and wept too and then she went back to her counter and played Bix, smelling the hamburgers cooking on the barbecue, feeling sand beneath her feet, seeing the hops on the bines. She thought of the cheeses she had clutched to her, Jack's bruised face in the van, Frank's struggle with the LA and she knew she'd have to go on. She wouldn't let herself lose, not now, not ever and this is what she told Jack, when he came in, but although his smile touched her pain, it didn't make it go away.

When she returned that evening, Grandpa was ill; he had the same cold as Lee had struggled with. She sat by his bed all night and every night for ten days and though he was better he was not the same, and she knew that she couldn't go on with her plans. Not yet.

He needed her at lunchtime and when she finished work and during her tea breaks, and she was there because she loved him, not because Norah shouted at her, 'You've got to. It's only fair.'

She was young, only seventeen, she told herself as she brushed her hair, tucking it behind her ears. There was plenty of time. She would wait, but waiting was so hard.

The next day she made Norah queue at lunchtime while she came home and sat with Grandpa because Norah had shouted at him this morning.

When Norah complained she said, 'You're not fit to be near him. You're cruel, you always were and you still are. But you'll do the goddamn shopping. It's only fair.' She no longer felt guilty where Norah was concerned. The feeling had faded when Rosie had begun to look after Grandpa day and night, out of love but out of duty too. She and Norah were equal now and there was no room in her life for guilt any more – or almost no room. Besides, there was too much pain in the darkness of the night and she wondered how many tears a person could cry.

It was on Friday that they went to the jazz club again, and Jack told her he had won twenty pounds when Pearl Diver won the Derby and that the bookmaker had been Mr Jones. She laughed but stopped when he said she must have the money to go towards a ticket to America, to see Frank and Nancy. To go back for ever, if that is what would take the shadows from her eyes. Maisie had said she would look after Albert, and Jack would too.

The smoke was all around them in the club. A man in the corner was rolling a reefer, his girlfriend was smoking hers. The smell was sweet.

'Go on, you use it,' Jack said, pushing it across to her. 'It's your birthday present. A bit late, I know.' He was drinking his beer, not looking at her, and Rosie thought of the sweater she had knitted him for his birthday, out of two of Grandpa's old ones, and here he was, offering a way of life back to her.

He looked tired too, and she felt like a spoilt child who had kicked and screamed because she had been hurt, ignoring him. Thinking he couldn't see what she was feeling.

She pushed the money back. It was held together by a rubber band. 'I couldn't leave you,' she said. 'I couldn't leave any of you. And anyway,' she said, leaning back and drawing circles in the beer which had spilled on the table, 'now my plaits have gone, where would I put the rubber band?'

He laughed, very loud, and the boy rolling his reefer looked across at them, nodding his head at his girlfriend, licking the cigarette paper, lighting it, breathing it deep into his lungs.

Rosie drank some of Jack's beer and knew now that she loved him, more than anyone else, and the pain receded and she slept each night and woke to sunlit days.

Since Rosie would not use the money, Jack took them to Butlins in August instead, after a summer of austerity with rations reduced yet again. Mr Attlee said, 'I cannot say when we shall emerge into easier times,' and Rosie nodded as she read these words. She was already emerging.

Grandpa was pleased because Marshall Aid appeared to be a possibility.

'I knew humanity would prevail,' he said.

But Frank had written to tell her that in the spring President Truman had embarked on an American crusade against Communism. He wanted the West strong enough to buffer the US and Rosie wondered if this was the only reason they were receiving aid. She didn't tell Grandpa that. She didn't tell him either that Frank had been visited again by the Local Administrator because Nancy seemed to think it was just a nuisance not a problem. And maybe she was right.

Only Norah, Rosie, Ollie and Jack went to Butlins. Not Grandpa, he was still weak but feeling much better, and not Maisie, who stayed behind with Lee to look after the old man. She wanted to, she had insisted when Rosie went round. Lee's too young. You all go and enjoy yourselves. And I don't mind about the sheets either.

They travelled by charabanc past verges sown with barley which were now being harvested. They saw a man scything an entry for a reaper-binder into a field of wheat. They stopped and watched him rake up the wheat he had cut. It was too precious to waste.

As the charabanc engine started again they began to sing on the back seat, Jack and Ollie drinking beer, and soon the whole coach was joining in, even Norah. The camp had rows of flat-roofed chalets, a swimming-pool, a gym, a dining-room, and over on the edge where the hedge leaned over from too many years in the path of the wind, there was a fun-fair.

She and Norah shared a chalet and Norah walked around touching the wardrobe, the dressing-table, the basin.

'This is what a prefab must be like,' she said. 'Nice and clean, fresh and new. That's what I want. My own new prefab. You can win competitions for the best gardens, you know.'

Rosie sat on the bed and nodded. Norah had never gardened in her life. She looked around. She preferred Grandpa's house with his books, the fireplace, bricks which had been there for years. Bricks which had housed him, and her.

Jack and Ollie had a chalet in the next row.

In the morning the tannoy woke them, shouting 'WAKEY WAKEY', but she didn't mind because she had no sheets to wash and wring. They straggled with the other campers past rose beds clear of greenfly into the dining-room, to eat beans and bacon, and Ollie wondered whether the roses had been there when the services took over the camps in the war. Rosie felt in her pocket for her matchbox. It was there. Why had she brought it? Would Maisie remember to catch the ladybirds for Grandpa?

She drank her tea and smiled at Jack. They were here together for a week and it was as though the years had fallen from her and she needed nothing else. Just him. They ran to the pool when breakfast was finished. She stood in her swimsuit on the edge of the pool, the tiles cold beneath her feet. She felt Jack's eyes on her. She flushed and dived into the cold water. Jack's body was strong and as pale as hers was now. Her lakeside tan was gone.

She hauled herself up on the edge, then stood and dived again, hearing the water gushing past, kicking out, reaching the other side. It was as good as the lake and it was fun. She hauled herself out, dived a third time, heard the water again. Yes, it was just as good. She surfaced, wiped back her hair and smiled at Jack.

Now the Redcoats were blowing whistles, and they were formed into teams for racing. Jack's team won. Again and again they plunged into the water, throwing balls, racing when the whistles blew, then filing into the dining-room again for lunch.

At three Rosie went with Norah to keep fit in the gym, throwing her arms up and down, feeling the sweat on her face. Again and again until she was too tired to think of Frank and the LA, Grandpa, even the journalism, but not too tired to think of Jack.

That evening they danced in the ballroom. She and Jack did not jitterbug but held one another close while the lights caught the chandelier and the MC called out numbers, giving prizes to those who won.

Jack smelt of chlorine, and his hands were cold and dry against her skin. She wore nylons he had bought for her, for Norah too. He pulled her closer and she felt him down the length of her body and they danced as though they could never be apart.

'I love you, Rosie,' he murmured, his breath warm in her hair.

'I love you too,' she said and she did. She always had, she always would.

The band struck up now, loud and fast into the Hokey Cokey, and they both laughed as they formed a circle, Rosie holding Ollie's hand, Jack holding Norah's, and it was like the ship's dance as they sailed away from Liverpool. But tonight she was home, her pain had been faced and this was better than the Lake Club had ever been, better than the barbecue with Joe.

That night she dreamed of Gallagher in Lower Falls. The next day she wrote to Frank and Nancy, asking them if there was any danger that Frank would have to give up the paper because of this LA. It was his life.

She wanted to know what they were facing because she could think of them without pain now. She licked the envelope as the tannoy called 'WAKEY WAKEY'. Breakfast was an egg, a soft-boiled egg, and she dipped her soldier into it, remembering the egg cosies her mother had knitted, asking Norah if she did too. She nodded and smiled.

They swam again, watched by other campers in deckchairs, some with knotted handkerchiefs on their heads, and Jack put Ollie's name down for the Knobbly Knees Competition in the afternoon.

At twelve-thirty they rushed to queue for lunch because the food was put on the tables exactly on time and yesterday it had been cold but that hadn't mattered to Rosie, because she hadn't had to buy it, or cook it, or wash up afterwards. Rosie wrote a postcard to Grandpa and Jack sent him one of a fat lady and a thin man doing something with a banana and Rosie was glad Grandpa needed new glasses.

Ollie didn't win the Knobbly Knees Competition, a sandy-haired young man with a moustache did. He was on holiday with his mother. Jack gave him a wolf whistle and Rosie gave Jack a slap.

They swam again though it was cloudy and cool but she liked to feel the water around her.

'Do you remember the stream at the bottom of the hop-yards?' Jack called over from the other side.

Oh yes, she remembered it. The pebbles beneath her feet, the water lapping around her calves, Jack lying on the grass, his hair hanging over his forehead, his sleeves rolled. Oh yes, she remembered it.

She put make-up on that evening, wearing lipstick for the first time. It felt sticky and tasted of peppermint. She wiped it off again. They went to the Tyrolean beer garden before dinner, singing along to an accordion player. Jack bought Ollie a beer while Ollie went to phone the local pub back in London, where Maisie had said she would be.

He was angry when he came back, throwing his jacket on the back of the chair, furious that she hadn't been in the bar.

'You said you'd ring Monday and Friday, didn't you? Maybe she got muddled. Or maybe Grandpa's cough's not so good?'

'Maisie said she'd ring us here if he wasn't, didn't she?' Norah said, looking over Jack's shoulder at the sandy-haired young man, primping her hair, pulling out her mirror and checking her lipstick, which had smeared on to her teeth.

Rosie looked at Jack, then at Ollie who was sipping his beer, his eyes dark again, his foot tapping beneath the table, on to the tiles, clicking, clicking.

'No, only if he was very bad. She'll be there on Friday night.' She wanted to slap Norah because Jack's eyes were darkening now and she remembered the months following her return, the shouting, the pain and anger in the boy she loved.

The accordion player was near them now, playing 'Roll Out the Barrel', and Jack bought another drink and they talked of how they used to collect tat for the rag and bone man and keep it in the old barrel at the bottom of Ollie's yard, but the laughter in Jack's voice was forced.

'You remember, don't you, Dad?'

Rosie watched as Ollie looked up from his beer, wiping the froth from his upper lip.

'You remember the tat, don't you?' Jack repeated and Rosie watched the accordion squeezing in and out, the fingers pressing the buttons and keys. Where the hell was Maisie?

'Yes, I remember.' And now at last Ollie was smiling. 'What about you two finding those dog-ends and selling them? Bloody cheek, that's what it was.' He was laughing now.

Rosie remembered the saliva-limp ends which Jack had made her tear off and which made her feel sick. She remembered the man on the train on her way back from Liverpool, stamping out his cigarette end. She remembered the Lucky Strikes Maisie had been smoking in the hop-yards. She looked at her hands.

Ollie had stopped laughing and was just staring into his beer. Rosie spoke again because she wasn't going to let Ollie and Maisie ruin Jack's holiday. They'd already hurt him enough.

'We sold them for twopence. Pinched your cigarette paper too.' She paused as he looked up. 'I bet Jack never told you that.'

Now Ollie laughed again and Rosie looked at Jack, who smiled, but his face was still tighter than it had been. She took his hand and as they hurried to dinner with the rest of the campers she said, 'It'll be all right. She got the time wrong. We're together. We're safe together. Forget about everything. Now come on, catch me.'

She dodged ahead of Norah, weaving in and out of the people streaming to the dining-room, doubling back round the rose bed and then up to Norah again. He hadn't caught her, though it had been close and he was really laughing now.

After dinner they sat in the ballroom and shook hands to left and then right as the compère directed. The young man with knobbly knees was on their right, sitting with his mother. Norah shook his hand, and Rosie watched as she smiled, her head tilted, her mouth pursed.

'Good evening,' Norah said.

His reply was lost in the chorus of 'Hi di hi' from the campers to the compère. What would the Lakeside Club think of all this? Rosie thought, laughing, happy, free. Frank and Nancy would love it.

The band played Glenn Miller numbers most of the night and Rosie tapped her foot to 'Little Brown Jug'. At the Ladies' Excuse Me she watched Norah, who stayed in her seat, her neck rigid, her eyes lowered. The young man had not yet asked her to dance.

Rosie nudged her sister, who ignored her but turned to Ollie and said, 'I think I'd like to try one of your cigarettes please, Ollie.' Her mouth was rounded, her vowels careful.

Ollie turned, his hands red from clapping to the music, his forehead sweating in the heat.

'Eh, what's that?' he said.

Rosie stood, walked round the table and tapped Knobbly Knees on the shoulder, drawing him to his feet. Norah's neck became even more rigid.

'Well, hi there.' Rosie's voice was more of a drawl than it had ever been. 'Sure is a great little dance hall.'

She was leading him on to the floor now. His hands were sweaty, his nose was too and the pores of his skin were big. His glasses were steel-rimmed and glinted beneath the chandelier. She stood with him, her hand on his shoulder, waiting for the beat, feeling Norah's eyes drilling through her, to him.

'Say,' she said, 'I guess this dance is way beyond me. You come on over and we'll get Norah to show me how it's done.'

She pulled him behind her. He still hadn't spoken.

'Say, what's your name?'

'Harold Evans.' His voice was high-pitched.

They were almost at the table now and Norah turned from them. Jack was looking down at his drink.

'So, Norah,' Rosie said. 'This is Harold Evans. We can't seem to get the hang of this dance. How about helping us out?' Rosie pulled at her arm, hauling her up.

'Harold Evans, this is Norah Norton. Naughty Norah for short. That's Jack and Ollie Parker. Now off you go, before you miss the music.'

Rosie stepped round them, walking off to the bar to buy a cool drink, not watching to see if they danced. She had done her bit. It was up to them.

Jack was still laughing when she got back, his head down, his shoulders shaking.

'I didn't recognise him with his trousers on,' he said. 'And where do you get the brass nerve?'

Rosie sipped her drink, winking at Ollie. 'I just pretended I was Nancy. I didn't want Norah's long face all week anyway and it would be nice for her to have someone. I have.' She touched his hand.

The dancers wouldn't leave the floor that night, even when midnight had been and gone, so the Redcoats formed a crocodile and danced them out in a conga and had to do that each evening from then on.

The next day Norah met Harold and sat on the deckchairs around the pool, watching as others swam. His mother sat with them, knitting, but Norah looked happy.

'He's a clerk in a bank,' she had told Rosie the previous

night. 'An office worker, not just someone selling things off a stall.'

'I expect he likes prefabs too,' Rosie had said, not showing her anger.

Rosie went to the gymnasium on her own, Norah was too busy sitting round the pool. She met Jack and Ollie and they walked to the fairground and shot at pitted yellow ducks which flapped up and down on a revolving belt. Jack and she pulled ropes in swinging boats and the wind rushed through her hair and Jack whistled as her skirt blew up. Ollie laughed and went to watch the Beauty Competition.

Jack and she sat on the ghost train. She screamed when the cobwebs dangled in her face and she remembered the Polyphemus moth and screamed again, glad that it was Jack's arm around her, not Joe's. Glad that it was his lips which touched hers, clung to hers, and his hand that now stroked her breast, but gently on top of her blouse.

They looked ahead as the train burst through the rubber doors, out into the daylight, past laughing campers, past a Redcoat who called 'Hi-di-hi'.

'Hi-di-ho,' Rosie yelled back and Jack too and they looked at one another as they walked away, their hands touching. His closed round hers and squeezed and now they smiled. 'I love you,' they said together.

They stopped again at the yellow ducks. Jack shot three down out of four. He tried again and shot down all four.

The Redcoat behind the counter handed him a pink teddy bear.

'When your turn comes, you should do well on the ranges. I was bloody hopeless.' He was fair-haired and hazel-eyed. Jack handed the teddy to Rosie.

'What was it like?'

'Not so bad if you like being kicked around a square, having no sleep, and peeling spuds until your arms drop off.' The Redcoat picked up his cigarettes from the counter, flicked one out to Jack who shook his head. 'Just put one out.'

The man laughed. 'You'll be smoking sixty a day before you're through your first week.'

Rosie knew what he meant and she gripped Jack's arm. She

had forgotten about National Service. She had forgotten that Jack would go.

'It's not dangerous though, is it?' she asked.

Jack jogged her arm. 'Come on, don't be daft. We've got loads of time anyway.'

Rosie didn't move. 'But it isn't, is it?' Because they were talking about Jack and this was important.

'No, you have to volunteer to go to the hot spots. Most of the time.' He nodded and winked at Jack. 'Go on, have a free go.'

Jack picked up the air gun. 'You sure?'

'Well, can't nick any money with these jackets coming down over me trouser pockets so you have the perk instead. Even have to keep me fags on the counter so I don't need to reach in me pockets.' He shrugged. 'Go on. Won't hurt anyone.'

Rosie paid anyway and gave Norah the second teddy.

The weather held up all week and Rosie wouldn't think of him leaving her. It was so far away. Conscription might be stopped by then. By Friday her tan was deeper and his lips were on hers and nothing else mattered.

That night Harold sat with them and told them about his brass-rubbing weekends. He told them how he travelled round churches and was always losing his cycle clips. Norah laughed, her finger dabbing at the corner of her mouth.

'Yes, fascinating hobby. I used to do some in Somerset.'

Jack spilt his beer and Norah frowned at him.

'We have some very old churches near us in Middle Street, you know,' Norah continued. 'I should think you might find some rather nice things to rub.'

Ollie coughed, then stood up. 'Must go,' he said hurriedly, 'need to phone.'

Rosie said, 'Why don't you come over, Harold? You live near Putney, don't you? Could be a change of scene for you.' She was shaking Jack's leg. 'That would be nice, Jack, wouldn't it?' It would be lovely, she replied to herself. It would be 'real swell' to have Norah happy and away.

They rushed to dinner as usual and Jack said that Norah had never been near a brass in her life, let alone rubbed it.

Ollie didn't come for his meal. They found him in the Tyrolean Bar when they had kicked their legs out in the last conga, singing, whistling out of the dance hall with streamers draped round their necks, and hats lopsided on their heads.

He was drunk. Maisie had not been in the local as they had arranged and his anger was frightening.

CHAPTER 8

When the charabanc dropped them Maisie came to the front door and pushed aside Ollie's hands which were shaking from the beer of the night before. She pushed aside his muttered oaths and questions and took hold of Rosie who had been bracing herself for the row that would come, wanting to shield Jack from the tensions of these two.

Rosie watched Maisie's lips, heard her words, then dropped her bag, turned and began to run, up the road, past the grocer's down First Street, then Wellington Avenue, past the glue factory and through the smell which always hung so thickly in the air.

'Grandpa's very ill,' Maisie had said. 'He wouldn't get the doctor. It was too expensive. He made me get medicine from the chemist but it wasn't enough. The doctor came in the end. I fetched him. It's his chest and his heart. He's in St Matthew's. He's never going to come home, Rosie, but he wouldn't let me bring you back. He wanted you and Jack to have that time together.'

He's never going to come home, come home, come home. Her feet were beating it out now and the breath was harsh in her throat. He must come home. He's Grandpa. He mustn't leave me. She was dodging round people, leaving them staring. One man pulled at her arm. She shook him off.

'It's me grandpa. He must come home,' she shouted at him. 'He mustn't leave me.'

Then Jack was with her, running alongside..

'It's all right. It'll be all right,' he said, his voice coming in bursts as he ran, but how could anything be all right now? she wanted to scream at him. I left him alone and now he's dying. But there was no breath left and at last she had to slow down and walk, bent over, the stitch digging into her side, her mouth dry, her shoes scuffed and dirty from the street dust. Then she was off again as it eased, Jack alongside. Norah hadn't come and she was glad.

There were long tiled corridors in the hospital with green ceilings and notice boards on chains, like the swings in the park.

'But they're not rusty,' she said, walking quickly, her shoes clipping along the floor, hearing the squeak of the swings, remembering the smell of rust, the scent of summer.

Jack pulled her back. 'Slow down, calm down.' But she pulled away. Grandpa was in here, alone. Didn't he understand? She had left him and now he was in here, alone.

They found his ward but the Sister stopped Rosie at the doors, her cap starched and upright, her face thin.

'Visiting hours are between three and four or six and seven,' she said. She held a clipboard in one hand and her watch was upside down. Why was that? So that she could see it of course. There was another sign hanging outside the ward. WARD 10. Would that squeak?

'It's my grandpa. He's been brought in and I've just arrived. I have to see him.' Rosie was calm now, her voice strong. She could see him down at the end, pale against the white pillow, the white sheets. He was her grandpa but somehow he wasn't. His eyes were sunken, his chin had dropped and his mouth hung open. She looked again at the Sister. 'I must see him and then I must talk to you.'

The Sister looked at her, then down at the clipboard, tracing a pencil along a list of names and words and numbers. Rosie didn't move, just waited. She would wait all afternoon, all evening, all night. She was used to waiting. Didn't they know? All her life she had waited.

A staff nurse eased past carrying a covered bedpan. An old man sitting next to his bed in a checked wool dressing-gown was picking at the air with clumsy fingers, again and again.

She looked back at the Sister whose navy uniform drew the colour from her tired face. The woman looked up at her, smiling slightly.

'Well, Doctor has finished his rounds. Perhaps it would do Mr Norton good. But just this once, mind. And I shall be in my office just behind you, to the left.' She pointed over Rosie's shoulder and Rosie felt Jack turn, then saw him nod.

'Thank you, Sister,' she said and walked down the ward, alone.

She talked gently, quietly to Grandpa who smiled at her but did not speak. She told him that he was looking well, that he would soon be home. But he wasn't and she knew he wouldn't. She held his hand which was so much thinner. How could people become so thin so quickly?

She talked of swimming in the pool on holiday, telling him how it had been boarded up when the Navy had taken it over.

'It would have been more good to them as it was,' she said. 'They could have practised their battles.'

She told him about Norah's clerk, of the Knobbly Knees, of the fun-fair and all the time she held his hand and wanted to say, 'I love you, Grandpa, and I can't imagine life without you. I've just found you again and I can't bear it if you die.'

But part of her remembered the words Norah had shouted down the pavement after her. 'You'll be pleased. Now you can get on with your bloody job.' Was that true? She looked down at his hand in hers. No. She would rather there was never a job for her if he could come home again.

She kissed his hand, held it to her cheek and couldn't say how much she loved him because she would cry and then he would know how very ill he was. So she listened as he tried to talk of the roses but, halfway through, the words died behind lips which were too clumsy to be his.

'I'll look after them, don't worry. There are no greenfly,' she murmured, watching his face.

'There are no roses here,' he murmured, nodding at the dark and grimy yard outside his window.

She touched his hand. 'Just rest,' she said.

Though his eyes were sunken, they were the same. They were dark and kind and the eyes of the young man he had once been. The lids, though, were heavy and closing and she reached forward and stroked his cheek. He hadn't been shaved properly. There was stubble beneath his chin and it was this that made her weep as she walked home with Jack because Grandpa had always shaved each day.

Norah was sitting in the kitchen eating Spam and boiled potatoes. There were some left in the pan. They were overcooked and in pieces. Rosie drained off the cold, thickened water, tipped the potatoes on to a plate, cut a slice of Spam, then a tomato.

'It's his heart and his chest,' she said as she sat down. 'The Sister says that he might die tomorrow or in three months' time, or in six months' time.'

Norah took a drink of water. 'As long as we're not expected to have him home.'

Rosie looked down at her plate. 'No, he's too ill. But he misses his roses.' She was tired and the tears were too close to tell Norah that she had a voice like a goddamn saw and the soul of a witch.

As she lay in bed that night she thought of the bleak yard, the soot-stained walls, the emptiness of it all.

At lunchtime Mrs Eaves said she could leave half an hour early because Rosie told her she must sort some things out for Grandpa. She walked home and put two of the smaller roses which grew in pots into the wheelbarrow. They were not strongly scented but their colour was rich. She pushed them through the streets in her Woolworths uniform. The same streets that she had run along yesterday.

Her arms were taut, her shoulders ached and people stared at her again, but it didn't matter. None of this mattered. Didn't they know what had happened to her grandpa?

She passed the back of the terrace which fronted on to the rec and turned left down the alley, coming out opposite the slide. She pushed the barrow across the road along to the swings and the footworn grassless earth. She pushed a swing. It squeaked. She looked back at the houses, ripped apart, unrepaired. There was more wallpaper than ever flapping on the end wall.

The park in Lower Falls had been grassed. Picnic tables and ice-cream vans had spotted the ground. She preferred this one. She looked down. The rust from the chains had stained her hand again. She moved behind the swing and pushed the seat, sending it soaring, hearing their laughter from the long lost years.

She pushed the barrow in through the hospital gates and past an ambulance which was parked with its back doors open. She edged round to the left-hand side, walking beside the main building, checking where she was in relation to the annexe which housed Grandpa's ward.

She walked alongside the soot-blackened walls until she saw the peaked roof of Ward 10. She pushed open two gates which were set into the wall. There were dustbins in one yard and old trolleys in another. She moved on. There was no one else walking, or standing, or watching. There was just the distant smell of cooking; the distant clink of plates, pans, cups.

Rosie stopped. Her hands were blistered. There was a lower wall now and she looked back at the building, shading her eyes against the sun. Then back at the wall. This had to be where the yard was but there was no gate.

She clutched the handles, pushing the wheelbarrow on again, welcoming the pain in her hands because it deflected her grief. She wheeled the roses round to the other side. Here was a small brown gate with a rusted latch which she lifted and then brushed back her hair. She could smell the swings on her hands.

She eased open the gate, looking towards the ward. There was no face looking out but she could see Grandpa eating in bed with a bib on. She lifted first one, then the other rose, putting them where he could see, checking for greenfly though she knew there was none.

She pushed the wheelbarrow home and bathed her hands. The blisters were bleeding. She bound them and then she climbed the stairs, taking a chair from Norah's room and heaving herself up into the loft, searching through old boxes. At last she found his nailer's penny. Grandpa had looked diminished in other people's pyjamas, in a ward which was not his home and she wanted him to remember who he was. She wanted to remember who he was.

That evening she took it in to him and he held it, holding her hand tightly too.

'They call me Bert here, but my name's Albert.'

'I'll tell them, Grandpa.'

'I tell them all the time, but it doesn't make any difference.'

'I'll tell them now,' Rosie said, leaving him, feeling his hand about hers as she found the Sister and told her, and then found the Matron and told her also.

Grandpa was asleep when she returned but he still held the penny. She kissed him and started to leave but as she reached the end of the bed he opened his eyes.

'There are roses in the yard. They'll have a gentle scent.' He was smiling at her, his eyes full of love.

She came the next day and he gave her the penny to put away safely.

'They called me Albert today,' he said.

'Of course they did. They know that's what you like.'

It was hot in the ward and the water in the jug was warm but he didn't mind and sipped as Rosie held the glass and then he told her how hot it had been around the nail furnaces, how thirsty they had all become. Rosie stroked his arm and listened as he told her how he had made Flemish tacks, so small that a thousand weighed only five ounces, but he had made hobs, and brush nails, and clinkers too.

He sat up, and she straightened his pillows and he told her how the fire and the chimney were in the middle of the shop, how he used to watch the different colours in the flames when he was a child, how he had woven stories in his mind then, but once he was a nailer he didn't have the time.

He told her how he would take one of the three iron rods from the fire, turn it with one hand and hammer out the tang, or point, to make the iron harder. He told her of the special coke that was bought from the gas works. It had already been used but was good enough for them once it had been broken up.

Rosie asked him about the boy who had been nailed to the doorpost by his ear, the one he had taken down. Grandpa stopped smiling then and asked for more water. It was still warm and Rosie held the glass to his lips and now he was crying.

She stood up, putting her arm around him, feeling like the parent he had been, listening as he said, 'He repaid me, you see.'

He wouldn't talk any more about nailing and she left that night wondering if his heart had broken each time she had cried throughout the years, as hers had just done. And wondering why it was that the tears had come.

As August turned to September and September to October, Rosie and he talked of other things, other people, but never of the nailers. He told her of the books he would like to have written and how he had read them instead.

She told him of Norah's clerk who had ridden over on his

bicycle. How Norah had taken him brass-rubbing at St Cuthbert's, how she had come back with sore knees and a mouth like a sparrow's bum which had flashed into a smile the moment he looked at her. They were going again next week, and the next and the next.

'With a bit of luck and a following wind,' Rosie said, and Grandpa laughed.

She told him of the letters she had received from Frank and Nancy. They had asked her to write a feature for their paper because, Nancy said, it would cheer Frank up to think of her working at something like that.

'Why does he need cheering up?' Grandpa asked as the leaves swirled into the yard, over the wall, snatching at the roses, scudding into corners.

'Things are a bit difficult on the paper right now. You know how work gets, Grandpa. There are ups and downs.'

But it was more than that, she knew, as she slipped into the yard and pruned the roses before she left that night, putting the old blooms into the canvas bag she had brought. Frank had spoken up for the Anti-Nazi League during the war and the Local Administrator had discovered this. Frank had been questioned by two other guys now, Nancy had told her, adding that Commie-hunting was getting to be quite a sport.

Rosie put away her secateurs and waved to the nurses who were watching from the window. They hadn't minded about the roses. They had been pleased.

That night and for the rest of the week she worked on an article about Austerity Britain, telling America of the fuel cuts the Midlands would have to suffer, losing power for one day a week; of the imports which still had to be kept at a minimum; how Britain had to export or die; how in 1946 even the new cricket balls for the Test Match had had to be rationed.

She sent this off with a letter to Frank and Nancy telling them that Grandpa was a little stronger but really no better and that she needed to be able to delay her lunch-hour and visit at three, which Mrs Eaves allowed. Maybe another employer wouldn't and so her career would have to wait for just a while longer.

In October she read that the film star Ronald Reagan had appeared before a Congressional committee investigating

Communism in the USA. She read how he had opposed a Hollywood witch-hunt against Communists or anything which might compromise the democratic principles of America. She read that already there was evidence against seventy-nine Hollywood subversives but Nancy wrote and told her that none of these had been named and hysteria was the order of the day.

'Where the goddamn hell is it all going to end?' Rosie asked Jack as they walked to the hospital in the afternoon on 1 November. He shook his head.

Frank wasn't too well, it was the strain of being questioned about activities which were deemed patriotic during the war years. But now the enemy was different and she felt the anger rising again as the wind whipped through her coat.

She kicked the leaves, angry and confused that the world had broken into enemy camps again, before anyone had yet recovered from the last war, and even in America, the land which had always seemed so free, so happy, there were victims.

Nancy had also written to say that the feature was not what they had wanted. They could read that in any paper. 'What we want from you, my girl, is something from the point of view of the people and don't leave the new career in the air for too long.'

Rosie and Jack leaned against a lamppost, watching as children swung from a rope tied on the next one, playing chicken with the bikes which raced past in the gloom, listening to the curses of the riders who shook their fists and told the kids that they should be at home in bed.

'I'll try again,' she said to Jack.

That evening Grandpa talked of Bromsgrove again. He sat high up against his pillows, his eyes looking into hers as he told her of the foggers. His breathing was too loud tonight and the Sister had said he was not so well again. He was speaking quickly, as though there was no time, and Rosie felt the fear tighten within her.

He told her how foggers were middlemen who employed nailers and sold their products to the nailmasters. How the nailmaster liked them because the fogger could provide him with whatever he wanted at short notice. This meant that the nailmaster did not have to carry large stocks. It also meant that he did not have to supervise the nailers.

'The fogger did that, you see,' Grandpa panted.

Rosie gave him more water. 'Not now, Grandpa. There's no hurry.'

'But I want you to understand, little Rosie. Can't you see that?' He paused, coughed and she held a handkerchief to his mouth. 'Can't you see that?' he repeated when he could talk.

Rosie nodded. 'Yes, Grandpa.' But she couldn't.

'Those foggies could play tricks, you see. They could say them nails weren't a proper job. Give you less for them but charge nailmaster the same. They could bore a hole in the weight. Weigh up your nails light, so you gave him too many. They were smart. They made money. They were hard.'

Rosie patted his hand. 'Sshh now.'

There were screens round the bed next to Grandpa's and a doctor had gone in.

'But I want you to see how he made his money.'

Rosie looked at him. 'Who made his money, Grandpa?'

'Barney, the boy with the nail through his ear. Your grandma loved him, you see. That's why we came to London. He moved down here.' He was panting, leaning forward. His shoulders were so thin beneath his jacket. 'He moved with the money he'd made. That was when she wanted to come down here. It wasn't me at all. But he was married when we got here.'

Now Rosie couldn't see the screens, she could only see Grandpa's face as he picked hops in his beloved hills, his body easy, his eyes at peace. And then she thought of Grandma, whose eyes had seemed devoid of warmth. Could a woman like that ever have felt passion, love?

Grandpa was coughing again and it was longer before he could catch his breath this time and while he did she smiled and said, 'Oh no, Grandma loved you. You know she did.'

Grandpa lay back, his eyes closed. 'Maybe you're right.'

'Anyway, Grandpa, she was married when she met this Barney, wasn't she?'

'She met him the week after we'd wed. After she'd come over from Dudley, and somehow the light went out of her face, if you know what I mean.'

Rosie could say nothing because suddenly she saw Maisie and knew exactly what Grandpa meant.

His hand was clasping hers now. 'You must marry someone

you love, someone who loves you, Rosie. You wait for that person and don't you settle for anything less. Do you hear me, Rosie?'

The screens were being moved back now and the visiting bell was ringing.

'Do you hear me, Rosie?' His grip was firmer than it had been since he had come in here.

'I hear you, Grandpa, and I promise. But she loved you, you know.'

She kissed him, smoothing the sheeting around him, brushing his hair to the side with her fingers, smiling into his eyes.

He watched her walk up the middle of the ward, waited for her to turn and wave. She always waved, she always smiled and thought he couldn't see her tears. But he saw them, all right. He had seen them when he had taken her to Liverpool. He had seen them as she had walked up the gangplank and he had felt her gas mask in his hand and had wanted to run after her, push everyone else away and take her back with him.

But she had needed to be safe. That was what had been most important, that the children were safe. He lay back on the pillows, looking out into the yard, at the pruned rose trees. He remembered the children waving from the portholes, singing 'Roll Out the Barrel' as the tugs eased the ship out into the fairway.

He had still heard them singing as the ship moved away. He hadn't heard for four weeks whether she was safe and then each day, each week, each year had been empty without her. He loved her, like the air he breathed, like he'd loved Martha, like he'd loved Nellie, and Norah. He'd been down to Somerset to see Norah every three months but she'd been ashamed of him and had no more love for him than she'd ever had. She was her grandmother's child and had learned all her bitterness at that woman's knee and now there was no love left in him for Rosie's sister, none at all.

On 20 November Ollie said he would visit Grandpa while Rosie slept out overnight along the Mall with thousands of others to cheer as the King and Princess Elizabeth drove to Westminster Abbey.

Jack arrived at midnight and they lay side by side on old

blankets and newspapers and it was good to hear him breathing so close and to drink steaming tea together from thermos flasks as dawn came.

She wrote it all down, the bitter cold, the woman who sang 'Knees Up Mother Brown' at dawn and toasted the Royal couple with stout. She toasted Jack and Rosie too.

'Because, God bless us,' she said, 'I like to see some love in this bloody awful world.'

Jack's kiss had tasted of tea, his lips had been soft, and now, as she peered over the heads of the crowd and snatched a view of the Irish State Coach escorted by the Household Cavalry in their scarlet uniforms and riding black horses, she could still feel his body alongside hers.

She wrote of the tulle veil which hung from a circlet of diamonds and the coupons which had been needed. She wrote of Lieutenant Philip Mountbatten who had been born in Corfu, the son of a Greek Prince, and would now be known as Prince Philip, Duke of Edinburgh.

Rosie wrote of the cheers from the crowd after the service as Princess Elizabeth and the Duke of Edinburgh travelled to their wedding breakfast at Buckingham Palace, cutting the five-hundred-pound wedding cake with Prince Louis of Battenberg's sword.

She knew this because she and Jack had moved along to the Palace and she had listened to the reporter in front of her. Jack had laughed and said she'd go far with ears that could flap that well. Rosie turned to laugh with him and as she turned she thought she saw Maisie at the back of the crowd. The light was back in her face and she was looking up at a big man with red hair who stooped and kissed her mouth.

Rosie typed up the story that night and sent it to Frank, then visited Grandpa and wouldn't let herself think of Maisie, or Grandma and the fogger. She wondered whether to tell Jack but she couldn't bear to see the pain in his eyes return and besides, she might have been mistaken. Yes, that was it. It was a mistake. It wasn't Maisie, the crowds had parted and then closed, it could have been anyone.

At the end of November Frank wrote and said he loved the

piece and it would be used. He also said that the Russians had tested an A bomb which was putting some members of the town into a total sweat. But do they seriously think anyone would use those bombs? he wrote. Rosie didn't know because the world seemed crazy enough to do anything and she held Jack tighter that night as they walked back from visiting Grandpa because he would have to register for National Service in April.

A letter from Nancy arrived at the beginning of December, when there had been a flurry of sleet which had frizzed Norah's perm.

Lower Falls
November 26th, 1947

Dearest Rosie,

We think of your grandpop every day and wonder how things are. You know we send our love to you all and only wish we could be there to help.

Great things are happening in Lower Falls. Our Local Administrator is becoming positively peacockish with importance and self-righteousness. A deadly combination. The big boys of the film industry have blacked ten Hollywood writers and producers who were cited for contempt of Congress after allegations that they were Commie sympathizers.

They have said that none of these will be re-employed until 'he is acquitted or has purged himself of contempt and declares under oath he is not a Communist.' Many liberals feel that in America we should not have to declare anything at all. This should be a free country.

I guess I lie awake at nights now because all that work Frank did in the war to encourage people to support the Britishers against the Nazis is beginning to look as though it is going to cause him pain. It somehow makes him an automatic Red. He is very tired, very strained. But I can't believe that any of this can go on for long. Sanity will prevail, as my old mom used to say. I have to go. The old boy has bitten through another pipe. We will write soon.

Nancy

The next evening Jack and Rosie went to Soho, to walk down the street and hear the music pitching and soaring because she had dreamed all night that the jazz had become silent and the buildings were derelict brownstones.

They stopped to listen to banjos, pumping tubas, four-square rhythms. They leaned against railings and drank in the Chicago-style jazz which was drifting up from a basement window, closing their eyes at the solos with their riff backing, squeezed between snatches of the theme.

Later, back in Middle Street, they kissed in the yard and Jack stroked her breasts and kissed her neck, her shoulder, the soft rising flesh, and Rosie didn't feel the cold which had earlier chilled her. Then they held one another close, so close, because they were both new to such passion, such longing and wanted more, much more.

On 20 December Rosie took paper and glue to the hospital and together she and Grandpa cut and stuck paper chains. They gave some to the ward and some she took home, and could not forget those swollen hands which could barely hold the paper together as it stuck.

The next night they just sat and there was snow in the yard, settling on the rose bushes, and Rosie said that in no time at all the spring would be here.

'Not for me, my little Rosie,' Grandpa said as a nurse walked past with the old man who still picked at the air. 'Not for me.'

But Rosie wouldn't listen because she couldn't imagine a time when he wasn't there and so she talked of the jazz which had played in Soho and Lee who wanted a cart for Christmas. She talked of the pram in the shed which she and Jack had raced on and Grandpa just sat and smiled and listened until she fell silent, watching the clock, wanting to go, but not wanting to ever leave.

'It's because of Barney and your grandma that we got the house. I want you to know because you'll need to understand this when I'm gone.'

He shook his head as she interrupted. 'No, Grandpa. It's Christmas . . .'

'Rosie, listen to me.' It was the voice he had used when he was younger and firmer, and she knew she must listen, and so she did, holding a handkerchief to his mouth as he coughed, again and again before he could begin.

'You know that man Jones. The one who owns the warehouse. He owned our houses too. He was going to sell. To kick us out. Ollie and me and all the families.' Grandpa coughed again and Rosie poured a drink, holding the glass for him, then wiping his chin. There was still stubble and his hair was too long.

'We needed to buy the house and your grandma told me to go to Barney. To borrow enough and for Ollie too. I had to go with me cap in me hand. I can remember twisting the brim so much that I couldn't wear it again. The words sort of stuck in me throat but he lent us the money and that was what was important. Nothing else. Nothing else at all.' He was coughing again and Rosie didn't want to listen. She didn't want to see the tears smearing over his cheeks. This was her grandpa, and she didn't want to see him like this but she had to.

'Your grandma always said it was her house. Barney did it for her. She was right. I tried to think it was because I took him off the doorpost but it wasn't. He told me so. He said he'd had her on the foggers' floor. That she'd loved him, followed him to London. But he didn't love her. So he owed her something. He laughed, you know.'

Rosie wiped his face. 'Don't, Grandpa, please don't. It was probably just words, to hurt you. He was jealous that you'd got Grandma. That's all.'

'But you've got to understand that it was your grandma's house really. And you mustn't blame me. I've made sure you're all right.' He was gripping her hand now. 'Promise you understand. Go on, promise.'

'Sshh. It's all right. I promise.' But she didn't know what she was promising and before she left she said, 'But why did you go to him? Why not just find somewhere else to live?'

He was lying back now, his jaw slack, breathing through his mouth, his eyes following the movements of the nurse behind Rosie. He said nothing for a moment and then lifted his head, wiping his mouth with a clumsy hand.

'Your mum and dad were dead. How long would we live? I had to work hard and pay it off so you always had somewhere to live. It was for you children. It didn't work out quite like I wanted, but you'll be all right. I promise.'

Grandpa didn't die that night, or the next, but on Boxing Day, after Rosie had kissed him, and held him, then left. There had been the peace of Herefordshire on his face all evening and so she was not surprised, but that did not make it any easier.

CHAPTER 9

Rosie stood in the churchyard, hearing the vicar but not watching him, hearing Maisie's sobs, but not watching her, or Norah, Ollie, Jack. Instead she looked above the heads of all of them to the trees which lined the cemetery. There were no leaves, there was no sun. There was no Grandpa any more but she still could not believe that.

She picked up the handful of earth and dropped it on the coffin but it meant nothing. The vicar's words meant nothing. He was gone. That was all. He was gone.

At the solicitor's office she sat with Norah on raffia-seated chairs. A strand was broken and dug into her leg. It meant nothing.

In his will Grandpa left the house to Norah, in pursuance of his wife's wishes, the solicitor intoned. With Rosemary to have residence for so long as she required. The nailer's penny and his books were to come to Rosie, along with the letter which was now handed to her. It all meant nothing. Because he had gone.

Rosie walked with Norah towards Maisie's for sandwiches and tea and to accept the condolences of the neighbours. She listened to her sister, saw her smile, felt the letter in her pocket which she would read alone, because Grandpa had said that people needed their privacy.

They walked past the torn houses but she didn't feel torn, she felt nothing. When they reached Maisie's she smiled at Ollie and the people who kissed her with sweet tea on their breath and kindness in their faces. She drank sweet tea herself. She didn't take sugar. Had Maisie forgotten? But what did it matter? She didn't eat though. Even with the tea her mouth was so dry, her eyes were dry, her heart was dry.

She put down her cup, carefully, still smiling, still nodding, still thanking Grandpa's friends for their kindness as she walked out through the yard, past Jack, who didn't stop her because he knew she had to be alone. But there was love in his face and grief too.

Grandpa's yard was empty. The rose trees were stunted from her autumn pruning. She touched The Reverend Ashe, running her fingers along its thorns, remembering its summer scent mingling with the creosote of the shed, seeing the roses which she had left in the hospital yard to bloom for someone else.

She went up to her room, taking her jacket and her dresses back into the kitchen, fetching Grandma's green wicker sewing box from beneath the bottom of his bookshelves. She measured and cut the black tape she had bought from Norah's counter and then sewed, stitch by stitch, a black armband on the left sleeve of the jacket. And then there were the dresses.

The needle went in and out, in and out. The scissors cut the thread cleanly. One done. The needle went in and out again and again. The fire was burning low. She had wrapped the coal in damp newspaper last night. She had heaped the fire with ash before she climbed the stairs. She had riddled it this morning, holding up newspaper to draw the heat, but Grandpa would never sit here again.

Middle Street

Dear little Rosie,

Please try and understand. Your grandmother felt that Norah should have gone to America too. She felt it was unfair that it was just you. She felt the house was hers and when the bomb fell and she was dying she made me promise that Norah would have it in my will. She knew then that the impetigo would keep her from America.

I couldn't cry for her. Not after that. But I promised, you see. You must stay in the house for as long as you need to. That was the best I could do. I find it hard to forgive myself. I leave you my penny and my books. I loved them but not as much as I love you.

Grandpa

Rosie put the letter back in her pocket. She felt nothing. She picked up the needle again, in and out, in and out.

There were footsteps in the yard. They were not Jack's or Norah's but Maisie's and her arms were plump and warm as they hugged her, but Maisie's face was without light, and as Rosie let the last of the dresses fall from her hands she thought of the big red-haired man but it was all too distant. And what did any of it matter?

'I wasn't there with him, you see, when he died. And I left him for too many years. He was so alone and I even left him to die alone,' Rosie said.

Maisie's arms were no help. They didn't reach inside her. But there was a lavender smell in the crook of her neck and Rosie rested on her shoulder for a moment and wondered how you could take away the years and return to where the sun smiled and you shelled peas on the back step.

'Come to me next door whenever you need help or you want to talk.' Maisie stood up and Rosie didn't watch her but looked instead at the flames of the fire as Grandpa had watched the flames up in Bromsgrove.

'I know things are bad again but come. Don't be put off by the rows. We love you. All of us. Jack especially. And we all loved Albert. It won't be the same.' Now Maisie was crying and Rosie turned from the flames which were easing round the lumps of coal. Maisie's eyes were red and her skin was blotched and Rosie stretched out her hand.

'No, it won't be the same. But nothing's been the same for so long.' And she wanted to say, why are you quarrelling again? Who is that man? Did he exist or did I imagine it? But she wasn't imagining the pain in Jack's eyes.

She said nothing though, just watched Maisie walk away through the smog that was creeping into the yard, edging her hair and clothes with droplets.

She looked around the room, at Grandpa's books, at his ashtray bought in Malvern. At the slippers which still held the shape of his feet. At the table covered in oilcloth. At the back step where they had shelled peas. No, nothing was the same.

All this was Norah's and she couldn't believe this had happened. That she no longer belonged in the house she had been brought back to. She couldn't believe that Grandma could do this to her. That Grandpa hadn't fought her. But she shouldn't feel angry because Grandpa had told her why and she should understand. She should goddamn understand.

But there was a noise now from the yard and then another, sharp and loud. She saw through the window that the shed door was open and that Norah was pulling and heaving at something, her coat rising at the back and her petticoat hanging down beneath her frock.

It was the pram she was pulling out, dragging it to the alley, chucking it at the children waiting outside playing flicksies in spite of the fog.

'Have that, and good riddance,' she said and Rosie watched as she went back into the shed. It was Norah's house now. Rosie couldn't stop her, and she would stamp down on the rage which was making her head burst.

But then Norah came out with the saw which was rusted and hadn't been used for years. She took hold of the thick trunk of the peach trailing rose, The Reverend Ashe, which had held the warmth of the summer. She took hold, leaning down, her breath thicker than the smog, and now Rosie moved.

She wrenched open the door, calling, 'Leave that alone, you greedy bitch.' She didn't recognise her own voice as she tore through the yard, pushing Norah backwards, snatching at the saw, feeling the raw cut it made on the palm of her hand.

'Get away from his roses.'

She held it to one side as Norah grabbed at it, hitting and slapping Rosie, pulling at her arm, shoving her, shaking her, but she couldn't reach the saw. Rosie was on her knees now, forced back by Norah, who shrieked and gripped her hair, pulling it hard, forcing Rosie backwards, her eyes pulled into slits, pain searing through her.

Norah's face was close to hers now. She was bending over and Rosie felt the spittle which sprayed from her mouth.

'This is my house now, Miss bloody Hoity Toity. If I want those roses down, I'll take them down.'

Now Rosie twisted free, slapping Norah hard across the face and then again, hearing the saw crash to the ground. 'You leave them! You leave them or I'll tell that apology for a man you've got that you've never rubbed a brass in your life. That you sulked all through your time in Somerset because you didn't get a GI button.'

Norah came at her again, her hands like claws, fury, rage, hatred in her face, and Rosie held her wrists, keeping her away, forced back now on to the rose, the thorns digging into her scalp, her back and hands as Norah pushed back, harder.

Then Norah stopped, pulled away, stood there panting. 'This is my house. His roses can stay. You can't.'

Rosie eased forward, the thorns dragged at her hair, at her cardigan, snagging, pulling.

'His roses will stay and so will I. Go and look at the will again.'

Norah wiped her nose with the back of her hand.

'Then you'll be in the way. Harold will marry me now I have the house. Why don't you just get back to where you belong? Nobody wants you over here now that he's dead. Grandma never wanted you, only me. Now they're both dead. You haven't got him to stand by you.'

Norah turned, pulling her coat straight, walking into the kitchen, slamming the door. The light came on and Rosie cried in the yard that was empty and cold.

The fog was catching in her throat and her tears were warm. She'd never noticed that tears were so warm. She leaned against the shed and then Jack came and held her, saying nothing, just holding her until she walked to the bench where she used to sit with Grandpa.

'Will you go back to Frank and Nancy?' Jack asked, still holding the saw that he had taken from her. 'There's nothing to keep you here. Not now. It's the sensible thing to do.'

He propped the saw against the shed, squatting, taking a packet of Woodbines from his pocket. Rosie saw the match flare, smelt the sulphur. Saw the oast-houses, saw Frank striking a match against the kitchen tiles. Heard Nancy say, 'Get that goddamn thing out of here.'

'You must do what makes you happy, Rosie,' Jack said, smoke pouring from his mouth. His face was pinched, pale, alone. He didn't go to the Palais any more because the rows were so much worse, and Rosie held out her hands to him, watching as he pushed himself upright.

'You're here. That's what makes me happy,' was all she said because he was alone and she loved him and she couldn't leave him, not as she'd left Grandpa.

The next day she applied and was accepted for a job as a typist at a magazine and handed in her notice at Woolworths. The day after that she took the train to Herefordshire and watched the winter claw deep into the earth and into her body where there should have been pain, but there was nothing again.

She took a bus from the station to the village, driving along mist-draped roads which curled around the base of the hills, then up between them, weaving and turning. There were oast-houses drained of colour, their cowled vanes motionless. Sulphur would not sting anyone's eyes today.

The bus passed a broken wagon with its shafts upended at the entrance to a field. Cobwebs were moisture-laden in the hedgerows. No birds sang as she stepped from the bus and walked up the lane to the farm along the frost-hard track. The blackberry leaves were dark, torn, furled. Her fingers had been purple last year from the juice. Norah's face had been purple all those years ago.

She walked past the yard where manure steamed through the mist. A dog barked. She didn't stop until she reached the pigsties, the sties where Grandpa and she had slept. Where they had all slept and laughed and talked.

The cold was deep in her now, her hair was heavy and damp. She dug her hands deep into her pockets and turned towards the path to the hop-yards. The dog still barked but there were no other sounds.

The grass had overgrown the path and its wetness soaked her shoes, but it did not matter. The sloping yards were empty of bines, as she knew they would be. There was no sea of green, no Roman Candles of green sprays. She took her hands from her pockets, lifted them to her face and remembered the hop smell of sticky hands, the yellow powder under nails, Grandpa's last season.

She cried, standing in the long wet grass with snow spattered on the distant Welsh hills and his 'me dooks' echoing again and again. It was here, standing in the hop-yards, that she said goodbye and at last believed that he had gone.

She waited for the bus at the end of the track, next to the telegraph pole where no bines wound today. But in the spring they would grow again, twining up clockwise, always clockwise, two feet in a week, and the pickers would come. She could hear the bus now, lurching up the lane, and turned again to the hop-yards.

One day she would come again because this is where the sun had always shone. One day she would come back, with Jack. And in the meantime she would stay at 15 Middle Street, to be near him, to make something positive out of her life.

The office was pleasant to work in. She watered the flowers, typed all day, listened, watched, learned and asked how she could move into Features. The Editor laughed.

'Give it time,' she said. 'At least now we know you're keen.'

She wondered if Frank had liked her feature on the jazz clubs. She had heard nothing from him or Nancy.

She and Jack no longer went to the Palais for Jack had seen Ollie hit Maisie after the funeral and now he didn't like to leave them alone. So they spent their evenings walking up and down the alley behind the houses and listening for the sounds of angry voices.

In February Frank sent her twenty dollars for the feature, which had drawn letters from his readers. More, please, he said, when you have time. He didn't talk of the Local Administrator, just of Grandpa and how sad they were for her and would she be coming back to Lower Falls?

That night she sat in her boxroom and wrote, telling them that she would come back but only when Jack had gone for his National Service because she couldn't leave him. She didn't tell them she loved him and that he was her reason to breathe, to live. But he was.

Each night they would just be together. Sometimes they talked, sometimes they kissed, but it was enough that their hands were joined and that their voices mingled, that their lips touched and then drew away because they were both frightened of too much passion.

In March Frank wrote of his distress at the news that the Communists had staged a coup in Czechoslovakia, and journalists who had attempted to get through to the President's Palace had been turned back by police and militia wearing armbands and carrying guns. Coming only nine years after the Nazi takeover it chilled the blood.

Nancy also wrote and said that the Local Administrator had written a letter to the newspaper calling on all good Americans to be extra vigilant as the Communist Menace crept forward yet again. Frank had not published it, of course. 'And come when you can,' she wrote. 'We love you. We grieve for you. This Jack must be important to you. I'm glad. Keep going with the writing.'

On 23 March Harold and Norah were married in St Cuthbert's. Rosie wore a new hat and so did Maisie. There was to be a small reception at a local hotel which Rosie had paid for because Norah had cried and said that Harold's mother would expect one.

Rosie had nodded and given her the money as her wedding present as Grandpa would have done, and besides, it would stop her goddamn crying. Maisie made the cake, though she had wanted to use hemlock as the flavouring, she told Rosie as Norah came down the aisle while an elderly man played the wedding march. He had a drip on the end of his nose.

Norah looked almost beautiful but Jack said that was because the veil was thick and hiding her face. Rosie nudged him and then held his mother's hand because Maisie had begun to cry. Her tears were silent but Ollie saw and looked away. Rosie watched his hands tense, but then Lee wanted Jack to lift him so that he could see Harold put the ring on Norah's finger. They kissed.

It was the first time Rosie could remember Norah kissing anyone, even Harold. Usually they cycled to their latest rubbing or sat either side of the fire, neither speaking, while she sat at the table, working up a Feature, practising, always practising.

At the reception Ollie toasted them, his voice thick from the beer he had already drunk, while Maisie held Lee and kissed his neck and Rosie saw that there was no light in her face, and that her eyes were bleak and red.

Norah didn't thank Rosie for the reception, she just simpered to Harold's mother, who was cold and distant because her son was leaving her alone in her small flat for something bigger and better.

Rosie squeezed Jack's hand and moved through the people who were crowding around Maisie's cake. They were mainly

Harold's friends. Sam and Ted had already joined up. Dave and Paul too, and Norah didn't seem to have many. But Mrs Eaves was there and Rosie touched her arm.

'I'm so glad you could come,' Rosie said, leaning forward and kissing her powdered cheek.

Mrs Eaves smiled. 'I've missed you, young Rosie. Is it going well? The job, I mean.'

Rosie nodded. 'But I miss you and the girls.' It was true. She did.

'And will you stay over here, now your grandpa's gone?'

Rosie looked at Harold who was pushing cake into his mouth. There were crumbs on his chin and his glasses were crooked.

'Yes, I'll stay but when Jack goes I'd like to visit back there.' She wanted to go, but more than that, much more than that, she didn't want Jack to leave. She couldn't imagine life without him, not for eighteen months. But at least he would be safe. There wasn't a hot war now, only a cold one, and you had to volunteer for the dangerous postings.

She had another drink. She mustn't think of April, of losing him too. She moved from Mrs Eaves, back to Jack and the warmth of his arm as he held her closely to him.

In April Jack heard that he had to report to the Ministry of Labour and National Service. He woke up Rosie, throwing stones at her window because Norah and Harold would play hell if he woke them by banging on the door. It was still cold and Rosie, wrapped in her cardigan, stood at the back door and laughed while he held her, kissed her, because she thought he was just impatient to see her but then he told her the news.

She felt cold inside at the thought of the months without him. Haven't we all been through enough, all we children of the war? Haven't we spent enough time away from the people we love? What did their Lordships want – our souls too?

'Don't go,' she said. 'You can't go.'

She was holding his sleeve, tightening her grip, pulling at him.

His face was still pinched and pale as he kissed her, held her, and the lines from his nose to his mouth were deep but his smile was the same.

'Don't worry, my little Rosie. Trust me. I've got to go and

see someone I know to try and sort something out before I report. I'll come back later. Don't worry.'

But she did worry. She forgot to water the plants at work. She made mistakes. She couldn't eat and wasn't interested in the letter which had come this morning from Frank. Frank was worried about the turn events were taking in Europe with the Berlin Blockade and the possible murder of the Czech Foreign Minister, and, worst of all from an American point of view, Truman's guarantee that US troops would step in in case of Soviet aggression in Europe. What did she care what was happening out there in this crazy world when Jack might be leaving her?

But then all afternoon she did care because was Frank saying there might be another war? She was tired. The world was mad and Jack was leaving as Grandpa had done.

He was waiting for her in the garden on her return. He had been taken on as an apprentice by old Jones. A phoney apprenticeship but at least his National Service would be deferred and he could stay home and look after Maisie and Lee.

'And you, Rosie,' he said, his breath warm in her hair.

Rosie held him, breathing in the smell of his skin.

'But Jones, you hate him. He'll squeeze you dry, rub your nose in it.'

'I know, but it's worth it to make sure Mum and Lee are all right. Dad hit Mum again last night. I don't understand him any more.'

That night Rosie dreamed of Grandpa twisting his cap in front of Barney.

In June Ollie put money on My Love to win the Derby. It won and he gave money to Maisie for a new dress but still there was no light in her face and the quarrels continued.

Harold and Norah seldom took their cycles out now, because Norah didn't want to. They didn't quarrel though, they sat either side of the fireplace while she knitted and he watched Rosie and sucked his teeth just because she was there. But Rosie just looked back, because there was nowhere else she was goddamn going, not yet.

On the day that the Berlin airlift began and the Dakotas shuttled in the food that would break the Russian blockade, Jack had to attend for his medical, which he passed but he wasn't required to report. He was an apprentice, wasn't he, he told Rosie when he met her from work.

They picked Lee up and went straight to the rec to push him on the swing. The wallpaper was still hanging off the damaged houses but there was more and more grass pushing through the caked earth over by the slide.

'The bines will be growing,' Jack said, his voice lurching as he pushed. 'One day we'll go back.'

Rosie watched his hands on the back of Lee's seat, the muscles in his arms, his shoulders. His skin was tanned now and she wanted to reach forward and kiss him.

She remembered their most recent trip to Soho. They had listened to jazz and he had said that Duke Ellington was always changing, that was why he liked him. She had said that she was tired of change. That was why she liked New Orleans, Dixieland. Bix Beiderbecke. He was dead. He couldn't change.

She did move now, putting her arms around Jack as he swung Lee, wanting him close. Because soon he might go. How long could he get away with all this?

In August, the Olympic Games were held in London but without Germany, the Soviet Union and Japan. Frank and Nancy had written to her asking for a feature on it from her point of view. They sent money for her travel expenses to Henley for the rowing, to Bisley for the shooting and to Cowes for the yachting. She arranged for some time off work and they said that she should show them her work and they would consider it for publication.

Norah was jealous and angry and told her as she slopped potato out of the pan on to her own plate that she should go back to America with her superior ideas and leave them in peace.

At Cowes she loved the feel of the wind in her hair and as she leaned on the rail of the ferry leaving Portsmouth she thought how Grandpa would have enjoyed this. She had Lee with her to give Maisie and Ollie a bit of peace.

They stayed the night at a small cottage where they ate scones and homemade jam. The landlady's son was in the Army, a National Serviceman who was fighting the Malayan Communists. His friend had been killed next to him, three weeks ago, in the jungle, Mrs Mallory said, but so far her son was fine.

The tablecloth was crisp and white and Lee picked up the crumbs he had made. His hands were like Jack's and Rosie held them and kissed them, wanting to catch the ferry back to Jack. Not for the first time she was grateful to the man whose cheeses they had stolen.

Lee pulled away, and reached for another scone, so she stroked his hair instead and looked at the horse brasses on the wall, the black beams across the ceiling and thought that one day she and Jack would have a home like this, but within scent of the hops.

The next day they watched the yachts and the crowds and Rosie described the gulls which wheeled and dived on to a bald man's head. She wrote of the blazers, and the women in sleek dresses who burst into cheers as Britain won a gold medal, of the ice-cream which tasted almost as good as maple walnut, of the trees around Osborne which were almost as tall as the white oaks. She wrote of all this but thought of Frank disappearing out round the point to fish. One day she would see them again because Frank was still stressed, but there was no time now. Each moment must be for Jack.

She took Lee to Wembley too and wrote of the thirty-year-old Dutch housewife who was cheered on by the British women because, though she was world record holder in both the high and long jump, she competed in neither and won four track events instead.

She wrote of how the cinder track seemed to beat back the heat and the disappointment when Britain failed to win an athletics gold. She lifted Lee on her shoulders to watch the Czechoslovakian Emil Zatopek win the 10,000 metres and thought of Frank and his love for that small country as the crowd rose to cheer the runner. Tears were pouring down her own face and Lee laughed, bent over, digging his heels into her arms, and wiped them for her with his sleeve.

She bought him a drink and a sandwich from a stall, and they sat on some steps, Lee tucked in next to her in her shade, laughing as he pushed some bread into her mouth. The egg was warm. The sun was hot on her neck. She put her arm round him and held him to her.

'I love you,' she said, rubbing her face on his hair.

'Love you, and Jack,' Lee said. 'Still will when I go to school next year.'

'And we'll still love you, even though you'll be really big.' Rosie unwrapped some biscuits she had made and poured him some milk from the flask. The ration had gone up to three and a half pints.

Lee turned his face away.

'Go on, it's good for you.' Rosie held the mug for him, hearing the crowds cheering in the background. He wouldn't drink it.

'Why should you?' Rosie murmured as she poured it back into the flask. 'There's too much you have to do because someone tells you to.' She thought of Jack and the landlady's son in the Malayan jungles. He must have volunteered. How crazy.

She watched Lee eat his biscuit and then took him by the hand because she wanted to watch the Americans running in the relay. It reminded her of Lower Falls School somehow, the heat, the ice-creams, the fun. They pushed their way up, squeezing on to seats, looking down at the track. Maybe there should be majorettes. She saw her old room, the Cougar pennant, the programmes.

It was hot and she pulled Lee's hat from her pocket, and made him wear it although he wriggled. She sat him on her knee, holding his legs, knowing her dress would crease but not caring because he was Lee and she and Jack loved him.

The crowd were noisy, the relay hadn't begun. People were still going up and down the stairs, seeking seats. Rosie wiped her forehead. It was so goddamn hot. She shielded her eyes. The race must begin soon. The athletes were limbering up, shaking their arms and legs. She could almost hear the cinders crunch.

But then she saw Maisie walking down the steps between the seats twenty feet away. She watched her turn, and stretch out her hand towards a big red-haired man and her face was full of life and full of love and Rosie could not breathe, but held Lee tightly. It was a mistake. She looked away, then back again, and knew it was no mistake. The man was the same one who had been at the Royal wedding, and there was still the same love on both their faces.

Rosie didn't watch the race, only those two people who walked on and disappeared, and then she took Lee down the steps too, pulling his hat even further on to his head because his hair was the same red as that man who had looked with love at Maisie.

That evening she heard Maisie carrying washing into the yard and left the roses she had been dead-heading, throwing the faded blooms into the compost in the corner, opening the yard gate, shooing away the children that played in the alley, entering Jack's yard.

'I saw you today,' she said, not looking at Maisie but helping to peg up the sheets, smelling their freshness, hearing the dogs and children further down the alley, knowing that Lee would be out there soon kicking a football with his friends.

'I saw you, Maisie, and you've got to decide. You can't go on like this. It's not fair on Jack. Or on Ollie. You're tearing them apart and yourself.'

She still didn't look but heard Maisie throw her pegs back into the old cocoa tin and lean against the back wall, her face to the sun.

'I can't decide, you see, Rosie. That's just it. I'm torn between two worlds. But don't tell them. Please.' Maisie moved now and took her arm. 'Please. I'll sort it out. I'll make it all right. Just don't tell anyone. Albert always said you had a right to privacy.'

Rosie shook out the last sheet. Lee's laughter was loud as he ran past her and out into the alley, dribbling the ball, kicking it to his friend. She and Jack had done that.

She turned now. 'Of course I won't say anything but just don't hurt them. Especially Jack. Please don't hurt them.'

Maisie touched Rosie's hair. 'I won't. I promise I won't. I'm glad you know. It will help me to be firm.'

Rosie's magazine didn't take her pieces because they were geared to the American markets, but they thought she had talent and when there was an opening they would give her a chance. They celebrated because Jack came round to say that Maisie was being nice to Ollie again. She seemed more settled, he told Rosie.

'It's strange. I don't know what's happened but something has,' he said.

They went up West and ate in Lyons Corner House while a small band played and then they danced and she felt his body next to hers, dancing in step, always in step, and the evening was warm and long and that night they kissed in the yard, and his mouth was as urgent as hers, and his hands were strong on her body.

'I love you, Rosie. I love you and I want you. But we must wait.'

He drew back and his face was beautiful in the light from the moon and there was the fragrance of Grandpa's roses all around. It was not the place for words, and so Rosie said nothing about Maisie and the man. She could not break her promise.

There was a letter on the hall floor for her next morning, which Norah and Harold had not picked up. They never did, if it was for her.

It was from Nancy enclosing sixty dollars.

Lower Falls

My dearest Rosie,

I do hope that perhaps soon we shall see you. It would cheer Frank up so much. He loved your features. They were published last week. Again to great enthusiasm.

Our local band of defenders against the Commies is in full cry yet again because two Congressional committees have been set up to investigate allegations that 30 US officials belong to a spy ring. Thank God most people don't believe it but there are two men, Karl Mundt in the House and Senator Joe McCarthy, a Wisconsin Republican, who most certainly do.

It would be laughable if it wasn't so serious. A manhole blew up in the street yesterday and Frank yelled, 'It's those Commie bastards.' Some people believed him.

But he is kind of down. He's got himself all worried about Korea now. I keep telling him it's all getting too stupid. He's seeing a new war where there is none. I'm kind of worried about him. The paper's readership is suffering. We have had a brick through the office window, but he won't stop writing common sense. The LA doesn't like that of course.

The Lake was great. Sandra sends her love and that young guy Joe too. Do you remember him? He's doing quite well on the paper now. Wish it could have been you.

All our love,
Nancy

Yes, Rosie thought as she folded the letter and brushed her hair. Yes, she did remember him but like a distant shadow because Jack filled her life now. She put down her hair brush and read the letter again. How serious was all this?

That evening Jack came home, straight to her, his eyes angry, his lip swollen. Jones had wanted him to deliver stolen meat. He wouldn't. He was sacked. He was no longer an apprentice. Jones would inform the Ministry of Labour and the Army would send for him. But when?

CHAPTER 10

January 1949 was cold but there was still no call-up for Jack and so they didn't feel the wind which cut into their chapped skin as they walked to the Palais. Sometimes they walked because it was better to be alone than with either family.

Spring came. The clothing ration ended and there was still no call-up but now, with each day, their kisses were getting stronger, their bodies pushing closer because it could not be long and there was so much love between them, and so much that was beautiful when they were together, so much that was dark when they were apart.

They walked to the rec on the last Saturday in April, when all the plates had been sold, and Ollie had gone to the pub, yet again. Rosie wouldn't think of that as Jack swung lightly, his face tense. Instead she watched the shadows of the clouds scud across the park. There were buds on the clubbed trees. She heard the scrape of his shoes on the earth, the shriek as the chain jolted to a halt, felt him reach out and pull her to him.

'Look after Maisie and Lee for me. Promise me. Promise me,' Jack said as he sat on the swing and she moved to stand between his legs. He always asked her this. He pressed his head against her belly and held her tightly.

'I will, don't worry. It will be fine,' Rosie said, looking at the fence which was being erected around the bomb-damaged houses. Work would begin soon. Then all this would be changed. She hugged him. Everything would be changed.

They'd had a letter from Sam this morning. He had only another six months to go before he came out.

'See, it went quickly,' she said now, listening to the foreman shouting as one section of the fence fell down.

'He'll be home soon. Nothing can happen in eighteen months. You wait and see. It'll all be fine. Maisie and Ollie will sort it out. It's already better.' And sometimes it was, but not always.

She could feel his back lifting and falling with his breathing, feel his body heat, smell him. She didn't need to say that each day for her would be endless without him. He already knew. She didn't need to remind him that there were twenty-four hours in each day, seven days in each week, fifty-two weeks in a year.

She wouldn't tell him that Norah was longing for him to go, so that she would also leave. That Frank and Nancy had written to her telling her to come when Jack had left. But she must stay here for now, alone, without him, without Grandpa, because she had promised him that she would. She would just hold him because he ached at the thought of the future too.

In May his call-up still had not come but the Berlin Blockade ended. Again there was a letter from Nancy talking of Sandra's new hairstyle, Mary's new Hoover. The target on the garage door which Frank had repainted for when Rosie came back out. She mentioned Frank's stress again, but that was all.

The summer was hot and blistered the pavements. The stall did good business and Jack's voice was hoarse at the end of each day but his lips were as soft and warm as always, his hands as gentle, his words of love as tender as they had always been.

And she wrote and told Nancy again that she would not be coming, not yet.

In July the sugar ration was put down to eight ounces a week, the sweet ration was back at four ounces and there was a further cut in tobacco supplies. Another letter from Nancy told her that Truman had tried but failed to dampen the hysteria which was spreading across America after the latest Soviet spy conviction. And had Rosie heard about the attempt to screen all school books by the House Committee for Un-American Activities? Didn't they know that Goebbels had burnt books in the streets? Did this always happen after a war? Boy, is that goddamn Local Administrator having the time of his life!

It's great that Jack hasn't been called up. We're sorry you can't come. So sorry. But maybe later?

But Rosie wouldn't think of this, she pushed it all from her because each dawn so far had brought the knowledge that Jack was next door, so close, so dear and nothing could spoil this love they had. Nothing. Not even absence, nothing.

They went to Southend with Maisie, Ollie and Lee. They ate winkles and she felt the wind in her hair and heard the laughter of the children who pushed go-carts, racing them, screaming as they won, screaming as they lost and she remembered the feel and smell of the old pram which Grandpa had kept and she missed him. But then she missed him every day.

She sat with Maisie, their skirts held around their knees, the wind tugging at their hems and sleeves, and they laughed as Jack rolled up his trousers to his knees, then ducked Lee down into the sea, then across to Ollie, who took him and held him.

Rosie looked at Maisie. 'So, it's all right?'

Maisie took a Marmite sandwich from the OXO tin, squashing the bread together, eating it with small bites. There were teethmarks in the bread. 'Of course it's all right, Rosie. Just you wait and see. You mustn't worry your head about us.'

But behind the dullness of her eyes there was pain. And Rosie did worry. And all any of them seemed to do was wait. She didn't ask about the man. She didn't want to know; all she wanted was for it to be all right.

She watched Jack again, his strong back beneath his shirt, his pale legs in the rolled-up trousers. She wished they could both be by the lake, lying in the sun, tanned. She wished she could see his body. She wished they could lie together and she could feel his hands on her, his kisses on her breasts.

That night she clung to him in the yard, tasting the salt on his skin as she kissed him, seeing the pallor of it clear in the late evening light. She gripped his jacket, searching his face. She never wanted anything to come between them. Their love must never die and pain take its place as it had done with his mother.

'I want to sleep with you,' she said, holding his head close to hers, talking against his mouth, and she felt his arms tighten.

'I want to sleep with you.' His mouth was on hers. 'But not yet. There's time, my love. There's time.'

But there wasn't time. His call-up papers were in the hall when he came down the next morning and in her hall was a letter from Nancy telling her that the last American occupation forces had left South Korea. What would happen now?

She screwed it up and threw it across the yard because Jack

was there, beside The Reverend Ashe, reading out his enlistment notice, and what the hell did she care about Korea, or Truman, or bloody witch hunts which were so far away and which had nothing to do with her or the boy who was now holding her, the lashes of his brown eyes throwing shadows on his cheeks?

They both cried, there, within the scent of the rose, and Jack felt he couldn't bear to go and leave her here where he couldn't touch her, hold her, love her. He couldn't bear to go and leave his mum whose pain he could still see deep down but couldn't understand, or Lee who would start school in September without him. What if the shouting began again?

He left two weeks later, on Thursday, from King's Cross. Rosie came, but only Rosie. There were couples kissing, crying. There was the rail warrant in his jacket pocket. There were doors slamming, porters pushing through them. 'Mind yer backs.'

The station smelt of dirt and heat and loss and he held her to him. Breathing in her smell, which drowned out all else, holding her face between his hands, kissing her lips, her eyes.

'Be careful. Come back soon. Come back,' she said, tasting his lips, but the whistles were blowing now and he heaved his case into the corridor, scrambling in after, leaning out of the window, sharing it with another boy, holding her hand, bending to kiss it, but the train was moving and he was leaving and he let her fingers slide from his grasp.

'Stay with Mum. Look after Lee. Promise me.'

She was running along the platform now and her lips were smiling and she was nodding but there were tears all over her face, dripping down on to her blouse.

'I love you, Rosie. I love you, little Rosie. I'm sorry I have to leave you.' He gripped the window. Had she heard?

The station was still busy, there was another train leaving from the next platform, there were whistles, doors, calls, the tannoy, but all she could hear were his words. I love you, little Rosie. And they were Grandpa's words too and now she was alone.

The train picked up speed as it left the station. Jack still waved, though he could no longer see her. The wind was too strong in his face, it made his eyes water. It had made his eyes water when he left for Somerset, leaving his mum behind in the bombs. He was leaving her again, with Ollie. He was leaving Rosie but there was nothing else he could do. He had to go. He had been told to go.

He drew his head back in, pulled up the window. It was quiet except for the voices along the corridor. He rested his head on the window. There was nothing else he could do.

He shoved his case back against the sliding door which was open then eased himself into the compartment, between two other boys. The air was thick with Woodbine smoke. He drew out a cigarette and struck a match, cupping his hands, sucking, smelling the sulphur, trying not to think of the oast-houses, the stream where she had paddled, her legs so slim, so brown. Trying not to hear Lee's laugh, or see Maisie's smile, Ollie confused, angry.

He leaned back, feeling the heat of the conscripts either side, hearing their jokes, their coughs, their laughs, and at last he was talking too, pushing them all down deep inside because there was nothing else he could do. Just nothing and it hurt too much.

And so he listened, but did not really hear, and laughed, but did not really mean it, and talked, but only with his mouth, not his mind. The train lurched and rattled over the points and a boy who spoke with a plum in his mouth sat by the window and told them how he had been a sergeant in the OTC and was going to apply for a commission.

'Frightfully good management experience you know,' he said. The compartment door slid shut, then open again. A boy looked in.

'Seen Joe?'

'Who's Joe?' asked the lad next to Jack, stubbing out the cigarette with his foot.

The boy walked on. There was laughter in the corridor and a packet of cigarettes was thrown past the door, caught and thrown back and still the train travelled on, roaring through tunnels, shafting out into sunlight, further from Rosie, from Maisie. And he didn't want to leave them. Didn't want to be sent to God knows where to do God knows what. He wanted to get on with his own life. But he had no choice, had he? Had any of them? He closed his eyes. There had to be more to life than all of this.

He thought of the sign, ABSOLUTELY NO JITTERBUGGING ALLOWED. thought of the sign, 12 YEARS AND UNDER ONLY. thought of Ollie slapping Maisie, of himself pulling at his father, heaving him out into the yard, wanting to shout at them all to stop.

But it was all right, he told himself, as he drew on his cigarette, feeling the heat in his lungs, coughing, stubbing it out, leaning back. It's all right, Rosie's there. She's strong, she'll take my place. She'll always love me. I'll always love her.

He shut his eyes, shaking the thoughts from his head, making himself listen to the talk which was flowing past him. Really listen, hanging on to the words, the jokes, the questions, taking a newspaper when it was offered, reading it, passing it on.

He talked to Sid, next to him. He was just eighteen, never left his mum before. Never been evacuated. His hands were shaking. Jack, at nineteen, felt old. But they were all the same. None of them wanted to be here. They all had other lives.

The towns had gone, there was wild free country, not the sloping hills of Herefordshire, or Somerset. He remembered the picture he had unscrewed and sold, the milk chocolate they had been given, the corned beef. He had been sick.

'I mean to say, basic training is absolutely nothing. When you're experienced, as I am, it's a doddle.' The boy with the plum was speaking again.

Sid leaned forward. 'What'll we do then?'

'A bit of marching, a bit of polishing. Getting fit, improving ourselves, you know.'

But they didn't, not yet. All Jack knew was the ache inside, the loneliness of it all, the missing. What was Rosie doing now? What was Maisie cooking for tea? Had his bed been folded and taken from the kitchen? Was Ollie drunk?

The train pulled into the station at a platform which held kiosks selling books and sandwiches and tea, but Jack moved past with the others, his case heavy in his hand, banging against his leg, but this time there was no gas mask.

They hurried along, Sid beside him, skirting through the others, keeping ahead of Nigel, the OTC Sergeant, trying to lose him in the crush. They headed towards the branch line and the train full of conscripts. They tried one door. A boy with a crew cut and no front teeth leaned out.

'Sorry, cock, full up.'

They moved on to the next and the next and by now Nigel was with them again and Sid cursed. Jack winked, opening a door, throwing his case in, Sid's too, Nigel's too. Whistles were blowing, boys were leaning out of windows whistling and shouting, and then they were in but there were no seats. There was singing though, and rampaging up and down the corridor, and Jack remembered how they had pretended to cry on the evacuee train as they passed through stations so that the onlookers got their money's worth.

The moors stretched either side and there was beauty in the sky, in the bleakness of the dales, the scattering of sheep, the heather, the short-cropped grass. But Rosie wasn't here, Maisie wasn't here, and it was fear as well as loneliness that stirred him now because Sam and Ted had told him too much about the Army.

In the station yard there were lorries backed up with their tailboards down. They heaved their cases into these now and Sid lit a cigarette, his hand shaking.

A Corporal pacing backwards and forwards glanced at his millboard, then shouted at Nigel to 'get his bleeding legs working and hurry over'. Then he turned.

'Put that ruddy fag out, you ruddy nig.'

Jack turned, and his eyes met those of the Corporal.

'Got anything to say, nig?' the Corporal shouted at Jack. 'Got any comments to make, any suggestions you would like me to send back to Mother?'

Jack shook his head as Sid stubbed out the half-smoked cigarette, put it back in his packet.

'You see,' the Corporal shouted, stabbing a finger at Jack and Sid, 'we don't like dirty 'abits in the Army. We don't like people bringing their nasty little ways in with them. Put that bleeding fag over there, in that bin.'

He pointed towards a bin fastened to a lamppost over by rusty railings near to the station entrance.

Sid stumbled towards the tailboard, jumped down, ran across, and picked out the cigarette from the packet, but his hands were shaking so much that they all fell into the bin. He reached down, then saw the Corporal, looked again at the cigarettes, and ran back, pushing himself up and into the truck.

'You'd better get yourself back down and go and fetch those cigarettes, hadn't you? You forgotten there's shortages? Or maybe Mummy lets you have hers.'

Sid moved to the tailboard again, hunched down beneath the lorry roof. He ran back, picked the cigarettes out, brought them back. They were stained, dirty, smelling of old fruit.

The Corporal nodded and turned, calling, 'Come along please, Mr Sanders, Mr Nigel Sanders, or Nanny will be cross. Come along. Don't be afraid. You're only leaving civilisation behind. You're not humans any more, you're nigs.'

Sid was shaking and Jack felt anger drown his fear as when the Billeting Officer in Somerset had separated two sisters, sending one to the town, the other to a village. There was nothing any of the children could do. There was nothing he could do now. Nigel hoisted himself up and the lorry rumbled away from the station yard.

They drove into the camp and a wooden barrier fell behind them. Jack felt trapped, lost, but so did the others, he could tell from their faces, even Nigel. They passed bleak married quarters, barracks, squares, huts, black stencilled notices, and then they stopped, jumped out, listened to the shouts of the Corporal, watched the spittle on his chin, the red cheeks which reddened, the eyes which narrowed.

They were lined up, their suitcases still in their hands. They were marched, out of step, to their barracks. They left their cases, turned, marched to the quartermaster's stores.

There were counters, Corporals shouting, battledress, beret, boots – some that fitted, some that did not.

'What a shame, poor little boy wants Mummy to change them? Tough shit. Wear 'em.'

More kit was slapped down and they stuffed it into drab-green kitbags, collected their mattresses, which they draped over their heads, then hauled the bag and blankets to the barracks. Heard a siren. Reported to the cookhouse for tea as their Lance-Corporal ordered. Were sent back for wearing civilian clothes. They changed. The Lance-Jack laughed, standing in the corridor to his room. They were too late for tea.

Jack felt anger come again but it mingled with strangeness, fear, loneliness, all of which he had felt before in Somerset. Rosie had felt it too. Little Rosie.

They marched back again to the barracks, to the thirty wire-framed beds, to the windows which were nailed down and unopenable. To the stove which would have been too small to heat Grandpa's shed, to the tall metal lockers beside each bed, to the stone floor which struck chill into them, although it was August and hot.

They were given pen and paper to write to their families.

'To say that you're having a lovely time,' the Lance-Jack said, walking up the centre of the room, looking them up and down. They were hungry, lying on their beds in prickly khaki, feeling in their pockets for change to go to the Naafi.

Jack wrote home, saying he was having a lovely time, saying his clothes would be sent back, saying it was just like being evacuated and that had turned out all right, hadn't it? No problems, he wrote.

He wrote to Rosie, saying that he loved her, that he would be home for two days at the end of basic training, in two months, that she must look after Maisie, please, and Lee, and herself. Please.

As he, Sid and Nigel walked to the Naafi and bought a sandwich and a beer, he thought of Elsie, the fat farmer's wife in cords who had lit an oil lamp each evening so that he would not be afraid of the shadows in the old farmhouse. The smell of it had eased into his room from the landing. The others were silent too, sipping their beer which dripped on to the formica table. Their thoughts were elsewhere too.

They bought boot polish before they returned to their billet and all night long they bulled their green-corroded brasses, rubbing with emery paper for hours. Their hands grew cramped and stiff, their necks too, from bending. There were Woodbine stubs in the tin ashtrays on the two tables, there was a sourness in their mouths, a loneliness in their eyes which were heavy-lidded, tired, unsure. And always there was the radio playing, but there was no jazz.

Sam, from Liverpool, brought out a candle and a spoon, and heated the handle, rubbing it over the dimples of the boots, squeezing out the oil, rubbing away the waterproofing with it, but who cared? It would make them shine.

He showed them how to spit, then rub the polish which they had all bought in the Naafi round and round. It produced a shine. A bloody shine, and so they all did the same or ironed their boots. They laughed and swore and said they weren't afraid of the Lance-Jack, or the Corporal, or the Sergeant, but they were. Finally at 0400 hours, they slept, though the radio still played through speakers controlled by the Lance-Jack. In their sleep they rocked to the rhythm of the train, to the lurching of the truck, to the voice of the Corporal.

They were woken at 0530 hours. The Sergeant screamed 'Wakey Wakey', and thumped his swagger stick along the end of each bed, swearing, tipping every other metal locker over, standing over the spilled contents, calling them whores who had turned the place into a bordello, telling them their kit would be stacked properly or they wouldn't live long.

Jack shaved in cold water, and dabbed at the cuts which ran red. He thought of Butlins but he didn't smile. Hi-di-bloody-hi, he thought. His eyes were red and sore, his hands and shoulders ached and he hadn't even dreamed of Rosie in that brief hour of privacy, he had been too tired.

Nigel's face was without cuts. He had no need to shave. The cat calls followed him out but he flicked his towel over his shoulder and smiled, walking away, giving a royal wave. They had to fold their sheets and their blankets just right. Put back the lockers, just bloody right.

Then they were out, into air which smelt sweet, into a summer day where birds sang, and Jack had forgotten for hours that anything pleasant existed. They marched with knife, fork and spoon held in one hand behind their backs as the Corporal ordered them to, but were screamed at because they were not swinging the other arm. No one had told them.

'You should have known,' he screamed again.

They marched, out of step, into the cookhouse, drinking sweet thick tea, eating greasy tinned tomatoes, and bacon, then tipping the remains into slop bins whose putrid smell reached out into the steamy hall. They moved along, sluicing their cutlery in the lukewarm tank. Bits clung to the forks and the knives.

Then back to the barracks and the lavatories. The floors were swept, the windows polished. Jack took the ablutions instead of Sid because Sid was shaking and pale. He had called out for his mother just before dawn.

Jack handed him his window cloth, and with Sam from Liverpool hurled buckets down the clogged stinking pans so that the inspecting officer wouldn't complain, wondering all the time how this mad-house could be allowed to exist.

They had their hair cut, the shears pulling and scraping far up their necks. They had a medical inspection in the afternoon, sitting on benches in a building which stank of urine and disinfectant and gleamed with green and white paint. They all passed and all groaned.

That night they blancoed their webbing, pressed their clothing, ironing over a sheet of brown paper which had been wetted with a shaving brush. They breathed in the pungent smell of steam and scorched paper, feeling the heat on their faces, their heads already bursting with the ache of tiredness. There were only two irons between the thirty of them. The night was endless. The music blared. Sid slept and Jack pressed his then wrote to Maisie asking her to send spare pyjamas and underpants so that he could keep the Army issue ready at all times for inspection.

He wrote to Rosie, sitting on the floor because the bed was laid out for inspection. He told her that all he could smell was scorched, damp, brown paper, all he could hear was cursing, all he could feel was the ache of tiredness. The ache of missing her.

'God, I'm bushed,' groaned Nigel.

They spent the last hour of the night on the floor, to avoid messing up their beds, Sid and Nigel too. They were scared, Jack was scared, of the Sergeant with the swagger stick and eyes like bullets and for the second night he was too tired to dream of Rosie.

They were right to be scared. The Sergeant tipped their pressed clothes, their lockers out on to the cold stone floor but they didn't turn and look. They stood to attention at the foot of their beds, their faces set, their minds raw with anger, with despair, with the confusion of tiredness.

'You're a bloody shower,' the Sergeant shrieked.

They had their injections that day then they polished the studs on the soles of their boots, the brasses again, the windows, the tables, the buckets, the floors. They polished the words off the lid of the boot polish tin, set it to one side for inspection and bought another for use.

They pressed the military frieze into sharp creases again. They covered everything in newspaper so that nothing would get dirty between the evening and the morning. They moved by numbers, they didn't think, they didn't feel, they didn't dream.

'God, I'm bushed, exquisitely bushed,' Nigel groaned.

'Go to sleep then,' Jack murmured. 'Give us all a break.'

The next day they drilled. The rifles were heavy, their shoulders were sore from them. They marched, they halted, they turned, they about-turned. Sid stumbled on the turn, every time. The Corporal swore. They stopped for a smoke break, Jack, Nigel and the others, but Sid was marched up and down, up and down, and still he stumbled and his face looked like the faces of the sisters who had been separated in Somerset, like Lee's when his father turned from him.

Then they all marched, again and again, and their boots rubbed but they were not allowed to stop for lunch because Sid still couldn't turn and that night Sam cursed Sid, and the others did too, and tipped him out of his bed and threw his locker over because the minutes had ticked away for tea break too, and still he had made mistakes.

'Get out of it,' Jack shouted and Nigel helped him push them away.

They picked up Sid's things, turned their backs to his tears, giving him privacy, shielding him so that the others couldn't see either. They were tired, dog tired, but they laid out their beds for inspection, then Sid's, and walked him to the Naafi though their feet were raw and burned with each step.

'Just a quick one,' Jack said.

'Builds up the sugar level,' Nigel murmured, his lids drooping.

They bought Sid beer and listened as he told them that he got so worried he couldn't think and it was then that he made mistakes and he didn't think he could bear it.

They bought him more beer so that he would feel too ill to think and the next day he didn't stumble or the next, or the next, and he bought them the beers those nights. But the next week the Corporal shouted at him, rode him, cursed him again until he stumbled on the turn again the next day and the beers in the evening didn't help.

Jack watched as the boy's hands began to shake, and the taunts began again as the whole squad was punished, missing lunch, missing tea. He watched as the light faded from Sid's eyes and felt anger above his tiredness.

So when the Corporal lined them up and the Sergeant marched with clipped strides down the ranks, pointing his stick at Jack, he moved it to one side, his eyes hard like the Sergeant's, his hands sweating with the fear he wouldn't show. He didn't want Sid to suffer any more.

He could cope. He was stronger, he was nineteen, a man. Much older than the sister who had been killed by a car when she ran away from the town to the village to see her Sarah. Much older than Lee who had been pushed aside by Ollie.

He was marched away, sworn at, cursed, pushed, his head yanked back by his short hair.

'Got a nice little job for you,' the Corporal said, his voice low, his lips thin. 'You're not going to know what day of the bleeding week it is when you've finished, sonny.'

He was handed scissors and spent the afternoon on hands and knees cutting the grass around the parade ground. The ants scrambled amongst the grass, the dandelions were acrid, their milk spilling white on to the ground. His thumb and finger were blistered. He changed hands. That thumb and finger became blistered too.

He changed again, the sun sharp on his neck. He could hear the Corporal, and the boots.

'Forward march.

'Halt.

'Turn.

'About turn.

'Smoke Break.

'Forward march.

'Halt.

'Turn.

'About turn.'

His thumb and fingers were bleeding, he padded them with grass he had cut. It was cool but with each cut the pain dug deep.

He didn't break for tea. He worked on until the ants and the sun had gone. And then in full kit, he doubled around the tarmacked square on blistered feet which bled warm blood into his boots. But Sid was left alone and that helped the pain of his hands and feet as he lay on the floor all night because there was an inspection in the morning.

The next day he was told to shin up, then jump from gym ropes he could hardly clasp by a sweating instructor who moved the mat as he jumped and laughed as the rope burned his hand and then the mat burned his shins. He laughed as his elbow, then his shoulder crashed on to the hard polished floor.

'Think you know more than the Army, do you?' the instructor ground out. 'Think you can cheek a Sergeant, do you? We'll see about that.'

He was put on fatigues because he was last out of the changing rooms when the instructor hid his boots, slapping his rubber slipper in his hand as he laughed, whipping it across Jack's back. But he wouldn't show the pain, or the anger.

The next day he drilled with raw feet, threw his rifle against his bruised shoulder and held the butt in a hand that throbbed and bled but he showed nothing. There was no smoke break for him and he winked at Sid and Nigel as he marched, looking at the sky, the clouds, thinking of Lee, of Rosie.

He scrubbed the walls in the cookhouse all evening and watched the cockroaches scuttling out from behind the pipes. But none of this mattered. He was tough, he could take it. He was alive. He was nineteen. Rosie loved him. Lee was all right. Maisie and Ollie were all right. Rosie had written and said so.

The next week the Corporal found a speck of dirt on the back of Jack's buckle and grinned as he extended his punishment. He spent the evening syphoning petrol then rubbing graffiti off the lavatory walls with it, tasting it, smelling it. He vomited all night in the latrines.

But he could take it, he told Sid and Nigel who came and stood by him. It was Sam's bloody handwriting.

'How exquisite,' Nigel said.

They laughed, all of them, even Sam, who polished Jack's boots for him that night, and bought him a beer, while Sid stayed behind and laid out his kit. Nigel bought him another and because he was such a tight arse Jack wondered why.

'You're keeping that bastard off our backs. We're extraordinarily grateful, you know.'

He didn't understand why Jack laughed, why he laughed even when he lay on the floor beside his bed, and neither did Jack himself, especially in the dead of night when the laughter choked into silent tears and he churned between images of the sisters and Lee and Rosie.

He peeled potatoes when the Corporal decided his locker was a disgrace, though there was nothing wrong with it. He watched the squad run to PE in baggy shorts and singlets, carrying their plimsolls, wearing their boots, their pale hairy legs thickening already from the drill. He thought of Butlins, of Harold, and cut into the potato once more. Rosie had written, she still loved him. Lee was happy. Maisie and Ollie were fine. And he was fine. He was nineteen. He could take it.

Sid shared his food parcels with Nigel and Jack. They were all fitter by the fourth week. The Corporal still shouted, still punished, but Jack hadn't broken. The men were his friends, they cheered as he cut the grass, yet again. They helped him off with his pack after he had been doubled round the square, yet again.

They woke him when he slept too soundly during the education talks in a room thick with smoke as they were told, yet again, of the Empire, and the pox, and they grinned when he winked at them. But he was nearly finished. He was nearly broken. He had no dignity left, no power to save himself. No nothing. Just Rosie's letters and the thought of the hand that had written the words.

In the fifth week the Corporal left his bike outside the hut when the Sergeant had ordered it to be put away and the Corporal left their squad with the Sergeant's language still thick on the air. The men blew up johnnies bought from the barber and let them fly from the door as he passed.

The Lance-Jack took his place, a new stripe on his arm and a voice which was not so loud, not so cruel, and now the fatigues ended and Jack slept at night. At last he slept and had the time and the privacy to dream of Rosie.

In September his squad cursed and swore on the assault course, feeling the skin scrape off their stomachs as they scrambled up and over the nets carrying packs filled with bricks, feeling the straps cutting into their shoulders, humping Sid up before them because last one home got fatigues.

They plunged from logs into murky water-filled ditches, spitting out filth, pushing against the weight of the pack, forcing their heads up and the panic down. They raced and beat the squad from Waterloo barracks in the cross country and the Lance-Jack bought them all beers.

They sat up that night and cheered as Nigel sang and danced and Sam called, 'You'd make a lovely tart.'

Jack wrote to Rosie and told her. They watched new squads arrive and stumble and scramble, and tossed them cigarettes and told them it would be a bleeding picnic.

They shot on the rifle range, feeling the Yorkshire breeze in their hair, the first hint of winter in its coldness, lying full stretch on their stomachs. He wrote to Rosie and told her of the smell of the ground which still had the summer tight in its grasp, of the men, who were now moulding into a team, almost in spite of themselves.

They were paid.

'One pace forward.

'Two, three, salute.

'Two, three, take pay.

'Take paybook.' Open top left pocket.

'Pay and paybook correct, sir.' Place pay and paybook in pocket.

'Two, three, salute.

'Two, three, about turn.

'Left right, left right.' Three bags full. Sir. There were drinks in the Naafi. Only a few days more then a transit camp. Postings came in. Sid was a clerk, Nigel a Sergeant in Education. He didn't want a commission now. He was one of the men. Jack was a squaddie.

The next day, the last before the passing-out parade, they squatted on the grass with the weak late summer sun on their faces around a Sten gun which was taken to pieces by a dirty-fingered NCO.

Jack said, 'Be gentle with the grass, Corp. It's been very carefully cut.' The squad laughed, the Corporal too.

The Corporal put the gun together, then took it apart again. Jack could smell the oil, see it beneath the Corporal's fingernails, and he remembered Ed in that Somerset village. The oil beneath his fingers as he threw the ball to Jack, the drawl as he shouted at him to pitch it higher next time, the sun shining on his red hair. Where was he now? Why had he never written?

The gun was in pieces again. They tried to put it together and failed. They tried again and succeeded and the smell of the oil was heavy and it was the same as the smell on Ed's hand as he had ruffled his hair and asked when his mom was coming down again.

'The aim of war,' said the Corporal, 'is to kill the enemy.'

Sam murmured, 'Don't tempt me, sunshine.'

The others laughed and the Corporal called the comedian out to the front, standing Sam there, pointing to his head.

'Don't aim at his head. You'll miss, and if you hit it, you'll find there's no brain, just air if it's like this specimen.'

Jack pulled at the grass, floating it down in the faint breeze.

'Don't aim at his legs. You won't kill him.'

Had Ed killed anyone? Had he sat in the sun and listened and learned. Ed had needed to. They didn't. The war was over. Frank got over-worried. There was the bomb now. There wouldn't be another war.

'Aim at the body. That'll get them.'

Jack had applied to become a clerk. It was a cushy number but he had been refused. The officer said his schooling was incomplete though his IQ was high and that he would be directed towards the Infantry because his rifle range report had been good. Jack looked at the Corporal and then at the Sten. At least he'd never have to kill anyone. And nothing mattered now, because basic training was over. He was going home after passing out tomorrow. For two whole days he would be home, with Rosie.

CHAPTER 11

The carriage was as full of smoke as it had been on the journey up to Yorkshire, and the floor as littered with cigarette stubs, but now it was different. They had passed out. They would not have to go through anything like that again. Nothing as bad ever again.

They were to be clerks, teachers, wireless operators, or squaddies and then their lives could begin again. And for the next thirty-six hours they were going home. They all laughed again, as Sid won a hand of cards and Nigel dealt another on the table they had made by heaping a coat over a kitbag.

Jack looked out of the window, the cards worn and slippery in his hand. Rain raced down and across the glass, jagged from the slipstream, and he could see little, but as they drew near London the houses grew thicker. There were chimneys belching smoke, there were the same damaged buildings. Nothing had changed in two months. But what about the people? What about his family? Were they all right?

The train was drawing in, shunting, slowing, stopping. They hauled kitbags out on to the platform, then up on to their shoulders, walking in a group. The smell of London was the same but Jack felt as he had done when he returned from Somerset. Strange, different. And his home had been different too. Was it now?

They took the Underground or other trains, waved, slapped shoulders and couldn't say to one another how they felt. This had been a family, and now they might never see one another again. So they waved, laughed, looked away, looked back, and Nigel, Sid and Jack stood still, looked, nodded then drifted into the crowd. What else could they do?

Rosie was waiting at home, at the entrance to his back yard. The rain had stopped, the fog had settled, raw, close. He saw her as he walked down the alley, leaning against the wall, her scarf round her mouth, her coat belted, the collar up. He watched her straighten and run and heard the thud as his kitbag rolled from his shoulders into the drain and then she was there, in his arms. He pulled down the scarf, kissed her warm lips, searched her mouth with his, felt her against him, her arms around him, and the strangeness was gone. She was here. He was home.

'They're all right,' she said into his neck. 'There's been no rows. No trouble.'

Then there was the sound of running feet, panting breath, and Lee was there, clasping his leg, crying, laughing, punching, and Jack picked him up, threw him into the air, caught him, hugged him. He hadn't changed. It had only been weeks. It seemed like years.

Ollie and Maisie bought in beer from the pub, and Rosie ate with them because Maisie said every minute was precious when you were in love. Rosie looked away from the bleakness of her eyes, back to Jack who sat balancing on two legs of the chair. He was broader, fitter. A man. And when he had held her she had felt shy against his strength, against the roughness of his stubbled chin, against the voice which was deeper, stronger.

'Do you still love me?' she had asked.

'More than ever. You are what I dreamed of at night. You are my world. You keep me going and you keep my family safe for me. I shall never love anyone else.'

She had felt the pulse in his throat as she touched his neck and then his hands where the scissors had scarred. She picked up his hands and kissed them.

The two days passed too quickly. Rosie waved from the back yard. He wouldn't let her go with him to the station where they would be pushed and pulled by the crowd, where he would see her face as the train left.

She watched as he walked up the alley, listened as his footsteps grew fainter.

She wrote to him at the transit camp, and then to the Barracks when he moved on there. He wrote to her of guard duty, the inspections, the charging of his friend because of a dirty buckle.

He wrote of the Corporal who read out the Guard Duty orders, issued them with bicycle lamps, whistles and pick-axe handles, allocated the stags, or shifts. He drew second stag – 2030 to 2230 then 0230 to 0430. He wrote of the route they walked, the huts they guarded. He wrote of the hours they spent guarding nothing against nobody.

As November became December he wrote of rifle practice. How he would lie on a groundsheet, feeling the iciness of the earth seeping up into him, seeing his breath white before his face, feeling his fingers hurt with the cold as they held the rifle, then the numbness.

He told of pushing home the ammunition clip with the palm of his hand, seeing a red and white flag for a miss, but more often it was a bull.

He told her he loved her, missed her, and knew that she must love him because she stayed for his sake to help Maisie and Lee, when she could be in America.

On 20 December Rosie made paper chains with Lee, but in Lee's house, not Norah's because Norah would not allow the mess, and she was glad that Jack was lying on groundsheets firing at targets because the British were launching the biggest drive yet against the rebels in the Malayan jungle and that could have been Jack, but it wasn't. Thank God, it wasn't.

She strung the paper chains around Norah's kitchen, though she had not wanted any, but Grandpa had always liked them. She helped Maisie do the same. Balancing the step ladder while Maisie reached up, pushing the drawing pin in, laughing because Lee was laughing, and soon they all were, even Ollie who came through the door with a bottle of wine for Christmas and a message from the pub that Jack was coming home for two days' leave.

They ate the turkey at Maisie's because Norah and Harold were going to his mother's for two days. She looked at Jack, and he at her, and she barely tasted the turkey, because he was back. This year there was no perfume for Maisie, no need for Rosie's lies, and she drank her wine, her shoulders easing, because soon perhaps she could go to Nancy and Frank. 1950 promised to be a good year.

Jack walked her back, into the empty house, up the silent

stairs into the boxroom where ice crept up the inside of the windows and the chill dug even through their coats. He wouldn't let her stay up here where it was so bleak and carried her mattress, her bedding, and laid it where Grandpa had slept, where he slept next door.

She watched the muscles in his back beneath his shirt as he stirred up the fire, straightened the blanket made of cardigans. She watched his arms as he tucked the blankets under the mattress. She watched his face as he turned and held out his arms to her and the bed was soft and warm now as they lay together, and his hand undid her blouse, traced the shape of her breast, and his lips too touched her flesh and his tongue licked her skin and it was the right time where Joe had been the wrong time and the wrong person.

She undid his shirt, pushing it back from his muscled shoulders, remembering the boy who had played flicksies, the boy who had raced in the carts, the boy who had pinched the cheeses, the boy who had been beaten by Jones's man. They were not children any longer. They were nearly twenty.

'I want you, Jack. I love you.' She was breathing in the smell of his body, kissing his shoulders, his chest, his arms.

His voice was soft as he drew her close. 'I want you too, but there might be a baby. We must wait.'

But she was kissing his words away because she was alone and soon he would go and she couldn't bear it.

His kisses were stronger, his leg was between hers, his hands on her skirt, but then he moved, pushing her back, sweat on his face and chest.

'No, not now. Not yet. We must wait.' He stood up and drew on his shirt, turning from her, doing up the buttons, looking into the fire, stooping, scooping out the ash, banking it up. Then just standing, watching the greyness that was all that was left of the smouldering fire.

'We must wait, little Rosie. Wait until we're married.' He turned now and sat with her, pulling up the blanket, wrapping it round her.

'I've never seen your body. I've never felt your skin against mine. I don't need marriage. If you do, we'll marry now.' She leaned against him. Didn't he know what it was like, living with a sister who wanted you to go? The snow would be crisp now in Lower Falls. Frank was under pressure because things had become much worse for liberals in his town. She could go back, lean into Nancy's arms. But more than this, she longed for him and his love.

Didn't he know that, though she had promised to stay for his sake, she was lonely? That the days were long and the nights longer still? But then she looked at his hands, the scars, and knew that it was a time they both had to live through.

January pushed into February and she heard little from Nancy and Frank. She wrote to say that she missed them, loved them, and would have come but Maisie and Lee needed her help and support, but maybe she could come in the summer. Did they understand? Were they angry?

Nancy wrote saying that of course they understood, but they had been a little busy. Mao's victory in China and the friendship pact between China and the Soviets had caused a bit of an upsurge in the Reds under the Bed campaign. McCarthy had launched a true blue Red Crusade, saying that he had the names of over two hundred Communists working in the State Department. Three more of their friends had been fired – one had had his house burned down. Another had killed himself. Frank was still fighting through his paper, through letters to other papers, and he was becoming a target.

But she also said that this was only a wrinkle and Rosie mustn't worry. It was just that it was taking a lot of their time. Maybe it would be better if she didn't come for a while anyway.

Rosie chose to believe her, because there was nothing else she could do. She went next door to Maisie. It was Saturday and they took Lee up West, had lunch in a Lyons Corner House and Maisie held her hand and said, 'It's easy when I have you.' Her smile reached her eyes and Rosie squeezed her hand. What else could she do? And things were getting better for Maisie and Ollie, she was sure they were.

Jack wrote telling her about the trench digging they were doing. And then the trench refilling they were doing, day after day.

In March Norah heard that there was to be a new town built in Corby, Northants.

'If you weren't here then we could go. Why don't you get out and find a place of your own?'

'Because this was Grandpa's house and I can stay as long as I goddamn need to. I don't enjoy it. I just have to stay here.' Rosie sat at the table, watching them both sitting in the armchairs, looking at the space where her mattress had been when they were away, and Grandpa's had been before that. Yes, for now she had to stay here, she had promised Jack.

In April she laughed because customs men raided a liner and seized thousands of pounds' worth of smuggled nylons and Jack wrote to say it was a crime, all those stockings being kept from the streets.

At the end of May the sun was hot and on the first Whitsun since petrol rationing ended Maisie and Rosie took Lee to Southend by train, and walked from the station past streams of cars. Rosie held her face up to the sun. Jack was more than half way through. The sun was out, the world was good today. They would marry when he left and had sorted out a job. He had written and asked her. Soon, all the grey years would be over.

But on 25 June North Korea invaded the South and Rosie wrote to Frank because she wanted to know what it meant. He had always said Truman was afraid of appeasement. Would the United States become involved? Was this the conflict he had dreaded? Come on, Frank, she wrote, tell me what's going to happen. Jack's a soldier now.

She didn't have to wait for his reply because on 26 June President Truman offered military aid to South Korea and Attlee endorsed his actions in the House of Commons. On 27 June the UN backed the opposition to the Communists, making it a police action, not a declaration of war. But did that make any difference? Boys would die anyway, wouldn't they, she wrote to Jack. It was not a question.

The Soviet Union was boycotting the United Nations and was unavailable to veto the motion. On 28 June British ships were placed under the command of US General Douglas MacArthur, the same day that the South Korean capital, Seoul, fell to the North Koreans, and that night she didn't sleep. But so far British troops were not being sent. And anyway the boy at the Butlins fairground had said the only conscripts who went into action were volunteers.

She wrote to Jack in the first week of July, sitting out in the yard as dawn came up, breathing in the fragrance of the roses, sure that England would not send troops into yet another conflict. They had done enough. Yes, here, with the yellow roses unfolding and dew thick on the petals, she told herself that England had done enough.

For God's sake, the houses still hadn't been rebuilt, food was still rationed, unexploded bombs were still being found. Yes, they had done enough. And so she wrote not of the conflict in Korea but of Sinatra's visit which she had written up as a feature and would send to Frank.

She wrote of the new Zephyr that Jones was driving and how she had let his tyres down because of the beating he had given Jack, and the apprenticeship he had terminated. But before she could finish the letter the post came, and a letter was brought out by Norah because it was from America, and not in Frank or Nancy's handwriting.

Norah waited as Rosie peeled it open, looking at the address. It meant nothing to her, neither did the writing. She turned it over. It was from Joe. She looked up at Norah standing beside her. Rosie stared at her, then walked from the yard, remembering his blond hair, his tanned skin, his lips on her breasts, but he meant nothing to her. She leaned against the wall which was not yet warm from the sun and read the letter.

Lower Falls
27 June

Dearest Rosie,

I'm writing to you because I feel you should know that Frank has been ill for some considerable time. It's his heart. They didn't want you to know, which is why they were glad you couldn't get over. The pressure of the last few years, the rise in the anti-Red feeling – though for God's sake Frank isn't a Commie, just a liberal – were giving him problems. They didn't want to tell you. Felt it was better not to.

But Korea was the last thing really. Frank kind of takes all this to heart. He is so scared it will make things much tougher over here for those guys already in trouble with this un-American thing as well as involving our boys in war again. I guess he feels that with MacArthur in Japan it could get real nasty. That guy's such a hot head.

Anyway Rosie, Frank has had a heart attack. He isn't well. He could die. He thinks of you as his daughter. I know that it would do him more good to see you than anything else. I work for him now. I know him. Please come if you can. I'm sending you a ticket. Pay me back later if you can. I still remember that summer before you left. It was really great to be with you. Do you remember?

Yours,
Joe

Rosie folded the letter, putting it back into the envelope, taking out the ticket. Hearing Frank's voice, his laugh, seeing his broken pipes, seeing the love in his eyes for Nancy, for her. She mustn't cry. There was no time for tears. She must go now. She had waited too long already. She had neglected them.

'I've got to go, Maisie,' she said, wiping Lee's chin with her finger and licking it. Her finger was sticky. It had been sticky with hops that first summer back here, when her heart was so raw at leaving the lake and the Wallens.

'I've got to, Frank's ill.' She looked at Maisie who was cutting bread, holding the loaf to her body, against her apron, sawing a slice from the top. There were crumbs on the table.

Maisie stopped, her face paling. 'Don't go. Don't leave me. I'm not strong enough.' She threw the knife down. 'Don't leave, Rosie. Don't leave us. Not with Jack gone too.'

She hurried round the table, took Rosie by the arms, shook her, looking at Lee who had gone quiet, and stopped eating.

Rosie smiled at him, at Maisie. 'It's not for long. I have to go. I have no choice. I'll be back. Soon. Hang on. Please, let me go. Promise me you'll stay. Jack loves you so. You and Lee and Ollie. Promise me. If it gets very difficult, I'll come back. Just write.'

Maisie promised to stay, promised to write if it became too hard, and kissed her, held her tight, and there was the smell of lavender on her neck.

Rosie wrote to Jack too. She said that she knew she had promised but she had to go. It was only for a while. You'll understand. He's ill, they've written. I'm needed. I love them but I love you more. Write to me. I love you, I love you.

She forgot about Korea. She forgot about everything but informing the office, packing her clothes, posting Jack's letter, taking the train which rattled from the station, and now she cried because she feared that she would be too late.

CHAPTER 12

On the ship, Rosie thought of Jack receiving her letter, reading it on his bed, the only private space he had. She stood by the rail, watching the gulls wheel above the wake as they left Southampton, and wished that he was with her to take her in his arms and tell her that he understood. Surely he would when he knew that Frank was so ill?

She thought, too, of Grandpa standing on the dock so long ago as the children sang 'Roll Out the Barrel' and her voice broke so that no words came from her. Had he heard them as the ship moved out? She would never know now.

As the days went by and England faded, she remembered the leaves on the north shore of the St Lawrence as the ship carrying the evacuees at last drew into Canada, of their colours which she could not believe even now. She thought of the three cheers on deck when they docked, the high arched dining hall where they were taken, the lights in the streets, the food. But most of all the lights because England had been so dark.

On board now, she wrote to Maisie, talking as she would have done had she been there, pulling her back to them all, talking of days gone by; the good times. She would be back soon, she said, and Jack would finish with the Army next year. She wondered to herself how long it would be before Maisie had no more need of their support. They had their own lives to lead, their own love to enjoy. Their futures to explore and work towards.

She wrote to Jack, explaining again, telling of her love, again. She wrote to Norah.

She sat in deckchairs, feeling the breeze on her face, breathing in the air which was free of London smog, free of smoke, thinking of the balls which Frank used to throw to her to catch, the mitt that was warm on her hand, thinking of the balls which he threw for her to hit, the bat which she could swing as well as any boy. Thinking of Jack because she was sailing far away from him and already it was hurting her.

She ate food which was plentiful and fresh and sweet, and felt again the guilt which she had felt as a child a million years ago. But this time she had chosen to come. It was her decision – and she could have made no other. Jack would surely understand that.

She rested in the day because she didn't sleep at night, and each morning asked the purser how much longer, until at last he smiled and said they would dock within thirty-six hours. But she knew that because the gulls were back over the wake again and as they moved along the Hudson River the next morning she saw the cars on the Brooklyn Shore Road, the Staten Island ferries passing the ship. She saw the towers of the city glittering in the morning sun from the starboard side.

She moved to the other side. Here there was the Statue of Liberty, Ellis Island and the low outline of the New Jersey shore. She was back, she was almost home and she was crying.

Merchant ships lay at the piers, steam was surging up from the streets beyond, streets filled with new shining cars. Britain could not afford to keep its goddamn cars, they were exported, and she realised she was gripping the rail, taut with anger.

She took a cab to Grand Central Station and there were no damaged streets, no queues outside the shops, and the tears came again now because she was going home, but she had left home too. She belonged in both, but really she belonged with Jack.

The cab plunged in and out of the shadows of apartment blocks and sped along the double highway of midtown Park Avenue which Frank had said covered the New York Central and the New Haven railroad tracks.

'You a Britisher?' the cab driver asked, his jaws never ceasing to chew gum. He flicked her a piece.

'Yes, but I spent six years here. I'm glad I'm back.'

The gold lettering was still on Grand Central. She walked through the pillared hall, bought a ticket from a booth, thought of all the cleaners, looked up at the zodiac on the ceiling. No, she couldn't see what was wrong with it. She remembered Frank's face and hurried. She didn't stop to look at the Oyster

Bar, or the movie houses, and there was no one meeting her beneath the clock. She felt alone and longed for the feel of Jack's hand in hers.

She moved straight towards the bronze doors, checking her watch. The train would go at one minute past the scheduled time. There were redcaps wheeling trolleys to the silver grey trains, conductors standing by the doors. There was air conditioning on the train. It hummed like the ice-box would hum in the kitchen in Lower Falls. She sat down, she looked at her watch. Come on, for Chrissake. Frank was ill.

But he wasn't at the house. No one was. The blinds were drawn and it looked smaller than she remembered. She walked round to the back. The target was painted as Nancy had said. The rhododendrons were glossy, the lawn was green except where the hose wouldn't reach. There was no jazz sweeping out across the lawn. She stood with her hand to her mouth and longed for Jack because she couldn't bear to think that Frank was dead.

But he wasn't. A neighbour rang the newspaper for her because Frank and Nancy had gone to the lake, and it was Joe who came, driving across in a silver grey Buick which flashed the sun into her face. He drove her to the lake, the hairs on his arm still bleached, his watch still golden against his tan. His voice was deeper, his shoulders broader, but she couldn't look at the hands which held the steering wheel, or the lips which had kissed her breasts.

Instead she listened to the swing music on the radio, and longed for jazz. She looked out at the small towns they were passing through and the petrol stations with their pumps right beside the road and longed for Jack, only for Jack.

'Frank's getting better,' Joe said, reaching forward, pulling out the lighter, drawing on his cigarette. 'He doesn't know you're coming. But I sort of guessed you might use the ticket. I left word with the neighbours.' He was looking at her and she nodded.

'I know. I should have wired to tell them. It was stupid. I was busy getting ready, saying goodbye.'

'Uh huh. So how's little England?'

It was hot, and her legs stuck to the seat. She wound down

the window. There was a smell of petrol, diesel and dust. Heat hazed the distant mountains. She thought of the soft hills of Hereford, the stark dales that Jack spoke of. She looked at Joe's hands now. There were no scars on his fingers and thumbs.

'England's just fine,' she said. 'It was good of you, Joe, to send me the ticket. I'll let you have the money when we get to the lake.'

'Say, no hurry. We know things are tight with you Britishers right now.'

She wound up the window, feeling in her purse. She had the money. It was her savings.

'Things aren't tight with us little Britishers,' she said, putting the money on the dashboard, swallowing her anger. She closed her eyes, pretending to sleep as the next four hours crept by. Pretending to sleep until they drove in amongst the walnut and the ash trees and then the rhododendrons which were purple in June.

Just wish there was still the wild plum and the white oak like my dad knew, she mouthed, as Frank had always done at this stage of the journey, and wondered if Frank had been well enough to do it this time.

She was sitting up now, leaning forward, as the sun went down below the hills and the earth was oozing out the last of the heat. She heard the crunch of the gravel beneath the tyres, saw the wood-lapped house, smelt the lake. Yes, she was sure she could smell it.

She opened the door before the car stopped, ran across and up the steps, opening the door, and then stopped. She hadn't told them she was coming. How different would they be?

But then Nancy was running across the cool pine floor.

'Where the goddamn hell have you sprung from, my darling little Rosie?'

And her voice was the same and the arms that held her, but the face which looked closely into hers was older, so much older, and thinner and the lines were deep from the nose to the mouth and there were shadows beneath the eyes.

'Joe sent me a ticket. I've paid for it. I came. I love you both so much, so I came.' Rosie reached for the hand which was smoothing her hair and kissed it. 'How is he?'

They were walking across the floor and then she stopped and turned, looked back as Joe brought in her bags.

'I owe you, Joe. Thank you.'

He was still so tall, so strong, so tanned, but she longed for Jack, his slighter body, his smile, his pale skin, his drawn face. Her Britisher.

'Thank you,' she said, then turned and climbed the stairs because she had already forgotten the boy who had kissed her breasts after the barbecue.

She sat with Frank all evening, holding his hand, laughing when he chewed his empty pipe, listening as Nancy read him *Gone With the Wind.*

'It makes him fall asleep,' she said.

Rosie sat with him until he fell asleep, then she walked without shoes down the stairs, feeling the coolness of the floors, breathing in the smell of pine from the furniture, from the shellacked logs, from the very air which was cool as she stepped out on to the verandah. She walked with Nancy across the lawn, into the shadows of the trees, and neither spoke as they approached the lake.

She could hear its ripples slapping against the shore, smell it on the breeze, feel the mulch of the woods beneath her feet. She lifted her head. She could not see the star-strewn sky through the branches.

Then they were out on to the shore and the moon lit the air and the water and she dug her shoes into the sand, reaching down, scooping some into her hand, letting it fall through her fingers. Jack would be happy here. She would bring him one day and they would make love here, while the sand was still warm.

She put her arm through Nancy's. They walked down to the water, letting it lap their feet.

'So how is he really?' Rosie asked because they hadn't spoken of this until now.

'Thank God, he's going to be fine. They think anyway, as long as he doesn't get a lot of pressure again.' Nancy looked up at the sky. 'It kind of makes you feel the world's gone mad, Rosie. Here you have a good man, then things change and suddenly there's a suspicion he's a bad man because of the company he keeps or kept. Because of the words of reason he writes.'

She turned and they walked towards the boathouse.

'And what's even more crazy is when that company isn't bad either, but just had or have Commie connections. It kind of makes me want to puke. But it makes me goddamn frightened too because it's happening here, in our "free" country.'

The wind was gentle, there were no waves now, just a swell. It would be a good fishing night for Frank.

'Will he get completely well?' Rosie looked towards the point. Frank had looked older, like Nancy, thinner too. The lines were deep and his eyes sunken. He had no tan.

Nancy hugged her now. 'Sure, honey. Especially now that you're here. He is just so pleased and he knows it must have been hard to leave Jack and Maisie, especially now that they're sending British troops to Korea.'

Rosie drank hot chocolate in the sitting-room, talking about Uncle Bob, about Norah, about Grandpa, watching the moths beat against the glass, hearing their thuds, feeling the cold fear which Nancy's words had brought, but not being able to speak of it, because Frank was ill and needed her. Because Nancy did too.

It was only when Nancy had kissed her at the bedroom door that she could think. She moved to the window, opened it and breathed air which was so different to London. Then she wrote to Jack, thinking of the landlady at Cowes and her son's friend. You only have to go if you volunteer, the man at the fairground had said. She told Jack again now. She also told him again and again that he must not, but then, why would he?

The next day and the next and every day in July and August she sat with Frank beside his bed, with the windows and doors wide open, the drapes billowing in the breeze, playing records on his gramophone. They talked, but never about Korea, or McCarthy or his three friends who now had no jobs, about the 'hate' letters which Nancy said they had begun to receive in far greater quantities since North Korea invaded the South. Neither did they talk about the falling readership.

There were many hours when they just sat silently together listening to the piano of Erroll Garner, the voice and trumpet of

Armstrong, or the record by The Gang, Bob's new band, that had a tension and an urgency which Rosie liked and so did Frank.

She tapped her foot, poured him iced drinks and thought of the reports in the US papers of the American soldiers who were being mauled as the North Koreans pressed home their advance, and of the British 27th Infantry Brigade who were travelling to Pusan from Hong Kong. She thought of all the United Nations troops that were still being pressed back into the South Eastern coastal tip and thought that the world had gone mad.

Each of those days she walked down the gravel path to the mail box and once a week Jack wrote. His first letter was angry – worried about Frank, about Maisie – but she replied, telling him that Maisie was fine. She had seemed better, had promised that if there was trouble she would write and then Rosie would come back. Trust me, she wrote. I'm only here because I had an urgent letter. But she did not tell him that it was from Joe.

After that he sent her love and news of the assault courses they were clambering over, the football match his team had won, and she was glad that his letters were filled with news such as this. Not of battle which seemed to be in every paper that she read.

Nancy and she went to the Club and Sandra screamed and rushed over, her brace gone, her hair permed, her lipstick bright. She was in her first year at College, majoring in English. She was tanned, a gold watch hung loose on her wrist. They sipped vermouth from chilled glasses which stuck to the tables. They slid them to the edge to break the vacuum, and could only talk about the old times because their lives were so different now – Rosie was not at College, she did not have a gold watch – there was nothing between them and all she longed for was Jack.

Nancy held her hand as they walked to the car and Rosie told her then of her love for him, but Nancy knew already.

'Maybe it would have been Joe, if you'd stayed. He's a good man. Pretty ambitious, but a good man. He got you over. That was kind.'

Rosie nodded. Yes, it was kind, but he wasn't Jack. He didn't go back all those years, like Jack. Jack was her childhood, he was England. He was her life.

*

By September the leaves were falling from the trees and Frank was well enough to sit in the back seat while Nancy drove and Rosie looked back at the house as they left, wondering when she would come again. Because she would be back, but next time she would come with Jack.

In her room in Lower Falls her skis still stood, and the Cougar pennant hung as she had left it. The patchwork quilt was still on the bed and she sat and felt the ridges, then traced her hands along the pine headboard which Frank's grandfather had carved. It was the same, all the same, but she had grown.

The next day Mary returned from holiday and they kissed and hugged and Nancy built up the barbecue to catch the last of the mild autumn. As the light faded and the moths were dragged towards the lanterns, Rosie sat with Frank on the glider and listened because now he was home and there had been a stack of hate mail in the box, and he needed to talk.

His words were calm, slow, but his jaw was clenched as he spoke of the fear and suspicion that was rising in America. He wanted to be back where the trees and the lake hid him, but that wasn't possible. Someone had to print some sense.

He gripped his empty pipe with one hand and her fingers with the other, carving points out of the air as the smell of steak rose with the charcoal smoke.

'The fear and suspicion really got going when America heard that Russia was making headway with its own A bomb. Then there was China. How could the nationalists, supported by our wealth, go down to a peasant army? Now there's Korea. The North with Commie backing sweeping us aside as though we were flies.'

He was swinging the glider gently and his voice was calm. Tired but calm. 'They're frightened that another war will take all this wealth from them. Or maybe it's "we", hey, Nancy?' he called. But Nancy shook her head.

'You've never been afraid of poverty. You made all this, you could make it again. You might *have* to make it again if this goes on.' She flipped over a steak and laughed. Frank laughed too and Rosie felt the love flow between them and thought of Maisie and Ollie.

'That guy McCarthy, he's cunning. He wants re-election.

He picked out a hot chestnut to get in the papers. He's telling us he knows over two hundred Commies in the State Department. He hasn't named them. He can't name them, but some people want to believe what he says.'

'Steak'll be ready in five minutes,' called Nancy. Rosie nodded and Frank waved his pipe.

'But why?' Rosie asked.

'There was a backlash after the First World War. We had the Ku Klux Klan then. Now we have the Red Menace.' Frank rubbed his face with his hand. There were age spots on the back. 'And it's like I said before; it's hard for people to believe that this great big country of ours can get beaten by Mao, or Korean peasants. Look at our troops in Korea, pinned down by fire power. Cut off, whole battalions surrounded, thousands of our boys captured. It can't be the way we handle things, can it? It has to be betrayal from within. That's the only answer for some.' Nancy called them over now and Rosie helped him to his feet.

'Look at Hiss, a Harvard Law School graduate from a WASP family under suspicion of spying. McCarthy loves that. He tells the people that we are being betrayed by the high-ups within. He tells them that we red-blooded Americans could wipe our boots on the Commies, except for this betrayal.'

The barbecue was hot on their faces, the smell rich and sweet, and it seemed a world away from the harassment and fear of which Frank spoke, but that night there was a phone call, which Nancy took, and it was only when Frank went up to bed, his feet heavy, that she told Rosie that Uncle Bob had just been interviewed by the FBI. He had been reported last week for speaking out at an isolationist meeting back in 1940 and shouting that the Nazis must be beaten. It had been the day after Rosie had yelled at him from the stairs.

The doctor came the following week and now Frank was able to walk down the block, and drive into work for a few hours, and he came home with Joe, who stayed to dinner, his shirt white, his teeth white, his hair bleached. They talked of the jobs Frank had given to two of his blacklisted friends and Joe frowned as he drank from the crystal glass.

'I guess we should be seen to be even-handed,' he said. 'There should be a leader column alongside yours taking a more normal view. We'll be closed if we take too much of a liberal stand.'

Rosie put her own glass down. 'Frank's paper is even-handed.' Her voice was sharp.

Frank laughed. 'He's got a point. I haven't been publishing any of the crazy letters. I guess we'll let them roll. Maybe it'll shake some of these burghers up, make them see what's going on outside their picket fences. And maybe it's time Joe had a column. We'll give it a shot.'

They moved to the sofas and sat in front of a fire which flickered and swept heat into the room, and Rosie thought of the small banked fire, the queues, and Jack. She looked at Joe. He was so big. She wanted to be back in England, to feel Jack's arms around her, his lips on hers, to feel safe. There had been no letter from him last week, or this week, so that night in bed, she read all that she had received and slept with them beneath her pillow.

There was no letter from him the next day either but there was one from Maisie.

California
USA
7 Sept. 1950

Dear Rosie,

You will see from the letter that I am in America too. I couldn't manage any longer. I love him you see. He came over for me again and this time I had to go back with him. Lee is Ed's boy. Forgive me. Jack left, you left. Ollie is a good man. I've hurt him so much. It was never his fault, always mine. Jack loved Ed too. I wrote to Jack but he didn't write back. Go to him.

Maisie

She left that day, throwing clothes into her cases, kissing Nancy and Frank, saying she'd come back. She had to be with Jack. She flew. The ship was too slow. Frank paid. She didn't mind. She had to get back to Jack and all the time she cursed the red-haired man and the woman who smelled of lavender because they would bring pain back into Jack's life and he might blame her.

She took a taxi down the narrow streets. They had still not rebuilt the houses round the rec. Why hadn't Maisie written? She would have come back. Rosie had known the man was Ed. Deep down she had known.

She jumped from the taxi, paid, tipped, and ran down between the houses to the alley, her cases banging into her legs. She dropped them in Jack's yard. He wouldn't be there, but Ollie would.

Ollie was sitting at the table, drunk. His face was unshaven. He smelt of stale beer. There were dishes in the sink. Lee's toys were heaped in the corner of the room, broken and hacked apart. Maisie's clothes were with them. There was no fire in the grate and it was cold.

Rosie walked over to him, putting her arms around him, holding him, rocking him, but he didn't cry, he just moaned.

'I'm so sorry,' Rosie whispered. 'I'm so sorry, Ollie.'

He was silent at last, then pushed himself away from her, turning back to the beer, pouring it into his glass, drinking again. She stooped to pick up the clothes, the toys.

'Leave it. I'm going to burn them.' His voice was cracked like an old record.

She moved to the fire then, cleaning out the grate, emptying the ashcan into the dustbin, feeling it in her eyes and throat. She laid wood, then coal, lit it. Held a paper to draw it, heard the crackle then felt the heat.

She boiled a kettle, washed the dishes, made tea. Came and sat at the table with him. She poured him a cup, and one for herself. It was hot and strong. He didn't drink his. He didn't even look. He just drank his beer. She should have stayed in England, but how could she? How the hell could she?

'I knew it was that GI,' he said as Rosie poured another cup. 'Bastard.'

He pushed his chair away, kicking at the toys, standing there, his hands limp by his sides.

'I just knew,' he repeated then he walked into the yard. Rosie followed.

'I loved her, you see. It drove me mad. If I'd been kinder maybe she'd have stayed. But it burned inside me. She wouldn't let me touch her, not after she met him.'

Rosie held his arm. It was dark now. There were lights in Norah's house.

'The boy was his. I knew. It was the hair. They both had the same hair. I used to buy ham off him. I liked him. Trusted him, but only in the beginning. Now they've gone.' He turned and looked at the house.

'Your granddad and me bought these two houses. Things were all right then. Now I've got nothing and he's dead.' He was looking at her now, in the light from the kitchen. 'It's you bloody Yanks. You knew, didn't you, and you never said. Maisie told me. You bloody Yanks, you stick together. Well get out of here. You don't belong. Just get out.' He was shouting, moving towards her, and Rosie backed away from him, out of the yard, because he was right. She had known and there was nothing she could say. But then he called, 'There's a letter here for you. From Jack.'

She stood at the gate, the latch was rusty, there was a slight fog, the dampness made her cough. Why was Jack writing to her here?

Ollie went into the house, came out. The letter was white in his hand. He thrust it at her, then pushed the gate shut. It was dark, too dark to read. She walked to the end of the alley, to the lamppost where Jack and she had swung. She ripped it open.

Rosie,

Norah told me someone called Joe wrote to you. Who the hell is Joe? Is that why you went? Is that why you left Maisie? You promised. You said if I wasn't there, you would be, but one letter from a man I've never heard of and you're rushing back to the Wallens. Was Frank really so ill?

I trusted you and all the time you knew about Ed. She's taken Lee. He was Ed's. You Yanks think you own the bloody world. Go to hell. Go back, you seem to like it so much. Don't let me see you again.

Jack

CHAPTER 13

Rosie spent the night at Norah's. Not speaking to her, or to Harold. She couldn't. She couldn't sleep, eat, think. All she could do was feel.

She travelled to Yorkshire the next morning, her mouth dry. She must see him, talk to him. She must make him understand. The leaves were down from the trees, the wind buffeted the train. There was a view of Harrogate screwed to the wall. What had happened to the one that Jack had taken and sold in Somerset? What had happened to her world?

She turned from the glass-framed picture, from the man who sat reading his paper, blowing his nose. She stood, left her paper in her place and walked up and down the corridor to dull the pain. Everything was dark. There was no colour. He couldn't leave her. He was her life. He was her childhood, her future.

She leaned her head against the window, letting it bang against the glass as the train rushed through long sweeps of countryside, watching the rain jerk down the pane. Yes, she'd known. But she couldn't tell. It would have made it worse. Or would it? She didn't know, for Chrissake. She didn't know. All she knew was that she had promised Jack, and Maisie too, and there was anger added to the pain. Why couldn't people live their own lives? Why reach out and destroy hers? Why, Maisie? For God's sake why?

She changed trains, buying a roll which she couldn't eat from a kiosk, buying stewed tea, feeling it coat her teeth; feeling despair. She had to wait two hours for a connection. This part of the journey was slower, and she wanted it to roar and rush. She had to talk to him.

The camp was large. Squat buildings lined the roads. Nissen huts stood behind barbed wire. White notice boards held stencilled letters. The taxi took her to the duty room. It was six p.m. He was out.

'Where?'

They wouldn't tell her.

She held the taxi, gripping the door as though it would drive off, asking each soldier who passed, ignoring the winks, the whistles. No one knew. But still she waited. Still she asked.

'In the pub, in the village,' a boy with a shaved neck told her. He looked a child.

'Which pub?' She still held the taxi door. The meter was ticking over.

He didn't know. But it was one in Little Somerton.

They drove there along unlit roads. Sheep were huddled on the moors and the trees were stunted and crouched before the wind. Faster for Chrissake, she thought, but she said nothing.

She paid the taxi, standing in the centre of a village which was more like a town and watching it leave. It was dark and cold. The grey stone of the buildings funnelled the winds in off the dales. There were soldiers in the streets and girls who smiled, their lipstick bright in the light from the street lamps and the windows of the houses. There were railings, sharp pointed, newly painted. She could smell it.

Rosie walked up the street, looking at the men, and they looked back, walking towards her, but they were not Jack. She moved on, shaking her head. There were catcalls.

'Give us a knee trembler then.'

She pushed open the door to The Red Lion. It was crowded, full of smoke. Soldiers were playing darts, the juke box was loud. There were girls at the tables, their laughter high, too loud. A man in front turned, he was drinking beer with a cigarette in the hand which held the glass. There was froth on his upper lip. He grinned at her, wiping his mouth with the back of his hand.

'I'm looking for Jack Parker.'

He shook his head. 'Never 'eard of him. What about me?'

She looked past him, at the man behind, the men to the left and right, all of them, but none was Jack.

She turned and left. The man followed, holding open the door, calling after her.

'Come on, sweetheart, I'll buy you a drink.'

She didn't turn, she just walked on. She had to find him, had to talk. She couldn't live without him. She couldn't live with this despair. It made her breath shallow, her skin clammy.

In the second pub there was the same smoke, the same juke box music. Lights pulsed from it, on the men, the women, the ceiling, but not on Jack. He wasn't there.

In the third pub there was no music. There was a pool table down one end and dominoes too. There were girls at the tables, soldiers right up to the door.

She pushed through them, looking, asking. Their khaki was rough and damp. It smelt. Was that the smell Jack had meant when he told her about pressing his clothes?

A man caught her arm. She pulled away. He spilt his beer.

'Bloody 'ell,' he said, shaking his head, 'I'm only trying to tell you, Jack's over there.' He jerked his head behind him and she gripped his arm.

'I'm sorry, so sorry.'

Then she was past him, sliding through another group, smelling their beer, their sweat, and he was there, sitting at a table flicking a beer mat over and over, his arm round a girl with blonde hair and black roots, and it was as though she was split apart, jagged and bleeding, as she heard a moan. It was her. It was like the noise that Ollie had made.

But no one else heard. No one saw her. No one was looking. Not the men round the table, not the girl who was leaning into his neck, not Jack whose lashes were still too long, whose face was still too pale, too drawn, so sad.

She didn't hear the others, see the others. Those that pushed her, jostled her, those that sat around his table. They were laughing. Their mouths were open, their shoulders were heaving but she couldn't hear them.

'Jack.' It was her voice. It sounded the same, not as though it came from the pain which was slicing through her body.

She watched as he looked up, his face changing. He moved, then stopped. His face became set, his arm gripped the girl. He turned from her. But for a moment he had loved. She had seen it.

She moved closer. 'Come and talk to me, Jack.'

He was turning to the others, his shoulder towards her, then his back. The girl looked over him, to Rosie, and laughed. There was lipstick on her teeth.

'Talk to me, Jack.' Rosie leaned forward, picked up a glass of beer that the Lance-Corporal who sat opposite him had just put back on the table. It was three quarters full.

'Talk to me,' she shouted and the laughter stopped around the table. But Rosie couldn't hear anything other than her own voice. Now he turned. 'Come outside and talk to me or I throw this goddamn beer over him.'

She nodded to the Lance-Corporal who sat still, doing nothing, saying nothing. There was quiet all around them. She could hear that now. The glass was heavy, and wet. The beer was sticky. The hops had made her hands sticky too.

She said, 'Remember the bines, Jack? Remember how sticky the hops are? How the dust gets beneath your nails? Come and talk . . .' She did not need to go on because he rose.

The girl caught at his hand. He shook her off.

Rosie kept the beer in her hand until he had passed and then she handed it to the Lance-Corporal, but wanted to throw it over the girl. Into her eyes, her hair, her mouth, because Jack had held her and she had leaned into his neck where the smell of him was strong.

She pushed through the crowds, those who were still talking, those who hadn't noticed. The rest opened a path for her, not looking, their eyes busy, and everywhere there was the smell of damp khaki.

She opened the door. It was cold, dark. Jack was down the street, leaning on the wall, his foot up against it, a cigarette in his hand then his mouth. He had done this when she had come home the first time. But then it had been different, he had wanted her.

He watched her come. Her walk, her hair, curling around her face, her neck. Her eyes which were heavy with pain, her lips which were trembling and he wanted to reach out and hold her, love her, but she had gone away. Joe had written and she had gone. Maisie had gone. Rosie had known about Ed, all that time. And now the love washed away and the anger came again, as it had done every day since Maisie had left, frightening him by its savageness.

He turned and walked on, hearing her footsteps behind him, just behind, never at his side because he walked too fast. She would never walk beside him again.

He would never let her. He had trusted her, loved her above all else. But she had rushed to Joe, to Frank, to America, and because of that Maisie had gone to Ed. His heart was full of pain, his eyes too, but she mustn't see that. No one must see his pain again. He pushed it away until only the anger was left.

Rosie followed him, out of the town, to a crossroads where the only sound was the wind, but when it dropped she heard the sheep too. He stopped now, sitting on the rocks off to the left, lighting another cigarette.

'I'm sorry, Jack. I'm sorry I left.' She wanted him to reach out and hold her but he didn't and so she put her hand out. He knocked it to one side and threw his match away. It fizzed in the damp grass.

'I had to go. Joe wrote. To say Frank was ill. He works for him, you see.'

Jack sat slumped on the rock, his head down, his cigarette glowing. 'Is that so? Norah gave me the letter. You left it in your room. You knew him well. You had a summer together. You never told me. Maisie knew Ed well. She never told me either. You knew though. But you didn't tell me.'

Rosie put her hands in her pockets, bunching them. This was all wrong. Joe meant nothing. How could he come into this? How could he touch her life with Jack? This was about Maisie and Ed, not her and Joe. The panic was rising, she wanted to hold him, kiss him, tell him she loved him, only him, but there was such anger in him. It changed his face, now, as she looked at him.

She spoke slowly, carefully. 'It wasn't like Maisie and Ed. Joe works for Frank. I knew him, that's all. Long ago. We dated. He wasn't important.'

Jack didn't look up and his voice was dead. 'I told you about the girl in Somerset. She wasn't important. I wanted you to know. So that you could trust me. So that I could trust you.'

Rosie wanted to reach out, make him look at her, make him see her love. She said, 'I don't know why I didn't tell you, Jack.' But she did know why. It was because Joe had touched her breasts and his tongue had found her mouth and she was ashamed, but how could she tell him that?

He flicked his hair with his hand. It was longer now. She wanted to reach out and stroke it, stroke his face, see him smile.

'Anyway, what about that girl? What about the trust I have in you?' she asked, her hands clenched tighter now, with anger as well as pain. The red lipstick, the mouth, the hair, all in her mind.

Jack shrugged. 'What about her? She's here. You aren't. You went to America. Maisie left. You knew about Ed. You didn't tell me. You deserve nothing better. I thought I could trust you.'

He was standing now, shouting at her, screaming at her. 'Don't you understand? It was Ed. I loved Ed. Ed was like my father. But he wasn't mine, he was Lee's. After all that he's Lee's father and Lee has gone.' He was gripping her shoulders, shaking her until her head jerked backwards and forwards. Then he stopped and turned.

'Tell me you didn't know, Rosie. Please. Tell me it was a mistake.' His voice was tired. The anger was gone in her. She knew his face would be drawn but he wouldn't turn for her to see.

She couldn't tell him. She stood there as the cold wind caught at the trees behind her and at her hair and wanted to be back in Middle Street, back with Grandpa and Jack, back with the roses, with the life they had had. Back where she could understand why this was happening.

'I did know. I saw them. I didn't know it was Ed then, or I didn't think I knew. But when Maisie told me in her letter it wasn't a surprise. She had said she would give the man up. She made me promise not to tell you. I said I would help. I stayed as long as I could. But then I had to go. Frank was ill. I love him.' Her hands were out of her pockets now, reaching for him. 'I didn't tell you because I didn't want to hurt you. I thought it would be all right. She promised when I left.'

He hit her then, turning, slapping her across the face, then pushed her backwards, and again, gripping her coat as she almost fell.

'But you promised me, Rosie. You promised me that you would stay. Then you get a letter from this bugger and you go. What have you done? What has Mum done?'

He was holding her now, hugging her, crying because he had wanted to cry like this when Ollie had rung, when he had caught the train home, gone into the empty house. But Maisie had already gone and Rosie wasn't there and she was his friend and his love and he needed her.

She held him close, though her mouth was bleeding and her face throbbed. She held him because for this moment he was hers again and there was so much sorrow, so much love. 'I did nothing with Joe. I've let you down though. Lee's gone. I can't bear that either but I had to go.'

She felt his breath in her hair, the wetness of his tears. 'I love you. I thought I'd helped. I thought it was safe to go. I had to go.'

But now she felt him stiffen again and tried to hold him as he pulled away.

'I know. You went. Maisie went. Lee went. Over there where Ed is. I trusted you all. I loved you all and now it's just Dad and me.'

He walked back to the road. He could hear the wind in the trees. He could hear his voice, Ed's voice. He had lent him his bike. Ed had given him sweets. They had laughed and talked and Jack had told him that his dad was changing, becoming mean and strange, and Ed had put his hand on his arm. Don't worry, he had said. It's the war.

'And all the time he was laying my mum,' he shouted, laughing, turning to Rosie who was dabbing at her mouth. 'Is that what you were doing with Joe?'

He didn't know where the words were coming from. He didn't know what to do with the anger which filled him, spilled over, made him crazy, made him hurt her. Made his head go round until he felt ill.

Her mouth was bleeding. His Rosie's mouth was bleeding and he went to her again, holding her, telling her he was crazy. He didn't know what he was doing. He loved her, he hated her. He hated them all. He loved them all. She wasn't here when he needed her. She was with Joe, and Maisie was with Ed. He loved her. He loved his mother, and Ed. But he hated them. Christ, how he hated them. They had taken Lee. They've . . . taken . . . Lee.

He was howling now and he could taste the blood on her mouth as she kissed him. She drew him to her, stumbling, falling, taking him with her on to the soft grass, and he kissed her, his tongue in her mouth. He pulled at her coat but she stopped him and, he undid her buttons. Then he ripped at her blouse, he wanted her to tear, to feel his lips hard on the softness of her skin. Had Joe done this too, while Ed took Maisie and Lee from him?

'I love you, Jack,' Rosie said. 'I'm sorry. I'm so sorry.'

He looked up at her then. 'Has Joe done this to you?'

The wind was clawing at the branches, the clouds were whirling across the sky. Rosie looked at him, deep into his eyes, into the pain that all the lies had brought.

'Yes,' she said. 'But long ago and it was not what I wanted. I was confused.' She held his face between her hands, making him listen, making him look into her eyes. 'It was long ago. I love you. I've always loved you. All my life I've loved you.' She was kissing his lips, his eyes, his skin. There was blood on his face and the warmth of it in her mouth and she didn't know that it was hers. Slowly he began to kiss her back.

But the anger hadn't gone. It took hold deeper, stronger. Other hands, American hands, had touched her. Touched his Rosie, the girl who had played flicksies, the girl he had pushed on the swing. The girl he had taken to fetch the cheeses. American hands had touched his mother, taken his brother. Christ, it was all too much. It was all too strong. The rage was too strong.

He pushed up and away, but she pulled him back.

'Don't leave me,' Rosie said against his mouth.

He pushed away again, because he wanted her, but he hated her, loved her, wanted to hurt her, wanted to hold her and the rage was still there; his head felt as though it would burst.

She pulled back at him again.

'Don't leave me,' she said again and now her kisses were on his lips and her hands were on his back, and the wind was all around and he couldn't think, he couldn't see her, and he held her, moved on her, dragged at her skirt, her pants, hauling them down, pushing her legs apart, heaving at his own clothes. He sank down on to her, and she cried out as he tore and entered her. And he cried out as he came because all the love and the hate were still there, and the rage too. And then it was over.

Suddenly it was cold, and they moved, pulled at their own clothes, neither helping the other. Then they sat with their backs to the wind, separate, alone, and he wanted to wipe the last minutes from their lives, but it was too late and he was glad that he was leaving England, taking this rage away from her.

They moved without speaking into the trees where the wind was not as strong. The damp had soaked into their coats. Jack lit another cigarette.

'I'm going to Korea. I've volunteered.'

The branches were cracking, shaking, twisting, and the sheep across on the other slope were moving, baa-ing, Rosie saw them, heard them. He couldn't go. No, he couldn't go.

'You can't. I love you. You can't leave me.' She felt the ache between her legs, the feel of him inside her. He couldn't go. Those were the only words left in the world – he couldn't go.

'You love me,' she insisted, catching at his arm as he lifted the cigarette to his mouth, watching as he drew its nicotine deep into his lungs and then out again, his lips pursed, his eyes on the trees in front.

'I do love you and I hate you and if I stay I'll do what Ollie did. I feel as though I'm going mad inside. Everything's gone bad. I'll destroy us both.' He took her hand. 'I've got to go. I've got to get the anger out of me. It's been building since she went. Ollie cried and I held him and then I held him while he tried to tear the house apart. I wanted to do it too.' He pinched out the cigarette. 'I can't think. There's so much hate. I miss Lee so much. I missed Ed so much.' He dropped her hand.

'I've got to get away. That's all.' His voice was angry again. He stood up. 'Let's get you back.'

He walked in front of her, down the road. There was no train that late so she had to stay in a hotel, alone. He left her there, outside. Not touching her, not smiling.

'I'm sorry,' he said. 'About . . . well, you know. If you're in trouble, let me know.'

She gripped his arms. He couldn't go. Not out there. He couldn't leave her. They loved one another. She knew they did. This anger would pass . . . wouldn't it? But then she thought of Ed and Lee, of Maisie, of Joe, of America and she didn't know.

There was light from the hallway, falling out on to the street, there were soldiers walking past, one being dragged. He was singing 'Roll Out the Barrel' and she wanted her grandpa.

She said nothing. She let her hands fall, made herself watch as he walked down the street, made herself nod as he called back, 'I'll write. When I've sorted myself out, I'll write. If I sort it out. If there is anything worth sorting out between us any more.'

Then he was gone and there was no one left in her life. 'Oh, Jack,' she called, but it came out as a whisper. 'You and your goddamn anger. Your pain. What about mine. What about mine?' She was shouting now but he didn't hear.

CHAPTER 14

Jack sailed from Liverpool at the beginning of October on a troop ship with Regulars, Reservists and National Servicemen, and he was glad to be amongst them, to be leaving England, to be leaving Rosie and the memories. He was glad to be leaving for The Land of the Bleeding Morning Calm as the Sergeant had called it when he marched them up the pier.

He was glad to be on board, to be drilled, to be exercised. He enjoyed the orders, the bull, because it was familiar, like the scar on his hand was familiar. Like the other men were familiar, though he knew none of them. He just knew their language, their style, their habits, because they were like him. He was Army now.

There were no women. There was no tenderness. No betrayal, because if anyone broke the trust, out there on the hills of Korea, they all died.

He enjoyed pushing the ammunition into his rifle, hearing the click. It was cold, final. He enjoyed the storm which lashed the ship for four days, pitching and tossing, throwing him from his bunk, making him sick, making him wheel and fall, because it stopped him thinking and feeling.

He enjoyed the lectures, because then he could not hear her voice in his head. He learned how the North Koreans with Russian-built tanks and weapons had poured across the 38th parallel into South Korea in June.

'Will the West really resist the spread of Communism? is what the Russians will be asking themselves,' the instructor said. 'And I can tell you that we will. They've challenged the UN. They must be stopped.'

Jack listened when Captain Norris said that the Korean War had come when the international outlook was already bad, how the cold war was at its height, how Eastern Europe was under Russian domination. How West Berlin had just escaped this fate. How the Chinese Communists had triumphed in China. He knew all this from Frank's letters to Rosie. But, no, he wouldn't think of her.

He took out a cigarette, smelling the match, thinking of the oast-houses, the fag-ends they had collected as children. But he wouldn't think of that. He must listen to the officer with the moustache now, standing as Captain Norris sat. He must look at the Padre sitting upright, one leg crossed over the other. He must not think of her.

The second Captain was pointing at the board where a map hung.

'In June the South Koreans had a small army, no tanks or heavy artillery and only a small airforce. The North would have conquered South Korea if the United States hadn't had access to their occupation forces in Japan. These, though under strength and ill equipped, were mobilised but were still pushed back to the South East Corner along with our men when they also reached Korea.'

The officer slapped his cane down into his hand. Jack pinched out his cigarette. The Corporal next to him sighed.

'Get a bloody move on,' he murmured. 'I want me bleeding lunch.'

Jack grinned. The Captain was looking at his notes, the men were stirring. The man in front of Jack rubbed his neck. His hair was very short. L O V E was tattooed on his fingers. But there wasn't such a thing, was there?

'As you know, men, General MacArthur launched an invasion in September at Inchon while those in the Pusan perimeter, in the South East, went into the offensive. Now the North Koreans are on the run. We have pushed them back almost as far as their capital Pyongyang. Well over the 38th parallel. The border.' Captain Mackin coughed and looked up as another officer left, papers in his hand.

'It was a hard slog, don't think it wasn't. The harbour was mined, the roads were mined. There are still mines. That took a toll of tanks and men. The casualties have been heavy, but General MacArthur has turned down an order from Washington cancelling their issue of one can of beer a day.'

He stopped for laughter. There was some but the reservist

Tom, on Jack's left, was quiet. He had served in the Far East. He had been a POW at Changi. His war should have been over, he told Jack as they went for food. His wife thought so too.

'It's worse for the girl you've left behind,' he said.

Jack didn't reply. He hadn't left anyone behind, had he? But he didn't want to think about it. He couldn't get past the anger, the hate, to the love. He didn't want to any more. Not now, not yet. It was easier this way.

They sat through another lecture that afternoon and the sea was calm, there was only the vibration of the engines, the smell of diesel, and the Captain's voice again as he told them that the biggest fear was that Communist China would become involved.

But then he swept on quickly, telling them of the country and its people, but all Jack could think about was whether the Chinks would come in, because if they did, it would be tough. Very tough. Tom's hands were shaking and Jack wondered how the Government could send people back into the ring who had already been through so much.

Would the Americans send Ed over here? He had done a lot, hadn't he? They should send him. He should be killed. But he was too old.

'Old enough to be my father,' he said that night as he leaned on the rail and spat into the waves and wondered when the ache inside his head and chest would fade.

The days wore on. They listened, they trained, they wrote to their families, their lovers, their friends, but Jack only wrote to Ollie. He had no lover. But in the darkness of the night, when the only sounds were the grunts of men and the throb of the engines, he felt her warmth, her passion, and turned away from the memory of his own savagery. He wanted to feel love again, as it had once been. But he could not. And so he didn't write.

They arrived in Korea at the beginning of November. It was cold. They could see their breath on the air as they stood at ship's muster. They could see the buildings, the jeeps. They could see the hospital ship too, moored alongside. At Pusan they heard that the Chinese had come in, fiercely, briefly, but everyone knew they would come again. It was only the UN Command who refused to believe it, a Sergeant said as he passed them, grey and tired.

They entrained for Seoul but not before the Red Cross hospital train drew in from the forward battle areas. Tom watched and so did Jack. The red was sharp against the white of the bandages. The orderlies carried the drips beside the stretchers, the nurses checked labels, soothed, gave drinks, listened to a man shout that he could still hear the bugles.

A GI hobbled past. 'Yes, it's the bugles. You know it's them then. It's the bloody Chinese, they attacked us near the Manchurian border. Your turn next, buddies.' He was smiling but it didn't reach his eyes.

'Bloody Yanks,' said Jack. The GI had been big like Ed.

He pushed Tom on. 'Come on, let's go.' But he didn't want to. The Chinese were involved now, up on the border, but they wouldn't stay there. He wanted to go home. This wasn't drilling, exercising, smoking, drinking. This wasn't a scarred hand. This was vivid, stark, shocking. The fear made his voice rough.

'Come on, Tom, get on.'

The wooden seats were slatted, dusty. But he didn't want to go forward. He wanted to go home. This was real. God, Rosie, this is real. He slung his kit on to the floor. The dust caught in his throat. More were heaped on top. Tom was close. He could smell his sweat. But what was there at home any more? Who was there?

Seoul was damaged, bombed like London had been. But Jack wouldn't think of London, only of Korea and the tents they lived in, the mobile Naafi, the mist which changed to sharp cold almost overnight. It was all right, they were told, they weren't moving forward.

They stayed, smoked, bulled, smoked, trained. Felt nothing but boredom. Filled days which went too slowly, watched American troops lurch by in jeeps and Jack felt nothing but hate. In Seoul the hotels were functioning. There were drinks at night, Korean bar-girls who sat on stools with slits up their skirts, but he didn't want them. He didn't want anyone's lips against his. He didn't want anyone near him ever again.

Tom didn't want them either. These girls were Koreans. Koreans had guarded his camp. Their cruelty had been worse than the Japanese and so they bought drinks only for themselves. They sat sipping the beer, watching the flares in the sky. Watching the refugees pulling carts piled high, their faces numb.

The men wore white robes, baggy trousers and straw hats similar to the women who dragged their long hair back into buns. They drank another beer. There had been no more talk of the Chinese and it was 20 November. MacArthur had said they would be home for Christmas. He had to sort himself out before then. He had to write. But he didn't know what to say. He didn't know what he felt.

On the 22nd ten of them were sent north to the forward position as Infantry replacements, along roads girded by frozen paddy fields, and on either side were snow-dusted mountains and hills; shrub-covered, desolate.

Troops were dug in. Smoke rose from the fires. There was a wind. Always a wind and as they travelled the squad talked, but of nothing because they all remembered the boys on the hospital train.

'But the Chinese haven't come and MacArthur said we'd be home by Christmas, didn't he?' Jack repeated.

He shifted on the seat, peering out of the canvas-covered truck, listening but hearing only the wind. He laughed, they all laughed because they had all been listening too. For bugles.

They smoked, looked out at the cottages made of wood and mud and thatched with straw. Three were scorched and ruined. Even in this cold they could smell the human excrement used to feed the soil.

They passed peasants who carried loads on A-shaped frames, women who carried loads on their heads and babies on their backs. The roads were dirt tracks with pot holes which were frozen over. The truck cracked the ice, splintering it, frosting it. Jack threw out his cigarette stub. It arced away, bright in the cold air.

Tom sat, his hands loosely between his knees, his rifle leaning into the crook of his arm.

'I wish I wasn't here,' he said.

'No good saying that when you're sitting on top of a bleeding hill.' The Sergeant opposite nudged his leg. 'You just remember to keep your head down, your eyes open, and pray you get home. You've been in it before. You should know. Help this lot of nigs. Anyway, we're here. Home sweet home.'

The truck stopped at the base of Hill 12. They hauled their kit up on foot, catching on to shrubs, pulling themselves along, slipping, their rifles clattering. A stream ran from the top to the river below and ice crusted the overhang.

The unit they were to join catcalled them at the top. A Lieutenant met them. They saluted. He was grey and lined too, although, they learned, he was only twenty-two. The Sergeant led them to the field kitchen. Others were there before them, warming their hands around their mess tins, moving from foot to foot, nodding as they dug out their tins. At least the beans and stew were warm.

'More shit-diggers. Just what the Chinks want for tea,' a Lance-Jack grinned.

Jack nodded, laughed, and when they had eaten they were shown the hoochies they would sleep in, fight in, shit in. They were shown the machine guns, the mines, the booby traps. That night he and Tom slept in sleeping bags. Dave, John and Simon didn't.

'We've been here too long,' they said. 'You might need to run. Those buggers are like a bloody avalanche.'

The hoochie was heated by an ammunition box into which petrol dripped from a copper tube fed from a can fixed high on the outside. The chimney was made from shell cases, and prodded up through the roof made of branches. It was still too cold for Jack and Tom but there was no firing. There had been none for many days.

But there was the cold and it ate into him. He zipped up his sleeping bag, pulling it over his head, but the cold eased through the ground, the air. It kept the sleep from him and he thought of the ice on the inside of Rosie's boxroom, the damp of the ground when he had held her, driven harshly into her, felt her warmth, her love, and he felt ashamed.

But she had left Maisie, she had gone when Joe had written. Joe had kissed her breasts. Ed had taken Maisie and Rosie had let him and he turned again and again but he couldn't find warmth, he couldn't find sleep and neither could Tom because the Chinese might come. But they didn't. Not then, and not the next day or the next.

'And they probably won't,' Jack said, digging another

perimeter fox-hole, cursing the frost-hard earth, the ice-cold pickaxe.

'Get your bleeding weight behind it,' the Sergeant growled. 'A Chink would shoot your backside off in that pathetic little hole.'

So he dug further and so did Tom, hearing the clatter of stones, looking out across the valley, the river, the hills. Seeing nothing. No Chinese, no birds, just the cold which stabbed into your lungs but didn't stop you thinking. He dug again. He wouldn't think of her. He wouldn't write. He wouldn't write to Maisie either.

On 24 November it was Thanksgiving Day and they watched as trucks brought out turkeys, and planes dropped the trimmings to US troops, and he wondered if Maisie was eating turkey too. He pushed the thought of her from him, but for a moment he stopped and leaned on the barricade he was building from the rocks, not seeing the planes, not seeing the trucks or the snow-frosted world. Just remembering Lee's laugh, the feel of the little boy's arms around his legs in the back alley on his first leave.

Still the Chinese didn't come but there was no sense of ease. Only of waiting. He had spent his life waiting. Should he write? No, he couldn't.

They went on patrol that night as the snow started to fall, heavily, silently. Five of them, the Sergeant leading, Tom second. He knew so much about survival. He had fought the Japs, he had survived the camps. He was quiet, calm, except when his hands shook.

They slid down the slope, digging in their heels, not speaking, not clinking, looking, listening, and Jack's hands were wet inside his gloves and his breathing was rapid.

He was frightened out here, beneath the sky, away from the holes, the others. And no, he wasn't thinking, he was breathing with his mouth open, tasting the snow, straining to hear the enemy, if they came. He was looking, always looking, but what could you see through all this snow which drove in and around him? Christ, he was frightened. These weren't manoeuvres. This was real. And what the hell was he doing here?

He put his feet where Tom's had been, he slipped, recovered. His feet hurt with the cold but that was all right. It was when they didn't hurt that you had frostbite, it was then that you lost your feet.

He looked and listened. His throat hurt from the cold air. There was nothing, just the sound of breathing, and soon the hill had flattened and the going was easier as they crept to the shore of the river.

They set up a listening post behind scrub and rocks where they could sometimes see the river as the snow hurled itself in a different direction and the curtain lifted. Tom linked up a field telephone. They spent three hours watching, listening, feeling the cold bite through their clothes, their balaclavas, their gloves, feeling it stab into their lungs with each breath. It had been minus thirty-five when they left. They could hear the snow cracking the branches of the shrubs and the Sergeant's breath froze on his moustache.

The next patrol came down to relieve them at 2300 hours. They edged up the hill again. Watching, scrambling. Christ, be quiet. Using their hands, shaking the snow which caked their gloves and faces, and always they listened, even as they thawed in the 'warm tent'. But the enemy didn't come and no one relaxed, though MacArthur had said they would all be home for Christmas.

The sound of firing woke them the next night, it was down by the river.

'Thank God, thank God,' he whispered when he woke. 'That could have been me.' Now there were bugles, rattles, whistles and drums, grenades and small arms fire.

But his hands were too cold to unzip his sleeping bag and he wept as John and Dave and Simon ran out, rifles in their hands, ducking and weaving as the Sergeant shouted, 'Take that side and keep your heads down.'

'Christ, I can't get out.' He was going to die. They were coming for him and he was going to die. But Tom was there, calm, leaning over him, unzipping the bag for him, helping him as Ollie had done when Jones's man had beaten him at the warehouse, as Rosie had done with the cheeses. Tom gripped his shoulders.

'It's OK, Jack. You're OK. They're not here yet. Remember what you've been taught and stay with me.' He turned and moved out into the snow. There was firing all round, from the hills ahead and around them.

The fear held Jack still. Dad, where are you? Rosie? He wanted to run. Just run and hide because he could hear screams and shouts and the bugles at the base of the hill and they were getting nearer, the firing was louder. The snow was heavy, and he couldn't see. He hadn't been able to see in the fog either. Dad, where are you?

But the barricades were there. They would keep them away. Jack was out in the open. Following Tom, running, the snow in his eyes, his nose, his mouth. The breath was sharp in his chest. He slipped, scrambled up again, ran to where the Sergeant pointed, heaving the Sten gun up on to the wall he had built, firing down at men who fell as the ducks in the fairground had fallen, but more took their place. For God's sake. More took their place.

His gun was hot. Tom was firing. There were tracers in the air. Flashes from grenades were bright against the snow. Still they came. On up the hill. And he wasn't killing men, he was killing ducks. Ducks which flipped back up, no matter what he did.

They were closer now, scrambling where he had scrambled, firing, blowing their bugles. The Sergeant was behind them. They were much closer.

'Stand your ground,' the Sergeant shouted, but they were so close. He would see their faces soon. They were at the first barricade, leaping over, shooting, stabbing, killing. This was real, for Christ's sake. People were dying. There were screams and groans all round and there was sweat on his face, dripping on to his coat. But he was cold. How could he sweat?

The Sergeant screamed, 'The buggers are through. Over here, you two.'

They crouched and ran back to the next fox-hole. Jack lay down, fired again, heard Tom do the same. It was cold, for Christ's sake. The ground was cold but the Chinese were coming on, falling, dying. Jack fired, Tom lobbed grenades, but more came.

'Where the hell are they coming from?' It was Tom. He was standing, his body exposed. Jack pulled him down.

'Keep firing.' His mind was cool now. It was Tom's hands that were shaking, not his. There was no hate, no love. Just the gun, just the Chinese, and they were closer. For God's sake, they were so damn close.

'You've got to hold.' The Lieutenant was behind them, his breath short. He was shouting. 'Got to hold, let Hill 16 complete their manoeuvre. Then we can go, if we have to. But hold.'

John was with them now. They dug their knees in deeper. It didn't matter that it was cold. They wanted to live. They held for five hours.

At 0300 hours the Sergeant slapped Jack on the back, took over the Sten.

'Get out now, over there.' He was pointing to where other men were leaving, stumbling and running, while others still fired, still fought. Jack took his rifle, crouched, ran. Tom was with him, passing him a Luger he had taken from a fallen soldier.

The Chinese were breaking through. They were fighting. He saw arms lifted, guns and knives which twisted and plunged. Tom turned, his head down, his gun up.

'Get out, Jack!' His voice was faint against the noise but Jack heard him, stopped.

'Come on, Tom. Your wife. Get home.' He grabbed him, pulled him, turned him and they ran on together.

They skidded down the hill, ducking and weaving, looking forward, behind, to the side. There were others, friends and enemies. A Chinese lunged for Jack, he dodged, drove home the rifle butt, felt the jolt through his body, but they went on, down the slope, slowing, easing, creeping at the base, sidling off to the side of the road, but there were more and they were firing and Jack felt a punch high up in his arm.

He turned. Tom was down too. There was blood on his chest, on his stomach. He had been shot four times. His mouth was open, his eyes too. He was dead. Snow was already settling. He was warm and Jack took him in his arms, tried to lift him, carry him home to his wife, away from all this, because he had been in too many wars.

But the punch had been a shot and he could only move one arm and the pain was beginning now. He tried to drag Tom, but he had no strength and so he had to leave him, there, in the snow, alone but not alone for there were other dead around him.

Jack felt the anger and the pain rage and he screamed, 'Rosie.'

The Sergeant was there then, pulling, dragging him towards the road where tanks were retreating. He shoved Jack up on to the body of one.

'Hang on or you'll die. Hang on, son.'

There were others clinging, hurting, panting, and he did cling on but not for long because the road was blocked by blazing vehicles and a tank which had lost its track.

He dropped to the road. His coat was too heavy. It dragged at him. He pushed at the tank with the other men but there was too much fire from the hills each side and behind them and so he walked, and another man took his rifle, struggling on ahead.

They passed a soldier on fire from burning phosphorus. How could he burn with so much snow? The flames were so bright. How could he burn when it was so cold? Jack felt as though his head were bursting.

'Shoot me,' the American was screaming. Jack shook his head, stumbled on. Christ, that could have been him. Oh Christ. Dad, where are you? Rosie. He stopped, turned back.

'Shoot me,' the man whimpered now, holding out a blackened claw. 'Shoot me.'

The snow was still falling. The man carrying his rifle had gone, walking on, not waiting. There was just this man here, crying, burning. There was no war, no firing, just the two of them, and one was dying, slowly, and his whimpers seemed so very loud.

Jack did shoot him, with the Luger. The whimpering stopped but pain blossomed in Jack and he cried as he walked because he had shot a man with a blackened, burning body and he would never be free of the smell or the sight of it.

Many others straggled back as the days went by. The UN were in retreat again. He didn't mind the pain in his arm. He didn't mind the throbbing, it was better than being dead. Tom was dead and he had a wife. Jack had no one and he was glad. There was too much pain in loving. Tom's wife would know that now. There was always too much pain. He was glad it took all his strength to put one foot in front of the other. He was glad it took all his mind to breathe in and out. In and out because he didn't think of Rosie, or the burning man, or Tom.

They passed blazing villages, and always the enemy was close behind and to the sides of them in spite of the US airstrikes. There were mortar bombs arcing through the freezing sky. They walked with refugees, then passed a burned out field hospital. A jeep came, doling out hot chow. 'Hurry up. For Christ's sake, hurry up,' the Corporal said, ladling hot cereal and powdered eggs into their helmets because they had no mess-kits any more.

The firing was as close as it had been before, but no closer. Why was the Corporal panicking? He wasn't dead. It was all the others that were dead. Jack dropped his helmet. He was hot, so hot. The food spilled on his boots, into the churned snow.

He sank to the ground. It wasn't cold as it had been when he was shooting the ducks on the hill.

Jack felt the jerking of the jeep, the rattle of the train, and it was like the one that had taken them hop-picking and he knew he must think, he must write to Rosie. But what would he say? He didn't know. He was too tired. Too hurt.

The field ambulance carried him from the train to the ship. A stretcher took him from the ambulance to the gangway. The Medical Officer and Wardmaster lifted the blanket, looked at his shoulder. He screamed as they touched him.

'No gangrene. Those maggots have done a good job,' the Medical Officer said, not looking at Jack, just at his arm. The Wardmaster wrote medical instructions on a label which he tied to Jack's wrist. He was sick of labels. They had tied one to him when he went to Somerset. He wasn't a parcel, he was a person. Rosie hadn't liked hers either. But he wouldn't think of that.

He was carried on a stretcher by South Koreans to the ward on the water line, one deck below the air-conditioned quarters for those seriously injured. They didn't see a doctor on the trip to Japan. There were too many operations needed. Too many amputations because of gangrene.

Jack wouldn't think of the maggots which had been cleaned from his wound. He couldn't bear to think of them in his body. He lay and listened to the throb of the engines, felt the vibration in his wound, his arm which was hot and swollen. He talked to the others as they limped, or sat, arms bandaged, heads bandaged, but they all had their limbs, they all had their lives. Tom hadn't any more and soon his wife would know.

Love hurt.

It was hot. So damn hot. He sat up, but he had no strength, so he lay again. It had been so cold up there on the hill and as they ran away. Pyongyang was burning now. The UN troops were scorching the earth, burning the supplies, stopping the enemy from gaining anything. They were retreating to the 38th parallel. How much further would they go back? Would it all have to be done again?

The trip took three days because the channels could not be guaranteed free of mines and the heat grew worse. The wards were over the main generators. The portholes were secured when at sea.

There were no washing facilities. They were dirty, they were in danger of dehydrating. There were large jugs of water and lime-juice and the boy next to Jack poured him some because he couldn't stand. The ship's engines were so loud. They throbbed in his head, in his wound. All over his body.

He was given more penicillin. He knew there were more maggots but he must wait until Japan to have them scraped away.

An American died and the boy next to Jack told him that they were going to store the body in ice which had to be replenished every two hours, because the Americans returned the corpses to their homeland. Jack turned away from him. They took too many things back to their homeland. They had taken his mother, his brother.

They drew into Osaka and Jack thought that perhaps it was better that Tom was dead, not here with him, because these were the people who had beaten and struck him. These were the people he had hated. As Jack hated Ed. Did he hate Rosie?

The dead went off first, covered with the flag of their country, while the band played. Then the wounded, but not the walking wounded yet. They waited but when it came to their turn Jack still couldn't walk. He was carried on a stretcher and shared an ambulance with a man who had been burned but Jack wouldn't look because he had shot a man with burns. He had been an American. He had pleaded to die.

Jack felt the gun in his hand again. He had shot him. He had looked into a man's face and killed him. Seen the agony go from his eyes, but the light too. An American had asked that of him.

An American had taken his mother. An American had kissed Rosie's breasts, and as the ambulance drew away from the docks towards the hospital he knew he still couldn't write to her.

CHAPTER 15

Rosie walked into the hotel when Jack left, lifting her head and ignoring the gaze of the woman behind Reception, taking her key, climbing into the bed which had not been aired. There was frost on the inside of the panes. He had left her, goddamn him. God damn him. And now she was crying.

Jeeps passed, their headlights flashing into the room, across the ceiling, lighting up the pictures which hung from thin chains. She couldn't sleep. She wouldn't cry. She could scarcely breathe. She lay with her hands on her breasts where she could still feel his mouth.

She wanted to go from the bed, out into the town, to the camp, find him, make him love her, make him push his hate away, her anger, her pain, but she stayed, watching the sky through the window, feeling the throbbing between her legs which had become an ache by the morning. There were drops of blood on the sheet. She sponged them. Each breath hurt. She didn't speak as she paid for her room. She didn't nod. She couldn't.

At the station were the same kiosks selling rolls and newspapers, but she bought nothing, not even tea, and she didn't turn as the train took her away from him. But everything was dark.

She took a Tube and bus and then walked to Middle Street. She walked slowly. She put one foot in front of the other carefully because she ached inside, and she was going home and there was no point to it. And he might come running up behind her, catch her arm, pull her round. Tell her he was wrong. He was sorry. He loved her. But he didn't. And still it hurt to breathe.

She entered the house before Norah and Harold returned from work. The fire was banked. There was a faint heat. She dropped her coat on the floor, her bag too. She dragged the tin bath from its nail on the yard wall.

She smelt the gas before it lit, she heard it hiss as it heated the water in the boiler, she saw the steam beating up to the ceiling, layering the room, clouding the window.

She tipped the water into the bath, poured in cold. There were only two inches. She poured in more cold. Then she peeled off her clothes, leaving them where they fell. It didn't matter that the water was cold. She barely noticed, but she knelt in it, feeling the ridges of the bath on her knees, heaping the water into her cupped hands, splashing it over her body, between her legs, because she had to remove the smell of him or she would die, from anger and from loss.

She splashed again and again, wetting her hair, her body, her arms, her legs, everything. Soaping, rinsing, crying because they had loved but it had not been as she had dreamed. They had loved, but there had been hate, and love without tenderness, only pain. And he might have gone for ever and she didn't know how this had happened. She didn't know how her world could change like this. She didn't know how she could love someone as much without them loving her back.

She dropped her head to her arms, and sniffed. Then to her legs. There was none of him left. Would that help the minutes, the hours, without him? She would not think of longer, of for ever. Now there were more tears, racking sobs which dug deep into her chest and still it was difficult to breathe.

She dressed in fresh clothes, dragged the bath to the yard, tipped the water down the drain. She washed her clothes, hung them on the line where they dripped. She set out the candy she had brought back for Norah on the kitchen table. She hung the scarf she had brought for Harold on the chair and looked at the shirt which had been for Jack, the blouse which had been for Maisie, the car which had been for Lee.

She carried round the bourbon which she had bought for Ollie and left it on the doorstep. What did it matter if he drank it all too quickly? What did anything matter? There was only anger, only pain.

Norah came back at six-thirty and Harold too.

'You're back then. So, how's lover boy? Ollie said you'd gone up there. He said you know all about Maisie's man. Bet

Jack didn't like that.' Norah shrugged out of her coat, nodded towards the candy. 'It'll make me fat.'

Rosie made tea, slicing up the tin of ham she had brought back, boiling potatoes, cutting tomatoes into quarters. She put a fruit cake that Nancy had made on a plate in the centre of the table.

She couldn't eat but she made herself put food in her mouth. She made herself chew until the plateful was finished because Norah was watching.

'So, Jack's volunteered?' Norah was smiling, looking at Harold who pushed his glasses up on the bridge of his nose.

'Yes,' Rosie said, and felt Jack's weight on her body, inside her, but she wouldn't cry, not now. Not here.

'Left you, has he?'

'He's going to Korea. For a while. Only for a while.' Rosie took her plate to the sink. Washed it, dried it. She could smell the soda but not him. At least she could not smell him.

'Have you still got your job?' Norah was wiping her plate with bread she had torn off the loaf.

'Leave the girl alone,' Harold said as he stood up, leaving his plate for Norah to clear, moving to Grandpa's chair, opening his paper, stretching his legs out.

Get out of my grandpa's chair, Rosie wanted to shout, but he had been kind. For a moment he had been kind. She stood with her back to the sink. She had given Lee's present to his friend, who had been playing footie in the alley. He was lonely, he had said.

'Don't know why you don't get yourself a live-in job.' Norah pushed a crust that was too large into her mouth.

'This is my home, for as long as I need it. Don't you ever goddamn forget that. I have a right to be here.' Rosie moved to the back door, lifting her coat off the hook, putting it round her shoulders. 'I'm going out.'

'Where to, now Jack has gone?'

Rosie turned the handle, opened the door, walked out into the cool of the evening and the fragrance that still hung on the air from the last of the roses. She didn't answer. She didn't know. Jack wasn't there, nor Maisie, nor Lee. What *was* there, without them all?

As she passed the yellow rose she stooped, smelt its scent,

touched its petals, picked it, held it to her cheek. It was soft, fragrant. Some things never changed.

She walked to the rec. She sat on the swings and heard the laughter of their childhood. She leaned against the chains. His hands had held these. She pushed lightly, her feet rocking against the ground. He had to come back. In spite of everything. He was her life. He must see that. He must see that she couldn't have stopped Maisie. One day his mother would have had to live her own life. Or could she have stopped her? Perhaps she could.

She pressed her forehead against the chain, hard, rocking sideways now, crushing the rose, the stem with its thorns, but nothing helped the pain then, or that night or any night, or the anger.

Nothing helped the panic which caught and held her, pushing her up from the bed, making her walk, rubbing her hands up and down her arms at the thought that he might never want to hold her again. He might never want to look at her smile. How could all that love go, so quickly? How could all that love be pushed aside by hate? How could such anger and pain live inside her too?

The next morning she walked to see Mrs Eaves and thought she saw his head amongst the crowd. But it wasn't him and the pain was too sharp and she turned, looked in the tobacconist's window and cried but the tears didn't make anything better.

The store was bright and warm in a world that was cold, empty and dark. Glenn Miller was being played by a girl with neat peroxided hair and Mrs Eaves saw her, waved, took her by the arm to her office. Her keys jangled as she walked. They talked and Rosie cried again and said that Frank was better but Jack had gone. Hating her, loving her, unable to decide.

'But he'll write. I know he will,' Rosie said, watching as Mrs Eaves nodded, pressing out her cigarette in the ashtray which had Margate written on the edge.

'Of course he will, but it'll take time. And if he doesn't it's not the end of the world.'

But it would be. Rosie knew that, though she said nothing.

She did still have her job, though, and they liked the piece she had written about small-town America. Its fears, its guilts. Its hysteria. They edited it down to half and ran it. For a few days that took her mind from the ship that was taking Jack to Korea but for no longer than that. But now at least she would not hope to see him come towards her as she walked to the bus. Now he had gone but he would be back. She had to believe that, she told Mrs Eaves.

She wrote to Frank and Nancy, telling them that Jack had volunteered, that he was on his way.

She didn't tell them that he might never come back to her because she didn't dare to write the words. She loved him in spite of the pain, the anger. She would never love anyone else and all his love couldn't just disappear, could it?

The day she wrote her letter to Frank she received one from them and read it in her lunch break sitting on a bench in the park.

Lower Falls
26 September

Dearest Rosie,

We miss you so much. How are things? Is it sorted out with Maisie? How did Jack take it? You must not think it is your fault. You couldn't babysit the situation for ever, you know. I trust that Jack understands that.

Here's good news anyway. Frank has had details through of the Inchon landings. It seems MacArthur got it right. He came in strong, surprising the North Koreans but had to ride out a typhoon on the way. They had to time it exactly to land during high tide or they would be wading ashore in mud. As it was, some Marines had to do just that as they attacked Wolmi-do which guards the approaches to Inchon.

There were fierce battles as other forces landed on the mainland but they advanced rapidly, as you will know. Those in the South East are on the offensive too.

This success seems to have quietened down the zealots in our area which is a good respite for us both. Frank continues to do well. McCarthy is still stirring things up nationally.

Come back, my dear, whenever you can, whenever you want to. We love you so very much. We miss you. Give our love to Jack. Bring him too. Joe sends his regards to you.

Nancy

Rosie tore it up, dropping it into the bin over by the seats. She didn't want to read about the war, not now, not ever, because Jack would be there soon. She wanted to go back to Frank and Nancy, to their arms and their gentle voices, but not yet. Not until she heard from Jack. He might write. He would write. He might be injured. She must know. She must stay, and fear began, at last, to dull the anger.

In the second week of October, Sam and Ted were buying a record of Frank Sinatra's in Woolworths when they saw her. They came over, laughing, joking. They were older, much older. They were men but Jack was a man too.

'Ollie says he's gone, the daft bugger,' Sam said, his smile wide but his eyes serious.

Rosie took the ribbon the salesgirl handed her. It was blue and wide.

'Yes, he's gone. He is a daft bugger.'

'Ollie says his missus has gone?' Ted was looking at her now. 'Wasn't your fault. Everyone knew. You couldn't stay with her for ever, you know.'

Rosie touched the ribbon. It was soft and cool. Write to Jack, tell him, she wanted to shout but couldn't. She knew now that he must realise that on his own.

'Come up the Palais. It'll be like old times,' Sam said, looking at the ribbon. 'Not your colour,' he added.

They went that night but it wasn't like old times. Sam and Ted drank beer. She drank sherry. It was too sweet. They danced but Sam and Ted met girls they knew and she was one too many but they had been kind and they knew Jack and for a moment it had been good.

At the end of October she received a letter from Nancy telling her of the UN advance in Korea, and how the North Korean forces had crumbled in the face of the UN forces. In the space of a few short weeks the UN had occupied virtually the whole of Korea.

'Frank is worried that MacArthur cannot now be reined in. He might try to end the threat that Communist China poses to American interests in the Far East by not stopping at the frontier. Truman has to insist that this is a "limited action" against a specific Communist act.

'Maybe it will be over by Christmas. If so, Jack won't fight. He won't be there long enough. Keep hoping, my dear.'

The Features Editor had been working her hard. She typed, took shorthand, read the slush pile, wrote short pieces and slowly the career that she had always striven for was within her reach, and that, at least, gave her pleasure, gave her purpose.

She took the letter into the park and read it again. Even though it was cold she brought her lunch here every day. It gave her some peace. An elderly woman sat next to her, eating ham sandwiches. She wondered where the pig had come from. There was almost no bacon or pork left in the country, or so it seemed. She looked at the snoek between her bread. The Government was pushing these tins of fish at a protein-hungry public but the smell made her feel sick. The taste was rank and salty. It had upset her for days. So had the whalemeat which Norah kept for sandwiches. The taste of cod liver oil was too strong.

The old woman saw her looking, smiled, patted her leg and passed her one.

'Thanks,' Rosie said. 'But no. I'm not very hungry.'

But the old woman insisted and she took it and tasted the fresh ham, but she felt the nausea begin again. She waited until the old woman had left the park, then fed it to the birds, watching as they flapped their wings, listening as they squawked.

The next morning she woke early, eased herself from the bed, put on her coat, crept down, heated the kettle, and ate a biscuit, but it didn't work. She rushed to the privy, leaned over the pan, and vomited. She leaned back against the wall, sweat-drenched, cold; the sickness was in her stomach, her throat. She vomited again and again, but quietly. For God's sake be quiet. She pulled the chain to drown the noise.

She dressed, and made bread and marge for her sandwiches, ignoring the snoek tin with its blue fish, ignoring the whalemeat and the cheese. She worked, and came home through the fog which was sulphur thick. Slept. It was the same all that week and the next but there was no letter from him. Still no letter.

There was one from Frank though.

Lower Falls,
1st November

My dear Rosie,

I got it wrong. I thought things were cooling down a bit. I've been pulled up before the Un-American Activities Committee. Interviewed, hectored, treated with contempt, shouted at until I couldn't think straight. It's this Anti-Nazi League thing and because I know a Hollywood screenwriter who's been blacklisted. You know. You met him.

They wanted me to name friends of his and mine that we knew at College. How can they do this? How can people believe all this garbage about good people? He claimed the 5th Amendment. He hasn't worked for four years as far as they know. But he writes for me under another name. They don't know that of course. Thank God. But am I a coward for saying that?

I thought things were improving. I guess they're not. McCarthy is still fuelling the fire with that goddamn bulging briefcase of his which never actually pulls in any 'spies'. Just ruins good folk. Thank God I don't have an employer. I would have been sacked. People think you're guilty if you stay silent. Have they all gone mad to believe this bunch of lunatics? Haven't we just spent years fighting this in Europe?

Have you heard from Jack? Things still seem to be going OK out there. You are our bright spot. My health is OK so don't worry. I'm just mad.

Maybe you can come out for Thanksgiving, or Christmas? The fighting will be over by then, the troops will be home.

Our love always,
Frank

But Rosie couldn't go. Two days later, on 17 November, she fainted as she shopped at Woolworths, and Mrs Eaves took her into the office and pushed her head between her legs.

'When did you last have a period, Rosie?'

She was stroking Rosie's hair, her other hand was on Rosie's wrist. It was a plump hand, like Nancy's, and now Rosie leaned her head against this woman and wept but said it was only the snoek because that had to be the truth.

That afternoon they took two hours off and travelled by

taxi to a doctor that Mrs Eaves knew. There was a brass plate on the wall, polished so that the letters were smoothed almost to flatness. The bell didn't sound outside but a nurse opened the door, showed them upstairs, and gave them magazines to read while they waited on amber-covered chairs.

Mrs Eaves didn't come into the consulting rooms with her. She went alone. There was a large desk, a letter rack, a blotting pad. There was no ink on it. It was white, pure white. The man who rose and shook her hand was Ollie's age. He had a bald head, a moustache, and kind eyes beneath full, bushy brows. How could someone with no hair on their head have so much above their eyes? Rosie wondered, sitting down, feeling too tired to be here. To be anywhere.

'So, we have a problem, eh, Miss Norton?' The man steepled his hands, rested his mouth on his forefingers, pressed his lip up into his moustache.

'I don't know,' said Rosie, bunching her hands inside her coat pockets. She felt nausea rising. She swallowed, watching the signet ring on his little finger.

'Let's have a look shall we?' he smiled, pointing to the back of the room. 'Just leave your petticoat on. The nurse is there waiting.'

She lay still on the couch behind the curtain at the back of the room, looking up at the coved ceiling, feeling strange hands pressing her. She lifted her legs as he asked. She answered his questions, not looking at him. Tracing the crack which wound up the wall, beneath the coving, then on to the ceiling until it was finished. This could not be happening to her. This man wasn't real. The nurse, who would not meet her eyes, wasn't real.

She dressed, and walked to the chair again.

'Well, my dear. You are almost certainly pregnant. We'll run a test, just to confirm, but there's really no need.'

His hands were steepled again. He tapped his teeth this time. She watched that, listened to that. She didn't think of the words which had been in her own mind for six weeks. It wasn't possible. It couldn't be possible. What would she do? For God's sake, what would she do?

She stooped to pick up her bag from the floor. She said nothing. She couldn't speak. There was too much fear.

'There are things that can be done.' The man was playing now with a paperknife, turning it over and over, the light flashing on its blade. He stopped, looked up at her. 'You aren't married?'

Rosie covered her left hand but then said, 'No.' He knew that already. He had called her Miss Norton. Oh God. What would she do?

'How will you support the child?'

She shook her head. Until those words she had not thought of a child, only of the shame.

'I don't know.'

The doctor hesitated, looked at her, then down at the desk. 'I can help but you realise it must be discreet. It would be quick and painless. Not in a seedy room in some dirty street. But it will cost a hundred guineas.'

Rosie thought of the hop-yards, the sticky smell on her hands, the gypsies who brewed potions. The Welsh girl who had drunk some on a hot and heavy night and then screamed in pain all night but smiled for the rest of the picking because there would be no disgrace, not this time.

But Jack had been at the hop-yard, Jack had smiled and held her. Jack had thrust himself inside her on the cold damp moors and she had wanted him. Not like that, not in that way perhaps. But she had wanted him and she loved him, even if he no longer loved her. This child was part of him. She counted the breaths she was taking, they were in time with the clock on the mantelpiece.

'No, thank you.' Rosie stood up, handing him his consultation fee. The movement made her feel faint. She sat again. He came round the desk, put his hand on her shoulder.

'Will the father marry you?'

'I will be quite all right, thank you,' Rosie said, rising, but slowly this time.

She went to the GP. The next week she collected iron tablets from the chemist in her lunch hour and nodded to Mrs Eaves.

'The baby is due at the end of June,' she said quietly.

Mrs Eaves told her she must sit with her feet up and rest as much as she could at work. She must carry nothing heavy, but a shorthand pad wasn't heavy, neither were the articles she had to sift. Mrs Eaves also said she should go back to America but Rosie said she couldn't. Frank and Nancy had enough to worry about and she couldn't face their disappointment, the ending of all their hopes for her.

'How would Jack find me, when he comes home?' she said and wouldn't allow herself to see the doubt in Mrs Eaves's eyes or acknowledge the same doubt herself.

It was at night that the fear grew and cut the breath in her throat, when she was away from the lights of the office and the smiles of the other girls. It was when she was alone that she allowed herself to think of the child that was growing and she didn't know if Norah would let her stay until Jack came back at Christmas. Because she had to believe that he would, just as she had to believe that he would write. Goddamn it, Jack, write. You must write. Because there was still an anger that swept her as well as fear and love and it helped to keep her strong.

In the first week of December Frank wrote with the details of the Chinese assault which had pushed the UN forces back, slaughtering them in the narrow valleys, even though they marched on only a handful of rice. How Mao's men had marched on through the snow, capturing, fighting. How the British Forces had carried out rearguard duties. How brave they had been. Had she heard from Jack? Was he all right? They would not now be home for Christmas.

Rosie went round to Ollie who opened the door, his face setting when he saw her.

'Is he all right?' she asked because there was no place for anger or her own fear. There was only the thought of Jack and Korea.

Ollie looked at her. 'I'll let you know if he isn't.' He shut the door.

That night she fainted as she stood to take her plate to the sink. Her cheese was still on the plate. She hadn't been able to eat. Harold carried her to the armchair by the fire, Grandpa's chair, and Rosie cried, her head down in her hands, because Grandpa wasn't here and neither was Jack. But Norah was, standing in front of her, her stockings rolled down round her ankles, her slippers trodden down at the back.

'You're pregnant, aren't you?' Norah's hands were on her hips.

Rosie wiped her face with the back of her hands and nodded.

'Does that Jack know?'

Rosie shook her head.

'Then you'd better write and tell him.'

'I can't.'

Norah slapped her face then hard, catching Rosie's hair, jerking her head to one side.

'You're a bloody little slut. Why not? Isn't it his? Is it that Joe's?'

Rosie gripped the arms of the chair. She pushed herself back into it, away from Norah who was leaning forward, her face ugly. She would stay in Grandpa's chair, then she would be safe. It would all go away. All of it. It would roll away to the time before all this.

'Go on then, whose is it?' Norah insisted.

'It's Jack's, but I can't tell him. He's left me. He wants to make up his mind whether he loves me. He'd come back if I told him, but I'd never know whether he wanted to.' Rosie reached out her hands. 'Can't you goddamn understand? I love him. I can't do that to him.'

Rosie looked at Harold now. He was kind sometimes but now his face was filled with contempt.

'So you're alone. Lovely little Rosie hasn't anyone to love her. Now you'll know what it's like.' Norah was reaching down, pushing at Rosie, pulling at her, forcing her from the chair. 'I was left with you and Grandpa. I was alone.'

Rosie clutched at her, she felt sick again. 'But Grandpa loved you, and Grandma. You know they did. Grandma most of all. What the hell are you talking about?' Norah was still pushing her out of the kitchen, towards the hall, and Rosie didn't have the strength to stop her.

Norah shouted in her face now, pulling her back, jerking her to a stop. 'But you had the best. You still have. You go to America, you bring back candy. Push it in my face. You little slut. Well, you've got more than you bargained for out of all this love, haven't you? You're an alley cat.' She pushed her towards the foot of the stairs.

Rosie felt her legs growing weak, her head heavy. The blackness was gripping her again. Sweat drenched her body. She clung to the banister, sank on to the stairs.

'Get out by the morning,' Norah hissed, standing above her, watching.

'I can stay as long as I need to,' Rosie said, anger driving the sickness back, but only for a moment. She leaned her head down on her knees. 'Grandpa said.'

'And what do you think Grandpa would say to this bastard you're bringing into the world? You don't think he'd want it in his house, in his neighbourhood. Where it'd bring disgrace. Where his rose growers would know.'

Norah left her, went back into the kitchen, shut the door. There was no light left. Just darkness. And Rosie knew Norah was right. There were too many memories here. There was too much of the past which needed to be guarded for Grandpa. She must go. It was Christmas in three weeks and it was time for her to go. To find some privacy.

CHAPTER 16

The hospital was clean and white and light. And so cool. Jack was eased on to the bed. The pain was all over him now, sweeping, cutting, and he groaned, turned his head, watched the naval nurse as she smiled. Looked at the bag on top of his locker which contained toilet necessities, playing cards, cigarettes and sweets. There was writing paper too.

He looked away. He wouldn't need that. Not to write to Rosie. Not now, not ever. He wouldn't write to Ollie either. Why tell him?

'You'll be going up to theatre soon. There'll just be a small prick now.' The nurse smiled at him again but his lips wouldn't work to smile back.

It was two weeks before the pain left him and then only in snatches in which he watched the ward, heard the clatter of trolleys, the murmur of voices. But then it claimed him again so that he didn't know which was morning, which was afternoon. He didn't know which was night, which was day.

All he knew was that Korea seemed further away than a three-day boat trip. There were no flares, no bugles. There were no screams. There was no Tom. There was no American dying of burns. No American he had to shoot.

But there was the smell of disinfectant, the gentle hands of the nurses who soothed the boy across the way when he groaned, who soothed Jack when he woke screaming from dreams in which he shot the American, again and again, but the flames kept burning, the hand kept reaching out and the face which called to him was Ed's. Yes, Korea was far away and England even further.

But now the times without pain were longer. He watched the clock move round and the nurses with charts, and smiles, and soft voices, and it was all so clean, so ordered. There were no decisions to be made, no questions to be asked except, 'What day is it?'

'It is December eleventh. Now rest.'

Each morning he was a little stronger and each day and night the dreams faded until at last he did not sleep in the day, or cry out at night.

That morning he ate breakfast, biting into crisp toast, and smiled at the boy opposite who smiled back. There had been no groans from him either.

He watched as the doctor did the rounds, first one bed, then the other. The sheets were starched and correctly turned, the pillowcases too. The Sister coughed, the doctor nodded and then they came to him and he felt the tension rise in him. He was better. He knew that. The doctor would know too. He would send him back, into the battle.

The doctor checked his bandage, talked to the Sister, laughed when Jack said he would be ready to do the town by the evening.

'Maybe next month. Maybe,' the doctor said.

Jack touched the bandage, feeling the tension relax, feeling his face smile. Thank God, he would be here for that long at least. He wouldn't be returning to the snow, the cold, the fear. He could stay here where there was no life outside the ward, outside the cool drinks, and the kind nurses, and the ache of his arm.

The Staff Nurse smoothed his sheets as the doctor moved on. 'A little bit longer then,' she said.

'You knew I was frightened?'

'You all feel the same. Why not? I would.'

'Each day,' the boy across the ward shouted, 'there are letters delivered. I bet my girl sends me one.' Jack had written none. He would receive none and so he turned from the Sister who stopped at each bed but his. Everywhere there were letters, three for the boy across the ward. All his had SWALK written round the flap.

Now there was silence as they read them and further silence as the letters were replaced in the envelopes and visions of home came too close.

He had none of that. He had none of their pain. The ache that he felt deep inside wasn't love. He had told himself that. It was anger. There was no love any more. He knew that. He remembered Tom. His wife must know by now.

He watched instead the Japanese flower girl who came to the ward with a trolley heaped with flowers and foliage. She wore bobby sox, and a skirt and blouse, and she almost looked American, but not quite. There was the golden skin, the lowered eyes, the small steps.

He wished that she wore a kimono like the girls he had seen on the way to the hospital. He didn't want anything American in here.

She took flowers and leaves to the central table. Her hands were small and quick. She undid the copper pulley, and lowered the existing arrangement which hung above the ward's central light. He hadn't noticed it before.

She tipped the faded blooms into a basket, emptied the water into a bucket on the trolley, refilled the vase, arranged the flowers, slowly now, and the foliage, then raised the arrangement back up above the light. That night, a small blue spotlight illuminated the flowers and he dreamed of the hop-yards and heard the bees, smelt the hops. Then the scent of roses, the scent of the past, filled the air and he woke crying, but he told the Sister it was the pain.

With each day he grew stronger and the nurses began to decorate the wards as Christmas approached. He and Bill from the bed across the way held the ladders while the nurses climbed and pinned streamers and foliage and the other men whistled and cheered.

That night he dreamed of Rosie making streamers because it was 20 December and in the morning he was running a fever and his wound had become infected. He was too ill to notice Christmas, too ill to open the presents forwarded from Ollie; the tie from Maisie, the letter from Lee, the shirt with no card, which he knew was from Rosie.

'I'm too ill,' he shouted to the nurse and pushed them all from the bed, making her take them from the ward, but keeping Ollie's card and the money he sent and looking up at the flowers which glowed throughout the night.

It wasn't until the middle of February that he was able to move to the convalescent ward and now he knew, they all knew, that though the Communists were pushing them back in the centre, the Chinese supply lines were in doubt.

In the west of Korea US and British troops had recaptured the port of Inchon which had been taken when the Communists carried forward their attack. UN troops were also shelling Seoul which was yet again in the hands of the Communists. On the east coast the South Koreans, supported by naval bombardment, had driven up the coastal highway to the 38th parallel.

They all knew this, but they didn't talk about it. They didn't want to remember, nor did they want to go back.

The next week they had a private in who had been injured when the Allied forces took up positions in a twenty-five-mile arc to the south of Seoul. He told them that Communist resistance had stiffened. That the fourth battle for Seoul was about to begin. That he hoped it would be over before he was returned as fit for active service. He was a conscript. He was nineteen. Jack felt old at nearly twenty-one. He didn't want to go back either, but neither did he want to go to England.

The flower girl came to this ward too while letters were delivered and so Jack heaved at the pulley for her with his right hand. His left was still bandaged, still in a sling which dragged at his neck. Each day he pulled it and smiled and they spoke of the coldness of the weather, the beauty of the flowers, and her voice was sometimes harsh as voices were in the Japanese tongue she told him. But her lips were shaped and gentle, her eyes demure and black. And he didn't have to look at the men opening their mail.

They talked of the summer and the sun that would come and she told him of the giant fish fashioned from bamboo and covered with painted cloth which is launched each July by Toyahama fishermen in honour of the ocean gods. She told him how the Japanese people bore gifts of rice to the dead in the graveyards and he thought of Rosie taking roses to her grandpa, but he didn't want to think of her. She was the past. She was where the pain was.

So he listened again to the flower girl, whose name was Suko, and she told him that their language could mean different things, that their symbols had many meanings. How the white dots of flowering plum and the red dots of camellia keep the

Japanese winter from ever being quite dead. He should travel to one of the unbombed cities, she said, when he was more able, and search for the outward signs of the Japanese spirit which had survived defeat and Hiroshima and Nagasaki. The spirit which had sought and found peace.

'For, Jack-san, you have need of that spirit,' she said as she lifted each leaf, each petal, and put them into the bag before pushing the trolley from the ward.

Jack did not help her again. He walked down the corridors, into other wards, talking to the men, looking out at the deep snow, sensing the cold which crackled in the air. He had no need of peace. It was the others who struggled and lashed and betrayed.

In March he took a small Japanese cab into the town and the cold was still sharp in the air. He had three weeks' Rest and Recuperation and would return to a hostel each night, the Sister had said, smiling, unless, of course, he found something more pleasurable to do.

'Sort yourself out, soldier,' she said as he stopped and looked back at her. She was Australian, big and kind, but Jack walked away from her and did not look back. There was no room for that sort of pleasure in his life now.

He looked out from the cab windows at the snow which had been pushed from the road and the pavements. He saw the street walkers, the Cadillacs, the Buicks, the American enlisted men who stood in groups on the street corners, chatting to the Japanese girls, kissing them, linking arms. He turned from them.

He paid the cab driver as they pulled up outside the hotel where he was to meet Bill, and was glad that Tom wasn't here to see this wealth amongst the people who had imprisoned him. Glad that Ollie wasn't here because there were no new cars available in England.

He climbed the marble steps, nodded to the Japanese bellhop, walked through to the bar. Bill was there, he was drunk, and there was beer on the counter where he had slopped it. There was a glass chandelier above them, soft music playing, nuts and crisps in bowls on the bar. Whisky lined the wall behind the barmen. There was no hint of a war being played out on their doorstep. Was there any hint in England?

'Let's eat,' Jack said, taking Bill's arm, steering him through the tables where beautiful people sat, staring.

'Don't you know there's a bloody war on?' Jack said to one girl with blonde hair and a wide mouth sitting with an American Captain. Their hands were linked. They both wore wedding rings.

'Sure, honey, but not in here,' she drawled and laughed. 'And not back in Iowa either.'

Bill lurched and Jack steadied him, walking him through, past the Japanese head waiter towards a spare table. There were flowers on the thick white tablecloth. There was an arrangement carved out of ice up near the stage. A band played a selection of Frank Sinatra's songs.

They ate a steak which was tender and rare and rice cooked in saffron and Jack didn't order wine, only water, and watched as Bill ate and then drank, slowly, carefully, and only when his plate was empty did they leave.

Jack drove him back to his room. Put him to bed, sat with him because the boy was laughing, then crying, and it was only when he slept that he returned to his own bed.

The next day he drank beer in the town with Bill, but not much, and then they walked past underwear shops full of GIs buying lingerie for the Japanese girls on their arms. They stopped at a restaurant which smelt of beer and fried fish.

They climbed narrow stairs and sat on large cushions, cross-legged. There were other soldiers there, laughing, drinking. There were geishas with white corn-starched faces and sticky hair who danced with them when they had eaten the fish which the chef had cooked in a deep pan of oil, swishing it round with long chopsticks.

The Sergeant who sat at the end told them that these girls were 'after the war' geishas who were not trained but who bought a kimono and pretended for the Americans.

Jack left then. He wanted nothing that the Americans sought or had possessed.

He borrowed a jeep the next afternoon and drove to the address that the Australian sister had given him when he called on her first thing that morning. She had kissed him on the cheek too, saying again, 'Just sort yourself out.'

As he drove he looked at the paddy fields pressed up against the tarmac, seeing through the thawed and muddy snow that every space had been cultivated, even the tiny gap between the ditch and a filling station where GIs were buying petrol for their jeep which was full of Japanese girls. He remembered Suko saying that there were too many people and not enough land.

There were no straggling copses, no hedges. In Japan, Suko had said, there were only disciplined, trained trees. There was no space for wanton growth. He passed small paper-windowed houses which soon became jammed together as he approached a village which was more like a town. They were jammed too tightly for fields, too tightly even to breathe it seemed. There were people walking, so many people. As the road narrowed and the houses took the light from the street he looked at the piece of paper in his hand. He stopped the jeep. He asked directions of an old man dressed in black, slowly, in English.

The man pointed. 'Leave jeep. Walk. Ask. Police.'

Jack did, passing tiny shops with paper doors, all with lights which shone through the paper, out into the street. There was a police box on the corner. Jack asked again.

'Keep on. Don't turn. It on right.'

Children ran past in quilted coats, shrieking, laughing. Was Lee doing that in the cold of America?

There were restaurants on either side of the narrow alleys he walked along. One opened on to the street, revealing people eating fish at small tables. So many people and they were all so small, like Suko.

He was there now. He stopped but the door was paper. How did he knock? He couldn't so he called out instead, 'Suko, it's Jack.' He waited, then called again. 'Suko. It's Jack. I've been rude. I ran away from you. In the ward. I'm sorry. I've come to say I'm sorry.'

The door slid back, and Suko was standing there in a kimono, not bobby sox. Her blue-black hair was pulled back. She bowed, three times.

'Jack-san, this is an honour.' She stood to one side. 'Please put your shoes here.' She pointed to the left of the door.

Jack stopped, looked at her. She wore no shoes. There was a Shinto shrine in the room. He stooped, unlaced his boots, placed them next to hers and entered.

He felt too big, too white. He nodded at the old lady who came forward and bowed. He bowed too. Christ, he was so *big*.

They sat on tatami cushions and his ankles hurt as he crossed his legs. Suko laughed, then covered her mouth with her hand.

'You will eat with us?'

Jack nodded and watched the old woman cut each item carefully. The brazier exuded heat, the charcoal had a sweet smell. She tossed and turned the fish and the vegetables, and Jack could find little to say, but Suko didn't speak either. They both watched her grandmother.

They ate with chopsticks and Jack was awkward and clumsy but no one laughed and so he tried again and it was good.

'Perhaps you would come with me tomorrow to find that unbombed town?' Jack said, but Suko shook her head.

'No, Jack-san, that is for you alone. But I take you to see Japan. I take you to puppets, to Osaka with its canals. I take you to the theatre.'

Her voice was soft but the harshness was still there. It always would be. Was there still that faint drawl in Rosie's voice? But what did it matter? She meant nothing to him now.

The next day they drove to Osaka and then along the roads where the piled up snow was melting. Men trudged up and down alleys with wicker baskets on their back. Women passed with babies strapped to their backs. An old battered car passed with Japanese bobbysoxers singing.

What would Tom think?

The next day they watched a puppet show where the Punch and Judy he had remembered from Southend paled into insignificance. These puppets were life-size with their puppeteers alongside, visible. There was no laughter, only tears. No farce, only tragedy, and Jack sat back and waited to be bored. But Suko sat still beside him, her golden skin smooth and pure, and soon the puppets took over the puppeteers and became savage, harsh, too strong, and Jack clenched his hands and believed.

They ate at a restaurant and Suko smiled and nodded and her hands were as delicate with the chopsticks as they had been with the flowers.

As they drove back alongside the fields she told him that in the spring the farmers would pull harrows and the women would dig, then sow. She told him how the farmers had always sold their daughters, in order to have fewer mouths to feed, in order to survive.

'Where are *your* parents?' he asked.

'They were in Nagasaki,' she said. 'They did not survive.'

Jack didn't visit Suko for a week. He didn't know what to say, what to do, but when he called outside her house again she slid back the door and smiled, took him in, gave him green tea. As they sat cross-legged on the floor he said, 'I'm sorry. I couldn't come. I didn't know what to say about your parents.'

Suko nodded. 'I know. One day you will be able to face pain, even that of others. For now you cannot. You must wait.' That was all.

They drove to the theatre, where actors took over the role of the puppets, and Jack listened to Suko explaining as they roared and laughed and cried that the message of this play was blind loyalty, whatever cruel and bloody acts this might require.

Jack watched the disembowelling and could not understand the pleasure it gave the audience, the pleasure it gave Suko. He watched the dancing and was glad when they returned to her small house, away from the colour of the pageant, away from the turbulence, and as he drew up to her house he turned and kissed her mouth. It was soft, small, and so was the body he held and stroked, and so was the hand which smoothed his hair and touched his lips and brought feeling back into his life.

'I've only one week left,' he breathed into her hair.

'You will come tomorrow and we will love,' she said.

Suko's grandmother was not there in the house when he arrived and Suko led him into the room, holding his hand in hers, not kissing him, not allowing him to kiss her.

'Not yet, Jack-san. You are in Nippon now. You must be slow. You must take time.'

He sat down on the cushions and she smiled and bowed, then left the room, and he watched her move with her short steps, one in front of the other. He watched the neatness of her body and wouldn't think of Rosie. She was dead to him now. The ache in his heart was anger, not love.

He drank the saki that Suko had left, first one glass and then another, and then another until there was softness in the room and an easing of his body.

It was then she called.

'Jack-san.'

He rose, his mouth dry, and walked into a small room which was filled with steam from a bath in the centre and the damp heat smothered him, but she was there too, in a white bathrobe, beads of sweat on her face, on her neck, beads which ran down on to her breasts.

She undid his buttons, slipped his clothes from his body, washed him down with soap, her hands gentle, probing, and he wanted her but she kissed his mouth, then pointed towards the bath. He climbed into the water which was almost scalding.

She rubbed his back with soft bark and it was as though there had been no past, there would be no future. There was only the present.

He rose from the water and slid her bathrobe from her shoulders, letting it fall from her body, and the heat he felt was not from the steam, but from within. She was golden, soft and smooth. So small. So very small.

He held her to him, wetting her, kissing her, tasting her sweat, tasting his on her. Then he carried her out into the room where the futon was already laid on the floor, and there, in the heat and smell and the light of the charcoal fire, he made love to her, gently, softly and then with a passion which swept him from the paper house to the cold hillside in Yorkshire, and when he cried he knew why, but he pushed his knowledge away.

He was to spend his last days at Suko's house, she told him. Her grandmother was not there. She had left because Suko asked her to, she told Jack at dawn as they sipped tea from the cups without handles.

'For us to be together, Jack-san,' she said, then set her cup down, took his from him, and they made love again, and again.

Suko worked each morning and wouldn't stay in the village with him.

'I make the flowers bring joy. It is my peace, Jack-san,' she said, her eyes lowered as she stood before him. 'You go to your friends. You return at night.'

Jack drove again to the theatre, walking over the bridge, looking down into a stream with ice clusters at the edge. He looked back down the path. There were cherry trees.

An old man stopped. 'In the spring the blossom blooms. Life begins again.'

Jack nodded and made himself walk into the theatre. He sat and listened and shrank from this culture which was Suko's.

They made love that night and the next and there was nothing that was savage, only everything that was gentle. They had four nights left and he whispered that he would come back when the war was over. He would never leave her.

'You're so beautiful.'

Jack held her, feeling her slightness against him, seeing the blackness of her hair against the pillow. She shook her head, then told him of her childhood, of her life with her grandmother as the bombs rained down. She told him of the American who had come with the occupying forces and he stiffened. He could smell the charcoal, feel its heat.

She kissed his mouth. 'I loved him. He loved me. He went back. He died on a plane which crashed as he landed. I loved him. I will always love him. You love someone. You will always love them. We find comfort with each other, that is all, Jack-san. You will not come back to me.'

He was standing now, standing over her, seeing her golden skin against the futon. Had her American seen her like this?

'Has he?' he screamed at her.

She stood now. 'Come and lie with me. We are happy together because we both have a heart which belongs to another. We give comfort.'

She was stroking him now. 'We give comfort, Jack-san. We cast the shadows from our lives for a while, the pain deep inside is soothed.'

He felt her hands, her lips on his chest, his belly, his thighs and knew why he had been back to the theatre. It was there, watching the Kabuki, watching the warrior, his face contorted, his limbs stiff and cruel, that he had recognised the savagery that was in his own heart.

The next day he travelled to Kanazawa, where there was no sign of bombing, where it was as it had stood for centuries. He walked. He stood and looked at the mossy stillness behind an ancient wall. Children were laughing and playing in the distance but he barely heard them.

He walked on to a cottage, and stood in the doorway as a peasant bowed. He smelt the sweetness of the rush matting, and saw the white of an early-flowering plum set as a symbol of stillness in a world which was mad.

He walked in the garden which nestled against the base of the eastern hill. It was walled, self-contained, still. There was an ordered stream, a bridge and no wind stirred.

He could smell again the hops, see the bines, trace the initials on the gate with his fingers. He could see Rosie.

He drove back to the village, back to Suko, back to her arms and her bed and she held him as he slept and that night it was as though he was a child again and the next night, and the next.

He flew back on Monday. His shoulder was stiff but what did that matter? He strapped himself into the bucket seat. All around was the smell of the disinfectant that had been sprayed on the plane's arrival. He clutched the seat belt as the engine roared, swallowed as the plane clawed through the sky. He looked down at the Straits of Korea, and thought of Suko, her body, her sweetness. He thought of the hills he was returning to and then the hills where the bines grew. He had a letter to write.

He looked at the sea again, and heard a distant echo of Chinese bugles.

CHAPTER 17

Norah did not say goodbye the morning Rosie left but Harold came to the end of the yard while Norah dressed in the bedroom. He took Rosie's arm and told her that he would forward any mail if she let him know her address. He gave her two pounds towards her fares.

She took it, kissed his cheek, remembered Butlins and told him that he must keep on with his brass rubbing.

'You mustn't let her take that away from you.'

Now, as she walked to Woolworths, she remembered how Grandma had tried to stop Grandpa's visits to the Rose Club, how Norah had tried to cut down his rose bushes. She dropped her cases and ran back, down the street, down the back alley, into the yard, into the kitchen. Harold was packing his rubbing wax into a grip. He wore cycle clips.

'Harold, what about the roses? Can you stop her?' Rosie was holding the door. She felt the nausea rise but she wouldn't be sick. Not here, not now.

He did up the buckles on the bag, walked to the doorway, then into the yard, strapping his bag to the back of his bike, looking round at the roses then back at her.

'I think so. I like them too. Don't worry. I'll think of something.'

He nodded, pushed his bike out into the alley, stopped, looked back.

'I don't agree with what you've done. With the baby and all that. It's a disgrace. But good luck.' He mounted the bike, then nodded towards Ollie. 'Don't worry. We won't tell him. Norah doesn't want anybody to know.'

He was off then, and Rosie left, looking back, remembering Grandpa shelling peas, his big fingers pushing their way up the pod, her small ones too. And Jack's hands taking five, throwing them up into his mouth. For a moment she could smell Maisie's bread and dripping and hear the echoes of the past.

At the store Mrs Eaves wanted to come with her to look for a bedsit but Rosie shook her head.

'No, I must do it alone but would you ring my office, please? Just tell them I'm ill and I'll be in tomorrow.'

She left her bags though, then caught a bus to Soho because that was where she had been with Jack. That was where the music still played, where there was still hope, warmth. It was a place where she would not be judged as she would be elsewhere, down each street, in each shop.

On the bus she felt sick, she felt alone, because Jack had always been with her before. She took slow breaths, pushing her hands against her mouth, feeling the clammy sweat on her forehead, the cold which swept through her before the vomit. She pushed herself from her seat, out on to the platform, ringing the bell, stepping off, ignoring the shouts from the clippie. She walked into a side street, and leaned against the wall, breathing, counting till at last it passed.

She caught another bus and this time the nausea did not reappear. She walked down Berwick Street where they were putting out the rubbish from the restaurants. She stopped, asked if they knew of any accommodation. They shook their heads.

It was so different in the day. There was no music sweeping out of the cellars, no tarts touting for custom. Instead they were collecting the milk from their doorsteps along with old ladies doing the same. She passed the baker's where people were queuing for their morning bread and barbers who were already open, already snipping.

A violinist played in the alley which connected the two street markets. A man stood opposite shouting that Jesus Saves. He grabbed at her arm, pushed a leaflet into her hand. She dropped it like others had done amongst the rotting vegetables and the woodshavings. She walked along the stalls, listening to the woman in a headscarf shouting.

'Christmas is coming, the goose is getting fat, but what about bleeding me if you don't buy me spuds?' The woman was digging into the money pocket of her apron, she wore fingerless gloves, her skin was shiny from the coins, her nails dirty, and

Rosie turned away. Jack had been able to charm the birds out of the bleeding trees, one woman had said.

She walked along the dirty streets, climbing steps to the peeling front doors of four-storeyed houses, knocking on doors but always there were no rooms. She stopped and had Camp coffee in a café. The teaspoon was chained to the counter. The sugar was clumped on the spoon. It was warm, it was sweet. What more did she need?

She walked in the other direction. It was lunchtime, the pubs were open. Music came from them and laughter. A newspaper seller was packing up for the day.

Rosie was hungry, tired, but she had nowhere to sleep for the night. She walked on past a newspaper shop. There were advertisements in the window. One was for a room to let. She wrote down the address, asked in the shop for directions.

'Just down the road. Second on the left,' the man said, serving a Cypriot with a packet of pipe cleaners.

She found it. Climbed the steps which were crumbling at the edges. There was a basement beneath her, a blanket strung up on a string. The courtyard smelt of tomcat. There were three dustbins. She looked away towards the door which was opening.

A small woman stood there, with neat hair, neat clothes and a smile which she flicked at Rosie when she asked to see the room.

They climbed the brown-painted stairs to a room on the top floor at the rear that looked out over the backs of other houses, pubs, and clubs. But she could see the sky. She took it.

Mrs Eaves came back with her to carry her bags. It was cold and dark as they left the bus but now music was soaring from the basements, castanets from one, swing from another, and Rosie smiled. They used the key that the woman had given her. The light went out before they reached the first landing and they switched it on again but again it went out before they reached her room. Rosie laughed. Mrs Eaves didn't.

'Come to us, Rosie. Please. You can't stay here. You might fall. Does she know about the baby?' She dropped her voice to a whisper.

Rosie felt the laugh die. 'No.'

Mrs Eaves put down the cases while Rosie unlocked the

door. 'Well, she said no children on the card. She might throw you out when it begins to show. Come to me then.'

Rosie nodded, but she wouldn't. She was alone now. She would be alone until Jack came back.

There was only a forty-watt bulb in the light and no shade. There was one blanket on the bed but Rosie had brought her jumper-blankets, and her own sheets.

There was a sink and a wooden draining board that was sticky with other people's soap and mess. There was a gas ring and a gas fire which Mrs Eaves tried to light, but the meter had run out. They put money in and it plopped as Rosie held the match to it, flaring blue, then yellow. Its hissing filled the room. There was a table covered in oilcloth, only one chair.

Mrs Eaves took her to an Italian café for tea. She knew the owner and his wife. They had met in the war when she had come here with her GI.

They ate baked beans and chips but could smell nothing but coffee. There were onions hanging against the pine-covered walls but Rosie wouldn't let herself think of Jack and the onion seller in the pub. The other tables were full. Young men with scarves trailing on the floor, wearing old coats, laughing, talking, flicking out rhythms on the tables, talking jazz.

There was a phone on the wall. It rang. The small Italian who had served them threw his teacloth over his shoulder, grabbed the receiver, and, waving his hands in the air, shouted across the room.

'Luke, for you again. You give them my number. Always my number. You all give them my number. I try to feed you. How can I when you make me your office too?' He dropped the receiver, it swung on its wire.

Mrs Eaves laughed and called across, 'Just the same, Mario, eh?'

'Worse, Anne. Much worse.' Mario was shaking his head.

'You need more help.'

'I know, I know. You'll come then, Anne?' He laughed, and walked through to the back.

Rosie moved the Worcester sauce and the salt and pepper into a neat line.

'Everyone is so young,' she said, looking round, moving the sauce bottle behind the pepper then back again.

'You're young, Rosie.' Mrs Eaves's hand was plump and warm and Rosie clung to her for a moment and then sat back, watching Luke at the telephone, laughing, putting his thumbs up to his friends at the table.

'We got the gig. Five pounds!'

They cheered.

'Not any more,' Rosie said, touching her stomach.

That night as she lay in the room, moonlight came in through the gap in the curtains which didn't meet. She listened to the noise of the house, the banging doors, the shouting from the room next-door. There was a smell of cabbage everywhere.

She pulled the blankets around her head. The bed was damp. She was alone. But at least she had her job and that would enable her to go forward, to carve out a future for herself and the baby.

There were shadows as clouds passed in front of the moon. There was the faint sound of a trumpet and she thought of his arms around her, holding her. She ran her own hands across her shoulders, held her arms, pretended they were his hands.

The next morning she took the bus back to Middle Street and left her address with Ollie and with Harold, then rushed in to work, travelling back to Soho in the evening. She wrote to Nancy and Frank, telling them she had found a place of her own, giving them her address, telling them she wanted her freedom, telling them she was happy. They mustn't know of the baby. They would be worried and they had enough.

At eleven the next morning, the Editor called her into the office to offer her the job of Assistant Features Editor. Rosie felt the sudden thrill of success, the pleasure which those words brought, but she knew, clasping the arms of the chair, that she would have to tell the elegant woman in front of her that she was pregnant.

'Will it matter, Miss Stephens?' she asked.

It did matter. She was sacked on the spot and told to take her things from her desk and leave at once.

She did. She packed her shorthand pad and her pencils and walked out of the office and it was not until she was walking in and out of the Soho shops, asking for work, that she really believed that her future had been snatched from her and she had to lean against a pub wall and turn her face to the bricks, because it was all too much.

It seemed hours that she stood there, but it was only minutes. Then a man came up and asked her for sixpence for a cup of tea and she dragged one out of her purse, and gave it to him. He was dirty and old. At least, she thought, she was young, and so she pushed herself away from the wall, repeating that to herself.

She asked in more shops, more pubs for a job.

'We need a washer-upper,' said a man with a moustache, flicking his ash on to the floor. 'You'd need to clean the lavs too.'

She said she'd call back. She walked and asked again, crossing Archer Street where musicians were gathered outside the doorways of the agents' and managements' offices.

She stopped outside the Italian café where it was warm and clean and light. It was lunchtime. There was jazz oozing out of a cellar two houses away. She listened, holding the icy railing, putting her hand to her mouth, pushing back the nausea.

The café was full. She pushed through to the counter. Luke was there again, buying coffee for three tables, laughing, throwing shillings on to the counter.

'And one for this girl too,' he shouted to Mario, nodding at Rosie, who flushed. He smiled and she wanted to say, you might not want to, I'm pregnant. But she didn't because there was warmth in his look and in Mario's as he wiped the counter and winked at her.

'I don't know. A bit of success. It goes to their heads.'

Rosie nodded, taking the coffee. 'Thanks.'

She sat by herself on the bench near the counter, watching the ebb and flow of the young men, and young girls. She couldn't join in. She wasn't young any more. How could you be young if you were pregnant? She remembered the contempt in Harold's eyes and in Miss Stephens's too.

Luke sat with the others, then stood up, raising his coffee.

'First gig tomorrow. First bloody gig.' He was laughing, waving to the others at his table to stand. They did. There was a girl with them, long-haired. She hugged a boy with a beard and he kissed her on the mouth and Rosie turned away, burning her tongue on the hot coffee, but it didn't matter.

She ordered toast but with no butter. It made her retch. Mario looked up at her.

'Can you wait? We're so busy. It gets worse and worse. You no want a job?'

She did want a job but she leaned across and said, 'Yes, I need a job. But I'm – '

Mario interrupted. 'I know. Mrs Eaves tell me. I no mind. My wife no mind. You come. She say you good worker. I trust her.'

Rosie looked down at the sugar clumped on the spoon. Jack had trusted a lot of people.

She started work on the spot. She walked through the streamers into the back room piled high with old tables and boxes. On into the kitchen where Mrs Orsini smiled at her, her eyes sweeping down her body.

No, it doesn't show yet, Rosie wanted to scream at her, her face rigid as she looked at the small fat woman, not lowering her glance, though she wanted to.

'Oh, these things happen,' Mrs Orsini said. 'Mrs Eaves, she tell us you are a good girl. You love this man. He leave you.' Her arms were folded, she leaned against the table piled high with rolls. Toast was grilling, spaghetti simmering in a large pan.

'No,' Rosie said as she hung her coat up on the hook along the wall and washed her hands, scrubbing them hard, and then scrubbing them again. 'No, he hasn't left me. He's gone to Korea. He'll come back. He'll write. I know he will.' There were tears running down her face but they didn't reach her voice. That was calm, but not calm enough, for Mrs Orsini held her, patting her back while Mario called from beyond the swing door.

'Where my spaghetti bolognese? You women. Where my spaghetti?'

Rosie wrote to Nancy and Frank that evening when the café had closed and she had made tea in her room, that she had taken a job as manageress of a restaurant and that she would freelance for the magazine.

She walked to the window, pushing up the bottom sash, listening to the jazz, to the shouting, to the drunken singing. Her legs ached, her back ached but she had a room of her own and a job. At least for now, she was all right. She wouldn't look into the future, there was no point.

On 20 December she heard from Frank and Nancy.

Lower Falls
December 1950

Dearest Rosie,

Have you heard anything from Jack? We worry about him.

It's been so cold out there. The frost was 45 at its worst. Rearguard duties fell to the new British brigade just arrived in Korea. That would be Jack.

Over here it is cold too. Joe has suggested that Frank writes under a pseudonym. We are losing readers. The reversal in Korea will not help. McCarthy is shouting louder each day. Our Local Administrator has an alarmingly large chest filled with importance. I just hate him.

Let us know your news about Jack. Let us know how the new job is going. It must be good for you to give up the magazine. We understand that you can't leave right now but come when you can. Frank is fit. He's fighting back. He's angry but not strained, if you know what I mean.

All our love darling girl.
Nancy

PS. The enclosed $40 is your Christmas present. It comes with love.

Rosie went into the café early that day and Mario nodded as she asked him about the decorations. She cut strips, coloured them, stuck them and wouldn't think of the fighting. Mrs Orsini helped and it was almost like being with Maisie again. They pinned them up. Customers came in and helped. Luke held her waist, steadying her beneath the holly which Mario had rushed out and bought in the market.

They drank coffee, and ate toast and omelette in the kitchen when the lunchtime rush was over, and Rosie walked to the post office for Mario at three in the afternoon, looking at the people walking past. Looking at the market traders shouting, dipping their hands into their aprons. The religious man pushed another leaflet into her hands and she turned.

'Don't you know there's a goddamn war on in Korea? Tell them all about that instead of pushing paper in people's faces.'

He turned from her, thrusting his leaflet at an old man. She grabbed him. 'There's a war on and nobody cares. Go on, get your mouth round that.'

But he pulled from her and she dropped the letters. An old man helped her pick them up. They were dirty and she was crying, standing in the street crying. The old man patted her hand and walked away. Everyone walked away in the end.

But then Luke came with Sandy, the girl with the long hair, and they walked back with her to the café, and then on home because the tears would not stop, because the world wouldn't stop either. Because life was too difficult.

She lay on the bed, and felt pain sweep across her back, and then her belly. She breathed slowly, and watched Luke boil the kettle on the ring and Sandy put tea into the pot, smelling it brewing, watching the milk being poured from the bottle, and the pain was still there and she was wet between the legs.

They called a doctor. He came and asked what she had taken. Luke held her hand as she thought of the consultant and his brass plate, his hundred-guinea offer. She thought of the gypsies and their brew and knew she might be losing the baby. All this could be over. She looked round the bedsit. She could go to America. She could stay here. Anything. She could be as young as Luke again and free.

Luke was squeezing her hand. It should have been Jack but he had gone, though her love for him had not. It never would. She turned to the doctor, who was standing over her. No one was taking the baby from her. No one had taken her career. She had done that. She had become pregnant. No one had taken Jack. She had helped to bring that about. It was time she got angry. It was time she began fighting again. It was goddamn time.

'I fell. This baby's part of Jack. It's all I've got of him. Just do your goddamn job. Please.'

Luke squeezed her hand again and Sandy smiled but the pain was too bad. She watched as Luke went to phone for an ambulance from the box on the corner, digging into his pockets for pennies, then looking in her purse. The doctor had to give them the money in the end.

She was in hospital, there were more doctors. There was Mrs Orsini and Mrs Eaves and there were days of rest when Christmas came and went and there was no card from Jack, though she had sent a present to Ollie for him back in November. But she wouldn't grieve because she was back in there, fighting.

In January she was back in Soho and Mrs Eaves and Mrs Orsini had put flowers in the room, and the baby was still inside her. She was fit, the doctor said, but mustn't leap over windmills. She had laughed because for now the world was good. Her baby was alive. She was alive and so was Jack because no telegram had come to Ollie.

There was a letter from Frank and Nancy when she got back to her room, and she returned to work knowing that the Chinese offensive had been halted. The United Nations were on the attack, but no one else that she passed seemed to care.

She served coffee, cooked, smiled, and laughed when Mario pushed a chair beneath her as she cut up the vegetables and asked if she had taken her iron today.

'And what about that soldier?'

He banged the pans when she shook her head.

Luke and Sandy made her sit too when she went out with them on a January evening to hear Luke's band's first gig and the warmth of these people made it seem as though the sun was shining through the fog which drifted and froze on the paintwork.

They sat at candle-lit tables in the basement of Chloe's and Sandy pushed her long hair back from her face, as Luke and the band worked their way down through the tables to the small stage.

'They've worked hard for this, all of them.' Her nail varnish was black. It was chipped. She was smoking in quick sharp bursts.

'Are they good?' Rosie asked.

Sandy smiled. 'You wouldn't know about jazz; I suppose. But yes, they're good.'

It was becoming crowded now. Rosie moved her chair closer to Sandy as a young man squeezed another round the table. Sandy was stubbing her cigarette out in the ashtray.

'It's hard, though, for them. They have to work too *and* fit this in. They need more time to practise. They need a place to practise. The flat's too small. The landlord doesn't like it.'

Rosie bought a beer for Sandy, a lemonade for herself from the girl behind the bar. But then the band was playing and Luke blew a trumpet as Uncle Bob had always dreamed. He explored the middle range, digging out melancholic tones, drawing pictures in the air, dredging feelings out of each person who sat and listened.

His eyes were closed, his foot tapped. He blew bends which broke her heart, he played a break while the others rested, improvising, soaring, growling, the sound beginning in his throat and forcing itself up through the instrument and out into the tone of the note. She smelt the steak on Frank's barbecue, saw Uncle Bob moving towards his band and had to turn from Sandy because of the tears in her eyes.

Luke played, Stan and Jim too, the clarinet and the trombone picking up the rhythm, Jake on the saxophone sliding in but he needed to be more mellow, throaty. She made herself listen again, watching the group through the spiralling cigarette smoke from the young man next to her.

Dave played block chords on the piano which was effective in small doses, but Dave knew that, she could tell, because he used it sparingly. Luke played a solo.

'Maybe he improvises too much,' Rosie said to Sandy, who looked at her through the hair which had swung back across her face.

Yes, Jack would think so, Rosie thought, because he liked Duke Ellington. Did he still?

When they broke for a beer and the clapping had died she spoke to Luke, telling him that she thought he used too much verbal agreement on the arrangements. 'It needs to be written out at this stage. It would be smoother, clearer.' And Jake, on the saxophone, needed improving. But the band was good, very good.

She felt the excitement rise in her as Luke looked at her and nodded.

'You know about jazz, don't you?'

'Yes, Frank taught me. Uncle Bob too. And Jack.'

She looked round as the band left to play another set. The excitement was there in everyone. One day they would be good enough for Bob, she'd make sure of that, but there was a great deal to be done before then.

The next day she poured Luke a coffee, Sandy too, as they came in for their lunch, and then she talked to Mario in the kitchen about the back room. She pointed to the packing cases, to the tables, to the extra space that could be used to bring in customers. She spoke to him about a Jazz Night where the bands could practise in front of an audience who would buy coffee and food.

Mario shook his head but Mrs Orsini nodded, slapping him on the back.

'Why not? Rosie knows what she's doing. That young Luke. He is good, is he not? You will hear all bands and decide. OK.' Mrs Orsini looked at Rosie and then at Mario who spread his hands wide.

'I will go upstairs when it starts. I will lie with my head beneath pillow. You are satisfied?'

'Not quite,' said Rosie, putting the dishes in the sink, talking as she washed. 'The boys are getting calls. They are being taken for a ride. They play for too little money. I want to take the calls for them, act as their manager, their agent. If they agree.' She turned.

'So you want to set up another business. Why not? They use my phone already, why not my staff? You would like a small dance floor. You would like me to swing from the ceiling in a tutu?'

Rosie laughed and so did Mrs Orsini.

'Yes, why not?' Mario said. 'For once there is a light in your eyes. Your Jack should see that. And don't forget you have clinic appointment this afternoon.'

Rosie went along. The nausea had almost stopped. There were mothers with young children in the waiting room. They clung to their mothers' legs as Lee had clung to hers and Jack's. As she had clung to Grandpa. She had forgotten that. She smiled at a blonde child and then at the mother, who looked away and tutted.

She was given iron by the doctor and told by the nurse it would be sensible to wear a curtain ring. Her voice was cold, correct. She gave Rosie details of a Home for Unmarried Mothers.

Rosie bought a ring from Woolworths. She went back to her room, climbed the stairs, breathed in the cabbage. Her legs ached, her back ached, but there was still the jazz.

She stood at the window. The sky was grey, full of snow. There would be snow on the mountains of Korea and he hadn't written. She lay on the bed. It was cold. He still hadn't written. She pushed the ring on to her finger. God damn you, my darling love.

She didn't go into work again that day. She lay on her bed but didn't sleep. All she could see and feel were his arms, his lips, his smiling eyes. All she knew was that she loved him. That night she allowed herself to cry, but only that night because she had his child to work for, to protect. A child who would put his arms around her legs. A child she had not pictured until today.

The next day Mario, Luke and the boys turned out the back room, and set up the tables while she and Mrs Orsini wiped the tables, chairs, the walls that she could reach without stretching. Luke would do anything high.

She stood behind the counter and served coffee and tea and food, listening all the time to the banging, the heaving, telling the customers that Thursday was to be a regular Jazz Night. The playing was free, she said, smiling, but the refreshments were not.

Over thirty came the first night and as people left at midnight a man approached Luke to play a gig at Chertsey on 1 March and offered him five pounds. Luke beckoned to Rosie.

'You'd better talk to my manager, Rosie Norton.'

The man smiled. 'Well, Mrs Norton, I'm Tom O'Toole. So, you manage these boys. Strange job for a woman, isn't it?'

Rosie brought out her drawl. 'It runs in the family. You might have heard of Bob Wallen from Pennsylvania.' She didn't wait for him to acknowledge the name which he might or might not have known. 'These boys can't work for that sort of money. Not now. They were offered twice that last week. I turned it down.'

She waved at Mr Orsini.

'Mr Orsini has had to pay ten pounds tonight and he got them for that because I know him well.'

She nodded to Mr O'Toole.

'Give me a ring sometime. On this number.' She handed him a card. 'But I can't stop now. I have to arrange their itinerary with them. Nice meeting with you.'

She shook his hand, and walked past him to Luke and Mario, gathering the boys around her until Jake said, 'He's gone. You've lost us five pounds.' He was smoking grass and she took it from him, and ground it into the floor, taking him to one side. Her back hurt, her legs ached, she had served coffee until the steam had dampened her hair, until she could stand the ringing of the cash register no longer. She was angry.

'If you ever smoke that goddamn stuff in here again you're out.'

'You don't own us.' Jake's head was down, his shoulders hunched, and it was like Sam again in the rec when she had first come home, but this time there was no Jack to stand by her. This time she was alone but it didn't matter, she was still angry.

Rosie looked round, called Luke over. 'He's smoking grass in here. Mario's been good to us. He could be in trouble. I've told him he's not to do it again or he's out. This is your band. Your decision. But if you want to play here again, smoking is out. Right?'

They had no choice. She knew that. They couldn't practise anywhere else. Luke took Jake to one side. She waited. She saw Luke pat Jake on the shoulder then look round and nod. She smiled, and she knew that there would be good days and bad days, but for now, she was strong enough to carry herself through.

'He'll be back. Don't worry. He'll phone. I know he will.'

He phoned back in March when her skirt was too tight to be done up any more. He offered the band twelve pounds to play in Surbiton, expenses on top of that, and so one night Rosie asked Luke to stay late at the café and told him that they must practise much harder. They were in the real world now. They could go on, even to the US, but there was a great deal of work to be done.

She told him that he should write out more arrangements, then maybe he should try the cornet. Luke agreed, kissed her cheek, said he was sending another band along to see her.

The next day the baby moved, for the first time, and a call

came through from Stone's Club near Birmingham. She talked the fee up to fourteen pounds and now she took a ten per cent cut which the band agreed was really not enough, but she wouldn't take more.

That night she wrote to Frank and Nancy and told them of Luke, glad that at least there was one lie less. But as she sat in front of the gas fire which plopped and hissed, the room seemed empty and bare. There had been no letter from the father of the child that had fluttered inside her and no one to share her pleasure.

CHAPTER 18

A truck took Jack straight towards the North. The enemy were in flight, the Sergeant told him and the twenty others who sat either side of the vehicle, lurching and bouncing past refugees and burnt-out tanks from the earlier United Nations retreat.

Jack leaned on his rifle, looking out at the snow which still covered the rice fields. He would write when he arrived. He would tell Rosie that he loved her, that he always had and always would. That he was coming home, when this was over.

'Shouldn't be long before we're home then, Sarge?' he called out to Sergeant Rivers.

'Who knows? Let's hope you're right,' the Sergeant answered.

They travelled for hours jolting along in the wake of the enemy, passing supply trucks returning empty from the forward positions. There were ambulances, too, but they didn't look at those. Jack flexed his shoulder. It was stiff but that was all. He looked out again at the hills splashed with snow. He wouldn't think of Tom either. He had to get home to Rosie.

He lit a cigarette, the match flame was fierce in the cold. He lit Bert's too, then tossed the box along to the Sergeant. There was a heavy smell of sulphur. He and Rosie would go to the hop-yards when he returned. He drew on his cigarette, jigging his feet to keep warm. Christ, it was cold. But it would be cold for the Chinese too.

They reached camp, leaping down and moving in single file off up the track to Hill 81, hearing the revving of the truck, the grinding of gears as it reversed then turned, leaving them, heading back to Pusan to pick up more troops, more supplies.

'Get on up that hill,' the Sergeant barked. 'Might be a bit of nice digging to welcome you back, work you little invalids in before you go running off towards the border doing your good deed for the West.' He was pointing, jerking his hand, his eyes red with tiredness, his voice hoarse. He looked old.

They headed on up the hill, straining their heads forward, carrying their rifles in both hands across their body, then, as the going got steeper, in one hand as they dug in their boots and their rifle butts, cursing, sweat pouring down their backs.

'Great to be bloody back,' Bert groaned in front of Jack, his boots thick with mud where so many feet had thawed the snow. The sun had gone by the time they reached the top. They went straight to the field kitchen, eating where they stood, looking round at the supplies piled up; the ammo, the Stens, the mortars.

There were look-outs on all sides and there was staccato firing in the distance, to the right and left and dead ahead.

'We move out in the morning. Chase the little buggers. Get your 'eads down where you can,' the Sergeant said, pushing past, cleaning his mess tin with a crust of bread.

Jack did the same, then swilled it with water, put it back in his pack, heaved that up on to his back again and headed towards the fox-hole where Bert was standing, beckoning to him.

At least there was no digging. That had all been done on the last advance and their hole was crowded but there was room against the sides. He didn't sleep in his sleeping bag. He had thrown that away. It was cold, bloody cold, but he slept. But not before he had thought of Rosie and the words he would write when the sun came up.

The Sergeant called them at first light and Jack ate breakfast, heaved at his pack, hearing the thuds and clinks all around. He could hear firing and now there were Mustangs high overhead.

'Keeping the pressure on,' an older regular said, nodding at Jack as he wrote his letter, standing up, pressing on Bert's pack, telling him to stand still for Christ's sake, while he told Rosie that he loved her, that he was coming home when his National Service was over. Begging her to forgive him, sure that she would because he knew she loved him too.

'Come on, get over here,' the Sergeant called and Jack stuffed the letter into an envelope, then pushed through the men to the Padre who had held a service as the field kitchen was packed up. He took letters from the men, waving to them as he set off in one direction and they in another, down the hill, taking up the pursuit, heading towards the firing.

It was then, as he dug his heels into the slope, looking out towards the peaks and snow-shrouded shrubs, that he felt a hand grip his shoulder and heard Nigel's voice say, 'Well, you old reprobate, here we are again. Bet you wish you were back cutting the grass with those scissors.'

Jack swung round, stepped out of line, gripped Nigel's arms, wanting to hug him but their eyes said it all and it was enough. Jack saluted then, heard the Sergeant shouting, 'Come along, if you don't mind, Sir.'

Nigel grimaced, and moved on down the hill as Jack fell back into line.

'Catch up with you later, Private,' he called back.

Jack laughed. 'Yes, Sir.'

And it was not until that evening, when they set up camp, bivouacked between boulders, crouching into the existing hoochies, taking two-hour watches, straining their eyes, cursing the men behind who stumbled on old tins left by the previous occupants, that they had time to talk, pressed up against the perimeter look-out.

'Too much pressure, dear boy. Simply had to take a commission.' Nigel was grinning but he didn't turn, he didn't take his eyes from the land around.

'Yes, Lieutenant Sanders. The pips look exquisite. How long have you been out here?'

'Just two weeks.'

Jack knew it could not have been longer. There was no fear in Nigel's eyes and there was still youth in his face.

'We'll soon clear those gooks,' Nigel said.

'Maybe, but they can march on rice, oatmeal, dried peas. They've been fighting with Mao for years. They plan and execute. They're professionals, mobile, take advantage of the terrain. They may be poorly armed but they take weapons from the dead. And they keep on coming.' Jack remembered the bugles, the screams. He remembered Tom and the burning man. 'Just keep your head down, especially now you're leading my platoon.'

They were whispering, listening. There were tracers in the distance. There were flares but he felt better now that Nigel was here, especially with Tom gone.

Nigel looked at him now. 'You're different, Jack.'

'I've been here longer than you and I've grown up a bit. That's all.'

He punched Nigel's arm when their relief came and crawled into his hole, thinking of Rosie, thinking of Suko, thanking her for all that she had shown him.

They set off the next morning as dawn broke. There had been no bugles, but then there wouldn't be. They were the ones chasing this time, weren't they? They marched all day, between hills, alongside paddy fields, the snow and mud clinging to their boots, their thighs sore from the slapping of their wet trousers. Patrols were sent out. The way had been cleared by the troops up ahead. They marched, they slept, they listened.

On the fourth day they were up with the forward troops and the firing was closer and all around. As evening came they straggled through dark hills. There were trees, there were shrubs and large boulders, and Jack looked to each side, straining his eyes.

The Sergeant came along, speaking to them all, but quietly. 'Seems like a good place for a bloody ambush. Keep your wits about you.'

Jack looked ahead to Nigel, who turned. 'Did you tell them, Sergeant?'

'Of course I bloody told them,' the Sergeant said under his breath and then, more loudly, but not too loudly, 'Yes, Sir.'

No one spoke, they were all listening, walking, praying. So far so good. Jack was breathing through his mouth. The air was cold. There was enough light to see his breath. It was crazy. No one would hear his breath over the noise his bloody feet were making. And over the noise the Centurion tanks that had joined them this afternoon were making as they came up the pass behind them.

He turned. He could see their antennae waving. He looked ahead at Nigel, his head turning from side to side. His shoulders were rigid. Jack's were too. Everyone's were.

Then the firing started, small arms thwacking into the ground around them, mortar thudding, screaming.

'Return fire, get some cover. Keep your heads down,' the Sergeant was shouting, waving his arm towards the paddy fields. They were wet, cold. Jack ran, then sprawled down, full length. The tanks were firing, but one was hit by mortar and exploded. The track was slippery and another tank keeled over into the paddy field.

The Chinese were swarming down the hill now, firing burp guns, throwing grenades, and the bugles were blowing. The endless bloody bugles. Jack looked across at Nigel.

'Get your head down, Sir,' he called and Nigel spun round, then ran crouching towards him, throwing himself down beside Jack. Firing as he did so. The rifle butt rammed hard against Jack's shoulder as he fired, again and again, but he couldn't even feel the pain.

The barrel was hot. He reached for more ammunition. Nigel moved along the line of men, talking, helping to reload the Sten. The Chinese were falling but more were coming in their place.

'Don't they know they're supposed to be retreating?' Jack ground out.

Bert lay on his side reloading. 'Bloody little buggers,' he said again and again, but now they were fading. Fewer came to replace them, and Nigel called, 'We're to make our way across the base of the hill on our left. Orders from HQ. Meet up there with a US Infantry Brigade, or what's left of them. Take casualties with us.' He was speaking in short bursts, as though he'd been running, but Jack was panting too. It was fear.

The first squad moved east while Nigel stayed with the rearguard. Jack ran with the first squad, then set up a rearguard under the Sergeant while Nigel and his men broke out, and ran past them. Now Jack, Bert and six others held the Chinese again who faded and left.

'That's what the book says should happen,' grunted Bert.

'Make the most of that piece of perfection then, sonny,' shouted the Sergeant as he passed.

They marched through the night towards the US Infantry Brigade and ate breakfast with men who drawled and looked like Ed, and Jack, though he loved Rosie, could not speak or eat with them.

The UN forces pushed north relentlessly day after cold day and Jack's platoon slept, ate, and marched, forcing the Communists back, seeing the airstrikes on the hills in front, the burning napalm, and he turned from that, feeling sick.

At night he watched the mortar scoring across the cold sky and wouldn't smoke the American cigarettes which Bert had been given.

It became commonplace to storm an enemy-held hill, firing, gripping the shrubs, pulling themselves up, hurling grenades, fighting hand to hand, plunging their rifle butts into heads, hearing screams all round, Chinese and British. Each time they took the hill, they herded prisoners into lorries then sat, their legs weak, vomiting, their stomachs churning from the smell of death. But at least Rosie would soon have his letter and, at least, soon, this war would be over.

At the end of March the Chinese were pushed across the 38th parallel and Jack's unit dug in on a hill which was scattered with the debris of previous battles. They stepped over abandoned Chinese and American equipment, they picked up pay books and identity tags and the Captain sent these back to Seoul which was once more in the hands of the United Nations.

Digging in was difficult in the sandy, frost-hard ground but none the less they tried.

Nigel and Jack talked on watch and Nigel said that the UN and Truman would be looking for a political settlement after throwing back the enemy, but MacArthur wanted to carry the war to Manchuria.

'He'll have to go,' Jack said. 'Or there'll be another war, with atom bombs this time.' He stared across the quiet sky, thinking of Nagasaki, and Suko's parents.

In April they watched the hills bloom with a profusion of colour which he had never dreamed could exist in this land where there seemed only harshness and poverty.

They watched from the hill as the transport became bogged down in the spring mud, they cleared out the fox-holes and cursed it. Their uniforms were wet from the rains, their skin sore from the chapping, but the war was as good as over, they would be going home soon. So they laughed and smoked, leaning on the stone-built barricades, hearing the rain on their tin hats, on their capes, and thought of England. Of its greenness, its rain, its fog, its rationing, and longed to be there.

They heard that the Gloucesters held the most exposed position on the direct approach to Seoul across the Imjin River but surely the Chinese wouldn't come again. They were beaten. There would be peace, MacArthur had been sacked on 11 April.

But they did come again, at the end of April as green was sprinkling the rice fields and new life was beginning all around. They came with their bugles blowing and the Gloucesters saved the left flank of the UN Corps and held up the advance of the Chinese so that the line could be reformed and held. Out of a force of 622, forty-six officers and men returned.

But Jack didn't have time to grieve, because the Chinese were storming his hill, too, and the air was rent with bugles and cymbals and screams, but Jack wasn't screaming, he was lining up the Sten, hearing it clink against the stones of the barrier, and now he was firing it, as the first wave of Chinese rushed up the hill.

How did they move so fast, for God's sake? He heard the gun, felt it judder, concentrated on that, not the bugles, nor the cymbals. He just fired, while Bert fed in the ammunition and threw water on the barrel to cool it as the night wore on, and there was no sense of surprise any more. He was getting used to all this.

He saw four Shooting Stars scream into the valley and bombard the enemy with rockets and cannon fire and napalm and this time he didn't feel sick. He was angry because he should be going home to Rosie. Not firing through showers of mud thrown up by mortar, not lifting a water bottle to his parched lips, not looking at the men he killed, feeling nothing because more would come in their place to kill him and he would never see Rosie again.

They fought all that day, keeping them at bay, waiting for reinforcements but none came. There were too many Chinese storming the whole line. There were supplies though.

'Thank God,' Nigel said as he slapped Jack's shoulder, telling him he would send a relief to take over the Sten soon.

Jack could see the parachutes with ammunition cases dropping amongst the Chinese instead.

'Oh Christ,' Nigel groaned.

They fought into the evening. They fought as the sun dropped, brilliant red, behind the hills and now, in the dark, they fired by the light of flares, picking out the Chinese, who were still crawling across the valley and up the base of the hill, getting closer to them now.

Nigel came running out to him, crouching, looking at the rain-sodden maps. 'Can you both hold out for a while longer? They're coming up three sides. No relief teams to spare.'

Jack nodded. 'Keep your bloody head down, Nigel.' He turned. He hadn't called him Sir. They looked at one another and smiled. There was no time for anything but friendship now.

Bullets were thwacking into the mud in front of them as Nigel ran back, dodging, shouting to the Sergeant, 'Get that man down.' But he was too late. Jack saw the radio operator fall, blood spurting from his chest, his radio set blown apart on his back.

There was so much mud flying into the air from mortar explosions, and there was the noise. So much noise and so many Chinese.

At midnight the order came through to pull out, down the hill, deploy six hundred yards to the rear.

They moved, each acting as rearguard, each doing as they were ordered without question, each saving the lives of their friends, and the parade ground flashed into Jack's mind as he skidded down the hill, taking up position as others slid past, then moving again.

They took up positions along the further side of a stream, wading through the water, holding their weapons above their heads, spreading out, flanking the valley, waiting because they knew the Chinese would keep on coming and that their own reinforcements would not.

The enemy came with the dawn. The machine gunners found their targets, and now the British counter-attacked, roaring towards the Chinese as they forded the stream, bogged down in the mud. The rain was in Jack's face, he could taste it, but his mouth was still dry as he ran towards the enemy, firing.

There were no bugles now and the British pushed back towards the valley again, yard by yard, until the day passed and the evening came again but the Chinese rallied and stormed, wave upon wave, as the last of the sun lit the spring flowers, and Bert was killed and Nigel dropped, wounded, his arm useless, and the Sergeant didn't shout any longer, for he was dead.

Jack dragged Nigel towards the base of the hill, ignoring his screams. There were too many all around to listen to just one.

'Break out, all of you that can,' the Captain shouted.

Jack heaped Nigel on to his back, but he was too heavy. He slapped Nigel's face. There was a bullet graze on his forehead and a flesh wound on his arm. He stirred.

'Stand up or die, Nigel,' he shouted, holding his face, looking around, then back at Nigel. 'Stand up, damn you.'

Nigel stirred, groaned. 'Stand up,' Jack repeated. Nigel stumbled to his feet, and Jack slung his arm over his shoulder, taking his weight, moving through the mud, slipping on the stones, but they were moving. At last they were moving.

He dragged Nigel, hearing his breathing, feeling it on his neck. His mouth was still dry from fear and exhaustion. His eyes were sore as he peered into the moonlight. God, Nigel was heavy.

He stopped, and lay down with Nigel beside him at the edge of a paddy field. He could smell the mud, the generations of excrement, and so he thought of the hop-fields, the gentle hills, and when he had rested he moved again. But this time small brown young-looking men loomed up in front of him in the moonlight and the green lush fields of Herefordshire were gone as they shouted and pushed and made Jack walk with his hands on his head in front of Nigel.

When he turned to look at his friend he was prodded with a rifle butt and he was afraid because he had heard of the cruelty of the North Koreans and this is what these men were.

Nigel moaned with every step and Jack breathed in time with his moaning. They could barely see the ground but there was enough light from the cloudless night to avoid the boulders, to stay with the track, and now there were others with them and Chinese soldiers too and Jack breathed more easily.

They were allowed to drop their hands but their fear remained. He stopped and looked back at Nigel, whose feet were dragging, who dripped blood with every step, and the Chinese guard nodded. Jack took his friend's weight and the man behind stepped forward and eased his arm round Nigel's body.

'Let me give you a hand, soldier.' It was a drawl, but Nigel needed help and so Jack nodded but didn't look.

They walked all night and came to a village as dawn broke. They were lined up in the courtyard and there were other Chinese soldiers there. They were given sweetened rice to eat and Jack pushed it into Nigel's mouth, waiting while he gagged, then giving him more.

'Prop him up between us,' the American said, nodding to a cart which was taking other wounded. 'We've heard that they're never seen again. They shouldn't know that he's wounded.'

So they pulled Nigel up, tying the sleeve of his shirt round his arm, needing water to wash the wound, but not daring to ask.

They were searched. Mirrors, scissors, knives were taken by the Chinese who didn't speak and who didn't notice Nigel's arm with the American's jacket slung over it. All the time the North Koreans loitered at the edge of the courtyard, watching.

A Chinese officer came into the courtyard in the cool of the morning sun. He stood before them.

'You are prisoners of the Chinese People's Volunteer Forces in Korea. You have been duped by the American imperialists. You are tools of the reactionary warmongers, fighting against the righteous cause of the Korean people.' He paused, looked around.

Jack tightened his hold on Nigel's good arm. He saw the American clasp his arm more tightly round his body. There were ten men in front of them. Nigel's head was lolling.

'Hold your head up,' Jack hissed and Nigel did.

'You are hirelings of the Rhee puppet government but you will be given the chance to learn the truth through study and you will correct your mistakes. We shall not harm you. At home your loved ones await you. Obey our rules and regulations and you will not be shot.'

They were allowed to sit down and Jack found some shade near the edge of the compound. The mud was deep. It soaked through their clothes but all Jack thought of was Rosie reading his letter, waiting for him, and it gave him strength. But only until a peasant came and struck two prisoners in front of Jack and then turned, hitting him and Nigel with a stick, again and again until blood burst from their lips and heads, because his family had been killed in a raid.

The American, whose name was Steve, stood up and took the stick from the Korean, then the North Koreans moved, pushing through the seated ranks. The mud was in Jack's mouth and nose and he pushed up with his hands and saw the North Koreans take the Yank, pushing him before them towards the edge of the village. He looked for the Chinese but they had gone.

Jack rose, staggered and almost fell but then he was on his feet. He followed Steve and clutched a guard. 'Leave him,' he croaked. 'Leave the Yank.' He was grabbed too. He pulled away but was hit again by the peasant and the blood was running down his face. He turned, called, 'Look after Nigel,' and thought of Rosie as they hauled him, shouting, their breath sour, in his face.

'Hang on, bud,' the American shouted over his shoulder.

They were hauled to a pit, pushed in and there was white blossom on the branch of a tree which hung between them and the sky. Rifles were fired at the walls so that the bullets ricocheted around them, but they were not hit. The North Koreans laughed and the earth smelled of urine, of faeces, but Jack didn't look at the base of the pit, or into the dark flat faces. He thought of Rosie and the bines which swung as though in the sea. And white blossom.

Steve was silent. He stood with Jack, unmoving, until the bullets ceased, and still he said nothing and Jack had no voice with which to speak. Fear had taken it from him.

They were hauled from the pit and a revolver was placed at the American's head.

'Confess your crime, imperialist dog,' the largest North Korean said.

The American said nothing and the hammer clicked but the chamber was empty.

The North Korean opened the chamber and showed Jack. There were two bullets. He spun it, closed it. He held it to Jack's head.

'Confess your crime,' he said again.

Jack looked across the space to the other men, some of whom were visible between the village huts. He thought of Rosie, her mouth, her eyes, and said nothing because there was nothing to say.

But there was no bullet, only the noise of the hammer striking the empty chamber reverberating along the barrel, through the skin into his mind, but Rosie was there, and there was no room for the scream which wanted to leave his mouth.

The Chinese came then, pushing the North Koreans to one side, shoving Steve and Jack before them, back to the village square, and they sat on either side of Nigel and neither spoke because now their legs and their hands were trembling.

They drank the water that the Chinese soldiers passed round and when they had gone Jack cleaned Nigel's wound with the sleeve he had soaked, and dripped water into his friend's mouth, careful not to let the guards see because one man had been beaten for washing his face with the water. He had insulted the guard by using it in that way.

They stayed in the village during the day, pressed up against the hut walls in case the US planes strafed the village. Jack lay listening to the bullfrogs, listening to Nigel's groans, but Steve said little, especially when the North Koreans were near because, he explained, he was American, and the gooks hated them above all else. Jack was glad of his silence. He didn't want to speak to this man.

Each soldier in turn was taken to a hut and interviewed by a high-ranking Chinese officer who asked his rank, name and number, and asked why he supported the Wall Street warmongers who had helped South Korea invade North Korea in July 1950. Jack didn't answer.

'We Chinese believe in a lenient policy to preserve lives so that you imperialist tools can learn the truth. The North Koreans are different. Do not try and escape. They wait for you to do so.'

When Jack came out the North Koreans were there, waiting.

They took Steve too and now they knew that he was American, but there were others who were aircrew and they became the targets of the interrogation instead.

The day passed and at six p.m. the guards came round with

sorghum which Jack and Steve ate from cigarette tins because they had lost their hats in the mêlée. A British Sergeant came round too and said that more marching was expected tomorrow and there'd better be a better exhibition than there was today or he'd want to know the reason why.

It raised a smile, it raised morale, and Jack watched the flares and the tracers in the sky, and wondered how this could have happened when they thought they were going home, when he thought he was going home to Rosie.

CHAPTER 19

The landlady stopped Rosie in the hall in March as she searched the wire letter-box for the letter that just might be there. The woman's hair was newly permed and smelt as Norah's had. She wore lipstick and an overall and crossed her arms over her sagging breasts. There was a cigarette in her left hand and the ash drooped, then fell on to the linoleum.

'You've put on a lot of weight. You must think I'm daft. You'll have to leave when that baby you're carrying's due. I wouldn't have that sort of thing here, even if you were married.'

The woman sucked on her cigarette again. There were lipstick marks against the white of the paper. 'This is a decent establishment. No place for the likes of you. You've got to go before it's born.' She exhaled smoke as she spoke, nodded and turned, dropping more ash.

It was the ash that Rosie watched, not the woman who walked back into her room which opened on to the hall. As she opened the front door she watched it blow, then crumble to nothing. She shut the door behind her. She wanted to slam it against the words which she could still hear. Mrs Eaves had said this might happen.

She walked down the steps to the pavement, then turned and looked back at the house, at the peeling balustrade, at the door with its bubbling paint. Where could she go? Fear swept through her. She tugged at her skirt, easing it around her swelling waist where two safety pins were now clasped together. Who would take her and a baby?

The pavement was damp and footsteps were muted all around. She couldn't go to Mrs Eaves; it wasn't fair and there wasn't room. She called in to the butcher's where the smell of meat made her want to retch. There was a queue, there was always a queue, and the woman in front of her wearing a headscarf knotted at the front over her curlers laughed when the butcher brought his cleaver down on to the scarred and stained wooden block and shouted, 'It's 1951 and it'll take three books this morning, ladies, to buy a pound of meat.'

We know that, Rosie wanted to shout. But where can I find somewhere to live and what about the boys fighting out in Korea? Who knows about them, or even cares? And now the Chinese have been routed, will they come home? Oh God, I wish he'd come home. I wish he was safe.

She picked up Mario's order, and carried it to the shop, heaping it on to the table, laughing as Mrs Orsini shouted upstairs to her husband, 'So now the meat is here, Rosie is here, a customer is here, but you are not.'

Yes, she laughed but the laughter was empty because the fear inside her was building, making her weaken and she mustn't do that. She eased herself through the streamers between the kitchen and the café, smiling as she poured coffee for the three young men who stood waiting, knowing that there would be no tips from them. They were in worn coats and shapeless sweaters.

One of them stirred his coffee at the counter. His hands were red and chapped. He looked up at her. His glasses were steamed up and she smiled again as he took them off, rubbed them, replaced them.

'Luke said you might be able to help,' the boy began. 'We play New Orleans style.'

The others at the table behind weren't drinking, they were listening, and Rosie nodded. She mustn't think of Jack coming home, she must think only of fending for herself and the child. 'Tell me about yourselves. What have you done so far? Where have you played?'

As she listened the panic subsided. Yes. It was all right again. She must always believe that Jack was safe. She must concentrate on the new life. That was her job. She must work now, that was all, harder than she had ever done in her life before. She must save enough to tide her over for the birth and a few weeks afterwards and then she would manage. Mrs Orsini hadn't said yet that she could bring the baby to work with her, but she might.

But where to live while she had the baby? She pulled herself away from that thought. It was March, she had until June and she must listen to this boy because bands like these were her future. She would be like Bob, manage, guide, but always care. That's where she must put her energy; not into thoughts of Korea, not into fear for herself.

'We're playing at a club two blocks away tomorrow,' the boy told her.

'I'll come and listen.' Rosie smiled. 'We'll talk some more after that.'

She served all morning and in between made bookings over the phone, dropping in her coins, holding a hand to one ear, haggling, always raising the offers to something better while Mrs Orsini clucked and made her eat sandwiches because now she was eating for two.

'But it's too much. I haven't got an army in there.' Rosie smiled at the plump Italian woman. She wasn't hungry but she ate because this was Jack's baby and hers.

After the lunchtime rush she took a bus to Middle Street, slipping down the alley, letting her scarf hang down over her body because no one must know, least of all Ollie whom she was going to see. Perhaps Jack had written and Harold hadn't forwarded the letter.

She pushed open the gate into Jack's yard. Paper had blown into the corners. Lee's old bike was rusted and broken, lying on the ground with the wheel at an angle. The curtains were drawn. The door was locked but she knocked anyway. She wanted to hear some sound, and to touch something that Jack had touched. She wanted to stay where he had been, just for a moment, and hear the echoes of their laughter.

Harold came then, out through Grandpa's yard. He stood at the entrance to Ollie's. 'I thought I heard something.'

He was looking at her body and Rosie held her scarf in a bunch. 'Hello, Harold. I just wondered if any mail had come?'

He looked up at the house where the windows were like blank eyes. 'No. I'd bring it to you, honestly I would.' He was looking at her face now, not at her body, and she believed him, and everything hurt within her. But how could there be so much pain when she knew deep inside there would be no letter? Was she very stupid?

'It looks so empty.' She looked back at the house.

'Ollie's gone. He's got a job building the new town outside London. Norah wants to go when it's finished.' Harold nodded his head towards Grandpa's house. 'I don't though. It grows on you.'

Rosie nodded. 'What about the mail, though? What if it comes to Ollie, not to Number 15?'

Harold nodded. His moustache needed a trim. 'She's picking it up. Don't worry. I'll see you get any news.' He turned, then looked back over his shoulder. 'I'd ask you in but . . .'

'She still feels the same then?'

'Yes. Says your grandpa would too.' Harold shrugged. 'You're OK, though, aren't you?'

'Oh yes, no worries. I'm fine.' She walked out of the gate, watching as he turned back into the yard where she could no longer go. She could see that the roses were still there.

'Prune them for me, Harold,' she called softly and he nodded.

'I will. I like them. It's the scent, you know.'

Yes, she did know.

She walked to the rec, sat on the swings and wanted to go to Herefordshire again, paddle in the stream or go back to Pennsylvania and swim in the lake, let it soothe, listen to the ripples, but now was not the time. Now she must work. The wind was cold, too cold, and so she walked back to the bus, past the warehouse where she and Jack had walked with the cheeses and she could hear their laughter again, feel his closed-mouth kiss.

Back in Soho there was music coming from the basement clubs and she pushed her way through to the bars of the pubs which lined the road to the café. She took a job as barmaid three nights a week, starting when the café closed, leaving the other evenings free to listen to groups, practise with them, build up the business.

It would be good for her, she told herself. There would be less time in the bedsit, less time listening to the hissing fire, to her own breathing, to her loneliness. Less time to worry about where she would live, because so far none of the landladies she had asked would take a child.

The next night she listened to the new band and the pale young man who played the banjo. She heard its sharp tones cutting through the collective improvisation, through the murmur which continued from the dimly lit tables all around, and later they talked over glasses of beer and he told her that he played the guitar too and Rosie was glad.

'It's more flexible, but keep the banjo too. You can play well. Come to Mario's Club on Thursday. I'll have fixed you a few gigs by then. I take ten per cent.' She looked away as she said this. His coat was so shabby, all the musicians were poor, but so was she, and so would her baby be, unless she charged the rate that Luke said was fair, unless she worked until she dropped.

The boy smiled, and shook her hand, and they sat up talking about the clean and emphatic rhythmic backing that the banjo had always given, about the Big 25 Club in New Orleans where he had always wanted to play. Rosie nodded, her eyes sore with tiredness, but she needed to know her groups, to care about them, to find out their strengths and their weaknesses.

She worked at the bar the next night, pulling pints, smiling, wearing loose clothes to hide her shape, but her legs ached and her arms and her face from the smile that had to be there.

There was a letter in the wire rack on her return but it was not from Jack, it was from Nancy. She read it by the light from the small table lamp Mario had given her, hearing the plop of the gas, smelling it. Sipping cocoa, which was all she could face after an evening of beer-laden breath and nicotine-heavy air.

Lower Falls
March

My dearest Rosie,

Do hope that all is well with you. Your groups seem to be coming along well. Uncle Bob tells us you've written about this guy Luke and his band. Sounds interesting. Maybe if he comes over, you could come too. Perhaps with Jack when the war's over.

I hope to God it comes soon. It might take some of the panic out of things over here. Then 'pinkoes' like us might just be able to get some sleep at night without some nut ringing up and shouting – Reds go home – over the line! Then we might get back to being fifty instead of ninety.

It's not being helped by the Rosenberg trial in New York City. My God, how tempers are rising all around.

It would cheer us both so much if you could come out to see us. But maybe you need to put in time at work, especially when you're just trying to get the restaurant on the road and the groups too. We understand.

All our love,
Nancy

The paper was cold. The heat didn't reach across to the bed and Rosie wanted to read of the maples and oaks at the lake, the target on the garage, the barbecue, Mary. She didn't want to hear of tension, of heartache, because she couldn't go back. All she could do was lie to the people she loved. The people who needed her right now.

Her legs were throbbing, her head ached. She lay down and pulled the knitted blanket up round her head. She wanted to be in her bedroom at Lower Falls, she wanted to be back where Nancy's arms could take away the pain, where her laughter broke into her loneliness. But she wanted to be here more, waiting for Jack, in case he came, in case he wrote.

That night she dreamed that he wrote, but March became April and there was no letter. There was just work, but the money was mounting and she sent in an application for an Unmarried Mothers Home. She was accepted but the letter was cold and the list of garments and equipment required was long.

So she worked on Sunday at the pub also and they said they would take one of her groups on a Friday night, unheard, because her reputation was growing. She slept well that night but couldn't face more than cocoa.

Towards the end of April, the UN forces retreated as the Chinese poured in reinforcements, and the newspaper ink came off on her hands as she read the piece again and again at the Orsinis' kitchen table and cried because now he wouldn't be coming home soon, the UN forces would have to go on fighting and there had been no letter.

She cried and couldn't stop and Mrs Orsini held her.

'He won't be coming home yet,' she whispered as she felt the heat from the older woman's body.

'One day he will. I know he will, if he loves you as we do,' Mrs Orsini said. 'You are a good girl. He cannot fail to love you. You must wait. You must be patient. You must not give up.'

That night as she lay in bed she wondered how long hope lasted. How long she could bear such loneliness. And how could she bear it if he died and she was never told? But Mrs Orsini said that Ollie or Harold would tell her and Rosie knew that she was right.

She worked throughout April, barely noticing the leaves sprouting on the clubbed trees, barely noticing the blocks of ice melting outside the French restaurants along the back streets. She listened to groups, listened to booking managers, and always increased the fees so that the ten per cent she took left the boys with the original offer.

She and Luke spent one evening a week with Jake, coaxing, nagging, drawing him on, because now they were both convinced that his playing could be brought up to the standard of the others, but still it was not quite right. She wrote again to Uncle Bob, telling him that Luke's group was almost ready. That he would want them when he heard the middle range, the melancholia, the dexterity, the heart.

She went to the clinic and they said she was underweight but the baby was strong. They gave her more iron. Mrs Orsini gave her soup, sandwiches, salads, but she was too tired to eat and Mario couldn't understand the circles under her eyes and neither could Mrs Eaves. She didn't tell them about the bar work, they wouldn't understand how necessary it was. She said nothing to Luke either, or to Sandy, who made her sit down now when she phoned because her legs were trembling for much of the day and so were her hands.

She still pulled pints though, in the evening, and it was here one night that Luke found her, pale, tired, bending, stretching, and he waited outside until the doors were locked and the customers had left. He waited beneath the street light, his leg crooked up behind him, until she came out of the side door and for a moment she thought he was Jack and ran towards him, but then stopped.

'Why are you doing this?' Luke said, his arms crossed, his voice hard. 'You're more than seven months pregnant. Are you mad?'

The light cast shadows on his face and Rosie walked past him. She didn't need this. She needed money for her baby. She needed a future. Not this. Not now. She didn't turn but he followed her, grabbing her arm.

'Are you mad or just greedy? Why this on top of everything else? What do you want to do? Go back to America a rich woman? Show off to your friends about how well you've done? You're killing yourself. You're killing the baby.'

She pulled from him. The stars were clear in the sky. There was no cloud, no breeze. She would think of that, not his words.

'I'm going home because for now and for now only it is home. When the baby's born I have to leave. I have nowhere to go, no one to go to.' She wasn't looking at him, she was looking at the sky above the rooftops. 'That's why I'm working. I've got to pay for the goddamn Home, I've got to survive afterwards until I can work. I'll see you tomorrow, Luke.'

She walked on, back to the house by herself, climbed the stairs by herself, but then the baby stirred and she smiled. No, not by herself.

Luke didn't come into the café the next day, or the pub in the evening. Neither did the rest of the group, or Sandy. They didn't play on Thursday night but it didn't matter, because the new group did and the applause was loud, though Rosie had been too tired to tap her foot. Too tired to feel the hurt of Luke's rejection, because that is what his absence meant.

Mrs Orsini was quiet too, and busy. There didn't seem time for her to smile and Mario was in and out. Rosie served coffee, made phone calls, took phone calls, added gigs in the book, totalled up the figures. Served spaghetti bolognese to Mrs Eaves who came and smiled but left quickly with Mrs Orsini, and Rosie told herself it didn't matter.

She served in the pub that night and she had never been so tired. The Chinese and the North Koreans had been held on a line to the north of Seoul and the Han River. Where was Jack? Was he safe? Would he write?

As she left the pub she looked towards the lamppost but Luke wasn't there and the walk home was cool and quiet and empty. But the wire box for letters wasn't.

There was one from Frank saying that Joe was coming over to cover the Festival of Britain which had started at the beginning of May. He was also coming to hear Luke's group and to see her, to put their minds at rest that she was well and happy. Frank wanted her to write a feature on the Festival as well since she was doing freelance features in Britain.

Rosie read it again, lying fully clothed on the bed, then she tore it up, into smaller and smaller pieces. How could she hide this baby now and why was there no letter from Jack? And she hadn't written anything since she had left the magazine – her skill had gone, absorbed by the life she now led.

She slept, dragged herself from the bed when the alarm rang at seven a.m. She made tea and toast but couldn't eat, she was still too tired. She pushed her swollen feet into her shoes, and took her coat because the wind was still cool. The landlady was by the front door, holding it open for her.

'Made other arrangements yet?' she asked.

'You've had my rent until the end of May,' Rosie said, pushing past her, buttoning up her coat, knowing that the hem rose at the front and dipped at the back because she was so large.

When she arrived at the café the Closed sign was still up though the door was unlocked. The chairs were still upside-down on the tables and she moved slowly, setting them down, thinking of Joe, working out the letter she would write to stop him coming, the extra lies she would tell, but then Mario came into the room, his white apron smudged, and Mrs Orsini was behind her with Mrs Eaves.

Mario took the chair from her, set it down, took her by the hand, led her behind the counter, through the kitchen, up the stairs. Past the Orsini flat, right up to the top where the attic was. He said nothing and Rosie was too tired to ask.

He opened the door to the rooms which had housed packing cases, old chairs, rubbish. Luke and his band were there, with Sandy too. There were no packing cases any more. There was a carpet on the floor. There were chairs, a table, a cooker. Mario showed her this and the bathroom with the white suite. Light flooded in through the eaved windows.

There was another room with a white-sprigged muslin bedspread draped over a bed. There was a dressing-table. No one spoke. Rosie turned. Mrs Eaves had followed them up and stood with Mrs Orsini.

Luke said, 'This is yours, Rosie.'

Rosie stood but her legs were trembling, and now Luke moved over to the side of the bed where a sheet hung over something. He pulled it back and there was a cot with blankets cut down and freshly ironed sheets.

'And this is the baby's,' he said.

She walked over to the cot, stroked the bedclothes then the headboard. Frank's grandfather had carved the headboard on her bed at Lower Falls out of maple. She heard again the jazz from the open window flowing across the shadowed lawn.

She turned. 'I don't deserve it.' She laid her hand on her stomach. 'I can't take it.'

The sky was blue behind the rooftops and the chimneys. There were white clouds. How strange. There had only been darkness for so long.

She said again as they all stood, silent but smiling still, 'I can't take it.' But how she wanted to be able to.

Mr Orsini spread open his hands. 'Then you look for another job, my Rosie, because the person that works with us now has to live above. It is better for business. We are putting a phone up here.' He turned, the others were grinning now. 'But, you want to leave. You leave. We want you to stay. We want the baby too. We want you live here. Work here, with baby.'

Mrs Eaves came then, took her arm, moved her through into the other room, pushed her towards the chair beside the fire which had been hidden beneath an old sheet up to now. It was Grandpa's.

'We brought it over from Norah's. Harold helped us.'

Rosie sat. She looked at her own hands clutching the arms of the chair which his had held and now she looked up. His books were here too, on shelves along the wall.

'Thank you.' It was all she could say, but it was enough because there were so many tears in her eyes and everyone else's and she wanted to hug them, tell them how much it all meant to her. Mrs Eaves stooped and kissed her head.

'We know, my dear,' she murmured.

Mr Orsini clapped his hands and laughed. 'Good, good. Now downstairs, everyone. The café should be open. There is much to do. You too, Rosie, and there will be no more job at pub. There will be no more nasty woman at house. There will be no talk of Home for you and baby.'

He was taking her arm, helping her up while Mrs Orsini nodded and Mrs Eaves smiled. They followed Luke and the group down the stairs and everyone was talking at once but Rosie listened to Mr Orsini. 'You will go now to clinic. You will have baby in nearby hospital. You will come home to us.' He put up his hands. 'No arguments. That is as it should be. We help until Jack comes back.'

Rosie walked to the clinic and there was blossom on the trees, there were children running in the streets, laughing, shouting, as she and Jack had done. As their child would do, and one day they would take her to the hills of Herefordshire and the lake in Pennsylvania.

On 20 May Rosie went to the market for vegetables. She chose spring greens, with the dew still on the leaves, carrots, onions but left the potatoes for Luke to bring later. She listened to the man who sold crockery, dipping his hands into the money pocket of his apron. He wasn't as good as Jack.

She stopped, bought a paper and read of the British and Australian troops who had defended their positions and thrown back the Chinese. People pushed past her. They didn't care that there was a war on. Rosie put the paper into the litter bin and looked up and down the street. Was there fresh spring growth where Jack was? Was there blossom against blue skies as there was here? Was he thinking of her?

She walked on. She knew he wasn't dead. Ollie would have had a telegram and so she thought of him as she had known him, selling his plates, laughing, throwing the cheeses over the wall, and the sun was warm on her face and she didn't see the dog until it was too late.

It ran at her, caught her behind the knee. She fell, the carrots bursting out of their newspaper as her bag fell with her, and for a moment there was no pain, just surprise, just dirt on her hands and in her mouth. Then there were hands lifting her, voices, faces that cared, that were worried, shocked, and now the pain came, passing over her in waves.

'Sit down, missus.' Someone brought a chair out of a shop and an ambulance was called but the carrots were still all over the pavement. Someone must pick them up. The newspaper was lifting and flapping. It was dirty. Her hands were dirty and her mouth. She could taste the grit.

At the hospital she held out her hands through the fog of pain. They were dirty, so dirty, and the Sister smiled and washed them and asked how they could get hold of her husband.

'Jack's in Korea,' Rosie whispered because there was too much pain to use her voice properly.

The doctor tried to stop the baby coming because it was four weeks too soon, but the contractions were stronger, coming too quickly, and Rosie lay on the bed and called for Jack, again and again, because his baby was coming too soon. Mrs Eaves and Mrs Orsini came and patted her hand, soothed her forehead but they weren't allowed to stay.

'We'll be in the corridor. We'll wait,' Mrs Eaves said and there was a smile on her face, but not in her eyes.

The pain came again. 'Don't go,' Rosie called. 'Everyone goes.'

Lucia Anne was born at one a.m. She was small, but strong and beautiful, so very beautiful, and Rosie held her before they took her to an incubator. She stroked the small hands, the perfect nails, the soft hair, the skin. She kissed her cheek. Mrs Eaves and Mrs Orsini saw the baby too and cried when they heard the names because they were theirs.

The Sister came into the ward the next day, her face stern, her lips thin. She pulled the screens round the bed. 'There is no husband, is there?'

Rosie shook her head.

'Then you should have the baby adopted. It would be better. There would be two parents, a settled home.' The Sister straightened her apron. 'You're young enough to start again. Forget all about this.'

'I have a home. The father will come back from Korea. I know he will.' Rosie turned away to face the screen and would say nothing else.

At visiting time the husbands came and she looked away, out of the window at the blue sky. She was glad she had been to see Grandpa when he lay in hospital. She was glad she had carried the roses until her hands were raw because there was a loneliness here like no other.

Mario came, and Luke, and then Mrs Eaves and Mrs Orsini and they said they had told Norah. She did not come. The doctor spoke to her the next day about adoption but Lucia Anne was hers, she told him. She loved her.

'But my dear, love is not enough,' the doctor said.

'Love is everything,' she replied.

She took Lucia home and there were flowers in the flat and light, so much light. And there was love. So much love, from them all. But Jack wasn't there.

And Joe was coming soon and what would happen then?

CHAPTER 20

Jack's long march to the 'safe rear' began at seven p.m. as spring edged into the summer of 1951.

'To prevent strafing from UN planes,' the Chinese guard said.

They carried sacks of sorghum and Jack and Steve helped Nigel, who was stronger now but his arm was swollen and stiff. Jack still couldn't smile at the American, because he was a Yank like Ed, but he took the help he gave because the Yanks had taken so much from him.

They marched through mud and the Sergeant at the head of the column set up the rhythm and it helped, it made them feel human after the Korean children had giggled and stared and the North Korean guards had spat.

The mud dragged at their boots, Nigel lost the rhythm. Jack chanted left right, left right, and the Korean guard lunged at him with his rifle butt, screaming.

'OK, buddy, keep your shirt on,' Steve drawled and the guard turned on him and thudded the butt into his ribs.

Jack kept silent because the American had taken the blows which should have come to him. The bruises would have been easier. Steve kept silent too and now Nigel was back in rhythm, they were all in the rhythm, cursing with each step, cursing, counting, cursing, counting, but only in their minds, and Jack thought of this, not Steve and his long loping strides in which he saw echoes of Ed.

Trucks passed them, their lights picking out the road, spewing up mud, leaving the sickening smell of gasoline hanging on the air. Planes sometimes soared above, dropping flares which illuminated the road and adjacent hills, and each time the men had to break and scatter into the roadside ditches, sinking into the stinking mud as rockets hit the hills and the road. Then, as the planes disappeared, they clambered out again, marching on in sodden clothes, which rubbed against their skin. Christ, how they rubbed.

All along the hilltops bordering the roads the Chinese air-raid wardens fired rifle shots into the air when other planes were sighted and again and again they were back in the ditches, cursing the American air crews but cheering them too, if only in their minds.

They crossed bridges and were made to run for the length of them, their breath jerking in their chests, the sorghum sacks breaking their backs, deadening their legs. Jack could hear Nigel groaning but the guards couldn't hear above the thud of boots.

'Better than the assault courses,' he said as they ran. 'Do you remember? Just keep going.' And Nigel did.

Their mouths were dry. There were no drinks, but the guards had nothing either and they carried packs too.

They halted in a village before it was light, crouching in the centre, their bodies cooling quickly in the morning chill. Nigel was groaning but Jack gripped his good arm.

'In your mind, Nigel. In your mind.' Because the prisoners who had been in the Japanese camps in the last war could understand the North Koreans. They understood that the ox-cart which followed them meant death for the injured placed upon it.

Steve checked Nigel's wound. 'It's OK. The maggots are in it now.'

Jack nodded, swallowing. He couldn't have lifted the bandage, seen the writhing mass, but he wouldn't think of that. He would think of his mouth which was dry, of water which had not yet been given. He would think of the stream below the hop-yards, of Rosie standing, letting the water ripple about her legs.

The Chinese officer was shouting at his men and there were bullfrogs in the paddy fields which lay all around them. They were given water to drink and hot watery sorghum to eat, then herded up into the hills before dawn broke and there they lay during the long daylight hours.

They slept on the sandy ground, sheltered from planes by rocks and shrubs, and in the village he could see trees with white blossom bursting from their branches, symbols of stillness. He thought of Suko and the avenues of trees he had not stayed to see in Japan. But most of the time he thought and dreamed of Rosie and hated himself for hurting her.

But then the Chinese would come and sit and talk of their sins, of their crimes against the Korean people, of the right of the Chinese people to Formosa, and all the time the North Korean guards sat and lay on the perimeter, watching the men, fingering their guns, their knives, and no one tried to escape on that first night or day, or indeed the whole journey.

They marched again at seven p.m. when the rain was pouring. It was in their eyes, their fatigues, their mouths and so they weren't thirsty, but tired.

'So goddamn tired,' Steve drawled and Nigel nodded, but Jack looked straight ahead.

They stopped in the morning and this time there was room to stay in village shacks but it enabled the Chinese to talk to them more easily. A smooth-faced lecturer in well-pressed olive greens came by truck and harangued the prisoners as they slumped with knees crossed on the floor, looking out of the door at the blossom.

For two hours they sat and listened and their backs ached, their heads too, and then they were allowed to rest but the children of the village threw stones into the shacks, then beat sticks on the walls so there was no sleep for any of them. They marched again at seven p.m. and the lice were itching.

By ten p.m. they were lying in ditches, scattered before a strafing plane, its roar filling the air which was full of flying cartridge cases. One guard was killed and two prisoners. They were so tired, they barely noticed, but when they arrived at the next village they turned their clothes inside-out and squashed what lice they could between their fingernails.

There had been lice in Middle Street before they'd bought the houses. He and Rosie used to crush the lice there too. Steve checked Nigel's arm again, because Jack could not, and it was then that Jack said, 'Thanks. I couldn't do it.' It was the first time he had said thank you to an American since Maisie had left, but he couldn't look at him when he said it. And it was for Nigel that he spoke, not himself.

That day, they heard a cuckoo call as they lay on the hills

which were drenched in colour. Jack eased himself on to his back and thought of the Somerset village, the hill, the May blossom, the camp he and the other evacuees had made. He thought, too, of the cuckoo which he and Ed had heard. But then he thought instead of Rosie.

Each night they marched, each day they hid, drinking boiled water, eating sorghum, rice. Each day all the prisoners cracked lice and Steve checked Nigel's wound. They listened to the Chinese and wondered how long this would go on for.

For weeks they marched with the ox-cart trundling behind and more prisoners joined them until there were eighty of them. They brought news, but it wasn't good. The Chinese were advancing.

Dysentery had killed fifteen of them after four weeks and still they marched. The heat sapped their energy and now the flies were thick around them as they hid on the hills, resting, lying on the dry ground. They crawled in their ears, their eyes, their noses, their mouths.

When they covered their faces with squares of shirts they felt them crawling on the surface, heard them buzzing, but Nigel's arm was better, the maggots were gone, and he carried his own sack of sorghum. They had no need of Steve now, but he continued to march with them, though Jack barely spoke.

In the second week of June they entered a camp which was set on a peninsula, in a valley between two hills beyond which was the sea. There were barely any soles left on their boots. Their skin was burnt, their hair and clothes were thick with encrusted dirt. Their lips were cracked.

'This is exquisite,' Nigel said, bracing his shoulders, marching in step.

Jack laughed, looking up at the blue sky.

'Hardly exquisite, dear boy,' he answered, looking down now at the single strand of wire which marked the perimeter of the camp, knowing that the geography was the real restriction. He, too, braced his shoulders and marched in step to the huts, then gave news to the prisoners who had been there over the winter; who were thin, bruised, hungry, but who said the regime was kinder now. Indoctrination was the order of the day. It wasn't very successful. Jack looked at Nigel and they smiled. Steve smiled too.

They ate corn and millet that evening. They wanted to sleep but were taken out into a large hut and lectured and Jack looked at his thumbs which were black with the ingrained blood of the lice, but still he itched, still he scratched. They all did, but tomorrow they wouldn't march. At least there was that.

In the morning they were put on a wood rota and Steve and Jack went up into the hills with eight others but Jack talked to the others, not to Steve. They collected wood, brought it back, boiled water for drinking, but it was too late for some. Five of their men died of dysentery in the camp that first day.

They were broken down into companies by the Chinese for daily political study sessions. Nigel, Steve and Jack were kept together and there was nothing Jack could do about it. They sat in rows, cross-legged, trying not to listen.

'You soldiers have come here as dupes of the imperialists, the warmongers, the Wall Street big-shots who have tricked you to leave your countries and fight this war to increase their profits,' the lecturer told them. His voice droned on and on.

There were flies everywhere. Jack dropped his head on to his chest and thought of the cool breeze of England, Rosie's soft hands.

They were given paper to write an essay on the lecture they had received. Nigel wrote, and Steve and Jack copied his words. They were all sent for that evening. They stood before the Commandant and confessed their copying crimes as the Commandant insisted they must. But Steve and Jack couldn't write the essays that the Commandant now insisted upon because they had not been listening. They were taken to cells in the village.

The North Korean guards pushed them inside the clay and wattle building which smelled of excrement, urine, and the gasoline which was stored in drums at the end of the passage. There were doors either side. It was dark. Steve murmured, 'This looks kinda fun.'

Jack looked at him now, really looked, because there had been no fear in his voice and he wondered how that was possible. But now he saw the fear in the American's eyes. There was youth too, and kindness, and Jack smiled but then he was pushed alone into a cell.

The uneven dirt floor was soaked with oil. It was dark. So dark. The door opened and he turned. A North Korean guard stood there, a pistol in his hand.

'You come.'

Jack left and Steve called, 'Good luck, buddy.'

He was taken to a wall which flanked the square outside the cells. His arms were tied with wire. He was turned to face the guard. The sun was too bright, the shadows so sharp. For Christ's sake! He was going to be shot. Shot, now. Jack put up his hand. *No*, but the word was silent. There was no time. The guard had levelled the pistol, pulled back the hammer. The gun fired into the wall behind him and Jack's legs shook and he nearly fell.

The guard returned him to the cell and Steve tapped on the wall.

'You OK?'

'I'm fine. Just fine. What else can you do on a quiet afternoon?' But he wasn't OK. He sat on the floor, his arms round his knees, trying to stop the shaking and the tears, listening as Steve in his turn was taken, but he also returned and so the shaking stopped and the tears too. Because he hadn't died today and he wasn't alone.

The guard handed in a blanket, rice bowl and spoon and took their boots, and he couldn't sleep that night because he didn't know when they would come again to take him. The cells were full, and he knew the others couldn't sleep either because they tapped and talked in whispers. So, although there was no light, there was comradeship, and that kept the fear from all their voices.

The next day the guards came and took them one by one, barefoot, to the earth latrine at the end of the passage, then back to the cells. They were made to sit bolt upright from five-thirty a.m. onwards. Jack's back stiffened, burned. He slouched. The guard looked through the grille and shouted. He sat up again, back rigid now, until eleven a.m.

There were no more trips to the latrines. A young American air navigator had dysentery and Steve told the guard, who hit him in the face with his fist, and Jack wondered how he could ever not have liked this man.

The navigator used the corner of his cell.

'That is good. You need to learn humility,' the Chinese officer called through their doors.

At eleven breakfast arrived. They stepped three paces outside the cell to collect the food, but one at a time so they saw no familiar face. Jack forced it down. Boiled water was brought. Jack filled up his bowl, sipped it. Tipped a little on to his fingers, wiped his face, his hands.

At midday the flies and the heat rose. The Chinese bugles blew and the guards shouted that they must lie down for one hour. Jack pulled the blanket over his face, lying on the dirt floor. He heard and felt the flies, felt the sweat soak into the blanket, but it was better than having them in his mouth, crawling heavy and bloated across his skin.

They were then made to sit again, bolt upright, and there was comfort in the knowledge that others were having to do the same. There was such comfort in not being alone.

Each minute seemed an eternity. He thought of Rosie, of the coolness of the bines, the softness of her lips. He didn't think of the cold ground in Yorkshire because it made him feel so disgusted with himself, and so grateful that she could still love him. The shirt had shown that and it was more than he deserved. But at least there had been no child for her to struggle with alone. She would have told him.

At twilight they were ordered to lie down and sleep. They were inspected at nine p.m. A torch was shone in his face. He pretended to be asleep. He pretended to be asleep when Steve tapped, and when he spoke, because the disgust was still with him.

As he walked to the earth latrine in the morning he watched a guard carry a bucket towards a sheet of wrought iron on the ground. He saw him kick the sheeting to one side. An American officer emerged wearing flying boots. He was white and haggard and stumbled to the latrines ahead of Jack.

Jack's guard laughed. 'He not confess to crimes.'

'Good luck, buddy,' Jack called and the man turned, dazed, his eyes deep sunken. He smiled before Jack felt the blow of the rifle, felt it thud into his ribs, felt the dust in his mouth as he fell.

He was dragged back to the cell before he could use the latrine. He was made to sit all day without food, without water, and there was only the corner of his cell as a latrine. But it was worth it to have reached out, for that one moment, to a boy, an American, who was suffering more than he.

That evening, after twilight and after inspection, he talked to Steve about Ed and Maisie and Lee because all the anger and the bitterness were gone. They had disappeared when Steve had spoken without fear and when the American had crawled from the pit.

They were out of the cells within a week and at the end of June the Chinese danced as evening came, swaying in weaving columns to the discordant sound of a drum and clashing cymbals in celebration of a festival only they understood.

'How exquisite,' Nigel murmured and Jack nodded.

'Kinda strange, out here,' Steve said. 'Can't quite catch the tune, but I've heard those cymbals before.'

They had all heard them, but then they had been almost drowned by bugles and guns.

There were fewer North Koreans now and less brutality. They were allowed to wash but there was no soap or towels. They were given anti-malarial tablets and louse powder. They were fed twice a day from the Chinese troops' kitchen. They knew it was all to re-educate them through leniency but by now Nigel had dysentery and none of this helped that.

So each day they listened to lectures, wrote essays, but thought their own thoughts and clung to their own dreams, their own memories, and longed to be home.

In July the Commandant spoke to them. He smoked Dragon cigarettes from China and shouted when Nigel had hiccoughs and couldn't stop.

He told them that some of them were righteous progressive men who were self-consciously learning the truth.

'You are our friends and we will help you to struggle free from the toils of the warmongers.' He looked at Nigel who was still hiccoughing. 'Others of you are semi-righteous, uncertain. You are swayed by every wind that blows. You listen to both sides but cannot make self-conscious decisions.'

Nigel was still hiccoughing, clenching his hands into fists, holding his breath. Men were laughing now, but not the Commandant.

'Others of you are bad men. You believe slanderous things.

You close your minds against the truth. You distract others from learning.' He motioned with his swagger stick to Nigel and the guards came and took him and now there was no laughter.

Steve looked at Jack. 'He's too weak. That dysentery. He ain't fit enough to take that cell, or the pit.'

Jack nodded. He began to stand but Steve pressed him down.

'That won't help. We'll have to wait.'

They didn't take Nigel to the pit though. They took him to the Commandant's hut where he spent the evening writing a self-criticism which he had to read the next day to the camp.

It was clever, very clever, Jack thought, grinning. It was a criticism of the Commandant, not capitalism, but written in a way which made this impossible to grasp. Afterwards Nigel told him that he wanted to go to university when this mess was over.

At the end of the week they were given paper to write a letter home, c/o The Chinese People's Volunteers' POW Corps. Jack wrote to Rosie, telling her that he loved her, that his friend Nigel was here, and Steve, an American. That all the anger was gone, that he would survive. That he was ashamed. That he hated himself for hurting her. That this couldn't go on for too long and he would be back.

They handed them in but an American who knew Korean heard the guards say that they would never be sent and home seemed very far away.

The wood-gathering parties had to scavenge further afield now but suddenly the trips became more popular because Mexican POWs had discovered marijuana growing on the hillsides and now they rolled the leaves between book pages and smoked them to ease the boredom of the days. But Jack and Steve refused to smoke because they needed to care for Nigel who was weaker each day from dysentery and beri-beri.

There were no medical supplies, though there was a doctor who tried to help. The Chinese had no drugs for themselves either.

They still sat through lectures, listening just enough to be able to answer questions, but they also talked to the Puerto

Ricans who knew and understood the herbs which could save lives. Steve and Jack used the remains of the paper which they had been given for their essays to write down descriptions of the plants.

The following week they strayed from the wood-gathering party, searching, picking, stuffing the herbs into the pockets of their trousers, remembering to carry wood under their arms as well. They brewed the mixture up behind the hut and no guards stopped them because boiling up water was common. Nigel drank it from his cigarette-tin and he seemed a little better and they talked of home, and of Oxford where he would go when the war was over.

They did the same the next week, and the next, and then it was the beginning of August and new prisoners said that talks were being held in a tea-house in Kaesong on a ceasefire in Korea. That this must almost be the end, and that day the wood party looked up at the hills, felt the heat and the dust, and because the war would be over soon it didn't seem so important to stretch themselves beyond endurance. They were late mustering, slow in leaving and Jack watched them straggle in on their return. He watched the Commandant too, standing frowning, and waited for what he knew would happen.

The Chinese herded all the prisoners into the square. They were lectured on their negative attitude to labour and made to sit in the sun for the afternoon and Nigel became worse as the heat increased. The herb gatherer had forgotten to gather.

Jack and Steve went out on the wood detail the next morning, even though they were tired and weak and it wasn't their turn, but Nigel was worse. They needed herbs, they needed to make sure the squad were brisk and that Nigel didn't need to sit in the sun again.

They took the sloping paths, lifting the wood which was already hot though it was only eleven a.m. They found the herbs, bitter, sweet. The smell clung to their hands. They moved further from the others, picking, leaning over for wood, glancing behind, checking the guards, picking, always picking. And others did too now for their own friends.

They came out the next day too, and the next, picking for Nigel, and for others, but on the Sunday afternoon Jack and Steve were not cautious enough as they searched and picked.

They didn't check how close they were to the squad. Jack heard the shouting of the guards first, then the warning from Steve, then bullets thwacked into the ground at their feet. There was the sound of running feet and they were pushed face down and kicked, then dragged back to the camp.

They were brought before the Commandant, who accused them of trying to escape. They said nothing. The scent of herbs was still on their hands. Steve looked at Jack who shook his head. They couldn't admit to the herbs in case others were stopped too. In case the marijuana smoking was discovered and men punished.

'You must admit your error,' the Commandant said.

'I'm kinda sick of admitting to errors,' Steve said. 'Why don't you go take a powder.'

The Commandant didn't speak, he just nodded and the guards took Steve across the square. He dropped the herbs on the ground. They were picked up by another prisoner and taken to Nigel.

Jack saw this. He also saw the flies around his head. Then he watched the smoke rising from the Commandant's cigarette and there were no flies near the smoke. Power brought advantages, that was for sure.

'And you. You will admit your error? Your attempt to escape.'

Jack stood to attention. He rubbed the scar the scissors had made. He was tired too, of obedience, of humility. Yes, he was tired and the war was nearly over anyway.

'I have made no errors,' he said.

He also dropped his herbs on the ground and they were picked up too and the soldier who did so said, 'I'll get them for Nigel until you're back out.'

He was thrown into the pit near the latrines and Steve called out from the other, 'You'll like the privacy, Jack.'

He didn't, though, and neither would Grandpa, he thought, smiling wryly. It was dark, it was hot, so hot. The sun beat down on the iron, the guards banged with sticks and he sat crouched, hugging his knees, feeling the sweat rolling off his body. He stripped off his clothes, held his head in his hands while it ached enough to burst.

As the heat of the day beat on the steel covers he took shallow breaths, panting, seeking air, lifting his head, but there was none. He rolled on to his side. The earth was cooler. He buried his face in it but the dust entered his mouth, his nose. He crouched, he wept and the tears were salty and then he sat, still and straight, as Suko had done before the Shinto shrine. He thought of white blossom, of the cool of the stream about Rosie's legs.

They lifted the covers at twilight. He staggered to the latrines, heard Steve's voice as he returned. It was cracked and dry.

'Kinda like a long holiday, eh, Jack?'

Jack slipped down again into the pit. The guard handed him sorghum in a tin and half a can of boiled water. It was warm. They pushed him down. Some of the water spilt. They slid the sheeting over again.

He heard Steve being taken now and when he returned he called out to him.

'Better than a deckchair at Southend, eh, Steve?' His voice was cracked and dry too.

The next night was cold and the morning took so long to come, but then the heat came too and the flies and the noise of the sticks and because they had spoken to one another their arms were tied behind their backs after they had been taken to the latrines. Food was still passed in, though, but they had to bend over and lick it from the tin like animals.

They didn't call to one another again, but they shuffled their feet or they coughed and that was enough. And it was enough, too, for Jack to sit still now and hold his body upright, to ignore the bindings and think of blossom, Rosie and the cool of England.

After two days the guards untied their arms, but pushed them back down again into the pit. There were deep raw grooves in their skin from the rope but these didn't touch the thoughts inside Jack's head, the memories, the echoes of the life he had lived, the people he had loved.

In the second week he pictured the pebbles in the stream below the hop-yards. He picked them from the water. The water was cool, the pebbles wet. He built a pyramid. The pebbles dried. He walked amongst the cool green fountains of hops, and saw the yellow dust beneath his fingernails. He picked the hops, flicking them into the bin. He smelt them, felt them. Kissed Rosie, laughed with Ed, smelt the lavender on Maisie's neck, threw Lee up into the air, heard his laughter. Heard Ollie's too.

In the third week he breathed slowly, emptied his mind, and on each trip to the latrine he coughed with a dry throat, and each time he heard Steve do the same he knew he could go on. They were released at the end of August.

Jack could barely stand. The light hurt his eyes as it had hurt them each time he had walked to the latrine. He was marched back to the compound, through North Koreans who threw stones at him and called him a murderer.

They did the same to Steve, whose beard was dark against his white skin. Jack rubbed his own beard. He watched the stones hit his friend. But Steve didn't notice. He was thin, his legs trembled as Jack's did. They met at the gate, nodded, smiled, held one another's arms.

'The war must be nearly over,' they called to a prisoner who brought them water. They lifted the cans to their lips.

The young boy shook his head. 'New POWs in say the talks will go on and on, maybe for years. There's no truce, only more fighting.'

They felt sick with something deeper than anguish and couldn't move as they watched the boy walk on, his head down, dust scuffing up with each step. The hop-yards were fading. Jack couldn't hold on to them.

They walked towards Nigel's hut but he wasn't there. He had been moved to the officers' camp, another prisoner told them.

'He didn't want to go. He wanted to wait for you, but he had no choice. They're trying to destroy the old leadership system, demoralise everyone, so the officers have been separated from the ranks. He died there last week. We've only just heard.'

CHAPTER 21

Joe came at the beginning of June, when Rosie had only been home a week. He walked into the café as Lucia slept in her pram outside the kitchen door in the small sunswept courtyard. Rosie was talking on the phone to a promoter who wanted Luke at whatever cost.

'Though within reason, my dear.'

Rosie laughed. 'Twenty pounds. Excluding expenses. I don't think I can be more reasonable than that, Harry.' She knew he would take far more in profit for she had been to the function room behind his pub, seen his gold rings, his expensive watch.

Rosie grinned as he sounded her out about a national tour for the band. She turned to write the date in the book. Joe moved and she looked up, saw his blond hair, his tanned skin, his white teeth. She saw the watch which gleamed against his skin. It was new. Everything went quite still and then jogged into motion again as she put her pen down, carefully. There was ink on the nib. It had smeared her finger.

She didn't kiss him but shook his hand, feeling cold, wishing he hadn't come. Her world had been intruded upon. The lies were about to be exposed and she was ashamed. For the first time for weeks she was ashamed.

He grinned, looked around. 'So this is it?'

'Yes, this is it.' She poured him coffee, nodded towards Luke. 'We're on for Saturday. Expenses excluded. Twenty pounds!'

Luke whistled and Joe looked at her. 'From what Frank said I imagined the restaurant would be bigger.'

'Remember you're in little old England now,' she said, wiping the counter.

'You're looking good.' He sipped the black coffee as he leaned against the counter.

Rosie didn't know what to say to this man who didn't belong here. Who shouldn't have come. 'You must meet Luke,' she said, her voice cold and crisp, because she could remember that the hand that lifted the cup had stroked her breasts. It had been a mistake.

Joe arched his eyebrows. 'Have I said something wrong? Burst in on you? I should have rung. I didn't think.' He looked unsure suddenly. She hadn't seen this in him before and she smiled, reaching out her hand, touching his.

'No, I'm just busy. Too much to do, too little time.' She had pushed the thought of his trip away, unable to think of any lies strong enough to make Frank change his plans, too engrossed in Lucia. And now she relaxed. What did it matter? Lucia was with her, safe, beautiful. That was what was important.

'Luke,' she called. 'Meet Joe. Uncle Bob's scout.' She laughed and Joe relaxed, shook hands and passed Camels round while Rosie collected cups, took orders, and passed them through to Mrs Orsini.

She then took Joe out to the yard. There was no point in wasting time but she had to make sure he didn't tell Frank and Nancy.

She walked to the pram, and pulled back the blanket. 'This is my child. Jack's child,' she said.

She watched Joe flush. He looked from the baby to Rosie but said nothing. He just stood, his hands in his pockets, and then he murmured, 'Quite a surprise. No wonder you didn't want to visit Frank and Nancy. They've got quite a bit on their plates already. This might shake them up a bit.'

Rosie touched her child's hair. It was always so fine, so soft, so warm. 'I'll tell them when things are easier for them, but you must say nothing. You must promise me that.'

She waited, wondering whether he would agree, wondering how she could make him, if he refused. But he agreed and she was surprised, but why should she be? He was kind, wasn't he? He had sent her money to go over to Frank. But she was still surprised and didn't know why.

Joe touched the baby, who woke.

'I thought you hadn't heard anything from Jack?'

'I haven't. He doesn't know, but I'll tell him, when he writes, because one day he will.'

He laughed as Lucia gripped his finger. His shirt was so white against the tan of his skin and he had promised he would say nothing. Rosie was grateful. He had touched her child and smiled and she was pleased.

He didn't stay long but came again in the evening to hear the band. Luke played while Joe drank Coke and listened, his finger tapping on the glass. Luke's band played for an hour and the music was good, mellow, haunting, penetrating. They listened to the chord held at the end of the chorus, heard the crescendo as Luke led the band into an all-in section. They heard the growl, heard his improvisation but it was a carefully planned one. He was so good, and Jake was better. So much better, but he still needed to go a little further.

'He'll get there though,' she told Joe. He nodded.

Luke sat with them in the interval. There was smoke in the air and candle wax on the table. Rosie checked her watch. Mrs Orsini was looking after Lucia but she would need a feed at ten.

'Great, really great. This club is good too, better than I expected,' Joe said, and Rosie winked at Luke, who sat back in his chair and smiled. 'You're right, Rosie. Bob'll really go for this. It's what he's been looking for. The guy on sax will have to go though.'

Rosie felt cold. It was as though there was no laughter in the room, no murmur of voices. Hadn't he heard her? Hadn't she just said that Jake would make it? Joe was still smiling, lifting the glass to his mouth, and she could picture him at the Lake Clubhouse, smart, adored, arrogant, ruthless. But he had agreed to keep her secret. There must be some softness there, maybe?

'But Jake is almost there. He's getting better every day,' Luke protested, and Rosie nodded, looking at their clothes, looking at Joe's. But no matter how slick he was, he was wrong.

'He'll make it. I'll stake my reputation on it. I'll pull in favours from Uncle Bob,' she added quietly.

Joe put the glass back on the table, and looked towards the group who were edging their way back through the tables.

'Look, Luke, you're a commodity. Bob can package you but you've got to get rid of the weak link. There's no room for feelings in this game.' He turned to Rosie. 'This is business. You need to toughen up, Rosie.'

Rosie stared at Joe, then at Luke. She waited.

'No,' Luke said getting to his feet. 'Thank you, Joe, but no. We all go, or no one goes. No package without Jake.' His smile was ironic.

Joe shrugged. 'I think you're wrong.'

Rosie put up her hand to stop Luke. She could fight for Luke now that he had made his decision. And she would fight because there was more than one way of doing business. You didn't have to be hard, just fair, and Joe could be fair. He had shown her that this afternoon.

'He's not wrong. Bob thinks of his bands as people. You're wrong, Joe. Think of the group who played at the barbecue, Bob nurtured them. Jake needs confidence, that's all, and a little time.' She wanted to shout at him, but she kept her voice calm. 'Bob wouldn't thank you if you passed this group over and they made it elsewhere, because they will.'

She watched him as he crossed his legs, picked at a thread on the sleeve of his jacket, rolled it between his thumb and forefinger. His nails were short, clean and square.

'Have you a lot invested in these guys?' Joe asked her quietly, leaning forward, talking behind his glass.

'A lot of time, a lot of effort, a lot of pleasure. Why not give them until you leave England? See what happens.' Why did he equate everything with money? She thought of his family. How could he be otherwise? But he could learn. She remembered his hand on her child. She still held on to Luke's jacket.

Joe looked at her and grinned. 'Why not? Bob's in no rush. OK. You got a deal. Just one condition.'

Rosie felt Luke relax, she let her hand drop from his jacket, feeling the relief surge in her too. She nodded. 'What?'

'I've got to write a feature for Frank on the Festival. You're expected to send one back too. Show me round. Let's have some fun.' He was smiling, his voice was lazy again as it had been on the beach by the lake.

She didn't want to celebrate while Jack was fighting, but she nodded. He knew about Lucia. He was going to report to Bob and he had been fair. There was no choice, but they wouldn't be alone. She would take Lucia, Jack's child.

But before she went anywhere, with Joe or anyone else, she took Lucia to Middle Street one morning when Norah would be at work. She pushed the back yard gate open, and picked up Lucia, taking her to Grandpa's roses, their fragrance heavy on the mid June air.

She walked along by The Reverend Ashe, took a matchbox from her pocket and tipped out the ladybird she had found, easing it with her finger on to the underside of the bud where too many greenfly were flourishing. Poor Grandpa.

'This will never do, will it, Lucia?' she said softly, bending to kiss the head of the sleeping baby. She heard the back door open and turned. Norah wasn't at work, she was standing in the doorway with a mouth like a sparrow's bum. Nothing changed.

'Hello, Norah.'

Her sister looked her up and down and then the baby in the fine white crocheted shawl which Mrs Eaves had made.

'I heard you'd had it.' She stood with her arms crossed over her breasts.

Rosie moved closer. 'I thought I would bring her to see Grandpa's roses, and now to meet you.'

Norah shook her head. 'I don't want to see your by-blows and now you've fiddled with the roses you can go. That fool Harold spends enough time on them as it is.' Her face was tight.

Rosie gently brushed away a bee that was hovering over Lucia. No, nothing changed. 'I'm sorry I bothered you.'

She reached out and picked the dark red rose from the raised bed. It was loosely budded. She smelt it, put Lucia back in the pram, and laid the rose on her blanket. Before she left she turned. 'There have been no letters for me then? No news for Ollie about Jack?'

Norah shook her head. 'He won't come back for you. You're on your own now.'

Rosie nodded. 'I'm not on my own any more, Norah.' She looked at Lucia, then pushed her from the yard, towards the rec where she sat on the swing with Lucia in her arms and watched the children playing, the mothers sitting knitting, talking. Thinking of Lee and of herself. Of Jack, of Norah. Listening to the echoes.

*

Norah sat in the kitchen, stirring her tea. The door was shut against the sun and those bloody roses. Shut against the sight of her sister with the baby that she and Harold seemed unable to produce.

Yes, there had been a letter from Jack. She had destroyed it. Yes, there had been a letter to Ollie informing him that Jack was a prisoner of war. She had told Ollie that Rosie had been informed.

She sipped her tea, looking at the space where Grandpa's chair had been, at the shelves devoid of books. How dare she take things from this house? How dare she have a child and a new white shawl? How dare she be loved, because Norah had read Jack's letter before she had burnt it. How dare she be loved when Harold no longer sat opposite her in front of the fireplace, and instead went out rubbing brasses or pruning roses. How dare she?

It was a hot day when Joe and Rosie went to the Festival, and as they approached the South Bank and the Skylon that seemed to hang in the air above them, Rosie said, 'I wonder if this isn't some sort of paternalistic exercise in educating the masses. There are so many exhibitions here which seem designed to present British Society as a family divided, not by class, but by a rift between the imaginative and the practical.'

Why was she talking like this? she wondered. Lecturing and pointing towards the twenty-seven acres which lay between County Hall and Waterloo Bridge.

'Casson and the other architects have laid it out like a miniature wonderland. It's crazy when there's still so much hardship, so much ruin. There's still so much fighting in Palestine and Africa and Korea.'

That was why she was lecturing. Because she was with another man and that man was pushing her child. He had been kind, and it was good to have someone with her, but it should have been Jack.

There were thousands of others strolling with them, stopping, investigating here, by the red, white and blue awning, the role of the British in exploration and discovery. Over there, by the yellow stand, was the geology of the country. Over there by the brown was the history of the monarchy.

'This is some kind of a pat on the back, is it?' Joe said, cupping his hand round the cigarette in his mouth, protecting the match from the wind which lifted his hair. He stood with his back to the crowds, one of whom nudged him. He dropped the match. Began again.

'Yes, I suppose so. We deserve it. You just have to look around.' Rosie pushed Lucia on. 'You haven't got this kind of damage back in the States, have you? You don't have to queue for basic foodstuffs. You just call in your loans.'

Joe laughed, drew on his cigarette, flicked the match into a litter bin. 'Point taken. But this really is quite something.'

He was taking photographs now, of the piazzas, the terraces, the murals and modern sculptures. Rosie looked in one pavilion, saw the new design in furniture, the chairs with spindly legs and the spidery staircases rising into the air. They looked as though they would take no weight.

An exhibitor smiled and called her over. 'Come on, madam, try the chair.'

She looked at Joe, who nodded. 'Go on then.' He took a photo and she pulled a face and then another and he was clicking all the time and then they were laughing.

They looked at the plan of the exhibits, following the red dotted line with their fingers, and Joe said they must retrace their steps and start at the beginning or they wouldn't get any sort of an article out of all this.

They began then at The Land of Britain and Rosie took notes on how the natural wealth of the British Isles came into being. She told Joe that she was going to slant her feature by comparing the new architecture – the piazzas, the modern sculpture – with damaged Britain, utilitarian Britain, the Nissen huts, the pill-boxes. He called her a 'goddamn pinko'. They laughed and she waited but he didn't tell her how he was going to write his feature.

They moved along, listening, looking, writing, talking, and he told her that Frank was well, much better than anyone had hoped.

'More important, though, are the circulation figures. They're right up again now that he's started using a pseudonym. The money's rolling in again.'

Rosie looked at him, at his smiling face, his assured manner, the hands which carried his notepad. A woman was in the way of the pram and Rosie stopped, waited.

'Excuse me, ma'am,' Joe called. 'We're trying to get through here.'

The woman turned. Rosie smiled. 'Don't hurry, we're looking too.'

She was embarrassed that Joe had wanted to force his way through. They had all day, there was no panic. She looked at the small models of the Skylon, the symbol of the Festival, which a trader was selling. Rosie bought one, and put it on the end of the pram, and the woman came over, looked at Lucia and smiled.

'You're a lucky couple, she's lovely.'

Rosie nodded and Joe flushed. 'I know,' Rosie said and it was only later as they were looking at the photographs representing the wide range of British manufacturers that she said gently, 'You said that the circulation figures were more important than Frank and that the money is rolling in. I hardly feel that either of these things is more important than Frank. Now I must find somewhere to feed Lucia.'

She looked around. There was a tent for lost children with a red pennant on the top. Her breasts were full and heavy, they were aching. She was angry with Joe.

She pushed the pram into the tent, sat on a folding chair, put Lucia to her breast and thought of the woman who had looked at the baby and said how lucky *they* were. And though she had been angry with Joe it had been so good to pretend for that short moment that she was one of a pair. She looked at the ring on her finger. Was she always going to be alone, or would he come?

They ate sandwiches and tea at a stall and Joe said, 'I didn't mean to say that the paper was more important than Frank. I guess you must know that.'

Rosie ate the moist bread, the Wensleydale cheese.

'Do I?' she replied. 'I'm not sure that I know anything any more.'

Joe put down his cup and asked for coffee because he couldn't drink the tea. It was ninepence. 'Gee, that's a lot.'

He took it and turned back to her. 'It's just that it's everything he's worked for. He loves that paper. I love it. I work real hard now. It's coming up good. It's going to be a good investment.'

'And what about McCarthy? Do you write against that poison, Joe? Do you shout that it's wrong to victimise innocent people?'

Joe bought another coffee and they moved away to let others near. 'Frank writes against it. That's enough.'

They finished eating, then walked further but Rosie was tired and there was something wrong. She was still angry and she didn't understand why.

'I must get back now, Joe. I've some calls to make, some details for Luke's tour to tie up and the other bands too.'

He nodded, pushing a path through the crowds. 'You shouldn't have to work like this, not with a baby. It needs two.'

Rosie shrugged. 'I'm doing just fine.'

'You sure are but it's a lot to handle. You're just swell.' He leaned over and propped the Skylon upright, but it fell over again as she mounted the kerb on their way out.

'Is it still OK for this evening?' he asked.

Rosie nodded. They had planned to go with Luke and Sandy downriver to Battersea Park to see the open air sculptures and then on to the fun-fair. She hadn't wanted to go alone with Joe.

Mrs Orsini looked after Lucia that evening and they took a cab to Battersea Park which exuded so much light that it bounced off the clouds and for a moment Rosie was with Frank and Nancy in New York again.

As they arrived fireworks soared high into the air. They heard the bangs and the whizz and Joe said, 'Guess they knew we were coming and this is the welcome mat.'

Tonight he was different somehow, he talked of Frank's expertise, his kindness. He said how much he respected him, how empty life would have been if anything had happened to him, and Rosie looked at him and smiled, her anger dying.

'I'm glad you feel the same as I do.'

They linked arms with Luke and Sandy and marched in step to the fun-fair singing 'Roll Out the Barrel', and by the time they arrived Joe knew the words.

They sat on painted horses, clutched the spiralling poles, and couldn't talk because the music was so loud, but they laughed. They all laughed and then they swung in boats, the ropes slipping between their hands. They shot ducks and she wouldn't think of Jack. They threw darts and she won a teddy bear and Joe carried it for her. They laughed, sang, drank and she felt young again. So young and the lights were on the river and it was as though she was by the lake. She felt Joe's arm around her, felt his kiss on her cheek.

'It's sure good to see you again, Rosie,' he murmured, and she smiled.

'Yes, it's good to see a friend from America. It's been so long. You were kind to tell me about Frank, and send my ticket over. I shall always be grateful to you for that.' She touched his face. 'Thank you.'

Luke grabbed her, pointed towards a striped tent. 'This we have got to see.' He dragged her off and she laughed and touched his cheek too. It was good to have friends.

They tried to guess the weight of the fat woman in the striped tent and ate candy floss which stuck to their faces in melted strands. They stood and watched the horses again, then had another go, and another. In the hall of mirrors they pulled faces, stuck out their legs, lifted their arms, and laughed until they ached.

They went on to the Fairway of the South Bank and danced, she with Luke, Sandy with Joe. They jitterbugged, and there was no Palais MC to tap her on the shoulder, no forbidding notices pinned to walls.

Joe tapped Luke's shoulder and she danced with him. They jived and his arms were strong as he pulled her towards him, steered her back, moved with her and with the music. His wrists were dark against his shirt. He pulled his handkerchief from his pocket, wiped his face, threw back his head and laughed.

'This is just great.'

And it was. Then the music slowed and they danced cheek to cheek and he told her of the drive-in movies they had in the States now. How kids would drive in, take a bay, honk their horns to bring the girl car-hops to their windows, order their food, which was brought to them on a hook-on tray. How the kids kissed and loved and hooted their horns when they had gone all the way.

She didn't want to hear this. Not from Joe. He was too close. So she talked instead about the growing popularity of jazz in Britain. So many loved it and all the time she could feel his breath on her hair, the heat of his skin as he held her hand. All the time she could remember the feel of his lips and hands on her breasts and she was angry at Jack because he wasn't here. Because he hadn't written and she was lonely.

But then she was angry at herself because she was dancing to music, swaying with the rhythm, laughing, when there was a war on. And nobody seemed to care. And she didn't understand herself.

'The Gloucesters' casualty figures came in as the King inaugurated this Festival,' Rosie said against Joe's shirt.

'Speak up, Rosie, I can't hear you,' he said, quickening his pace because the music was faster now, but they were jitterbugging again and she didn't repeat her words.

They danced until midnight and she wasn't tired but her breasts were full again. They caught a cab, then walked home, all of them, and Soho was still awake and they all wanted to go on to a club, but her dress was wet from the milk and how could she tell them that? She asked them in for a coffee while she checked on Lucia, and asked Mrs Orsini if she would mind staying for longer. Mrs Orsini sat in Grandpa's chair and smiled.

'You look happy. You look twenty-one at last. That is good.'

Rosie said again, 'We'd like to go to a club. I know it's very late, but I'll do the kitchen in the morning.'

Mrs Orsini smiled. 'You feed her now then you go back down and you go to a jazz club with them and we will share the kitchen. I like to see you like this.'

She put down her knitting and held up a hand as Rosie thanked her. 'No. No thanks. You just do as an old witch tells you and be happy. Tonight you are young and you are free. Go and explore yourself. My Mario says the same.'

Rosie picked Lucia up, felt her suck the nipple and she stroked the head of Jack's child.

They went on to the 51 Club. Luke knew the man on the door. Joe bought champagne and the ice clinked in the silver bucket. Rosie ran her finger down it. It was so cold. Joe eased off the stopper with a light thud. He poured the brimming bottle, letting the froth subside in each glass, then topping them up.

'To us all,' he said and they lifted their glasses.

'To us all,' Rosie repeated and included Jack.

They listened to the jazz. The air was thick with smoke and with laughter, theirs included, and Luke said that perhaps there should be dancing at Mario's. It was happening in other clubs. He nodded towards the floor.

'Not enough room, unless we open up the annexe,' Rosie said. 'Still, no reason why not. I'll talk to Mario. But I want to talk to this group first. They're good.'

Luke laughed, but Joe didn't. 'Can't you leave your work behind for one night?'

Rosie looked at him. 'It's work I love. It's work I need. There's Lucia, you know.'

He paused, then smiled, lifting the glass to her. 'I understand,' he said, but she wondered if he did.

She worked her way through the tables, catching up with the saxophonist, a young man with glasses, as he led his group to the bar, and booked them for Luke's tour that she and Harry, the promoter, were organising. She had a full programme now and she and Luke bought the next bottle of champagne because life had been good to them this summer. Rosie nodded, she had eight bands to organise now. It felt good.

They joined the other dancers on the floor and the beat was insistent, the lights revolved, she was young, she was free and tonight she had friends and more than that, she had a partner to hold her, swirl her round, pour her drink, toast her, and the tiredness dropped from her as they danced until nearly dawn.

Joe walked her home, waving to Luke and Sandy, shrugging away their thanks. Rosie was quiet because it was different now that they were alone. It was not so safe, so easy.

The streets were emptying as they walked from one pool of light to the next and there were no ropes hanging on the lampposts. Rosie told Joe that when she and Jack had been children there had been some in Middle Street. They had tied them. She looked at her hands. She could still feel the rope.

He stopped then, caught her arms, held her to him, stared into her face.

'He's gone. He hasn't written. He won't come back. Surely you know that now. You must make a life for yourself.'

Rosie pulled away, looking up at the sky where the clouds still hung. 'I don't know that. I don't know anything. If only I knew where he was, what he's doing, what he's feeling, I would know where I was going. No, I don't know anything, Joe, only that I love him.' She wished Luke and Sandy were still here, that they were all dancing and laughing again.

She looked down again at her hands, then at Joe. 'You're going to Japan. Frank told me. See where he is. Find him for me?'

He took her hands in his. He was warm, gentle. 'We were friends, Rosie. It would have been more if you hadn't left. Do you remember the beach?'

She shook her head, but she did. Goddamn it, she did. She said, 'I know he'll write. I know he loves me. Find him for me, Joe.'

She walked back towards the flat, back towards Jack's child. Joe walked with her, his strides long, easy. He said nothing but kissed her cheek at the door.

'I'll be back in December. I'll find out what I can.'

CHAPTER 22

It had been hard to accept Nigel's death, to think that he would never go to Oxford or punt on the river as he had talked so often of doing. That he would no longer wake up in the morning and look towards the hills and say, 'It's quite exquisite.'

Jack and Steve sat against the hut wall together in the baking heat of early September and marvelled that it was still only 1951. It seemed a very long time since they had first arrived in Korea. They felt so old and they were only twenty-one.

As more days passed Steve talked of college, of the history course he would take. His parents farmed in the Mid-West and couldn't understand that he wanted to move to New York, to feel cluttered by the buildings, to hole himself up and write novels.

'They say, get a proper job. OK, so I will, but one day I'll get there.'

Jack threw pebbles at the marker Steve had dropped. He had struck twice. If he did it again it was Steve's turn.

'I've never really thought what I'd do. It was all going to wait until I finished the draft.' He threw again. The pebble missed.

'You got a lot of time to think now, bud.'

The next pebble hit. They heard the click, heard a man rush past them with his arms outstretched, his mouth pursed, roaring like an engine. Two more men came close behind him. They looked at one another and grinned. It was silly time. They stood up, kicked down the pile of stones and joined in the swooping and whirling, dodging in and out of the others. One Corporal became a helicopter.

The guards stood and watched, bemused. But then the planes started making staccato gun noises and the guards moved forward, pushing, shouting, and at a signal from the

Corporal the men stopped dead. Their arms still outstretched until there was another signal, the jerking of a head. They stood to attention, their protest made for today; confusion generated. It made them feel less powerless.

They were made to dig holes as punishment for the gun noises. The soil was dry and stony but they had all done this at basic training. There was nothing new in the world. They were ordered to fill the holes in. They had done this in basic training too.

The next week they watched a tennis match, all the men lining either side of an imaginary court in the compound. They moved their heads in unison, watching a non-existent ball, clapping as the scores were called. This time there was no punishment but it would have been worth it, even if there had been. Jack wrote it down on the extra paper that he stole during essay writing.

'Rosie might be able to make something of it,' he told Steve.

'You make something of it. I'll help.'

Jack shook his head. 'We won't be here *that* long. I'm better suited to the market stall.'

They were still there in November, though, when the cold crackled in the air. By then the ground was too hard for them to dig as punishment and so they were made to stand upright until what little sun there was had gone from the day and frost coated their clothes. A man laughed at the Chinese guards who walked by, holding hands.

Jack allowed Steve to help him draft out an article on the escapade because he wanted to discuss the confusion between cultures, the cruelty of laughter. They knew now that the fighting would go on for a long time and, therefore, they would be here for a long time too. They understood that now and were trying to stay sane, trying not to think of the news the new prisoners had told them when they had been marched into the compound.

The peace talks were being held up by the Communists who wanted all their captured men to be returned, irrespective of whether or not they wished to be. The West remembered Yalta, and would not agree to this. It was insane that they were all kept here, day after day. But they mustn't go insane, they knew that.

'It's like the First World War back there, mate,' a Lance-Jack had told them. 'We're ranged in two lines along a static front lobbing everything we can get at one another, while the politicians talk. It's a laugh a minute. Nice and quiet here, though.'

But that was before he had sat through two hours of indoctrination in Chinese, two hours of translation, then attended interviews, then written essays. They spoke to him two weeks later when he was thinner, bored, restless, longing for a home which was very far away, longing for a letter, though no mail had yet been distributed. No, none of them must go insane. They must have something to work towards, to hang on to.

A new Commandant arrived. He called each of them in for an interview. He smoked but Jack didn't. There was no tobacco any more, only that which was offered by the lecturers, the interrogators, to those who volunteered to give propaganda interviews.

The man had smooth olive skin. His voice was soft. He smiled. Jack smiled. Would it be the same as it had always been?

'What does your father do?'

'He sells vegetables.'

'What does your mother do?'

No, it was not the same.

'My mother does nothing,' Jack said, not knowing now what Maisie did. Was she still laughing with her head thrown back? Did she still make bread and dripping? Do Americans eat that? He must ask Steve. He smiled because it didn't hurt to think of her any more.

'Why you smile? You are proud that mother not work? That mother lazy?'

'My mother is not lazy. I'm smiling at something private.'

'There is nothing private. You are being cleansed here. All is open. Why you smile?'

'I smile because I love my mother.'

The Chinese looked at the interpreter, then back at Jack. Then down at his sheet.

'Why your mother not work?'

'She has a child.'

'She could work with your father.'

'Maybe.' Jack shrugged. He couldn't tell this man his mother had gone away with a GI. That she lived in the land where the capitalist warmongers thrived. That she had chosen to do this. He had learned here that truth was sometimes best avoided. Rosie had known that. She had been right.

'How much land your family got?'

'As big as this room.' Jack looked round. 'Yes, as big as this room.'

He could see the shed, the fence, Lee's toys. He could smell Grandpa's roses. Were they still there?

'How many cows your family got?'

'We get milk in bottles.' Yes, he could still smell the roses, and yes they would still be there. Rosie would make sure of that. And no, he wouldn't go insane, not when he had her to return to.

'How many pigs?'

'No pigs.'

'What jewels you own?'

'No jewels.'

'What coins you own?'

'No coins.' But there was the nailer's penny. Did Rosie still have that? He knew she would.

The Commandant wrote, his head down, dandruff on his shoulders, then he sat back in his chair. 'You poor peasant. You should like our ways. You should fight the capitalists.'

Jack shrugged. The questions had begun differently but the end had been the same.

He told Steve not to mention his horses, his acres, his cows. He told him not to be too generous with the truth, not to get angry, not to shout, because he knew his friend dreamed of the pit and woke groaning. Jack did too.

'Don't let him sting you into saying anything,' Jack said.

But the Commandant did sting Steve and he did shout and rage and was dragged to the pit, stripped to the waist when the cold was deep in their bones. He was there while the Americans celebrated Thanksgiving with a service and songs, not feasts.

Jack wrote about the service, about the handfuls of millet which they had cooked to eat that day, and most days. He wrote about the Pilgrims. He drew parallels between the two.

But it was muddled and that was how he wanted it to be because he would need it like that when Steve was released.

He showed it to Steve when he came out. He made him sit and read it, while others threw their jackets over him, and blankets too, all donated by the men who had heated water for him to drink.

'Get away, Jack,' Steve said, pushing the paper aside, trying to curl over. 'Just get away. I've had enough. It's never going to end.'

But Jack had known he would say this. It was what he would have felt and he also knew that if he took the paper away it would be the beginning of the end. So he dragged Steve upright.

'Come on, Steve, I can't get it right. It's confused. You can help.'

Steve was pushing him away again, but Jack came back, shoving the paper in his face. Steve took it, scrunched it up, threw it across the room, and lay down. Rob, another prisoner, brought the paper back to Jack and helped to support Steve.

'Read this, you goddamn give-upper. You bloody Yanks, you're all the same.' Jack wasn't shouting, but his face was close to Steve's. He wasn't angry either, but Steve wasn't going to be allowed to give up. Those who did so died and Jack wasn't going to lose this friend who was so like Ed.

He straightened out the paper but again Steve knocked it from him, and it took an hour to force him to look at it. He stabbed at the second paragraph with a dirt-choked finger.

'Take it out. Who wants to know that garbage? Ain't you got no sense, Jack?' His voice was tired, angry, but he was reading it. Jack rewrote it in the morning and again Steve turned it down and it wasn't until the evening of the second day that he nodded, but Jack didn't care whether it was good or not, Steve was back on side. That was what mattered.

They attended lectures as before, threw stones at markers, as before, and Steve said, 'No more pit for either of us, eh?'

Jack nodded. 'Yep, let's get to the end of all this, then go out and get blind drunk, once in England, once in New York.'

They rose. It was time for afternoon lectures and the young men who filled the camp wondered how the minutes could drag so slowly, how their bones could ache with boredom, but they did. Day after day after day.

The next week they were all called into the big hut and saw a prisoner sitting alongside the Commandant. There were Chinese cigarettes on the table in front of him. The Commandant rose.

'You not have group study this morning. You have morning to self because one has behaved with great satisfaction.' He pointed to the prisoner who stared ahead.

'This man has seen the truth. He will go now from the camp and he will tell the world on the radio of the crimes of the Imperialists. He will tell of the wrongness of his attitude which has given way to correctness.'

There was silence in the room.

'You too can leave this camp. You too can see the truth. Your countries are not interested in you. You are still here. The war goes on. You are behind wire, play foolish tricks while warmongers eat in restaurants. Your wives live well without you. The years pass. Even if you do go home, we can reach you. You are never free of us. It is better to be a friend than enemy.'

He took a cigarette from the pack and gave it to the man, who put it between his lips. He was thin, drawn and his eyes still looked straight ahead. The Commandant lit the cigarette, smoke spiralled up to the wooden roof. Jack watched it disappear.

There was still silence, even when they were dismissed. The words were the same as they had been on previous occasions and there had been silence then. No one booed, no one blamed the man. It was his way of surviving.

'Gets to you, though, doesn't it?' Steve said as they crouched on the ground and threw stones at the marker. Jack had won thirteen games, Steve eighteen. 'Guess the months could become years.'

Jack nodded, looking round at the hills dusted with snow. It was so cold. He looked up at the sky, it was cloud-heavy. There might be snow tomorrow. Where could they throw their stones? It was better to think of that.

But the next week they were told it was over. The guards herded them into columns, the Commandant stood before them, the snow falling on his cap, his pressed olive green uniform, his soft golden skin, as he told them 'All prisoners go home'.

It was too sudden. He could not believe it, but then he felt Steve's hand on his arm. 'We're going to make it, Jack.' And then the joy came, coursing through him from deep inside.

They were dismissed. For a moment they could not move, then they leaped in the air, whooping, cheering, some crying. They were going home, goddamn it, they were going home. Jack thought of Rosie, of running down the alley towards her, of her arms as she came out of Grandpa's yard. Then he thought of the prisoner who had taken cigarettes in return for survival. Would he go home?

Joy pushed the hunger and the cold away. It brought smiles to faces which had stiffened into grim endurance. It brought hope into faces which had been without for too long. They were going home.

They were marched to a train, the snow soaking into their worn uniforms and through the split seams of their boots, but they marched in time, their few possessions slung on their backs.

The Sergeant called out the drill orders. Their shoulders were straight. They took the walking wounded, helping them, bearing their weight, and Jack felt the stones he had thrown at the marker in his pocket. They could be kept with Grandpa's penny.

He turned and looked back at the mountains. 'How exquisite,' he said.

Steve nodded his goodbye to Nigel too.

They were marched to a train. There were no seats but it didn't matter. They would be home for Christmas. They headed south in the last of the daylight, looking out across the country, seeing the ruins, the devastation, the napalm-damaged hills. The people were living in dugouts, hovels. There was nothing but poverty, but they were working, stolidly clearing the snow, cooking over open fires, ignoring the train. Jack wrote about this for as long as the daylight lasted, asking what the fighting had been about, but soon it was too dark to see the page.

There was no light then, no food, no drink. They sat on the floor, moving with the train, huddled together for warmth.

'My mom'll be pleased,' Steve said, his voice a murmur like all the others.

'I'll write to mine but first I'll see Rosie,' Jack said.

Before daylight broke they eased into a tunnel and stayed there throughout the day to avoid the air strikes. So the fighting wasn't over, the Sergeant asked the guard, looking uncertain.

'No, you being exchanged,' the guard said.

They had water, they had food, but they were colder now and blew on to their hands, draping old blankets over their shoulders. But did any of it matter? They were going home. They were bloody well going home.

Bob sat with them, talking of the food he would cook on his wife's stove in their prefab.

'I don't know, you retreads. You've all gone soft,' Steve laughed. 'Let her do the cooking.'

Jack laughed too, wondering how reservists could bear to be called up, having already done their bit, and then he thought of Tom. He would not be going back. He thought of Suko too and hoped that she would find happiness.

Bob told them how he would cut the rind off the bacon, fry that until it was crisp, then the bacon, then the mushrooms picked the evening before from fields behind the house. He would take the sharp knife from the drawer, slice the tomatoes, grown against the wall behind the house, and fry them too. He would walk up the ash path to pick the warm eggs from the coop, the straw still on the shells. Soon the whole wagon was listening, hearing the fat spitting, tasting the bacon, the British not caring that it was the wrong season for tomatoes, not caring that bacon was still on ration. It was home, and that was where they were going, and now they cheered and laughed even when the guards swung back the door and said, 'Quiet. You should sleep. Quiet.'

How could they sleep? They were leaving here. The big man himself had said so.

They travelled on south as darkness came. On the fifth night they were shunted into a siding near Pyongyang where they stayed for a week, asking the guards each day when they would be released.

'When Captain come,' they said.

The men used a bucket as a latrine, pushing it far into the corner. They squashed lice which still bit them in spite of the cold, but none of this was for long and so it didn't matter.

On the eleventh day a Chinese Captain slid open the wagon door and they clambered to their feet, pushing towards the entrance. Other guards put up their rifles as the Captain said, 'You go north instead. Prisoner-of-war camp. A mistake has been made.' He smiled and slammed the door shut and there was only darkness, only silence. It had been a trick, but a darker trick than the ones they had played. It was a pitch black trick.

It broke three of the men. It nearly broke all of them. Hope had gone. Hate had come for many of them, but not for Jack. He had had enough of hate. He just wrote it down and Steve helped. They made Bob help too because he cursed and swore, beating the side of the wagon with his fists. He wasn't the only one who came close to despair as the train swept north again. There were tears too, in the darkness of the night.

'Funny trick, eh?' Steve whispered to Jack, his voice full.

'Capped our games in the camp, didn't it? Quick learners, eh?' The tears were dry on Jack's cheeks now, there would be streaks in the dirt. He rubbed his skin.

'The goddamn bastards.'

'Maybe we could try and escape,' Jack whispered. He couldn't bear to think of the train taking him further and further from Rosie. He wanted to break from it, hurl the guards to one side, rush for the South. 'Can't be too far from the lines now, but with each day, it's further. We'll talk as we march.'

A guard had told them they were leaving the train the next morning. They waited, sitting with their arms around their knees, resting their heads, but not sleeping. No one was sleeping. How could they when the disappointment was so sharp, the anger so raw?

They were marched from the train, out into a road cleared of snow.

'To another camp,' the guards said, pointing north.

The Sergeant lined the men up before they left, ignoring the guards who gestured for them to begin. He stood before them, looking as thin as they did, but ramrod straight, his eyes sweeping the men. 'You'll march in step. You'll remember who you are. You'll not let these buggers beat you, or I shall have your heads for my breakfast and your danglies for my lunch. Is that quite clear?'

The men smiled and nodded.

The Sergeant barked, 'About turn.' He ignored the guard who was pulling at his clothes and shouting at his men to hurry. 'Forward march.'

It was only then that the men moved, and they did so in perfect unison. It was only after the first mile that the pace slowed but they were still in time. They would be until they dropped now.

Before Steve and Jack could make their move, two Americans ducked out of the line as it passed between wooded slopes. They sneaked off into the undergrowth. Jack watched them snake across the snow-covered rice field to the base of the hill. They were stark against the white and their footsteps were clear.

Ten minutes later, the alarm was raised. North Korean guards found them two hours later and beat them to death.

Later Jack looked up at the condensation trails behind the shooting stars as the north-west jet streams pushed the planes home and nodded when Steve said, 'Seems kinda pointless. Might as well get through school, buddy.'

They both nodded, still marching, still watching the men in front, blocking out the two beaten bodies which had been thrown into the ox-cart. Those men would never go home now.

They marched until January, through deep forests where all sound was deadened, dragging their legs through thick snow, pulling their balaclavas low. Snow fell from branches, whooshing through the frost-laden air.

'It's quite exquisite,' Steve said and Jack nodded.

Finally, in driving snow, they reached the camp and were pushed into a large barn.

Their Sergeant was saluted by men who were already gathered in the building. One stepped forward.

'Fellow students, we welcome you to this college of correction. I am Sergeant Howe,' he said and bowed.

'How exquisite,' said Jack, bowing back, and they began to laugh, all of them, too loudly and too long, but it was a laugh.

They were given padded overcoats by the Communists which they thought was a trick, but which Sergeant Howe said was part of the 'lenient policy'. They waited in the barn for the interrogation which they knew must come, and then there would be the lecture and the translation.

It came and Jack looked at the Chinese who asked him how much land he had. What his mother did. What his father did. Jack answered him, wanting to ask in return, 'And what have your people just done to our hopes? Did you think it was funny?' but he just answered the questions as they all did, then sat and listened to the lecture, and to the translation, because this was their life now until they left it on an ox-cart or the war was over.

It was eight in the evening before they were released from the barn to their clay and wattle huts which were heated by tiny wood-burning stoves. The floorboards were covered by straw mats with a narrow aisle down the middle.

They slept shoulder to shoulder. The wind swept through gaps in the clay and their breath froze on their blankets, on their lips, as the night hours passed. No one talked, but no one slept either. They had been so close to escape and now they were back at the beginning again.

Early in the morning loudspeakers blared Soviet and Chinese revolutionary music over the compound and Jack leaned up on his elbow.

'I think I prefer Butlins, on the whole,' he said and pushed the despair away, because it was a new morning and he must live each day, if he was to return to Rosie. And he would return.

Before roll-call at seven a.m. the new men, including Jack and Steve, were put on the wood-collecting rota.

'I guess everything's back to normal now,' Steve muttered and he, like Jack, began again. They all did.

They ran across to the lean-to communal latrine in temperatures which were forty degrees below zero and ran back because it was too cold to walk. They had to stand, though, for roll-call and thought that they would die.

Then they did physical jerks as the Commandant ordered. The snow glistened at the edge of the compound and the twilight of the winter morning turned into daylight and the cold air cut into their throats and chests.

One hour before breakfast the squad leader, Corporal Jackson, read a Communist publication aloud in their hut with a guard at the door. He read without pausing for full stops, for correct pronunciation, but used his own. It lightened the morning.

Four men collected the food from the camp kitchen where it was cooked in pots, carrying it back to the hut in a large bucket. The men placed their rice bowls and cups round the bucket and millet was spooned out into each. They ate it standing or sitting on their straw mats, talking quietly.

Another four men drew water into another bucket and wash-pan from the kitchens, where there was a gasoline drum full of water which was kept full over a fire which burned from dawn to dusk.

A bell rang at 10.00 hours and they went with the other men of their squad to the lecture room, where they sat with legs crossed on the bare boards and listened while they were instructed on the Marxist philosophy in Chinese, and then again in translation whilst their ears and noses felt that they would drop off with the cold.

They broke at midday, ate rice which contained a few tiny pieces of pork.

'It's a better camp,' Steve said.

'The Commies have officially decided that they'll not convert us all by cruelty. They're trying kindness to turn us into eager little beavers who will spread the message back home, when we get back. Make the most of it. Who knows how long it will last,' the Sergeant said.

They sluiced their bowls, then walked in the compound, taking note of the sentry at the gate and the sentry posts at intervals around the perimeter. They watched the village life which went on outside the wire and Jack remembered the Italian prisoners and how they had given the evacuees apples and showed them pictures of their children. He thought of the hot meal he had eaten. The prisoners probably ate better than the villagers. The whole thing was crazy.

At 14.30 hours they were back in the unheated hall and now the prisoners were made to read aloud from Marxist books and they did so, with no regard for punctuation or meaning.

The lecturer then picked Jack out to give his opinion on the chapter that had just been read.

Jack had listened to the beginning and the end so he stood up and repeated, 'The philosphical basis of Marxism is dialectical materialism which is hostile to all religion. Marxists feel that religion defends exploitation and drugs the working classes.'

He sat down.

'Proper little swot, aren't we?' grinned Bob.

'But what is your opinion of it?' the lecturer insisted.

'Oh-oh,' whispered Steve as Jack rose to his feet.

'Love is an opiate, so is alcohol. They exist. Religion exists. It gives ease as the others do and comfort. Therefore my opinion is that as religion exists so does its use as an instrument of peace and comfort.'

There was silence as he sat.

'Didn't understand much of that,' Steve murmured.

'Neither did I,' Jack replied.

'Neither did he, from the look of him.' Bob was looking at the lecturer who looked at the guards, then shrugged and asked another man for his opinion of Jack's opinion.

The hours crept on and in the evening they were issued with Russian and Chinese papers, translated into English. They used the paper to roll marijuana cigarettes in the summer, the Corporal told them, tearing the outside edge of three of the sheets, but only three, because the guards took the papers back at the end of the evening.

The next afternoon they were issued with paper and pencils and ordered to write an essay on 'Why the unjust aggressor is in Korea'. Jack managed to take two pieces of paper and, writing on both sides of one, he kept the other so his lessons could begin again that night with Steve.

And so the hours and the days slowly passed. Sometimes there were letters though none from Rosie, but then many people had none. They wrote letters too, but doubted that any were sent.

January became February and then it was March which limped into April and the days were still filled with boredom, with hunger, with cold and nothing changed with the coming of spring but the weather.

CHAPTER 23

By mid December '51 Rosie and Mario had extended the club, using the annexe for tables, leaving space in the back room for dancing. Luke and Sandy had left to tour Britain, along with the Larkhill Boys Rosie had met in the club with Joe.

'Bookings are good,' Luke rang to say. 'Full houses everywhere. Harry's bought himself another gold watch. You'll be able to do the same.'

'Or maybe Father Christmas will do that for me,' Rosie laughed. 'See you in January. Take care, all of you.' She put the phone down and looked round her small flat.

The table lamps lit the room softly, illuminating Grandpa's books. He would like it here, not as much as in his own home, but he would like it. There was a small half-knitted cardigan lying on the workbasket. She reached for it, began knitting, listening to the fire which hissed in the grate. She missed Luke and the boys. She measured the length of the cardigan then decreased for the armhole. It was ten o'clock. She was tired. She should sleep but each day and each night she waited for Joe to phone with news of Jack. He hadn't yet.

She finished the armholes, caught the remaining stitches on a holder, cast on for the left front, knitted up to the armhole, but her eyes were dry and sore. Rosie looked at the clock again. Eleven. She put her knitting away and went to bed, hearing Lucia breathing quietly in the cot beside her. The baby hadn't stirred since her feed at ten. She would sleep through until seven. She was perfect.

On 19 December she received a Christmas card from Frank and Nancy together with a present of a $50 bill which she put into the bank with the rest of her money. There would be no gold watch for her. There was a long future to build. She read their letter as she waited for the spaghetti to cook in the café kitchen.

Lower Falls
15th December

Dearest Rosie,

Well, your skis are still in your room, the snow is here but you aren't. We understand though, really we do. Joe told us how busy you are and we can remember how hard we worked when we took over the paper. One day, we'll come to you.

Frank is well. He writes his columns, and edits the paper unofficially, makes his 'pinko' stand for common sense. Two of his friends still can't find regular work but pick up whatever they can. They will never write again, as long as McCarthy can stand up and give the performances that he does.

It is thought that maybe Eisenhower will throw his hat into the ring for the elections. Maybe he will be able to bring him to heel. Enough of that. We survive. I hope it isn't that which keeps you from us? But even as I say that, I know it can't be. Forgive me. It's just that you start leaping at shadows some days, so many friends have turned their backs.

It was so strange, wasn't it, the way the shooting stopped in Korea at the end of November following the establishment of the truce line along the 38th parallel. Joe filed his copy on it, saying no one ordered it, it just happened. For a moment there was peace.

I can't hold out much hope on a full armistice for a long while. The repatriation of the prisoners of war is the stumbling block. Have you heard from Jack? What is that boy playing at? How did you get on with Joe? He's a good reporter. He's sending back some good copy.

Have a wonderful Christmas, Rosie. The house will be empty without you, darling. Dare we say we will see you in 1952?

Your ever loving
Nancy

Nancy did not mention the feature Rosie had written about the Festival. Perhaps there was too much happening with them over there. Rosie wished she could go, but she couldn't.

Mrs Orsini, Mario and Rosie decorated the café and the club the next day, tying together holly with red ribbon bought from Mrs Eaves, pinning it up in corners, sitting Lucia up in her pram so that she could see, stringing streamers across the room. The customers helped. Mrs Eaves helped too and somehow there was enough laughter to wash away another Christmas without Jack, without news even.

On the evening of the twenty-second Rosie cut, coloured and pasted chains for her flat, showing Lucia who banged her rattle on the blanket in front of the fire, turning from her front on to her back, kicking her feet, pushing the rattle into her mouth, dribbling. Rosie kissed her cheeks, they were wet, pure.

She picked up her child and held her, seeing Jack in her movements, in her smile. She carried her to the window, looking out over the rooftops, hearing the jazz, the shouting and the laughter.

'Where are you, Jack?' she called, breath clouding the window.

A telegram came from Joe the next day, while she was serving customers and Mrs Eaves with mince-pies.

'Have news stop Be with you 24th stop Joe'

Rosie put it down. Mrs Eaves read it, folded it, put it away, then asked Mrs Orsini to babysit for Lucia while Rosie came with her to the West End.

Rosie looked at her, then started to put sugar into bowls. They were too full. There would be news tomorrow. It would be Christmas Eve and there would be news. How could she wait that long? Why was it so hard to breathe?

'Come on then, get your coat,' Mrs Eaves said, picking up her handbag and her gloves, pulling them on, pushing up between her fingers. 'Come on, get your coat, I said. Let's get you through this evening anyway. And don't worry. It can't be bad news or he would have cabled you earlier.'

They walked out into the crisp air. There was jazz all around, coming up from cellars, mingling with calypso, with swing. Tomorrow there would be news and she couldn't bear the minutes that had to pass until then.

Chestnuts cooked on braziers, sailors on leave entered the pubs, finding accommodation for their leave, amongst the homosexuals or the girls. Tarts lingering in doorways called, 'Merry Christmas, Rosie. I'll be in later for a coffee.'

Mrs Eaves took her arm and pointed to the Christmas tree outside the pub. There were streamers on it and candles which weren't lit. 'They'll light them at midnight on Christmas Eve, as they always do, now the war's over,' the publican said, as he waved to them from the doorway.

But the war wasn't over. Not the one Jack was fighting and the thousands of other young men.

They caught a bus, singing carols with the Salvation Army band as they waited. They went up to the West End, walked along Oxford Street, then, catching another bus, walked along Shaftesbury Avenue, looking at the billboards; and then they went back to Soho which they both preferred, which they both knew now. At least the evening was passing. There was only the long night to get through and some of the next day.

Joe didn't come until six p.m. on Christmas Eve when the café had closed. Rosie stood at the door of her flat, watching as he climbed the stairs. There was a small decorated Christmas tree fixed into a log in his hand. He held it out. Rosie's breath was shallow again.

'For Lucia,' he said. His mac was open, his belt dragged on the floor. It was dirty, muddy.

Rosie nodded, stood aside to let him enter. The tree smelt of pine. She placed it beneath the window. By the morning the room would smell too. It would be fresh and clean and pure but she couldn't wait any longer. She turned.

'Tell me,' she said.

Joe smiled, shrugged. He looked tired, there were bags under his eyes, lines across his forehead. 'Well, the good news is that he's safe. He's a POW. His father should have been notified. I don't know why he didn't let you know. Something went wrong somewhere. Anyway, Jack is one of the lucky ones. At least he's been named as a prisoner by the Communists. Thousands of them have just been sucked in and lost.'

Rosie turned to the bright sky, to the stars, to the jazz which she could hear drifting up, along with the steam from the clubs and pubs. It was going to be a good Christmas, she thought, as the joy surged within her. He was safe, he was out of the fighting. He had not come back because he couldn't, that was all.

'So that's why he hasn't written,' she murmured, putting her hand to her mouth.

Joe wrestled with his tie, pulling it loose, unbuttoning his collar. He looked around, saw the bottles on the table and asked, 'Can I pour myself a drink?'

Rosie came across the room, poured the bourbon Mario had found for her and then one for herself. Joe could have the crown jewels for bringing that news.

'I've no ice,' she said, feeling the smile broaden on her face.

'Drink up, Rosie. I said that was the *good* news.' Joe swirled his drink round in the glass. It was amber in the soft light. The fire was hissing. She looked at the tree. She shouldn't have smiled, that was it. Or made the streamers. If she hadn't made the streamers it would have been good news only. No, she didn't want to hear any more. She knew the important news, didn't she?

'Take your mac off, Joe,' she said, sipping the bourbon. It was harsh in her throat. The glass was cold. She put it down on the small table by Grandpa's chair, carried the mac across to the hook on the back of the door. It smelt of Joe, of America. It should smell of Korea. Why was it so hard to breathe? Why did her throat ache like this?

She walked back, sat in Grandpa's chair.

'Tell me now, then.'

She didn't look at him, but at the Christmas tree, at the chains she had made, but which would have been better left unmade. Then she looked at the fire as he told her that he had discovered in Japan that Jack had fallen in love with a Japanese girl called Suko. That they had had an affair, that he was to marry her on his return. That he would never be coming back to her and that was why he had never written.

She looked at the glass of bourbon on the table, she pulled it to the edge, tipped it, breaking the vacuum as they had done at the Lake Club when they were so very, very young. There was no vacuum, but what did it matter?

She drank, then looked at the tree, at the fire, at the chains, at Joe who stood there, looking down at her.

He moved towards her, knelt, touched her knee, her arm. 'I'm so sorry. So very sorry.'

'At least he's safe,' she said but she didn't want Joe there. She didn't want anyone there. She wanted to push him away, he was making the room dark. He was taking what air there was. She couldn't hear the hissing of the fire while he was there. She couldn't see the chains. She couldn't see the tree, but it was his tree. He had bought it for Jack's daughter. He had been kind. And there was no pain yet. For God's sake, the pain hadn't come yet.

'Come for Christmas,' she said. 'For lunch. You mustn't be alone. No one should be alone.'

She stood now, keeping the glass in her hand. She walked to the door, took the coat off the hook and gave it to Joe, because the pain was beginning and it was hard to breathe. So hard to breathe.

He left, walking softly down the stairs.

She called, 'There can be no mistake?'

He stopped and turned. 'No, Rosie, no mistake. I can vouch for that.' And what did it matter, he thought, as he moved down the stairs, what did it matter if he had lied. That man didn't deserve her. She was far more suited to him.

The Christmas meal was held in Mario's flat. Mrs Orsini drank sweet sherry and gave some to Rosie because the older woman had heard the news. They pulled homemade crackers and Joe gave her a gold watch and she smiled, felt its coolness against her skin, felt his fingers as he did up the catch. She held it up to the light.

'Luke will be pleased,' she murmured. 'Thanks, Joe.' She wished that Luke and Sandy were here.

She heard her voice from a distance, saw his smile. She gave Lucia Grandpa's nailer's penny, hung now on a silver chain. She pulled her cracker, ate turkey, ate Christmas pudding, found silver sixpences, fed Lucia, sat by the fire, listened to the King's speech but was dying inside.

Joe came the next day and the next and the next, helping, talking, comforting. He played with Lucia who laughed and held her hands out to him. He took the baby to the park, then hoovered the flat for Rosie, typing out his copy, talking to her about her writing, about the Cougars, about the tennis courts at the lake, about Frank and Nancy, about a world which did not include Jack.

She worked in the café, she played with Lucia, she wrote a letter of thanks to Frank and Nancy and on New Year's Eve she stayed up until midnight in the Orsinis' flat and Joe clicked his glass against hers when the clock struck twelve.

'Happy 1952,' he said, and smiled and both their gold watches glinted in the light from the Orsinis' lamps but Rosie wanted her own lamps, her own fire, and could bear all this no longer. She ran from them, taking Lucia, running up the stairs, laying her child down in her cot, stroking the hair that was Jack's, kissing the smile that was his too.

Now the pain broke and she stood at the window, hearing the music. And she cried, great racking sobs, because he wouldn't be in her life again, but how could he not be? He was part of her. His memories were hers. They had swung on the rope tied to the lamppost together. They had smelt the hops, they had stolen the cheeses. How could he do this?

Then she felt terrible rage, searing violent rage. He had shared her life, hated her, loved her, thrust himself into her, torn her, taken her in his confusion and now he had forgotten her and all their years together. Goddamn you, Jack. I hate you, I hate you.

She leaned against the window and hated him, loved him, wanted him, wanted Nancy, wanted the comfort of arms about her. And then Joe came. He held her, his arms were strong, and they had memories too. The lake was there as he soothed and stroked. The lake and the sun and the long sloping lawns where she had known peace and love. Where everything had been so much easier.

He carried her to the bed, he undressed her and undressed himself and she clung to him because he was part of Frank and Nancy's world. He was kind, he was here, he wanted her. Jack didn't. His hands had found someone else's body; his mouth, someone else's mouth.

But Joe was too fast for her, and it was as if they were at the barbecue by the lake again with his lips on her breasts, his hands on her body. She knew she only wanted comfort, nothing more than that, but what did it matter? What did any of it matter? She shut her mind to the face which loomed over her, to the body too close, too heavy. The body which wasn't Jack's and which was entering her, filling her, and now she held him, because passion of a sort was sweeping her too. Passion born of anger, of pain.

In the morning they walked Lucia in her pram across the frost-hardened grass, carving out patterns on the ground. Her hand was warm in his, her lips too, from the kiss he gave her, and it was good not to be alone. But Jack was still everywhere and her love for him was too, and her anger and her pain.

But as the weeks wore on and Joe was seconded to a Fleet Street paper it became easy to be with him. He laughed, he joked, he tossed Lucia in the air and took her back to the time she had shared with Frank and Nancy.

At night she forced herself not to think of Jack as Joe kissed her and held her, because Jack had held another, he loved another. The waiting was over. Their love was over.

But she dreamed of him. Each night she dreamed of him and woke up crying, wanting to clutch at the image, wanting to shake it, hurt it, as she was hurting.

In February the King died and Frank wrote asking for a feature from each of them. Separate ones please, he said, which Rosie thought was strange, because how else would they do it? She left Mario to take any messages and wrote about the black armbands the children were wearing, the adults were wearing, she was wearing. She wrote of the simple oak casket which was moved from Westminster Hall to St George's Chapel. She wrote of the thousands of subjects who paid their last respects to this man who had brought them through war and peace.

The coffin left Westminster on a gun carriage. Big Ben rang out one beat a minute to mark the fifty-six years of the King's life and many of the men and women who stood with Rosie wept. And Rosie wept too.

The Household Cavalry, in ceremonial dress, walked in slow time to Paddington station where the royal train was waiting. As the cortège passed Marlborough House, Queen Mary, the King's mother, stood at the window and bowed her head and the crowd wept again.

Rosie wrote about the woman who turned to her while she was writing and asked who all the words were for. Rosie told her. 'Tell them we loved him,' the woman said.

Joe was covering the story at the Windsor end and when he arrived back that evening he hugged her, kissed her, his lips eager, his tongue searching her mouth. His nose was cold from the frost-full air, and so were his hands as he slipped them beneath her shirt. She laughed and kissed his neck and felt his hands become warm as they stroked her back, her breasts.

'You had a good day then,' she murmured, glad that someone was coming home to her each day, glad that she was becoming used to it, welcoming it, wanting Jack to know that she was not alone either.

Joe kissed her forehead, tucking her shirt back in, moving away, laughing.

'I sure did, so let's have your notes, I'll put this together and then we have the evening left for better things.' He laughed again and reached forward, rubbing his finger around her mouth.

Rosie smiled. It was good to be wanted at last. 'No. I'll write mine. You write yours. That's what Frank asked for.'

She moved to Grandpa's chair and began to write. Joe came towards her. 'Oh, come on, Rosie. Let's put it into one. It'll make a better feature. Won't take me a minute.'

But she refused because George VI had been *her* king, not his.

'Perhaps you should write about the return of the Duke of Windsor for his brother's funeral. That might appeal to the Americans,' she said, wanting to soften her refusal.

'Trying to teach me my job?' His voice was cold.

Lucia called out from the bedroom Rosie had made for her out of the boxroom. She moved towards the door. She didn't want this row. She didn't want any rows. There had been enough struggle already, hadn't there?

'No, you know your job. I know mine.' She didn't want to talk about this any more. She was too tired.

'I still think it would make a better feature. We'll split the fee.'

Rosie stopped. 'Look, Joe. It's not the goddamn money. I don't need the money so much any more. It's just that I have something I want to say from the British point of view. You wouldn't understand.'

Joe moved towards her, pulling her back towards the chairs. 'Oh, come on. I don't give up easy. Let's talk this over.'

'I've told you. No.' Rosie pulled away. He had hurt her wrist. Her watch had dug into her skin. She rubbed it and returned to the door. Now she was angry. 'Goddamn no.' She was shouting. Lucia cried.

Joe left her then, picking up his mac, thudding down the stairs, pushing aside Lucia's pram, scoring the hall wall, and by the time he returned she had finished her feature and posted it. He was drunk. He was sorry. So was she, because he was a good man, a kind man.

Joe knelt by Grandpa's chair and kissed her and she kissed him back because he had soothed her, comforted her, and there was some sort of caring growing inside her for him, though she didn't know how much.

February grew colder and Rosie pulled the blankets up around Lucia's shoulders when they went out. Lucia was sitting up now, pulling herself forward, pointing, her nose red in the cold. Joe never again drank as much as he had on the night of the King's funeral. Instead he talked of the future, of Frank's paper, of the need to keep it in the family, of his love for her.

At night his body sought hers and she liked the feel of his hands and his lips and now she stroked him too, held him, kissed him, and the dreams of Jack were not so fierce. But still they came.

Lucia was pulling herself up, using the table, and it was good to share these moments with someone else. But Rosie still read the news about Korea.

Nancy wrote to say that she was sorry, so sorry about Jack, but it didn't seem like the boy Rosie had loved. Was she sure of her facts?

But Rosie wouldn't allow herself to think about Jack any more, at least while she was awake. She had been working harder in these last few months than she had ever done before. She took phone calls late into the night and made them too, adding to the stable of bands, moving more and more into the promotion side, enjoying the battles, enjoying the triumphs, pushing away the failures.

Joe didn't like it. He didn't like the phone ringing when he was stroking her hair, when he was kissing her mouth. He put on the radio too loud so that she had to strain to hear. But he was so kind and he comforted her, she told herself. He had found out about Jack for her. And it was better than being alone, wasn't it? And after all he had said he would listen to the band again now that Luke was coming home and send his final report to Bob. Rosie planned a party and Joe helped to lay out the drinks in Mario and Mrs Orsini's flat, because her own wasn't big enough. And then Luke was home and the gramophone played Bix Beiderbecke. Luke and Jake kissed her, held her, gave her a package. It was a gold watch.

She took it from the box, held it and couldn't speak but then Joe came up.

'Beat you to it, fellers.' He lifted Rosie's arm, pulled back her sleeve.

Luke and Jake flushed, then laughed, but Rosie didn't laugh. She took off Joe's watch and put it in her bag. She offered her wrist to Luke and he slipped the new one on.

'I'll wear one today, one tomorrow,' Rosie said, knowing that Joe had stiffened. Jack would have waited until he saw whether or not she could cope. But she mustn't think of him.

She took Joe's arm, kissed his cheek, led him away, poured him a drink and told him he was handsome, kind, loving. Soon he was laughing again and asking her to book Luke for Mario's club so that he could hear the group again.

The music was softer now and Luke came and danced with Rosie, holding her. He was familiar and he was safe. She told him that she was sleeping with Joe. She told him that the memory of Jack still hurt so much. He nodded.

'Don't rush into anything. Remember what your grandpa said.'

She didn't rush anywhere. She woke, worked, loved, slept and the days passed, but it always seemed dark. It had seemed dark since Christmas. She was tired. She ached inside. Joe was with her but the loneliness remained.

*

At the end of March Rosie received a letter from Frank enclosing $50 for the article on the King's funeral.

Lower Falls
20th March

Dearest Rosie,

Yes, this is what I wanted. All your own work. I didn't tell you that the paper spiked your feature on the Festival. You copied Joe's ideas about drawing comparisons between the new ideas and the Nissen huts, the austerity etc. I faced him with it. He'd been having some trouble handling domestic features, you know. He told me he had talked his ideas over with you. That you must have 'borrowed' them.

I was sorry you did that but he said things were tough, you might have become confused. I can understand that happening. I've done it myself. I was worried about you. You must have been real upset, real tired, but I guess things are better.

I wanted you to know I love you.
Frank

Rosie waited for the day to pass. Waited until Joe came home. She worked, she phoned, she cancelled one booking because the manager of the theatre was known to pass drugs. Her boys were too good for that. She took a taxi to Middle Street. She walked past 15 and 17 down to the rec. The wooden fencing was still up around the bombed houses.

'Will it ever be finished?' she murmured into Lucia's hair, sitting on the swing, hearing her laugh.

She cooked a meal for herself, not for Joe. Not ever again for Joe.

He came in at seven. Lucia was in bed.

Rosie stood by the window. He slung his mac over the arm of the chair, poured a bourbon with his strong tanned hands. His cuff was white against his skin, his teeth white too. His watch golden. He was such a golden boy. He belonged at the Lake Club, not here. He moved towards her, kissed her, put his arm about her.

She handed him the letter, not watching as he read it but knowing when he had finished because he moved away.

For a moment there was silence, and then Joe said, 'I know what this must look like.'

'You must go,' Rosie said, looking at him now. 'You really must go.'

There was no anger in her voice. Just as there was no anger in it when she was dealing with difficult promoters and managers. That was business. This was business. Nothing else now.

'I'm not going. I belong with you. I love you. Together we can do things. We can build up the paper. Take over from Frank. It's all I've ever wanted, you know that. Married to you, that's possible.' He moved to her now, gripping her arm. 'We need each other. Jack's gone. You need me.'

She looked at his hand on her arm and then at him. He dropped his hand.

Rosie said, 'I've packed your bags. They're in the café, by the counter. I'm surprised you didn't see them.'

His lips were thin now and there was no love in his face. There never had been, she could see that now. 'If you do this I'll tell them about Lucia. I'll tell Bob to turn down Luke.' Joe was shouting, gripping her arm again.

Such short clean nails, suitable for the Lake Club. So very suitable. She moved away and again his hand dropped as she picked up his mac. It was still cold, damp and smelt of Joe. It meant nothing to her.

'Get out, Joe. I can't trust you, so there's nothing left.'

'I only wanted you so I'd get the paper.' He was spitting out the words, his shoulders rigid, his hands clenched into fists.

'And I've used you too, and I'm sorry,' Rosie said, holding the door, nodding to him as he stood there, large in this small room where he was now an intruder. 'Please go now, Joe.'

He started to say, 'You're a bitch . . .' but then stopped, shaking his head. 'Rosie, can't we . . . ?'

She shook her head, handing him his mac. He snatched it from her, turned, flung it at the window, driving a glass ashtray to the floor. It broke and only then did he leave, his mac lying crumpled on the sill.

Rosie quietly closed the door, knelt and picked up the splinters. She wouldn't need an ashtray now. She didn't smoke. Grandpa was right. Second best was no good.

She carried the broken glass through to the kitchen in Joe's mac, dropped them in the bin, then stood at the window listening to the sounds of the streets, to a soft cough from Lucia. Yes, he was right, it was better to be alone.

Rosie wrote to Frank and Nancy, telling them that she and Joe had quarrelled, that the report about Luke would be bad, but that *she* vouched for the band. Please would they tell Bob that? She also said that the Festival feature had been her idea. Joe had copied it.

She didn't tell them about Lucia because Joe might not and they had enough heartache now. And she had enough too.

In April she went again to Middle Street and slipped in through the back gate at a time when Mrs Eaves said Norah would be out. She pruned the roses, cutting them back to the healthy buds. She returned to Soho, and bought three rose plants from the market, planting them out in pots in Mario's yard. These were in recognition that the past had gone. There was to be no more waiting for anyone.

In May Frank and Nancy wrote to her, full of love, full of guilt at what they saw as their betrayal of her. They could not write fully until Joe returned from the POW camps where the North Koreans and Chinese were housed. Things were supposed to be bad there, he said. When Joe arrived in Lower Falls in the summer they would tell her what had been decided for that young man.

In the summer Frank wrote to her:

Lower Falls
June 1952

My dearest Rosie,

We have spoken to Joe. He no longer works for the paper. I now write again under my own name. There has been enough subterfuge. It's time I got out there fighting again. McCarthy can't go on for ever. When the Korean war ends my guess is that he will lose his appeal. All this talk about betrayal by the leadership because of the reverses and then the stalemate is just too easy to spout.

God giving that man a mouth was like giving a lunatic a gun.

The report on Luke was bad. Yours has over-ridden it. Bob trusts you.

But now I write about really important things. The first being that I know now that I am a grandfather. Joe told us. How can you think that this would bring anything other than joy? How can you think that it would have made our problems worse? We love you. We shall love Lucia. But your pain is our pain.

Think carefully, Rosie. Joe vouched for the news he brought about Jack's love affair. I have checked the POW list. He is on that but that doesn't mean the rest is true. Give him the benefit of the doubt where love is concerned. Just wait until the end of the war when you will know one way or the other. Please. I know it is what your Grandpa would want.

Incidentally, we are coming over to see you in July.

Frank

CHAPTER 24

The year had passed slowly; tortuously slowly. The lectures didn't change as 1952 slipped into 1953, neither did the nature of the seasons. The cold was extreme, the spring came with its usual glorious explosions of colour.

'Exquisite,' Steve said and they remembered Nigel, but Steve couldn't really see the colour. The lack of vitamins had given him twilight blindness. He groped his way if Jack wasn't with him, and he didn't sleep because he thought he would never write now.

The Doc said he would. That vitamins would reverse the situation.

'But when will he be able to have those, Doc?' Jack had asked.

'When this lot is over.'

But no one knew when that would be. Sometimes they doubted that it would ever happen.

The peace talks continued. New prisoners, conscripts who had not volunteered, told them so. The newcomers told them about the guns which blasted from the trenches and showered shrapnel and earth on to the men of both sides. It was trench warfare again. In this age of great might, they had returned to static trench warfare.

Conditions improved again as the blossom bloomed on the trees. The men were given two larger meals a day, with rice and soya beans. Once a week they had a piece of pork. There was steamed bread, Korean turnip, cabbage leaves which Jack made Steve eat raw because Maisie had always said that cooking boiled the vitamins away. They also had potatoes now.

Jack told Steve how he had picked potatoes in Somerset, how Rosie's grandpa had grown some one year in a bucket in the yard. They had been small and translucent and good enough to eat on their own.

There were no letters from Rosie. Steve had none either though he was sure his mother would have written. Some men had letters, though, and between the news of births and deaths the words which cut deepest were those of everyday life. The sink that was cracked. The bulbs that had been planted before they left. The bike that was rusted.

Jack wrote about all this with a journalist's eye. 'Keep at it. You'll do well,' another American whose father was a Sub-Editor on the *Washington Post* said when Steve showed him.

Each day they threw stones at the marker, because why should they change the ritual of their life, just because one of them no longer saw clearly, Jack asked? He forced his friend to concentrate while he gave him instructions. 'Same direction, not so hard this time.' Jack told Steve that as long as he could still hit the marker he would also be able to write.

'Just you wait and see. You'll use all these months, these years. The times in the pit, the times when the blossom has bloomed and filled us with wonder, and one day you'll win the Pulitzer Prize.'

Steve threw another stone, hitting the target. He aimed in exactly the same direction for his next throw.

'There you are, and just you wait, it'll be over soon. You'll get those vitamins.'

But would it soon be over?

It was for Steve. In April 1953 the North Koreans agreed to repatriate a number of wounded and ill prisoners and they included Steve on the list that they called out at roll-call. They included Bob too because dysentery had taken its toll of the older man and a stomach ulcer was suspected.

Jack scribbled a note to Rosie and gave it to Bob to post. It was hurried because the trucks were already pulling in. The men had thirty minutes to grab their belongings and say their farewells. As the others were being helped to the truck Steve hugged Jack, slapped his back. They held one another and couldn't bring themselves to say goodbye until the guard started shouting at them, pulling at Steve to move.

'See you, bud,' Steve said. 'I almost don't want to go. Don't want to leave you. It's been so long. But I'll see you.'

'You will. You get those vitamins inside you and you goddamn will,' Jack said, helping him up into the truck.

They clasped hands as the truck jerked away. Jack ran along behind waving to Bob, waving to Steve, watching as the mud spun from the wheels, swallowing his envy and his loss, wondering how he could go on without his American who was more than a friend, who had known the horrors of the pit alongside him. Who had defecated in the corner of the same rail-truck, who had washed Jack's rags when he had dysentery. Whose rags Jack had washed in turn.

He turned away as the truck eased into the haze and now the Sergeant shouted at him and the others. He lined them up. Told them that they were a motley shower, a bloody disgrace to their countries and he didn't want to see any long faces. Their friends had left. Soon they would all leave this godforsaken country, and they would leave with their spirits intact, their health intact, even if he had to break their bloody necks.

'And don't you forget it,' he bellowed. 'Dismiss.'

Throughout April the routine remained the same as it always had been and the men stopped looking up each time the Commandant left his house outside the compound. Nothing had changed. They weren't going home, yet.

The days were lonely now for Jack. He threw pebbles at the marker. He sat through lectures, using them to sharpen up his précis. Using them to dream of Rosie. Using them to rest. They were all so thin and tired and more fell ill with beri-beri but no more were shipped out.

Jack remembered the train ride to Pyongyang and feared that the same trick had been played again and maybe Steve would be trucked back. He didn't return though as April turned into May. In the camp they were given sleeping bunks, chairs and tables. Razors, mirrors, combs, nail-clippers, toilet bags, cigarettes, wine and beer. They shaved away the unkempt beards and looked almost young again.

The food had improved so much that the British were more able to play soccer, the Americans to play baseball. Jack wondered if Frank still had the target on the garage that Rosie had told him about.

Each day he threw pebbles at the marker because it was part of his routine and then he squatted in the compound and listened as the Americans threw, batted, ran.

'Now whad'ya gonna do, batter, batter?' was the chant from the supporters.

'Stay loose, baby, stay loose.'

'Whad'ya say? Whad'ya say?'

But solitary confinement still continued too and manual labour outside the compound: hauling logs, unloading trucks, digging channels – and the wood detail, the never-ending chopping of wood.

Peking Radio's English broadcasts continued too, including interviews with those UN troops who had turned, and although most of the men in the camp scarcely listened, the tone of the reports was different and some of them became convinced that the end was near. But Jack, and those who had been with him, could not forget the train journey to Pyongyang and refused to think of home.

On 27 July their Sergeant lined them all up at 1400 hours and, as the sun beat down on the compound square, the Commandant addressed the camp in Chinese.

'The bugger,' breathed Jack, because he knew the Commandant spoke English well. There was a pause.

Then the interpreter said, 'Both sides in the Korean war have agreed to a cease-fire to take effect from now. You will be returned to your own side.'

There were cameramen with the camp staff and Jack knew that they were there to record the scenes of joy, but none of the prisoners moved. They looked at the Sergeant and waited.

He gave his orders. They obeyed. Attention. About turn, quick march. Back to their huts, denying their captors any emotion. Denying themselves any as they sat on their beds and wondered if this was another trick.

One week later, in pouring rain, trucks came and took them to the railhead. They travelled in cattle wagons until they reached another camp. They lived beneath canvas for another two days eating beans and rice. Jack would not believe that he was going home and neither would many of the others.

Small groups departed each evening. Red Cross observers

were there now. Jack watched the yellow moon push up over the mountain crest. Where were they going? Back to the camp? Even with the Red Cross he could not bring himself to believe.

But then it was his turn. He pulled himself up into the truck and wished that Steve was here and Nigel, Tom, Bob. And still he couldn't believe. He couldn't feel. A Chinese Captain stood in the rain, urging them to turn from the warmongering capitalists and stay where there was truth.

Jack said, for Steve, for Tom, for Nigel, 'Why don't you take a powder.'

They drove into Freedom Village three days later and passed lorry after lorry taking Communist POWs back north.

There's nothing left for you up there now, Jack thought, the ruined countryside still raw in his mind. It was the people that suffered, always.

They drove into the encampment beneath a 'Welcome Home' arch and slipped down from the lorry. Someone directed them towards doctors who examined them, then on to the interrogators, who examined them. Then on to the psychiatrists who gave them ice-cream, and examined them.

'I just want to get home,' Jack said, because now he believed it and the joy was racing through him. He had been asked to fill in too many forms, been asked too many questions for it not to be the truth. It was over. He was going home. He was bloody well going home.

A woman in WVS uniform came to him as he sat on his bunk. She gave him a shirt and sat and talked to him. It was too long since he had heard a woman's voice, too long since someone had done up the buttons on his shirt, and his eyes filled with tears.

'It's so long since I've seen Rosie,' he said to the woman and then he cried.

The next day he boarded the troop ship, felt the wind in his hair and stood by the rail, with so many others who were too thin, too old, to be twenty-three.

'It was exquisite,' he called out as the ship left, not caring about the looks from those at his side. He was saying goodbye to Nigel and to Tom. 'It was goddamn exquisite.' And he was crying again, the tears smeared across his cheeks.

*

The year had passed slowly for Rosie too. Frank and Nancy had come in the summer of '52. They had held Lucia, they had held Rosie. They walked in the park, they looked at the ruins, at the rosebay willowherb which covered some still-unfilled craters. They gazed at the re-building which was slow, very slow. They took her to shows, to restaurants where there was still a maximum price. They went back with her to Somerset but not to Herefordshire because she must go there alone one day.

They travelled through the Somerset lanes, visited Montacute, Martock, Crewkerne, Stoke-sub-Hamdon. They climbed the hill and looked across the Levels. They looked down on the orchard where Ed had camped. They stood outside the school where Jack had been taught. They heard the laughter through the peaked windows and Frank put his arm round Rosie, chewing his empty pipe.

'He'll come back,' he said, but none of them really knew whether he would or not.

Frank and Nancy had left for the States again in August and when they took Luke and the group back with them it was as though they had taken the sun. Winter had come and gone and Bob had sent for the Larkhill Band too. They were all playing in New Orleans which Luke said 'was heaven come early'.

There had been no letters from Jack though she had written. Nancy said that much of the mail did not get through.

In April 1953 Frank telegraphed her: 'Repatriated POWs arriving RAF Lyneham, Wiltshire. May 1st. Meet them. Ask them. Frank.'

He arranged for her to have admittance but when she arrived and saw the plane land, saw the men being helped to the ground, sick, tired, injured, she turned away. This was a time for the families that surrounded her, families that now held back tears that had been falling all morning.

She wouldn't intrude. She would wait. She would work.

Promoters started coming to her with propositions in spite of her youth and because of her honesty, her reliability. On 2 June she covered the Coronation for Frank's paper because it kept her in contact, it kept the paper in the family. She took two-year-old Lucia with her and she sat in the pushchair, waving a flag, turning and laughing at Rosie, with Jack's mouth, his laugh.

She wrote of the golden coach, the eight grey horses and wished that Lucia was old enough to remember it all. It was wet and it was cold but wasn't England so often wet and cold? Rosie laughed and so did Mrs Eaves who was with her.

'Will you go back to America?' Mrs Eaves asked.

'It depends if he comes back. And if he does, will he want the stall? It all just depends. Both countries are my home.'

They waved at Queen Salote of Tonga, that huge brown smiling figure whose open carriage, Mrs Eaves said, must have been filled with rainwater.

Each Commonwealth Prime Minister had his own carriage and that led to such a shortage of professional coachmen that, Rosie wrote, businessmen and country squires had dressed up and were now driving some of the coaches. Rosie and Mrs Eaves laughed again and moved to Buckingham Palace where the Queen and the Duke of Edinburgh waved from the balcony at midnight by which time Lucia and most of the other children around them were asleep in their pushchairs.

Rosie said to Mrs Eaves as the crowd roared, 'I missed VE Day. I'm glad I caught this.'

Mr and Mrs Orsini had been watching it on their new television and when Rosie and Mrs Eaves returned they toasted the new Queen in iced champagne which Mario had saved since the beginning of the war. They talked until two, with Lucia asleep in Rosie's arms. Life was good, she thought.

On 15 June the Chinese launched a new Korean offensive and she cried all night because there seemed to be no end to this waiting, this killing.

Then Frank rang her from America. 'It's me. Take no notice. It's these goddamn Commies trying to gain some sort of propaganda success before the armistice is signed. We're close, Rosie, very close. Hang in there, goddamn it. See you. Bye.'

The line was crackling, she had hardly been able to hear. But it was enough.

The roses in the yard behind the kitchen were blooming well by July and Lucia pointed to Rosie's pocket each time they went out, wanting to be shown the matchbox which they always took for the ladybirds.

On 27 July the armistice was declared and a few days later

Rosie rang her jazz groups and her contacts and told them she would not be available for at least two months. Mr Orsini would handle everything. She took a cab to Middle Street and dropped a letter in through Ollie's door. It said:

> Dear Jack,
> If you come back and want to see me I shall be in Herefordshire until the end of September. I love you.
> Rosie

She didn't go into Grandpa's yard because Norah was there, the windows were open. She walked to Woolworths and heard Frank Sinatra singing, felt the warmth, basked in the light, fingered the glasses, the jewellery, the same sort of ribbon which she had bought when she met Sam.

'I'm going to Herefordshire. I can't wait here. I shall give myself two months and then that's the end. I've left a letter. I haven't told him about Lucia. He must come because he wants to,' she said to Mrs Eaves, speaking in short sentences because it seemed to hurt too much to speak, to breathe.

Jack's troop ship arrived at dawn on 18 September. He felt better, he had eaten well and there was a little more weight on him now. All he could think of was Rosie and he rushed for the train, sat in the carriage looking out of the window at the greenness of this land. He had forgotten. Somehow he had forgotten how green it was. He leaned out of the window as the train rattled through fields which had been ploughed, through fields in which cows grazed. There was sweetness to the air. He was home.

A woman was knitting opposite. She looked at him as he sat down again. 'Been posted abroad have you? Must have been nice to get a tan like that. I don't know, you young people. Away from the shortages. You don't know you're born,' she tutted.

'I've been in Korea.'

'Oh, that's the one my Harry said was a waste of time.' She was looking at her pattern, tracing the line of instructions. It slipped and fell to the floor. Jack picked it up.

'Yes, you could say it was a waste of time,' he replied and

looked out of the window again. So many years had passed, so many men had died. There had been so much waiting, for them all. But there was Steve, there was Bob, and he had learned to write, learned about himself. He shrugged. 'Some of my friends will have thought it a waste of time,' he said. 'They didn't come back. They'll never come back.'

But the woman wasn't listening, she was counting her stitches. There was no point in talking any more. He just sat and watched the country unfold, the towns cluster, the suburbs of London approach. He ran down the platform, out to the taxi-rank. There was a queue. There was always a bloody queue. He was laughing and the man behind him smiled.

'Been away then?'

'Yes.' Jack didn't say where to. 'Going back to see my girl.'

'That's what makes it all worth while, ain't it, mate?' the man said.

Jack nodded, climbing into the taxi which drew up. 'Yes, that's what makes it all worthwhile,' he called back. 'Middle Street,' he said to the cabbie.

He looked out. The ruins were still there, but progress had been made. He smelt the air. It was the same old smoke, the same familiar skyline, the same streets which were becoming narrower. It wouldn't be long now. The taxi was turning into Albany Street, past Woolworths, down into Middle Street. Jack tapped on the glass partition. 'This'll do, mate.' He pushed open the door outside Rosie's house. He paid, tipped, ducked down through the alley, into Grandpa's yard, then stopped. Dropped his kitbag. He was home. At last it was all over. They could begin again, if she would have him.

He knocked on the door, pushed it open, calling, 'Rosie. I'm back.'

There was only Norah there, washing clothes at the sink, her hair permed, her mouth pursed. Grandpa's books were gone from the walls, his chair too. Norah turned from the sink and said, 'Thought you'd be here one day. She's gone. Back to America with that Joe. Gave you up a long time ago. Ollie's gone too, up north of London. Building the new towns.'

Norah didn't watch him go, she just heard his feet run out through the yard. She knew he'd try Ollie's house. She'd left the key there in the usual place but she'd burned the letter he'd got his friend from the camp to post. She'd taken the letter Rosie had pushed through the door. Thought I wouldn't see, I suppose, she thought, scrubbing harder at the dirt ingrained in Harold's trousers from kneeling on those church floors. Well, that'll teach her to tell my husband to go back to his hobby. That'll teach her to take him away from me. She turned back to the sink.

In Herefordshire, the sun was still warm, though it was nearly five p.m. Rosie paddled with Lucia in the stream, taking the pebbles as her daughter handed them to her. They were wet. She carried them to the bank, adding them to the pile of those which were drying.

Two weeks to go until the end of September and Jack had not come.

She looked up at the slopes above her. The bines were half picked. The pickers were using the last of the light, flip-flipping, not looking. Chatting, laughing.

When she had arrived the barley had still been in the fields all around the cottage she had rented. The combine had worked up until the end of August, shaving off the last tuft before the farmer sent in the plough. Seagulls had clustered over the furrows and Lucia had stood with her mouth open, waving at the birds, calling back when she thought they called to her.

Rosie had gone for a walk with her daughter the evening before the pickers came, and climbed the stile into the kale, hearing the partridges as they whickered in the hedge.

They had passed the blackberry bushes, still ripe with fruit, and looked across the sloping fields, down to the stream they were paddling in now. Seeing the thistles, the cows grazing, she had felt the peace of the place, the echoes.

She had waited, then walked her daughter through the bines which swung in the gentle breeze, telling her that one day they would all come and pick hops and then dance like she and Grandpa had once done. She had taken Lucia to the gate, shown her the carved initials. Her daughter had rubbed her hand over the letters her father had cut and laughed.

And each day they had waited.

Rosie turned back to the stream now, easing her feet through the water, over the stones, as Lucia, her dress tucked into her knickers, laughed and held up more pebbles, drips running down her plump arm.

Rosie turned and threw them towards the pile. Yes, they had waited but not for much longer. If he didn't come she knew now what she would do. She would spend half her year in England, half her year in Lower Falls and she would survive and prosper. But . . . But . . .

They waded towards the bank, ate sandwiches which were warm from the sun. Rosie remembered the lake, then Lee at Wembley, and touched the letter in her pocket which he had written, now that he was 'a big boy'. She lay back on the grass, pulling Lucia on top of her, hugging her, rocking gently, hearing the buzz of nearby bees.

There were moths at night, beating against the window, trying to reach the light. Didn't they know it was hopeless? She kissed Lucia fiercely.

'Water, Mummy, water,' Lucia said and laughed, pointing to the stream.

The water was cool against their legs as they waded in again and they scooped pebbles and threw, again and again, and the pile grew bigger as Rosie told Lucia how Daddy had lain on the bank and told her of Somerset and how Grandpa had picked hops that year as though he was a young man again.

Her hand was cold now but the pyramid wasn't high enough and so she threw again.

Another, larger pebble came through the air, hitting the pile before hers did. 'I hit the marker every time now,' Jack said.

Rosie saw his smile, his thin face, his thin hands that he held out to her and to his daughter. Then she was running with Lucia clutched to her, through the water, over the pebbles which bruised her feet, but which she didn't feel. Running as he came down the bank and into the water too, and at last his arms were round them both, his lips were on hers, the same soft gentle lips, the same skin, the same words.

'Mrs Eaves told me you were here. I love you, little Rosie.' And then, into her neck, 'Forgive me.'

'God damn you, my darling love,' was all she said, because the waiting was over.